UNMARRIAGEABLE

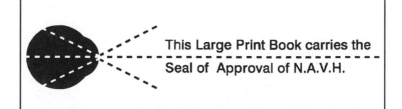

This Large Print Book carries the
Seal of Approval of N.A.V.H.

UNMARRIAGEABLE

SONIAH KAMAL

THORNDIKE PRESS
A part of Gale, a Cengage Company

Farmington Hills, Mich • San Francisco • New York • Waterville, Maine
Meriden, Conn • Mason, Ohio • Chicago

LIBRARY OF CONGRESS CIP DATA ON FILE.
CATALOGUING IN PUBLICATION FOR THIS BOOK
IS AVAILABLE FROM THE LIBRARY OF CONGRESS

ISBN-13: 978-1-4328-6263-3 (hardcover)

Published in 2019 by arrangement with Ballantine Books, an imprint of Random House, a division of Penguin Random House LLC

Printed in the United States of America
1 2 3 4 5 6 7 23 22 21 20 19

For Mansoor Wasti,
friend, love, partner,
and
Buraaq, Indus, Miraage,
heart, soul, life

Upon the whole, however, I am . . . well satisfied enough. The work is rather too light, and bright, and sparkling; it wants shade; it wants to be stretched out here and there with a long chapter of sense, if it could be had; if not, of solemn specious nonsense, about something unconnected with the story; an essay on writing, a critique on Walter Scott, or the history of Buonaparte, or anything that would form a contrast, and bring the reader with increased delight to the playfulness and epigrammatism of the general style.

— Jane Austen on *Pride and Prejudice* in a letter (1813) to her sister, Cassandra

I have no knowledge of either Sanscrit or Arabic. . . . I have never found one among them [Orientalists] who could deny that a single shelf of a good European library was worth the whole native literature of India and Arabia. The intrinsic superiority of the Western Literature . . . we are free to employ our funds as we choose, that we ought to employ them in teaching what is best worth knowing, that English is better worth knowing than Sanscrit or Arabic . . . that it is possible to make natives of this country thoroughly good English scholars, and that to this end our efforts ought to be directed. . . . We must at present do our best to form a class who may be interpreters between us and the millions whom we govern — a class of persons Indian in blood and colour, but English in tastes, in opinions, in morals and in intellect. To that class we may leave it to refine the vernacular dialects of the country.

— from Thomas Babington Macaulay's "Minute on Education," 1835

■ ■ ■ ■

PART ONE

■ ■ ■ ■

December 2000

CHAPTER 1

It is a truth universally acknowledged that a girl can go from pauper to princess or princess to pauper in the mere seconds it takes for her to accept a proposal.

When Alysba Binat began working at age twenty as the English-literature teacher at the British School of Dilipabad, she had thought it would be a temporary solution to the sudden turn of fortune that had seen Mr. Barkat "Bark" Binat and Mrs. Khushboo "Pinkie" Binat and their five daughters — Jenazba, Alysba, Marizba, Qittyara, and Lady — move from big-city Lahore to backwater Dilipabad. But here she was, ten years later, thirty years old, and still in the job she'd grown to love despite its challenges. Her new batch of ninth-graders was starting *Pride and Prejudice*, and their first homework had been to rewrite the opening sentence of Jane Austen's novel, always a

11

fun activity and a good way for her to get to know her students better.

After Alys took attendance, she opened a fresh box of multicolored chalks and invited the girls to share their sentences on the blackboard. The first to jump up was Rose-Nama, a crusader for duty and decorum, and one of the more trying students. Rose-Nama deliberately bypassed the colored chalks for a plain white one, and Alys braced herself for a reimagined sentence exulting a traditional life — marriage, children, death. As soon as Rose-Nama ended with *mere seconds it takes for her to accept a proposal,* the class erupted into cheers, for it was true: A ring did possess magical powers to transform into pauper or princess. Rose-Nama gave a curtsy and, glancing defiantly at Alys, returned to her desk.

"Good job," Alys said. "Who wants to go next?"

As hands shot up, she looked affectionately at the girls at their wooden desks, their winter uniforms impeccably washed and pressed by *dhobis* and maids, their long braids (for good girls did not get a boyish cut like Alys's) draped over their books, and she wondered who they'd end up becoming by the end of high school. She recalled herself at their age — an eager-to-learn though ultimately naïve Ms. Know-It-All.

"Miss Alys, me me me," the class clown said, pumping her hand energetically.

Alys nodded, and the girl selected a blue chalk and began to write.

It is a truth universally acknowledged that a young girl in possession of a pretty face, a fair complexion, a slim figure, and good height is not going to happily settle for a very ugly husband if he doesn't have enough money, unless she has the most incredible bad luck (which my cousin does).

The class exploded into laughter and Alys smiled too.

"My cousin's biggest complaint," the girl said, her eyes twinkling, "is that he's so hairy. Miss Alys, how is it fair that girls are expected to wax everywhere but boys can be as hairy as gorillas?"

"Double standards," Alys said.

"Oof," Rose-Nama said. "Which girl wants a mustache and a hairy back? I don't."

A chorus of I don'ts filled the room, and Alys was glad to see all the class energized and participating.

"I don't either," Alys said complacently,

13

"but the issue is that women don't seem to have a choice that is free from judgment."

"Miss Alys," called out a popular girl. "Can I go next?"

It is unfortunately not a truth universally acknowledged that it is better to be alone than to have fake friendships.

As soon as she finished the sentence, the popular girl tossed the pink chalk into the box and glared at another girl across the room. Great, Alys thought, as she told her to sit down; they'd still not made up. Alys was known as the teacher you could go to with any issue and not be busted, and both girls had come to her separately, having quarreled over whether one could have only one best friend. Ten years ago, Alys would have panicked at such disruptions. Now she barely blinked. Also, being one of five sisters had its perks, for it was good preparation for handling classes full of feisty girls.

Another student got up and wrote in red:

It is a truth universally acknowledged that every marriage, no matter how good, will have ups and downs.

"This class is a wise one," Alys said to the delighted girl.

The classroom door creaked open from the December wind, a soft whistling sound that Alys loved. The sky was darkening and rain dug into the school lawn, where, weather permitting, classes were conducted under the sprawling century-old banyan tree and the girls loved to let loose and play rowdy games of rounders and cricket. Cold air wafted into the room and Alys wrapped her shawl tightly around herself. She glanced at the clock on the mildewed wall.

"We have time for a couple more sentences," and she pointed to a shy girl at the back. The girl took a green chalk and, biting her lip, began to write:

It is a truth universally acknowledged that if you are the daughter of rich and generous parents, then you have the luxury to not get married just for security.

"Wonderful observation," Alys said kindly, for, according to Dilipabad's healthy rumor mill, the girl's father's business was currently facing setbacks. "But how about the daughter earn a *good* income of her own and secure this freedom for herself?"

"Yes, Miss," the girl said quietly as she scuttled back to her chair.

Rose-Nama said, "It's *Western* condition-

15

ing to think independent women are better than homemakers."

"No one said anything about East, West, better, or worse," Alys said. "Being financially independent is not a Western idea. The Prophet's wife, Hazrat Khadijah, ran her own successful business back in the day and he was, to begin with, her employee."

Rose-Nama frowned. "Have you ever re-imagined the first sentence?"

Alys grabbed a yellow chalk and wrote her variation, as she inevitably did every year, ending with the biggest flourish of an exclamation point yet.

It is a truth universally acknowledged that a single woman in possession of a good fortune must be in want of a husband!

"How," Alys said, "does this gender-switch from the original sentence make you feel? Can it possibly be true or can you see the irony, the absurdity, more clearly now?"

The classroom door was flung open and Tahira, a student, burst in. She apologized for being late even as she held out her hand, her fingers splayed to display a magnificent four-carat marquis diamond ring.

"It happened last night! Complete surprise!" Tahira looked excited and nervous.

16

"Ammi came into my bedroom and said, 'Put away your homework-shomework, you're getting engaged.' Miss Alys, they are our family friends and own a textile mill."

"Well," Alys said, "well, congratulations," and she rose to give her a hug, even as her heart sank. Girls from illustrious feudal families like sixteen-year-old Tahira married early, started families without delay, and had grandchildren of their own before they knew it. It was a lucky few who went to college while the rest got married, for this was the Tao of obedient girls in Dilipabad; Alys went so far as to say the Tao of good girls in Pakistan.

Yet it always upset her that young brilliant minds, instead of exploring the universe, were busy chiseling themselves to fit into the molds of Mrs. and Mom. It wasn't that she was averse to Mrs. Mom, only that none of the girls seemed to have ever considered traveling the world by themselves, let alone been encouraged to do so, or to shatter a glass ceiling, or laugh like a madwoman in public without a care for how it looked. At some point over the years, she'd made it her job to inject (or as some, like Rose-Nama's mother, would say, "infect") her students with possibility. And even if the girls in this small sleepy town refused to wake up, wasn't it her duty to try? How grateful she'd have been for such a teacher. Instead, she and her sisters had also been raised under their mother's motto to marry young and well, an expectation neither thirty-year-old Alys, nor her elder sister, thirty-two-year-old Jena, had fulfilled.

In the year 2000, in the lovely town of Dilipabad, in the lovelier state of Punjab, women like Alys and Jena were, as far as their countrymen and -women were concerned, certified Miss Havishams, Charles Dickens's famous spinster who'd wasted away her life. Actually, Alys and Jena were considered even worse off, for they had not enjoyed Miss Havisham's good luck of having at least once been engaged.

As Alys watched, the class swarmed around Tahira, wishing out loud that they too would be blessed with such a ring and begin their real lives.

"Okay, girls," she finally said. "Settle down. You can ogle the diamond after class. Tahira, you too. I hope you did your homework? Can you share your sentence on the board?"

Tahira began writing with an orange chalk, her ring flashing like a big bright light bulb at the blackboard — exactly the sort of

18

ring, Alys knew, her own mother coveted for her daughters.

It is a truth universally acknowledged in this world and beyond that having an ignorant mother is worse than having no mother at all.

"There," Tahira said, carefully wiping chalk dust off her hands. "Is that okay, Miss?"

Alys smiled. "It's an opinion."

"It's rude and disrespectful," Rose-Nama called out. "Parents can never be ignorant."

"What does ignorant mean in this case, do you think?" Alys said. "At what age might one's own experiences outweigh a parent's?"

"Never," Rose-Nama said frostily. "Miss Alys, parents will always have more experience and know what is best for us."

"Well," Alys said, "we'll see in *Pride and Prejudice* how the main character and her mother start out with similar views, and where and why they begin to separate."

"Miss Alys," Tahira said, sliding into her seat, "my mother said I won't be attending school after my marriage, so I was wondering, do I still have to do assign —"

"Yes." Alys calmly cut her off, having

19

heard this too many times. "I expect you to complete each and every assignment, and I also urge you to request that your parents and fiancé, and your mother-in-law, allow you to finish high school."

"I'd like to," Tahira said a little wistfully. "But my mother says there are more important things than fractions and ABCs."

Alys would have offered to speak to the girl's mother, but she knew from previous experiences that her recommendation carried no weight. An unmarried woman advocating pursuits outside the home might as well be a witch spreading anarchy and licentiousness.

"Just remember," Alys said quietly, "there *is* more to life than getting married and having children."

"But, Miss," Tahira said hesitantly, "what's the purpose of life without children?"

"The same purpose as there would be with children — to be a good human being and contribute to society. Look, plenty of women physically unable to have children still live perfectly meaningful lives, and there are as many women who remain childless by choice."

Rose-Nama glared. "That's just wrong."

"It's not wrong," Alys said gently. "It's relative. Not every woman wants to keep home and hearth, and I'm sure not every man wants to be the breadwinner."

"What does he want to do, then?" Rose-Nama said. "Knit?"

Alys painstakingly removed a fraying silver thread from her black shawl. Finally she said, in an even tone, "You'll all be pleased to see that there are plenty of marriages in *Pride and Prejudice.*"

"Why do you like the book so much, then?" Rose-Nama asked disdainfully.

"Because," Alys said simply, "Jane Austen is ruthless when it comes to drawing-room hypocrisy. She's blunt, impolite, funny, and absolutely honest. She's Jane Khala, one of those honorary good aunts who tells it straight and looks out for you."

Alys erased the blackboard and wrote, *Elizabeth Bennet: First Impressions?*, then turned to lead the discussion among the already buzzing girls. None of them had previously read *Pride and Prejudice*, but many had watched the 1995 BBC drama and were swooning over the scene in which Mr. Darcy emerged from the lake on his Pemberley property in a wet white shirt. She informed them that this particular scene was not in the novel and that, in Austen's time, men actually swam naked. The girls burst into nervous giggles.

"Miss," a few of the girls, giddy, emboldened, piped up, "when are you getting married?"

"Never." Alys had been wondering when this class would finally get around to broaching the topic.

"But why not!" several distressed voices cried out. "You're not *that* old. And, if you grow your hair long again and start using bright lipstick, you will be so pret—"

"Girls, girls" — Alys raised her amused voice over the clamor — "unfortunately, I don't think any man I've met is my equal, and neither, I fear, is any man likely to think I'm his. So, no marriage for me."

"You think marriage is not important?" Rose-Nama said, squinting.

"I don't believe it's for everyone. Marriage should be a part of life and not *life.*"

"You are a forever career woman?" Rose-Nama said.

Alys heard the mocking and the doubt in her tone: Who in their right mind would choose a teaching job in Dilipabad over marriage and children?

"Believe me, Rose-Nama," Alys said serenely, "life certainly does not end just because you choose to stay —"

"Unmarried?" Rose-Nama made a face as she uttered the word.

"Single," Alys said. "There is a vast difference between remaining unmarried and choosing to stay single. Jane Austen is a leading example. She didn't get married, but her paper children — six wonderful novels — keep her alive centuries later."

"You are also delivering a paper child?" Rose-Nama asked.

"But, Miss Alys," Tahira said resolutely, "there's no nobler career than that of being a wife and mother."

"That's fine." Alys shrugged. "As long as it's what you really want and not what you've been taught to want."

"But marriage and children *are* my dream, Miss!" Tahira gazed at Jane Austen's portrait on the book. "Did no one want to marry her?"

"Actually," Alys said, "a very wealthy man proposed to her one evening and she said yes, but the next morning she said no."

"Jane Austen must have been from a well-to-do family herself," said the shy girl, sighing.

Alys gave her a bright smile for speaking up. "No. Jane's mother came from nobility but her father was a clergyman. In their time, they were middle-class gentry, respectable but not rich, and women of their class could not work for a living except as governesses, so it must have taken a lot of courage for her to refuse."

"Jane Austen sounds very selfish," Rose-Nama said. "Imagine how happy her mother must have been, only to find that overnight the good luck had been spurned."

"It could also be," Alys said softly, "that her mother was happy her daughter was different. Do any of you have the courage to live life as you want?"

"Miss Alys," Rose-Nama said, "marriage is a cornerstone of our culture."

"A truth universally acknowledged" — Alys cleared her throat — "because without marriage our culture and religion do not permit sexual intimacy."

All the girls tittered.

"Miss," Rose-Nama said, "everyone knows that abstinence until marriage is the secret to societies where nothing bad happens."

"That's not true." Alys looked pained. She thought back to the ten years her family had lived in Jeddah, Saudi Arabia, where she'd studied at a co-ed international school and made friends from all over the world, who'd lived all sorts of lifestyles. Though she'd been forbidden from befriending boys, many of the girls were allowed, and they were no worse off for it. Like her, they'd also been studious and just as keen to collect flavored lip balms, scratch-and-sniff stickers, and scented rubbers, which she'd learned, courtesy of her American classmates, were called erasers, while a rubber was a condom, which was something you put on a penis, which was pronounced "pee-nus" and not "pen-iz." Alys's best friend, Tana from Denmark, stated that her mother had given her condoms when she'd turned fifteen, because, in Scandinavia, intimacy came early and did not require marriage. Alys had shared the information with Jena, who was scandalized, but Alys had quickly accepted the proverb "Different strokes for different folks."

"Premarital sex is haram, a sin," Rose-Nama said, "and you shouldn't imply otherwise to us, Miss Alys." Her eyes widened. "Or do you believe it's not a sin?"

Before Alys could answer, the head peon, Bashir, knocked on the door.

"Chalein jee, Alysba *bibi,"* he said, *"phir bulawa aa gaya aap ka.* Principal Naheed requires your presence yet again."

Alys followed Bashir down the stairs, past classrooms, past the small canteen where the teachers' chai and snacks were prepared at a discount rate, past a stray cat huddled on the wide veranda that wrapped around

25

the mansion-turned-school-building, past the accountant's nook, and toward the principal's office, a roomy den at the end of the front porch with bay windows overlooking the driveway for keeping an eye on all comings and goings.

The British School Group was founded twenty years ago by Begum Beena dey Bagh. The name was chosen for its suggested affiliation with Britain, although there was none. However, it was to be an English-medium establishment. Twelve years ago, Naheed, a well-heeled Dilipabadi housewife, decided to put to use a vacant property belonging to her. She sought permission from Beena dey Bagh to open a branch of the British School, and so was born the British School of Dilipabad.

Naheed had turned her institution into a finishing school of sorts for girls from Dilipabad's privileged. Accordingly, she was willing to pay well for teachers fluent in English with decent accents, and, just as she'd all but given up on proficient English-literature teachers, Alys and Jena Binat had entered her office a decade ago.

Alys entered the office now, settled in a chair facing Naheed's desk, and waited for her to get off the phone. She gazed at the bulletin boards plastering the walls and boasting photos where Naheed beamed with Dilipabad's VIPs. They were thumbtacked in place to allow easy removal if a VIP fell from financial grace or got involved in a particularly egregious scandal.

Naheed's mahogany desk held folders and forms and a framed picture of her precious twin daughters, Ginwa and Rumsha — Gin and Rum — born late, courtesy of IVF treatments. Gin and Rum posed in front of the Eiffel Tower with practiced pouts, blond-streaked brown hair, and skintight jeans. Naheed's daughters lived in Lahore with their grandparents; she'd opted to send them to the British School of Lahore rather than her own British School of Dilipabad because she wanted them to receive superior educations as well as better networking opportunities. Gin and Rum planned to be fashion designers, a newly lucrative entrepreneurial opportunity in Pakistan, and Naheed had no doubt her daughters would make a huge splash in the world of couture and an equally huge splash in the matrimonial bazaar by marrying no less than the Pakistani equivalents of Princes William and Harry.

Naheed hung up the phone and, clearly annoyed, shook her head at Alys.

"Rose-Nama's mother called. Again. Apparently you used the 'f' word in class."

"I did?"

"The 'f' word, Alys. Is this the language of dignified women, let alone teachers?"

Alys crossed her arms. Naheed would not have dared speak to her like this when she'd first joined the school. Ten years ago, when Naheed had realized that Alys and Jena were Binats, her tongue had been a never-ending red carpet, for the Binats were a highly respected and moneyed clan. However, once Dilipabad's VIPs realized that Bark Binat was now all but penniless — why he'd lost his money was no one's worry, that he had was everyone's favorite topic — they devalued Bark and his dependents. As soon as Principal Naheed gleaned that Alys and Jena were working in order to pay bills and not because they were bored upper-class girls, she began to belittle them.

"Alys, God knows," Naheed said, "I have yet again tried to calm Rose-Nama's mother, but give me one good reason why I shouldn't let you go."

Alys knew that Naheed had tried to hire other well-qualified English-speaking teachers but no one was willing to relocate to Dilipabad. The sole entertainment for most Pakistanis was to eat out, and the elite English-speaking gentry in particular believed they deserved dining finer than Dilipabad offered.

"Alys, am I or am I not," Naheed's voice boomed, "paying you a pretty penny? It is not as if good jobs are growing on trees."

The fact was, over the years Alys had been offered lucrative teaching positions in other cities, and then there was Dubai, where single Pakistani girls were increasingly fleeing to find their fortunes, but she was unwilling to leave her family, especially her father.

"It was a crow," Alys said. "Rose-Nama and her mother should educate themselves on context. A giant crow flew into the classroom and startled me and —"

"Alys," Naheed said, "I don't care if twenty giant crows fly into the classroom and start singing 'The hills are alive with the sound of music'; you absolutely may not curse in front of impressionable young ladies. Rose-Nama's mother is right — if it's not cursing, it's something else. Last year you told students that dowry was a 'demented' tradition. Could you not have used 'controversial' or 'divisive' or 'contentious'? You of all people should be sensitive to diction. Then you told them that divorce was not a big deal! Another year you told them that they should be reading

Urdu and regional literature instead of English. An absurd statement from an English-literature teacher."

"Not 'instead.' I said 'side by side.' "

"Yet another time you decided to inform them that if Islam allowed polygamy, then it should allow polyandry. This is a school. Not a brothel."

Alys said, stiffly, "I want my girls to at least have a chance at being more than well-trained dolls. I want them to think critically."

Naheed pointed above Alys's head. "What is the school motto?"

Alys spoke it by rote. " 'Excellence in Obedience. Obediently Excellent. Obey to Excel.' "

"Precisely," Naheed said. "The goal of the British School Group is for our girls to pass their exams with flying colors so that they become wives and mothers worthy of our nation's future VIPs. Please stick to the curriculum. I'm weary of apologizing to parents and making excuses for you. Also, I know you value your younger sisters studying here."

Alys gave a small smile. Qitty, in the eleventh grade, and Lady, in the ninth, attended BSD at the discount rate offered to faculty family, which, all the teachers agreed, was not as generous as it could be.

"I may not be able to protect you any longer," Naheed said. "Begum Beena dey Bagh's nephew is returning from completing his MBA in America, and things seem to be about to change. For one, the young man plans to abolish the uniform. Can you imagine our students turning up in whatever they choose to wear? Anarchy!"

Alys understood Naheed's concern. She and her husband had the monopoly over the British School of Dilipabad's uniform business — winter, spring, fall — and the loss would be an expensive hit to their income.

Principal Naheed's gaze fixed upon the driveway. Alys turned to see a Pajero with tinted windows and green government number plates driving in. The jeep stopped and the driver handed the gate guard a packet. Minutes later, Naheed tenderly opened a pearly oversize lavender envelope embossed with a golden palanquin. All smiles, she drew out equally pearly invites to Dilipabad's most coveted event: the Nadir-Fiede wedding, the joining of Fiede Fecker, daughter of old-money VIPs, to Nadir Sheh, son of equally important VIPs, though rumor had it that drug-smuggling was responsible for the Shehs' fast accumula-

31

tion of monies and rapid social climb and acceptance into the gentry.

"Such a classy invitation," Naheed said, tucking the invites back in.

Alys disliked the word "classy," a favorite of those who aimed to be arbiters of class. She knew that Naheed was hoping the Binats would not be invited, despite their pedigree, since Alys and Fiede Fecker, a graduate of the British School of Dilipabad, had been at loggerheads over incomplete assignments and projects never turned in.

"Alys, the *namigarami* — the elite of Dilipabad — have spoken," Naheed said, fingering her invite. "Our duty is to send their daughters home exactly as they were delivered to us each morning: obediently obeying their parents. We are to groom these girls into the best of marriageable material. That is all." Naheed signaled to Bashir, who had been dawdling by the threshold, to get her a fresh cup of lemongrass tea and, in doing so, dismissed Alys.

Alys rejoined her ninth-graders, bracing herself for Rose-Nama to demand her views on premarital intimacy. But Rose-Nama was busy scolding the class monitor, a timid girl Principal Naheed had appointed because her father had given a generous donation to renovate the science laboratory. Mercifully, the bell rang as soon as she stepped in, and Alys, gathering her folders and cloth handbag, headed to the tenth-grade classroom.

"Girls," Alys said to the tenth grade, "open up your *Romeo and Juliet.* Let me remind you that Juliet is thirteen years old and Romeo around fifteen or sixteen and that they could have surely experienced a happier fate had they refrained from romance at their ages, which may well have been Shakespeare's cautionary intent for writing this pathetically sad love story."

CHAPTER 2

When the final bell rang, Alys headed toward the staff room, nodding at girls giggling and gossiping around Tahira's engagement ring. In the staff room, teachers were enjoying the celebration cake from High Chai that Tahira's mother had sent. Alys beckoned to Jena, and both sisters headed toward the school van.

For a small fee, BSD provided conveyance to and from school for teachers and their relatives studying there. The Binats had an old Suzuki but Alys thought it wise to save on petrol, no matter how much more it embarrassed fifteen-year-old Lady to ride in the school van.

Lady and Qitty were inside the van, squabbling.

"Qitty, move over, you fat hippo," Lady said, elbowing the sketchbook her elder sister was drawing in.

"Shut up!" Qitty said. She was the only

overweight Binat sister, a blow she could never forgive fate or God. "There's no such thing as a thin hippo, so fat is redundant, stupid."

"You're stupid, bulldozer," Lady said. "You always hog all the space, hog. And stop showing off your stupid drawings."

"You wish you could draw." Qitty flipped to a fresh page and within moments had outlined a caricature of Lady. "The only talent you have is big breasts."

"Thanks to which, thunder thighs," Lady said, "I'm going to make a brilliant marriage and only ride in the best of cars with a full-time chauffeur. And, Qitty, you will not be allowed in any of my Mercedes or Pajeros, because I'll be doing you a favor by making you walk."

Qitty drew two horns atop Lady's caricature.

"Lady!" Alys said, avoiding the torn vinyl as she settled into the seat beside her best friend, Sherry Looclus, who taught Urdu at BSD. "Apologize to Qitty. Why do you two sit together if you're going to fight?"

The van driver was, as usual, enjoying the skirmish. The rest of the teachers ignored it.

"I pray your dreams come true," Jena said to Lady, "but that doesn't mean you can be mean to Qitty or to anyone. We are all God's creatures and all beautiful."

"Those who can afford plastic surgery are even more beautiful," Lady said. "Qitty, you fatso, stop sniveling. You know I call you fat for your own good."

"I eat far less than you, Jena, Alys, and Mari all put together," Qitty said. Lady was willowy and seemingly able to eat whatever she wanted all day long without expanding an inch. "It's not fair."

"It's not fair," Alys agreed. "But, then, who said life is fair? Remember, though, that looks are immaterial."

"Alys, you are such an *aunty,*" Lady said, taking out a lip gloss and applying it with her pinkie.

"You can call me an aunty all you want," Alys said, "but that doesn't change the fact that looks are not the be-all and end-all, no matter what our mother says. Qitty is a straight-A student, and I suggest, Lady, you pull up your grades and realize the importance of books over looks."

Lady stuck her tongue out at Alys, who shook her head in exasperation. Once all the teachers had climbed in, the van drove out of the gates and past young men on motorbikes ogling the departing schoolgirls. These lower-middle-class youths didn't have a prayer of romancing a BSD girl, Alys knew, despite the fantasies that films tried to sell them about wrong-side-of-the-tracks love stories ending in marriage, because there were few fates more petrifying to a Pakistani girl than downward mobility.

Alys watched Lady's reflection in the window. She was running her fingers through her wavy hair in a dramatic fashion. Lady was a bit boy crazy, but Alys also knew that her sisters were well aware that they couldn't afford a single misstep, since their aunt's slander had already resulted in the family's damaged reputation. She tapped her sister's shoulder, and Lady looked away as the van turned the corner.

Dilipabad glittered after the rainfall, its potholed roads and telephone wires overhead freshly washed and its dust settled. The manufacturing town claimed its beginnings as a sixteenth-century watering hole for horses and, after a national craze to discard British names for homegrown ones, Gorana was renamed Dilipabad after the actor Dilip Kumar. In more-recent times, Dilipabad had grown into a spiderweb of neighborhoods, its outskirts boasting the prestigious residences as well as the British School, the gymkhana, and upscale restaurants, while homes and eateries got shabbier closer to the town center. In the town center was a white elephant of a bazaar that was famous for bargains, a main petrol pump, and a small public park with a men-only outdoor gym. The elite, however, stuck to the gymkhana, with its spacious lawns, tennis and squash courts, golf course, boating on the lake, swimming pool, and indoor co-ed gym with ladies-only hours.

Mrs. Binat had insisted they apply for the Dilipabad Gymkhana membership despite the steep annual dues, and since the gymkhana functioned under an old amendment that once a member, always a member, the Binats were in for life. The amendment had been added on the demand of a nawab who, after gaining entry to the gymkhana once the British relaxed their strict rule of no-natives-allowed, had been terrified of expulsion.

Though Mr. Binat was seldom in the mood to attend the bridge and bingo evenings, Mrs. Binat made sure she and the girls put in an appearance every now and then. Once Alys had discovered the gymkhana library, she'd spent as much time there as she had in the school library in Jeddah, where she'd first fallen in love with books: Enid Blyton. Judy Blume. Shirley Jackson. Daphne du Maurier. Dorothy Par-ker. L. M. Montgomery's *Anne of Green Gables*, and S. E. Hinton's class-based novels, which mirrored Indian films and Pakistani dramas.

In the gymkhana library, Alys would choose a book from the beveled-glass-fronted bookcase and curl up in the chintz sofas. Over the years, the dim chinoiserie lamps had been replaced with overhead lighting, all the better to read Agatha Christie, Arthur Conan Doyle, Austen, the Brontës, Dickens, George Eliot, Mary Shelley, Thackeray, Hardy, Maugham, Elizabeth Gaskell, Tolstoy, Orwell, Bertrand Russell, Wilde, Woolf, Wodehouse, Shakespeare, more Shakespeare, even more Shakespeare.

Alys pressed her forehead against the van's window as they left behind the imposing gymkhana and passed the exalted Burger Palace, Pizza Palace, and the Chinese restaurant, Lotus, all three eateries shut until dinnertime. Only the recently launched High Chai was open and, going by the number of cars outside, doing brisk business — in local parlance, "minting money" — because Dilipabadis were entertainment-starved.

Alys gazed at the café's sign: High Chai in gold cursive atop pink and yellow frosted

39

cupcakes. It took her back to a time when their mother would dress her and Jena in frilly frocks, a time before their father and his elder brother, Uncle Goga, were estranged, a time when they'd been one big happy joint family living in the colossal ancestral house in the best part of Lahore: her paternal grandparents, her parents and sisters, Uncle Goga and Aunty Tinkle and their four children.

They'd play with their cousins for hours on end. Hide-and-go-seek. *Baraf pani.* Cops and robbers. Jump rope and hopscotch. They'd fight over turns and exchange insults before making up. However, Tinkle always took her children's side during the quarrels.

"Why is Aunty Tinkle so rude to us?" Alys would ask her mother. "Why does she act as if they're better than us?"

Pinkie Binat replied hesitantly, "Her children are not better than any of you. You have the same history."

Pinkie Binat made sure her daughters knew where they came from. The British, during their reign over an undivided subcontinent, doled out small plots to day laborers as incentive to turn them into farmers, who, later, would be called agriculturists and feudal lords, which is what the Binat forefathers ultimately became. These men then turned their attentions to consolidating land and thereby power and influence through marriage, and even during the 1947 partition the Binats managed to retain hold over their land.

It was infighting that defeated some of the Binats. After the death of his wife, Goga's and Bark's ailing father had increasingly come to depend on Goga and his wife, first-cousin Tajwer "Tinkle" Binat, a woman who spent too much time praying for a nice nose, thicker hair, a slender waist, and dainty feet. When Binat Sr. passed away, he left his sons ample pockets of land as well as factories, but it was clear Goga was in charge and not impressed by his much younger brother's devotion to the Beatles, Elvis, and squash. He was even less impressed by Bark's obsession with a girl he'd glimpsed at a beauty parlor when he went to pick up Tinkle.

"Please, Tinkle," Bark had begged his cousin plus sister-in-law, "please find out who she is and take her my proposal. If I don't marry her, I will die."

Tinkle knew immediately which girl had smitten Bark. She herself had found it hard to not stare at the fawn-eyed beauty and, in a benevolent mood, she returned to the salon to make inquiries into her identity:

Khushboo "Pinkie" Gardenaar, seventeen years old, high school graduate. The girl's mother was a housewife, overly fond of candy-colored clothes. Her father was a bookkeeper in the railways. The girl's elder brother was studying at King Edward Medical College. Her elder sister was a less attractive version of Bark's crush.

The girl's family claimed ancestry from royal Persian kitchens. Nobodies, Tinkle informed Goga; basically cooks and waiters. After the brothers fell out, Tinkle would discredit Pinkie's family by stressing that there was zilch proof of any royal connection. At the time, however, the Binats accepted the family's claims, and so it was with fanfare that Barkat "Bark" Binat and Khushboo "Pinkie" Gardenaar were wed.

On the day of the wedding, Tinkle lost control of her envy. Was it fair that this chit of a girl, this nobody, should make such a stunning bride?

"She is no *khushboo,* good smell, but a *badboo,* bad smell," Tinkle railed at Goga as she mocked Khushboo's name. "I'm the one who went to a Swiss finishing school. I'm the one who sits on the boards of charities. But always it's her beauty everyone swoons over. She calls a phone 'foon,' biscuit 'biscoot,' year 'ear,' measure 'meyer.'

She does not know salad fork from dinner fork. How could your brother have married that lower-middle-class twit? Doesn't Bark care that they are not our kind of people?"

Tinkle's jealousy grew as Bark and Pinkie delivered two peach-fresh daughters in quick succession. Tinkle's own children barely qualified for even *qabool shakal,* acceptable-looking. Goga tried to ignore his wife's complaints. He had bigger matters to trouble him, including the loss of the Binats' factories after a wave of nationalization. Goga was doubly displeased over Bark's welcoming attitude toward the government takeover. Could his bleeding-heart brother not see that socialism meant less money for the Binats?

In order to diversify assets, Goga invested in a series of shops in Saudi Arabia to capitalize on the newly burgeoning mall culture. He informed Bark he was needed to supervise the investment, and Bark and Pinkie dutifully packed up and, with their daughters, Alys and Jena, headed off to Jeddah.

Even though Pinkie had been reluctant to leave her life in Lahore, once in Jeddah, frequent visits to the holy cities of Mecca and Medina were a great spiritual consolation. Alys and Jena were enrolled in an international school, where their classes looked like a mini–United Nations and the girls made friends from all over the world. Pinkie's friends were other expatriate wives, with whom she spent afternoons shopping in the souks and malls for gold and fabrics. The Binats resided in an upscale expat residential compound, which had a swimming pool and a bowling alley, and Pinkie hired help.

Life was good; Jeddah was home. Bark grumbled occasionally about the hierarchy — Saudis first, then white people, no matter their level of education or lineage, then everyone else. Still, they might have remained in Jeddah forever were it not for a car accident in which a Saudi prince rear-ended Bark's car. In Saudi Arabia, the law sided with Saudis no matter who was at fault, and so Bark counted his blessings for escaping with only a broken arm and, fearing that he might be sent to jail for the scratch on the prince's forehead, packed up his wife and their now five daughters and moved back into their ancestral home in Lahore.

It took two years for Bark to unearth the rot. His elder brother had bilked him out of business and inheritance. Bark proceeded to have a heart attack, a mild one, but

Tinkle made sure Goga remained unmoved by his younger brother's plight.

Bark had nowhere to turn. His parents had passed away. Relatives commiserated but had no interest in siding with Bark or helping him money-wise. Alys, then nineteen, convinced her father to consult a lawyer. They were the talk of the town as it was, she said, and they needed to get back what was rightfully theirs. Too late, said the lawyer. They could appeal, but it would take forever and Goga had already transferred everything to himself. They would learn later that the lawyer had accepted a decent bribe from Goga to dissuade them from filing.

Tinkle wanted them gone from the Binat ancestral home, and Bark shamefacedly accepted the property in Dilipabad that Tinkle didn't want because of its ominous location in front of a graveyard. Bark told Pinkie that *she* could no longer afford to be superstitious and that they had to move as soon as possible, and so Jena and Alys were disenrolled from Kinnaird College and Mari, Qitty, and Lady from the Convent of Jesus and Mary school.

The Binats arrived in Dilipabad one ordinary afternoon, the moving truck unceremoniously dumping them outside their new house with its cracked sign proclaiming: BINAT HOUSE. Binat House was an abundance of rooms spread over two stories, which looked out into a courtyard with ample lawn on all four sides, gone to jungle. The elderly caretaker was shocked to see the family. As he unlocked the front doors and led them into dust-ridden rooms with musty furniture covered by moth-eaten sheets, he grumbled about not having been informed of their coming. Had he known, of course the rooms would have been aired. Cobwebs removed from the ceiling. Rat droppings swept off the floors and a fumigator called. Electricity and boiler connections reinstalled. A hot meal.

The Binats stared at the caretaker. Finally, Hillima, the lone servant who had chosen to accompany the fallen Binats — despite bribes by Tinkle, Hillima was loyal to Pinkie, who'd taken her in after she'd left her physically abusive husband — told the caretaker to shut up. It was his job to have made sure the house remained in working order. Had he been receiving a salary all these years to sleep?

Hillima assembled an army of cleaners. A room was readied for Mr. Binat. The study emerged cozy, with a gorgeous rug of tangerine vines and blue flowers, leather sofas, and relatively mildew-free walls. Once the bewildered Mr. Binat was deposited inside, with a thermos full of chai and his three younger daughters, attention turned to the rest of the house.

Mrs. Binat and Alys and Jena decided to pitch in; better that than sitting around glum and gloomy. They coughed through dust and scrubbed at grime and shrieked at lizards and frogs in corners, though Alys would bravely gather them up in newspaper and deposit them outdoors. Dirt was no match for determined fists, and Alys and Jena were amazed at their own industriousness and surprised at their mother's. They'd only ever seen her in silks and stilettos, fussing if her hair was out of place or her makeup smudged. Grim-faced, Mrs. Binat snapped that before their father married her, she'd not exactly been living like a queen. Soon floors sparkled, windows gleamed, and, once the water taps began running from brown to clear, Binat House seemed not so dreadful after all.

Hillima was pleased with the servants' quarters behind the main house — four rooms with windows and attached toilet, all hers for now, since the caretaker had been fired for incompetence.

Bedrooms were chosen. Alys took the

room overlooking the graveyard, for she was not scared of ghosts-djinns-*churails,* plus the room had a nice little balcony. In their large bedroom on the ground floor, Mrs. Binat brought up to Mr. Binat — as urgently as possible, without triggering another heart attack — the matter of expenses. Pedigree garnered respect but could not pay bills. There was the small shop in Lahore that Goga had missed in his usurpations, which they still owned and received rent on, but it wasn't enough to live on luxuriously. Gas bills. Electricity bills. Water bills. The younger girls had to go to school. Mr. Binat's heart medicines. Food. Clothes. Shoes. Toiletries. Sanitary napkins — dear God, the cost of sanitary napkins. Gymkhana dues. Hillima's salary, despite free housing, medical, and food. They also needed to hire the most basic of staff to help Hillima: a *dhobi* for clean, well-starched clothes, a gardener, a cook. How dare Mr. Binat suggest she and the girls cook! Were Tinkle Binat and her daughters chopping vegetables, kneading dough, and washing pans? No. Then neither would Pinkie Binat and her daughters.

It was Alys's decision to look for a teaching job. She and Jena had been in the midst of studying English literature, and their first stop was the British School of Dilipabad. Principal Naheed pounced on them, particulary thrilled with their accents: The soft-spoken Jena would teach English to the middle grades, and the bright-eyed Alys would teach the upper grades. Alys and Jena were giddy with joy. Newly fallen from Olympus, they were inexperienced and nodded naïvely when Naheed told them their salary, too awestruck at being paid at all to consider they were being underpaid. What had they known about money? They'd only ever spent it.

Alys and Jena had returned home with the good news of their employment only to have Mrs. Binat screech, "Teaching will ruin your eyesight! Your hair will fall out marking papers! Who will marry you then? Huh? Who will marry you?"

She'd turned to Mr. Binat to make Alys and Jena quit, but instead he patted them on their heads. This was the first time he'd truly felt that daughters were as good as sons, he attested. In fact, their paychecks were financial pressure off him, and he'd happily turned to tending the overgrown garden.

Alys was always proud that her actions had led their father to deem daughters equal to sons, for she had not realized, till then, that he'd discriminated. However, looking back, she wished he'd at least advised them to negotiate for a higher salary. She wished that her mother had asked them even once what they wanted to be when they grew up instead of insisting the entire focus of their lives be to make good marriages.

Consequently, Alys always asked her younger sisters what they wanted to be, especially now that there seemed a cornucopia of choices for their generation. Qitty wanted to be a journalist and a cartoonist and dreamed of writing a graphic novel, though she said she wouldn't tell anyone the subject until done. Mari had wanted to be a doctor. Unfortunately, her grades had not been good enough to get into pre-med and she'd fallen into dejection. After copious pep talks from Alys, as well as binging on the sports channel, Mari decided she wanted to join the fledging national women's cricket team. But this was a desire thwarted by Mrs. Binat, who declared no one wanted to marry a mannish sportswoman. Also, Mari suffered from asthma and was prone to wheezing. Mari turned to God in despair, only to conclude that all failures and obstacles served a higher purpose and that God and good were her true calling. Lady dreamed of modeling after being discovered by a designer and offered an opportunity, but their father had absolutely forbidden it: Modeling was not respectable for girls from good families, especially not for a Binat.

Alys had fought for her sisters' dreams. But wheezing notwithstanding, Mari was a mediocre cricket player, and, as for Lady, no matter how much Alys argued on her sister's behalf, their father remained unmoved, for he hoped his estranged brother would reconcile with him and he dared not allow anything to interfere with that. Whatever the case, Alys was adamant that her sisters must end up earning well; now if only they'd listen to her and take their futures seriously.

The school van drove into a lower-middle-class ramshackle neighborhood with narrow lanes and small homes, where some of the teachers disembarked. Unable to afford much help, they shed their teacher skins and slipped into their housewife skins once they'd entered their houses. They would begin dinner, aid their children with homework, and, when their husbands returned from work, provide them chai as they unwound. They would return to the kitchen and pack the children's next-day school lunches, after which they would serve a hot dinner, clean up the kitchen, put the children to bed, and then finally shed their housewife skins and wriggle back into the authoritative teacher skins to grade papers well into the night.

Alys and Jena had heard the weariness in the staff room as teachers wondered how long they could keep up this superwoman act. Yet their jobs provided a necessary contribution to the family income — a fact their husbands and in-laws frequently chose to downplay, ignore, or simply not acknowledge — and afforded them a vital modicum of independence. The trick, the teachers sighed, was to marry a man who believed in sharing the housework, kids, and meal preparations without thinking he was doing a great and benevolent favor, but good luck with finding such a man, let alone in-laws who encouraged him to help.

The school van entered the Binats' more affluent leafy district and stopped at the entrance to the graveyard. The Binat sisters had only to cross the road to enter their wrought-iron gate and walk up the front lawn lined with evergreen bushes to their front door. They'd barely stepped into the foyer when Mrs. Binat flew out of the family room: "Guess what has happened?"

CHAPTER 3

Mrs. Binat was in the family room, praying the rosary for her daughters' futures, when the mail was delivered and in it the opportunity. Hearing their voices in the foyer, she rushed to them, asking them to guess what had happened as she waved a pearly lavender envelope like a victory flag.

Alys immediately recognized the invite to the NadirFiede wedding. Lady whooped as Mrs. Binat rattled off the names of all the old and new moneyed families who would be attending: Farishta Bank, Rani Raja Steels, the British School Group, Sundiful Fertilizers, Pappu Chemicals, Nangaparbat Textiles.

Mrs. Binat was still dropping names as her daughters followed her into the family room, where they settled around the electric fireplace. Alys climbed into the window seat that overlooked the back lawn. She tossed a throw over her legs, making sure to hide her feet before her mother noticed that she wasn't wearing any nail polish. Qitty and Lady sat on the floor, beside the wall decorated with photos of holidays the Binats had taken once upon a time: Jena and Alys at Disneyland, Mr. Binat holding toddler Mari's hand next to the Acropolis, Qitty nibbling on corn on the cob in front of the Hagia Sophia, the whole family smiling into the camera in front of Harrods, a newborn Lady in a pram.

"Alys, Jena." Mr. Binat rose from his armchair. "Your mother has been eating my brains ever since that invite arrived. I'm going to the garden to —"

"Sit down, Barkat," Mrs. Binat said sharply. "We have to discuss the budget for the wedding."

Alys sighed as her father sat back down. She'd been looking forward to finishing her grading and then reading the risqué religious short story, "A Vision of Heaven" by Sajjad Zaheer from the collection *Angaaray*, which Sherry had translated for her from Urdu into English.

"Discuss it with Alys," Mr. Binat said. "She knows the costs of things better than I do."

"I'm sure Alys and everyone else knows everything better than you do," Mrs. Binat said. "But you are their father, and instead of worrying whether the succulents are thriving and the ficus is blooming, I need you to take an active interest in your daughters' futures."

"Futures?" Mr. Binat beamed as Hillima brought in chai and *keema samosas.*

"I want," Mrs. Binat announced, "the girls to fish for husbands at the NadirFiede wedding."

Alys gritted her teeth. She could see before her eyes a large aquarium of eligible bachelors dodging hooks cast by every single girl in the country.

"Aha!" Mr. Binat said, taking a *samosa.* "Nadir Sheh and Fiede Fecker are getting married so that *our* daughters get married. So kind of them. Very noble! I suggest you also line up, Pinkie, my love, because between you and the girls, you are still the most beautiful one."

"I know you are mocking me, Barkat, my love, but a compliment is a compliment! However, once a woman births daughters, her own looks must take a backseat."

Mrs. Binat gazed at each of her daughters. From birth, Jena was near perfect, a cross between an ivory rose and a Chughtai painting, her features delicate yet sharp, good hair, good height, slender, and the disposition of an angel. Lady was a bustier, hippier, pug-nosed version of Jena and towered over her sisters at five feet nine inches (thankfully height had gone from impediment to asset!). Mari was a poor imitation of Lady, with plain features, a smallish chest, and without Lady's spark. Qitty was exceptionally pretty, except her features were lost amid the double chins. And Alys. Oh, Alys. If only she wouldn't insist on ruining her complexion by sitting in the sun. If only she wouldn't butcher her silky curls. If only she'd wear some lipstick to outline those small but lush lips and apply a hint of bronzer to her natural cheekbones. What a waste on Alys those striking almond eyes. And such an argumentative girl that sometimes Mrs. Binat would cry with frustration.

She extracted the cards from the invitation. "We have been invited to the *mehndi* and *nikah* ceremonies at the Dilipabad Gymkhana and to the *walima* ceremony in Lahore. Jena, Alys, Qitty, Lady, you'll have to take days off from school."

"Don't worry," Alys said to her mother. "Principal Naheed has been invited too."

Mrs. Binat's nostrils fluttered. "That means those scaly daughters of hers, Gin and Rum, will also be fishing. No doubt

56

they will be wearing the latest designer outfits and carrying brand-name bags. Everyone will. Alys, what is the budget for new clothes?"

"None," Alys said. "Anyway, tailor Shawkat overcharges us."

"How many times must I tell you that girls are only as good as their tailor, and Shawkat is worth every paisa he charges." Mrs. Binat glared, Alys's hair suddenly annoying her more than usual. "Honestly, if you wanted short hair, couldn't you have gotten a nice bob like a good girl?"

Alys ran her a hand over her cropped curls and exposed nape. "I like this. It saves me hours in the morning."

"I like it too," Mr. Binat said.

Alys smiled at her father. She'd grown up with her mother constantly telling her father what a *jhali* — a frump — she was, and over time Alys had realized that she was her father's favorite for that very reason. He loved that she'd always squat beside him in the garden and dig in the soil without a second thought to broken nails, dirty palms, or a deep tan.

"Barkat, you like everything this brainless girl does," Mrs. Binat said. "Thankfully Alys has a nice neck."

Mrs. Binat's ambitions for her daughters

were fairly typical: groom them into marriageable material and wed them off to no less than princes and presidents. Before their fall, her husband had always assured her that, no matter what a mess Alys or any of the girls became, they would fare well because they were Binat girls. Indeed, stellar proposals for Jena and Alys had started to pour in as soon as they'd turned sixteen — scions of families with industrialist, business, and feudal backgrounds — but Mrs. Binat, herself married at seventeen, hadn't wanted to get her daughters married off so young, and also Alys refused to be a teenage bride. However, once their world turned upside down and they'd been banished to Dilipabad, the quality of proposals had shifted to Absurdities and Abroads.

Absurdities: men from humble middle-class backgrounds — restaurant managers, X-ray technicians, struggling professors and journalists, engineers and doctors posted in godforsaken locales, bumbling bureaucrats who didn't know how to work the system. Absurdities could hardly offer a comfortable living, let alone a lavish one, and Mrs. Binat had seen too many women, including her sister, melt from financial stress.

Abroads: middle-class men from foreign countries like America, England, Australia,

Canada, et cetera, where the wife was no better than an unpaid multitasking menial, cooking, cleaning, driving, looking after children, and providing sex on demand with no salary or a single day off. An unpaid maid with benefits. Mrs. Binat had seen enough of the vagaries of life to know that getting married to a middle-class Western Abroad could mean exhaustion and home-sickness, and she would not allow her daughters a life of premature aging and loneliness. As such, she was unwilling to marry them off to frogs and toads, because she was too good a mother to plunge her girls into marriage simply for the sake of marriage. For that, she would wait until Jena and Alys turned thirty-five. There was also the small complication of the girls' reluc-tance to move abroad, since, for better or worse, they loved Pakistan. But, most im-portant of all, if she sent her daughters abroad, *she* would miss them.

The plan was to remain in Pakistan and wed a Rich Man. Of course, Mrs. Binat knew through her own sad experience that even rich men could turn into poor night-mares, for had she not married a Rich Man? And now where were her holidays, designer brands, and financial security? In her milieu, sons had been coveted for their income and thereby the security blanket they afforded retired parents, but, having married into wealth, she'd never cared to even pray for a son. Mr. Binat too had stopped hoping for a boy after their fifth child was a girl. How she wished now she'd prayed for sons, and kept trying in order to spare herself the worry of a destitute old age. Being financially savvy and ambitious was a vital component of a successful man, and often Mrs. Binat wondered whether she was to blame for not having had the upbringing to distinguish, in Barkat "Bark" Binat, the real from the impostor.

She would not allow her daughters to make this mistake. She clutched the Nadir-Fiede invitation. This was a real Rich Man fishing ground she was not going to waste.

"We must give a marriage present that rivals everyone else's. We must give thirty thousand rupees."

"Thirty thousand!" Mr. Binat glanced in alarm at Alys and Jena. "We are neither family nor close friends!"

"Thirty thou is petty cash for Fiede Fecker." Alys laughed. "Five thousand from us should suffice."

"We don't want to look like skinflints," Mrs. Binat said. "They are sure to tell the whole town who gave them what."

"Mummy," Jena said gently, "five thousand rupees is stretching it for us as it is."

Mrs. Binat sighed. "Okay. Gifit is done."

"Gift," Lady said. "Gift."

"That's what I'm saying. Gifit. Gifit." Mrs. Binat shook her head. "*Oof,* I'm so sick of the tyranny of English and accent in this country. Alys, Jena, go get the trunk."

Alys and Jena dragged in the metal trunk that housed the Binats' sartorial finery, collected over the years — *saris, ghararas, shararas, peshwas, lehengas, anarkalis, angrakhas, shalwar kurtas, thang pajama kameezs.* Most of the outfits had been tailored out of fabrics Mrs. Binat had purchased in Jeddah, aware that with five daughters to dress, they would come in handy. Thankfully she'd had the foresight to pick neutral colors that could be worn through any turn of fashion and brightened with accessories and jewelry. The smell of mothballs rose as she riffled through the trunk, only to announce that Jena and Alys were definitely getting new clothes.

"I want new clothes too," Lady wailed.

"After Jena and Alys are married," Mrs. Binat said firmly.

"Oh, hurry up and get married already, you two!" Lady said crossly. "And Alys, no one cares if you don't want to get married."

"I've been praying so hard for them," Mari said, looking up from her nebulizer. "Obviously God must have good reason for putting us in this predicament."

"I'm leaning toward new silk *saris.*" Mrs. Binat looked Jena and Alys up and down. "The other guests can wear brand-name *chamak-dhamak* razzle-dazzle from head to foot, but you two will have an understated, classic Grace Kelly look."

"Everyone," Lady said, "knows people go classic when they can't afford brands."

"People who depend on brands," Mrs. Binat said resignedly, "have no style of their own."

"Silk *saris* are going to cost a lot, Mummy," Alys said as she tried to calculate exactly how much.

"Cost-effective in the long run. The money can come out of your father's gardening budget" — she ignored Mr. Binat's huge, shuddering sigh — "and we'll spice up the *saris* with a visit to our special jeweler."

Ganju *jee* specialized in artificial jewelry that could rival the real thing. He was located in Dilipabad's central bazaar, in a pokey little alley where Mrs. Binat had stumbled upon him. After she smiled at him a little too kindly, he'd always been excited to oblige with wares at excellent prices.

"I want to wear a *mohti.*" Lady grabbed the current issue of *Social Lights* and flipped past the pictures of people who seemed to do nothing but brunch, lunch, and attend fashion shows. She stopped at the fashion shoot where her favorite model, Shosha Darling, was wearing the garment of the moment: *mohtis* — miniskirt *dhotis.*

"You can't wear that." Mrs. Binat peered at Shosha Darling's bare legs. "It must cost a fortune. Look at all the hand embroidery on the border."

"I don't have to buy it," Lady said. She turned the pages until she came to the weekly column "What Will People Say — *Log Kya Kahenge.*" This week's celebrity quotes concerned fashion designer Qazi of QaziKreations — Qazi had once designed an Oscar dress for a very minor celebrity, which had, back home in Pakistan, turned him into a very major celebrity — and Qazi's latest creation, the *mohti,* for which he was taking orders.

Shosha Darling: I'm always given gifts! Believe and you will receive.

"That's what I plan to do," Lady said. "Believe and I will receive."

"Please, Lady!" Alys said, laughing. "These stupid skirts are severely overpriced and Shosha Darling is an idiot."

"You think everyone is an idiot except for yourself." Lady scowled. "If I can't wear a *mohti,* then I want *saris* with halter tops."

"I wouldn't wear a *sari* even if I was paid," Mari said. *"Saris* are for Hindus. As Muslims, our ties lie in Arab culture. We should be attending this wedding in *burqas."*

"I'd rather die," Lady said, "than go in a *burqa* to any wedding, let alone Nadir-Fiede."

"Me too," Qitty said.

"Mari, have you gone crazy?" Alys said placidly, for after Mari's dejection they were all quite cautious, and even Lady dared not bring up her poor grades or medical school. "Pakistani roots have nothing to do with Saudi *burqa,* or any Arab culture. Muslims have worn *saris* forever and Hindus have worn *shalwar kameez."*

"I despise it when you use that teacher's tone at home," Mari said.

"It's that stupid club of yours, Mari," Lady said. "Each time you return with some holier-than-thou gem."

"Shut up, Lady," Mari said. "Alys, you know the club is just a bunch of us girls who want to discuss *deen* and *dunya,* religion and its place in our lives and the world. The last topic was menstruation, and we concluded it was probably a blessing for overworked women to be considered impure and so banished from cooking and other duties long enough to get a rest. We're also starting good works, and the first good work is my idea." Mari beamed. "A food drive for Afghan refugees. After that we're going to campaign for the abolishment of men selling brassieres and bangles and other purely female wares to women. It's shameful the way the bra vendors openly assess our breasts and the bangle vendors hold our wrists as if to never let go."

"That's truly admirable," Alys said. "And I think it's time you also got an actual job. Come teach. Or look for an administrative position somewhere. We could do with the money, and you could do with getting out and meeting new people."

"We can certainly do with the money," Mrs. Binat said. "Free *kaa* food drive! You'd better not take anything from the pantry without telling me. Good deeds! All this girl does is watch tennis all day long and wheeze whenever it suits her purpose."

Mari glowered. How she wished yet again that she'd gotten into medical school or that some pious man would marry her and take her away from her family. The first sister married. Then her mother would surely think the world of her.

"Since we can't afford brand names," Lady said, "the next best thing is to become as skeletal as possible. Hillima, can you make sure the cook prepares diet foods for me for the next two weeks before Nadir-Fiede?"

Hillima, sitting by them and gawking at European models on the fashion channel, nodded.

"I'm not going to NadirFiede." Qitty looked up from her sketchbook. "I'm sick of going to places surrounded by skinny girls fishing for compliments by complaining how fat they are."

"I'm not going either," Mari said. "I don't approve of these ostentatious weddings, when Islam requires a simple ceremony."

"I swear, Mari," Lady said, "no one is going to marry you except a gross mullah with a beard coming down to his toes, and once he finds out what a party pooper you are, you'll be the least favorite of his four wives."

"The only party worth worrying about," Mari said, "is the one after death, and if you don't change your ways, Lady, you're going to end up in hell."

Mrs. Binat slapped her forehead. "Mari

and Qitty, you're attending NadirFiede, whether you like it or not. Qitty, lose five pounds and you will feel much better."

Qitty glared at her mother. She hadn't had a single *samosa* so far, but now she popped one whole into her mouth.

"See, Mummy!" Lady said. "She doesn't want to be thin."

"Shut up," Qitty said. "You've had six. Mari is right. You're going to go to hell, Bathool."

Lady had originally been named after Mr. Binat's mother, but after bullies at school rhymed "Bathool" with "stool," "cesspool," "drool," et cetera, Mrs. Binat insisted Mr. Binat allow her a legal name change. Bathool chose Lady, from the animated film *Lady and the Tramp,* even though her sisters cautioned against renaming herself after a cartoon dog, no matter how regal.

"Sticks and stones may break my bones," Lady said to Qitty, "but names, hippo, will never hurt me."

Mrs. Binat half-suppressed a smile.

Qitty was livid. "This is why she calls *me* names, Mummy. Because you favor her."

"God knows," Mrs. Binat said, "I never play favorites. Qitty, I'm your friend, not your enemy, and I'm simply saying what is best for you. These days, you girls are expected to be the complete package. Gone are the days when a woman could get away with a single asset like a pair of fine eyes or a tiny waist. Now you have to be a bum-shell."

"Bombshell," Mr. Binat corrected her. "Bom, not bum."

Mrs. Binat flashed her eyes at her husband. "Please, Qitty, for my sake try to lose some weight before NadirFiede. No one wants to marry a fat girl."

"You wait, Mummy," Qitty said. "Bathool the Fool is going to do something so unforgivable one day that my being fat will be nothing in comparison. You should have seen the way she was making you-you eyes at the motorbike brigade outside of school today."

"Liar!" Lady said. "Why should I make you-you eyes at motorbike boys? Although some are so handsome, while too many Rich Men are ugly."

Mrs. Binat squinted. "The uglier and darker the Rich Men, all the better for you, because they are actively hunting for fair and lovely girls to balance out their genes."

"Mummy," Lady said, "would you have married Daddy if he was ugly?"

"Luckily for me," Mrs. Binat said, "your father was handsome as well as rich. Alas,

68

he was also unwise and so I became a tale of rags to riches, riches to rags. He let the corrupt Goga and Tinkle completely dupe him. Anyway, God is watching, and it is said the children will suffer for the sins of their parents."

"Pinkie, please." Mr. Binat sat up. "How many times must I say, Goga's and Tinkle's children did nothing to us; leave them out of it."

"Daddy, calm down." Alys got up to kiss her father's cheek. "Shall I get you fresh chai?"

"Daddy's *chamchee*, his toady," Mrs. Binat said. "Run and get him a bucket of chai, so he can drown of shame in it."

"*Hai*, Mummy," Lady said, "how shameful it will be when we arrive at the events in our *saddha hua* Suzuki *dabba*. That car is so embarrassing."

"Can you please," Jena said, "be grateful for the fact that we at least have a car? Anyway, Lady, why would you want to marry someone who cares only about the make of your car or the size of your house?"

"How is that any different from marrying someone because they are smart or nice?" Lady said. "Criteria is criteria!"

"Too many people marry for the wrong reasons," Jena said. "They should be looking for kindness and intelligence."

"Jena, my sweet girl, you are too idealistic," Mrs. Binat said. "On that note, Jena, Alys, if anyone asks your age, just change the subject. I so wish you'd stop telling everyone your real ages, but it is the fashion to think your mother unwise and never listen to her."

"But you're always telling the girls to be fashionable," Mr. Binat said, winking at Alys.

"Wink at Alys!" Mrs. Binat threw a dagger of a look at her husband. "Please, Barkat, wink at her again. Keep teaching her to disrespect her mother. Keep teaching all your daughters to deride me. You used to do the same in front of Tinkle. That woman wished she had one percent of my looks, and yet you allowed her and your brother to treat me like nothing. And what did they do in turn! They treated you like nothing."

"I'm going to the garden," Mr. Binat said. "If I sit here any longer, I'll have another heart attack."

"Please, go," Mrs. Binat said to his retreating back. "One heart attack years ago and constantly we have to be on best behavior. Who thinks of my health? I get palpitations at the thought of you five girls languishing in this house, never knowing the joy of marriage and offspring. *Hai,*" she said, suddenly wistful, "can you imagine Tinkle's face if even one of you manages to snag an eligible bachelor at NadirFiede, let alone all of you."

"Maybe Qitty can snag an eligible bachelor by sitting on him," Lady said.

Qitty picked up her sketchbook and whacked Lady in the arm.

"Jena, Alys," Mrs. Binat said, "shame on both of you if this wedding ends and you remain unmarried. Cast your nets wide, reel it in, grab it, grab it. But do not come across as too fast or forward, for a girl with a loose reputation is one step away from being damaged goods and ending up a spinster. Keep your distance without keeping your distance. Let him caress you without coming anywhere near you. Coo sweet somethings into his ears without opening your mouth. Before he even realizes there is a trap, he will have proposed. Do you understand?"

CHAPTER 4

Ten years ago, the evening Hillima declared the cleanup of Binat House complete, the Binats gathered in the study, wondering how to occupy their time. Jena began reading a pop-up *Alice in Wonderland* to her younger sisters. Mr. and Mrs. Binat quarreled about finances. Mrs. Binat segued into how she wished she'd gotten Jena and Alys married off before their banishment.

Alys escaped her mother's dire predictions regarding her prospects by fleeing to her new bedroom. She sat on her bed, made cheery with a yellow chenille bedspread and crewelwork pillowcases, and thought about what the hell she was going to do with her life in this small town.

She stared at her bare walls, livened up with a Pisces poster and a photo of herself amid friends during a school trip to the Red Sea. She remembered treading the ocean bed with Tana, laughing as they looked out for sea urchins, snorkeling under the hot sun, returning to land and sand fights. The future had seemed so limitless and bright back then.

Alys stepped out onto her small balcony. Evening had descended on Dilipabad, and the sun was setting in a sky pollution had turned milky. She wasn't sure when she began to cry. She wiped her tears and told herself to stop. She was crying because ever since they'd returned to Pakistan two years ago, all she'd heard was how, if she did not conform to certain beauty standards and demure etiquette, she was going to die alone. She was crying because she missed her friends in Jeddah and wondered if she'd ever see them again. When Alys had left Jeddah, she and Tana sent each other letters but, slowly, they petered out. In her last letter, Tana mentioned that her family was returning to Denmark, after which Alys's letter was returned saying "no forwarding address."

In Lahore, Alys and Jena had met some friendly faces in college. But sitting in the canteen and sharing greasy *naan kebabs* with girls who'd known each other since kindergarten and accordingly cracked ancient jokes just made them feel lonelier. So it was that the two sisters had turned to each other: "Do you remember Radhika in the Brownie troop getting into trouble for demonstrating how to play spin the bottle?" "Do you remember when we watched Madonna's Virgin Tour at Sahara's house?" "Do you remember when Tana showed us a condom and we thought it was a balloon?"

They'd been too young to say goodbye forever to friends, home, familiarity, and now they'd even left big-city Lahore and come to Dilipabad, where life seemed to revolve around marrying well and eating well. There wasn't even a proper bookstore or library. Alys's eyes filled up again. Any minute now, she was certain, her mother would come barging in to tell her that if she cried, then she'd ruin her eyesight, and if she started to wear spectacles, then no one would marry her.

Across the road, at the graveyard's entrance, a flower-cart vendor was putting away the marigold garlands and loose rose petals he sold to mourners to commemorate their dead. Alys blinked. The graveyard was the one place no one would follow her, because her family was terrified of ghosts, djinns, *churails,* and, thanks to Michael Jackson's "Thriller" video, ghouls, zombies, and monsters.

Alys tiptoed down the stairs and out of

the front door and across the street to the graveyard's entrance.

"As-salaam-alaikum," the vendor said, looking up from his flowers. "You are the new people who've moved into the house?"

"We moved two weeks ago," Alys managed to reply in her heavily English-accented, stilted Urdu.

"Chunga — good," he said. "No place deserves to remain empty for too long. From Ingland or Amreeka?"

"Jeddah."

"Mashallah. You must have gone to Mecca and Medina?"

"All the time."

"Mashallah. My cousin is working in construction there. Building malls. He doesn't like it. He misses home. But the money he sends has already gotten two daughters married off with full dowry, *alham-dulillah."*

Alys sighed. Did anyone talk about anything except marriage in this country?

"I want to go into the graveyard," Alys said. "There's no closing time, is there?"

"No. But most people are scared of the dead, and even more so at nighttime."

"If you ask me," Alys said, "it's the living who people should be scared of."

The vendor laughed. He handed her a

75

plastic bag full of rose petals. When Alys protested that she had no money, he smiled and said, "Today free, but next time buy double flowers."

Alys stepped into the cemetery and onto a paved path that wound through graves, some with plain tombstones and others with elaborately filigreed ones. Many headstones had epitaphs in both Urdu and English, the scripts of both languages shining like ebony jewels against the gray-veined white marble. She read random epitaphs, placing petals on strangers' graves.

A row of ashoka trees, vibrant and healthy, created a man-planted border, their roots feeding from blood and bones on both sides, and Alys slipped through the trunks and into, it seemed, another cemetery. Dirt paths wound through overgrown vegetation and eroded marble headstones with British names in faded lettering. She walked on, scared now that she was so deep inside the graveyard. Moonlight spread down her back like ice. All was quiet except for crickets and her footsteps, crunching twigs. She saw a form leaning against a wall, an unnatural fiery glow emanating from where a mouth should be.

Alys screamed. The form screamed.

A girl stepped out of the shadows, a lit

cigarette dangling from bony fingers, a scrawny braid curling down one shoulder to her waist. She was wearing red sandals and a purple-and-green *shalwar kurta* topped with a red cardigan with white plastic buttons. Not someone, Alys instinctively knew, her mother was going to think very highly of, for, as was the case with too many people who'd jumped class, Mrs. Binat was often the harshest critic of the class she believed she'd left behind.

"You scared me." Alys put a hand on her beating heart. "I thought you were a ghost."

"Hel-lo. You scared me." The girl spoke in Urdu. "I thought you were a rabid dog. What are you doing here? Are you from the family that has moved into the ruins in front of the graveyard?"

Alys nodded. "Not ruins anymore. It's cleaned up quite well."

"Aren't you Pakistani?" the girl said. "Your Urdu is very poor, even for a Burger."

Alys rolled her eyes at the derogatory term used to describe Pakistanis who predominantly went about their lives in fluent English by Pakistanis who predominantly went about their lives in fluent Urdu or a regional dialect. In local parlance, Alys was an English-speaking Burger and this girl an Urdu-speaking Chapati. Usually the two groups did not reside in the same neighborhoods, but that seemed to be the case here.

"Do you know any local languages?" the girl asked.

"English is a local language," Alys said, switching to English completely.

The girl replied in a stilted English, "Did you people buy the ruins?"

"We own it," Alys said.

"You are a Binat?" The girl switched back to Urdu.

"Yes."

The girl's eyes widened. "And what has brought the Binats to live in Dilipabad?"

Mrs. Binat had forbidden any mention of the family feud, but Alys felt they had nothing to be ashamed about. Also, who cared if people talked? People were going to talk anyway. So she told the girl the truth.

"They took everything?" The girl's face softened.

"Pretty much."

"Kismet, wheel of fortune, luck, destiny, what can one do? By the way, my good name is Syeda Shireen Looclus, but everyone calls me Sherry. What is your good name?"

"Alysba. Everyone calls me Alys."

Sherry held out her hand. Alys shook it.

"Married?" Sherry asked.

"I would be if my mother had her way. You?"

"Still unmarried, much to my mother's distress," Sherry said. "I am an Urdu lang-lit teacher at the British School of Dilipabad."

"A career woman." Alys beamed. "Do you know if your school is looking for English teachers?"

"You want to teach?"

"It just occurred to me."

"BSD is the best school here, and Principal Naheed is very picky. Education level?"

"Second year of undergrad in English literature."

"How old you are?" Sherry asked.

"Twenty."

"You look much younger," Sherry said wistfully. "How old are you really?"

"Twenty." Alys frowned.

"*Chal yaar* — whatever, friend. No need to lie to me, I won't tell a soul."

"I'm not lying. In March, I'll turn twenty-one."

"Really? Hasn't your mother ever told you that you need to pretend to be at least four years younger than your real age? That way you'll age much slower publicly and can stretch out your marriageable years."

"She has, but I think hiding one's age is

stupid, and the only way to defeat ageism is to not comply with it. How old are you?"

"Twenty-eight," Sherry said. "Forever twenty-eight."

"And your real age?" Alys asked wryly. "I won't tell anyone."

"I don't know you to trust you. And you'd better not tell a soul you saw me smoking."

Alys signaled for Sherry to hand over the cigarette pack. A smile spread over Sherry's face as Alys lit one and took a drag.

"There," Alys said. "Now you saw me smoking too."

"*Yeh hui na baat!* That's more like it!"

"Can you finish it?" Alys handed it back to Sherry. "I'm not really a smoker. Not fond of staining my teeth. Also, cancer."

"I'll risk that for now," Sherry said as she put out Alys's barely touched cigarette and returned it to the pack. "Do you want chewing gum?"

Alys took some cinnamon gum to freshen her breath. "I had a couple of friends in Jeddah who smoked — secretly, of course, like you — and I'd join occasionally."

"Will you join me occasionally? I come here every evening after the Maghrib prayers. My mother thinks I'm feeding birds."

"You're twenty-eight or something like

that. You have a job. Your own income and therefore independence. Surely *you* can smoke if you want."

"Good girls don't smoke." Sherry eyed Alys curiously. "Anyway, these mothers only stop dictating your life once you get married."

"True," Alys said. "And then your husband dictates it."

"I'd love to get married!"

"You would?"

"I'm tired of my parents worrying about me," Sherry said, "not to mention that everywhere I go, the first question I'm asked is: 'When are you getting married?' Everyone promises to pray for me. So far no one's prayers have come true, so I'm wondering if they really are praying."

Sherry smiled. Alys smiled.

"Anyway," Sherry said, "I don't want to die without ever having had a husband. I want that phase of my life to begin, but it might never happen. You see, proper proposals for me have dried up." She squatted behind a wide headstone. Alys sat crossed-legged beside her.

"I was engaged twice before," Sherry said, relighting the cigarette Alys had barely puffed. "First to a cousin. I liked him. He liked me. Then he went to Germany on an engineering scholarship and married a German lady for citizenship after convincing his parents that she was a good career move. They have five children now. Boys. They visit off and on. I avoid them completely."

"You're better off without such a person," Alys said, and feeling the intensity of Sherry's disclosure, asked for a cigarette.

"I managed to get engaged a second time, this time to a nonrelative, at my insistence." Sherry handed Alys a cigarette and struck a match. "He wanted to marry immediately, but my mother was undergoing knee surgery and we had to wait. Shortly after our engagement, he passed away. Turned out he'd had kidney problems, which his family had kept from us. His parents were very aged and they wanted a widowed daughter-in-law who could earn as well as look after them. I tell you, God saved me from that terrible fate. But as far as everyone was concerned, I'd driven one man into the arms of a foreigner and another into the mouth of death, so obviously I was *man-hoos,* an ill omen. Then we found out I couldn't have children. Useless Uterus, that's me."

"Don't say that," Alys said, flicking ash onto the path.

"Everyone else does. Basically, until I

started teaching, I was nanny to my sister and two brothers. They're much, much younger than me. After having me — a girl, unfortunately — my mother suffered from years of miscarriages. If my paternal grandmother had had her way, my father would have remarried for a son, but he refused to, and thankfully, through the miracle of praying and *manaats,* my mother was able to produce live births again and, finally, my precious brothers." Sherry took a long drag and looked out into the distance. "Anyway, I still pray that one day my *shehzada,* my Prince Charming, will come. I still get the odd proposal, but they're from either men who come with a dowry list as long as my arm, which my family is in no position to fulfill, or widowers with children looking for a nurse-plus-nanny in the guise of a wife, or divorced men known for domestic abuse or something similar. Listen, tell me, Ms. Burger, what is the English word for a man who is divorced? I know a woman is a 'divorcée,' because that's what everyone is calling an aunt of mine who left her cheater husband."

Alys frowned. "Actually, there's no specific label for a man. In English we apparently live in a world where we only keep track of whether or not a woman is a pigeon."

"Pigeon?"

"Virgin." Alys glanced at Sherry to see how she'd taken the use of the supposedly bawdy word. Sherry was chuckling. "Pigeon is my and my elder sister's code word for virgin."

"I love it!" Sherry said. "Pigeon. Let us pray that one day my pigeonly feathers flutter and I fly the coop."

Sherry and Alys gave each other shy high fives.

"By the way," Sherry said, "my real age is thirty-one. I'm thirty-one years old."

Ten years later, Sherry was forty-one, though as far as the rest of the world was concerned she wasn't a day over thirty-five. Over the years she'd begun dying her skinnier braid and plucking her chin and, when she laughed, which was often, her laugh lines deepened. Yet she still hoped her Prince Charming would come, if only because there was simply no other respectable way for a girl from her class in this country to have sex.

So Sherry reminded Alys as they slipped into the graveyard and headed toward the spot where they'd first met. Sherry cleared leaves off a stone slab and sat down. She lit a cigarette. Alys did too.

"I would," Sherry said, blowing a smoke ring, "like to experience sex before dying, and not just with my hand. *Rishta* Aunty —"

Alys groaned. *Rishta* aunties were the local matchmakers, a perfect job for professional busybodies. Paradoxically, the key to a *rishta* aunty's success was keeping the secrets she learned about prospective clients to herself. Her job was to get people married off, but she did not guarantee happiness or children and she was very clear about the fact that if marriages were decreed in heaven, divorces seemed to be too, and that even spouses in perfect health could die and she should not be made to give a refund for services rendered.

While *rishta* aunties were a regular fixture at Sherry's home, Looclus Lodge Bismillah, Mrs. Binat did not entertain them. Not because she cared that it embarrassed her daughters to be forced to parade the mandatory *rishta* trolleys, prepare cups of chai to display their domestication, or be picked apart by prospective mothers-in-law, but because Dilipabad's *rishta* aunties were not up to standard. To Mrs. Binat's disappointment, they did not have the network or connections to go beyond Absurdities and middle-class Abroads, categories that

Sherry's parents — Bobia Looclus, a home-maker, and "Haji" Amjad Looclus, a super-visor in a factory — were in rapture over.

"*Rishta* Aunty," Sherry continued, "told us this prospective groom-to-be is on the lookout for a nubile virgin. Pigeon I am, nubile I'm not, but *Rishta* Aunty believes this one is my stud of a Prince Charming. He's sixty-one and, despite managing a grocery store, apparently does not possess too big of a potbelly."

"Better to die a pigeon than copulate with a potbelly," Alys said solemnly.

"Clearly," Sherry said, "you're enjoying your hand."

"That I am." Alys laughed.

"Anyway, this particular potbelly has never been married, because he was looking after two unmarried sisters. The sisters recently married two brothers working in Sharjah, and so now he's looking for a bride of his own. He's probably as eager a pigeon to fly the coop as I am. He's fond of mas-sage and being read to, because his eyesight is weak but he doesn't like to wear specta-cles. *Rishta* Aunty told him I was strong and I'm a teacher, so I can read very well and earn. Let's hope that incentive seals the deal."

"Can you please meet the man first," Alys

said, rolling her eyes, "before agreeing to marry him?"

"Not up to me, is it," Sherry said. "I'll wheel out the *rishta* trolley with the expected cake, fruit *chaat,* and *shami kebabs.* I'll make chai for him and the rest of his relatives, who'll have accompanied him for free food. I'll confirm that I've cooked all the food from scratch, which, in my home" — Sherry looked archly at Alys — "*I* will have done. Unlike you Burger girls, I can actually cook and don't just bake for fun."

"Be quiet, Chapati," Alys said. "I don't even bake for fun."

"I'll sit there after having served chai to the potbelly and pretend to be a shy and opinion-less dummy. And on my wedding night I'll turn into a sex maniac, and then he'll divorce me on account of too much enthusiasm, since ardor will imply immorality."

"Or," Alys said, "maybe he'll appreciate that you can't get enough of flying the coop."

Sherry took a long drag. "I hope this prospect doesn't decide to poop in our toilet, like the last one did. Took forever to unclog that mess."

"Here's a mess of a different kind. We received the invite to the NadirFiede circus.

I've wasted all afternoon listening to what gift will make us look rich enough and what we're going to wear in order to captivate eligible bachelors. You know how despicable I think this whole husband-hunting business is."

"Yes," Sherry said, "I'm well aware. *Chalo,* best of luck. Let us hope you and Jena hunt good husbands."

"I don't even want to go," Alys said. "A bunch of himbos and bimbos showing off to each other about who enjoyed the glitzier holiday this year."

"Have you any idea how many people would die to be invited?" Sherry said. "I'd love to just see who in the world is marrying that pain in the bum Fiede Fecker. Do you think Fiede is a pigeon or have she and Nadir Sheh flown the coop?"

"It is a truth universally acknowledged that a good girl ought to keep her mouth shut about whether she's been keeping her legs shut."

"I bet Fiede's been humping and pumping night and day," Sherry said. "But at the wedding, like all good pigeons, she'll pretend her feathers have never fluttered."

"Come with us to the NadirFiede *mehndi,*" Alys said. "Come!"

It was quite acceptable in Pakistan to

bring an uninvited guest to a wedding, for in a gathering of hundreds, what was one more?

"Your mother," Sherry replied, smiling, "will not be happy to have me tag along."

"Mummy will be fine," Alys said, knowing full well that she'd be annoyed. "Please come. The NadirFiede spectacle will actually be fun with you there."

Sherry shrugged an okay.

"Yeah! You're coming with us! And who knows, you might very well meet your Prince Charming at the *mehndi.*"

The friends laughed. They ground out their cigarettes in the grass and popped chewing gum into their mouths. Then, linking arms, they strode out of the graveyard toward their homes.

CHAPTER 5

The Binats parked in the overflow lot and headed to the gymkhana gates for the Nadir-Fiede *mehndi* ceremony. The security guard at the gate beamed when he saw Alys, Jena, Sherry, and Mari. The four women had long been tutoring low-income children for free, and Jena asked the guard how his son's exams had gone.

"Excellent," he said, blessing them with happiness and long lives as he let them in.

"Such a good omen," Mrs. Binat chirped, "to enter such an event with the blessings of a menial. You watch, Alys and Jena, this wedding will end well for both of you."

"Mummy, shh," Alys said, as they joined other guests walking up the candlelit driveway toward the vast grounds and into the wedding *shamiana,* the huge multicolored tent shot through with gold thread. The scent of perfumes and colognes mingled with that of beef *seekh kebabs* and chicken *tikkas* cooking on coal grills. Guests stood in clusters, chattering, and children ran underfoot followed by ayahs preening in last season's castoffs.

The groom and his entourage had yet to arrive. A gaggle of young girls — Fiede's cousins and close friends — sat on the makeshift dance floor in front of the bride-and-groom stage with a *dholak* between them, though clearly none of them knew how to properly play the double-sided drum. Lady was an expert; she elbowed her way into the group, and soon she was play-ing the drum and bellowing Punjabi wed-ding songs — *"lathe di chaddar, chitta kukkar banere, sadda chidiyan da"* — with such gusto and to such ear-shattering whistles that several guests asked if she was Fiede's best friend.

Mrs. Binat spied Fiede Fecker's parents — Mr. Fecker, in a navy raw-silk *kurta,* and Mrs. Fecker, in hideous tangerine organdy — and she and Mr. Binat proceeded to congratulate them. Mr. Fecker shook hands with Mr. Binat. Mrs. Fecker's gargantuan eyelashes, supposedly imported from Milan, were apparently weighing down her eyes, because it took her a moment to recognize Mr. and Mrs. Bark Binat, after which she thanked them for coming before moving on to the next guest.

Mrs. Binat glowed as moneyed folk flitted around. She recognized acquaintances from when she too had been moneyed folk, and she chose to overlook the women's cool greetings. Instead, she basked at the welcome their husbands were giving Barkat. They were embracing him and exclaiming that they hadn't seen Bark-Bark in years, which was true, for Mr. Binat had chosen to become something of a recluse since his elder brother's betrayal.

In fact, Mr. Binat had been reluctant to attend NadirFiede, for fear that his brother and sister-in-law might be there. It was only after Alys reminded him that it was the perpetrators who should be mortified and stay away and not the victim that Mr. Binat agreed to come. As their father stood among old friends, a little bit of his former self returned, and all the Binat girls stood taller as he introduced them to uncles who remarked how much they'd grown and how lovely they'd become. Soon the wives steered their husbands away from Mr. Binat's daughters, and Mrs. Binat, refusing to allow any slight to upset her this evening, proceeded to lead her brood to one of the fuchsia velvet sofa sets arranged around coal stoves.

She was pleased to note the number of eyes following Jena as they walked down the Afghan rugs covering the lawn and into the seating area. She'd dressed her daughter well. Jena was in a dove-gray silk sari, the muted color enhanced with a darker gray sequined blouse and a *kundan*-and-emerald choker set — the gems fake, of course, thanks to Ganju *jee,* but no one was the wiser. At an event where everyone was dressed like a Brazilian parrot, Jena's under-stated elegance as the African parrot stood out. If it weren't for the wretched Tinkle's smear campaign, Mrs. Binat knew, women seeking brides for their sons would have been coming up to her in order to make inquiries about Jena's age, occupation, and intentions for marriage.

Still, Mrs. Binat knew beauty had the potential to defeat the slurs of a jealous relative. Jena had only to sink her hooks into a prospective Rich Man, who would subsequently be so besotted by her looks that he would ignore rumors about her family. Alas, Mrs. Binat thought as she smoothed a wrinkle from Jena's *pallu,* none of her daughters were proficient in the art of hook, reel, grab. In fact, except for Lady, her daughters were discomfited by the very notion of catching a husband, despite the number of times she'd told them that one had to seek out a good proposal as one would a promotion or a comfortable shoe.

It was all this nonsense about falling in love that was making catching a husband unseemly. Of course one must fall in love, but let it initially be the man who falls and then, once his ring is on your finger, you too may allow yourself to fall in love — though within reason, Mrs. Binat always cautioned, for the best marriages were ones where the husband loved the wife more. She sighed. It was her full-time job as a good mother to get her daughters married well, and she was determined to do her duty regardless of all obstacles, even Alys's obstinacy.

Despite Mrs. Binat's copious pleas for Alys to wear a new sari like Jena's, the disobedient girl had dived into the trunk and picked out a lackluster outfit. Couple that disgrace with barely any makeup at an event where women were wearing so much they would have to use scalpels to scrape off the cosmetics. Not that any of her daughters required any makeup, Mrs. Binat thought with pride, but, still, didn't all girls like enhancing their assets? Sometimes she feared Alys was serious when she said she didn't want to get married. What sort of girl did not want to get married? What sort of girl did not want children?

Mrs. Binat had, a few years ago, made Jena, closest of Alys's confidantes, put her hand on the Quran and swear that Alys was not a lesbian. Asking Alys directly would have been useless; she would have defiantly said, "So what if I was?" and given her a lecture. Mrs. Binat had also considered asking Sherry, but she did not trust friends and so did not want to give Sherry any ammunition to start rumors about Alys.

Poor girl, Mrs. Binat thought, as Sherry settled on a sofa. Did she have no other wedding wear but nylon satin monstrosities? The only plus going for Sherry was her skinny body, luckily for her in vogue. But a side effect of being so thin was also to be completely flat-chested, a setback given that even the most *shareef* — pious — of men wanted a wife with some breasts.

Mrs. Binat was rescued from further rumination by Principal Naheed and her two daughters, who were making a beeline toward them. The principal had on a decent Chantilly lace *sari* in a tolerable puce, but those stubby daughters of hers — why in the world had she allowed them to wear *patiala shalwars* with crop-top tunics that made their limbs look like cocktail sausages?

Mrs. Binat rose to air-kiss Naheed, and she decided it was just as well that Gin and Rum displayed zero sartorial sense and sensibility, for that meant even more opportunity for JenaAlysMariQittyLady to shine.

"*Salaain-lai-kum,* Principal Naheed," Mrs. Binat said. "Gin and Rum are looking like visions of perfection."

"*As-salaam-alaikum,* Pinkie," Naheed said. "They're wearing the best of the best. QaziKreations' new line, QaziSensations." Naheed turned to Mr. Binat. "Bark, I see Pinkie continues to look just as dazzling as your daughters."

"Hello, Naheed, yes, Pinkie outshines us all. And how are you? How is Zaleel?" Mr. Binat asked, referring to Naheed's husband, Khaleel, by his nickname.

"Zaleel couldn't make it today," Naheed said. "He was lifting weights this morning and dropped a dumbbell on his foot."

"That's dumb." Mr. Binat guffawed at his own joke. "But let's hope for a quick recovery." Then he returned to surveying the tent for his brother and sister-in-law.

"I must say," Naheed said, "Fiede has outdone herself with the classy décor and arrangement. So striking, so *mashallah.*"

"Striking, *mashallah,*" Mrs. Binat agreed.

Everything was very nice: the soft lighting in the tent, the fresh flowers, the low-backed sofas with faux pearl–encrusted sausage cushions, the heaters, the fairy lights looped around the tent poles, the arrangement of the buffet to be served in a separate tent.

Naheed said, "A friend of Fiede's has started event planning, and Fiede handed the wedding over to her — no charge, of course. But, then, this is how her friend will garner business in the future, for everyone will want Fiede Fecker's event planner to plan events for them. I have always said that the most troublesome students turn out to be the greatest assets, and Fiede Fecker is a true asset to the British School of Dilipabad. Hello, Alys, Jena. What an absolutely breathtaking sari, Jena, and such lovely jewelry."

Jena nodded thanks at the compliments.

"Qitty, have you lost weight? I was expecting a watermelon, but you look like a cantaloupe tonight. You have such a pretty face; why don't you try to lose some of your chunkiness? Look at Lady! Slim 'n' trim!" Naheed said approvingly as Lady rejoined her family. "But, Lady, aren't you cold in sleeveless? Mari, you look very un-fresh compared to your sisters. Sherry, oho" — Naheed gave Sherry a terribly sweet smile

— "*tum bhi pahunch gayee* NadirFiede. You've also managed to make it to Nadir-Fiede."

Sherry flushed, but before she could answer, Gin and Rum decided to greet everyone with air kisses and cries of *"Bon-joor, bon-joor, bon-joor."*

"*Hain?* What?" Mrs. Binat said, air-kissing the fidgety girls. They had so much foundation on, she could smell the chemicals.

"I'm so sick of the girls' French!" Naheed said, clearly not sick of it at all. "Ever since they've earned their fluency certificates from the Alliance Française, it's *parlez vois* this and *parlez vois* that."

"Not *vois,* Ama, *vous, vous,*" Gin and Rum said together. *"Vous. Vous."*

Naheed swallowed a withering reprimand to her daughters. "I keep reminding these two future Dilipabad superstars to stop the French talk with me and wait until they go to fashion school in Gay Paree."

"Gaypari?" Mrs. Binat asked. "*O kee?* What is that?"

"Paris, Aunty, Paris," Rum said. "Paris is also called Gay Paree, because it's fun time all the time and not because of any gay thing, in case you were wondering. Not that there's anything wrong with anything gay. It's becoming very fashionable these days to have at least one gay friend, and we hope to make one once we get there."

Everyone tried their best to look impressed, except Lady, who was genuinely impressed.

"Paris!" Lady squealed. "*Hai*, lucky! *Acha*, you had better give me discounts, because I'm already booking you both for making my *shaadi-ka-jora*, my only stipulation being that I want *motay-motay*, fat-fat, diamantés on the bodice."

"*Ah oui!* Oh yes!" the twins said. "Though we still have to apply to fashion schools in Paris and get in."

"You'll both get in," Naheed said tersely. "Lady, aren't you in a bit of a premature rush to book your wedding outfit? You have four unmarried older sisters ahead of you. Let's hope the next wedding we attend will be Jena's, *inshallah.*"

"*Inshallah,*" Mrs. Binat said. "God willing."

They were interrupted by the unmistakable *dhuk-dhuk-dhuk* of the hired drummers who always accompanied bride-and-groom parties and whose beating drums no one could resist, at the very least, tapping their feet to. Cries arose: "The boy's family is here!" Fiede Fecker's cousins and friends — including Lady, who merrily joined the bridal party — grabbed platters of rose petals and lined up by the entrance.

"Here come the eager pigeons," Sherry whispered to Alys as Nadir Sheh's family and friends entered, dancing to the drummers. Laughter broke loose as petals were showered left, right, and center. The drummers changed beat every few minutes as the family entered, some dancing, some carrying baskets of flowers and trays of mixed sweets, others candles in earthen *diyas,* the oil lamps illuminating excited faces. Nadir Sheh had invited a few of his London college friends, and all were keeping up well with the *dholak* beat.

The bridegroom's party was led to the reserved chairs with red bows in front of the stage, and Nadir Sheh climbed up the stage and settled on one of the two baroque armchairs as if it was a throne and this his coronation. He sat with arms akimbo and legs splayed in his dandy outfit: an orange silk *kurta* topped with a heavily embroidered red waistcoat above a starched-to-death cream *boski shalwar,* and his feet were clad in the pointiest golden wedding *khusse.*

The guests turned for Fiede Fecker's grand entry. Again the drummers drummed up a frenzy as the bride's cousins and friends came in with platters of *mehndi* embedded with bangles, candles, and flowers. They were followed by Fiede's male cousins carrying a palanquin, in which sat Fiede Fecker, peeping through a curtain of marigolds. They rested the palanquin at the side of the stage, and Fiede's father helped her out and led her to the armchair next to Nadir Sheh. Fiede was wearing a vermilion *shalwar kurta* and a yellow *dupatta* pinned strategically to accentuate her long, flat-ironed hair. Fresh rosebud and jasmine hoops dangled from her ears and matched her floral bracelets.

Once the groom and bride were seated side by side, their immediate family members proceeded with the *mehndi* rituals. Nadir Sheh's mother, aunts, and female cousins began to dance a *luddi* around the henna platters they'd brought, circling the platters to the drumbeat and changing their dance steps for each new circumambulation. The guests looked on politely, clapping and chatting among themselves and wondering when the synchronized dances would begin, after which dinner would be served.

There were quite a few BSD students with their families present at the wedding, and they kept passing shyly by Alys, Jena, and Sherry, giggling as students are apt to do when they see teachers out of context. The recently engaged Tahira introduced her fiancé to them. He had an open, honest face and duly informed them that they were all Tahira's favorite teachers. He looked like a nice person, Alys thought, and she hoped he was. She managed to slip in how nice it would be if Tahira might finish high school after marriage, perfectly doable, and she was glad to see that he did not dismiss the suggestion outright.

Rose-Nama, crusader for duty and tradition, was here too. She and her mother had taken one look at Alys, their faces going sour, and had begun to mutter among themselves, Alys was sure, about how the Feckers had invited every *aira gaira nathu khaira* — every Tom, Dick, and Harry — as if it was a *mela,* a funfair, and not the Dilipabad wedding of the year.

"If Fiede sits any closer to Nadir," Sherry whispered to Alys, "she's going to end up in his lap. Nadir's mother looks like she's going to faint over Fiede's lack of decorum."

"So does Fiede's mother," Alys said.

Fiede Fecker was clearly finding it hard to look down demurely, as befit a proper bride-to-be. She was whispering away to Nadir Sheh and boldly surveying the tent to check out who was in attendance. But, then, Sherry noted, she was Fiede Fecker, Dilipabad's honorary princess, and therefore whatever she did would be considered proper and, soon enough, fashionable.

"I hope," Alys said, "Lady doesn't get any ideas from Fiede Fecker. Do you remember how Fiede was supplying marijuana to those girls at school, and the only people who got in trouble were the girls, because Principal Naheed dared not cross Fiede's mother, who insisted Fiede was being framed?"

Sherry nodded. "Fiede's mother would let her get away with murder."

"The only thing they didn't let her get away with," Alys said, "was going to college."

Dilipabad did not have a quality girls' college, and Fiede's parents did not want to send her to a boarding college. Instead, after graduating high school, Fiede was sent on a consolation holiday to Amsterdam, to relatives who lived there. Out on the canal, Fiede's boat bumped into Nadir Sheh's boat. Nadir Sheh, attending college in London, was visiting Amsterdam on spring break. He was attracted to Fiede's long, bleached-blond hair falling prettily onto her big Chanel bag. That Fiede was not bothered about world affairs or feminist rhetoric was the clincher for him.

On her part, Fiede had been enjoying

Amsterdam very much — although the Anne Frank museum had made her very sad — but she was also missing her tribe terribly. Nadir Sheh's upper-class Pakistani demeanor made her feel back home, and his genuine Hermès belt — Fiede had an eye for impostors — signaled to her that he would be someone her family would willingly accept. Though a love marriage, officially, the Feckers were telling everyone it was a purely arranged marriage so that no one could accuse Fiede of being "loose" or "fast."

"That we should all have such happy endings," Sherry said, sighing, "if our boat bumps into someone else's boat. I tell you, Fiede Fecker is not a pigeon, though she's probably done everything but *it,* which makes her a part-time pigeon."

"I agree," Alys said. "Part-time pigeon."

The dances began. Wedding dancing was the one avenue where girls from good families were allowed to publicly show off their moves. Lady, who loved to dance, was having a hard time remaining seated but, since she was neither family nor a close friend, she was not supposed to join in the revelry. As a guest, her role was that of spectator.

Nadir Sheh's friends and family performed a synchronized dance they'd been rehearsing for weeks to a Pakistani number, *"Ko Ko Korina,"* which many guests would deem too obscure a choice for such a high-class wedding but, sigh, Nadir Sheh's family was new money, after all.

Then it was Fiede Fecker's family and friends' turn to perform a dance. They'd chosen the double-entendre Indian song *"Choli Ke Peeche Kya Hai"* — "What Lies Behind Your Blouse" — and were greeted with enthusiastic applause. This was a siren song for Lady, and in a sudden frenzy she leapt onto the floor. Other dancers stopped to stare. Alys yanked Lady off the floor and looked at her sister so ferociously that Lady remained glued to her seat through the remaining dances.

Once the synchronized dances were over, the DJ played requests. Fiede Fecker's friends and cousins started dancing, and Fiede decided, conventions be damned, this was her wedding and she was going to dance too. Who cared *log kya kahenge* — what people said — including her in-laws? And so she made history as the first bride in Dilipabad to dance at her own *mehndi* ceremony. Soon Nadir Sheh and his friends joined the freestyle dancing too.

Mrs. Binat and the other Dilipabadi

matrons looked on and tried to gauge if Nadir Sheh had delivered any fish worth hooking. Gyrating on the dance floor was a cement scion. An owner of a sanitary-napkin company. A hotelier heir. A sugar-mill proprietor — twice divorced, but so what? Money was money. Also dancing was the young owner of the British School Group, recently returned from America.

Naheed was dying to know who the BSG scion was, for Gin's and Rum's sake, but also because she planned to have a few words with him about the rumor that he was going to do away with school uniforms. Was the BSG scion the sweet-looking gangly fellow with a flop of sandy hair? Or the ballerina-looking guy dancing well enough to not be the laughingstock but awkwardly enough to draw chuckles? Who was the chap that looked like a cross-eyed polar bear and was jumping up and down as if he was at an aerobics class? And that elderly gentle-man who kept shaking his bottom too close to the seated young girls — surely he had to be Uncle Sugar Mill. And who was that tall, good-looking boy with the fine eyes?

The food was finally served close to midnight. Ravenous guests rose en masse toward the food tent, where they would serve themselves from either side of the chafing dishes, creating ideal conditions for boys and girls who longed to accidentally flirt and fall in love, eyes meeting over sizzling entrees, fingers caressing fingers as serving spoons were exchanged. The Binats entered the tent, a smaller rainbow replica of the larger one. Lady and Mrs. Binat headed straight for the buffet serving Italian food and loaded their plates with lasagna localized with green chilies and garlic bread infused with cumin. Sherry and Qitty headed for the Chinese buffet, piling their plates with egg fried rice and sweet-and-sour chicken. Alys, Jena, Mari, and Mr. Binat helped themselves to the Pakistani buffet, their plates soon full of beef *biryani,* grilled *seekh kebabs, tikkas,* and buttered *naan.*

At the dessert table, Jena, Alys, and Sherry wished they'd eaten a little less dinner. Still, they managed to sample everything: *gulab jamuns* in sweet sticky syrup, *firni* gelled in clay ramekins and decorated with edible silver paper, snow-white *ras malai,* tiramisu cups and lemon custard tarts, *kulfi* ice cream and sweet *paans* from a kiosk preparing them fresh on the spot, the bright-green betel leaves stuffed with shredded coconut, betel nuts, fennel, rose-petal jam, sugar syrup, and then folded into perfect triangles.

Jena was taking a dainty bite of an unsweetened *paan* when she was approached by two girls with cascades of highlighted hair. Some extensions, for sure, she thought, and a healthy amount of makeup, just shy of too much. They were dressed exquisitely in heavily embroidered *lehenga cholis* with their flat midriffs bare, and diaphanous *dupattas,* clearly the work of an established designer. Jena noticed their single-strap matte-silver heels. She'd been searching for shoes like these, but all she'd been able to find were horrendous wide-strapped glittery platforms.

"Where did you get your shoes?" Jena asked, smiling her admiration.

"Italy," one of the girls said. "I love the detailing on your sari blouse and border. Whose is it?" She rattled off a few designer names.

Jena shook her head. "No designer. My tailor, Shawkat. He has a small shop in Dilipabad Bazaar."

"Oh, I see." The girl's face fell for a second. "I'm Humeria Bingla — Hammy."

"And I'm Sumeria Bingla — Sammy," said the other girl. "Actually, Sumeria Bingla Riyasat. I'm married. Happily married."

"Jena Binat," Jena said. She proceeded to

introduce Alys, Mari, and Sherry. Hammy turned to Sherry with a huge smile.

"Are you Sherry Pupels from the Peshawar Pupels clan?" she asked. "The politician's wife?"

"No," Sherry said. "I am Sherry Looclus from Dilipabad, born and bred."

Alys would swear Hammy-Sammy's noses curled once they realized that Sherry was not the VIP they'd mistaken her for.

"Hi." It was the sweet-looking sandy-haired fellow.

"And this," Hammy said, turning as if the interruption was preplanned, "is our baby brother, Bungles."

"Fahad Bingla," he said.

"Bungles," Hammy said firmly. "Because, when we were children, he kept bungling up every game we'd play, right, Sammy?"

"Right, Hammy," Sammy said.

"And," Hammy said, "he'd still keep bungling up if Sammy and I didn't keep him in check."

Bungles laughed and shook his head. He held his hand out to Jena. Jena shook it and Bungles held on for a second too long. Jena blushed. Bungles shook hands with Alys and Sherry, but Mari wouldn't shake his hand, because, she said, Islam forbade men and women touching.

"Are you *all* very Islamic?" Hammy said.

"Clearly not," Alys said, a little annoyed, though she wasn't sure whether it was at Mari's self-righteous piety or Hammy's supercilious tone. "Anyway, this is Pakistan. You've got very religious, religious, not so religious, and nonreligious, though no one will admit the last out loud, since atheism is a crime punishable by death."

"What a font of knowledge you are, babes!" Hammy said. "Isn't she, Sammy?"

"She is," Sammy said, as she turned to a stocky man lumbering toward her with a cup of chai. "All, this is my husband, Sultan 'Jaans' Riyasat. He's thinking about entering politics. Jaans, all."

Jaans gave a short wave before plopping into a nearby chair, his stiff *shalwar* puffing up around him. He patted the empty seat beside him. Sammy glided over, perching prettily, ignored the fact that Jaans was taking huge swigs from a pocket liquor flask. She proceeded to take elegant sips of her chai.

The out-of-town guests had come to Dilipabad to attend the *mehndi* ceremony tonight and the *nikah* ceremony the next day and were staying at the gymkhana.

"So basically, babes, we're bored," Hammy said. "We got into Dilipabad two days ago, because Nadir wanted to make sure everyone was here, but there's literally nothing to do. We went to that thing this town calls a zoo, with its goat, sheep, camel, and peacock. And we went to the alligator farm and stared at alligators, who stared back at us, and I told them you can't eat me but I'll see you in Birkin. And Nadir and Fiede arranged for a hot-air-balloon tour over what amounted to villages and fields."

"The hot-air balloon sounds like fun," Alys said. "A bit of Oz in Dilipabad. You know, *The Wizard of Oz*?"

"Babes, for real, it was all green and boring," Hammy said. "What do you locals do for fun in D-bad?"

"We have three restaurants," Jena said. "And a recently opened bakery-café, High Chai."

"Oh dear God!" Sammy said. "Fiede took us there yesterday."

"There was a hair in my cappuccino," Hammy said. "A long, disgusting hair."

"And the place smelled like wet dog," Sammy said.

"We've been multiple times and everything was quite lovely," Jena said. "Nothing but the scent of freshly baked banana bread. And the staff wore hairnets and gloves."

"Oh my goodness, Jena!" Hammy took Jena's hand and stroked it as if she was speaking to a child. "The hair was bad enough, but the Muzak was some crackly throwback tape that played 'Conga' and 'Girls Just Want to Have Fun' on repeat. Get with it, D-bad. It's the year 2000."

Alys was suddenly offended on behalf of "D-bad."

"I'm sure the hair was an aberration," she said. "And you should have asked them to change the songs."

"Oh," Hammy said. "We abhor being a bother!"

"Yes," Sammy said. "We're guests. Passers-through. If you locals are happy with the state of things, why should we try to change anything? We can live without fun for a few days. Right, Hammy?"

"Right, Sammy," Hammy said. "Boredom is a bore, not a killer."

"And what," Alys asked, "according to you constitutes fun?"

Before Hammy-Sammy could answer, Lady, Qitty, and the fine-eyed guy on the dance floor descended upon the group at the same time. Alys glanced at him. His eyes were intensely black, with thick lashes their mother always claimed were wasted on men, as was his jet-black hair, which fell neatly in a thick wave just below his ears. He was taller than Bungles and had broader shoulders. He frowned and glanced at his expensive watch, and Alys noted that he had sturdy forearms and nice strong hands. Lovely hands.

"Hello," Lady said. She was carrying a bowl full of golden fried *gulab jamuns.* "Have you tried these? To die for. Isn't this the best wedding ever? I have a good mind to tell Fiede to get married every year."

"Is that so?" Hammy said. "I'm sure Fiede will be thrilled at your suggestion. And who are you?"

"Aren't you," Sammy said, "the girl who crashed the dance floor?"

Lady nodded, unabashed, even though her sisters cringed.

"I'm Lady, their sister." Lady pointed to Jena, Alys, and Mari. "And this is our other sister, Qitty."

"I can speak for myself," Qitty said. "Hello."

"But a moment ago," Lady said, "you told me you'd eaten so much you could no longer speak."

"Because I didn't want to speak to you," Qitty said.

"Qitty!" Alys said. "Lady!"

"Ladies' Room," Jaans called from his

chair. "Everyone wants to go to the Ladies' Room. Is it open?"

"Oh, you!" Sammy smacked her husband on his hand. "Such a joker."

The guy with the intense eyes and lovely hands, Alys noted, was watching as if he'd decided the entire world was a bad comedy and it was his punishment to witness every awful joke.

"Bungles," he said, "if you're done entertaining yourself, can we —"

Bungles interrupted him. "This is one of my best friends, Valentine Darsee."

"Valentine," Hammy said, "say a big hearty hello to the sisters Binat and their friend Cherry."

"Sherry," Sherry said, flushing.

"Sherry," Hammy said. "My sincere apologies."

Darsee seemed to be taking his time giving them a big hearty hello, Alys thought, but before he could get to it, Lady began to laugh uncontrollably.

"Valentine!" Lady doubled over. "Were you born on Valentine's Day?"

Spittle sprayed out of Lady's mouth, and Darsee and Hammy jumped out of the way, revulsion on their faces.

"Lady!" Jena said, mortified.

"Oops!" Lady wiped her mouth with the

back of her hand. "Sorry. Sorry."

"I'm sure you are," Hammy said. "But I'm not sure I'm getting the joke. Valentine is such a romantic name."

Everyone waited for Darsee to say something, but after several moments Bungles spoke up.

"Valentine's late mother," Bungles said, "was a big fan of Rudolph Valentino, and she named him Valentino. The staff at the hospital mistook it for Valentine and, by the time anyone checked, the birth certificate was complete and so that was that, right, Val?"

Valentine Darsee gave a curt nod. It was unclear to Alys whether he couldn't care less if they knew the origin story of his name or whether Lady's spittle had caused him severe trauma.

"Same thing happened with Oprah," she offered in a conciliatory tone.

"Pardon me?" Darsee said, as if he was seeing her for the first time and not liking what he saw.

"Oprah. She was named Orpah, after a character in the Bible, but her name was mistakenly recorded as Oprah." Alys added, "I read it in *Reader's Digest,* I think, or *Good Housekeeping.*"

Darsee turned to Bungles. "I'm going to

check in with Nadir for the night and then head back to our room."

He left without a smile, without a "pleased to meet you," without even a cursory nod. Hammy at least nodded at the group before running after him. Lady decided to get more *gulab jamuns* and dragged Qitty with her. Sammy and Jaans turned to each other. Bungles explained, sheepishly, that Darsee had recently arrived from Atlanta, where he'd been studying for an MBA, and was still jet-lagged. Alys and Sherry exchanged a look: Valentine Darsee was the British School Group.

"Jena," Bungles said. "Can I get you some chai? Dessert? Anything?"

"Jena," Sherry said, "why don't you and Bungles Bhai go get chai together?"

Bungles thought this a fabulous idea, and Jena, with no reason to refuse, walked with him to the tea table, where teas, pink, green, and black, were being served.

"That was obvious," Alys said. "A great 'grab it' move. My mother will be so proud of you."

"You and Jena need to listen to your mother once in a while," Sherry said. "Clearly Bungles Bhai is interested in Jena, and she needs to show a strong interest in return."

"She just met him," Alys said. "Two minutes ago."

"So?" Sherry said. "If she doesn't show interest, a million other girls will."

"If he's going to lose interest because she's modest, then perhaps he's not worth it."

"Of course he's worth it. And aren't you the sly one to use the word 'modest.' "

"Huh?"

" 'Modest sanitary napkins for your inner beauty, *aap ke mushkil dinon ka saathi,* the companion of your hard days,' " Sherry said, spouting the jingle that played during the animated advertisement for Modest sanitary products. "Bungles, Hammy, and Sammy are Modest. They own the company. I recognize them from interviews. And soon our Jena will be Mrs. Modest."

"You'll be naming their children next." Alys shook her head. "They barely know each other."

"Plenty of time for them to get to know each other once they're married."

"I think," Alys said, "better to get to know each other before deciding to get married."

"Big waste of time," Sherry said. "Trust me, everyone is on their best behavior until the actual marriage, and then claws emerge. From what I've gleaned, real happiness in marriage seems a matter of chance. You can marry a seemingly perfect person and they can transform before your eyes into imperfection, or you can marry a flawed person and they can become someone you actually like, and therefore flawless. The key point being that, for better or for worse, no one remains the same. One marries for security, children, and, if one is lucky, companionship. Although," Sherry laughed, "in Valentine Darsee's case, good luck on the last."

"I can't believe Lady!" Alys said. "No one deserves a spittle spray. Actually, I take that back. Hammy probably does deserve it."

Ten minutes later, Alys believed Darsee deserved it too. She'd gone to congratulate Fiede and was about to climb down off the stage when she heard Bungles's and Darsee's voices. Their backs were turned to her and, despite knowing it was a bad idea to eavesdrop, Alys bent down to fiddle with her shoe.

"*Reader's Digest*?" Darsee was saying. "*Good Housekeeping*? She is neither smart nor good-looking enough for me, my friend."

"I read *Reader's Digest*," Bungles said, laughing.

"Yes," Darsee said, "sadly, I know."

"You have impossible standards in everything," Bungles said. "Alysba Binat is perfectly attractive. But you've got to admit, Val, her elder sister is gorgeous."

"She is good-looking. But, please, stop foisting stupid, average-looking women on me."

In the car on their way back home, Alys announced what she'd overheard. She laughed as she recounted Valentine Darsee calling her "stupid," "average-looking," and "neither smart nor good-looking enough." However, Alys was not one to lie to herself: His words had stung. Valentine Darsee was handsome and he was wealthy, but obviously his upbringing had lacked classes on basic manners and etiquette: He was rude, he was disdainful, and he thought altogether too much of himself.

Mrs. Binat agreed. She was most indignant. Never before had a single person doubted the beauty of her girls.

"I hate Valentine Darsee," Mrs. Binat declared, and proceeded to inform everyone of the Darsee family's less-than-stellar background. Valentine's mother was a dey Bagh, this was true, the crème de la crème. But his father's family was another story. Although the Darsee clan had accumulated an immense fortune via the army, they did not come from noble stock. They were neither royalty, nor nawabs, nor even feudal landowners like the Binats. The Darsees descended, Mrs. Binat announced, from *darzees* — tailors — and at some point their tradesman surname of Darzee had morphed into Darsee, or else, she suggested, squinting, an ancestor must have deliberately changed Darzee into Darsee on official certificates.

"I wish you wouldn't bring up everyone's lineage all the time," Alys said. "Who cares?"

"Good society cares," Mrs. Binat said. She turned from the passenger seat, where she sat in Qitty's lap, in order to glare at Alys. "Let this be a lesson to you to never attend another function not looking your absolute best. And don't you dare sit in the sun any longer."

"I like my complexion dark," Alys said decisively.

Mrs. Binat sighed. "Gone case."

"Oh God," Qitty groaned. "If Valentine Darsee thinks Alys is not pretty and a frump, he must think I'm ugly and a lump."

"I can assure you," Lady said, "Valentine Darsee was not looking at you. No one was."

"No one looked at you either," Qitty said, "except when you laughed like a hyena or embarrassed yourself by spitting or gallivanting onto the floor like a dancer-for-hire."

"Shut up, *behensa* — buffalo," Lady said.

"You shut up, *'Choli Ke Peeche,'* " Qitty said.

"Both of you, shut up," Mrs. Binat said. "For God's sake, is this why I went through pregnancies and labor pains and nursed you both and gave myself stretch marks and saggy breasts? So that you could grow up and be bad sisters? How many times must I tell you: Be nice to each other, love each other, for at the end of the day, siblings are all you have. Qitty, you are older than Lady. Can't you just learn to ignore her?"

"I'm barely two years older than her," Qitty sputtered. "We may as well be the same age."

"Stop laughing, Lady," Alys said. "Between spitting and dancing uninvited, what you did was unacceptable."

"But *'Choli'* is such a good song," Lady said.

"All it takes is a good song for you to lose self-control?" Alys asked.

"What about Fiede Fecker?" Lady demanded. "She crashed her own dance floor."

"She's Fiede Fecker," Sherry said. "She can do whatever she wants to do."

"I want to be Fiede Fecker too," Lady

said, angry tears appearing in her eyes.

"Fiede Fecker's mother-in-law looked most unhappy," Sherry said.

"I was unhappy," Mari said, "at the dancing and singing, especially in an unsegregated gathering."

"Oh God!" Lady said. "The high priestess has begun!"

"Mari, if Allah forbade mixed company," Mr. Binat said, without taking his eyes off the road, "then holy pilgrimages would be segregated."

Mari decided to use her inhaler because she didn't know what to say.

"Live and let live, Mari," Alys said encouragingly.

"You're such a hypocrite, Alys," Lady said. "You don't let me 'live and let live.' "

"You humiliated us, Lady," Jena said quietly. "You humiliated me. What must Bungles and his sisters be saying about us."

"Jena, don't be angry with me," Lady said. "I apologized, didn't I? Which is more than that fat man, Jaans, did after calling me 'Ladies' Room.' "

"Jaans is hell-bound for sure," Mari muttered.

"So is that arrogant Darsee," Mrs. Binat said, "*darzee ka bacha,* son of a tailor."

"The truth is," Sherry said, balancing on

Alys's knees in the cramped car as Mr. Binat swerved to avoid a donkey in the road, "whether Darsee descends from *darzees* or *dhobis* is immaterial because, at present, he is A list, and who can blame him for being proud and thinking no one is good enough for him?"

"I'd allow him a smidgeon of an ego," Alys said, "if he hadn't destroyed mine."

"He was having a private conversation, Alys," Jena said. "Not that any of what he said is true, but you weren't meant to hear it, and I'm sure he'd be upset to know that you had and were hurt by it."

"Jena," Alys said, "can you please stop supposing people are nicer than they are?"

"Our Jena is such a sweet soul," Mrs. Binat said.

"Doesn't Darsee know pride comes before a fall?" Alys asked. "Who the hell does he think he is!"

"Your boss's boss," Sherry said solemnly, "as it turns out."

"I'll resign," Alys said.

"You'll do no such thing," Mrs. Binat said sharply. "Barkat, tell your brainless daughter that she'd better not do anything impulsive. If anything, she should be asking for a raise."

Mr. Binat caught Alys's gaze in the rearview mirror.

"Alysba, my princess," he said, "why are you letting some spoiled rich boy cause you a single second's upset? You are not stupid. You are not unattractive. You are so smart. You are so beautiful. Let him look down on *Reader's Digest* and *Good Housekeeping*. You should be proud that you are an equal-opportunity reader and will read whatever you can get your hands on — highbrow, middlebrow, lowbrow."

"Prophet Muhammad, peace be upon him," Mari said, "is said to have said, 'He who has in his heart the weight of an atom of pride shall not enter paradise.' In my humble opinion, pride is a fairly common sin, because everyone thinks very highly of themselves. And vanity is no different. We are vain because we want others to regard us as highly as we regard ourselves. He's hurt your pride, Alys, because you are vain. In that respect, you and Darsee are the same."

"Be quiet, Mari," Mrs. Binat said. "How can you compare your sister to that egotistical descendant of tailors, no matter how elite his schooling. But, his friend, Fahad Bingla — *ahahahaha,* perfection. All the girls were looking at him, and he was looking at you, Jena."

Jena blushed.

"Bungles seems very sweet," Alys said. "But his sisters are not as nice as they pretend to be."

"I disagree," Jena said. "I thought Hammy and Sammy were very nice."

"They were very nice to *you*," Alys said, "and when someone is nice to you, of course you are bound to think they are nice."

"Bungles's parents," Mrs. Binat said, having gotten the full story from gossiping matrons, "live in California. His mother is an anesthesiologist and very active in the Pakistani community, and his father made a fortune in start-ups. Fahad Bingla's elder brother, Mushtaq, works with their father and is married to a lawyer named Bonita-Hermosa."

Years ago, the Bingla family had made a trip to Lahore to get in touch with their roots, and the parents had decided to leave behind the eight-year-old Hammy-Sammy and seven-year-old Bungles, under their grandparents' tutelage. The siblings had returned to America for college, but after graduating they'd returned to Lahore, because that was home for them.

Hammy and Sammy had long noticed a need for affordable feminine hygiene products in Pakistan and, with Bungles on board, the three siblings "borrowed" money from their parents and set up Modest. The company soon outperformed their modest expectations, thanks to God's blessings, their hard work, and the demand for good-quality, reasonably priced sanitary napkins and adult diapers. Also, Mrs. Binat had been told, they regularly threw good parties and get-togethers and thus became popular on the social scene.

However, not hailing from a pedigreed background could have its drawbacks, no matter having attended the best of schools, and so Sammy had married Sultan "Jaans" Riyasat, a shabby-chic nawab — meaning he came with a coveted surname but zero money. The union turned Sammy and her future children into Riyasats and, thanks to her, Jaans came into money once again. Hammy was on the lookout for an equally illustrious catch.

"As for Fahad Bingla, he has chosen Jena." Mrs. Binat beamed. "And mark my words, by tomorrow, *inshallah,* she will be engaged to him. We'll throw a fancy func—"

"Pinkie," Mr. Binat said. "Can you please wait until this Bungles fellow proposes before planning functions."

"You proposed to me at first sight," Mrs. Binat said with quiet pride. She had lucked out on looks alone, and it was the defining moment of her life.

"That was a different era," Mr. Binat said. But he smiled blissfully, for he was forever tickled at having pulled off a love-at-first-sight marriage in a time where arranged marriage was the norm.

"You watch," Mrs. Binat said, with a knowing nod. "Fahad 'Bungles' Bingla will propose to Jena tomorrow during the *nikah* ceremony. I am certain of it — otherwise, I promise you, I will eat my shoe."

CHAPTER 6

The next day dawned sunny but cold. Mr. Binat decided that he needed to recover from the previous night's stimulations and was not going to attend the *nikah.* Mrs. Binat did not argue, for if she allowed him to miss this, then he would have to agree to attend the final ceremony, the *walima,* in Lahore. Mr. Binat, oblivious to his wife's calculations, happily went into the garden to inspect his spider plants, his fingers tenderly smoothing the variegated, long leaves as he wiped them free of debris.

The Binat girls spent the morning beautifying themselves in the courtyard. Mrs. Binat was very strict when it came to beauty regimens and only allowed homemade products. She'd risen early and whipped up face masks of rosewater and ground chickpeas for Jena, Alys, and Lady, who had oily skin, and for Mari and Qitty, who had dry skin, she added a drop of almond oil into the mixture.

Mrs. Binat sat her daughters before her and vigorously massaged their hair with organic cold-pressed mustard oil, on which she'd spent a pretty penny. Jena wordlessly took the special hand mask made for her from oatmeal and lemon juice, which would soften her hands since, her mother insisted, they were going to be the focal point tonight on account of the soon-to-be-acquired engagement ring. The waxing woman arrived and duly waxed each girl, gossiping the whole time, whether they cared for it or not. Tailor Shawkat arrived in case their outfits required last-minute alterations.

Mrs. Binat's choices for the girls' attire this evening were long flowy chiffon *anarkalis* with *mukesh-* and *zari*-embroidered bodice and hem, matching *dupattas* paired with matching silk *thang pajamas* and jewelry courtesy of Ganju *jee,* and topped with expensive shawls. Mrs. Binat wanted Jena to once again stand out as the epitome of purity and had picked for her white chiffon — paired, however, with a real diamond set. Hillima was handed the five outfits to iron and, because she wanted the girls to dazzle, she diligently pressed out each wrinkle.

After she was done, Hillima laid out each

girl's outfit on her bed. Jena was finishing up her prayers, and after folding the prayer rug, she thanked Hillima. She was terrified, she said. She should be, Hillima replied; grabbing a man was much harder than it sounded, but all their combined prayers should deliver positive results, and, reciting a quick prayer, she blew it over Jena.

Closer to midafternoon, as the girls began to bathe, Mr. Binat scrubbed the soil off his hands and prepared to drive his daughters to Susan's Beauty Parlor for their hair appointments. Although Mrs. Binat had been willing to spend money on a driver's salary, she'd ultimately decided against the hire, because having Mr. Binat drive the girls around was one of the few ways she could compel him to leave the house. Alys was the only one not going to Susan's for a blowdry. Anyway, Alys seldom went to Susan's for anything. In fact, Mrs. Binat was quite sure that her silly daughter would discard the teal chiffon she'd picked for her and instead choose something dowdy. Clothes were women's weapons, Mrs. Binat often told Alys, but God forbid that girl heeded her words. And so Mrs. Binat was enormously surprised and delighted when she saw Alys take an interest in her appearance for the first time in a long time and hand

Hillima the teal chiffon to iron.

Alys found herself slipping into her mother's chosen outfit, jewelry, and black *pashmina* shawl, one of ten in various colors Mrs. Binat always thanked God she'd had the foresight to purchase when she'd had money to spend on pure *pashminas* and *shahtooshes*.

Alys sat before her dressing table and applied liquid cat-eye liner on her upper lids, a nice flick of mascara, and painted her lips with a red pencil that deepened her tan. Unlike her sisters, who were getting their long hair blow-dried into the desirable waves or straightened, Alys rubbed lavender-scented gel though her hair and finger-dried her tight curls. Lady, returning from the parlor in big hair, took one look at Alys and whistled, a compliment she usually reserved for Jena, who was looking ethereal in her white chiffon ensemble and diamonds.

Come evening, Alys drove them through a thick fog to the gymkhana. Since Mr. Binat and Sherry were not going — the potbellied suitor was scheduled for a look-see that evening — there was plenty of space in the car, which automatically quelled a few spats between Lady and Qitty. Also, the sisters had tacitly agreed to get along tonight on account of it being the night one of them was finally going to get engaged.

At the gymkhana, a red carpet led the Binats to the main entrance, where Mr. and Mrs. Fecker welcomed guests into the great hall. The hall was festooned with curtains of golden gauze and marigolds galore, and illuminated by bright yellow lighting. Round tables were topped with pleated cream cloths and crystal and yellow rose centerpieces. A perk of the Binats' punctuality was being able to choose a good table, and Mrs. Binat headed for one close to the wedding stage, where the nuptials would take place. Once her daughters were seated, she caressed Jena's cheek and declared that it wouldn't be long now and she was sure it would be a big and sparkling solitaire.

Waiters in white uniforms with gold buttons were serving fresh seasonal juices, and soon the Binats were sipping foamy pomegranate juice. Slowly, the hall began to fill up. Men arrived in suits and ties and women in multitudinous loud hues, their ears, necks, wrists, and fingers drowning in gold, diamonds, rubies, sapphires, and emeralds. As Mrs. Binat suspected, her daughters once again stood out, this time like graceful nymphs among the gaudy and the gauche.

"There should be a mandatory note," Mrs. Binat mumbled to her daughters, "on wedding invitations, saying: 'Please do not try to outbride the bride.' "

"Mummy," Lady said, starting in on her third glass of juice, "you are always so right. We will put that note on Jena's wedding invite and also on mine."

A ripple went through the guests at the news that the governor, or at least one of his family members, was to make a special guest appearance, as was a general who might or might not be harboring dreams of coups and presidential palaces. But Mrs. Binat had eyes only for Bungles's arrival.

The groom and his retinue arrived respectably late, amid the customary fanfare of beating drums and rose-petal shower. Nadir Sheh, in a custom-made *sherwani* with a tall crimson turban, graced the stage and sat on a velvet sofa. Fiede Fecker, soon to be Fiede Sheh, had all this while been secreted away in a bridal waiting room with her excited friends, impatiently anticipating Nadir's arrival. When Fiede made her grand entrance, everyone fell silent.

"Someone must have had a few words with Fiede Fecker," Lady whispered to Qitty, because Fiede was walking with her head bowed like an obedient bride, or else the bulky crimson *dupatta* she had pinned to her bouffant was weighing her down.

Flanked by her parents, Fiede took her time walking down the red carpet all the way to the stage, because one only walked this walk once. The usual murmurs from the guests accompanied her: "beautiful bride," "stunning outfit." Though the truth was, Mrs. Binat muttered to Jena, Fiede's crimson-and-gold *gharara* was too ornate for her small frame. She looked like a child hiding in a pile of brocade curtains.

Fiede's mother picked up her daughter's voluminous skirt and helped her up the stage steps and seated her next to Nadir Sheh. It was announced that Fiede had not asked for the right of divorce on her marriage certificate, since to ask for this right was to begin one's marriage inauspiciously. It was also announced that Fiede had agreed to an amount of *haq mehr* equivalent to the sum given during the Holy Prophet's time by grooms to their brides and that she had agreed to this now-paltry figure because she was a pious woman and not at all money minded.

"Easy to accept pennies and not be money minded when you have money," Mrs. Binat snorted, "especially when you are the sole heir to your parents' fortune."

As soon as the bride and groom were seated and professional photographers began taking group shots, members of Nadir Sheh's entourage were free to do as they pleased, and Bungles's eyes sought out Jena.

"Here he comes," Mrs. Binat said, squeezing Jena's arm as she nodded at Bungles striding toward them with his sisters at his heels. "Here he comes with the ring."

Such was their level of expectation that all the Binats were shaken when Bungles did not drop to one knee and ask Jena to be his wife. Jena was so disoriented that it took Bungles saying hello thrice before she was able to respond.

Hammy and Sammy, looming behind their brother, took Jena's delayed response as an obvious lack of interest and hoped this would jolt Bungles out of his crush. Last night the sisters had made inquiries into Jena's family. Jena's own reputation was blemish-free, but unfortunately, thanks to her parents, she still came stained. Jena was a Binat from her father's side, but they were the penniless Binats of the clan; her father was ineffectual at business and estranged from his successful elder brother, which implied that Jena's family did not value family ties. As for Jena's mother's lineage: beyond disastrous.

"How was your day?" Alys asked Bungles

and Hammy-Sammy in order to give Jena a moment to recover.

"Excellent," Bungles said. "Darsee and I played a game of squash, enjoyed a very nice Continental breakfast by the gymkhana lake, and I took a nap."

"Sammy and I," Hammy said, "were recommended some horrid beauty parlor, where the girl flat-ironing my hair didn't know what she was doing and nearly burned off my face."

"Where did you go?" Qitty looked up from the paper napkin she'd been doodling on.

"Best Salon."

Mrs. Binat made a face. "Whoever recommended Best Salon must be getting a commission."

"We had a good mind not to pay," Sammy said, "but that girl probably never received any training, so not her fault. But, still, you have to send a monetary message, and so we didn't leave a tip."

After a second of silence, Lady said, "Next time go to Susan's. She's the best."

Susan's was Dilipabad's premier beauty parlor, run by a family whose patriarch had fled to Pakistan during the Chinese Cultural Revolution and never returned.

"Thank God there'll be no next time,"

Hammy said. "We're out of D-bad first thing tomorrow morning. Bungles can't wait!"

"That's not true." Bungles gazed at Jena.

"That's what you said," Hammy said. She happily observed that Jena was playing with the beads on her handbag and seemed not at all bothered by who was going and who was coming.

"All I said was it will be nice to be home again," Bungles said.

"Tomorrow morning?" Mrs. Binat said very loudly, as if the decibels of her voice alone might compel Bungles to propose. She quieted at the announcement that it was *nikah* time.

Everyone in the hall hushed as the maulvi read out loud the relevant verses from the Quran. He turned to Nadir Sheh: "Do you accept Farhana Farzana Fecker for your wife?" Nadir said *qabool hai* — "I accept" — thrice and signed the marriage certificate. The maulvi turned to Fiede Fecker: "Do you accept Nadir Nauman Nazir Nizam Sheh for your husband?" Fiede Fecker said *qabool hai* thrice and signed the marriage certificate.

The Feckers and Shehs embraced to cheers of congratulations, and Nadir's mother and Fiede's mother hugged with tears in their eyes. Turning to the newly-weds, they immediately demanded a grand-child. Nadir said that could be arranged. Fiede blushed on cue. Everyone laughed. How cute!

"A few naughty uncles," Lady whispered to Qitty and Mari, "must surely be imagining Fiede in her wedding lingerie."

Qitty began to sketch a naughty uncle on a napkin.

"Disgusting!" Mari hissed at Lady and Qitty. "You both need to get your heads examined before you really head to hell."

Bungles returned from participating in the rituals of *doodh pilai* — in which Fiede took a ladylike sip from the glass of milk meant to give the couple fertility and strength on their wedding night and Nadir guzzled down the rest — and *jhootha chupai* — in which Nadir had ended up distributing a lot of money to Fiede's friends and cousins in order to get them to return his shoe, which they'd hidden — and dragged a chair as close as he could to Jena's. Hammy and Sammy also rushed to sit close to Bungles. And here came Jaans, who was regaling Darsee with tales of recent financial scandals that had befallen otherwise-upright Pakistanis.

"Valentine," Hammy said, jumping up,

"take my seat."

Alys watched in amusement as Darsee took her seat. He did not say hello to anyone.

"You look dashing," Hammy said to Darsee, and he did, in a raw-silk ivory *shalwar kurta* with a teal mirrored waistcoat. "I swear, you should think about modeling just for fun. I can already see you on a Times Square billboard."

Alys longed to say that instead of modeling, it might be better if Darsee enrolled in an etiquette class or two.

Lady whispered to Qitty, "Hammy is making you-you eyes at Darsee."

"Gigantic you-you eyes," Qitty whispered back. "Her *dailay* — eyeballs — are going to pop out."

"Hammy is right, Valentine," Sammy said. "Times Square. Modeling a watch. Or underwear."

"*Oye, Begum,* Wife, stop talking about other men's underwear!" Jaans said. "I'd look dashing too if it wasn't for you."

Apparently Jaans was wearing ill-fitting attire because Sammy had packed his preweight-loss suit by mistake and, even worse, handed away his brand-new custom-made suit to their driver. Sammy had asked the driver to return it, except he'd already sent it to his village, to a cousin who was leaving for a job in Hong Kong.

"That will be one happy bastard strutting around in my suit," Jaans said. "Who can train my wife in housewife skills?"

"Not a housewife," Sammy said testily. "I run a company."

"Jaans, dude," Bungles said, "company or no company, pack your own clothes."

"Bungles *beta*," Mrs. Binat said, "isn't Jena looking lovely tonight?"

"Yes." Bungles turned red. "She is."

"Mummy! Stop it!" Jena said.

"What stop it? If a mother cannot point out the obvious, then who can? Bungles, you must stay in Dilipabad for another few days. And if you need anything . . . but why should you need anything? God has blessed you with everything, except . . ." And she glanced at Jena.

If Jena wished to turn invisible, Alys did too.

Darsee's mouth fell open. Never in his life had he heard such a blatant hint. Neither had Hammy and Sammy. Darsee could tell the sisters were stunned. His eyes traveled across the table and connected with Alys's, who just happened to be looking in his direction at that very moment.

Now that Darsee had, for the first time,

looked directly in Alys Binat's face, it occurred to him before he could stop it that she had luminous eyes. It occurred to him that even though she was the opposite of everything that was considered beautiful in these parts — an alabaster complexion, long hair, light eyes, a simpering femininity — she was uncommonly attractive. Alys held his gaze for a moment and then, blinking in obvious disinterest, turned away to talk to some girl.

Darsee was well aware of all the ruses gold diggers practiced these days. The most popular, Jujeena, his only sister, had informed him, was a pretense of disinterest. Although it seemed to Darsee that Alys Binat truly did not care. He found himself stepping a little closer to Bungles and, as it so happened, in eavesdropping range of Alys's conversation.

Alys was talking to an ex-student, Sarah, one of her pride and joys, who'd badly wanted to go to college abroad. Her parents had set the condition that she could go only if she got a full scholarship, and Alys had helped Sarah get one. Sarah was in her final year and diligently studying economics plus literature. At the moment she and Alys were discussing potential thesis topics.

"You can," Alys suggested, "ask if friendships in Austen are more complex between friends or sisters. Or explore who jumps class in Austen and whose class cannot be forgiven, overlooked, or worked around. Or compare colonizer Babington Macaulay and Kipling's 'England's Jane' with a 'World's Jane,' a 'Pakistani Jane,' a 'Post-Colonial Jane,' Edward Said's Jane. What might Jane make of all these Janes? Discuss empire writing back, weaving its own stories."

Alys could ignore it no more. She turned to Darsee. "You're clearly enjoying our conversation. Care to join in?"

"No," Darsee said, "but I would like to know, how do you know all this?"

"*Reader's Digest*," Alys said, "and *Good Housekeeping*."

Darsee stared at her. Principal Naheed had arrived to say hello in the last seconds and she said, "Alys, don't be silly! Valentine, have you met Alys and Jena yet? Jena teaches English to the middle grades at BSD and Alys the upper grades."

Gin and Rum, dressed again in QaziSensations and looking like disco balls, had been told by their mother to sound their most intelligent in front of Valentine Darsee, and so they proceeded to show off their knowledge of international books with titles they'd memorized.

"Miss Alys, do you remember," Gin said, "when you made us join that summer book club? I still recall Leslie Marmon Silko's story 'Lullaby' and Bi Shumin's 'Broken Transformers.' "

"You made us read," — Rum squinted — *"The House on Mango Street* by Sandra Cisneros, 'Désirée's Baby' by Kate Chopin, and 'Everyday Use' by Alice Walker. And then you made us read that novel *The Blackest Eye."*

"The Bluest Eye," Gin said.

"Yes." Rum beamed. *"The Bluest Eye.* We were all so disturbed by the incest in it."

Naheed changed colors.

"What my brilliant daughters mean," she stuttered, "is that Alys is such a forward-thinking teacher who never shies away from any subject."

"I see," Darsee said.

Alys had no desire to know what Darsee saw. Taking the gift envelope from her mother, she strode to the stage. Horrid man! Listening to her with that mocking look. And thoughtless Gin and Rum for mentioning that particular novel, over which Naheed had very nearly been forced to fire her because so many parents had turned up at the school. Thankfully the author, Toni

Morrison, had won a Nobel Prize in Literature, and that had calmed them down.

Darsee watched Alys leave, and he allowed Principal Naheed to distract him with her view on school uniforms. By the time dinner was served — a buffet to rival the fare at the *mehndi* ceremony the night before — Alys was barely on his mind. As he ladled a fragrant mutton *biryani* onto a plate, Hammy joined him.

"Babes, you must try the *rogan gosht,*" she said, "before Lady and Qitty gobble it all up. I've never seen greedier creatures. Jaans thinks Alys is a lesbian. Agree?"

"*Why* would Jaans think that?"

"Her hair, babes, her hair."

"That's ridiculous," Darsee said. "I happen to think her cut accentuates her eyes."

Hammy's rather ordinary eyes grew wide. Darsee instantly realized his mistake and, nonchalantly popping a mutton *boti* into his mouth, waited for Hammy's response.

"My heartfelt congratulations," Hammy said, "on finding your soulmate in D-bad."

"So, so predictable," Darsee said, shaking his head.

Hammy gave a feeble laugh. "I'm beginning to wonder if the Binat girls really do practice magic. First my brother is bewitched. Now you."

"I'm not bewitched or any such thing."

"Your future mother-in-law," Hammy said, "the oh-so-charming Pinkie Binat, will be so thrilled to have not one but two sons-in-law to paw."

Darsee grimaced. "Not prime mother-in-law material."

"Nor are those creatures sister-in-law material!"

"Agreed," Darsee said.

Hammy was relieved not only that Darsee had not complimented Alys further but that he'd acknowledged the appalling nature of the Binat family.

"I wish Bungles would wake up from Jena's spell or whatever you want to call it."

"It'll pass," Darsee said. "His crushes, unlike mine, always do, which is why I've learned to not fall as easily as he does."

"And who is your current crush?" Hammy asked, a little too quickly.

"No one," Darsee said. "I'm too busy with Jujeena. I should not have gone to do my MBA. I neglected her."

"Don't be so hard on yourself," Hammy said. "I bumped into your sister a few times this last year and she seemed happy living with your aunty Beena.' "

"Beena Aunty took excellent care of her,

but" — Darsee stopped — "she has her hands full with Annie."

"How is Annie's health?"

"So-so," Darsee said. "Anyway, I'm back now, and my top priority is my sister, as well as getting involved with the British Schools. No time for crushes."

"Please knock the same sense into Bungles, at least when it comes to Jena Binat."

"I'll try," Darsee said.

However, when it came time to leave the *nikah* ceremony, Bungles asked Jena if her family was planning to attend the *walima* ceremony in Lahore. When Jena nodded, Bungles instantly turned to Mrs. Binat: He, Hammy, and Sammy were going to a charity polo match for breast cancer at the Race Course Park, and could Jena accompany them as their guest?

CHAPTER 7

The next morning Sherry visited the Binats and, over chickpea *chaat* and chai, Lady and Qitty excitedly informed her of Jena's invitation to the polo match. They'd been discussing, nonstop, Bungles's failure to propose to Jena, juxtaposed with the fact that he must really like her to have invited her to the polo match, to which Mrs. Binat had so readily and graciously given her permission.

"Of course he likes Jena," Mrs. Binat said, fishing out a spicy potato from the *chaat.* "Likes, my foot. He loves her. He's just a shy boy, but, then, not everyone can be bold and daring the way your father was when he asked for my hand in a heartbeat."

Mr. Binat entered with one of his wife's shoes in hand.

"But, Pinkie," he said gaily, continuing a previous conversation, "you guaranteed this Bungles fellow would propose last night and that if he didn't you would eat your shoe.

Come on now, eat up."

"Oof." Mrs. Binat pushed away the shoe her husband was thrusting at her. "Barkat, you really must get out more. Your attempts at humor are becoming third-class. Put down that filthy shoe. He's taking her to the polo match in Lahore, where, I guarantee you, he will propose."

"Mummy," Jena said, "you led me to believe he was going propose yesterday, and I was so nervous I could barely look at him or speak to him properly. I'm going to go to the polo match with no expectations."

"You'll see," Mrs. Binat said. "You'll return from the polo match with a diamond ring so big your finger will fall off."

"Tauba," Mr. Binat said, helping himself to the *chaat.* "Dear God, what a thing to say."

"Look, Jena," Sherry said, pouring extra tamarind chutney into her bowl, "you need to steer Bungles Bhai."

"Steer him?" Jena said. "Is he a bull?"

"Jena, you need to do no such thing." Alys scowled.

"She does." Sherry looked from Jena to Alys. "Jena, trust me. You need to drop little hints such as 'I'm getting so many proposals' or 'I'm scheduled for a look-see and if it works out I'll be getting married.' You know, hints to hurry him along."

148

"Vomit, puke, *ulti,*" Alys said.

"Alys is a fool," Mrs. Binat said. "Sherry, you are a girl after my own heart and know well the game of grab-it."

"Thank you, Khala," Sherry said. "Although if I knew how to grab it that well, wouldn't I have grabbed a husband by now?"

Everyone observed a moment of contemplation.

"Jena," Sherry said, sipping the last of her chai, "follow my advice and if Bungles Bhai has got any smarts, he'll realize that you are hint-dropping, and then he'll be in no doubt that you like him."

"How about *I* just propose to *him*?" Jena said, annoyed. "That should clear up any confusion."

"In Islam," Mari said, looking up from the tennis match on the sports channel, "women can propose, since Hazrat Khadijah proposed to the Prophet Muhammad, peace be upon him."

"Hai!" Mrs. Binat slapped her chest lightly. "No one follows religious example properly in this country. If only girls from good families could propose, how easy everything would become. Instead, we have to wait until the man decides it is time."

"May I remind everyone," Alys said,

squashing a chickpea with her fork, "that Jena and Bungles literally met a day ago. They don't even know if they like each other, much less love."

"Love at first sight, followed by rest of life to sit around falling in like. That is the farmoola," Mrs. Binat said.

"Formula," Mr. Binat said. "Form-you-la."

"Far-moo-la. That's what I said." Mrs. Binat extracted a hairpin from her bun and used the looped end as a cotton swab. She ignored her daughters' aghast looks. "How long does it take to fall in love? Your father looked at me, instant love" — she snapped her fingers — "and immediately he sent Tinkle to find out who I was and, the very next day, proposal."

Mrs. Binat regaled them with a detailed account of their honeymoon in Chittagong Hills and Cox's Bazar beach in current-day Bangladesh. It had been her dream to go there, and their father had made it come true.

"He was such a hero," she preened. "Every day, flowers, frolic, and I love you, I love you."

"Daddy was a lover boy," Lady said, her eyes shining. "A romantic hero."

"I was indeed," Mr. Binat said bashfully,

150

for he quite loved to hear what a hero he'd been.

"Times have changed," Alys said. "No one gets married like that anymore. Love doesn't work like that anymore, if it ever did."

"Love is love and will never change its nature," Mrs. Binat said. "One look is all love needs. One look."

"I can't wait to fall madly in love," Lady said. "*Acha,* Jena, do you love Bungles?"

Jena tossed a cushion at Lady. "Mind your own business. And forget love-shove — why aren't you studying your algebra? Your teacher at school told me you're very good with equations if only you'd apply yourself."

"Who cares about equations?" Lady said. "I don't need equations to be happy. I need love to be happy. I'm not going to marry anyone unless I fall in love, love, love. First comes love, then comes marriage."

"First comes marriage, *then* comes love," Mrs. Binat said sternly as she summoned the giggling, eye-rolling Lady to snuggle with her on the sofa, after which mother-daughter switched the TV channel from sports — despite Mari's outcry — to the Indian film channel, where Sridevi and Jeetendra were dancing-prancing-romancing around trees to the ludicrous love song "Mama Mia Pom Pom." After a few sullen minutes, Mari curled up on her mother's other side, even as she asked God's forgiveness at wasting her time over frivolous fare. Qitty joined at the far end of the sofa and opened up *Drawing on the Right Side of the Brain.* Jena took out some grading. Alys and Sherry murmured that they were going to feed birds and headed toward the graveyard.

In the graveyard, Alys and Sherry took a path that led to a cluster of family tombs in a roofed enclosure. They sat in a patch of late-afternoon sunlight on the cracked marble floor. Alys told Sherry she'd caught Darsee looking at her a few times.

"*Oof* Allah, he likes you," Sherry said, taking out her cigarettes. "He loves you. He wants to marry you. He yearns for you to have his arrogant babies."

"Ho ho ho. Ha ha ha. You should become a comedienne." Alys shook her head. "He was, no doubt, checking to see how crooked my nose is, how crossed my eyes are, and whether I have all thirty-two teeth intact. I was talking to Sarah —"

"How is she?"

"Good. Her mother is adamant that she drop future PhD plans, because, she insisted, no one wants to marry an overeducated girl in case she out-earns her husband, which will drive him to insecurity and subsequently divorcing her. I told Sarah to forget her *khayali* nonexistent husband's self-esteem and work toward her dreams. We were talking about thesis topics and Darsee asks me, 'How do you know all this?' Literally. As if I'm some ignoramus."

"What did you say?"

"*Reader's Digest* and *Good Housekeeping*."

Alys and Sherry exchanged high fives.

"How did it go with the potbellied Prince Charming?" Alys asked.

Sherry gave a small laugh. The potbellied prince had brought along sixteen family members, for whom Sherry and her younger sister, Mareea, had to scramble to fry up double, triple batches of kebabs. Then, after serving everyone chai, which took a good hour, Sherry was told she had to take a reading test. The potbellied prince produced a conduct book of Islamic etiquette, *Bahishti Zewar* — "Heavenly Ornaments" — and made her read out loud, in front of everyone, the section on how to keep oneself clean and pure before, during, and after sex.

"My father left the room, lucky him." Sherry exhaled a smoke ring. "But no one thought to stop the reading. I suppose they were picking up tips."

"You should have just stopped," Alys said.

"The reading was the easy part," Sherry said. "Next test was massage."

She'd had to massage his ropy, sweaty, oily neck for several minutes while he shouted, "Left, right, upper, lower."

"You should have pinched him," Alys said.

"I did," Sherry said. "I even dug my nails into him. But he seemed to enjoy both."

The real shock came when he was leaving. He'd looked straight at her, removed his dentures, which *Rishta* Aunty had neglected to inform them he wore, and wiggled his tongue in an obscene manner.

"Anyway, he rejected me." Sherry lit another cigarette with trembling fingers. "He telephoned to inform us that, although I'm a competent reader, my fingers do not possess the strength he, at age sixty-one, requires, and also I'm too thin and don't earn enough to compensate for my lack of a chest."

"Would you have married the potbellied pervert if he'd said yes?" Alys asked quietly.

Sherry sighed. "There's no dashing Bungles waiting to de-pigeon me. I'm down to either perverts fluttering my feathers or a lifetime of listening to my brothers groan and moan about having to look after me in my old age. These are the same brothers whose diapers I changed, snot I wiped, whom I taught to walk and talk. I'm tired of them treating me like a burden and I'm sick of my parents' morose faces, as if every day I remain unmarried is another day in hell *for them.* Honestly, Alys, Jena needs to *chup chaap,* without any frills, make her intentions clear to Bungles, before it's too late."

"It is a truth universally acknowledged," Alys said, "that hasty marriages are nightmares of *bardasht karo,* the gospel of tolerance and compromise, and that it's always us females who are given this despicable advice and told to shut up and put up with everything. I despise it."

"Me too," Sherry said. "But I'd rather *bardasht karo* the whims of a husband than the scorn of my brothers. Not that I blame my brothers. It's my duty to get married and I'm failing. I'm a failure."

"It's not your duty and you're not a failure." Alys planted a kiss on Sherry's cheek. "You and I will live together in our old age, on a beach, eat *samosas* and scones, and feast on the sunsets. We won't need anyone to support us or feel sorry for us. Your brothers and everyone else will instead envy our forever friendship."

"Outstanding fantasy." Sherry inhaled the

last of her cigarette. "You won't believe what my mother did after the potbellied pervert telephoned. Instead of thanking God that I'd escaped a fate of being reader and massager in chief, she starts berating me for not massaging him properly and so losing another proposal. I swear, I wish my mother would just disappear for a while."

"Better yet, I know how to make you disappear." Alys put her arm around Sherry. "We're going to Lahore for the NadirFiede *walima,* and you're coming with us."

CHAPTER 8

Mrs. Binat would have been utterly displeased about Sherry's inclusion in the Suzuki for the two-hour trip to her elder brother's home in Lahore, but she was so excited about Jena's and Bungles's future nuptials that she did not complain too much. Before they knew it, they were parking in the driveway of the six-bedroom house located in Jamshed Colony — unfortunately no longer a fashionable part of town, much to Mrs. Binat's chagrin, but thankfully not one of the truly cringeworthy areas either.

When they heard the Binat car honking at their gate, Nisar and Nona Gardenaar came rushing out to the driveway with their four young children — a daughter, Indus, and sons, Buraaq, Miraage, and Khyber.

"Now, this family," Alys said to her mother, "is what liking your spouse and compatibility look like."

"It was love at first sight, is what it was," Mrs. Binat said.

Years ago, Nona's older brother, Samir, had been cohorts with Nisar during their medical residencies. Nona had been studying at the National College of Arts, and one day Samir's motorbike broke down and he borrowed Nisar's to pick her up from college. As thanks for lending his bike, Nisar was invited to their house for dinner. The somber boy with a shy smile found Nona's family — her parents, her brother, and Nona herself, with her freckles and sugar smile — a very pleasing contrast to his younger sisters, Falak and Pinkie, who seemed obsessed with fashion, celebrity gossip, and who's who.

Under one pretext or another, Nisar began to frequent Nona's home. He wanted to be a doctor. She wanted to be an artist. Her father worked at a travel agency, and her mother was an art teacher in a government school, and Nona wanted to teach art too. Her goals were to earn enough for art supplies and, once in a while, to go out for a nice meal. Nisar warned his sisters that they may not be impressed by Nona, but, to his pleasant surprise, Falak and Pinkie fell in love with Nona and her total disinterest in where they came from and who they were now.

By then Falak was struggling to find some happiness with the bad-tempered under-achiever she'd married, who was very proud at having no ambition other than playing cards and carrom and smoking charas and who knew what else with his equally feck-less friends, and finally she'd been forced to look for a job. Through a friend's recom-mendation, she joined a bank as a teller and felt forever guilty at not being a stay-at-home mother to her only child, Babur.

In turn, Pinkie died a million deaths whenever Tinkle and her friends openly mocked her name, Khushboo, by calling her "Badboo" and laughed at her mispronunci-ation of words or brands — "Not paaanda, darling, pan-da." "Not Luv-is, dear, Lee-vize." "Goga, you must hear Pinkie's latest gaffe. Pinkie, say 'Tetley' again. What did I tell you, Goga, 'Tut-lee!' " How utterly lost and stupid Pinkie would feel as Tinkle and clique conversed about Sotheby's and Ascot and the Royal Family and "oh, how very mundane it all was at the end of the day." Pinkie derisively referred to her in-laws as *Angrez ki aulad* — Children of the English — even as she envied them their *furfur* flu-ency in English and swore to herself that

159

her children would also master the language and customs and never be mocked on that score.

"Both my poor sister and my rich sister are unhappy in their own ways," Nisar had told Nona one evening as they sat on the metal swing in her parents' garden. "After our parents passed away, as their brother, I vowed to take care of them whenever needed, and, Nona, I want to continue with that vow once married."

That had been the beginning of Nisar's proposal to Nona, and she said yes. Nona's parents cautioned her that marrying out of one's religion could be extra-challenging, but having had their say they welcomed the Muslim Nisar. Falak and Pinkie did not care that Nona was Christian. They did care that she adored their brother and was kind to them.

It was Nona who babysat Falak's son until she was promoted to bank assistant manager and was able to hire a reliable woman to look after Babur during the day. It was Nona who dropped the high-end fashion magazines into Pinkie's lap and told her to study them, until Pinkie, with her killer figure, could confidently out-style anyone — especially Tinkle, who Nona had disliked on sight, what with her ample art collection but scant knowledge of who she'd had the disposable income to collect.

Over the years, Nona would get annoyed over Falak's lack of pride in being a working woman and her rants against her husband but refusal to subject Babur to a "broken home," as well as over Pinkie's obsession with marrying her daughters into great wealth, but overall she loved her sisters-in-law and all their children.

Nona hugged the Binats and Sherry, then put her arms around Jena and Alys, and they all headed into the living room. The house smelled of vanilla and chocolate. The maid, Razia, brought in tea and the mini-cupcakes Indus had made especially for them.

"Your daughter is going to outdo you one day, Nona," Mr. Binat said, wagging his finger before following Nisar into the garden to take a look at a guava tree.

"She must!" Nona proclaimed. "That's what children are for, aren't they? To become better versions of their parents. Girls, what news?"

"*Hai,* Nona *jee!*" Mrs. Binat said, shaking with excitement. "We have struck gold. Gold! Such a good boy! And sisters are also mod-run, but in a good way."

"Not mod-run, Mummy," Lady said.

161

"Mod-ern."

"Modrun. Modrun. That's what I'm saying," Mrs. Binat said. She proceeded to inform Nona that she was sure Bungles had chosen the upcoming polo match as the proposal venue so that he could ride up to Jena on a horse, just like a prince in olden-day films.

"*Hai,* Mummy," Lady said, as she took the hairbrush Indus brought her and began to French-braid her young cousin's hair. "I also want someone to propose to me astride a horse."

"Me too," Qitty said as Khyber dropped crayons into her lap.

"Not me," Mari said as she, Buraaq, and Miraage opened up the Snakes and Ladders board game. "Imagine the man is proposing while the horse is pooping away."

The kids started to giggle at the thought of a poopy horse.

"Jena," Nona asked gently, "are *you* expecting a proposal?"

Jena glanced at her mother. "I know he likes me."

"Likes you!" Mrs. Binat said. "Any sane person can see he is badly in love with you."

"And his family?" Nona said. "Are they also badly in love or might they have some other girl in mind?"

"If they have some other girl in mind," Mrs. Binat said indignantly, "then Bungles will be no better than that hoity-toity Darsee, who insulted Alys's looks."

"And intelligence," Sherry said, adding five spoons of sugar to her milky tea.

"But," Mrs. Binat said, "Bungles is not like Darsee. Girls, tell Nona how Bungles is one in a million."

The girls proceeded to tell her.

"*Chalo,* okay, Jena, good for you," Nona said after she heard them out. "If I could bake a magic cake that would make him propose this very minute, I would."

Three years ago Nona had baked an Arabian Nights cake for her daughter's birthday at school. The children had fallen silent at the sight of the fondant bed with yellow marzipan pillows, the strawberry pantaloons–clad storyteller, Scheherazade, and her blueberry pantaloons–clad sister, Dunyazade, on the bed, surrounded by crystal-sugar characters from the stories: Aladdin, Sinbad, Ali Baba, and Prince Shahryar turned chocolate giant with licorice whiskers. The teachers cut the cake carefully, a little apprehensive that, like many things in life, it would look beautiful from the outside but would turn out to be tasteless from the inside. It was delicious.

163

Word of mouth spread so fast that Nona was soon inundated with orders.

"You need to charge," Falak and Pinkie urged Nona. Soon, white boxes with lace calligraphy saying NONA'S NICES were being sold to weddings, birthdays, graduations, anniversaries, Quran starts and finishes, Eids, Iftars, Christmases, Holis, lawn launches, fundraisers, et cetera. Nona and Nisar were, Falak and Pinkie often marveled with dazed pride, minting money.

"I'm doing more charity cakes," Nona said. "Birthday cakes for orphans at the Edhi Foundation, at Dar-ul-Sukun for the disabled, and I've added Smileagain Foundation for acid-attack survivors."

"Aunty Nona," Mari said as she rolled the dice, "you are surely going to heaven."

"Truly," Sherry agreed. "You are."

"You live the life I'd like to lead," Jena said softly. "To be able to contribute happiness to the less fortunate."

"Jena," Mrs. Binat said, "concentrate on grabbing Bungles, and, once you're married, you can do whatever you want."

"That's a lie." Alys gave a derisive laugh. "The dangling carrot to lure us into marriage."

"Lost cause," Mrs. Binat muttered, gazing sorrowfully at Alys. "You will die of loneliness if you don't get married."

"I'll never be lonely," — Alys gave a satisfied sigh — "because I'll always have books."

Nona smiled.

"Nona *jee,* don't encourage this *pagal larki,* mad girl," Mrs. Binat said, and she turned to Jena. "Jena, *beta,* I'm sure Bungles will allow you to —"

"Allow!" Alys shrieked. "Vomit, puke, *ulti.*"

"Yes, allow," Mrs. Binat said firmly. "And don't you dare ever encourage your sisters to disobey their husbands. You want them divorced and also relying on books for companionship and God knows what else! Jena, as I was saying, Bungles will *allow* you to aid every charity under the sun, because that's what begums do in order to keep themselves busy and give purpose to their lives. Do not scoff, Alys! Their need to keep busy is what helps those in need. I too was going to be a busy begum, devoting my life to good causes; instead, here I am, a nobody."

"Pinkie," Nona said, exchanging a glance with Alys, "even nobodies can devote their lives to charity."

"Yes, but when you are somebody, then you have the satisfaction of being told how wonderful you are," Mrs. Binat said, long-

165

ingly. "Look at that *kameeni,* horrible Tinkle. People think Tinkle is such a great humanitarian, but I know what she really is — fame hungry, her road to importance paved with carefully calculated good deeds. Nona *jee,* the polo match Jena is invited to is tomorrow afternoon, and I'd rather she arrive in your good car than in our crap car. Will yours be available?"

The next morning a winter sun shone down on Lahore as Jena and Alys climbed into the good car and Ajmer, the driver, backed out of the driveway. He was a sweet man with a weak memory for addresses, but Nona and Nisar could not muster the heart to replace him.

"*Aur,* Ajmer," Alys said, sitting back in the car, "how are you?"

"Very good, *baji!*" Ajmer smiled, his henna-dyed red mustache swallowing his upper lip.

"Your children?" Jena asked.

"My son is beginning his medical degree in Quetta and my daughter is finishing up tenth grade. Her dream," Ajmer said proudly, "is to become a doctor like her brother, and Nisar Sahib promised to help her get into medical school too."

"Every girl should have a father like you,"

166

Alys said. But she also wondered how benevolent Ajmer would have been had his daughter wanted to be an actress or singer or model. She sighed as she recalled how bitterly Lady had cried at their father forbidding her to model. For the truth was that behind every successful Pakistani girl who fulfilled a dream stood a father who allowed her to soar instead of clipping her wings, throwing her into a cage, and passing the keys from himself to brother, husband, son, grandson, and so on. Alys felt a headache coming on.

"Ajmer, turn the music on please," she said, and within seconds the car filled with an exuberant "Dama Dam Mast Qalander."

As they entered a busy thoroughfare full of cars, rickshaws, motorbikes, bicycles, everyone honking madly, Alys straightened Jena's hoop earring. Since Bungles, Hammy, and Sammy had already seen Jena in plenty of Eastern wear, thanks to NadirFiede, Mrs. Binat had declared it was time for some Western wear. They'd settled on boot-cut dark-denim jeans, a black-and-white striped turtleneck, and a chocolate leather jacket, which Jena had seen in *Vogue* and had tailor Shawkat replicate. Jena wanted to wear sneakers, but Mrs. Binat had handed her a pair of chocolate pumps originally brought for Qitty and so slightly large for Jena but still a decent-enough fit.

"I'm nervous," Jena said to Alys as the car inched closer to the Race Course Park. "I wish you were coming with me."

"You'll be fine," Alys said. "I plan to walk for an hour or so before returning home. Do you want me to send Ajmer to you before I head home? That way, if you want to return, just make an excuse that an emergency has come up and he's come to get you."

"Yes!" Jena said. "I'd rather face Mummy's wrath than sit there if I'm feeling awkward."

The car glided through leafy suburbs before turning in to one of the park's back lots and, from there, taking another turn onto a wide dirt road. The dirt road led up to Aibak Polo Ground, where privileged children learned to horse ride and some of them grew up to play polo on the impeccably mowed green ground.

The polo match had begun, and Alys and Jena could see majestic horses galloping at full speed toward goals, their coats polished by the sun, their riders in crisp whites wielding their mallets as they went after the wooden ball. Jena got out of the car and teetered for a moment on her shoes before turning resolutely toward the polo ground and clubhouse.

Ajmer drove back down the dirt road and parked amid a row of other good cars. Alys got out and told him she'd be back soon. Ajmer nodded. Pressing PLAY on her Walkman — she and Jena had recorded English songs on one side of the tape and Pakistani songs on the other — she hummed to "Material Girl" and jogged to the clay track that ran around the periphery of the Race Course Park. Once an actual racecourse, until betting on horses was banned for political expediency in the name of Islam, the course had been converted into a sprawling public park.

Alys passed the Japanese garden and pagoda. Every few steps the park gardeners pruned leaves and deposited seeds, their *shalwars* pulled up over ashy knees, their sun-wrinkled legs planted firmly on the earth. She nodded a greeting as she walked by, and they nodded back. She thought of her father and the calm and refuge he'd found among flora and fauna. She passed by a couple seated on a bench, eating oranges in front of impeccably manicured flower beds. The veiled woman was feeding the bearded man with her fingers, and a citrus scent floated over the jogging track from the orange peels gathered in her lap.

Stopping to stretch her calves, Alys gazed at some boys playing cricket. The wickets were red bricks set upright on their narrow ends. The fielders stood waiting in their jeans and knockoff T-shirts. The bowler was good; the batsman was nervous; the rest was history. She switched the tape to side B, and Nazia Hassan's seductive "Aap Jaisa Koi" came on, followed by "Disco Deewane." Nazia and her brother, Zoheb, were the first Pakistani pop singers Alys and Jena had heard and loved in Jeddah. Nazia had died earlier that year, and the sisters had mourned her passing.

Alys jogged by the artificial lake with paddleboats chained to one end for the winter and climbed up the steep man-made hill. Standing at the summit, she caught her breath as she looked out at the landscaped park, at the children in the playground, at groups of young men studying or napping, at the flock of sparrows in the blue-gray sky.

A little over an hour later, as she neared the polo ground, Alys hoped Jena was having a good time. She wiped sweat off her forehead and stepped into the parking lot. Where was the car? Her eyes swept over the rows. Ajmer had parked by the turnstile entrance. She was sure of it.

"*Suno,* bhai — listen, brother," she asked a driver leaning against a Civic, "have you seen a black Accord? A driver with a red mustache?"

The man shook his head. He called out to another driver, who informed Alys that the man she was referring to had driven away ages ago. In fact, right after she'd gotten out.

Alys stared. "Did he say where he was going?"

"Not to me."

"Oh my God," Alys said to no one in particular. Hadn't she told Ajmer to remain here? She had. Didn't he know he was supposed to wait for her to return from her walk? He did. Maybe he went to buy some cigarettes. Or to the toilet. But why would he take the car to drive to a toilet when the park had public toilets?

Alys bit her thumb. Even if she caught a rickshaw and went home, she could hardly leave Jena stranded and frantic when she wouldn't be able to find the car, or Ajmer. And Alys couldn't call Jena once she got home, because she didn't have the polo club's phone number. She shook her head in frustration as she marched up the dust road toward the polo ground. She knew she looked a sight, with her hair plastered to her face, her sneakers caked with mud, armpit sweat stains, and no *dupatta,* because she didn't believe in wearing one — men should avert their eyes from women, rather than women being forced to cover themselves — and oh, she must stink.

Still, Alys was taken aback at the degree of hush that fell over the polo-match spectators when she appeared. A solid block of designer sunglasses looked her up and down, saw she was not one of them, and turned back to the field.

Alys scanned the bleachers.

"Excuse me," she finally said loudly, "I'm looking for Fahad, Humeria, and Sumeria Bingla."

And who should rise, in culottes and a Swarovski-embellished cardigan, but Mrs. Nadir Sheh — aka Fiede Fecker.

"They're in the clubhouse," Fiede said like a queen addressing a peasant. "You may enter from the back, or the front."

Alys chose the front entrance. If the spectators wanted to gawk at her, then she would give them ample opportunity to do so. Past the bleachers, past the chairs, past sponsors' banners, past overdressed youth, past oily uncles and grande dames with facelifts, until she arrived at the front entrance and went down the steps into a hall.

She immediately saw Jena. She was perched on a sofa, her bare foot resting on a stool. Bungles squatted beside her, holding an ice pack to her ankle. Hammy and Sammy hovered over them. Jaans was sipping from his liquor flask. Darsee towered over them all.

"What happened?" Alys said, hurrying to her sister.

Everyone turned at her voice. Relief flooded Jena's face.

"Alys! Babes! Oh my goodness," Hammy said, "are you all right? You look like a horse dragged you through a swamp."

"I was walking," Alys said. "In the park."

"Walking?" Sammy said. "In the park? Without a *dupatta*?"

"Jena," Alys said, ignoring them, "what happened to your ankle?"

As it turned out, a divot-stomping session and Jena in Qitty's heels.

"Her entire ankle turned," Bungles said, worry etched on his face. "She needs an X-ray. I went out a couple of times to look for your car in the parking lot but couldn't find —"

"Alys, where is our car?" Jena managed to ask through her pain.

"I don't know," Alys said, baffled. "Ajmer is MIA. I hope he's okay. Is there a phone here?"

"I've been trying to call Uncle's," Jena said. "Busy signal."

Darsee took a flip phone out of his pocket and held it out to Alys. "Use this. Everyone should get one. Very convenient, especially in emergencies."

Alys had seen a few people carrying them. Principal Naheed had one. Alys had not used one before and looked at it for a moment.

"Dial zero-four-two," Hammy said, "and then your home number."

"Hammy doesn't have one yet," Jaans said, "but she knows all about it."

"You don't have one either," Hammy snapped back.

"I'm waiting for Sammy to buy me one."

Sammy said, "Why don't you go to work and earn it yourself?"

"*Oye,*" Jaans said, "don't get too uppity or I'll spank you."

"And I," Sammy said, "will withhold your pocket money."

"Anyone can make money," Jaans said. "Your company could go down the drain, baby, but my lineage will always remain. In this marriage, I contribute everlasting gains."

"You can take your lineage," Sammy said, "and shove it up your rear end."

Jaans flushed. "You better not get fat. Ever."

"Fuck off, Mr. Potato," Sammy said, jabbing her husband in his spare tire.

"If I'd known you were capable of such vulgarity, I would've never married you."

"You knew," Sammy said. "You need to stop drinking for two minutes in order to realize how lucky you are I married you."

"It's bad wives like you who cause good men like me to turn to drink. I know it's Hammy who's been poisoning you with all this women's rights crap."

Hammy hissed, "Sammy has a mind of her own, you know."

"Oh, shut up, Jaans," Sammy said. "I was no different when we were dating."

"Quit it," Bungles said. "Both of you. Jaans, don't speak to my sisters like that."

Alys returned Jena's quick pleased look. She too was heartened to see that Bungles had defended his sisters.

"Dating is different, Sammy." Jaans scowled. "Once you are lucky enough to become a wife, the rules change."

"Oh, come on, Jaans!" Darsee said. "That

mentality really needs to change."

"It does," Bungles said, "and in the meantime, Jena is in pain and does not need to be subjected to you two fighting. Alys, please call your home."

Alys took Darsee's flip phone as fast as she could, making sure to not accidentally touch him. Stepping outside, she was relieved when her mother answered on the first ring.

"Thank God you picked up. Jena has been trying to call for ages."

"Why?" Mrs. Binat said. "Has he proposed?"

"No! And Ajmer has disappeared."

"I know," Mrs. Binat said gleefully. "I told him to drop you both off and come back home so that Bungles has ample time to propose."

"What!"

"And, Alys, you too are aging by the day. You also need to get married, and plenty of eligible bachelors must be at the polo match to come to your rescue when they find out you need a ride home."

"For your information, Mummy, Jena has twisted her ankle and is in a lot of pain. We need to come home immediately. Send the car back."

"Tell Bungles to drop you. *Allah keray*,

176

God willing, he proposes in the car."

"If he proposes while she's in extreme pain, then he's a sadist."

"Who cares when and how a proposal comes. Foolish girl. Sit there and make sure that he asks her to marry him," Mrs. Binat said, and hung up.

Alys returned indoors. Jena was looking paler and her foot more swollen.

"Thank you," Alys said, returning the phone to Darsee. Why was he staring at her so intently? If he'd deemed her not good-looking when she was dressed up for a wedding, he was probably having conniptions at how she looked after a strenuous walk.

"My pleasure," Darsee said, slipping the phone back into his pocket.

"Valentine always comes to the rescue," Hammy said, not pleased with the way Darsee was looking at Alys. "Don't you, Valentine?"

"No, I don't." Darsee turned to Alys. "Were you able to get through?"

"Yes," Alys said, and murmured that Ajmer had misunderstood her directions and gone home. "Bungles, could you please drop us? Our uncle lives in Jamshed Colony."

She ignored the look Hammy-Sammy shared. Jamshed Colony had once been a

177

very prestigious residential area of Lahore and had only seen a sharp decline in the last fifteen years, as commercial enterprises turned it into one big shopping center.

"I think we should take Jena straight for an X-ray," Bungles said. "There's a first-rate private clinic ten minutes away."

"It's a good facility," Darsee said.

"Thank you for the offer," Alys said to Bungles, even as she stopped herself from informing Darsee that no one had asked his opinion. "But I think we should go home."

"Look," Bungles said, "the swelling is getting worse even as we speak."

"I want to go home," Jena said. "My uncle is a doctor —"

"Doctor of?" Darsee said.

"Pulmonology," Alys said.

"Your sister doesn't need her lungs heard," Darsee said. "She needs her ankle X-rayed."

Alys said coldly, "My uncle knows the best doctors for every ailment."

"Jena," Bungles said, pleading, "what if something is broken? You'll just be wasting time going home. Let the clinic take a look. Clearly your pain is unbearable."

"It's not that bad," Jena said, even as she groaned.

"Okay," Alys said. "Clinic."

She stared as Bungles proceeded to lift

178

Jena in his arms and carry her out of the clubhouse. It was like the scene in Jane Austen's *Sense and Sensibility* when Marianne Dashwood slipped in the rain and Willoughby carried her home in his arms. It was not a good omen, Alys thought, as she snatched her sister's shoe off the floor and hurried after them. Marianne and Willoughby did not enjoy a happy ending, no matter how promising their start. Worse, everyone outside was now going to witness Bungles being a gallant knight, and Jena, who had not asked to be swept up in his arms, was going to be the talk of the town.

Hammy waited until the club door shut behind Alys before saying, "What did Bungles just do? Jena could easily have walked. It's all a big act."

"I did see her ankle twist," Jaans said. "I think she's really hurt."

"It's a ploy," Hammy said firmly. "What do girls like this call it — catching a man, trapping a man, grabbing a man. Right, Sammy?"

"Right, Hammy," Sammy said. "In the olden days they'd get pregnant. These days they sprain their ankles."

"Everyone must have seen him carry her," Hammy said.

"So?" Jaans said.

"So," Sammy said, "they'll think something is going on."

"Something is going on," Jaans said.

"Nothing," Hammy said, "had better be going on unless Sammy and I approve. And, in this case, we disapprove. There's the cheapster mother's family reputation to consider and the family itself. A loser father. A fundamentalist sister. A fat sister. A spitting sister. A decorum-less sister. I thought I was going to die when Alys appeared looking like a swamp creature. Can't they afford private gym memberships?"

"Lots of people exercise in public parks," Darsee said. "The Race Course Park was one of my mother's favorite places to walk."

"Of course," Hammy said. "It's a very respectable park, and I'd surely love to walk here too. But I'd wear a *dupatta,* and I'm quite sure, Val, your mother did too. Being modern does not mean being inappropriate."

"Jaans," Sammy said, "would you let your sister gallivant half-undressed in a public place?"

"My sister," Jaans said, scowling, "has a treadmill in her bedroom. No need to even leave the house."

"And you, Valentine?" Hammy said.

"Would you want Jujeena going around like that?"

"Up to Juju," Darsee said.

"Juju would never do that," Hammy said. "I bet Alys Binat's eyes weren't so great today in that sweaty, blotchy face."

"Actually," Darsee said, "I think the fresh air made them even more luminous."

Hammy pouted and headed outside the clubhouse, where a million amused voices rushed to inform them that Bungles had left with his damsel in distress and her disheveled sister and that they were instructed to follow. Darsee, bothered by exactly how radiant he'd found Alys's eyes, had planned to go home. Instead, Hammy, Sammy, and Jaans climbed into his Mercedes and he headed toward the clinic.

CHAPTER 9

The clinic was an excellent facility, as all facilities that cater to excellent people tend to be, because excellent people demand excellence, unlike those who are grateful for what they receive. A nurse flipped Jena into a wheelchair and took her for an X-ray. The verdict: a mild ankle sprain. Even though the nurse said that an overnight stay was unnecessary and Jena agreed, Bungles immediately booked her into a VIP suite. Alys wondered how much the room was going to cost as Jena was lifted into a plush bed, where she lay elegant in her jeans and turtleneck, fiddling with the controls to elevate her foot. She'd been given a nice painkiller and was beginning to look relaxed.

Hammy and Sammy arrived. Their faces grew pinched at Bungles's insistence that an overnight stay was vital, no matter who said what.

"I'm not budging till Jena is discharged,"

he said, gazing at her with overwhelming concern.

"You have to budge," Hammy and Sammy said simultaneously.

Alys was enjoying the show that was the sisters trying to separate their brother from Jena, until she realized that Bungles intended to spend the night. Did he mean to completely obliterate Jena's reputation? As it was, there were already going to be vicious rumors over Jena *allowing herself* to be carried by him.

"Only I'll be staying with Jena," Alys said firmly. She went to the reception to call home and give her mother the news that Jena had been admitted for the night.

"Good girls!" Mrs. Binat said. "Jena immobile in bed. Bungles by her side. If this isn't a recipe for a proposal, I don't know what is."

"Jena is in no state of mind to receive a proposal," Alys whispered furiously into the phone. "And if Bungles proposes while she's drugged up, I'll doubt his state of mind. Now, please ask Qitty and Mari to prepare an overnight bag with a change of clothes for me and also pack the books on my nightstand."

A little later, Mrs. Binat breezed into the clinic with a bag for Alys and pillows galore, as if Jena had been admitted for the next month. Mari, Qitty, and Lady were right behind her. Lady was declaring it most unfair that nothing fun ever happened to her. Mrs. Binat kissed Jena, all the while exclaiming what a first-class champion Bungles was to be "taking such wonderful care of my terribly injured daughter."

"It's a mild sprain," Alys said, drowning out her mother. "We wouldn't even be here if Bungles had not insisted Jena be kept for observation."

"*Chup ker,* be quiet," Mrs. Binat said. "Oh, Bungles, look at my poor daughter, how frail, how helpless —" She stopped abruptly. Perhaps Jena as Invalid Supreme might turn Bungles off. "But my Jena is a fighter. When my daughters were little they got malaria, vomit everywhere, though Jena's vomit was of a very dignified hue, and within days she was up and back to normal. *Haan, jee!* Yes, sir! My womb has produced those rare creatures: girls who are dainty but also tough. And their wombs will produce just as well. Not to worry! Even Qitty's womb is in tip-top shape; all she needs is a bit of dieting."

Alys braved a peek at the company. Bungles was smiling awkwardly. Hammy-Sammy and Jaans snickered behind their hands. Darsee was simply staring with terrible fascination.

"Oh, but," Mrs. Binat said, "if one is going to get infected and die, it should be in a facility such as this —"

"Mummy," Alys said, interrupting her, "why don't you go to reception and settle the bill?"

"I've taken care of it," Bungles said.

"First-class gentleman," Mrs. Binat said.

"But you can't," Alys said to Bungles. "Absolutely not."

"Please," Bungles said. "Jena was our guest at the polo match, and my sisters and I insist that we take care of this."

Alys glanced at Hammy and Sammy. They were insisting no such thing.

"No," Alys said.

"Aunty" — Bungles turned to Mrs. Binat — "I will take it as a personal insult if you do not let me foot the bill."

"Hai," Mrs. Binat said, "that we should die before insulting you. May Allah grant you the pocket and power to foot a million such bills."

"Jena," Lady said, "you should stay a whole month now that we are not paying."

"Lady!" Alys glanced at a tight-faced Darsee.

"It's a joke!" Lady said. "Alys, you have

185

no sense of humor. So boring all the time."

"Alys is not boring," Mrs. Binat said. "Not all the time." She dug her eyes into Darsee, who was looking sullenly at the black-and-white-tiled floor. "She is also very attractive, and anyone who can't see that should get their eyes examined. Smart too, in her own way. At her school debate club, Alys was two-time gold medalist, and she was also backstroke champion, though I'm not in favor of girls playing sports. Take swimming. It makes the girls' necks very beefy, and goodbye to wearing necklaces. Bungles, are you in favor of girls swimming-shimming? You watch Olympics?"

"I do." Bungles nodded even as he made eyes at his sisters and Jaans to stop laughing.

"You must come watch Olympics with us in Dilipabad," Mrs. Binat said. "Our cook makes the best Chinese food. Humeria-Sumeria, Jaans, you must also come." She smiled at Jaans, who gave her two thumbs-up and said, "Go D-bad," and then she said curtly to Darsee, "You also come."

"Mummy," Alys said, standing up, "Jena needs to nap."

After managing to send her mother and sisters home, Alys disappeared into the attached bathroom to shower and change. As she slipped out of her T-shirt and track pants and shoved them into the bag, she hoped that everyone else would leave too. She'd love an evening alone with Jena, the two of them discussing Bungles at the match, and everything else. She emerged a half hour later, after a hot shower, smelling of gardenia-scented shampoo, water dripping off her curls and onto her red V-necked sweater and jeans, delighted to find that Sammy and Jaans had left in her absence after, apparently, quarreling yet again over whose contribution to their marriage was more vital: her money or his pedigree.

Alys took her *Kolhapuri chappals* out of her bag and slid her feet into them. She hoped that Bungles, Hammy, and Darsee would leave too. She did not relish the idea of having to endure Darsee's and Hammy's company, and she wished that Bungles, sitting beside Jena and looking as if he was going to burst into poetry, would propose soon so that Jena would no longer require chaperoning. Why was Darsee looking at her? Hadn't he seen a girl with messy hair and no makeup before? She flushed and ran her fingers through her tangles.

Bungles declared Jena was craving Chinese food, and he proceeded to place a dinner order for everyone.

"Jena," Bungles said when he hung up the phone, "do you want anything else? Shall I turn the TV on?"

Jena shrugged. Alys could tell she was being extra-cautious and acting all the more aloof. Good. Until she and Bungles were officially engaged, Jena's reserve was smart.

Hammy took the remote control from Bungles and switched on the TV. The clinic's movie channel came on. "Ooh! *Pretty Woman*." She gazed at Darsee, who stood by the window, gazing at the moon. "Val, I love this film."

"Every woman does," Darsee said in a not-too-kind tone.

"How presumptuous." Alys matched the snooty look Darsee gave her. "I don't. It sets up unrealistic expectations."

Alys was not a fan of updated Cinderella stories, *Pretty Woman* being a version in which a prostitute cleans up well and ends up earning herself a rich *roti* — a rich meal ticket — because she has a great figure and a heart of gold. Another version, readily available via Pakistani dramas, was a girl from the lower middle class who earns the respect and love of a rich *roti* because she's virginal and, no matter how smart or accomplished she is, allows her husband to put her in her place. Mari approved of these silly dramas, for she believed they were excellent propaganda for teaching women their role in society. Lady and Mrs. Binat were big fans too but more for the romance and fashion than the lessons espoused. Qitty watched them in order to people her caricatures.

"Unrealistic expectations!" Hammy frowned. "I'm surprised you don't like rags-to-riches stories."

"I don't like rags-to-riches *love* stories."

"Where did you learn to dismiss romance?" Hammy scoffed. "Jeddah?"

"Jeddah?" Darsee said.

"You don't know," Hammy said. "The Binats lived in Saudi Arabia for a while, where they attended, I believe, the Pakistan Embassy School."

Alys glanced at Jena. Surely she'd caught Hammy's scorn. But Jena was too busy assuring Bungles her ankle was in a comfortable position.

"The Pakistan Embassy School was quite all right," Alys said. "However, we attended an international school."

"I went to an international school too," Darsee said. "In Bangkok."

Alys feigned disinterest, though she wanted to ask him about his experiences.

"How was your experience?" Darsee said. "Do you miss it?"

"I miss California," Hammy said.

"Your parents still live there," Darsee said. "Going to school-in-transit, so to speak, is different. Would you agree, Alys?"

"Yes," Alys said. "I've lost touch with all my friends."

"I wish," Darsee said, "there had been a better way of staying connected back then, instead of just letters."

"Technology makes it easier these days," Alys said. "There is the email thingy."

"The email thingy?" Darsee smiled.

Alys gave him a cold stare. "You should read *Reader's Digest* and *Good Housekeeping*. Keep you updated on technology."

"Babes," Hammy said, "Val is a tech genius."

"I take it, Alys," Darsee said, "you believe I'm not impressed by these two publications that have impressed you."

"Have you ever read either one?"

"Nope," Darsee said. "The covers —"

"The covers!"

"Covers don't lie," Darsee said.

"That's not true."

"A risk I'm willing to take," Darsee said.

"Of course you are," Alys said, and seeing Bungles rip himself away from Jena in order to send his driver to pick up the Chinese takeaway, she took the moment to flee Darsee for her sister's bedside.

When Bungles returned to the room, he was carrying a bouquet of narcissuses sold by flower hawkers outside the clinic. A nurse followed him with a glass of water. Bungles put the flowers in and placed them by Jena's side. A delicious scent pervaded the room.

"My favorite flowers," Jena said, caressing a yellow center surrounded by cream petals.

"I know," Bungles said. "You mentioned it at NadirFiede's wedding."

"Bungles is so thoughtful to everyone," Hammy said, an exasperated smile on her face as she turned up the volume to *Pretty Woman.*

In ten minutes, the driver was back with the food. Alys and Bungles took out the containers and paper ware. Bungles leapt to fix Jena a plate. Hammy was eager to serve Darsee, except he dashed her desires by helping himself. Alys took a bowl of chicken corn soup.

Everyone ate in silence — except for Bungles, who kept asking Jena if she needed anything. Finally Hammy said, in a saccharine tone, that Jena had sprained her ankle and not her mouth and that if she

191

required his services, she would no doubt ask him. Bungles sheepishly distributed the fortune cookies.

"Jena," he said, "what does yours say?"

"A new beginning is on the horizon."

"Mine is so stupid," Hammy said. *"Karma is a witch."*

"You don't believe in karma?" Alys asked. She put her fortune cookie into her bag to give to Qitty, who was creating a food-and-word sculpture.

"If you don't remember anything from a past life," Darsee said, "then how can you avoid making the same mistakes in your present life?"

"I don't know," Alys said, taking some lo mein. "I suppose some people will be born with the same flaws, such as pride, and therefore be prone to repeating history."

"Pride isn't a flaw," Darsee said.

"It's just another word for smug," Alys said.

"Pride is a strength. Smugness opens one to mockery."

"Sometimes," Alys said, "one can be mocked through no fault of one's own."

"If you don't give cause, you will never be mocked," Darsee said.

"Let me guess — you've never given cause!" Alys turned to Hammy and Bungles.

"You need to mock him; otherwise, he really will think he's perfect."

"Oh my God, babes," Hammy said, "Valentine *is* perfect."

"I'm not perfect," Darsee said to Alys. "Far from. My biggest flaw in this day and age is that I don't suffer fools gladly. I hate sycophancy, nepotism, cronyism. I don't care to be diplomatic."

"You can afford to be undiplomatic," Alys said. "People let people like you get away with anything."

"You know what your glaring fault is?" Darsee said.

Alys glared at him. "Do tell."

"You take great pride in hearing only what you want to hear, and then you're smug about your interpretation." Darsee scowled at his watch. "We should leave."

"Yes," Hammy said eagerly. "Jena's been yawning away."

"Jena, are you sleepy?" Bungles asked. "Should I go?"

Jena, far from being rude enough to say yes, hesitated, and Bungles beamed.

"Val, you and Hammy go," he said.

Hammy flopped back onto the loveseat, and it was clear to Alys that she had no intention of leaving Bungles alone. Alys dragged a chair close to Jena. Darsee offered to help, but Alys said she could manage by herself, thank you. Curling up in the chair, she took out several books from her bag.

"I see you read more than *Reader's Digest* and *Good Housekeeping*," Darsee said. "My mother read books one after the other, as if they were potato chips."

"Alys reads like that," Jena said, as she took the water Bungles insisted she drink.

"I love to read, Valentine." Hammy rose to hover between Darsee and Alys. "I'm the world's biggest bookworm!"

Alys began to separate the books into two groups. Darsee glanced at the titles.

"For class?" he asked.

"Analogous Literatures. I'm pairing Rokeya Sakhawat Hossain's *Sultana's Dream* with Charlotte Perkins Gilman's *Herland* for utopias. Khushwant Singh's *Train to Pakistan* with John Steinbeck's *The Grapes of Wrath* for family stories alternating with sociopastoral chapters. Gloria Naylor's *The Women of Brewster Place* with Krishan Chander's short story "Mahalaxmi Ka Pul," comparing women's lives. And E. M. Forster's *A Passage to India* with Harper Lee's *To Kill a Mockingbird* for similar racial issues and court cases."

"I've read *Wrath* and *Mockingbird*," Darsee said. He skimmed *A Passage to India.* "I haven't read much local literature, not that *Passage* is local per se, though it's up for debate whether it's the nationality of the author or the geography of the book that determines its place in a country's canon."

"Val" — Hammy gave him her most dazzling smile — "have you read *Love Story*? It's really short and belongs everywhere, for love knows no boundaries." She sighed theatrically. "Love transcends country and geography."

Alys and Darsee both gave Hammy equally amused glances.

"I believe," Alys said to Darsee, "a book and an author can belong to more than one country or culture. English came with the colonizers, but its literature is part of our heritage too, as is pre-partition writing."

Darsee said, "My favorite partition novel is Attia Hosain's *Sunlight on a Broken Column.* Have you read it, Alys?"

Alys shook her head.

"That book made me believe I could have a Pakistani identity inclusive of an English-speaking tongue. We've been forced to seek ourselves in the literature of others for too long."

Alys nodded, adding, "But reading widely can lead to an appreciation of the universali-

"ties across cultures."

"Sure," Darsee said. "But it shouldn't just be a one-sided appreciation."

"I know what you mean," Alys said. "Ginger ale and apple pie have become second nature to us here, while our culture is viewed as exotic."

"Precisely," Darsee said. "At the wedding, you talked of a Pakistani Jane Austen. But will we ever hear the English or Americans talk of an equivalent?"

"Let's hope so," Alys said.

"You teach Austen, right?" Darsee said. "My mother adored Darcy."

"Oh my God, babes, I love Mr. Darcy," Hammy squealed. "Especially the part with his wet shirt. I could read that scene all day."

Alys's and Darsee's eyes met.

"Darcy is overrated," Alys said. "Mr. Knightley from *Emma* won my heart when he defended Miss Bates from Emma's mockery."

"I see." Darsee pointed to a bookmarked book. "What are you reading?"

"Virginia Woolf's *To the Lighthouse.*"

"According to my mother, Woolf captured the essence of time plus memory."

"She does," Alys said. "I discovered her in the British Council library. She has an essay on Jane Austen."

"You mean Shakespeare in *A Room of One's Own*?" Darsee said.

His supercilious tone cut Alys. Instantly, she recalled that she wasn't talking to a fellow bibliophile but to Valentine Darsee.

"Just because," she said sharply, "you are ignorant about something does not mean that I'm wrong."

Darsee looked at Alys. He stood up. They were leaving. Yes, Bungles, right now! As Hammy and a reluctant Bungles followed him out, Darsee resolved not to say a single word to Alys the next day. In fact, he wouldn't show up.

The next morning, Bungles arrived alone, and despite his pleas that she needed to stay on, Jena was adamant that she was absolutely fine. Would Bungles please drop them to their uncle's house?

Mrs. Binat was devastated when Alys and Jena returned home without an engagement ring. Mr. Binat was delighted his daughters were back. He, Nona, and Nisar were longing to talk about something other than who had dressed like a complete clown at Nadir-Fiede, who like a partial clown, and how massive a ring Jena should expect from Bungles.

"Jena, Alys!" Mrs. Binat said. "You barely

gave Bungles a chance to propose. Nona, have you seen any more dim-witted girls than these two? Instead of practicing grab-it, they are mastering push-it-away. Even the likes of Benazir Bhutto and Lady Dayna did not push it away."

Nona, knowing it was no use refuting Pinkie Binat when she was in this mood, did not answer.

"Not Dayna, Mummy, Diana, Lady Diana," Lady said. "Had I stayed with Alys and Jena, I would have made sure Jena did not leave without a ring."

"I should have left you there," Mrs. Binat said. "You are the most sensible of the lot. Don't you dare serve me a shoe, Barkat! If these two nitwits would have stayed, that boy would have proposed, I guarantee."

"Mummy," Qitty said, looking up from pencils she was sharpening. "There's still the *walima.*"

"*Chup ker.* Be quiet," Mrs. Binat said. "*Beheno ki chumchee.* Defending her disobedient sisters."

"We couldn't stay there forever," Jena said quietly, "waiting for him to propose."

Mrs. Binat was about to correct her on that score when Sherry returned from her overnight visit to her aunt — the divorcée, who'd thrived despite social stigma, thanks

198

to a very well-paying job — and offered a sympathetic ear.

"Of course you are one hundred percent right, Pinkie Khala," Sherry agreed. "Jena should never have left."

Mrs. Binat was so gratified, she declared they would order Sherry's favorite meal for dinner: mutton *tikkas, keema naan,* and *bhindi* fry.

"Qitty," Mrs. Binat added, "don't you even look at the *naan.*"

By meal's end, during which Qitty defiantly ate half a *naan,* Mrs. Binat had calmed down enough to start preparing Jena for the NadirFiede *walima,* where, she guaranteed everyone, Bungles would propose. Mr. Binat pulled Alys aside and reminded her of her meeting with the lawyer the next day to sort out the matter of the land fraud.

CHAPTER 10

Alys parked her car and stepped out into bustling Mall Road, ignoring the whistles and catcalls of loitering men. She hurried past Ferozsons bookstore, glancing at the window display, past Singhar, the beauty shop fragrant with sandalwood, and, turning into an alley, arrived at the law offices of Musarrat Sr. & Sons Advocates.

Once upon a time, Bark Binat had purchased an acre of land. When he was forced out of the ancestral home, he'd turned to the acre, only to discover that he, along with others, had been conned. The acres sold to them were government land, and the government refused to compensate anyone for being gullible. Mr. Binat had been hesitant to hire a lawyer yet again — after his brother's betrayal, he had no gumption to bring strangers to task — but Alys had not let it go. Even if they never saw a penny returned, they had to at least try, and she'd hired Musarrat Jr. on a friend's assurance that he was honest and trustworthy. The Binats' initial petition concerning the Fraudia Acre case had been filed a decade ago and, since then, there'd been no real progress.

Alys stepped into the tube-lit office. She could hear Musarrat Jr.'s booming voice from inside his office, saying, "Trust in God." The receptionist looked at the recent letter Alys had received from them and told her to proceed into the office.

Musarrat Jr. was hanging up the phone, and he beamed when he saw Alys.

"Alysba Sahiba, it's been a while! Please sit!" He settled his paunchy self into his swivel chair. "Mr. Binat is hale and hearty, I hope?"

Alys assured him he was. She wished her father had not begged off coming just because money matters gave him palpitations.

"Alysba Sahiba," Musarrat Jr. said, "as it says in the letter, the con man has reentered the country and, because one of the claimants' sons is a police officer, he is being questioned aggressively. *Inshallah,* soon there will be some resolution." He pressed a buzzer. A peon entered. "Check if Jeorgeullah Wickaam Sahib is back from court."

A few minutes later a young man entered.

Alys blinked. He was movie-star gorgeous, with chiseled features, dark-brown hair, and sleepy eyes the color of rich chai. His white shirt tucked into gray pants perfectly fit his well-muscled build. What good fortune, Alys thought as she sat up straighter and smoothed her floral sky-blue *kurta* over her scruffy jeans, that she wasn't the sort of person who would be taken by looks alone.

Musarrat Jr. introduced Alys and, with a proud smile, turned to the man.

"Alysba Sahiba, Mr. Jeorgeullah Wickaam, the lawyer newly assigned to your case and a rising star among youngsters."

Alys gave a polite, shy smile.

"Wickaam grew up in Lahore, did a stint at a military academy, realized it was not for him, went to New York for studies, returned, and here is he willing and ready to serve the wronged citizens of his country."

Jeorgeullah Wickaam gave Alys a courteous nod, which also seemed to imply that while he perhaps deserved this flattery, it was nevertheless embarrassing.

"First steps first," Musarrat Jr. said. "I suggest, Alysba Sahiba, you show Wickaam Sahib your disputed acre."

When they reached the Suzuki, Alys took

out her keys from her bag and Jeorgeullah Wickaam sprang to open the driver's-side door for her before he headed to the passenger side. Alys smiled to herself. Handsome, a rising star, polite. She could think of worse ways to spend an afternoon.

As she expertly reversed the car into an onslaught of traffic, he turned toward her with a friendly smile and informed her that though the arrested man was being questioned thoroughly, the chances of monetary recompense were bleak.

"Honestly," Alys said, stepping on the accelerator, "at this point a heartfelt admittance of guilt and a sorry would be very nice."

"Knowing how these rascals operate, I wouldn't bank on heartfelt anything." He shrugged regretfully. "By the way, please call me Wickaam."

"Call me Alys."

"A-L-I-C-E?"

"Pronounced the same but spelled A-L-Y-S."

"I had a *kebab* roll recently," Wickaam said. "It came wrapped in a magazine page with the photo of an elderly woman, and her name was A-L-Y-S. . . ."

"That's Faiz Ahmed Faiz's wife." Alys stopped at a light and glanced at him. He gave her a blank look. "Faiz? Poet, leader, communist, agnostic. His wife, Alys, was from England but she became a Pakistani citizen. Your meal came wrapped in her column."

"My apologies," Wickaam said.

"No need to apologize," Alys said as the traffic light turned green.

"True! It was a very good *kebab* roll."

Alys laughed.

"*Bol ke lab azad hain tere:* Speak, your mouth is unshackled," Wickaam said, quoting Faiz. "Of course I know who Faiz is. I was just playing with you."

"Thank God," Alys said. "I was like, oh no, a lawyer ignorant of his country's heritage."

"I think," Wickaam said, "you'll be pleased to know that historical preservation is one of my great passions. Have you been to England?"

"When I was much younger."

"With every step one is met by monuments to scientists, artists, thinkers. We Pakistanis have zero appreciation for anything except bargains and deals."

"Easier to commemorate history when you've been the colonizer and not the colonized."

"Whoa. I just meant history, not our

purchases, should define us."

Alys gave a small smile. "I wrestle with how to incorporate history. Can any amount of good ever merit the interference of empire? Do we never speak English again? Not read the literature? Erasing history is not the answer, so how does a country put the lasting effects of empire in proper context? Not deny it, but not unnecessarily celebrate it."

Wickaam shrugged. "Best to concentrate on the future."

"But the future is built on a past, good *and* bad. It's troubling when someone takes a book and makes a shoddy film out of it and then comes the day when no one has read the book and everyone thinks the shoddy film is the original."

"Come now." Wickaam winked. "You have to admit that films are better than books."

"Never!" Alys said fiercely.

Wickaam raised his hands, surrendering. "Tell me about yourself, A-L-Y-S. What is your great passion? Are you single? Married? Children? Am I getting too personal?"

"It's all right. Single. Happily single, much to the disappointment of many who prefer that single women be miserable. And I don't know if it qualifies as a great passion, but I teach English literature."

"I knew I should have said I loved books! Now you'll hate me!"

"I won't hate you!" Alys exclaimed. "You were honest when most people would just say what's expedient."

They arrived at the acre. Alys parked by a ditch next to a meadow. The late afternoon had grown chilly, and she took her black shawl with silver lining, which she'd flung onto the back seat, and wrapped it around herself. She and Wickaam walked onto the land, an expanse of grass with the scent of fresh earth.

"What did you plan to do with this?" Wickaam said.

"My father was going to build his retirement home and homes for me and my four sisters. One big happy family till death do us part sort of a thing."

"That sounds so nice," Wickaam said. "It is a blessing to belong to a loving family."

"Happy families are all alike; every unhappy family is unhappy in its own way."

"*Zaberdast!* Wow!" Wickaam said.

"It's from *Anna Karenina.* Tolstoy's novel? Russian author?" Alys smiled. "There is a movie, I believe."

"I will watch it."

Laughing, they walked on, stopping at a small pond. A couple of boys were scrubbing buffaloes deep in muddy waters, shrieking as they flicked water at each other.

"Photo op," Wickaam said. "Poor little naked brown children bathing with domesticated beasts of burden in beatific nature: an authentic exotic snapshot of rural health and happiness. I should sell such pictures abroad to make my fortune."

"I'm sure the idea has already been signed, sealed, and delivered," Alys said. "And won the Pulitzer."

"Oh well," Wickaam said, "I'm too late to every party. Mediocre luck."

"Mediocre luck is what I have too and I'm quite happy." Alys's gaze followed a flame of a butterfly as it settled on a buffalo. "I mean, you might not be able to fly to London and Dubai for healthcare, but at least you're not suffering because you can't afford any."

"A-L-Y-S glass half-full. I like that you're content. Very lucky."

Alys blushed. "As content as a single girl in this country can be when all anyone ever asks her is why she isn't married yet, and they tell her she better hurry up before her ovaries die. It's you men who are lucky. You might be asked about your marriage plans, but everyone leaves you alone the second you mention career. If we women mention career, we're considered aberrations of nature or barren."

"That's because we bring home the bread and you bring home the baby and there's no biological clock on bread and there is one on baby."

"We can do bread too," Alys said. "And as for baby, science allows for babies at any age now."

"A-L-Y-S, surely you don't have to worry for a long time about any such thing."

"Flatterer!" Alys laughed. "I'm thirty, soon to be thirty-one."

"You are not."

"I am!"

"You don't look it."

"Good, but I don't really care. Age is just a number."

"That it is. I'm twenty-six."

They were quiet for a moment as they registered that he was younger than she.

"Well," Alys said, "now that you've seen the acre, I guess we should head back."

As they walked to the car, Wickaam said, "If you're free, Wagah border is not far from here, and if you haven't had the pleasure yet of witnessing the Pakistani–Indian closing-of-the-border-gates ceremony, it's truly an experience I recommend."

"My father took me as a birthday present

ages ago," Alys said, "but I'd love to go again."

Alys and Wickaam chatted amiably about films and foods as she drove out of Lahore and entered the border village of Wagah, where the ceremony took place on the Pakistani side. On the Indian side, it took place in Attari village, which connected to the bigger city of Amritsar, home of the Sikh Golden Temple. Alys drove past sun-wrinkled women slapping dung patties to dry onto the outer walls of their mud huts, and she and Wickaam waved back at matte-haired children in bright sweaters who paused their play to wave at them.

At the venue, Alys parked outside the red-brick amphitheater overlooking the border gates. Last time she'd come, the bleachers had not been segregated, but now Wickaam entered the men's enclosure and she the women's. Climbing the stairs to the back-most row, she sat down at the end of an aisle beside a woman whose elaborate *mehndi* patterns on her palms and up her gold-bangled wrists indicated that she was a newlywed. A crow swooped over their heads, startling them. Together they watched it fly between the trees on the Indian side and the trees on the Pakistani side, its guttural *caw-caw-caw* reverberating freely in the open air.

The Pakistani and Indian spectators were sitting a stone's throw away from each other — or a flower's toss away, depending on international relations between the two countries on any particular day. The ceremony began. On the Pakistani side, a soldier beating a drum walked from the gates toward the audience. He was followed by mascot Chacha Pakistani, with his pristine white beard, holding aloft a Pakistani flag, the green representing the Muslim majority in the country and the white stripe the minorities. On this side, hand-held flags fluttered green and white. On that side fluttered the tricolored green, white, and saffron flags. The crowds on both sides cheered and roared their patriotism.

"Pakistan Zindabad!"

"Jai Hind!"

Two giant soldiers from either side, rendered taller by their plumed turbans, stamped past each other in a mutual display of power. The two countries' flags, hoisted over their respective gates, were rolled down in unison, until the next morning, and, with that, the gates to the Wagah–Attari border crossing closed for the evening.

After more cheering and slogans, the audience headed out of the amphitheaters. Alys was milling outside the men's enclosure, on the lookout for Wickaam, with a crowd swarming around her, when she bumped into somebody.

"Oh, hello," Darsee said, his momentary confusion replaced by a quick smile. "What a surprise."

"I happened to be in the vicinity, believe it or not," Alys said, also flustered for a second, "and decided to see the ceremony."

"Bungles and I," Darsee said, nodding at Bungles, who appeared beside him, "are in charge of sightseeing for Nadir's wedding guests from abroad."

Alys exchanged congenial hellos with the guests: Thomas Fowle, Harris Bigg-Wither, and his girlfriend, Soniah. She asked them if they were enjoying Pakistan, and they assured her that they were loving it. Pakistan was beautiful, Thomas Fowle said. The people were so friendly, Harris Bigg-Wither said. It was far from the mess they saw on the news, Soniah said. Alys smiled. She pointed to the shopping bags in Soniah's hand.

"I see you managed to squeeze in my mother's favorite activity."

"Yes! We went to handicraft stores and open-air shops in A-naar-kaa-lee Bazaar.

Darsee and Bungles were very helpful with the bargaining, they tell me. I got *choo-naaree doo-pa-tuss,* embroidered wallets, velvet-coated glass bangles, and some pure henna, different from the one I get back home in Addis."

"We've been to the Badshahi Mosque and the Sikh Temple," Bungles said. "Shalimar Gardens, the Wazir Khan Mosque, and now here."

"All in one day! I'm impressed!" Alys said. "But you must be exhausted."

"Our feet," Soniah said, pointing to her sneakers, "are killing us, but so worth it."

Bungles peered over Alys's shoulder. "Are your sisters with you?"

"No," Alys said, grinning at his supposedly subtle inquiry about Jena.

"There you are, Alys." Wickaam appeared, holding two bottles of chilled Pakola. "I was looking for you outside the women's section."

Darsee and Wickaam set eyes on each other. Darsee blanched. He looked as if he'd been kicked in the stomach. Wickaam turned red. He squawked a hello. Darsee turned and marched away. Bungles mumbled a weak hello in response to Wickaam's greeting and then, telling Alys he was looking forward to seeing her sisters at the

NadirFiede *walima,* he hurried after Darsee, the visitors in tow.

Alys took her Pakola and sipped slowly from the neon-green soft drink. Clearly something was amiss. Should she ask Wickaam directly? But how to ask without being intrusive?

"Out of all the places to meet my dear cousin."

Alys nearly choked on her Pakola. "Valentine Darsee is your cousin?"

"My first cousin. Our mothers are sisters. How do you know him?"

Alys told Wickaam about meeting Darsee recently in Dilipabad at the NadirFiede wedding.

"I see," Wickaam said. "I went to school with Nadir too, you know. I'm invited to the *walima,* but I'm not sure I'll attend what with Darsee being there. There's the myth of close cousins and then there's Darsee and me. I bet you found him wonderful at the wedding."

"I certainly did not," Alys said. "No one did."

Wickaam brightened. "I'm not surprised. Darsee is a dreadful person who pretends to be a saint. He betrayed me. The betrayal is hard to talk about, though I'm perfectly happy to tell you."

"It would be my honor," Alys said, "to hear your story."

"Are you hungry?" Wickaam said. "Pak Tea House café is close to the law offices on our way back. Have you ever been there?"

Alys had always wanted to go to the illustrious Pak Tea House, established in 1940, and she eagerly followed Wickaam through the doors and into a snug hall. Men were seated at a few of the wooden tables. One was reading a newspaper, a cigarette smoldering in a glass ashtray. Another two were playing chess. Alys and Wickaam settled in a corner and Wickaam ordered chai and chicken patties. Alys gazed at the walls lined with photos of famous male novelists, poets, and revolutionaries who had once congregated here.

"Where are the women writers?" she asked.

"Upstairs, I think," Wickaam said. "So, how does it feel, Miss English Literature, to be sitting here surrounded by Local Literati Legends?"

"A little sad that they might have as much, if not more, to say to me than Baldwin or Austen, Gibran or Anzaldúa, but since I can't read Urdu fluently, though I do try, that's that. Anyway, hurrah for translations."

"Too much is lost in translation," Wick-aam said. "I used to have an ayah, Ayah Haseena, whom I affectionately called Ayah Paseena. But while in Urdu the riff on Haseena/Paseena made perfect sense, in English trying to rhyme 'Beautiful' with 'Perspiration' was nonsense."

"You gain in translation by opening up a new world unto others," Alys said. "Anyway, a translation is better than nothing. We ourselves are works in translation, in a way."

"You sound like Valentine Darsee."

"Do not insult me." Alys frowned.

"My cousin *is* an insult!" Wickaam grinned. "I'm planning to write a novel to expose him, and not because it's fashionable these days to be a writer, ever since that Indian woman won the Booker Prize for the *Small Thing* something —"

"*The God of Small Things.*"

"Yes, that one," Wickaam said. "I haven't read it. I don't think I've read a novel since, oh, I don't know, years."

"You're planning to write a novel but you don't read them?"

"How hard can it be?" Wickaam said. "We all jot down words. Just a matter of finding time."

"Since we all have a brain, I plan to perform brain surgery as soon as I have a

215

spare moment."

"You're funny," Wickaam said.

The waiter arrived with their order. Wickaam poured chai into their cups and Alys added a splash of milk to hers. She bit into the rich flaky pastry with the spicy chicken filling.

"Delicious! Listen, Wickaam, if you'd rather not tell me about Darsee —"

"I have nothing to hide. I'm an open book. In fact, I believe it's my duty to tell everyone what my cousin has done to me." He took a deep breath. "My maternal grandparents, as you know, are dey Baghs, descendants of royal gardeners and luminaries of this land. They had three daughters. The eldest is Beena, then Deena, and lastly Weena.

"BeenaDeenaWeena attended Murree Convent School, followed by a year of finishing school in Paris and then a year in London. When they returned to Pakistan, they married within months of each other. Beena married a first cousin, Luqman 'Lolly' dey Bagh, whom she'd always had her eye on. Deena married the son of a family friend her father held in great regard, Fauji Darsee, an army officer in the intelligence. And my mother, Weena, married a Pakistani-British man she'd met in London during an exhibition at the Serpentine Gallery. My father was not wealthy, but he'd studied philosophy and dreamed of becoming a great playwright, and my mother was happy to support him.

"BeenaDeenaWeena got pregnant within months of each other, and soon Weena had me, Deena had Valentine, and Beena had Annie. I have pictures of the three of us cousins in identical tartan dungarees, in a tree house, playing the piano, riding horses, that sort of thing. Our life was so nice; we used to say we never wanted to grow up. BeenaDeenaWeena were also happy, and they decided to fulfill a dream they shared — of being educators — and so they established a private school for girls, British School Group. Now it has branches all over the country. What! You teach in a British School branch! Small, small world.

"Do you remember the Ojhri arms-depot explosion in 1988, which killed and injured scores of civilians?" Wickaam blinked. "Both my parents and Valentine's father had been in the vicinity together. They all died.

"Valentine and I were fourteen years old. Deena Khala kept insisting she was my mother now, but no one can replace a mother. Beena Khala comforted Valentine and me as if our losses were equal. But

Valentine had his mother and his four-year-old sister, Jujeena. I was the full orphan. Still, Valentine and I found ourselves crying shamelessly together and wishing revenge on everyone who told us boys don't cry and certainly not in public.

"Deena Khala was going mad with grief, just weeping all the time. She decided Pakistan reminded her of loss, and that a change of scenery would benefit us, and so we all moved to London. London was nice, except Valentine was growing sickeningly jealous of both his sister and me, for he couldn't bear to share his one remaining parent's love with anyone. Adding to Valentine's rage was his mother's frenetic dating, if 'dating' is what you'd call Deena Khala's revolving list of lovers. Darsee calls them 'unsuccessful relationships.' One day, Deena Khala declared she was in love with Ricky from Thailand and married him. They moved to Bangkok, and Deena Khala decided to take only Jujeena and Valentine with her.

"I was hurt, but I'd survived the death of both parents on the same day so this was nothing. I was sent to Bradford to live with my father's family. Everyone was very kind, but it was more out of duty than love.

"After three years, Deena Khala divorced

Ricky because he wanted a second wife, and she came back to Pakistan. I also returned to live with them. But it was not the same. The closeness Valentine and I had once shared was gone. And Jujeena barely remembered me. Then we found out that Deena Khala had an advanced stage of cancer and had months to live. I was so sad. I thought this would bring us all closer. Instead, for all of their supposed love for my mother, both Beena Khala and Deena Khala tampered with my mother's will. I received no share in the British School Group, or anything. God only knows why they did this; I believe this question will haunt me forever. I am not materialistic, Alys, but to be cheated out of one's inheritance is a hard thing to bear. It's why I decided to be a lawyer. To make sure that others are treated fairly.

"My father's family had no clout compared to the dey Baghs, and everyone on my mother's side preferred to remain in Beena Khala's good books. I'll never forget one moment: I'd come to pay my last respects to Deena Khala on her deathbed. Beena Khala was there too when Deena Khala said, 'Jeorgeullah is our sister Weena's son. Let us give him his due.' But Valentine roared, 'Never!' And that was that.

My own cousin, my buddy, my brother, if you will, betrayed me."

"I'm so sorry," Alys said, mortified. "I'm so sorry about the loss of your parents. Everything. I don't know what to say. My father went through a similar betrayal with his elder brother, and I understand your devastation."

"Thank you. Thank you very much. Your sympathy means so much to me."

"Darsee is even worse than I imagined," Alys said. "I can't believe he thwarted his mother's wish on her deathbed!"

"Believe it," Wickaam said, gazing into her eyes.

"I do!" Alys said, earnestly. "I most certainly do. But doesn't Darsee realize that money, power, prestige, it's all ephemeral, and that eventually we go to our graves with nothing and leave behind only memories?"

CHAPTER 11

Alys returned from her day with Wickaam in time to hear Nona sighing about having to make a night delivery and Ajmer being unwell. Alys volunteered to deliver the cake with Jena. Jena was making origami ornaments for the Christmas tree with the children, but she took one look at Alys and rose.

Alys backed the car out of the driveway and took a turn into the main street. She filled Jena in as fast as possible. Jena was thrilled that Alys had met Bungles and that he'd asked about her, but she was troubled at the report Jeorgeullah Wickaam had given of Darsee. If Darsee was as vile as his cousin claimed, then why was Bungles friends with him? Surely he must know about Darsee usurping Wickaam's inheritance.

"Perhaps," Alys said as she glanced at the address Jena was holding, "all decent people think Darsee is a decent person because he chooses to treat them decently."

"But, Alys," Jena said hesitantly, "just because a relative says something doesn't make it true. We know that!" A beggar tapped on her window and she rolled it down and handed him money. "I don't want to believe that Darsee is devious *or* that Wickaam has some ulterior motive for maligning him."

"You never want to believe ill of anyone," Alys said, driving around a bullock cart. "In a country where the national sport is back-stabbing and one-upmanship, I don't know whether to hand you a trophy for sainthood or for stupidity."

"I don't want trophies," Jena said. "Take a right from here. All I'm saying is that we have no proof to back Wickaam's accusations and that a person should be innocent until proven guilty."

Alys rolled her eyes. "What was the house number again?"

At the house, Alys delivered the solar-system cake to the kitchen and took the remaining payment. She returned to the car and turned back onto the main road. A car cut in front of her. She honked. The man inside yelled, "Bloody lady drivers!"

Alys gave him the finger. "Jena, Wickaam has nothing to gain by lying to me about

222

Darsee. And I trust him."

"How can you trust him? You just met him," Jena said, puzzled. "That's very unlike you, Alys."

"Wait till you meet him," Alys said, blushing. "You'll see."

Alys invited Wickaam to Nona and Nisar's Christmas party on the pretext that her father wanted to meet the man representing their Fraudia Acre case, but in her heart she wanted Jena to vet him. Wickaam accepted the invitation with an enthusiasm that surpassed mere lawyer-client relations, and Alys eagerly awaited his arrival.

On the morning of the party, the Gardenaars opened their Christmas gifts, attended church service, and returned to a festive house. A regal Christmas tree graced the drawing room, its boughs cheery with homemade baubles and store-bought trinkets, its fresh pine fragrance competing with the scents of roast lamb, leg of mutton, chicken *pulao,* mixed-vegetable *bhujia, aloo gosht, nargisi kofta,* shepherd's pie, and macaroni salad. Dessert was *seviyan,* vermicelli in sweet milk, and *zarda,* the saffron-yellow rice bursting with nuts, raisins, and orange peel, and, of course, Nona's Christmas cake, with the three wise men on

caramel camels bearing their gold, frankin-
cense, and myrrh, and pointing to an edible
silver star, which would take them to baby
Isa and his mother, Maryam.

At the party, Alys kept an eye on the door
even as she and the children belted out
"The Twelve Days of Christmas," followed
by an improvised "The Twelve Days of Eid."
A petite man entered. He stood at the
threshold, one hand behind his back like a
picture of Napoleon Bonaparte in a textbook. The man's dinner jacket hung off
sloping shoulders, and his checkered tie lay
lopsided over a satiny shirt. He scanned the
room, his soft hooded eyes resting on teenage girls preparing a synchronized dance.
He frowned before quickly composing his
face into a benign smile and heading toward
Nisar.

Nisar greeted the man, embraced the
three children tagging behind him, and led
them to his sisters for an introduction: Farhat Kaleen and his children — eighteen-
year-old Fatima, fifteen-year-old Musa, and
seven-year-old Isa.

Mrs. Binat and Falak were seated in front
of a coffee table, and they paused their
merry munching on dry fruit in order to
smile benevolently at the man and his
children. Mrs. Binat squinted. What in the

world was he wearing? Polyester, if the patina on that shirt was anything to go by. The children were better dressed and greeted her and Falak politely.

"Pinkie, Falak," Nisar said, "surely you remember Farhat Kaleen, our cousin nine times removed from the branch of the family that moved to England so many moons ago."

Kaleen beamed brightly. Upon returning to Lahore, he'd made it a point to reconnect with relatives and so had begun the arduous process of winnowing out the worthy from the worthier. He was very pleased with Nisar Gardenaar's worth, and because Nisar was worthy, Kaleen was willing to overlook Nisar's sisters' unworthiness for having married losers. Still, better to be safe rather than sorry, for fortunes could literally change overnight. Apparently Falak's son, Babur, was intelligent and had applied to prestigious colleges abroad, albeit as an agriculture major. His plan was to get in as a farmer and then switch majors.

Since Kaleen deemed it religiously inappropriate to shake hands with let alone hug women, even if they were his relatives, he proceeded to give Pinkie and Falak the most congenial of nods. He was, he told them, overjoyed to be reunited with them. He had a few memories from childhood, in particular visiting Lahore one summer when he was a young boy of ten and Pinkie sixteen and Falak seventeen. Did Pinkie and Falak remember being put in charge of babysitting him while his mother went to Ichhra Bazaar? Did they remember he found their lipstick-kissed posters of film stars and he'd threatened to tell their mother unless! "Unless what?" both sisters had cried. Unless, he'd replied, they let him tear out the picture of the girl in the red bikini in the lewd Western fashion magazine he'd also found tucked away in the drawer.

"That picture," Kaleen said, "allowed me an early window into the different types of women available in the world, and so I was able to see clearly at a young age which women were worthy of my time, attention, and earnings."

Mrs. Binat and Falak exchanged looks. So this is what had become of that snooping tattletale! Mrs. Binat vividly recalled his drawing-room preacher of a mother repeatedly proclaiming that if only Kaleen were a few years older than ten and Pinkie a few years younger than sixteen, then she would have gotten them engaged.

Kaleen, as if reading her mind, reminded Mrs. Binat of the same, and she giggled in embarrassed horror at the thought of ending up the wife of this balding, sartorially dismal man. Catching Mr. Binat's eye, Mrs. Binat shrugged coyly, for it was hardly her fault if admirers from the past popped up to remind her that she may very well have been their wife.

"And your wife is where?" Mr. Binat said, taking a step closer to Mrs. Binat even as he exchanged a bemused look with Alys. Alys and her sisters and Sherry had joined the circle around Kaleen, who seemed to be basking in the role of pistil to their petals. Mari, recognizing a kindred spirit with his talk of lewd magazines, was, for perhaps the first time in her life, experiencing the urge to make you-you eyes.

"Alas, my wife!" Kaleen put a hand on his heart. "My pious wife, Roohi, the good mother of my three children, passed away last year. She and I had gone for our evening stroll and she stopped to smell the flowers, and we suspect some insect entered her nose and from there her brain. Three days sick and on the fourth, poof, gone."

Amid a chorus of commiserations, Sherry's condolence rang out. She ruffled the seven-year-old motherless Isa's hair, smiling at him with all the kindness she contained.

"*Inna lillahi wa inna ilayhi rajioon.* From God we come and to God we return." Kaleen glanced resignedly at his daughter and sons. "But we miss her, and my poor children are left bereft of a most splendid mum."

He explained that he'd returned to Pakistan because it was difficult to raise obedient and virginal children in the promiscuous English *mohol,* atmosphere, with no motherly guiding light among the temptations of pubs and clubs. Also, he'd received a job opportunity too incredible not to accept, from a big-name patroness. She'd even introduced him to the most select of the select crowd, who in turn, all, by the grace of God, required his services in one capacity or another. Kaleen stood erect, hands clasped behind his back, and it was clear from his expectant expression he was waiting to be asked what he did.

Mr. Binat obliged. "What do you do?"

"I am," Kaleen stood tall on his tippy-toes for a second, "a physiatrist."

"A psychiatrist?" Lady said. "You'll have lots of business in this town, though no one will admit coming to you."

"Not psychiatrist!" Kaleen snapped. "Physiatrist. It is not the soul's trials I fix but the body's tribulations. Don't ask how much I make, because you will all faint."

"Faint in a bad way?" Alys half-smiled as she looked at her father, then glanced at the door. Where was Wickaam? He was quite late.

"In a good way." Kaleen frowned. "In a very good way. Is that not true, Nisar?"

"It is." Nisar nodded. "There is such high demand for physiatrists and pain management that Kaleen is setting up his private practice."

"Oh," Mrs. Binat said. She and Falak exchanged glances, acknowledging that if Farhat Kaleen was going to be an important member of society and mint money, then it was unwise to dismiss him. Mrs. Binat and Falak simultaneously moved to the edges of the sofa, and Mrs. Binat patted the center.

"Kaleen, you sit here and tell us all about your dearly departed wife, God rest her soul."

Kaleen perched between the two sisters; Mrs. Binat ordered Lady to introduce his daughter to the other teenage girls in the room, and she urged his sons to enjoy the appetizers, as long as they left plenty of room for the scrumptious dinner Nona had planned. The elder son settled on the edge of the couch and took a handful of pistachios. Sherry marched the younger son over to the children rehearsing carols for the show they planned to perform.

A sudden hush came over the room as all eyes turned to the entrance, where a dashing man stood with a bouquet of glitter-sprinkled red roses.

"Is that him?" Jena's eyes widened at Alys. "You told me he was decent, nice, and trustworthy, but I suppose you forgot to mention that he looks like a film star."

"I didn't forget," Alys said. "I just didn't see how it was relevant."

Alys hurried to greet Wickaam. He apologized profusely for being late — friends had coerced him into accompanying them to see the fairy lights strung all over town. Nona assured Wickaam he was not late at all, and Nisar added that he'd taken his own kids to see the city dolled up, although the decorations were for Pakistan's founding father, whose birthday fell on the same date as Christmas, a happy coincidence.

Wickaam complimented Nona on her bungalow, the Christmas décor, the tree, the lovely color of her walls and even lovelier shade of her burgundy lipstick, and, upon gleaning that the art on the walls was her own, he complimented Nisar on being the luckiest of husbands to have secured such a multitalented wife.

Alys introduced Jeorgeullah Wickaam to everyone. Wickaam could tell a good joke, and soon Nisar and the menfolk were slapping him on his back as if they were all old friends. Wickaam watched the children's Christmas show attentively. Afterward, to their delight, he mesmerized them with coin tricks. He helped the cook bring out dishes from the kitchen and arrange them on the dinner table around the green-and-gold-candle centerpiece. He praised Nona's menu, praised the cook's cooking, praised even the grocery stores from where the ingredients had been purchased. He was full of compliments for all the women. Someone's voice was angelic. Someone's hairstyle perfectly framed her face. Someone's shoes reminded him of royalty. He told Mrs. Binat that she was a stunner.

Mrs. Binat's heart fluttered. What a handsome man! What a solicitous man! What a gracious man! So conscientious of Alys! Thank God Alys had started to take a little more care of her looks. Bronzer dusted her cheeks and eyelids, and she was wearing a fitted embroidered *kurta* with bell sleeves that accentuated her bonny shoulders and waist. And, miracle of miracles, high heels.

When Lady put on film songs, every young person rose to dance. Mrs. Binat noticed that Kaleen did not look pleased at his daughter's participation. Mrs. Binat, in turn, was most gratified to see Wickaam force Qitty up. Considerate man! Amazing human being! True hero! In any case, Wickaam was paying special attention to each of her daughters, and Mrs. Binat prayed fervently that one of them would win the lottery of becoming Mrs. Jeorgeullah Wickaam.

Kaleen was feeling a bit green over having his thunder stolen by this smooth-talking fine-looking devil. It occurred to him that perhaps the devil might be a suitable match for his daughter. He asked Wickaam where he worked and how much he made. Wickaam informed everyone that he'd studied in New York, that he was back in Pakistan and was working as a junior lawyer, and that he was just starting out but he hoped, prayed, and planned to go places.

Hoping, praying, and planning to go places did not guarantee getting anywhere, and Kaleen immediately lost interest. He wanted to see his daughter married off as soon as possible, as per her dying mother's final wishes, but he had standards, which did not include struggling, penniless lawyers no matter how charismatic.

In her turn, Mrs. Binat tried to calculate

how many years before Wickaam would become a bigshot lawyer and which daughter of hers might be able to wait for this inevitability. Such a beautiful man was sure to ascend in the ranks based on looks alone. She concluded Qitty was the perfect age and that Wickaam needed to stop hovering over Alys and return to dancing with Qitty. Mrs. Binat's machinations were interrupted by Kaleen's whispered disclosure that he was on the lookout for a wife. He chucked his head diffidently and informed her that he found her daughters bedazzling.

Kaleen had privately pondered why the Binat girls were still unmarried and concluded it must be because, given their great good looks, they would only deign to entertain the most stellar of matches. Rocking himself to his full height of five foot six, he believed that with his promise of a thriving medical practice and immediate access to the best of society, courtesy of his benefactress, he was on par as a match with the best of the best.

"Your eldest daughter," Kaleen said, "is a vision of the houris in heaven promised to men after death."

"My Jena," Mrs. Binat said proudly, "is getting engaged any day now to Modest. You know, Modest *wallay.* The owners of

233

Modest Sanitary Company. Surely your daughter must be using their products? But . . ." Her hungry gaze settled on Alys. It would not be a match to crow about, given that Kaleen was neither prince nor president; however, getting this daughter married off to a future VIP would be nothing to scoff at.

"My second daughter, Alys" — Mrs. Binat gave Kaleen a congenial smile as he rapidly morphed from nuisance into prospective son-in-law — "is free for the plucking. Let me assure you she loves children and will treat yours as if they dropped out of her own womb. Frankly, you would be hard-pressed to find a more timid girl in all of Pakistan. Also, she's a schoolteacher with excellent earning potential."

"No need for a wage-earning wife." Kaleen waved his fists. "A woman's duty is to look after the children and run the household. The only drawback to my success is that I am too busy and so require a mother for my children. But, you see, I must marry someone who will be kind to my children not just in front of me but also behind my back. My children have grown up in an English atmosphere and so they only know stepmothers from 'Cinderella,' 'Snow White,' 'Sleeping Beauty,' and other rubbish fairy tales in which stepmothers want to murder the children. I tell them not to fear, for I will only marry a quality Pakistani girl. Also," Kaleen confided, grinning ruefully, "between you and me, we know men have needs that good women simply do not, and I am but a man."

"I believe Alys will prove to be exceptional with manly needs as well as motherhood," Mrs. Binat said. "But, Kaleen, you know how even in arranged marriages these days, young girls first want to get to know the boy. Therefore, I suggest that for the time being we hold off mentioning marriage to Alys. Instead, I recommend you endear your good self to her. In fact, if you have no New Year's plans, you must accompany us to a most coveted *walima.*"

"New Year's!" Kaleen's toothbrush brows bristled. "You mean Satan's special holiday, barring Halloween. New Year's is a festivity that encourages the triumvirate of 'B's: *Beygarithi, Behayai, Besharmi,* Immodesty, Indecency, Shamelessness."

"True," Mrs. Binat said, blinking, for she quite enjoyed a New Year's get-together and the subsequent welcoming in of the new year. Alys had lectured her one year about how time was a manmade concept and that no miracles were going to occur simply because a clock announced that December 31 had turned into January 1. Mrs. Binat prayed that, once wedded and bedded, her daughter would turn into a less opinionated and more cheerful person.

"Oho! Not a New Year's party but a *walima* on New Year's Eve," Mrs. Binat stressed. "After that we will be returning to Dilipabad, and you must visit us at your earliest convenience and stay with us."

"Done deal," Kaleen said, pleased.

"Also, my daughter, Mari, suffers from asthma, and I would be so obliged if you would check her."

"My pleasure," Kaleen said. Occupational hazard, and she'd not even cursorily mentioned payment, but then that was relatives for you.

"Oh, but Alys's health is superb. Do look at her." Mrs. Binat settled her eyes on Alys, and so did Kaleen. "How decorously she laughs. How daintily she crosses her legs. Such a meek creature, my little Alys, no one meeker to be found in Pakistan — therefore, I urge you again that until I give you the green light, not a word about your intentions."

"Of course," Kaleen said, proceeding to the dinner table with sudden gusto. "I understand and I approve of Alys's shyness, as well as the fact that in today's world it is right and fitting that she must get to know me before marriage. But for me, Pinkie, your assurance that Alys is demure and decent is enough of a guarantee that she will make a righteous wife and mother."

After the guests departed, the family settled down over fresh cups of chai to subject the evening to a postmortem. It was decided that Wickaam was the great hit of the evening — a pity about his lack of wealth but, oh, those dashing looks — and Kaleen was the great miss of the evening, income galore but a dud looks-wise.

"Farhat Kaleen has his own appeal," Mrs. Binat stressed to Nona and Nisar until they deigned to nod. Mari agreed with her mother, but she kept quiet.

"Mummy!" Lady said, "he's yuck-*thoo*! His nose looks like a popcorn! And he's so unstylish. Why did his kids let him dress like a clown?"

Mrs. Binat reminded Lady that sometimes parents did not listen to children and — she looked sharply at Alys — children also refused to benefit from their parents' wisdom.

"Qitty," Mrs. Binat said, "did you see how much attention Wickaam paid to you?"

Qitty nodded shyly.

Lady snorted. "He told me that I was a glamour queen destined for tremendous things."

Hopefully, Mrs. Binat thought as she rose to go to bed, the wait for Wickaam to become a Rich Man and propose to Qitty would not be too long, and at least Alys would not die in waiting for her Prince Charming, because Farhat Kaleen was truly eager to make her his blushing bride-to-be sooner rather than later.

CHAPTER 12

On the evening of the NadirFiede *walima,* Mrs. Binat opened the door to Farhat Kaleen arriving a full hour earlier than departure time. He was ablaze in sickeningly sweet cologne and looking, he believed, very sexy in a khaki suit, fuchsia shirt, and a white-and-fuchsia-striped tie.

Alys had chosen to wear the sari she'd refused at the *mehndi* ceremony. It was the color of Kashmiri pink tea, and Mrs. Binat couldn't help but conclude that the coincidence of Farhat and Alys both wearing shades of pink was a sign from God that they were a match made in heaven.

Jena looked striking in a peach *zardozi kameez* and seed pearl embroidered open front gown paired with a white silk *thang pajama,* a *shahtoosh* shawl, and Ganju *jee*'s rubies. The rest of the girls looked their best in lavenders, yellows, and greens, though, on second thought, Mrs. Binat decided she was never going to dress Qitty in green again. She looked like a raw mango.

So it was just as well that Wickaam had sent Nona a thank-you note for the Christmas party with the message that, unfortunately, he would be unable to attend Nadir-Fiede's *walima.* Qitty was understandably upset, and all the girls were miffed. Mrs. Binat herself was quite peeved at being deprived of his company, and she kept snapping at Mr. Binat to stop whining about not wanting to go: Even if his brother and sister-in-law were at the *walima,* he was to merely nod at them and move on.

When it was time to leave, Mrs. Binat put the Quran on Jena's head and read the Ayatul Kursi — not that there was doubt in anyone's mind that tonight, at NadirFiede's final event, Bungles must propose. Since Kaleen had his driver and car — the latest model of an excellent make, Mrs. Binat was gratified to see — she instructed Jena and Alys to ride with him. To her annoyance, Sherry climbed in with them — not that it really mattered, because no one in their right mind was going to give Sherry Looclus a second look, despite the poor thing having dressed up as best as she could in those tacky puffed sleeves and that greasy lipstick.

Mr. and Mrs. Binat, Lady, Qitty, and Mari got into Nisar's car with Ajmer, directions in hand, and they set off for the *walima,* which was to be held at Nadir Sheh's family's farmhouse. In this case, "farmhouse" meant a country villa surrounded by meadows without a single animal, barnyard or otherwise, to speak of. Since the Binats were arriving in good cars, Mrs. Binat insisted on idling at the gate in order to be noticed. Alys finally got out of Kaleen's car, grateful that the ride was over. Kaleen had talked at her the whole forty-five minutes about how many lives he'd saved, when all she'd wanted to do was mourn Wickaam's decision to stay away on account, no doubt, of horrid Darsee.

As soon as they entered the gates, Mrs. Binat saw Principal Naheed on the red carpet leading up to the farmhouse, with her husband, Zaleel, and Gin and Rum dressed in flapper-style long frocks. Dear God, Mrs. Binat thought, the twins looked like shredded streamers.

"Girls look great!" she said, greeting Naheed. "QaziKreations?"

Naheed nodded and complimented the Binat girls' attire. Formalities complete, everyone marveled at the abundance of flowers wherever they looked. The villa's main gate and boundary walls were strung with thick floral ropes. A tunnel of candlelit flowers engulfed the brick path from the gate leading to the driveway and a mini-fountain awash in petals. Guests turned from the mini-fountain into a dazzling floral pergola, which took them to the garden and into a tent of flowers, an Eden within an Eden, which meant, Alys couldn't help but think, there must be snakes too.

"This is what being in a bouquet must smell like," Mrs. Binat said as she made her way under the floral canopy toward forest-green velvet sofas.

Nadir and Fiede were wearing matching yellow-and-black ensembles designed by Qazi, for which, it was rumored, the designer had charged enough to enjoy at least five sumptuous holidays.

"Are NadirFiede supposed to be bumble-bees?" Lady asked as she took an effervescent mint drink from a floral tray.

"I think," Mrs. Binat replied, squinting, "the newlyweds are sunflowers."

"Mummy," Alys said, "I think you just might be right."

"I'm always right," Mrs. Binat said, "even if you and your father seldom acknowledge it."

Mr. Binat barely registered his wife's

242

complaint, on the lookout as he was for Goga and Tinkle, his ears buzzing so badly he could barely hear Kaleen's prattle.

Kaleen was admiring the fortune the Shehs must have spent to create this plucked paradise. That the Binats were invited to this VIP to-do had duly raised Barkat "Bark" Binat in his esteem. This was proof that Pinkie's family were not absolute nobodies, and Kaleen shed any doubts over his upcoming nuptials to Alysba Binat. He glanced at Alys. His bride-to-be looked like a rosebud tonight, one he could not wait to have and to hold. She was a little on the dusky side, but no matter; secretly he thought wheatish women equally as attractive as whitish ones. He wished he hadn't promised Pinkie Binat to keep his betrothal to Alys a secret, for he wanted this illustrious gathering to know that she belonged to him. He wondered what sweet nothings Alys was whispering into her friend's ear — what was her name?

Alys noticed Farhat Kaleen giving her another syrupy smile. The thought alone that he may have a crush on her was disturbing, and she focused on the stage. It was fashioned like a bower, on which Nadir and Fiede sat enthroned as if they were Shakespeare's fairy royalty, King Oberon and Queen Titania, greeting their florally smitten guests. Alys looked around for other characters from *A Midsummer Night's Dream.* There were Bottoms galore, wearing ass heads, a category into which she dropped Kaleen. Pucks abounded too, looking for mischief to spread between married couples, be they happy or unhappy, simply for their own amusement. Alys was sure she spied a couple of Helenas, the plain young girl who longs for love but can't find anyone to woo her. She pointed them out to Sherry, who was quick to remark that she was a Helena and she was sure Qitty felt like one too.

"I wonder," Alys sighed, "how many Emma Bovarys are here, sick of their rash marriages, and how many of Wharton's May Wellands, guarding their 'property.' And how many girls here are tomboys like Jo March in *Little Women* and what will happen to make them realize they are only women in a man's world. And how many of those women will then seek justice for that unfairness in the occult, like the mother in Zora Neale Hurston's story 'Black Death.' "

Alys pointed to the gathering of Daisy Buchanans, that spoiled little rich girl from *The Great Gatsby.* How many Myrtle Wilsons were here, nursing the wounds left from a Daisy Buchanan's emotional hit-and-run? Alys remarked that too many of the men in this room were Tom Buchanans and Meyer Wolfsheims, who believed they owned the women and most of the men, and ruled the world.

"As for Jay Gatsby," Alys said, "he's obviously a Wickaam."

"Jay Gatsby is a crook," Sherry said.

"He is a man turned crooked by society."

"And who are you?" Sherry asked as they made their way on the red carpet–covered lawn to congratulate the bride and the groom.

"I'm the omniscient narrator and observer in Austen's novels."

"I think," Sherry said, smiling mischievously, "you're that character who says no but ends up falling into a yes despite herself: You are Elizabeth Bennet."

"Elizabeth Bennet," Alys said, "had to marry Fitzwilliam Darcy, and he her, because Jane Austen, their creator-god, orchestrated it so. And there would be no Charlotte Lucas today because marrying for financial security is no longer the only choice she'd have. Thankfully we don't live in a novel, and in real life if I met someone as stuck-up as Mr. Darcy, I'd tell him to pack his bags, because there would be nothing that could endear me to such a snob, least of all the size of his estate. My views would frighten away a man like Mr. Darcy, who ultimately wants a feisty wife but also one who knows her place —"

"Excuse me —"

Alys stilled at the voice. Turning, she came face-to-face with Valentine Darsee. She reddened. Had he heard her? Not that she cared.

"May I help you?" she asked.

"You certainly may," Darsee said, nodding a polite hello at Sherry. "I wanted to give you this," and Alys, momentarily flustered, accepted the book he handed her, his fingertips brushing hers.

"*Sunlight on a Broken Column*," he was saying. "You said you hadn't read it, remember?"

"I don't remember," Alys said, though she remembered very well.

"I'd like to know what you think about it," Darsee said.

"I don't know when I'll be able to get to it," Alys said, and then added stiffly, "Thank you."

The girls walked on and, as soon as they were out of earshot, Sherry propelled Alys toward a secluded spot under a lantern fashioned of flowers.

"That man is definitely interested in you," Sherry said.

"Oh please." Alys was thankful Sherry hadn't caught their accidental touch. "Who cares."

"If you play your cards right, and he marries you, that would be the greatest coup."

"*I* wouldn't marry him. He's unmarriageable."

"You'd become the owner of the British School Group, and instead of Principal Naheed hauling you into her office, you'd get to tell her to behave."

"Even vengeance could not entice me to marry that man. Were Darsee to suddenly declare I was the most attractive woman in the world and not stupid, I would still not marry him."

"You've really got to get over that. He's a *real* catch and Jena is right, you weren't meant to hear what he said about you. Had you not heard it, you'd be delirious with joy that a fish like him is swimming toward your hook."

"I would not," Alys said. "You didn't see the way he cold-shouldered Wickaam at the border ceremony. For all Darsee's assets, he's still a jerk."

"I wish a jerk like that would fall in love with me." Sherry sighed. "You and Jena are so lucky. She'll marry Bungles and you'll marry Darsee. Your mother is right: All you need is one rich man to become besotted with your looks and, *jantar mantar,* abracadabra, your destiny is changed. Takes so much more for those of us without looks. So unfair."

"It is unfair. Especially when good-looking people complain how unfair it is that no one sees beyond their looks." Alys laughed dryly. "*Inshallah,* Jena will certainly marry Bungles. But there will be no such ending for me."

"I know why you are saying that," Sherry said. "It's that Wickaam. *You* are besotted by *his* looks."

"I don't get besotted by looks," Alys said. "You should know that much about me after ten years of friendship, Sherry."

"I know that you are human. But as your friend and well-wisher, let me advise you to put Wickaam aside and focus on grabbing Darsee."

"Will you please not use that disgusting word? You sound just like my mother."

"Grab it, grab it," Sherry joked, half seriously. "Grab Valentine Darsee because, trust me, he wants to be grabbed by you. Alys, listen to me: Wickaam seems nice, but Darsee has a lifestyle that only real money can buy."

"Money is not everything. And too many rich men have a tendency to be horrid because they think money stands in for character, decency, and smarts."

"Money is a safety net for everything that may not work out in life."

"Not if your husband is a control freak or a stingy hoarder."

"I really don't think Darsee is either. You two even share a love of reading."

"I don't want to share a love of anything with him, thank you," Alys said. "And luckily for both Wickaam and Darsee, I'm not a gold digger. I refuse to seek a rich *roti.* I'm going to make my own money and live happily ever after on my own terms."

"Tch," Sherry said. "I can understand why your mother is always so irritated by you. You're a teacher. In Dilipabad. And I know you don't look it or care, but you are getting older by the day."

"Would singledom be acceptable if I were still twenty and owned my own thriving business?"

"No."

"Thought so." Alys dropped *Sunlight* into the large cloth bag she was carrying instead of a delicate evening purse, much to her mother's exasperation.

Dinner was announced and the two friends joined the surge of guests going toward the buffet in the garden. It was a feast of prawns, by far the most expensive delicacy in Pakistan at the moment. *Tandoori* prawn. Prawn skewer kebabs. Grilled prawns. Prawn *pulao.* Penne prawns. Deep-fried prawns. Prawn *jalfrezi.* Prawn *korma.* Sweet-and-sour prawns. Butterfly prawns. Prawn fried rice. Prawn-stuffed *paratha.* Prawn cutlets. Prawn salad.

"Okay, Nadir Sheh, we get it!" Alys said as she and Sherry joined the buffet line. "You can afford all the prawns in the ocean. And I'd thought the flowers ostentatious."

"I love prawns," Sherry said, taking heaping spoonfuls of each entrée. "I've only ever eaten them once, and even then we only got four each. This is why you marry rich: an endless array of prawns whenever you want and prepared however you want."

"I think it's selfish!" Alys spooned a small serving of prawn salad onto her plate. "What about the people who don't like prawns? Or have allergies?"

"How sad to be allergic to prawns," Sherry said, as she followed Alys to the seating area, where guests were having trouble setting their plates down among the floral table décor.

Kaleen came to their rescue and led them to a table he'd already cleared of flowers as best as he could.

"Aha," Kaleen said, pointing to Sherry's full plate and then to his own, "I see we have prawns in common."

"Yes," Sherry said, "we do."

"Dear sweet Alys," Kaleen said, "your plate is shamefully empty. Allow me to pick prawns for you in the hope that my choice will please your palate."

"Oh!" Alys stood up abruptly. "Many thanks for your offer, Kaleen Sahib, but I see a friend I must talk to. Sherry here will be more than happy to keep you company." Alys smiled wickedly at Sherry. "Please do discuss all the prawns you have in common."

Valentine Darsee, in the buffet line, choosing a single prawn from each entrée, watched Alys rise from a table and stride across the tent. How gracefully she walks in her sari, he thought, and balances her plate at the same time.

"What are you thinking, babes?" Hammy said, appearing by Darsee's side as she and Sammy and Jaans cut the buffet line to stand with him. There were a few murmurs but, since everyone hopes to cut some line sometime in life, no one made much of a fuss.

"Not thinking anything," Darsee said.

"I love prawns," Hammy said, happily ladling penne prawns onto her plate.

"I'm quite partial to prawns myself," Darsee said, "but what about the people who are allergic or don't like them?"

"Sammy doesn't like prawns," Hammy said.

"Shame on you, Sammy-whammy," Jaans said to Sammy, "to dislike prawns in the face of such abundance. Darsee, did you hear Nadir's honeymoon plans? I told him, '*Cheethay,* leave some countries for another time,' but, no, he wants to take Fiede on a world tour she'll never forget. Wife, when are you taking me on a tour I'll never forget?"

"When you deserve it." Sammy glared at Jaans. "I hate seafood."

"Eat the *naan.*" Jaans shoved bread at her. "Since you're being ungrateful, it's all you deserve."

"I'm getting dessert." Sammy flung the bread onto Jaan's full plate. "Thankfully, you can't force prawns into desserts."

"Let's check on Bungles first," Hammy said. "The mother might have devoured him by now. Fortunately, Jena herself is standoff-ish; otherwise that brother of ours seems ready to be a doormat."

"Jena is just shy," Jaans said. "I've known girls like her. Too scared they might say something wrong and end up losing the proposal."

"There is no proposal," Hammy said.

"And," Sammy added, "don't you dare put such a notion into Bungles's head, Jaans."

"I don't have to," Jaans said. "He's not a child. What Brother Bungles is, though," Jaans made a rude face, "is a doormat, a *zun mureed,* a woman worshipper who will be perfectly happy to be a *joru ka ghulam,* a slave to his wife. He'll put her on a pedestal and expect them to be best friends."

Sammy made a wistful face; she wouldn't mind an uxorious husband for herself.

"So what?" Darsee asked Jaans.

"So," Hammy said grimly, "all the more reason Bungles needs to marry someone we can mold to our liking."

"That's disgusting," Darsee said. "Would you like to be molded?"

"I'd like to see someone try," Hammy said, gazing into Darsee's eyes.

"Brother Bungles," Jaans said, "is fully aware how lucky he is to have found a girl as beautiful as Jena Binat still single."

"Have you ever wondered," Sammy sneered, "why Jena the Beautiful is unmarried?"

"Why?" Jaans asked.

"Yes, why exactly?" Darsee said.

"Far be it for me to indulge in gossip," Hammy said, looking up at Darsee, "but Sammy and I have it on excellent authority that her mother belongs to a very bad family."

"What are you talking about, Hammy?" Darsee frowned.

"They say," Sammy said, "Pinkie Binat's ancestors come from a background of prostitution. Pre-partition, but still."

"Who says?" Darsee said.

"Everyone," Hammy said. "They say it wasn't even at the level of a courtesan but, rather, a cheap back-alley tart. Honestly, before I began investigations into the mother's family for Bungles's sake, I didn't even know there was a hierarchy of prostitutes. I thought they were all equal."

"Where's the proof they come from that?" Darsee said.

"Tinkle Binat told me. Why would she malign her own family?"

"Because," Darsee said, "the Binat brothers are estranged."

"Estrangement," Sammy said, "doesn't mean you concoct dirty ruinous rumors about your relatives."

"Where's concrete proof," Darsee said, "that any of us truly descends from our claims?"

"I'll give you proof in the Binats' case," Hammy said. "That mother of theirs might dress well, but the second she opens her mouth her style of talking, her demeanor, everything, speaks of an unsavory ancestry. She's all raspy and graspy like vamps and prostitutes in films. Like mother like daughters, I say, though you can detect the lack of breeding the most in Lady."

"Tone of voice is hardly proof," Darsee said. He put down his plate.

"It's not *not* proof," Hammy said. "There's nothing to disprove they aren't slut spawn."

"What a pleasant phrase," Darsee said. "Is it original?"

"Thank you! Yes!" Hammy said. "Now you'll understand why Sammy and I have always felt so sorry for the Binat sisters. They can dress like Audrey Hepburn as much as they want, but it's not going to confer class on them. Tinkle Binat told me" — Hammy lowered her voice for effect — "that Pinkie's lineage was the real reason for the brothers' rift. Goga Binat demanded his brother divorce her, but Bark Binat refused on account of his five daughters, and so what choice did Goga and Tinkle have but to disinherit them and banish them to D-bad."

"Honestly," Sammy said, "you should always tell the truth about your origins, especially in matters matrimonial, or be ready to face the consequences."

"If this is true," Darsee said, "then it was good of Bark Binat to stick by his wife and daughters even if it meant losing his inheritance. They're not her daughters alone. They're his too."

Hammy and Sammy exchanged a look.

"That puts a nice spin on the whole wretched business," Sammy said.

"Look, Val," Hammy said, "you have to knock some sense into Bungles's head. Jena will not do. Even if my entire family was willing to overlook Jena's hailing from a low-class prostitute, which we aren't, her family has issues. They are unsuitable girls from an unsuitable family."

"True." Darsee pursed his lips. "True."

Alys fled Kaleen's cloying overtures, only to find him following her and Sherry following him. Before she'd even set her plate down at her family's table, he was inquiring yet again if he could select her prawns. Alys's annoyed gaze met Jena's beseeching one: Bungles was sitting next to her. He was talking about whale-watching off the California coast and the aurora borealis in Alaska, two destinations on the NadirFiede honeymoon itinerary, which was available at each table in lamination for everyone's viewing pleasure. It was clear from Jena's face that he had yet to propose and that she was beginning to panic.

Dinner was fast coming to an end and the *walima* ceremony to a close; if he did not propose soon, there would be no more events at which he could do so. Yet Bungles did not seem like a man about to propose. He was busy eating *falooda,* taking dainty bites of the vermicelli in rose syrup and milk, all the while smiling at Jena with what anyone would only describe as utter devotion. No wonder Jena was losing her mind. Their mother was frantic, Alys could tell, from the way her eyes were darting all over Bungles, as if darts could prick him into action.

And then there was her father. Goga and Tinkle Binat had indeed arrived with great pomp and show but, luckily, boasting to all of the million weddings at which their appearance was vital, had left early. Mr. Binat had been terrified at encountering them and yet, when they'd completely ignored him, he'd become despondent. He sat now, his hand cupping his chin, utterly dejected and asking, every so often, what he could possibly have ever done to deserve his brother's conduct.

Alys would have ignored her family's behavior as usual were it not for Darsee, who kept walking by them to get to the buffet. Each time she saw him, she thought of the book in her bag, his fingers on hers. Why did he keep coming this way? The one time Bungles had gone to the toilet, Mrs. Binat loudly instructed Jena that, the second she became Mrs. Bungles, she was to search for equally suitable boys for her sisters. Another time Darsee passed them, Lady's soda spilled down her bosom, which she'd patted dry most indecorously. The last time Darsee had descended on the buffet, Mari was giving yet another female guest with a bare midriff a lecture on how women should not be upset over Islam's injunction to dress chastely, because the same was commanded of men.

From the corner of her eye, Alys spied Darsee coming their way again, this time with Hammy, Sammy, and Jaans.

"Hello, all." Jaans waved at the Binats. "How is everyone? Enjoying the prawns?"

Kaleen turned to the new arrivals. "My good name is Farhat Kaleen. I am a recent England return. I am a physiatrist."

"Psychiatrists are more than welcome in this loony bin of a Lahore," Jaans said.

"Physiatrist," Kaleen stressed. "Physiatrist. I deal with rehabilitation of the body in the event of accidents and chronic pain, and I am setting up private practice."

There was a lull before Bungles took it upon himself to introduce his group.

"Valentine Darsee?" Kaleen's eyes grew huge. "Nephew of Begum Beena dey Bagh?"

"Guilty as charged," Darsee said.

"I have been longing to meet you, sir!" Kaleen grabbed Darsee's hand and swung it vigorously. "Your 'unty Beena is my great benefactress. Have you guessed who I am? I am your cousin Annie's doctor! Dr. Farhat Kaleen. It is thanks to me that she has made startling improvements. By God, when I first saw her I thought she would not last the night, and now she sits upright and is showing an interest in fashion shows again. I've been encouraging her to return to modeling — why not, why should a cane stop her or anybody? Your dear cousin Annie calls me her miracle worker. Though I must say I have a model patient in Annie. Ha-ha. Model patient, no pun intended. Valentine Darsee! Such a pleasure to meet you! Had I known I was going to meet you here, I would have . . ." Kaleen stopped for a second, unsure of what he would have done differently. "I trust we will be seeing much of each other, for, given Annie's health, I am frequently at your 'unty's most grand estate, the Versailles of Pakistan."

Darsee extracted his hand from Farhat Kaleen's grip and perfunctorily announced, "It's time to go."

"Say goodbye to your friends, baby bro," Hammy said. "Up. Now."

"What's the rush?" Bungles said, gazing at Jena, who was staring dully into her lap.

"The rush," Sammy said, "is we have to get ready for Fazool and Moolee's New Year's party."

Bungles rose, but before relief could settle permanently on Hammy and Sammy's faces, he invited Jena to the New Year's party: Could she go?

CHAPTER 13

Hammy smacked Bungles's shoulder once again for good measure and mimicked Mrs. Binat, who'd risen like a peacock spreading its fan: " 'Of course Jena may go; she's all yours. But surely you cannot expect young Jena to go without a chaperone, so she will be happy to be accompanied by all her sisters.' " And then she imitated Bungles's response to Mrs. Binat: " 'But of course, I meant to invite them all.' "

"Why the hell did you invite Jena to begin with?" Sammy snarled. They were in Darsee's car on their way to the New Year's party, having gone to their homes to change out of their wedding finery and into party clothes, which, for Hammy and Sammy, meant the skimpiest outfits the current state of their slim figures would allow.

"Your puppy-like behavior is bad enough," Hammy said, "but that mother has apparently been informing the world that there is soon to be a wedding."

"You're stringing Jena along, Bungles," Sammy said, "and that's not very nice."

"Let Brother Bungles have his fun," Jaans said. "Jena's an adult!"

"Jena *is* an adult!" Hammy said to Bungles. "She's thirty-two years old to your twenty-five. Seven years' age difference."

"She could be a hundred years older than me for all I care," Bungles said, a bit cowed by the glares his sisters and even Darsee were giving him, though he glared back. "And I certainly don't care who her mother is or where she comes from."

"We care," Hammy said, "so that's that."

"It's not just the mother factor," Darsee said. "I don't believe Jena Binat is interested in you. She sits there without a smile. She barely says two words when you ask her a question. If she's a gold digger, she's not a very good one."

"Perhaps," Bungles said in a hesitant voice, "she's not a gold digger at all."

"Her mother is a gold digger!" Hammy said. " 'Like mother, like daughter,' they say."

"Why should I listen to 'they'?" Bungles asked. "Who is 'they'?"

"*We* are they," Hammy and Sammy thundered simultaneously.

"But I like Jena," Bungles said. "I like her very much."

"That's because the mother has put a hex on you," Hammy said. "I can't believe you invited Jena and her sisters to the party. Fazool is going to freak. You know how exclusive and classy she keeps her parties. The Binat sisters probably can't believe their lucky stars. Let's hope their car gets a flat tire and we are spared all five frights."

For perhaps the first time in his life, Ajmer did not get lost on the way to an address, and so it happened that the Binat sisters arrived at the party at the same time that Darsee's car did. As Bungles's and Jena's eyes met, Alys was finally convinced that her mother was right: Bungles meant to propose at the stroke of midnight. There could be no other meaning behind the tender look he was giving Jena, who, in her turn, looked away from him, clearly overcome.

The group entered the gate to the mansion and walked to the front door, behind which music was playing. The door opened and Hammy and Sammy were air-kissed by a slinky woman in a silver halter top and QaziKreations' most expensive *mohti,* the miniskirt *dhoti* shimmering with semiprecious stones; a man beside her grinned toothily when he saw them all.

"Amazing outfits! Love the shoes!" the woman said, looking Hammy and Sammy up and down as they tottered in red-soled black platforms. Hammy was in black leather biker shorts, a red lace bustier, and a black mesh bolero, and Sammy was in red leather biker shorts, a black lace bustier, and a red mesh bolero.

"Thank yous, thank yous," Hammy-Sammy said, complimenting Fazool's *mohti* and her red-soled nude Louboutins in return. Hammy introduced her to the Binats.

"Sisters Binat, these are our darling friends, Fauzia 'Fazool' Fazal and her husband, Hamid 'the Moolee' Fazal," Hammy said. "Friends, these are the five Binat sisters. Bungles graciously invited them. I hope you don't mind."

Fazool's eyes narrowed as she took in Mari's local garb, so out of place at such a happening event as her New Year's bash, at Qitty in a crushed-velvet black tent, at Lady in white jeans and a T-shirt that said UNMARRIAGEABLE in glitter and showed off her ample cleavage. Fazool glanced at Alys, whose chest also caused her envy. As for Jena — why did God bless some girls with so much beauty? Oh well, Fazool was rich and up there in the social register and clearly they were not, so she gave them the vapid smile reserved for nobodies who could not be completely ignored and said, "Do come in."

"Yes! Do!" Moolee ran his fingers through the curly chest hair crawling out of his half-buttoned Versace shirt. "The more girls, the merrier. Bungles, Darsee, Jaans, good to see you all. Hammy-Sammy, as usual — looking ready to mingle and tingle."

Moolee gave Hammy and Sammy lingering hugs. He turned to the Binats with thirsty eyes. "We look forward to mingling and tingling with you all, don't we, Fazool? Now, which one of you pretty sisters wants to hug me first?"

Before the Binat sisters could reply, Fazool laughed as if Moolee had cracked a great joke and then she adroitly turned her husband around, pushed him inside toward the party, and led everyone else indoors.

"What delights has Moolee been smoking?" Darsee asked Fazool as they entered the marble entrance with its winding staircase next to a piano with a vase full of blue twigs.

"Who knows?" Fazool said. She led them through the entrance and into a glass-paneled corridor alongside the garden and toward the music. "Since it's Happy New Year, I've let him off the leash a little." She smiled gallantly. "And he has let me off my leash too. Fun! Fun! Fun! For me, for him, for everyone. Anyway, he's harmless, Valoo, you know that!" Fazool linked arms with Darsee.

"Val, you've become way too somber," Jaans said tipsily, linking arms with Fazool. "You need to learn to live and let live."

Darsee shrugged. "Live and let live does not mean living consequence free."

Jaans sighed. "You used to be so much fun before you went to America, *behen chod,* sisterfucker."

"Mind your language, Jaans," Darsee said, as Bungles rested a calming hand on his shoulder. "I don't care how much you've had to drink."

"Ja-ans!" Sammy pouted. "How many times should I tell you not to not say *behen chod,* sisterfucker. It's so insulting to women. Use your own gender and say *bhai chod,* brotherfucker."

Alys glanced at her sisters. Lady was thrilled. Mari looked about to faint. Jena and Qitty looked shaken at how casually such expletives were being bandied about. Even Bungles was looking embarrassed and Darsee's jaw was clenched.

266

"Come on now, people," Fazool said, laughing, "no fighting on New Year's. That's a rule. The party is in the living room, the drawing room, and out by the swimming pool."

Alys watched as Bungles whisked Jena away and Sammy, Jaans, Fazool, Moolee, and Hammy, pulling Darsee along, gamboled toward a room pulsing with disco lights. Lady and Qitty followed them, as did Mari, who'd only come in order to observe firsthand the misguided partiers of Pakistan, so that she would know exactly which preaching methods to employ in the future to return them to the *sirat-ul-mustaqim,* the path of the righteous.

Alys followed her sisters into the disco room. It was full of men and women lounging on settees. All nursed obese glasses of wine, cigarette smoke clouding every face. A few shimmied on the makeshift dance floor. Clusters of friends hung out by the bar, the bottles of scotch, vodka, gin, and wine twinkling under the bright bar lights.

The Binat sisters ordered orange juices from the bartender, a Punjab Club waiter in his white uniform with plumed turban. Once they got their drinks, Alys seated them on a sofa. Then she left to explore the other rooms, where it was all the same, except hip-hop played in the dimly lit drawing room, where billiards was in full swing, and techno pulsed by the aquamarine swimming pool, where the guests lolled under the starlit sky.

Alys looked for Jena but couldn't find her. She wished Sherry had agreed to tag along; they would have had a fine time deconstructing this social circus. Alys circled back to the disco room. Mari and Qitty were on the sofa, watching Lady dancing by herself to ABBA's "Money, Money, Money." After Alys decided Lady was in no harm or doing any harm, she went in search of a toilet. She passed by walls full of the most insipid art: pastoral paintings of mustard fields, watercolor sketches of rowdy-haired men on horses, and Quran calligraphy, which, according to Nona, was all the rage these days for both the pious and the not-so-pious art collector.

Alys passed by one young man instructing another young man on how to most effectively snort the cocaine he'd been guaranteed was going to be the time of his life. A young woman was complaining about how her bootlegger was charging her more for alcohol than her male friends *just* because she was a woman. A few steps on, a cricket star Alys had only seen on TV was politely listening to a mediocre but well-connected musician telling him that, though a dud at the game himself, he had advice for the cricketer's bowling. Passing by two men, Alys realized that one was Qazi of QaziKreations and the other was another fashion designer frequently featured in *Social Lights*. They were engaged in debate: "You're awesome, you're awesome," "No, you are, no, you are." Then she stumbled upon Sammy and Jaans in a passionate embrace, whispering urgent terms of endearment — "parasite," "upstart" — and Alys tapped Sammy on the shoulder: "Where's the toilet?"

On the way back, Alys passed by a room with the door half-open: a library. Curiosity overcame her. Which books graced Fazool and Moolee's shelves? She was skimming a cherrywood shelf of leather-bound classics, which she found were hollow —

"We meet again."

"Shit!" Alys spun around, a hollow book almost falling out of her hands.

It was Darsee. He was stretched out in a chaise longue, a tumbler of scotch by his side.

"You scared me," Alys said, annoyed. "What are you doing in here?"

"What do you think I'm doing?" Darsee

held up a tome: *Betty and Veronica Double Digest*. "I just got back to the country, and I'm in no mood yet for Jaans and Moolee, et cetera. Their entire life's purpose has begun to boil down to 'drink until you drop, preferably daily,' while Sammy and Fazool, et cetera, are getting PhDs in congratulating themselves on being amazing. Ridiculous. Prefer it here, reading."

Alys gazed at him for a long second, then said, "Looks like you and I seem to share this preference, given that we're both in here instead of out there making fools of ourselves."

"I don't know if I'd say you could ever make a fool of yourself. As for me, I think definitely not."

Alys blurted, "I hear it's more your scene to force your relatives into becoming fools."

"Excuse me?"

"Jeorgeullah Wickaam. Your cousin. The cousin you've treated abominably."

"*I* treated abominably!" Darsee's face turned livid.

"Wickaam told me everything."

"I know you have a very high opinion of yourself," Darsee said, "but you don't know anything about Wickaam and, trust me, you don't want to know. My advice to you is stay far away from that guy. Far, far away."

"Why? Oh, but of course, because he didn't salute your highness and kiss your ass!"

"Salute me! Kiss my ass! I find such behavior repellent."

"How could you cheat your own cousin out of his inheritance? How could you betray someone who is like a brother to you?"

Darsee got up and strode out of the library.

After Alys regained her composure, she rejoined the party, keeping one eye out for Darsee in order to stay far, far away from him. In the disco room, Lady was dancing on a tabletop to Donna Summer's "Love to Love You Baby." She was dancing with Shosha Darling, who kept yelling to no one and everyone, "Be a winner, baby, don't be a loser."

Both Lady and Shosha were sandwiched between a geriatric socialite Alys recognized from *Social Lights* and the host Moolee. Fazool was clapping and encouraging her husband to give Lady all his tingling-mingling.

Alys yanked Lady off the table. Lady gave Alys a murderous look as Alys plonked her beside Qitty, who was browsing through a coffee-table book on Islamic art history.

Alys whispered furiously to Qitty, "Didn't you see how those men were dancing with your sister? Why didn't you stop her?"

"I tried," Qitty said crossly, "but she started calling me fat in front of everyone, and then that senior citizen looked me up and down and said, '*Mashallah, sehatmand* sister' — healthy sister."

"Tch!" Alys looked around. "Where's Mari?"

She spied Mari standing behind the refreshments table, nibbling on mini cheesecakes, her *dupatta* chastely spread over her chest, her smug expression suggesting she was witnessing hell to her heart's content.

Alys was about to go to Mari when Hammy came upon her.

"Alys," Hammy said, "may I speak to you for a second?"

Alys followed Hammy into the entrance, where it was a little quieter.

"Listen," Hammy said, "I just want to let you know that Valentine left the party in a huff. I know you brought up Wickaam, and so I say the following to you with the best of intentions: There is bad blood between the two cousins, and it is not Val's fault. I don't know the exact details, but I do know that Wickaam is a dishonorable man and that he's done something truly unforgivable to Val, and it's unfair that you should annoy Val like this. Of course, Val requires no defense, but still I thought it my duty to speak up for him."

"I'm sure you thought it your duty," Alys said.

"Wickaam is a scoundrel."

"According to whom?" Alys said.

"Valentine!" Hammy said. "Valentine!"

"I see," Alys said. "Darsee speaks and you believe."

Hammy squinted. "It seems to me that Wickaam speaks and you believe."

"Yes, I do," Alys said.

"Suit yourself." Hammy raised her brows. "Well, do enjoy the party, and see you around, I guess. Happy New Year."

Alys watched Hammy head toward the pool. She certainly didn't sound the way the sister of a man who was about to propose should sound to the sister of the girl he was going to propose to.

"Alys!" It was Jena. "I've been looking everywhere for you."

"I was looking for you," Alys said.

"I want to leave. We need to leave. Why did we even come?"

"What's wrong?" Alys frowned. "What's happened?"

Jena's eyes filled for a second, but she

hardened her face. "Darsee dragged, and I mean dragged, Bungles out of here ten minutes ago. After which Sammy tells me that they're all so exhausted attending NadirFiede that she, Jaans, Hammy, Bungles, Darsee, and his sister, Jujeena, are going to the Maldives for rest and relaxation. She hopes to announce Bungles's engagement to Jujeena Darsee when they return, and she'll send me an invite."

"She's bluffing."

"He didn't propose, Alys." Jena's voice cracked. "All these days, all these opportunities. I want to go home. I'm so tired. I never thought I'd say this, but I want to return to grading papers and making lesson plans and ot dreaming about more."

Alys and Jena quickly rounded up their sisters, despite Lady's objections to leaving minutes before the New Year was going to be rung in, and they wished each other a Happy New Year in the car, quietly, without knowing when the stroke of midnight officially arrived and when it officially passed.

■ ■ ■ ■

Part Two

■ ■ ■ ■

January–August 2001

CHAPTER 14

What Will People Say
Log Kya Kahenge

PARTY SEEN: Fazool and Moolee Fazal of Cockatoo Interior Designs pulled off yet another rocking New Year's Partay for 151 of their closest friends. The hip and happening crowd reveled till dawn. Funtastic music and a poolside countdown under the stars made this the scene to be seen. Eat your hearts out, the rest of you.

RIP MELODY QUEEN OF PAKISTAN: A little bird tells us that tempers were high in some quarters over the televised tribute to the late and great Madame Noor Jehan, whose sonorous voice has been wooing hearts for over six decades. "It should not," said one wannabe songstress, whose voice routinely scares the alley cats, "have been scheduled at the same time as my live concert."

BIRTH OF A STAR: Demand is so high for up-and-coming designer Boobee Khan's Nangaparbat Lawn Collection, we hear two eager customers slapped each other to be first in line. Congrats, Boobee! Watch out, Qazi! There's yet another contender in town for the crown.

CHARITY POLO MATCH: Every lady should have a knight as gallant as eligible bachelor Fahad "Bungles" Bingla to come to her rescue. Wouldn't you agree, Jena Binat, damsel du jour?

The long school day finally ended, and Alys sat in the school van between Jena and Sherry. Outside, a late January drizzle abated, and Alys wound down the window for fresh air, only to be assaulted by the stench of burning garbage. Jena was sitting with a hand to her head, her eyes shut tightly, and she barely shifted.

Principal Naheed had called Alys in today. Alys thought Rose-Nama's mother had lodged yet another grievance or was demanding yet another apology. Instead, to Alys's shock, Principal Naheed said she was getting complaints about Jena. Jena was zoning out during class, and, at times, leaving class altogether and not coming back.

Was Jena okay? Naheed had asked, her

teeth gleaming. Did it have anything to do with that delicious fellow mentioned in *Social Lights*?

They'd been back in Dilipabad right after New Year's and Alys — in fact, all the Binats — had hoped that with the school semester starting and life returning to its usual routine, Jena's sadness would subside, but that had not been the case. Even worse, teachers would bring celebratory sweets to the staff room every day, and Alys wondered if, each time Jena was offered a *ladoo* or a *barfi* for a son's promotion or a grandchild's birth or some other happy occasion, it reminded her anew that, had things turned out differently, she'd also have been offering teachers celebratory sweets.

Jena had not cried or railed, at least not in front of them, but she'd been inordinately quiet on the subject, except to say that it was their mother who had promised that Bungles would propose and that he himself had never promised her anything. Mrs. Binat was one minute full of ill will for Bungles, who, she claimed, had toyed with Jena, and the next minute upset with Jena, who, she accused, had thoughtlessly let him slip off her hook.

The van went over a bump and Jena's eyes fluttered open. Alys gave her a big smile.

Jena replied with a tiny smile. There were dark circles under her eyes and she looked beaten. Alys sighed as she recalled how Jena had blanched at seeing her name, fodder for a gossip column, in *Social Lights.* She wondered if girls from Jena's classes might be asking her invasive questions and if this was the reason for her erratic behavior. She glanced at Qitty and Lady. Had anyone said anything to them?

Alys caught Sherry's gaze. Sherry continued to insist that Jena should have asked Bungles point-blank: "Am I just a time pass or are you planning to marry me?" While Alys believed in being up-front, she was glad that Jena had not debased herself, and she was sure that Jena too was relieved to have not embarrassed herself.

The only bright spot in these bleak weeks was Wickaam's visits. The first had been on the pretext that Mr. Binat's signatures were required on the Fraudia Acre case papers and Wickaam did not trust the mail. He'd used a similar excuse for his second visit. But the third was simply the result of Mrs. Binat's open invitation to visit them anytime. In fact, she'd since urged him to stay the night, given how tiring a four-hour round trip from Lahore to Dilipabad could be, and he'd cheerfully accepted: a sleep-over!

More time for Wickaam to captivate all with the story of his childhood, his becoming a full orphan, BeenaDeenaWeena, Valentine Darsee's betrayal. He'd been amused and appreciative when Lady began to call Darsee "Dracula," and before long, all the Binats were referring to the traitorous cousin as Dracula.

Wickaam was installed in the cozy guest room, and the only awkward moment was when Alys had to send Lady to change her night-suit, with the admonition that she was not allowed to wander around the house in such a sheer nightie when they were hosting a male guest.

"Jeorgeullah is no mullah," Mari had said gravely. "Be careful, Lady."

"You be careful, weirdo," Lady said. "Mullahs aren't all saints, and I know you have flutters for Fart Bhai."

Lady pronounced Kaleen's first name, Farhat, so fast she'd transformed it into "Fart."

"I do not." Two bright splotches appeared on Mari's face. "Alys is right about the negligee. It's obscene. Go and change."

Lady had gone weeping to their mother. Mrs. Binat told Alys and Mari to mind their own business. Lady wasn't naked. A nightgown was a nightgown. When Alys had appealed to her father, Mr. Binat had declared, red-faced, that he was gladly relegating all matters of nightwear and nighttime activities to Mrs. Binat's expertise.

The school van stopped outside the graveyard, and the Binat girls and Sherry got out and sprinted to their homes to avoid the sudden downpour. In the Binat living room, Hillima laid out steaming chai and deep-fried *pakoras,* always a staple comfort food on a rainy day. Mr. Binat rose from the crackling fireplace, where he'd been reading a book on ornamentals, and kissed each of his daughters on the forehead.

The girls kicked off their shoes and settled onto sofas. Alys climbed into the window seat, enjoying the dark bubble of a sky. For a long minute, there were few sounds but the rumble of thunder, the sipping of chai, and the chewing of piping-hot *pakoras.* Mari finished up her prayers in the corner of the room and blew blessings of prosperity and peace on each of her sisters, spending a few seconds longer on Jena.

Mrs. Binat came into the living room. She beamed as she replaced the cordless on its cradle. She hadn't beamed like this since they'd returned from Lahore. Sometimes she felt she'd never recover from Jena's failure to grab Bungles, and she was beginning to believe that truly of what use was beauty without a brain that could plot and scheme.

"We are to receive a special visitor," Mrs. Binat said. "He will be arriving tonight in time for dinner and plans to stay for a few days."

Everyone smiled.

"It's not Wickaam," Mrs. Binat said. "It's Farhat Kaleen."

Everyone's smile faded. Except Mari's. Her heart pattered at the thought of being under one roof with the good doctor. Perhaps, together, they could inject some righteousness into her sisters' heads. Then he would see how perfect she was for him, and he would propose to her, and they would live happily ever after. Mari shook herself and asked God to forgive her the Farhat fantasy, in case it was untoward of her. But, God, she bargained, if you make me the first sister married, then I swear to thank you by starting to wear a *hijab.*

"Fart *Bhai!*" Lady said. "Fart *Bhai* is the big surprise? Is this a joke?"

"What's there to joke about?" Mrs. Binat said. "He is an up-and-coming EIP, extremely important person."

"He's a purity pervert," Lady said. "He told me that I shouldn't wear skintight shirts."

"He's right," Mari said. "And don't dare insult pious men by labeling them purity perverts."

"Women like you are the biggest purity perverts of all."

"Now, Lady," Mrs. Binat said, "do not disrespect Kaleen in any way. He's coming to check Mari's asthma, as well as other patients in Dilipabad, and I would like all of you girls — and you too, Barkat — to make yourselves amenable to him."

"He is a popcorn-nosed yuck-*thoo,*" Lady said. "I'm not even going to come downstairs while he's here."

"I will," Mari said.

"I bet," Lady said, "you're looking forward to Fart Bhai's stethoscope roaming all over your chest."

"Lady," Alys said, "have you lost all sense of decorum?"

"Aunty Alys, who made you the Superintendent of Virtue and Vice? At the New Year's party I was dancing with Shosha Darling — Shosha Darling! — and you dragged me off the table like a *paindu,* a yokel. Bungles —"

Jena left the room.

"Thanks for bringing him up yet again," Alys said.

"I didn't mean to," Lady said. "You provoked me. You always do."

"Honestly, Lady," Qitty said. "You are so inconsiderate."

"Shut up, baby elephant."

"You shut up," Qitty said, "Miss See-Through Nightie You-You Eyes while Wickaam was here."

"*Tauba,* you girls are too much for me," Mr. Binat said, also leaving the room.

"I wish," Mrs. Binat sighed, "that I too could be the sort of parent who can walk away from my daughters. Alys, go see that the guest room is ready for Kaleen. Why are you staring at me? Go. Do as you are told."

Farhat Kaleen arrived at Binat House exactly on time. Punctuality was a good habit no matter how un-Pakistani, he said, as he exited his car and his driver took out his bags. He beamed at all the Binats standing in the driveway to greet him, a gesture he found befitting his stature. He gave Alys a once-over and approved of her white wide-leg pants, white eyelet tunic, and the sunset shawl thrown around her shoulders. His nose wrinkled at Lady's tight jeans and tight T-shirt saying GALZ RULZ on her plump bosom. Ever since his wife's death, his daughter's attire had begun to lapse for lack of proper supervision, but — Kaleen smiled at Alys — that would soon be remedied. He was pleased to see Alys avert her eyes from him and proceed indoors. Such was indeed expected of a girl from a good family, and it warmed his loins.

After Kaleen freshened up from his journey, he checked Mari, recommending she continue her breathing exercises. As soon as that formality was finished, he requested a tour of Binat House and, assessing each room with the eyes of a future son-in-law looking to impress colleagues and clients — especially Begum Beena dey Bagh — he was pleased with what he saw.

Dinner was served after the Isha prayers, and Kaleen was delighted at the Binats' generous spread of mutton *karahi,* beef *seekh kebabs,* ginger chicken, eggplant in tomatoes, creamy black *dal,* potato cutlets, cucumber *raita,* and *kachumber* salad.

"You girls," Kaleen said as Mr. Binat invited him to begin, "must have spent all day in the kitchen."

"We have a full-time cook," Mrs. Binat said tersely. "And when he's on holiday, Hillima takes over. My girls never set foot in the kitchen unless they want to for fun."

"I meant no offense," Kaleen said. "My late wife was an exceptional cook, and I only wanted to pay my compliments to the chef of such delicious fare."

The cook, Maqsood, was called from the kitchen, and Kaleen, pressed into a corner to perform social obligations, tipped the fellow. Hillima appeared on the cook's heels, touting her contributions to the meal, and Kaleen delved back into his pocket with a forced smile.

Later, Maqsood and Hillima shared notes and concluded that Kaleen had not been as stingy as Wickaam but they prayed that the next visitor to grace Binat House would not only have money but also be bighearted.

Kaleen filled his plate to the maximum as Mrs. Binat handed him entrée after entrée. He was happy to see that Alys ate sparsely and with sophistication. By contrast, Lady had a robust appetite and kept licking her lips.

"My late wife," Kaleen said as he tore apart a *roghni naan,* "believed women who eat freely find it hard to control their desire in other matters too."

"What other matters?" Lady asked naughtily, her fleshy lips glistening with ghee.

Kaleen glanced at her distastefully. "Begum Beena dey Bagh also believes gluttony

287

is unappetizing in a woman."

Alys wished she'd overfilled her plate like a glutton supposedly might, however she had little appetite. The phone had rung earlier that evening, and she'd seen Jena's face light up and then fall when it had turned out to be Mari's friend. Now Jena played with a teaspoon's worth of food on her plate, and even though their mother had instructed the cook to prepare Jena's favorites round the clock — spaghetti *keema* and Kashmiri mustard greens with white rice — she barely ate.

"Beena dey Bagh was not at the Nadir-Fiede wedding?" Mr. Binat asked.

"Rest assured," Kaleen said, "she was the first luminary to whom an invitation was sent. Unfortunately, Begum Beena dey Bagh has been unable to attend many functions this winter on account of Annie suffering a setback. Far be it from me to ever brag, but they are lucky to have discovered me — otherwise, who knows what state Annie may have been in by now. She could even be dead. In which case, I tell mother and daughter, I am not just a doctor but also a savior, Annie's hero."

"Is such self-praise," Mr. Binat asked with a straight face, "spontaneous or practiced?"

"Both," Kaleen said. "For example, the

food on this table deserves spontaneous praise, and so I gave it, but in homes where the food is tasteless, practiced praise is required. Same rule applies for the accomplishments of men and the looks of ladies."

"The looks of ladies?" Mrs. Binat said.

"Yes," Kaleen said. "Praising plain and ugly girls makes their day, so they tell me. I now regard it as *sawab ka kaam,* God's own good work."

"What's wrong with Annie?" Alys asked, for she was curious about Wickaam's and Dracula's cousin.

"Sad story," Kaleen said, ladling a hefty amount of ginger chicken into his plate.

Annie was once a vibrant girl standing five foot eleven in her bare feet and studying at Berkeley, after which she'd planned to return to Pakistan to join her mother's business. Along the way, Annie was discovered at an airport by a fashion designer, and next she knew it, she was walking runways. One weekend she'd gone on a camping trip, after which her health began to fail rapidly. She'd sought Kaleen out at a medical conference where he was a guest speaker on autoimmune afflictions. "I'm Pakistani," she said, "you're Pakistani. Please help me. Not too long ago, I was walking in stilettos, and now here I am with a walking stick. Nothing shows up in my blood work and doctors insist it's all in my head. Please help me."

"I helped her," Kaleen continued. "Within days, thanks to the guidance of Almighty God, she was better. But once the conference ended I returned to England, and next I know, Begum Beena dey Bagh is offering me a dream package to move to Pakistan, and here I am."

"*Inshallah,*" Mari said, once Kaleen was done, "may Annie dey Bagh and every other human being suffering from disease and illness be fully restored to health."

"*Ameen,*" everyone at the table said, cupping their palms and looking skyward.

"*Summa ameen,*" Kaleen said, invoking a double blessing as he appraised Mari anew. His eyes lingered on the gold Allah-in-Arabic pendant nestling in her cleavage and visible beneath her muslin *dupatta.* Perfectly pious but, compared to Alys's striking looks, quite insipid.

Dessert was brought out — a vibrant beetroot *halwa* and chai, after which Kaleen asked to retire for the night. He gave Mrs. Binat a special look, which she rightly interpreted as his wanting to be fresh for the life-altering event the next day. After bidding him sweet dreams, she sent everyone to their rooms for an early night. They should all rest, she decided, for tomorrow would bring one long celebration.

CHAPTER 15

Farhat Kaleen came down for breakfast with his heart beating fast. He'd never thought in his wildest dreams that he'd have to propose twice in his lifetime, but this was obviously God's plan. He entered the dining room and was pleased to see that the Binat girls were still at breakfast. His eyes glanced at the food first — fried eggs, Pakistani omelet brimming with cumin and green chilies, potato *bhujia,* French toast, and cornflakes — and then at Alys, who was nibbling on a boiled egg and sipping black coffee.

She was reading the newspaper, which was all right by him — being a good woman did not mean being uninformed. But he frowned for a moment at her tracksuit bottoms and T-shirt that read NOT YOUR AVERAGE BEHEN JEE. Then he smiled. The casualness of her outfit at this most momentous of events for her would be but their first sweet memory.

Best, Kaleen decided as he looked for a place to sit, to do the deed on a full stomach. Mr. Binat was not present. Alys was at the foot of the table, flanked by Mari, drinking the herbal tea he'd prescribed, and Qitty and Lady, who sat in a nightie too flimsy for his comfort. He glanced at the empty chair beside Jena. Best not to sit next to her either, since she was getting engaged and so belonged to another man. He finally settled beside Pinkie Binat and took hefty servings of everything.

Mrs. Binat gave Kaleen an encouraging maternal smile, even as she wished he'd dressed differently. He was wearing a skintight red T-shirt and pale-gray pants. This ensemble may have looked snazzy on the K-pop musicians Lady and Qitty watched on MTV Asia, but on Kaleen it failed. For one, his nipples were pointedly on display through the fabric. Lady and Qitty were smirking and Mrs. Binat glowered at them to stop, as did Mari. Mrs. Binat wished Kaleen would hurry his breakfast before Alys left, and as soon as he swallowed his last bite, she scrambled up and ordered her daughters to come with her.

"Except you, Alys *meri jaan,* my darling, you stay," Mrs. Binat said. "Best daughter of mine, I've given my blessings to Kaleen, but it is only fitting that in this brave new world you get to say yes yourself."

Alys stared at her mother. Things fell into place. How could her mother believe that she and this man could be a match? Her sisters exited with sympathetic looks — even Lady looked sad — and, before Alys knew it, she was alone with Kaleen. She abruptly rose from her seat, and Kaleen rose too. He plucked a droopy gladiolus from the vase on the table and held it to his heart.

"Alys," he began, even though Alys raised her hands to stop him, "my sweet Alys, you are the sweetest creature. And believe me, my late wife would have agreed. Sweet chaste Alys, make me the happiest man in all of Pakistan, in the world, and marry this humble servant of yours?"

"No!"

"I know good girls are trained to say no at first, for eagerness does not become them —"

"Stop! Please stop! My no means no."

"Sweet, sweet Alys, unsullied Alys." Kaleen tried to hold her hand. "Demureness becomes you, my sweet!"

"I am not demure." Alys clasped her hands behind her back. "Trust me."

"Sweet, sweet Alys, with such sweet, sweet

lips, from which emanates such sweet bashfulness, stop playing with my heart, my sweetheart, and agree to be my virtuous wife."

"Please stop proposing!"

"So coy. So coy. This was my late wife's reaction at first too."

"Kaleen Sahib" — Alys took one step toward the door — "I have no idea why your first wife changed her mind, but I'm not going to. We are incompatible, and I genuinely apologize if anyone in this family has led you to believe otherwise."

"Sweetest purest Alys." Kaleen took two steps toward her, thrusting the gladiolus at her. It fell to the floor. "Even your pretend denials are sending shivers through my heart and other regions. How dearly my late wife would have approved. Our union will be blessed by Begum Beena dey Bagh herself, and we will make a power couple the likes of which Pakistan has yet to see. Were I younger, indeed, sweet innocent queen of my heart, I would be proposing to you from astride a stallion, but —"

Alys burst out of the dining room, only to bump into her mother, whose ear had been glued to the door. Pinkie Binat reached out to seize Alys, but she dodged her mother and fled to her father's study. Mr. Binat was in his armchair. He was toasting his toes at an electric heater, the double rods glowing a fiery orange, and he glanced up at her from a compendium of Rumi's ruminations.

"Why are your feathers aflutter, Princess Alysba?" he said. "What's wrong?"

"Daddy, did you know *why* Mummy invited that odious *uncle* to our house? Did you know?"

"Know what?" Mr. Binat sat up at the distress in his favorite daughter's voice.

"She wants me to marry that buffoon."

"Not a buffoon," Mrs. Binat said, entering and banging shut the study door. "He's a first-rate catch for the likes of you!"

"He's hardly a first-rate catch for a clown, let alone for the likes of me," Alys said.

"What is going on?" Mr. Binat asked.

"Farhat Kaleen wants to marry this ungrateful fool," Mrs. Binat said, "and she is refusing."

"Daddy, how can I marry that man?"

"How can you not?" Mrs. Binat roared. Alys was nearly thirty-one years old. Soon her waist would thicken and she would grow stout. Her hair would thin and what would be left would turn to gray wires and she'd be dependent on hair dye for the rest of her life. Her skin would wrinkle, her neck would droop, and her eyes would go from being beautiful to just another pair of fine eyes. A woman's curse, Mrs. Binat reminded Alys, was to age, no matter what Alys believed.

"Barkat, you'd better make your daughter marry Farhat Kaleen, or I swear I'll never talk to her again."

"Alysba is not going to marry him," Mr. Binat said. "And perhaps, Pinkie, my love, it might be best for your nerves if you do stop talking to her."

Alys gave a sigh of relief. Her father had ended the matter, for had he sided with her mother, she would have faced a formidable battle. Alys turned victorious eyes on her mother and, fleeing to her bedroom, she cried in relief.

Mrs. Binat's heartbroken shrieks must have surely reverberated all the way to Sherry's house, for Sherry, who'd been preparing breakfast for her family, decided that she must pay the Binats a visit. Farhat Kaleen was visiting them, and she wanted to request he take a look at her diabetic mother's swollen feet.

As soon as breakfast was done and she'd washed and dried the utensils and fed her cat, Yaar, Sherry grabbed the translations Alys had requested of Manto's story *"Khol Do"* and Ghulam Abbas's *"Anandi,"* and she hummed her way to Binat House.

Lady and Qitty opened the front door. Sherry thought she could hear shouting coming from inside the house.

"You're in for a treat," Lady said, pulling her in. "The house is in an uproar."

Sherry had never ever known the fifteen-year-old Lady to whisper.

"Has Bungles, thankfully, finally proposed to Jena?"

"Fart Bhai has proposed to Alys," Lady cut in.

Sherry blinked. Alysba and Farhat Kaleen?

"And Alys," Qitty said, "has point-blank refused. Our parents are yelling so loudly I'm sure Fart Bhai, who slunk into the guest room after Alys's rejection, can hear them too."

"I thought it was going to be yet another boring day Chez Binat," said Lady, linking arms with Sherry and Qitty as they walked to the living room. "But this is better than my wildest dreams. Fart Bhai and Alys up a tree, K-I-S-S-I-N-G. Fart Bhai told Alys that if he were younger, then he would have come for her on a stallion. Can you imagine that purity pervert on a horse? *Waise himmat dekho popcorn naak ganje ki,* Alys *se shaadi*! Imagine the popcorn-nosed baldy's boldness in proposing to Alys!"

"He's a decent catch, Lady," Sherry said, sighing.

"You and my mother always think alike," Lady said.

Sherry shrugged. A marriage was a marriage and Farhat Kaleen was no ordinary frog, and Mrs. Binat, poor woman, could see that, even if her daughters refused to.

They stepped into the living room. Mrs. Binat lay on the sofa while Mari gloomily applied headache balm to her mother's temples.

"*As-salaam alaikum,* Pinkie Khala," Sherry said, sitting beside her.

"*Walaikum-asalaam.*" Mrs. Binat managed an anguished smile. "Have you heard what your foolish friend has done? I ask you, if something was wrong with Kaleen, would I insist upon my daughter marrying him?"

Mrs. Binat took a moment to blow her nose into her *dupatta* — not a very classy thing to do, she knew, but given the circumstances who could blame her? Such a decent proposal, and Alys had broken her heart by not only snubbing it but also running to her father for protection. The same father whose family was the reason they were stuck in Dilipabad with no worthy proposals to begin with.

"Is not Farhat Kaleen marriageable material?" Mrs. Binat implored of Sherry. So what if she herself would never have considered him back in her day? That was then, and this is now.

Sherry nodded. "Any sensible girl would deem him a great grab."

"My daughters are not sensible." Mrs. Binat gazed with hurt eyes at Sherry. "You must make your friend see sense, Sherry. It is all up to you now. Promise me you will make your foolish friend marry him."

Before Sherry could promise anything, the living room door swung open and Jena and Alys entered.

"Sherry," Alys said. "I heard you'd come."

"Here she is!" Mrs. Binat flared her nostrils at Alys. "The most thankless daughter in the universe. God knows I love my daughters equally, but you, Alys, have always been my least favorite, for you put yourself before the well-being of this family. It's your father's fault. Always indulging you. What's your life plan now? To become Teacher of the Year and die an old maid? Oh God, better to remain barren than birth a disobedient child."

Sherry flinched at the word "barren." Alys shrugged an apology to Sherry for having landed at their house in the midst of this mess. Mrs. Binat continued telling Alys what she thought of her until the man of the match, Farhat Kaleen himself, entered the room.

Mrs. Binat quieted. "Girls," she said, adjusting her eyelet *chador* prettily over her shoulders, "be quiet now. Kaleen and I have important matters to discuss."

Kaleen pointedly ignored Mrs. Binat and turned to Sherry: How were her parents, brothers, sister, cat? Alys took the opportunity to slip out of the living room. Jena, Mari, and Qitty followed her, and though Qitty tried to pull Lady along, Lady would not move. Once Sherry satisfied Kaleen that her family and cat were well, she glided toward the window and pretended to busy herself checking the growth of the money plants on the sill. Like Lady, Sherry was tuned in to Mrs. Binat and Kaleen and so she was witness to Mrs. Binat's utterly doleful "*Hai,* Kaleen! Believe you me —"

"Pinkie, please." Kaleen pressed his palms together. "Let us forever be silent on the utter anarchy plaguing this house."

He settled ramrod straight on the Victorian chair adjacent to Mrs. Binat and proceeded to shatter the silence by assuring her that he did not resent Alysba. Why waste his time, he asked in a grave tone, resenting a woman whose favor he was beginning to be glad had been withheld after all? Obviously, Alysba would not have proved to be a perfect companion for him, let alone a good mother for his children, for he needed to marry a woman who knew her place, and Alysba had exercised displacement.

His first impulse had been to leave the Binats' home for a hotel, but in remaining, he hoped to protect the family's reputation from gossip. Pinkie was to rest assured that he did not hold her or Mr. Binat responsible for their daughter's behavior. He was a father and knew how hard it was to control one's children these days, although Alysba was no longer a child but a very aged woman. Alysba was lucky that he was not the sort of man who'd respond to her insult of a refusal by throwing acid on her. In fact, he was firmly against such retaliations.

Mrs. Binat felt faint as Kaleen's speech came to an end. Excusing herself, she fled to her bedroom and sobbed. Lady left the living room in order to give her sisters a rundown of Fart Bhai's speech — not the type to resort to an acid attack! — and she glanced down at him with horror before flouncing out.

Kaleen scowled at Lady's back and decided that this *behooda* — vulgar girl —

not ending up his sister-in-law was a blessing in itself. And Alysba too, he decided, was no doubt pretending to be pure and pristine, for she was far too sexy to really be a good girl. As Sherry turned from the money plants, the midmorning sunshine bathed her in its golden glory and it suddenly occurred to Kaleen that Alysba's friend looked like a spotless sturdy sapling of some spotless sturdy tree. For the rest of the day, he paid great attention to Sherry, partly in order to pointedly ignore the Binats and partly, he hoped, to annoy Alysba.

The next day, Sherry arrived yet again to aid the Binats by keeping Kaleen occupied. Alys thanked her best friend for doing so, but Sherry had an ulterior motive. If Alys did not want Farhat Kaleen, then he was fair game for her. That evening, the Binats and Kaleen dined at the Loocluses', and Sherry was dismayed to hear Kaleen proclaim that his late wife believed women who smoked possessed loose morals.

"My late wife," Kaleen said, "God grant her a place in heaven, agreed with me that cigarettes are different from the hookahs our foremothers used to smoke, for hookahs do not possess the indecent shape of a cigarette."

"Your late wife," Mrs. Binat said spitefully, "seems to have missed the fact that tobacco is tobacco no matter the receptacle."

Mrs. Binat was most unhappy at Mr. Binat forcing her to attend this dinner at the Loocluses' when all she felt like doing was pining away in bed. She darted a poisonous eye at Alys, who seemed truly unaffected, and at Kaleen, who seemed to have recovered all too fast. Why was he praising Bobia Looclus's décor? Pinkie cast a baleful glance over Bobia's tiny drawing room, the discolored cheap lace curtains behind a sagging plastic-covered sofa, the wobbly coffee table, the fraying artificial flowers atop an outdated TV, which, gallingly enough, reminded Mrs. Binat of the fact that, growing up, her family had barely been able to afford such a one. The only redeeming feature of this entire evening, she granted, was the delicious dinner poor Sherry must have spent the entire day preparing.

At the dinner table Mrs. Binat flinched when, after a few bites of the feast, Kaleen exclaimed that it was by far the best meal he'd eaten for days.

"Compliments to your cook, Bobia *jee*," Kaleen said, raising an appreciative eyebrow at the perfectly round puffed *chapatis* in the bread basket.

"Sherry is our cook, *mashallah,*" Bobia Looclus said. She pressed upon Kaleen the mutton *pulao* and *achaari* chicken. "There is magic in her hands."

"Indeed! Magic!" Kaleen liberally helped himself to these dishes as well as the *chapli kebabs* and *shahi korma*.

From across the table, Sherry refilled his glass with sweet *lassi.* The extravagance of the meal had cost them a good amount of her paycheck, but she was determined to show off her cooking skills.

Alys was dismayed when her mother rudely interrupted Kaleen's praise with the prayer that the Loocluses be able to hire a cook so that poor Sherry could see the last of the hot kitchen and stinky dishes.

"Pinkie," Bobia Looclus replied in a pinched voice, "I hope we never see the day where we can afford a cook if it means our daughters forgetting how to cook. Girls who cannot cook are destined to be divorced."

"Then," Mrs. Binat said, "all the upper-class women should be divorced."

"Trust me" — Bobia Looclus glanced keenly at Kaleen — "if husbands had to choose between wife or cook, cook would win hands down."

"Bobia" — Mrs. Binat glanced archly at Kaleen — "cooks may be irreplaceable for you, but for me wives are."

Kaleen was too busy eating to give either woman attention and, anyway, he wasn't in the business of giving the bickering of elderly housewives much thought. Instead, he complimented Sherry on her cooking again, much to Bobia Looclus's gratification and Pinkie Binat's chagrin, as the desserts — a green jelly trifle and a red carrot *gajar ka halwa* — were brought out. By the evening's end, Sherry was sure that if only Farhat Kaleen were to remain in Dilipabad long enough to eat her meals for a few days in a row, she might stand a chance.

The next morning, Sherry awakened for dawn prayers in the bedroom she shared with her younger sister. After praying, she stretched her arms in a yawn and, glancing out of her tiny window, she saw Farhat Kaleen shuffling up the lane. Sherry dressed as fast as she could and set out to meet him by accident.

Kaleen turned into Sherry's narrow lane. Though stirred by Alysba's spurning of him, he was not so shaken that he did not, the morning following Sherry's divine dinner, decide, after his prayers, to slip out of Binat House and make his way toward Looclus Lodge Bismillah. Stepping on weeds grow-

306

ing out of the dirt road, he continued rehearsing the very speech he had laid at Alysba Binat's feet. To his tremendous delight, Kaleen saw Sherry walking up the lane.

Sherry and Kaleen stood at the edge of the empty lane in the early morning under a mango tree that had grown not by design but due to littering. After exchanging shy *salaams,* Kaleen plunged straight into affairs of the heart. Sweating profusely, he hung his head and spoke of recently proposing to Alysba, of which Sherry was well aware.

"A terrible mistake," he exclaimed.

Sherry assured him that although she and Alys were friends, in too many respects she and Alys were opposites; one was not the company one kept. Minutes passed as Kaleen enumerated why Alys would not make an ideal wife. Sherry began to worry that Alys or one of the Binats would venture out to the lane and see them or the school van would arrive. Kaleen was assuring her he had lofty roots. His ancestors had owned carpet factories in Kashmir. When his side of the family had left the Kashmir Valley for the Punjab plains in order to further the family trade, they became known as simply *kaleen wallas,* carpet makers. Over time, the carpet trade had fallen away, and now all the connection that remained to their once-prestigious status in Kashmir was their name, Kaleen, "carpet."

Kaleen told Sherry that he'd grown up in a half-loving home, with a stern, unaffectionate father who owned a small handicraft shop and a stay-at-home mother who, amid constant hugs and kisses, never let him forget that he was the most handsome and intelligent son in the galaxy. His late wife, he informed Sherry, had held the same opinion. Sherry glanced at the rising sun as Kaleen branched off into the virtues of a good wife: cooking skills; a natural shyness combined with a cultivated modesty; could have opinions but must not voice those opinions, especially if they are in opposition to a husband's opinions; serve in-laws; cleanliness, punctuality, innocence; sacrificing self and career for children's well-being; sacrificing self for husband's well-being; sacrificing self for everything.

"I can be a good wife," Sherry blurted out. "The best."

It was out, and she was relieved. Let the likes of Jena Binat leave the likes of Fahad Bingla wondering whether she wanted to marry him. Sherry had meant it when she'd told Alys that a woman should not leave a man in doubt of her interest. If Kaleen laughed at her, she would survive. There were worse things in life than being laughed at, and one of them was being a poor spinster. She glanced at her cat slinking down the gutter along the sidewall, a large ball of gray fur. Why was Farhat Kaleen not saying anything? Was he appalled by her directness? She badly needed a cigarette. Two cigarettes.

"You can be a good wife," Kaleen repeated. He wasn't sure what to make of such straightforwardness. He'd promised his late wife that he'd remarry a woman as worthy as her, and just as she'd begun to instruct him on what exactly constituted worth, she'd taken her last breaths, which had sounded like a cat meowing. Now here was a gray cat meowing at him. Suddenly Kaleen knew this was the clue his pious wife had given him for recognizing a worthy woman; that it should be a cat's meow made perfect sense, because the Prophet Muhammad's favorite animal was the cat, and righteous people received signs in religious terms.

Kaleen would have fallen to his knees in a prayer of gratitude had the dirt road not been excessively strewn with stones. God had known Alys was the wrong woman for him all along and thus her shockingly unexpected refusal. Instead here was Sherry Looclus, the woman who was to be his wife, and God again had blessed him by making her reveal herself to him by her boldness, for there were certainly times when natural shyness needed to take a backseat. *Meow-meow* came again from behind him, and Kaleen took a giant step forward. Taking Sherry's hand in his, he declared:

"You, my sweet, will be *my* wife, for, trust me, it has been ordained."

Sherry's knees nearly buckled. She caught herself. Until a moment ago she'd been sure Kaleen was going to spurn her. Instead, the opposite. Would she truly never have to work again unless she wanted to, or fret about bills again, or worry about whether a sister-in-law would turn her into an unpaid maid? Best to get Kaleen inside and announce the unbelievable proposal to her parents and legitimize it before he had time to reconsider. As for smoking, she would try her best to quit. But the fact was, she had a bigger secret than smoking, and though she could have hidden it from him, Sherry did not want to dupe anyone into marriage.

"I have something to divulge," she said nervously.

"Tell me, sweet, sweet Sherry."

"I am unable to have children."

"Truly," Kaleen said, "God is showering me with blessings."

Her lack of a working uterus suited him perfectly. He wanted a mother for his children, he told her, but he did not want any more children.

Sherry hurried her beau into her house, where he proceeded to formally ask Haji Looclus for his daughter's hand. Sherry shivered the whole time. She could hardly believe that her spoiled uterus had not ruined her prospects, having constantly heard that grim verdict over the years, and now she promised God a gratitude Hajj, extra prayers for the rest of her life, and even more alms for the poor.

Her younger sister, Mareea, shed happy tears that no one could ever mock or dismiss her hardworking elder sister for being barren. As for Sherry's brothers, Mansoor and Manzoor, their delight was unparalleled: They loved their sister, but they were beyond relieved that someone was finally marrying her and that she was going to her "real" home.

Bobia Looclus chortled with pleasure — Bobia 1, Pinkie 0 — as she retrieved her Quran and blessed the future couple by touching the holy book to their heads. Whatever his reasons for marrying her, she informed Sherry in the kitchen as they quickly prepared chai, Sherry was not to worry — *Allah nigehbaan,* God was watching over her. Sherry was going to prove to Farhat Kaleen that he'd made the best decision. Why should they care that Kaleen had only days ago proposed to Alys. Every man was allowed his blunders. Alys's loss was Sherry's gain. The Binat girls were spoiled, and their mother was to blame for always telling them that they deserved no less than princes and presidents.

"*Agar uski betiyan ghar behtee reh jayen* — if her daughters rot at home for the rest of their lives," Bobia muttered, "it will be Pinkie Binat's fault for giving them standards instead of teaching them to make do." Bobia kissed her daughter's forehead. "I cannot wait to tell snooty Pinkie our good news."

But Sherry made her family promise that they would keep this a secret until she told Alys herself. Everyone agreed, though Kaleen wished he could go straight to the Binats and inform them that he was marrying Alysba's friend. Instead, when he returned to the Binats' house, he packed his suitcase to immediately leave for Islamabad and

312

surprised the Binats by his graciousness and promise to return very soon. As his car drove away, Mrs. Binat mentioned to Mr. Binat that she was sure Kaleen meant to turn his attentions to Mari, since she seemed to actually enjoy his sermons.

Sherry avoided telling Alys her big news during the school day on the pretext that it was the wrong venue but that evening, as they had their smoke in the graveyard, she could no longer stall.

"Alys," Sherry took a deep breath, "Alys, I'm engaged to Farhat Kaleen."

"What?"

"I'm engaged to Farhat Kaleen."

Alys had wondered whether Kaleen might be interested in Sherry, but she'd failed to imagine that Sherry would reciprocate.

Sherry lit a fresh cigarette with trembling fingers. "Stop looking at me like that."

"When did this happen?"

"This morning," Sherry said. "Before the school van came."

"I see."

"You see?" Sherry said. "That's all you're going to say?"

"Congratulations on a fine catch," Alys said. "If he could, he would come for you on a stallion, did he say?"

"Tch! Don't be like that! He doesn't care that I can't have children, and because he doesn't care, perhaps one day I *truly* won't care. Alys, the biggest attraction in marrying him is that his children will be mine. I will become a mother. I swear, his youngest already looks at me with so much trust and affection."

Alys wanted to tell Sherry yet again that she was more than a childbearing and child-rearing machine. But what was the use? Perhaps you truly could not make someone disbelieve what they'd been so thoroughly conditioned to believe.

"You know," Sherry said, "if you had accepted his proposal, you could have resigned from British School today without having to listen to Principal Naheed and Rose-Nama's mother's demands ever again."

"I'd rather be accused of imaginary crimes my entire life than become that man's wife."

"He has shortcomings. He's human! No one is perfect. Not even people like Darsee, or you."

"You're taller than him," Alys said feebly as she looked up at Sherry.

"I don't care, and he hasn't said anything," Sherry said. "And, anyway, only by one inch."

Alys took a deep breath. "Listen, Sherry,

I'm happy for you if this is what you really want."

"I want." Sherry took a long puff. "Of course I want. Children. Hel-lo: S-E-X. Car, driver. And he's a British citizen because of which I will become a British citizen. And then I will be able to sponsor my parents, my brothers, and my sister. This will change our lives. Do you understand that?"

"Love? Like? Respect? Or do only the material things he can provide count?"

Sherry shook her head. "You want to call me a gold digger? Go ahead. But my name should be Budgeting, Saving, and Serving. I've been working outside the home ever since I can remember, as well as inside cooking and cleaning, and I want to be in a relationship where duties will be shared. My husband-to-be may say ridiculous things like 'Dignified women do not work outside the home' and 'Men who expect their wives to earn are losers,' but I am perfectly capable of being content in a traditional marriage. He will be an excellent provider and, I guarantee you, I will be the best mother and homemaker in the world."

Alys sighed. "Sherry, people marry for money, for security, for children, then get stuck in crappy financially dependent relationships."

"Alys, stop being dramatic. I'm not saying I won't ever work outside again and earn my own income. When I choose to, I will."

Alys raised a brow. "And you think your husband-to-be will give you that choice?"

Sherry took a moment to answer. "I am practical, Alys. I am not you. Please try to understand. Please. For me marriage is not a love story; it's a social contract. *Inshallah* you'll get your love story and never have to compromise, and I sincerely pray you find a man who'll respect and appreciate you exactly as you are, and you a man you respect exactly as he is. But let me tell you, if Farhat Kaleen talks about me half as affectionately and respectfully as he talks about his late wife, I will be a very lucky woman."

"Affection and respect," Alys said, "increase exponentially once one is dead."

Sherry spluttered on her smoke. Alys patted her on the back.

"I've said it before," Sherry said when she could speak, "and I'll say it to my dying day: There is no guarantee of happiness in any marriage, and being in love with your prospective partner is not going to solve that. People change, relationships change."

For the first time since their friendship

had begun in this graveyard ten years ago, they walked out in an awkward silence. But it was done, thank God, and when Sherry returned home she told her parents that they were now free to spread the good news.

Duly, Bobia and Haji Looclus arrived at the Binats' with a box of heart-shaped *barfis.*

"Wah jee wah," Mrs. Binat said taking a *barfi.* "To what do we owe this celebration?"

Bobia Looclus spewed the news like water out of a high-pressure hose.

"Our Sherry and your Farhat Kaleen are getting married, *mashallah, inshallah.*"

Mrs. Binat's *barfi* fell into her lap.

"Please, Aunty Bobia," Lady said. "*Itni bari gup,* such a tall tale. Don't you know Fart Bhai is madly in love with Alys and dying to marry her?"

Bobia Looclus sucked in her cheeks. Her husband gave her a calming look and she contented herself with huffily adjusting her *dupatta* over her head.

"They are marrying," Alys confirmed. "Sherry told me herself."

"Aunty, Uncle." Jena got up to hug them. "*Bohut mubarak,* my sincere congratulations. Congratulations from all of us."

"Yes, heartiest congratulations, Bobia Behen, Haji Sahib," Mr. Binat said, even

317

though he was surprised that poor Sherry had agreed to marry Alys's reject. Mari's, Qitty's, and Lady's congratulations followed, and, eventually, Mrs. Binat managed a congrats.

"Oof Allah," Bobia Looclus informed her husband once they left Binat House and proceeded to another neighbor's, "if Pinkie Binat's looks could kill, Alys would be a dead girl." She let out a big happy sigh. "Dear God, protect my Sherry from *buri nazr,* the world's evil eyes and ill wills."

The very next day Sherry fulfilled a dream. She marched into Principal Naheed's office and handed in her resignation. Naheed was about to make a big stink about a week's notice when she looked at Sherry's form.

"You're marrying Beena dey Bagh's daughter Annie's doctor? That Farhat Kaleen?"

"Jee, Principal Madam."

Naheed's mouth fell open. How in God's good name had this gangly nobody managed to snag what was for her a stellar match, a doctor, despite the fact that Kaleen was a widower with three children? She had to tread carefully, for she did not know exactly how close Kaleen was to Beena dey Bagh, but it would not bode well if he informed Beena that Naheed had been rude to his wife-to-be. And so it was that Naheed accepted Sherry's resignation with courtesy and told her that she was not to worry about finding a replacement — Urdu teachers were a dime a dozen — and proclaimed that she looked forward to attending the wedding.

Sherry left Naheed's office stunned. She'd been expecting fury, and suddenly the full force of her coup hit her: She wasn't just getting married; she was marrying a *somebody*. A somebody who mattered so much that Principal Naheed had been forced into politeness. Sherry did not know why the universe had, after years of insult, decided to smile upon her now, but she went straight to the toilets, where she allowed herself a sob. She was late to her class but for the first time she didn't care.

The Loocluses fixed the wedding two weeks hence, *chut mangni pat biyah,* a quick engagement followed by a quicker marriage, lest Kaleen change his mind. There was not much to prepare because, per the teachings of Islam, Kaleen declared that he and Sherry were to have a simple wedding. Instead of weeks of *dholkis,* a *milad,* and a *mayun* leading up to the bankruptcy-inducing three main events of *mehndi, nikah,* and *walima,* Sherry would hold a Quran recital at her humble abode, Looclus Lodge Bismillah, where they would read the good book in order to begin the marriage auspiciously. The recital would be followed by the marriage vows, followed by a nice lunch for close family and a handful of friends, as well as sweet and savory *deyghs* prepared to feed the poor.

Once back in Islamabad, Kaleen would host a decent *walima* in a nice wedding hall, where Begum Beena dey Bagh and all his important clients would not hesitate to be seen. As for dowry, Kaleen hated the concept and would not hear of it. There was no dowry in Islam. Rather, the groom was required to give *haq mehr,* the mandatory monetary gift to the bride, and he planned to hand over to Sherry a generous amount on the very day of their nuptials. Sherry wanted to ask for the right of divorce, but her mother forbade it.

"An ill omen," Bobia stressed, "to begin a marriage with provisions for divorce. A good girl stays married for life no matter what, and only silly girls believe that making compromises toward lifelong commitment is old-fashioned. Sherry, if you want to be happy and successful in your marriage, then forget all the nonsense that bad influence Alys has been putting into your head." Sherry silently comforted herself with the thought of *khula,* no matter how much more difficult that method of procuring a divorce could be — not that, God forbid, the need for divorce would ever arise.

Bobia and Haji Looclus were overjoyed that Kaleen had not turned out to be one of those greedy men who expected his bride's family to fulfill material demands. Nevertheless, they could not stomach sending Sherry with zero dowry, lest anyone taunt her for arriving at her husband's house empty-handed, and so they prepared the minimum: a gold jewelry set, a bed and matching wardrobe plus dressing table, a wristwatch for Kaleen, and suit pieces for his children and close relatives. Thankfully, Sherry's *haq mehr,* which she would dutifully hand over to her parents, would defray the cost of the dowry. As for wedding outfits, Sherry was reluctant to spend a fortune on clothes that would never be worn again. Alys came up with the solution. Sherry could wear her mother's wedding clothes from back in the day.

"If someone asks," Alys instructed, "just say you're wearing them because of senti-mental reasons and also: vintage."

Other than conferring over wedding outfits and *mehndi* designs for her hands and feet, Sherry did not spend much time with Alys. Visiting the Binat household meant enduring Mrs. Binat's comments about friends who stole their friends' paramours and, when Alys visited Sherry at her house, the chasm between them was palpable: Where before they had discussed every topic freely, now they skirted around the one topic they knew was futile to discuss. Sherry missed Alys, but she was growing increasingly excited as her wedding day approached, and she was loath to let Alys's silent reproach dampen her enthusiasm.

Then the wedding day was upon them. The guests proclaimed that Sherry was glowing in her pink *gota-kinari gharara,* and Farhat Kaleen, dressed in a white suit and green tie and looking like a Pakistani flag, was overjoyed at his lovely bride. They signed the wedding papers, and Sherry was married, and before she knew it an entourage was walking her to her husband's tinsel-decorated car, with her parents holding the Quran aloft over her head, and her siblings and Alys walking behind her.

The car door opened, the real moment of impending *rukhsati,* of bridal departure, and everyone started to cry. Sherry clung to her parents and siblings for a long minute, and then she hugged Alys farewell. "I truly wish you happiness," Alys said. "I know," Sherry said, and she made Alys promise that she would visit her in Islamabad. In fact, her family was planning to come during the summer holidays and Alys was to accompany them. Alys, overcome by this moment of transition from home to home that most every Pakistani girl dreams of and dreads in equal measures, agreed to the visit, *pukka* promise.

CHAPTER 16

The wedding was done, there was no undoing it; Sherry Looclus was Mrs. Syeda Shireen Kaleen, and Pinkie Binat came undone, stitch by stitch, and she was determined to unravel her daughters too. Always critical, in her despair she turned cruel: No one would marry Jena, because she was a guileless nincompoop. Qitty was a mustached walrus. Mari was asthmatic and dim — that's why she hadn't gotten into medical school — and she had no sex appeal. No one would marry Lady, because who would marry the youngest sister at the tail end of four unmarried sisters. As for Alys, total loser.

"You are alienating your daughters," Mr. Binat said. "You are losing your mind."

Trying to make sense of how Sherry had pulled off this victory under her watchful eyes had put Pinkie Binat's very identity in a tailspin. She was a failed mother. She was a useless mother. How could Alys have been replaced by Sherry, of all people? Were her daughters not special after all?

The month of Ramadan at the Binat House was a subdued cycle of *sehris* and *iftaris,* with Mari leading her troubled family through mandatory prayers and plenty extra. The daily fasting and feasting were followed by a subdued *Chaand Raat,* the moon sighting leading into a quiet Eid lunch at which, to everyone's dismay, Mrs. Binat wanted to only lament Sherry's festive Eid as a new bride as per Bobia Looclus's boasts: Sherry's brand-new designer clothes for a gala Eid lunch, gold bangles and earrings and necklace set to match, three goats and three sheep sacrificed and the meat distributed to relatives, friends, and the poor. At each lament, Mrs. Binat eyed Alys with distraught rage. Alys's birthday came. She turned thirty-one. Mrs. Binat refused cake and wept. Jena turned thirty-three. Mrs. Binat wept even more and berated her daughters with new ferocity.

After weeks of their mother's haranguing, Alys grabbed Jena one afternoon and drove them to High Chai. They ordered cappuccinos. Jena was not hungry. Alys ordered baklava. The spring weather had turned warm and pleasant enough for High Chai to have opened their patio area, and the sisters sat outdoors. A vibrant fuchsia bougainvillea clambered over the red-brick boundary wall, and the scent of freshly mowed grass was in the air. Their mother was out of sight, though not out of mind.

"Mummy wants you to apologize," Jena said, poking a hole in the cappuccino's foam heart.

"Mummy, Principal Naheed, Rose-Nama's mother — is there anyone who doesn't want me to apologize?" Alys said. "Maybe I should tattoo a scarlet 'sorry' onto my forehead."

"Mummy just wants you to admit you made a mistake and that Sherry is a snake of a friend."

"I made no mistake and Sherry is no snake." Alys scraped a fork across the baklava's honey-soaked pistachio topping. "It's not as if I was about to walk down the aisle and she coiled herself around him. I had zero interest and Sherry knew that."

"I know," Jena said.

"Which is why I am never apologizing or accepting any of Mummy's unreasonable demands. I've grown up hearing, 'Who will marry you? Who will marry you?' Never once has she deigned to ask whom *I* will marry. She needs to apologize to me."

"You're both too headstrong."

"I swear," Alys said, "our mother would sell us off to the first bidder if she could. Who in their right mind abandons their daughter at a polo match so that she can be proposed to?"

"She's desperate to see us married, that's all," Jena said miserably. "It's not her fault, Alys. She's the product of her time and this system, and she can't see beyond it."

"She should try," Alys said. "She has a brain. And don't tell me that, no matter what, it's disrespectful to speak of one's parents like this."

Jena sighed. A sparrow hovered over one of the wrought-iron chairs. The sisters looked at it for a moment.

"We are," Alys said, "a society teeming with Austen's cruel Mrs. Norrises, snobby looks-obsessed Sir Walters, and conniving John Thorpes and Lady Susans."

"The whole world is full of these types," Jena said.

"Aren't you sick of everything, Jena?" Alys asked. "I'm sick of the hypocrisy and double standards. It's like they break your legs, then give you a wheelchair, then expect you to be grateful for the wheelchair for the rest of your life. How can you trust anyone? How

could anyone be happy with a Farhat Kaleen?"

"Everyone's standard of happiness is different," Jena said. "Sherry's settling down
and she'll be well settled."

"Settling down. Well settled." Alys laughed
derisively. "That's the golden ticket."

"Can I tell you something?"

"What?"

"I keep thinking," Jena said, "that maybe
if I'd worn something more flattering,
something more alluring, he might have proposed."

"Oh please." Alys swallowed back tears.
"Jena, it's not even just the men. We dress
to impress other women. Everything is a
competition, and the reward is the other
women's envy. But Mummy is wrong about
style and looks outweighing everything else.
It doesn't work that way. It *can't* work that
way. I won't let it."

"Maybe it's not my fault," Jena said. "If
he was meant to get engaged to Jujeena
Darsee —"

"Of course it's not your fault. And I'll bet
Bungles has no idea he's engaged to Jujeena
Darsee."

"Alys, stop it," Jena said. "His sisters were
very clear that he and Jujeena Darsee are to
be engaged."

"His sisters!" Alys stabbed apart the baklava layers. "Hammy *wishes* Bungles and Jujeena would get married. She thinks that will lead to Darsee marrying her."

"Alys, it makes complete sense to me that Hammy and Sammy would choose Jujeena Darsee for their sister-in-law. They've known her for a long time, and Bungles must want it too, for no grown man allows his sisters to impose their will on him. I was simply mistaken in his intentions. He thought of me as a good friend and that was all."

"You sound like a film star denying a love affair. 'We're good friends only, blah blah blah.' "

"I'd rather have mistaken his level of interest," Jena said, "than think he or his sisters are deceitful. Just let's change the subject." Moments later she said, "And, anyway, why would Hammy and Sammy try to sabotage their own brother's happiness?"

"Because," Alys said, "their own happiness is more important to them than his. They are selfish sisters, selfish girls, who manipulate their brother without any qualms. They hide their ugly hearts behind dressing well, and so manage to fool people like our mother, who believes clothes-style-accessories-grooming reflects character.

Hammy and Sammy think we are beneath them and so couldn't care less how much their brother likes you. And he does like you. Very much."

"If he liked me that much, he'd call me. He'd show up. He —"

"I'll bet he wants to, but his dragon sisters and Dracula —"

"Have they tied him up and gagged him? He's not a puppet."

"The problem is that he trusts that they have his best interest at heart. No one wants to believe that relatives and friends can betray them for their own selfish reasons."

"I'm sure Aunty Tinkle said something to them about us," Jena said, "and you know how crucial good reputations —"

"Stop," Alys said. "If you truly love and like someone, then nothing you hear about them should matter. Bungles is weak willed."

"Don't say that." Jena pushed away her cappuccino.

"Okay. And Sherry and I were going to spend our old age together, by a seaside, eating scones and *samosas,* two bachelor-ettes bingeing on the sunset forever."

"Don't be silly," Jena said with a wan smile. "Who eats scones and *samosas* at the same time?"

Alys grabbed Jena's hand. "You'll be all right. You'll be perfectly all right and Bungles will be a footnote of a funny story."

"Maybe I should have cracked some jokes?" Jena said, sadness settling on her face. "I was just being myself. I would be reserved with any man who showed interest in me. At least I didn't give him the satisfaction of knowing I was in love with him. But should I have? A little bit?"

Jena's eyes filled with tears. She laid her head on the table. Alys stroked Jena's hair, and by and by Jena dried her eyes and they sat together as long as they could, until it was time to return home.

A week later, Falak and Nona arrived with tranquilizers Nisar had sent for his sister. Mrs. Binat gave them an earful concerning Sherry. "*Kitni chalaak nikli* — what a schemer she turned out to be." "*Aastheen ka saanp,* a snake in our backyard." "*Budhi ghodi lal lagam,* an old mare dressed in youngster's red." She was supposed to have made Alys marry him, instead she married him herself! Then Mrs. Binat began on Alys yet again. Jena was obviously suffering from someone's evil eye, which had prevented Bungles from performing as expected, but Alys had let an already netted fish escape. Kaleen should have been theirs. Instead, he now belonged to the Loocluses. Pinkie 0, Bobia 1.

Mrs. Binat picked up her shoe and threatened Alys with a beating. Nona, her arms spread out, rushed between mother and daughter.

"Pinkie, *pagal ho gai ho*?" Nona asked. "Have you gone mad?"

"Nona *jee,*" Mrs. Binat yelled, "would it have killed her to marry Kaleen? Who will marry her now? Who will marry her?"

Alys strode toward her mother. Everyone froze. Then Alys hugged her mother tightly, not letting her go.

"Don't sell us short, Mummy," Alys implored. "Don't sell me short. I'm not useless or good for nothing. I don't want to get married just for the sake of it. I don't need to."

Mrs. Binat sobbed on her daughter's shoulder. Alys rocked her mother gently. Finally Mrs. Binat pushed Alys away, but it was not as rough a push at it could have been.

"Don't be so hard on the girls, Pinkie," Falak said, handing her sister a tranquilizer and a glass of water. "No matter what we do, kismet is the real decider of our fates."

"Kismet has nothing to do with anything," Mrs. Binat said. "It's all about looks."

"Kismet, fate, destiny," Falak said. "I was as beautiful as you, and look what became of me."

"You're still beautiful," Mrs. Binat said, because what else was one to say to a faded beauty.

"Good looks don't guarantee happiness or riches," Falak said. "Also, I've seen a thousand handsome and rich men marrying ugly women."

"True," Nona seconded.

"The only men who marry ugly women," Mrs. Binat said, "are men terrified someone else might find their wife attractive and tempt her into cheating. Proper men are proud to wear beauty on their sleeve. Look at Prince Chaarless and Lady Dayna."

"Charles," Lady corrected her mother. "Diana."

"Charles and Diana," Alys said, "are a perfect example of a mismatched arranged marriage."

"At least Dayna married a prince," said Mrs. Binat tearfully. "Tell me, Falak, how to flip my daughters' rotten kismets? How many more times should I read the Quran for their luck to change? How many more *wazeefays* must I pray? How many more fasts must I keep? How many more *manaats* must I make? Nothing is working."

Mrs. Binat turned to Nona's children, who'd been watching her with wide eyes. She kissed them and told them to go forth and play and make as much noise as they pleased. Indus, Buraaq, Miraage, and Khyber ran rampant through Binat House, their blissful laughter drowning out Mrs. Binat whenever she slipped back into a berating mood. The Binat girls began to unfurl. Lady gave Indus piggyback rides up and down the stairs. Mari bowled to Buraaq's bat. Qitty made paper planes with Miraage. Jena tossed Khyber up in the air and caught him, letting his mirth plant smiles on her face.

"The children have done wonders for Jena," Alys told Nona one morning as they sorted out gently used clothes to donate to charity. "I can't tell you how quiet and somber she'd become. I just know it's his sisters and that horrid Dracula that have kept Bungles away."

"In our culture," Nona said, "men flirt. They enjoy. They move on. They are brought up to believe that women are expendable. We are brought up to believe the opposite. One glance from a man and we readily give away our heart."

"Jena certainly did not mean to set herself up," Alys said. "It's all Mummy's fault. Dressing up Jena to be sold like a commodity. Convincing her that all she needs is the right outfit to get him to propose. Jena asked me if wearing something else might have made the difference. That's how insecure Mummy has made her feel. Did I tell you she keeps leaving her classes at school? Principal Naheed called me in again the other day to warn me that one more time and she'll have to ask Jena to take a leave of absence."

"A leave of absence?" Nona squinted. "Might Jena want to return to Lahore with us? A change of scenery may do her good."

"Being away from our mother will definitely do her good."

"I didn't want to put it like that." Nona smiled. "Lahore is Bungles's city too, but I'll make sure we have no reason to visit their part of town."

"I think being in the same city but with no contact will be good for her."

"Good. As for you, I want to talk to you about Jeorgeullah Wickaam. He's very popular in your household, I can see, and your mother is certain that he's going to marry Qitty, because he encouraged her to dance all of once, but I've heard the special way you speak of him."

"I don't speak of him in any special way." Alys folded a *dupatta* and added it to the keep pile.

"Sure." Nona flicked Alys on her nose. "Now, he's very handsome and magnetic, but I warn you, he's not marriageable material."

"How can you say that?"

"Believe me, I can tell. In my line of work, I come across all sorts of people, and Jeorgeullah Wickaam is a coaster. I would hate to see you end up with a coaster, Alys, and marriage has a way of turning coasters into burdens on their wives. Look at your Falak Khala."

"I have it on good authority," Alys laughed, "from Advocate Musarrat Jr. that Wickaam is a rising star."

"I'm serious, Alys," Nona said. "Wickaam's wife will be a star before he ever is. He'll be content at home, getting manicures, pedicures, facials, and massages all day long, a triumphant trophy husband."

"That's not true." Alys sat up. "Wickaam has faced much adversity, as you know —"

"Oh yes." Nona discarded a turmeric-stained sweater into the rags pile. "How could I not know? He is very eager to tell everyone all about his misfortunes. Look, Alys, it was my duty as your aunt to guide you, I have done my duty, and now I will keep quiet."

"Your duty is several hours too late!" Alys smiled at the alarm on Nona's face. "Wickaam called me this morning. He's recently gotten engaged to one Miss Jahanara Ana Aan."

"Engaged!"

"He met Miss Jahanara Ana Aan during a work trip to Karachi. Miss Jahanara Ana Aan is her father's only daughter and stands to inherit his accounting firm, and Wickaam intends to inherit it with her. Obviously well-off-enough people for him to see a good match."

"I see," Nona said. "You're very forgiving when Wickaam grabs it, not so forgiving when Sherry does."

Alys flushed. "I'm sure Wickaam's fiancée is not an ass-kissing social-climbing buffoon."

"Poor Qitty. Does your mother know yet?"

Alys shook her head.

"And you, my treasure, are you all right?"

"Too all right." Alys shrugged. "I believe that if Wickaam had money, or I did, I would have been his first choice. In any case, Miss Jahanara Ana Aan sounds like a smart and nice girl. I wish them well. Qitty and Lady were crying, but I thought, What's there to cry about? I'm telling you, Aunty Nona, I'm truly not cut out for marriage, children, that sort of thing. I'm actually quite pleased that Miss Jahanara Ana Aan has inadvertently resolved this 'situation' for me."

CHAPTER 17

Jena readily accepted Nona's invitation to come to Lahore. Principal Naheed was not thrilled at Jena's wanting to take off the remaining two months of the semester, but Alys volunteered to teach Jena's classes and Mari would substitute as a teacher-in-training. Mari was disgusted with the change in her lifestyle but, since it was for Jena's sake, she didn't grumble too vehemently.

Mrs. Binat prayed that fate would bring Jena and Bungles together in Lahore, and the thought cheered her. Satisfied that she might yet have her coup through Jena, Mrs. Binat inquired after Wickaam. Where had he disappeared? She was informed of Miss Jahanara Ana Aan. Her heart sank, but, then, she'd never truly believed Qitty would be able to attract such a gorgeous man, and neither could she blame Wickaam for grabbing a moneyed woman, and so she searched for a silver lining. Of course! Her daughters would be invited to Wickaam's wedding.

Immediately she began to discuss what outfits would be best for the events. Alys, Jena, Qitty, Lady, and Mari shared a glance and then looked at their father, who wore the same expression of dazed relief. Was Pinkie Binat back to normal and all right in their world?

Nona, the children, Falak, and Jena packed to leave for Lahore, and it was a tearful parting as the remaining Binats stood watching them drive away. Alys turned to Sherry's house for a cigarette, then remembered that Sherry too was gone.

Alys was not restless for long. Her days began with a whirlwind of a schedule as she managed her own classes as well as the workload for Jena's. Mari was turning out to be of little help, because she was more interested in preaching religion than in teaching the syllabus. Then there were the underprivileged children whom she, Jena, Sherry, and Mari used to tutor together, and now Alys insisted that Qitty and Lady get involved too.

Sherry called Alys frequently, and no sooner would Alys hang up than Mrs. Binat would inquire, "And what does your *friend* have to say for herself today?"

Alys would tell her mother the truth. Sherry was having the time of her life. Sleeping in. Car and driver at her disposal to go wherever and whenever she wanted. She'd joined a gym and had developed a yen for yoga and power aerobics. She was making friends, whom she met for brunches and kitty parties. She and Kaleen had dined at Beena dey Bagh's; both mother and daughter thought highly of Kaleen. Kaleen's elder son was respectful to Sherry, while the seven-year-old son said the cutest things and clung to her like a duckling. Kaleen's daughter was as friendly as she needed to be. Sherry's cat had also settled into the new environment as if she'd always been living there. All in all, all was good and Kaleen had only one request, which Sherry was beyond delighted to fulfill: that she cook for him.

"Hah!" Mrs. Binat said. "Even he knows all Sherry is good for is the kitchen."

"They have a cook, Mummy," Alys said. "All Sherry says she does is add spices."

"Let's hope," Mrs. Binat said, "Kaleen gets food poisoning and drops dead. Then Sherry will be a widow and that'll teach her to steal men interested in other women."

"*Tauba!* Dear God!" Mr. Binat said.

"What a thing to say!"

Alys did not share with her mother the prevailing awkwardness between Sherry and herself and how they had to force the closeness they'd once so easily shared.

It was Jena's phone calls Alys looked forward to. Jena called home daily to share news of her activities: shopping, films, restaurants, taking the children on outings. She would help Nona in the kitchen and they would make cake deliveries together. She visited Falak Khala once a week and was helping Babur prepare for an interview with a recruiter from Cornell.

Jena professed to be over Bungles. As proof, she planned to drop in to see Hammy and Sammy. No, she was not going to listen to Alys and stay far away from them. Bungles had been nothing more than a passing infatuation, pushed to extremes by their mother's pressure. Jena knew that now. She was merely going to visit Hammy and Sammy as she would any acquaintances of hers who lived in Lahore.

Jena dropped in one afternoon. Hammy and Sammy were at home. They were hosting a luncheon, and the maid, thinking Jena was one of the guests, led her into the drawing room where socialites were lining up to pose for a photograph. (The photo later appeared in *Social Lights;* Lady told Jena she'd seen it.) There'd been a hush when Jena entered the drawing room. Fazool said, "Ham, Sam, isn't that the damsel Bungs —"

Hammy and Sammy cut off Fazool. They hurried to Jena and hugged her and said what a nice surprise to see her and too bad it was not a good time but that they'd visit her in the next few days; they needed to see someone in Jamshed Colony anyway. She'd not asked about *him.* She'd not even looked for him at their house. The fact was, Hammy and Sammy had been very nice to her.

They were not very nice to you, Alys thought. They could have invited Jena to stay for lunch, a not-unusual courtesy in their part of the world; instead, she'd been sent off.

Three days later, Nona called Alys: "Jena needs to leave the house and stop waiting for them to visit. Who knows if they'll ever come?"

They came on the seventh day. Jena called home as soon as they left. For the first time, anger edged out her hurt.

"You were right, Alys," she said in a steely voice. "They are superficial and shallow and they never liked me. The person they were coming to see who lives in this part of town is their *dhobi*. They are attending a charity ball and need their gowns laundered according to specific instructions, which they didn't trust the driver to convey to the *dhobi*. I was the stop after the *dhobi*. They stayed for eight minutes and forty seconds and looked as if they expected spiders to descend on them the whole time. Basically they came to tell me that their brother knows I'm in town but he's busy with Jujeena Darsee and doesn't have a moment to spare on frivolities. I am a frivolity. They said they hoped I enjoy my visit to Lahore, and then they left. Good riddance to them. Hammy, Sammy, their brother — I will not let them spoil my mood for a single second more. You are right, Alys, I am too quick to believe people are nice. I am cured. I assure you."

The two months passed by. Alys set exams for her classes. She graded exams. She attended the staff meetings to discuss student promotions to the next grade level. She sat through end-of-term class parties, where students — who always discovered new-found love for teachers at the end of the school year — gave her gifts and handmade cards. Tahira hugged Alys and thanked her for the B-minus on her final exam. Rose-

Nama thanked Alys for her A grade too. Alys nodded, for she was not one of those teachers who settled scores through grades. Unfortunately, though, after the summer break, Alys would see Rose-Nama in her tenth-grade literature class, while Tahira was leaving to getting married. *Best wishes for the future!* Alys wrote on Tahira's uniform as students scampered about, getting their uniforms signed for posterity. Finally, the last bell for home time rang and everyone, including Alys and her sisters, headed to the gates, where they boarded the school van for the summer holidays.

Alys was leaving the next day for Islamabad. Sherry's family had rented a minivan so that they could travel in comfort. On the way to Islamabad, they were going to stop over in Lahore for a night, a prospect that had cemented Alys's decision to go, for she would get to see Jena and Nona.

"Don't forget your old father despite your change of scenery," Mr. Binat said as he hugged Alys goodbye. Mrs. Binat, Mari, Qitty, and Lady waved glumly, because they wouldn't have minded a trip to Islamabad and a change of scenery too.

The journey to Lahore took a quick two hours. The Loocluses passed the time with singing competitions, eating the homemade lunch of *aloo paratha* and *cheeni roti,* and marveling at how wonderful it was that Sherry *ne itna bada haath maara* — that Sherry had managed to marry so well. The Loocluses were looking forward to eating in good restaurants and sightseeing in style, for Sherry had assured them that they did not have to worry about the expense. She was going to foot all the bills, thanks to the generosity of her husband.

In Lahore, the Loocluses dropped Alys at her uncle's house for the night. Jena, Nona, and Nisar were eagerly waiting for Alys, and they insisted the Loocluses at least have chai before heading off to spend the night with their own relatives. Since it was the polite thing to do, and also because who would refuse Nona's *naan khatai* cookies, the Loocluses obliged.

During tea, Bobia Looclus whispered to Alys that Jena looked much happier, *mashallah.* Alys was grateful she'd said so, for she'd thought it herself. Later, Nona said that on occasion a cloud would yet pass over Jena but that she was determined not to wallow in it.

CHAPTER 18

The remainder of the journey to Islamabad was just as merry as the trip the day before, if not merrier for Alys, since Jena was on the mend. Hours later, they drove off the motorway and into the pristine capital city with its wide leafy roads, and eventually the minivan turned off the main road and entered a nice upper-middle-class neighborhood. Everyone in the van held their breath in anticipation of seeing Sherry's marital home. It was just as Sherry had described: a large two-story house with a decent driveway set in the midst of a pretty lawn. Farhat Kaleen and Sherry stood on the stoop of their home, waiting to greet them, Sherry with open arms, and Kaleen with a satisfied face that seemed plumper, no doubt courtesy of Sherry's cooking.

Bobia Looclus could not help but burst out in pride, "Sherry, *tum tho sitar say guitar bun gayee ho.* Sherry, you've transformed from the local sitar into an international-level guitar."

"Nothing lesser about the sitar or other local instruments, Aunty Bobia," Alys said, because it was not in her nature to let anything go. Sherry was looking very nice. Gone was her thin braid. Her new chin-length style suited her bony angles. Her skin had cleared up. She was clad in a well-tailored lawn *shalwar kameez* from one of the better brands and black ballet flats. Amethyst drops shone in her ears.

"Ammi," Sherry giggled, "if I tell you how much my haircut alone cost, you will faint."

"It's got nothing to do with that," Bobia Looclus admonished her daughter, "and everything to do with inner happiness. You are glowing."

"Of course she is glowing," Kaleen said as he welcomed Sherry's parents and awe-struck siblings to Islamabad. "Nothing but the best for my sweet blemish-free Sherry."

He gave Alys a wide smile. "Most welcome. Most welcome."

"You came," Sherry said, hugging Alys tightly.

"I came," Alys said, hugging her back, even as Kaleen urged them to part so that they could start the tour of his *gareeb khana*, his most humble abode.

Off they all went to tour the house. Like most standard upper-middle-class homes, it boasted multiple bedrooms — in this case five — with attached baths; a drawing-and-dining room looked out to the back garden, which was a haven for fruit trees. Bobia Looclus kept squeezing Sherry's hand. There were air conditioners in every room. Every room! And a backup generator to handle load-shedding. There was a cook, cleaner, driver, maid, gardener, gate guard, *dhobi,* tailor, and countless other amenities and luxuries at her daughter's disposal. Never had she imagined that her Sherry, whom everyone had written off, would be *so* well settled. This was proof that there was a God.

Alys noticed the glances Bobia kept giving her, which rivaled Kaleen's, signifying that all this could have been *hers.* Alys suppressed a smile and managed a suitably awed expression as they walked from the russet-tiled portico into a flourishing garden that also contained a large chicken coop and a milking goat lounging on lush grass.

Sherry's brothers, Mansoor and Manzoor, and her sister, Mareea, rushed to stroke the goat, and even Alys fell in love with its soft bleating and ebony eyes. The only goats she'd ever known were the ones inevitably

sacrificed at Eid for meat, and it was blissful to see this goat living its life, even if
tethered to the low water tap jutting from
the boundary wall.

Kaleen began to lecture on the benefits of
happy animals and fresh eggs and goat milk,
until Sherry gently ushered the party back
indoors to their bedrooms so they could
freshen up.

Alys was given a comfy room that overlooked the back garden. She opened the
windows to faraway goat bleats and a chikoo
tree thick with brown ripe fruit.

"It's a lovely room," Alys said. She plucked
a chikoo straight off the tree and inhaled its
sweet scent before handing it to Isa, who
was perpetually glued to Sherry's hip.

"It's a lovely life," Kaleen said jovially as
Sherry's cat contently circled his legs. "It's
a lovely house. Sherry couldn't be happier
or healthier. Right, Sherry?"

Sherry nodded and, kissing Isa and promising to peel the chikoo for him, she herded
everyone out of Alys's room.

Alys took a hot shower in, she had to
admit, a cozy cobalt-tiled bathroom and
then, as instructed, she returned to the living room. There, the maid, Ama Iqbal, was
serving a high tea and Kaleen was breaking
the great news: Tonight they dined at Begum

Beena dey Bagh's.

"Tonight?" Alys said. She'd been looking forward to getting in bed with a good book. "What's the hurry?"

"Hurry!" Kaleen scowled. He was beyond flattered that Beena dey Bagh had insisted Sherry's family's first dinner in Islamabad be at her table. "There's no hurry except that she wishes to do me a great honor."

"If you don't mind," Alys said, "may I be excused?"

"Excused!"

"Please, Kaleen," Sherry said, "your blood pressure will go up. Calm down."

"Number one, no one excuses themselves when Begum Beena dey Bagh summons," Kaleen said, seething. "And number two, Alysba, I expected your parents to have instilled some manners in you and some sense of protocol."

"Kaleen Sahib," Alys said, "number one, I'm assuming that Beena dey Bagh will honor you by inviting us at least once more in these next three weeks. And, number two, at my age I should hope I've taught myself how to exercise good manners and protocol of my own free will."

"Alys," Bobia Looclus said in a tight voice, "Begum Beena is Kaleen's employer, and we must not give cause for complaint."

"You're right, Aunty Bobia." Alys smiled sweetly at Kaleen, who was clearly squirming at being categorized as a mere employee. "I should have thought of this technicality myself. I would not like to be the cause of Kaleen Sahib getting into trouble with his employer."

Kaleen spluttered as he looked for something to say that would restore his full glory in everyone's eyes. Sherry squinted at Alys, a playful request that she cut it out.

Later that evening, Alys was the first guest ready and waiting to leave for Beena dey Bagh's estate, which was a good forty minutes away. Sherry was dressed in a brand-name silk *shalwar kameez,* and she was wearing new gold earrings that Bobia and Mareea were swooning over. Mareea had to borrow a silk outfit from Sherry's closet. Sherry told her younger sister that they'd go shopping the very next morning to update her meager wardrobe. Mansoor and Manzoor were dressed in ill-fitting suits with clip-on ties; they reminded their elder sister that they too required an upgrading, and Sherry promised them a shopping spree as well.

Kaleen entered in brown pants and a purple shirt. He glanced at Alys's *zari* embroidered *khusse,* white capris paired with a green-and-red *ajrak kurta* and matching *dupatta,* and the gray pearls dangling from her ears. He assured his guests that they were all looking decent and that none of them should worry anyway, because everyone's taste and style fell short compared to Begum Beena dey Bagh's and that — such a kind soul she was — she readily imparted her sartorial advice, as Sherry could attest.

"True," Sherry said with a glimmer in her eyes. "Begum Beena is enormously generous with her opinion to better people as she thinks best."

"Yes, she is." Kaleen beamed at Sherry as they all squeezed into his car, for the Loocluses' rented minivan was a rather tacky vehicle and not one Begum Beena dey Bagh deserved in her driveway. "You're so perceptive, Sherry; you're able to see things exactly as I would like you to see them."

Sherry twitched a smile at Alys in the backseat. Alys nodded. If such a marriage was working for Sherry, then so be it. As they drove out of Islamabad, the city fell away to increasingly rural surroundings until they were passing acres of land between grand houses nestled behind walls. Kaleen stopped at imposing gates with gold lettering, VERSAILLES OF PAKISTAN, and he honked politely until a guard opened the gate. They drove down a long driveway with peepal trees on either side until they arrived at a massive house with a huge fountain, water gushing out of the beaks of black and white swans.

The butler led the guests over black marble floors strewn with hand-woven Kashmiri and Afghani rugs and into the main drawing room. An Amazonian woman in a blue *ajrak shalwar kameez* and matching *dupatta,* though in a different pattern from the one Alys had on, looked up from the candles she was lighting on the mantel over the fireplace.

So this was the aunt, Alys thought, who was instrumental, along with Darsee, in robbing Wickaam of his inheritance. Beena dey Bagh's thick salt-and-pepper hair fell to her broad shoulders in a blunt cut. She wore diamond studs, a diamond Allah pendant, and several obese diamonds on her large French-manicured fingers. Her coral lipstick bled into the creases around her mouth. Above the fireplace was a blown-up Warhol-style photograph of a very striking girl. Kaleen had told Sherry, who had told Alys, that Annie was engaged to Darsee, and if it was Annie, Alys thought, then Darsee was in luck, looks-wise at least.

"You are on time, good," Beena dey Bagh said as she handed the candle lighter to the butler. Kaleen introduced everyone. Bobia and Haji Looclus nearly fell over themselves as they thanked Beena dey Bagh for her gracious invitation. Mareea, Mansoor and Manzoor were tongue-tied as they looked from glass ashtrays to porcelain vases to the myriad sculptures and figurines that adorned the coffee tables, side tables, and consoles of the four separate seating areas in the drawing room. Alys had grown up in a similar setting before Uncle Goga and Aunty Tinkle had kicked them out of their ancestral house, and she was not intimidated by expensive décor no doubt chosen by a costly interior designer.

Beena dey Bagh motioned to the sitting area with a minimalist arrangement, its angularity softened with plush cushions and a Zen tabletop waterfall with budding bamboos standing in black pebbles. She settled her imposing frame into a curved chair with spindly legs and invited them to seat themselves.

"My favorite corner," she said, peering at them one by one. "So peaceful. No, Mr. Looclus? Wouldn't you say, Mrs. Looclus?"

Bobia, who'd been wishing she could free

her inflamed feet from the confines of her good shoes, managed a fawning, "*Jee, jee, fuss class, fuss class.*"

"It is A-one setting," Haji Looclus said. "We are very sorry to be missing Lolly Sahib."

"Yes," Beena dey Bagh said. "My husband is in Frankfurt, attending a pen show, and then he heads to Switzerland for some skiing. Such an adventurer."

"Such an adventurer," Kaleen echoed.

"I remind him that, Lolly, you are too old to be going skiing, bungee-jumping, ziplining but he informs me age is just a number and he's not going to allow his knees, or me, to hold him back."

Haji Looclus threw in his trump card, for either you were rich or you elevated your status by claiming direct descent from the Prophet, which he did.

"We are Syeds, you know," he said with a magnanimous smile, "so we did not let age stop us from performing Hajj. Have you been for Hajj?"

"Hajj?" Beena dey Bagh said. "Seven, actually, and we're planning to go next year in order to give thanks for the miracle Kaleen here has managed with Annie."

Haji Looclus shrank into his chair. His single Hajj had left them all but bankrupt, and suddenly to have insisted on the title "Haji" on the basis of a lone pilgrimage seemed empty. Haji Looclus swallowed. To be a seven-time Hajjan! And still want more! Beena dey Bagh was a truly pious woman, and no wonder Almighty God had blessed her with so much.

Luckily for Haji Looclus, Beena dey Bagh was not interested in how many times anyone else had performed the holy pilgrimage and, instead, she pointed to the portrait above the fireplace and informed them that it was Annie at her best.

"And where is dear Annie?" Kaleen looked toward the archway that separated the drawing room from the large parquet foyer.

"As you know, Kaleen," Beena said, "if Annie cannot go to the salon, then the salon must come to Annie. She is so fond of mani-pedis, she gets them done as regularly as others brush their teeth. It so heartens me that my daughter remains interested in a few things."

A maid entered with a silver tray holding soft drinks. Mareea, Mansoor, and Manzoor excitedly chose from the array of colas. Alys took a glass of lemon squash.

"Ice, Alysba?" Beena said, and before Alys could answer, Beena had signaled to the maid, who whisked Alys's glass out of her hand, topped it with ice, and set it back down on a cut-crystal coaster. "Sherry has told me so much about you. Also I have Naheed's reports. I will say that the Dilipabad English-literature exam scores are consistently admirable."

"Thank you," Alys said, as she signaled to the maid to remove the ice.

Beena dey Bagh's eyes narrowed. "I hear other things too, Alysba. I'm not averse to progress, within reason, but I hear you like shocking students."

"I believe —"

"You teachers," Beena dey Bagh cut Alys off, "are such ardent believers in this, that, or the other." She looked up at a woman who entered. "Yes?"

"Madam," the woman said, "we're done with Madam Annie. Payment, Madam."

"Where is Nurse Jenkinudin?"

"Don't know, Madam."

Beena dey Bagh picked a walkie-talkie off the coffee table. Within minutes a woman in a starched white *shalwar kurta* came running in, apologized, and glared at the salon woman as she shepherded her out.

"I had such an efficient Filipina nurse for Annie." Beena dey Bagh threw up her hands. "Unfortunately her mother also got a visa to work in Pakistan and off mine went to join her in Lahore. A replacement is in the works, but visas can take time. Nurse Jenkinudin is my third local. The local domestics are shoddy compared to the foreign domestics. No work ethic. Of course, you pay through the nose for foreigners, but then you get the best."

Everyone nodded. Kaleen remarked that staffing his clinic with hardworking locals was a challenge too.

"Might you say," Alys said, looking at Beena dey Bagh even as everyone turned to look at her, "that if one were to pay the local servants the same wages one paid the foreign, then the local would be just as good?"

"Begum Beena dey Bagh," Kaleen said, grimacing at Alys as if she'd farted in public, "prefers the term 'domestics' to 'servants.' She believes it gives them an air of respectability that the term 'servant' lacks."

"Right you are, Kaleen," Beena dey Bagh said. "That is exactly how I feel."

"Of course, everyone deserves dignity," Alys said.

"Precisely," Beena dey Bagh said.

"But," Alys said, "were I a servant, I might be compelled to say, 'Call me by whichever term you want — "domestics" or "the help" is fine — but please pay me the same exorbitant salary as you would foreign servants.' "

"Are you a communist?" Beena dey Bagh hissed. "Surely you do not believe that everyone deserves the same salary if they have unequal qualifications. The foreign come trained, while I have to train the domestic. Anyway, inequality is ordained by God. Jew, Christian, Muslim, Hindu, Sikh, Buddhist — show me any religion or philosophy that does not speak of rich and poor. It is the rich's job to take care of the poor in their own way, often via charity, and it is the poor's job to take care of the rich in their own way, often through serving."

"But charity," Alys said, "is dependent on goodwill, and serving is a job that should be highly paid. If you ask me, even teachers' salaries should go way up."

Kaleen spluttered on his juice. Sherry gave a hint of a smile. Beena dey Bagh cackled.

"Everyone," she said, "ultimately thinks of their own skin."

"Yes," Alys said. "Everyone does perhaps think of their own coffers and comforts. But some people deserve and others simply hoard and exploit."

"Such confidence. How old are you?"

"I believe girls are not supposed to be

asked, or expected to divulge, their ages. However, I recently turned thirty-one."

"And the other teacher, your older sister?"

"Jena is thirty-three."

"And neither one of you is married yet, I hear." Beena dey Bagh gave an all-knowing smile. "Must be hard on your mother."

"It is," Alys said. "But I believe that as hard as it may be on our mother, it seems to be even harder on absolute strangers."

Beena dey Bagh geared up for a choice reply but, at that very moment, everyone turned to see Nurse Jenkinudin helping Annie walk in and sit down. Annie's tall frame wore well a white silk blouse and bottle-green jeans and gold Dior sandals, from which shone ten long toenails in pearly glittery crimson. The color rendered her complexion even sallower, Alys thought, but her hair was glossy and fell in a blue-black curtain to her waist and was cut in bangs above her pallid eyes.

"Sorry to have kept everyone waiting," Annie said, breathing heavily.

"My love, never any need for sorry from you," Beena dey Bagh said, as she signaled to the maid to set dinner. "How was this new mani-pedi team?"

"Fine, Ammi." Annie smiled at everyone. "Sherry, you must be so excited your family is finally here. So pleased to meet you all. And your best friend, it is Alys, right? Good to meet you. Sherry mentions you at least a hundred times each visit."

"All good mentions, I hope," Alys said, smiling.

"So far," Annie said, laughing. Alys laughed too.

Kaleen joined in the laughter, though he was miffed that Sherry would mention Alys at all. The maid announced that dinner was served, and they all rose and proceeded to the fourteen-seater dining table, where servers waited with three main dishes — *paya, nihari,* and *haleem* — and the many accompaniments that went with each of the delicacies — fresh coriander, chilies, lemons, julienned ginger, and crisp fried onions.

Beena dey Bagh asked Mr. and Mrs. Looclus to please begin. *Paya* was Haji Looclus's favorite dish, and he ladled the gummy hoof soup into the fine china bowl and sprinkled ginger and coriander on it. Bobia Looclus helped herself to choice chunks of meat from the *nihari.* Once they were done, the servers moved on to Beena dey Bagh and then around the table. Alys poured a little *haleem* into a bowl and squeezed lemon over the meat-and-lentil stew and topped it off with sliced green chilies. She dipped her buttered *tandoori* bread into it. Delicious.

Alys complimented the food, and Annie said that their cook should be declared a national asset.

"I do so miss being able to eat anything I want," Annie said as Nurse Jenkinudin placed a bowl of steaming chicken broth before her and cracked a fresh egg into it. "Did you know that in order to enjoy food one must smell it? So at least through smell, I get to eat. I had a friend back in college who developed anosmia — couldn't smell a thing — and lost all interest in eating. Once I fell ill, we'd compare notes about which was worse: no smell or not being able to keep anything down."

"Annie, you'll be eating everything you want in no time," Beena dey Bagh said. "Right, Kaleen?"

"Why not?" Kaleen said. "If God wills it."

"Life," Sherry said, "can change from good to bad so fast, and it follows that just as fast it can change from bad to good."

"You're so wise, Sherry. An angel to Dr. Kaleen's saint." Annie turned to Mr. and Mrs. Looclus. "Your daughter is an angel. Ever since she's arrived, she regularly reads the Quran to me, with excellent Arabic pronunciation. Neither of us understands the language, but just the rhythm is such a balm to my soul."

"It is very good," Beena dey Bagh said to Mr. and Mrs. Looclus, "that you people teach your children to recite the Quran by rote in Arabic regardless of whether they understand it or not. Of course, the best thing would be to learn Arabic, and if I ever had the time and inclination, I would be as fluent as any native speaker, possibly even better. Sherry has such a soothing voice and it brings such peace to Annie. In fact, Sherry, I'd like you to record the Quran for Annie so she has access to your voice at her convenience."

"Sherry does have a soothing voice," Alys said. "Sherry, you should sell the recordings."

"*Astagfiruallah,* God forbid," Kaleen said. "Selling the word of God!"

"Aren't Qurans sold?" Alys said.

Kaleen bristled. "There's no need for Sherry to earn a single penny. She's merely doing me a favor by helping me heal Annie through oral-to-aural therapy."

"I think every woman should have her own income," Alys said to Kaleen, "even married women."

"I agree," Annie said.

"Every woman should have the ability,"

Kaleen said, smiling at Annie and Sherry, "to earn her own income, but what will we husbands do if you women start to earn comparable incomes *and* have the babies? The lucky woman is one whose husband can provide well for her in his lifetime as well as after his death."

"We agree," Bobia and Haji Looclus said. "Sherry agrees too."

Sherry nodded politely.

"Alys," Annie said, "Sherry told me that you'd be the perfect person to ask: Can you recommend any stories with characters who are chronically ill and yet rise above it? But no *becharis,* no pitiable creatures."

"Have you read the short story 'Good Country People' by Flannery O' Connor? The main character, Hulga, is a non-*bechari.* Also there's Anne de Bourgh in Jane Austen's *Pride and Prejudice*."

"I've read *P and P,*" Annie said. "It was helpful in an unexpected way. Anne doesn't say a single word the entire novel, she just sits there, sickly and voiceless, and I decided that, no matter how ill I got, I'd never turn or be turned into Anne de Bourgh."

On the ride back, Kaleen wanted everyone to tell him their exact impressions of Versailles of Pakistan as well as of Beena dey

Bagh and Annie. Was Versailles not sophisticated? Was Annie not marvelous? Was Beena dey Bagh not majestic?

Bobia and Haji Looclus praised the estate and the pious Hajjan mother and her daughter to Kaleen's satisfaction, as did Sherry's siblings, their tongues loosening as soon as they left Versailles.

Alys, however, was not as forthcoming as Kaleen would have preferred. He did not like her tone at all when she said, "Beena dey Bagh certainly enjoys praise and compliments."

"Why shouldn't she?" he snapped, thanking his lucky stars yet again that he'd avoided marrying her, and he took over the exaltations until they were parked in his driveway.

Once Sherry settled everyone in for the night, she tiptoed to Alys's bedroom. Alys opened the door, her smile matching Sherry's. Sherry went straight to the almirah and extracted a pack of cigarettes from under a pile of spare quilts.

"This used to be Kaleen's daughter's bedroom before she returned to England, and now it's my smoking room." Sherry opened up the pack. "It's also the most remote room in the house, and I thought you'd like that."

Alys cranked open the window. A heady scent of night-blooming jasmine wafted in. The two friends discussed Beena dey Bagh and Annie. Annie seemed a nice-enough girl, they decided. Alys mentioned that Darsee would not be as miserable with her as she'd like him to be.

Alys informed Sherry about Wickaam and Miss Jahanara Ana Aan and assured her, as she had Nona, that she was quite the opposite of heartbroken. She entertained Sherry with tales from school and of Principal Naheed constantly gloating about how Gin and Rum had both been proposed to on account of looking irresistible in their QaziKreations outfits.

"I have a good mind," Alys said, "to tell her that maybe the proposals should be directed to the outfits. Anyway, Rose-Nama's mother is still demanding that I apologize for saying the desire for sex can lead to early marriages. You know better than most, Sherry, that legal sex is a big reason people in Pakistan get married."

Sherry told Alys that she was quite enjoying the conjugal duties of being Mrs. Kaleen, even though they slept in separate bedrooms.

"Kaleen snores like a truck, and apparently I snore too; thus he very shyly suggested that we should try separate rooms for sleeping purposes. I jumped on the offer. I've been sleeping alone for too many years to suddenly be comfortable with someone else in bed. Of course, I hop, skip, and jump to his bedroom for a visit when he asks, which is often, and I always return very satisfied. Since I don't have anyone else to compare my husband to, I'm quite sure it's as good as it can get. In fact, it is everything I'd dreamed of and more. I'm married, and yet I have my own space."

"I'm happy you are happy," Alys said simply.

"And how is Jena? Better?"

"Much better," Alys said.

"My mother was saying the same thing." Sherry dropped her cigarette butt into a bottle with water. "*Allah ka shukur hai,* thanks be to God. I was worried about her. No man is worth losing one's heart or one's looks over, especially if one looks like Jena."

"A lot of good her looks have done her."

"Kismet," Sherry said. "Look at me."

"You've always sold yourself too short."

"Now that Kaleen has bought me, I quite realize my worth."

"Yuck," Alys said, smacking Sherry on the arm. "What a way to put it!"

Sherry opened the cabinet and took out a

spray deodorizer. "This thing is so expensive. But I can afford it."

"Which reminds me," Alys said, "I would like to spend my morning in bed, lazing away, without being hauled off anywhere if that's all right with you."

"Fine by me." Sherry showed Alys how to buzz through to the kitchen. "If your majesty wants tea, breakfast, et cetera, in bed."

"I want," Alys said.

"Imagine," Sherry said. "This buzzer could have been yours, and I could have been visiting you."

"Be quiet," Alys said as she climbed into bed, "and good night and sweet dreams, before I remind you of my views on that."

CHAPTER 19

The following week was spent sightseeing and picnicking at Faisal Mosque, Daman-e-Koh, Rawal Lake, and shopping in Jinnah Supermarket. During the evenings, they would gather around a TV drama or a romance or action film before bedtime. Alys and Sherry would catch a quick midnight smoke and chitchat. Sherry hosted a luncheon for her new friends, who were the wives of Kaleen's friends. They were nice enough women, interested in being skinny, holidays and shopping, throwing costume parties, outdoing each other through their children's accomplishments, and bonding over the incompetence of their servants. When Alys teased her about her new best friends, Sherry was a good sport.

"Rather happy dimwits than a cynical crab like you," Sherry said, smiling. "Anyway, I have my translation projects to keep my brain oiled and, honestly, Kaleen encourages me to buy all the books I want."

That evening, when Alys made her routine phone call to Jena, she acknowledged that while Farhat Kaleen could be faulted for many a thing, being a miserly husband was not one of them, and both sisters were pleased for Sherry.

Alys sensed a returning melancholy in Jena's voice. Nona confirmed that Jena was certainly less lively than she'd been the previous week, and Nona suspected the cause. Had Alys seen the current issue of *Social Lights*?

"I recommend you suffer through this issue," Nona said. "Bungles, Hammy-Sammy, and gang are prominently featured."

After Alys hung up, she sent Sherry's cook to the market to buy the issue. The issue had a special section devoted to the luxe and snazzy vacations enjoyed by Pakistan's VIPs. The gang's week of rest and relaxation in the Maldives had a full page to itself. There they were, all smiles and sun and sunglasses and aqua, as if clueless that they'd left a heartbroken girl in their wake. Hammy, Sammy, Jaans, posing on a yacht. Darsee and his sister, Jujeena, in scuba gear. In another photo, Bungles in a pool with his arm around Jujeena, who was in a hot-pink bikini top with a gigantic waxy flower behind her ear.

Alys tossed the magazine into the trash. Nothing in life was fair. Nothing. Horrible people prospered and good, kind people did not, and there was no rhyme or reason to it. And for consolation, one attributed it to destiny.

Alys woke up the next morning still feeling dismal. She went for her morning walk-jog in the pretty park not five minutes away, determined not to let "Social Blights" ruin her day. She returned hot and sweaty. She bathed and changed into leggings and a T-shirt saying NOT YOUR AVERAGE BAJI. Then she proceeded to the dining room, where a late brunch was being enjoyed by all.

"As-salaam-alaikum," Alys greeted everyone. Taking a seat opposite Sherry, she poured herself a mug of instant coffee and cracked a boiled egg against her plate. She grabbed the newspaper no one had opened yet and flipped through the usual news of honor killings, dowry burnings, rapes, blasphemy accusations, sectarian violence, corruption scandals, tax evasions, and the never-ending promises by vote-grubbing politicians to fix the country.

Alys was on her second coffee when the

doorbell rang and, moments later, two men entered the dining room. Kaleen jumped up.

"*Aiye, aiye,* welcome, welcome," Kaleen said, his voice shaking as he led Darsee and his friend to chairs at the head of the table. "An honor! An honor! Sherry, have the cook brew a fresh pot of chai and fry up another batch of your superb *shami kebabs.*"

Darsee's companion was a friend from India, Raghav Kumar. He and Darsee had been in college together in Atlanta for their undergraduate degrees. No, he was not a vegetarian, Raghav said, as the cook brought in the piping-hot kebabs. Yes, many Hindus ate beef. Yes, he would very much like a cup of chai, with three teaspoons of sugar and plenty of milk.

Raghav was here on a twofold mission, one personal and the other a lifelong dream of climbing Pakistan's — nay, the world's — impossible mountain, K2. Last year he'd made it quite far up Everest. There were congratulations all around. Mansoor and Manzoor began to ask him questions about mountaineering, which was his hobby, and film editing, which was his job. Yes, he'd met quite a few superstars. No, he wasn't married. Yes, he was in a relationship.

"There's a lovely park just around the

corner from here," Alys said, "with a really nice jogging track but also an indoor climbing wall if you're interested."

"Interested. Thank you."

"And," Alys added, "just in case it's as big an issue for you as it might be for some people, a warning: It's not some fancy gym or exclusive climbing club but part of a public park."

"Exclusivity," Raghav said, "is a silly problem for silly people, for the most part."

Alys laughed. "Every segment of society here prides itself on being exclusive in some way."

"Such pride is a worldwide epidemic," Raghav said.

Darsee finally spoke. "How long are you here for, Alys?"

"A few weeks," she said a little curtly. "When did you come to Islamabad?"

"Last night," Darsee said. "We drove in from Lahore. Annie mentioned that you were all here. . . ."

"Did you happen to see my sister Jena in Lahore?" Alys asked. "She's been there these past few months."

Darsee cleared his throat. "No. Have you read the novel I gave you yet?"

"No. How was your time in the Maldives?" Alys asked.

"The usual."

"And what is the usual, for those of us not privy to your usual or to the Maldives' usual?"

"Hot and too commercial."

"Your party was featured in *Social Lights*. You seemed not too bothered by the heat and commerce."

Darsee scowled. "Hammy and Sammy had no right to release my sister's or my photos for public consumption."

"Some people," Alys said, "think it a great badge of social currency to be featured in social pages. I believe the term used is 'making it.' "

"Good for some people," Darsee said. "I find it crass. We're private people, not celebrities."

Alys groaned. "Please don't tell me you're one of those people who both love the exposure and complain about it."

Raghav raised his cup of chai to Alys. "If nothing else, *Social Lights* has catapulted Val into the role of even-more-eligible bachelor."

"Every mother, father, and daughter," said Alys, "has him in their sights now. There is no escape, thanks to his holiday in Maldives, drinking piña coladas at pools with bars."

Darsee rose abruptly. "Let's go, Raghav.

Thank you, Dr. Kaleen. Good to meet your family, Mrs. Kaleen. We actually came to invite you all to dinner tonight at Beena Aunty's, but I understand you must be unavailable at such a short notice, so —"

"Not at all. Not at all," Kaleen said. "For your 'unty I would break an engagement with the Queen of England. We'll be there."

After Darsee and Raghav drove away in a gleaming Pajero, Kaleen dropped into a chair with a self-satisfied look.

"That man, Valentine Darsee, has never thought it made sense to stop by my house, let alone exchange a word with me, in all this time. Yet here he was, come himself, drinking my chai, eating my kebabs. Clearly my importance for Annie is on the rise."

After Kaleen left for work, Sherry dragged Alys to the back of the garden in order to feed the goat and gather eggs. She duly informed Alys that her husband must be forgiven his flights of fancy for, clearly, dear Valentine Darsee had come for Alys.

"Don't be stupid," Alys said, flushing.

"He's aching to discuss the novel he gave you. Aching!"

"Shut up."

"Such an ache." Sherry lifted a squawking chicken and swayed it obscenely. "Such a deep ache."

"Too deep!" Alys said, laughing. "I thought you'd become all goody-goody once you married, and your sexual innuendos would end, but how nice that you've added flapping gestures to your repertoire. I don't know what Darsee's motive was for coming here. Last I saw him was at Fazool and Moolee's New Year's party, where we quarreled and he stormed out."

"And now he's stormed back in," Sherry said, and, singing "*Kabootar Ja Ja Ja,* pigeon fly, fly, fly," she impishly thrust the protesting chicken at a shrieking Alys before letting it loose.

The guests duly arrived at Versailles of Pakistan at the designated time and were once again ushered into the drawing room. Raghav and Annie were delighted to see them. Darsee was politely formal. Beena dey Bagh was, it seemed, a little put out. She was grumbling about her masseuse not showing up this morning for her daily rise-and-shine massage. However, it soon became evident to Alys that, when Darsee was present, Beena dey Bagh wanted him all to herself and had patience for no one else. Annie looked much healthier this evening. Her cheeks were flushed and her general mien vibrant, and Alys concluded it was on account of Darsee's presence. Although, since they'd arrived and been seated, Alys hadn't seen Darsee pay Annie any attention. If she ever got engaged, Alys thought, and her fiancé ignored her, she wouldn't put up with it.

"I loved Flannery O' Connor's short story 'Good Country People,' " Annie was saying. "Alys, the one you recommended."

The wretched mother, the gossiping neighbor, the angry daughter, the dreadful Bible salesman, the wooden leg. Annie could easily see this story set in Pakistan, and that made Flannery O'Connor an honorary Pakistani.

Alys laughed. "O'Connor, Austen, Alcott, Wharton. Characters' emotions and situations are universally applicable across cultures, whether you're wearing an empire dress, *shalwar kurta,* or kimono."

She recalled that Darsee had also said as much at the clinic and glanced at him at the bar, fixing a scotch for himself.

"I'm so glad you recommended her," Annie said. "Sherry, have you read it?"

"I've translated it into Urdu for a collection I'm putting together."

"How divine," Annie said.

Sherry smiled. "I've always wanted to

work on such projects but I've never had the time before, and now I have all the time in the world."

"Time for?" Raghav joined them with his freshened vodka. "You all look like you've been anointed. Tell, tell."

Alys told him about Sherry's undertaking and Annie's new love and that he should read it.

"It's not too long, is it?" Raghav said. "I'm more of a haiku person, short and punchy."

Alys shook her head. "You sound like a student asking how many pages an essay must be. You'll survive reading a short story. Imagine you're climbing a mental mountain."

"Yes, ma'am," Raghav said, giving her a mock salute. "Anything else, ma'am?"

Alys laughed. She was having a glorious time with Sherry, Raghav, and even Annie. Now if only Darsee would stop gazing at them from across the room as if they were worms. There was that look again, this time aimed at her.

"Instead of plotting our demise," Alys called out, "you may join us."

"I would," Darsee said, "but your figures look best from here."

"I'm sure they do." Raghav performed a pirouette. "Especially mine."

"Yes," Darsee said, "most especially yours."

"Oh, look," Alys said, "it has a sense of humor when it wants."

"It certainly does," Raghav said. They all laughed.

Beena dey Bagh, who'd been informing Kaleen and the rather baffled Mr. and Mrs. Looclus of the benefits of sashimi compared to sushi — *kachi machi,* raw fish, the Loo-cluses would exclaim for months — insisted that they share the joke. They did. Beena was not amused.

"Would any of you like to be referred to as 'it'?" she asked.

"Only," Alys said, much to Kaleen's consternation, "if I was being referred to as the 'It' Girl."

Beena clenched her fists. She would have forbidden them their laughter, except she was thrilled to see Annie enjoying herself. However, Beena was not happy with Alys. She clearly had no respect for Beena or her esteemed family. Perhaps time to seriously look into the parental complaints against her. Swearing. Promoting premarital sex. Her claims of marriage's being legal prostitution. Or some such nonsense, which Beena had so far ignored, at Principal Naheed's behest. Not that such views and impropriety were a surprising trait coming from a woman like Alysba Binat. Beena had heard all about Alysba's mother's family background. *Khandan* was *khandan,* after all, and sooner or later your pedigree showed. With the satisfying thought that no one could ultimately hide where they came from, Beena pressed the buzzer to the kitchen and ordered that the *khow suey* dinner be served.

Annie's entertainment being paramount to Beena dey Bagh, she saw no reason not to invite the Loocluses and, to her disgust, Alys — for there was no way to exclude her — night after night for dinner. Besides, Darsee and Raghav were also keen to have company over.

For his part, Kaleen felt he would explode at this nightly honor. Mareea, Mansoor, and Manzoor were thrilled to dress up and eat from such a splendid table in such luxurious surroundings and happiest when Kaleen's children joined too. Bobia and Haji Looclus compared, nonstop, the menus from the dinners as well as the sitting areas into which they'd been led. They felt that so much gracious chitchat with Beena dey Bagh must surely elevate their own social standing and that this change in their status must be reflected once they returned to Dilipabad. Perhaps a photo with Beena dey Bagh, which they would display prominently? And if a guest did not know who she was, well, then, that would prove the guest's insignificance.

Alys seemed the only one run a bit ragged by having to attend daily dinners, but it was nice to see Raghav and Annie. Darsee was tolerable enough given that, thankfully, they hardly interacted.

One morning, Alys found herself being joined on the jogging track in the park by Raghav.

"Hello, hello," Raghav said warmly.

"Hello!" Alys said, very pleasantly surprised.

"I checked out the climbing gym," Raghav said. "Thanks for the recommendation. Are you still walking? Join you?"

"Of course. So nice to see you."

"I also had to pick up some gear in town. I'm leaving tomorrow, earlier than scheduled. Big expedition going to K2, and my sherpa advises we should join."

Alys made a sad face.

"But let's do keep in touch," Raghav said. "And if you come to India, my home is your home."

"Thank you," Alys said. "Likewise, if you

ever come to my hometown, Dilipabad, my home is your home."

"Dilipabad." Raghav squinted. "Sounds familiar."

"Trust me," Alys laughed, "if you'd come to Dilipabad, you'd know. It's a tiny town."

"I did visit one small town, where my mother was born before partition. Last year, my mother passed away —"

"My condolences."

"Thank you, and she wanted me to spread some of her ashes in her childhood home here."

"So this trip is no ordinary visit for you, then," Alys said.

"Not at all. Valentine was instrumental in my getting a visa to come here as well as helping me locate my mother's childhood house. I am so grateful to him. My boyfriend couldn't make it. He's a photographer. He would have loved it here. Hold on! I know where I've heard of Dilipabad. I believe Darsee was there recently, for a wedding. Are you aware of any recent weddings that took place there?"

"Please," Alys said as nonchalantly as she could, "this is Pakistan. The home of the marriage-industrial complex. Always a wedding taking place everywhere. Weddings are our nation's bread and butter and foundation and flag."

"I believe Valentine recently saved a friend of ours, Bungles, from making a bad marriage or some such in Dilipabad."

"Saved?" Alys stumbled. "What do you mean 'saved'?"

"I think Bungles really liked some girl there, but Valentine didn't think it a good match."

"Who's Darsee to decide that? How do you know him and trust him so much?"

"Valentine and I were in college together in the U.S. for our undergrad degrees. He was serious back then too, the sort of person who feels compelled to tell someone to turn off a running water tap because waste-not–want-not. That's how he met Bungles. Bungles was a year junior and in our dorm. Bungles was brushing his teeth one morning and he'd left the water running, and Valentine descended upon him in the name of environmental enlightenment."

Raghav grinned. "I only met Bungles twice before I graduated — both times at a club, where Valentine was keeping a strict eye on him. Bungles is a decent but fun-loving guy and, if I recall correctly, Darsee steered him away from many a Miss Trouble back in college. Obviously he continues at it — hence the Dilipabad wedding rescue. Apparently the girl's mother is a mega–gold digger and kept flinging her daughter at Bungles, while the daughter herself showed zero interest. Valentine told me he was able to convince Bungles of her disinterest with concrete examples, until even Bungles could no longer deny that she'd probably even smiled at him only because her mother forced her to."

"Perhaps Darsee is interested in him for his sister?"

"No way! Val thinks women should be independent and know their minds before they get married. If Darsee has his way, Jujeena will be a double PhD, have solved world hunger, fixed the environment, brought wars to an end, and found the cure for at least three diseases before he recommends she marry."

"How nice for Jujeena."

"The fact is, Valentine is a good and sincere man and has been a great friend to Bungles and me."

A few steps on, Alys pled a sudden migraine. She assured Raghav she'd be fine and headed back to Sherry's as fast as she could. She was shaking when she got to her bedroom. By dinnertime, her head was pounding. Sherry gave her three painkillers, a strong cup of chai, and a plate of stomach-settling *khichiri* with homemade yogurt.

Alys did not eat. She stared at the plain ceiling and plotted Darsee's downfall. She abhorred him. He was singlehandedly responsible for Jena's misery. She would never forgive him, no matter how much he begged, were he ever to do so, which she prayed to God that by some miracle he would.

That evening Alys insisted she be excused from dining at Beena dey Bagh's. Kaleen, seeing how drained she looked, decided it was just as well that she stay behind. If she was coming down with something, he did not want her around Annie's immune system. When everyone left, Alys went to the living room, wrapped herself in a quilt, and switched on one of her favorite films, *The Terminator.* She tucked into a plate of her soul-settling comfort food — yellow lentils and white rice topped with cucumbers — and hoped that the machine-versus-man movie would at least soothe her for the duration of its running time. Oh, how she despised Darsee. If she ever saw him again she'd —

"Alys *baji,*" the maid, Ama Iqbal, poked her head into the living room. "There's a man to see you. Shall I bring him in?"

"A man?" Alys said.

"He came here once before. Ate all the *shami kebabs.*"

Alys nodded. Raghav. How sweet of him to come see if she was all right and to say goodbye before he left in the morning for K2. At least he wouldn't care that she was in her tatty pajamas and had oiled her hair. Perhaps she should tell him the whole tale and trust that he might tell Bungles the truth about Jena's feelings.

The door opened. Alys's smile disappeared.

"Hello," Darsee said.

"Is everyone all right?" Alys said. "Isn't there a dinner at your aunt's place?"

"All fine. No need to panic." Darsee glanced at the plate of half-eaten *dal chawal.* "I came to see how you were doing."

"How I'm doing?"

"Sherry said you've had a bad headache since this morning. Raghav said he and you had jogged together and it was humid. Could it be heat stroke? Is that oil in your hair?"

"Yes, it is. I was not expecting the Crown Prince of Pakistan to visit."

"I was worried." Darsee sat down. "You're watching *Terminator.* Is this your first time?"

"No," Alys said rudely.

"This is one of the only films with an even-better sequel. Have you seen it?"

"Listen," Alys said, "where does your aunt think you are?"

"Picking up emergency mountain stuff for Raghav. He leaves tomorrow morning."

Darsee rose. Then he sat back down. Then he rose again. He cleared his throat.

"What?" Alys said, as he looked down at her. "What's wrong with you?"

"Will you marry me?"

Alys stared at him.

"I *love* you."

This was so preposterous, Alys let out a hearty laugh.

"My admission is a joke to you?"

"Is this a prank?" Alys looked around. "Is there a hidden camera somewhere?"

"Don't be absurd." Darsee crossed the room. "I've tried to get you out of my head. I've tried so hard. I think about you all the time. Of how I want your opinion on this book and that film and this work of art and that play. I respect your opinions."

"*You* respect *my* opinions."

"Will you, Alys? Marry me? It's not the wisest of matches," Darsee said dolefully. "In fact, it's a disadvantageous match for me in all respects — well, except that you're smart, fun, and have a quirky personal style, which I like. And *you* are not a gold digger. This is the biggest plus of all."

"It is, is it?" Alys said.

"Beena Aunty will take some convincing, of course, but I'm sure I'll be able to win her over. Annie will help me too. I'm hoping that, once we're married, you'll agree with me that we need not meet your family with any regularity."

Alys had been in a daze this whole time. Now she stood up. Did Darsee think she'd agree to marry him? No doubt he'd been brought up to believe that he was a prince and all the girls everywhere were eager to be his princess and locked away in his castle.

"Aren't you engaged to Annie?" Alys flushed. She had not meant to ask this.

"Beena Khala would like that — consolidate property and the British School Group and all that — but Annie and I have grown up like siblings. It's gross. Anyway, Beena Khala's upset these days because Annie is refusing to break up with her Nigerian boyfriend. They began dating before she got sick. I like him. But why are you asking about Annie when I've asked you to marry me?"

"Marry you!" Alys said, even as she took in everything he'd told her. "Here's to bursting your bubble — I don't know what gave you the impression that I would marry you. I would never marry you under any circumstances. You are unmarriageable."

"I see." Darsee folded his arms. "I see. And why would you never marry me under any circumstances? Why am I unmarriageable? Do I stink or something?"

"Yes," Alys said. "You do stink. Of hubris. You are a pompous ass."

Darsee swallowed.

"You insult my family, tell me to seldom meet them, and then expect me to kneel in gratitude for the chance at being your wife? You think a way to a woman's heart is by calling her family coarse and crude?"

"I didn't use those terms, you did." Darsee scowled. "But they certainly are champions of what is called *ultee seeday harkatein,* bizarre behavior. You and I are both truth-tellers, and the truth is your family behaves disgracefully in public."

"*You* are uncouth," Alys said, "and unfeeling to expect me to not see my family. And if that's not bad enough, my sister Jena is in deep depression because of your interference between her and Bungles. That's why she left Dilipabad for Lahore. She was so upset she had to take time off from work to recover. She *really* liked Bungles and I know he *really* liked her, but you ruined it for them."

Darsee reddened. "She certainly didn't act as if she liked him."

"How stupid are you? My sister's reputation has taken a beating because of Bungles. She was even a gossip item in that stupid *Social Lights* column 'What Will People Say — *Log Kya Kahenge.*' Had Jena dared to openly encourage him, have you any idea what people would be saying about her then? Don't you know how people in this country talk? Show interest in a man and be called a slut. Don't show interest in a man and be called a tease or a prude or, as you'd say, disinterested. What's a girl to do?"

"It seemed to me that your mother was far more interested in Bungles than your sister was."

"Just come out and say it," Alys said. "You believe my mother is a gold digger. If we women decide to marry according to standards, then we are gold diggers, but when you weigh us in matters of looks and chasteness, then you're just being smart. I can't stand these double standards."

"Look," Darsee said, "it's terrible your sister is depressed, but based on what I saw, I was protecting my friend. Wouldn't you have protected your sister if it were the other way around? Have you any idea how many girls, how many women, throw themselves at Bungles all day long? At me?"

"It's not exactly you they're throwing themselves at," Alys said, "so don't unduly flatter yourself."

"Oh, I know," Darsee said grimly. "I was disillusioned ages ago. It's not me. It's my money, my family name, or both. Do you have any idea how hard it is to find someone who likes you for who you are? Marries you for yourself and not your assets?"

"Poor little rich boy Valentine Darsee. Such a hard life. Valued for what he has to offer rather than who he is. Welcome to a woman's world, where we are valued for tits, ass, womb, sometimes earning capacity, but above all else being servile brainless twits. Have you any idea what it feels like to want to be liked for your brains and instead be coveted for your body?"

"I like you for your brains."

"I don't like you for anything," Alys said. "I've refused your benevolent offer of marriage. Why are you still here?"

"So you've made up your mind."

"My God! You have more hubris than a Disney prince. I don't like you. At all. We have nothing in common. Nothing."

Darsee looked Alys up and down. "Yes we

do. We like reading and we have growing up abroad in common. We both grew up multicultural kids. We know no one person represents a group or a country in things good or bad. We know how to plant roots where there are none. We know that friends can be made anywhere and everywhere, regardless of race or religion. We know how to uproot. We know how to move on from memories, or at least not let memories bury us. Most of all, neither of us is a hypocrite, Alys. Neither of us would call an ugly baby cute."

"Even if we did have all this in common, I would never marry you," Alys said. "And you *are* a hypocrite. Or have you forgotten Jeorgeullah Wickaam?"

"Wickaam again!"

"Wickaam forever! You cheated your cousin out of an inheritance so that you could get it all for yourself. My father's elder brother did the same, and it damaged my family. Don't you think for a second that a betrayal of this type is something that I can ever forget or forgive. If you aren't a decent person, then your money and lineage mean nothing to me. Loyalty means everything to me, and you, Valentine Darsee, are not loyal to family or friends. You may have fooled the whole world into thinking otherwise, but you'll never fool me."

"I see." Darsee nodded. "You've spent time with me and with Wickaam, and your conclusion is that he is a saint and I am a materialistic disloyal villain. A good thing, then, that you have rejected me. Saves me from being with a person who has such a low opinion of me. I'm so sorry to have wasted your time, as well as my own. Good-bye, then, and best wishes."

After Darsee left, Alys did not move for a long while. She stared at the TV screen without hearing a word. The film credits rolled and the film turned off and the DVD self-ejected and she sat there still. Valentine Darsee said he loved her. That he valued her opinions. Valentine Darsee proposed to her despite all his objections toward her family.

He proposed.

She refused.

Alys heard honking at the gate. The party was back from dinner. Sherry would take one look at her and know something had happened. Alys did not want to discuss anything with anyone, not yet. She rushed to her bedroom, got into bed, turned off the lights, pulled the covers over her head, and fell into a deep and restful sleep.

CHAPTER 20

Alys woke the next morning and instantly recalled Darsee's proposal. She took a deep breath and decided that there was no need to tell anyone. Her mother would faint at her having turned down an offer of this magnitude. Sherry would tell her that she'd made a bad decision. Even Jena, she suspected, would scold her for having been too quick to refuse. But Alys was more than satisfied with her decision. The next order of business was to go about her day exactly as she would any other day, and what was so shocking now would in time turn ordinary.

Alys slipped on running clothes and left the house for the park. Not bad, Alys, she thought to herself as she embarked on her first lap. You must be doing something right for two proposals in one year, all the way from Kaleen to Darsee.

Suddenly Darsee appeared before her on

the path, holding out a letter.

"I didn't want this delivered at Kaleen's house, in case anyone else opened it, so I waited here, hoping you'd show up. Please read this and then, as I said last night, goodbye and best wishes."

Alys took it and watched Darsee disappear out of sight. She made her way to the nearest bench and slit open the sealed envelope.

Alys,

You made two accusations against me and I deserve a chance to explain. The first is about your sister. I've known Bungles for a long time, and he's always falling "in love." This time I did sense gravity in his feelings, but I honestly did not see those feelings reciprocated by Jena. I understand that in our society women play it safe until they get a proposal; however, there is a difference between showing restraint and showing indifference. I was beyond convinced your sister was showing indifference.

And then, your family. Look, you can't deny that your mother and Lady display no propriety. Even if a guy acted in private the way Lady does in public, I'd call him out. Lady and Qitty quarrel in public like they're hired entertainment.

Your sister Mari is Muslim fire and brimstone, and your father seems unable, or unwilling, to discipline anyone. Then there is the matter of your maternal ancestry. Alys, you must see that no true friend would recommend marrying into your family regardless of whether the girl showed great interest, which Jena did not.

I accept one wrongdoing. I did know Jena was in Lahore. I'm sorry I lied to you. I am not a liar. Bungles had no idea, because his sisters and I didn't tell him.

The second accusation concerns my cousin Jeorgeullah Wickaam. Wickaam gives everyone the sob story he gave you. My father and both his parents did pass away in the Ojhri arms-depot explosion; that much of Wickaam's story is true. We were all traumatized.

Wickaam became extremely clingy. No one blamed him given his circumstances. He needed love and stability. He could not sleep alone, so he and I shared a bedroom. When my mother, sister, and I moved to England, he came with us.

After a string of unsuccessful relationships, my mother remarried and we moved to Bangkok. It was Wickaam who decided to stay back with his father's family. As it turned out, he'd befriended an older woman; so began his philandering. When Wickaam's father's family found out about his "affairs," they didn't know how to handle it. My mother had divorced by then and so, after three years in Bangkok, we'd returned to Lahore, and my mother requested that Wickaam be sent back to us.

When he arrived at Lahore Airport, Wickaam was seventeen years old and turning every head. He targeted that most vulnerable of people, the adolescent maid. One, two, three maids came forward: Wickaam Sahib had seduced them by promising them marriage, money, gold earrings, etc. My mother was appalled. She tried to protect these young girls by sending them back to their villages and away from Wickaam's urges. And then one of the maids got pregnant. Mahira was adamant that Wickaam marry her and legitimize their child. Wickaam said she had no proof that he was the father.

Thanks to my mother and Beena Aunty, Mahira delivered a healthy baby boy. We paid for her and the baby's upkeep for life as well as his education.

My mother and Beena Aunty requested Mahira not disclose the arrangement to anyone but, next we know, another pregnant maid shows up.

My mother had recently been diagnosed with a late-stage cancer, and all this stress made her sicker. She felt she'd failed her late sister's son, and she worried about what would become of these poor maids, their children, and Wickaam with his inability to keep his pants zipped.

My mother and Beena Aunty decided to use Wickaam's inheritance to set up a school for underprivileged children, in which Wickaam's offspring would also study for free, as well as a facility for taking in abandoned infants who may otherwise be victims of infanticide. Wickaam was livid at his inheritance being taken away. He blamed me. Instead of taking his side like a "brother," I was some bleeding heart who'd sided with the maids.

After Wickaam visited my mother on her deathbed, my mother decided that he should receive tuition money for a college abroad, and Beena Aunty agreed. But what does Wickaam do? He uses the funds to travel the world of lechery in luxury.

My sister, Juju, is ten years younger than him, Annie, and me. Annie and I decided that Juju didn't need to know about Wickaam's sexual exploits. However, the minute I left for my MBA, that asshole began to prey on my sister, convincing her they were in love. Beena Aunty didn't even know the two were meeting, let alone what was going on. No one did.

One day I received a phone call from Juju. She was pregnant and Wickaam was insisting they elope. But she wanted me to be at the wedding. I booked the first flight back from Atlanta to Lahore. I told my sister to tell him they could marry but that I was going to cut off her inheritance and there'd be no money. Wickaam called my bluff. Next I took Juju to the charity school, where she saw Wickaam's children and had to believe what I'd been telling her. She was distraught. I told Juju to convince Wickaam she'd given up her inheritance to be with him. His response was to abandon my pregnant sixteen-year-old sister. Next I hear, he's in New York, where, while having a good time, he has purchased a fake law degree and is now going around telling people he went to a college in New York. He did — he literally walked through a college campus in New York City.

I told Juju I would support her no matter what she chose to do. After much agonizing, she opted for an abortion. I was unwilling to trust my unmarried sister's secret to doctors and nurses in Pakistan, and so I took her to Europe. She suffered so much, and all I could do was feel like shit.

Wickaam thinks Juju miscarried. Only she and I — and now you — know she had an abortion. I wish I could tell the world the truth, but I cannot without risking my sister's reputation as well as the reputations of others Wickaam has seduced.

He is my cousin, my blood relative, I'm sorry to say, but he is not my friend. He is no one's friend and does not know what the word "loyalty" means. Weena Aunty and Uncle Hassan, his parents, were so gentle, kind, and upright — they would be shocked to see how their son has turned out.

I'm sharing all this with you to tell you that Wickaam is not the victim here nor we conniving relatives, and I would advise you and yours to stay far away from him.

Alys, I wanted you to have a signed statement from me to prove that I trust you.

Valentine Darsee

Alys looked up. The sun was still shining. Bees buzzed over a bed of petunias. A group of elderly ladies power-walked past her. She could not believe what she'd just read. His explanation for his interference with Bungles and Jena had not appeased her, and she was furious that he'd kept Jena's presence in Lahore from Bungles. But he'd told her the truth. And if he'd told her the truth about that, then how could she doubt his account about Wickaam? But if Darsee was telling the truth, then Wickaam had lied.

Alys recalled Wickaam's face as they'd sat in Pak Tea House and he'd related his tale. He'd sounded so sincere. And yet here was this letter from Darsee. A letter in which he'd confessed to his sister having premarital sex that had ended in an abortion. In Pakistan, no one in their right mind would make up such a thing, let alone a brother about his sister.

It occurred to Alys that when Wickaam

had smiled at Darsee at the Wagah border, it had been a sheepish smile. That it was Wickaam who'd decided to back out of attending NadirFiede's *walima*. Wickaam who was always keen to demean Darsee.

Poor Juju! Poor maids! Should she warn Miss Jahanara Ana Aan that her fiancé was a heinous man and a father of children whom he did not acknowledge? "Father" was the wrong word. Wickaam was not a father. He was just a man who'd sired children. But what concrete proof could she offer without betraying Darsee's confidence?

Alys reread Wickaam's section. She read it several times. After she was done, she marched on the jogging path, trying to regain composure. She felt dizzy and sick. Wickaam must have seen the Binat name on the Fraudia Acre case papers and assumed they had money. Upon realizing they had none, he'd perhaps decided that if not marriage for money, then he could attain something else from one of them. He'd never tried anything untoward with her, but Alys recalled his attentions to Qitty, and she shuddered at the memory of Wickaam sleeping over while Lady pranced around in her nightie. Shame on their society, where maintaining unsoiled reputations was considered more vital than exposing scoundrels, for such secrets only allowed the scoundrels to continue causing harm.

Alys stopped walking and read the letter again. And then again. Each time, she felt a fresh pinch at "maternal ancestry," and anger that Darsee had believed this rumor as readily as everyone else seemed to. She also felt nauseous over his allegations about her family's crude behavior. The truth, as much as it stung, was that his charges were valid. And hadn't Sherry also feared that Jena's guardedness could be read as blatant indifference? But Alys was not going to blame Jena. She'd told Darsee that women were stuck in a bind, and they were.

Darsee had apologized for withholding word of Jena's presence in Lahore from Bungles. He'd written, *I'm sorry I lied to you. I am not a liar.* And from everything she could see, Darsee was a doting brother. Why had she so readily believed Wickaam?

Because she'd wanted to believe him. Alys swallowed her disappointment in herself. In Wickaam's case, she'd been favorably biased, and in Darsee's unfavorably prejudiced. She'd been flattered by Wickaam's attentions and offended by Darsee's initial dismissive assessment of her looks and her intellect. She'd readily welcomed Wickaam's — a total stranger's — derision of Darsee, and, even worse, she'd added to it.

Alys groaned as she recalled how she'd compared Wickaam to Darsee and told him he could never be loyal. His proposal had been conceited, there was no denying that, but she'd been petty in her rejection.

Alys wasn't sure how she was going to react when she saw Darsee next, but when she finally ended her walk and returned to Sherry's house, the Loocluses were discussing the day's events: Raghav had left this morning as scheduled for K2, and Darsee had suddenly decided to return to Lahore. Beena dey Bagh had telephoned to cancel dinner.

By and by, Kaleen decided that the cancellation was a stroke of good luck, since the Loocluses and Alys were scheduled to leave three days from now and this would allow them time to wrap up things. Three days later, the Looclus family and Alys set off for Lahore and from there to Dilipabad. As had been the case before, the Loocluses dropped Alys off at Nisar and Nona's and popped in for chai before heading to their relatives' house. They would pick up Alys and Jena the next morning.

Alys had hoped to have a few moments alone with Jena, but she quickly realized that a few moments would not be enough for what she'd decided to share with her sister and that, once they got home, privacy would be a dream. Consequently, she told the Loocluses that she and Jena had decided to stay an extra day in Lahore and that they'd take the Daewoo bus back to Dilipabad.

Two days later, Alys and Jena boarded a deluxe bus. The bus hostess introduced herself as Qandeel Baloch and, with a striking smile, distributed the boxed lunches and pointed out the toilets at the back. Once the bus started moving, Alys told Jena to brace herself for all she was about to hear.

"What?" Jena opened the box lunch to a chicken-salad sandwich, potato chips, and an apple. "What great secret has required us to spend money on bus tickets so we can get privacy?"

"Darsee proposed to me."

Jena's hands stilled on the apple.

"Darsee sought me out one evening when I was alone at Sherry's and informed me that he loves me and respects my opinions and wants to marry me."

"Dear God!" Jena said. "Oh my dear God!"

"I said no."

"Valentine Darsee proposed to you and you said *no*?"

"And that's not even the real explosive secret."

Alys took out Darsee's letter from her bag.

"Read from here." She tapped at the beginning of Wickaam's section.

"What's this above?" Jena said.

"You know what" — Alys bit her lip — "read the whole thing, except it's about you and Bungles."

Jena read it slowly, her expression going from wounded, to hurt, to puzzled, to resolute.

"Are you all right?" Alys asked gently as Jena came to the end of the part on Bungles.

"Yes and no." Jena shook her head. The fact was that of course friends asked friends for advice all the time, but Bungles should have trusted his own intuition about her rather than what his friend or sisters told him. They had not seen her looking into Bungles's eyes; he had. They had not seen her ensuring that his plate was always full of food; he had. They had not heard the tenderness in her voice for him when they were alone; he had. He should have trusted what he was seeing rather than what they were seeing.

He was weak willed and, the fact was, she did not want a weak-willed man.

Jena returned to the letter. As she got

deeper into Wickaam's section, she began to fidget. Often she glanced at Alys in agitation. When she was done, she folded the letter and handed it back to Alys.

"Can Wickaam truly be so two-faced? Can he hide his double nature so well?"

"Yes," Alys said, "and yes."

"But there's got to be some misunderstanding between Darsee and Wickaam. What Darsee relates here is just terrible."

"Doesn't make it untrue."

"My God, Alys, Wickaam spending nights, our mother offering any of us up to him for marriage, Lady in her nightie!" Jena's hand flew to her chest. "My God, do you think —"

"Lady is not that stupid," Alys said. "She's *zinda dil,* full of life, but even she knows the limits."

"Poor Jujeena. Do you think Bungles knows about this?"

"Darsee's clearly written that only he, Juju, and now I know."

"And now I know," Jena said. "Are you going to tell him you showed me?"

"No. Not yet. I don't know. I trust you."

"As he trusted you," Jena said, sighing. "I honestly don't know what to believe."

"I believe Darsee. I do. He's not the villain after all."

"I always told you not to judge so quickly."

Alys looked out the window at the orange grove they were passing.

"Jena," she said, turning to her, "ever since I read the letter, I knew you were right. And Sherry was right too. I was being unreasonable in my dislike for him, a dislike that started because he wounded my vanity and I let his judgment cloud my judgment. He's such a snob — you should have heard the dismal way he proposed to me — but surely snobbery is not equal to evil. I'm not saying he's suddenly turned into a saint, but I am cringing at all the times I agreed with Wickaam that Darsee was horrid. Cringing at all the times I defended Wickaam to Darsee."

"You didn't know any better." Jena squeezed Alys's hand. "You didn't have all the facts."

"Had Wickaam told me Darsee kidnapped babies and ate them for breakfast, I would have believed him."

"Oh, Alys."

"Darsee was right. I like to tell others the truth about themselves, but I'm not so keen to hear truths about me and mine. I'm ashamed that I'm not the person I thought I was."

"You should be proud that you possess the ability to revise your opinion and want to develop qualities you lack."

"Yes," Alys said wryly, "I plan to be very proud at being able to call myself out on my own prejudice. But, seriously, Jena, what should I do? Should I warn Miss Jahanara Ana Aan? Should we tell others about Wickaam?"

"It's not our secret to divulge," Jena said, truly troubled.

"Doesn't Wickaam need to be exposed so he can't dupe other girls? But this could truly ruin Jujeena Darsee's reputation for the rest of her life."

"Not just her life." Jena's voice was steel. "It would affect her children's reputations and her grandchildren's reputations. Is this not what we face? Thanks to Aunty Tinkle's slander concerning our grandmother's supposed profession, people malign us even though no one can furnish a shred of proof toward that rumor."

"I dare not imagine," Alys said, "what will happen to Jujeena's story in the hands of people like Rose-Nama and her mother and Naheed and Hammy and Sammy."

"I can," Jena said softly. "These people could be having premarital sex and abortions left, right, and center, but they'll put on such self-righteous airs you'll think they are the world's greatest *naik parveens,* pi-

410

ous women."

"Internal misogyny has made a mockery of female solidarity," Alys said, forlorn. "It's not even as if abortion is the issue. Married women here use it as birth control. It's all about premarital sex. Are you a virgin or not?"

"And these pigeon problems," Jena said in despair, "are only meant to preoccupy us while the men are free to focus their energies on the important things in life."

"Can you imagine the schadenfreude?" Alys said. "How gleeful people will be to hear of Jujeena and Darsee's scandal? In front of Jujeena they'll say, 'Poor Jujeena this, poor Jujeena that,' but behind her back they will call her a slut and blame her for becoming pregnant. All the while, even as they condemn Wickaam for being vile, women will try to reform him with their own true love, while men will slap him on his back for being such a manly man. This is the society we live in."

The sisters were still talking in hushed whispers when the bus reached Dilipabad, where they were met by their family, amid a cacophony of greetings.

"Missed you both so much," Mr. Binat said, hugging his eldest daughters.

"He did," Mrs. Binat said, giving Jena and

Alys pecks on their cheeks. "Your father wants to discuss his beloved flora and fauna, and no one else has the patience to hear him blather on about aeration and lime content. You look so relaxed and refreshed, Jena."

"Do I look like I've lost any weight?" Qitty tightened her *kurta* around her waist. "I've lost ten pounds since you left."

"You do look trimmer," Jena said.

"Shut up about your ten pounds, Qitty," Lady said. "It's not visible on your body, so it has to be your brains getting lighter."

"Lady! Behave!" Alys said as she hugged Qitty.

"Great," Lady said. "Aunty Alys is back."

"Qitty," Alys said, "I've brought you a bundle of used magazines I found, called *Mode,* for plus-size women."

"Did you get the things on my list?" Lady said.

"Yes," Alys said. "Such a long list of nothing but beauty products. Let me remind you: books over looks."

"I didn't have a single beauty product on my list," Mari said proudly. "I do not care about outer looks but rather the inner beauty of the soul."

"Inner beauty of the soul," Lady repeated, mimicking Mari in a squeaky voice. "Jena,

Alys, this is her new thing. Inner beauty of the soul. Mari, you have little outer beauty, so of course you are going to lecture on inner beauty. God, I want a long holiday away from this town and my family. We're dying of heat here. Jena, Alys, I went to see Mareea Looclus yesterday. She said Fart Bhai has air-conditioning everywhere and she was freezing all the time. I wish we could afford to freeze."

"We can't, thanks to Goga and Tinkle," Mrs. Binat said. "May God sprout warts on their privates."

"Pinkie, shhh!" Mr. Binat glanced around to see if anyone at the bus stop had overheard. "Your curses become more colorful with each passing day."

"Mareea also said," Lady grumbled, "that Sherry bought her everything she wanted and then some."

Mrs. Binat snorted. "I'm telling you, she must have bought clearance."

"No, Mummy," Lady said, "I told you I saw the full-price stickers. Also, she was crowing about how Fart Bhai has said that, as soon as she finishes college, she can move in with them. I say, good riddance. If Fart Bhai wants his fish-faced sister-in-law around, good for him. But, Jena, Alys, is it true? Did he really invite her to live with them? It's so unfair. Even Mareea will leave Dilipabad, while I will languish here and die."

"Hai!" Mrs. Binat said. "Why will you die? *Die karein tumhare dushman.* May your enemies die."

"They are not dying. They are prospering. Mareea said Fart Bhai is going to replace their shitty motorbike with a car, a very good car. Mummy, imagine those flamingo-faced Mansoor and Manzoor going from being motorbike boys to having a better car than ours. I can't stand it. Alys, it's not even as if they worked for it themselves, but you keep saying that us girls must earn everything for ourselves."

"Don't you listen to Alys. *Yeh tho pagal hai.* She's mad." Mrs. Binat's nostrils fluttered in her despair at Bobia Looclus's coup after coup. "Alys has done nothing for her family, while all that snake Sherry does is elevate hers via her husband's fat wallet. God only knows what spell she has put on that wife-worshipping Kaleen. Lady, my love, you watch — you will make the best marriage in all of Pakistan and have a million good cars."

"At this point," Lady said, "I won't settle for less than a private plane or two."

Mrs. Binat sighed helplessly. "Jena, Alys,

is Useless Uterus Sherry still giving herself airs and graces? How eager she was to call herself 'Mrs. Shireen Kaleen' as soon as she got married."

"But, Mummy," Jena said, "what else would she call herself?"

"Mareea swears," Lady said, "that Fart Bhai really does let Sherry sleep in for as long as she likes and that he insists she go to the beauty parlor daily and spend as much as she wants. Imagine! Before Sherry's marriage, visiting the 'porler,' as they pronounce it, was such a big deal for those two sisters, and now Mareea claims she's been so many times, she's tired of the very word 'porler.' "

"Lady," Mrs. Binat said, gently, "don't make fun of anyone's accent."

"I will!" Lady said. "Mareea Looclus is a show-off, and I hate her."

"You should not hate anyone," Mari said, "for hate will come back to haunt you, and envy will eat you alive."

Qitty added, "Don't be petty, Lady. Be happy for your friend."

"Mummy, High Priestess and Behemoth are ganging up on me again," Lady said.

"You're being very spiteful, Lady," Alys said as Jena nodded in agreement.

"Leave Lady alone, Alys," Mrs. Binat said,

frowning, as they walked to the parking lot. "It is thanks to your refusal of Kaleen that Mareea Looclus is in a position to preen in front of Lady."

"I just wish Mareea would remember," Lady said, "that, had Alys bothered to marry Fart Bhai, then I'd be the one going to the 'parlor,' but what's the use? No one cares about what could have been, and the fact is, Sherry grabbed Fart Bhai, and Mareea has lucked out. Jena, Alys, please, for the sake of my soul, please find someone outstanding to marry you. You've already reached your sell-by dates, and before you completely expire, I also want to see what it feels like to have a benevolent brother-in-law."

"Is Sherry hoity-toity all the time?" Mrs. Binat asked as they climbed into the car and proceeded homeward. "Or does she retain the good sense to remember where she comes from and to never forget her *pha-teecher* wretched home?"

Alys and Jena exchanged a look. They were home.

CHAPTER 21

Every year Nisar and Nona left their children with her parents while the two of them went on a holiday. This year they were supposed to have gone to New Zealand, but Nisar discovered his passport had expired too late to get it renewed, so they decided instead to retour Pakistan's Northern Areas. Alys had always been eager to see the breathtaking Lake Saiful-Muluk, Gilgit, Naran, Kaghan, Skardu, Hunza, Chitral. They weren't sure which lakes and valleys and peaks they would visit, but they would love for Alys and Jena to accompany them.

Alys agreed immediately. Jena declined. Their father's face had fallen at the invite and Jena decided that, having so recently spent so much time away from home, she would stay back. Everyone else's face fell too: Mrs. Binat, Qitty, Mari, Lady. There were shrieks and tears. Couldn't they have also been invited? In fact, Mrs. Binat and her three younger daughters would have happily invited themselves, had they considered hiking and staring at night stars the least bit fun. If only, Mrs. Binat kept lamenting, they could all afford a holiday the way they used to. How she longed to return to London! *Hai,* Lundhun! *Hai,* Oxford Street! *Hai,* Hyde Park!

Lady joined in her mother's longings. Holiday! Holiday! She'd been a toddler when they used to go abroad, and she didn't even remember these destinations everyone else had such fond memories of. Holiday! Holiday! It was all she would talk about, until even Mrs. Binat regretted mentioning the word "holiday."

"We have no money for even a week's getaway to a decent place," Mrs. Binat said. "We spent a fortune on clothes for the Nadir-Fiede wedding, and for what — nothing! Now, had Alys married Kaleen, we'd have spent the entire summer in Islamabad. And had Bungles married . . ."

But Mrs. Binat silenced herself. It was evident to all that no matter which smile Jena plastered on her face, she was still hurting, for she'd fallen in love and was now being forced to fall out of it. Even Mr. Binat had stopped cracking jokes about "eating shoes" in order to not cause Jena further pain.

Alys's holiday news was scarcely digested when the phone rang again. It was Lady's friend Hijab. Hijab's family had just this year relocated from Dilipabad to Karachi, and she was missing her friends so much that her mother had relented and allowed her to invite a close friend to visit for the remaining two weeks of the summer holidays. Hijab came from a good family — meaning, in local parlance, they were well off. Her mother fancied herself a journalist, having written a couple of recipes and New Year resolutions lists for *Social Lights*, and her father was in an executive position with the national airline, which meant Lady's ticket would be complimentary and all she would have to bring with her was shopping money.

"No," Alys said, as soon as Lady got off the phone and waltzed into the living room to inform everyone that she was going to Karachi. "You are not going anywhere by yourself, let alone to a different city hours away by plane."

Why couldn't she go? Lady screamed. Was Alys the only one in the family who deserved holidays? She'd barely returned from Sherry's in Islamabad and was now packing for Nona's and the Northern Areas. Alys hadn't even had to ask for permission, so why should she? Hijab had made plans for every day. Her family belonged to the Marina Club, and they were going to go sailing and crabbing and have bonfires on the beach! Her ticket was free! There was no force on earth that was going to stop Lady from going!

Alys did not even bother to appeal to her mother, who was already beginning to make a list of things Lady must pack. Instead, she marched to her father. Mr. Binat was in the garden, picking tomatoes off the vines. He smiled when he saw Alys and straightened up and stretched his lower back.

"These will make the best *red salan* yet," he said, pointing to the jute basket full of ruby fruit, which would be used to make one of the Binats' favorite dishes: tomatoes stewed in oil and spiced with turmeric, salt, and red chilies and topped off with hard-boiled eggs.

"Daddy," Alys said, "Lady's friend who moved to Karachi has invited her to stay with them for the rest of the summer. I don't think she should go."

"Here." Mr. Binat handed Alys a pair of gardening gloves. "Help me bag some for the few neighbors who remain in your

420

mother's good graces."

"Daddy, did you hear me?" Alys slipped on the gloves and stepped into the vegetable patch.

"I heard you," Mr. Binat said, "and I've been hearing Lady's shouting all the way out here. Why can't she go? You know she'll make our lives miserable if she doesn't and, frankly, your mother is enough to make life miserable already."

"Daddy, please be serious for a second," Alys said. She couldn't help think of Darsee's letter, which she never stopped thinking about anyway: *Your father seems unable, or unwilling, to discipline anyone.*

"I am being serious." Mr. Binat plucked another tomato. "I could not be any more serious if I was being paid."

"I don't think Lady should be sent anywhere by herself," Alys said. "I'm sorry to say this to you, Daddy, but she makes you-you eyes at everyone. I think the only man she's not made you-you eyes at is Farhat Kaleen."

Mr. Binat looked discomfited, as would any *ghairatmand* — principled — Pakistani father, but he was not one to pretend that girls did not go through puberty or did not have feelings for the opposite sex; his wife had made sure he was most comfortable around them while they discussed bra sizes and menstruation and, as a result, as far as he was concerned, making you-you eyes was just another thing women did.

"Princess Alysba," Mr. Binat said, lifting a green tomato to check its color on the other side, "let Lady have her fun and get it out of her system. She's just like your mother, a bit propriety-challenged, but neither means any harm."

"But harm is already done," Alys said.

Mr. Binat handed Alys a tomato for the basket. "Don't tell me Lady frightened away some suitor of yours? None of you girls need men like that in your lives. You've been given a lot of liberties in this home, which most Pakistani girls can only dream of, and a controlling man will suffocate you. Even Mari, though she may not think so, will not be happy with anyone who expects his to be the final word."

"I'm afraid for Lady," Alys said. She thought of Lady at the New Year's party, blissfully sandwiched between Moolee and his geriatric friend, and mocking Qitty in front of them. "I admire her high spirits, but she has no self-control over her actions, or her tongue."

"Alys, you're surprising me, *beta*. You are the last person on earth I expect to worry about *log kya kahenge.*"

"I don't care what people say," Alys said. "But I do care that Lady's carelessness could put her in a situation she can't handle. Please listen to me, Daddy — Lady is impulsive, too trusting, and lacks all sense of consequences."

"With such fine qualities, I think being away from us all will be excellent practice for Lady to learn self-discipline instead of always relying on us to provide it."

"She needs us."

"And we need some respite from her, especially Qitty, who could do with two weeks of no one making fun of her being fat." Mr. Binat stepped out of the tomato bed. "I think we're getting a bargain, Alys, with someone else paying for Lady's ticket to Karachi, which, may I remind you, is not cheap. Hijab comes from a good family. Hijab's mother will make sure that everyone behaves. In fact, if she reprimands Lady, it may have more of an effect than our doing so."

"Perhaps," Alys said, even as she shook her head, unconvinced.

"Perhaps we should have Wickaam keep an eye on her?" Mr. Binat said. "Now that he has moved to Kar—"

"No!" Alys stared at her father in horror.

Wickaam had telephoned them a week ago and spoken to her. He'd left Musarrat Sr. & Sons Advocates and was instead planning to remain in Karachi and seek new prospects. Frankly, he told her, law wasn't for him after all. Furthermore, he and Miss Jahanara Ana Aan had decided to break their engagement. He'd realized that she wasn't for him either. Her family had sent the distraught girl to Cairo, where she had relatives, in order to recover from a broken engagement.

"Is that so?" Alys had asked in a cold tone. "That's why her family has sent her away?"

Perhaps Wickaam had sensed her sardonic tone, because he asked her how her trip to Islamabad had been. Was not his aunt, Beena dey Bagh, a tyrant? And had Dracula been there?

Alys replied that Beena dey Bagh was who she was and that Darsee was who he was too but that, upon spending more time with him, she didn't think he seemed such a monster.

"Is that so?" Wickaam repeated.

Alys replied, "That is exactly so."

He'd wished her and her family well and, within seconds, he'd hung up.

"No," Alys said forcefully. "No, Daddy, there is absolutely zero need for Wickaam

424

to know that Lady will even be in Karachi."

"Oh dear," Mr. Binat said, "still upset Wickaam-of-the-rising-star left you for Miss Jahanara Ana Aan. He's free of her now and can return to you."

"God forbid," Alys said. "And I was never upset over anything. Simply put, Aunty Nona thinks Wickaam is a wastrel, and I believe her. As such, there is absolutely no need to socialize with the likes of him."

Mr. Binat shrugged. "Whatever you think is best, my princess. He's moved to Karachi anyway and we're in no danger of your mother inviting him to stay the night. Honestly, I think she's too generous with the guest room, but she means no harm and just wants to entertain herself."

Her father winked at her and, for the first time, Alys recognized her own complicity in her family's dynamics. She was her father's favorite daughter. His princess Alysba. And because she enjoyed her status as first daughter, Alys had chosen to overlook her father's ridiculing her mother. It was not that her father was wrong, but he should not have turned Pinkie Binat into a joke between them. Should not the husband-and-wife bond be more sacrosanct than that between a parent and child?

PART THREE

■ ■ ■ ■

August–December 2001

CHAPTER 22

Alys and Lady boarded the bus from Dili-pabad to Lahore, where Alys would meet Nona and Lady would fly on to Karachi. Mari waved goodbye with glee. She was looking forward to making some inroads into her Quran studies without Lady's taunts of purity perverts, high priestesses, and *hojabis*. Qitty also waved contentedly, for she was looking forward to poring over the *Mode* magazines Alys had given her, without Lady insulting every voluptuous body. Mr. Binat and Jena were looking forward to some quarrel-free peace and quiet, and they too waved gaily at Lady. Only Mrs. Binat moaned about how she would miss her youngest daughter as she blew kiss after kiss to Lady, seated in the bus by the window.

"I'll bet they are all so jealous of me," Lady said to Alys. "Are they going to stand here until the bus leaves?"

"Yes," Alys said, and she was right.

Once the bus left Dilipabad station, Lady immediately opened the box lunch, unwrapped the chicken-salad sandwich, and took a messy bite.

"Yum-yum," she said to Alys. "Are you going to have your sandwich?"

"Yes, I am," Alys said. "And for God's sake, try not to be greedy at Hijab's house. Display your best manners. Don't get overexcited about anything. Don't speak out of turn. Don't talk back to Hijab's parents. Say please and thank you to the servants. Remember to tip them when it's time to return. Do not use that tip money on yourself, Lady, I mean it. Imagine I'm right behind you, watching you the whole time."

"So creepy."

"Every minute my eyes will be on you," Alys said. "Did you hear me?"

"What do you think I'm going to do?" Lady said. "Run away with someone?"

"The fact that you'd even joke about such a thing scares me."

"Aunty Alys, I'd warn you not to run away too, except you're such a party pooper, I don't know who'd want to run away with you."

"*Khuda ke liye,* for God's sake, just don't make you-you eyes at anyone, okay?"

430

"What if someone makes you-you eyes at me?" Lady finished her sandwich, opened Alys's box, and took out her sandwich.

"I'm serious, Lady." Alys eyed her rapidly disappearing sandwich. "Please remember that the actions of one family member have repercussions for all family members."

"Oh, I know." Lady licked mayonnaise off her fingers. "Do you know how many girls at school saw Jena's name in *Social Lights*? Do you know how many asked me and even Qitty if we planned to allow guys to sweep us up in their arms?"

Alys looked at Lady in dismay.

"Qitty and I don't say anything, because we don't want to upset Jena but, trust me, we're suffering too."

Having gobbled up Alys's sandwich, Lady turned to her fashion magazine and a quiz on finding Mr. Right. Alys opened up *Sunlight on a Broken Column.* She'd started reading it after Darsee's proposal, curious suddenly about his "favorite partition novel" and his claim that it had allowed him a "Pakistani identity inclusive of an English-speaking tongue." So far, she was enthralled by the tussles between Laila, the headstrong, unconventional protagonist, and her cousin, Zahra, who wanted to marry well and enjoy her life.

Alys took out a pen and underlined a quote: *Do you know what is wrong with you, Laila? All those books you read. You just talk like a book now, with no sense of reality.*

She wondered what Darsee had thought about this line and whether he believed books led to an escape from reality or were windows into it. She recalled the animated look in his eyes when they'd discussed literature at the clinic, how he'd sought her out at the wedding to give her *Sunlight,* the feel of his fingers on hers, how he'd said he wanted her opinion on things. It was a truth universally acknowledged, Alys suddenly thought with a smile, that people enter our lives in order to recommend reads.

Such pleasant thoughts occupied Alys as the bus drove into the Lahore Daewoo station, where Nisar and Nona were waiting for her and Lady. They had good news and bad news. The good news was that Nona was being awarded a prestigious Indus Civilization Award for Women Who Make a Difference. Alys and Lady squealed in delight as they hugged their aunt. The bad news was that the award ceremony prevented them from visiting Pakistan's Northern Areas.

"I hope you're not too disappointed," Nona said to Alys.

432

"Of course not, given the reason," Alys said. Some of the other women being honored were a commercial pilot, a police officer, a comedienne, a CEO of a multinational company, an NGO healthcare worker, a human-rights advocate, and an environmental activist. Nona's award was for a home-based business entrepreneur, and Alys was extremely proud.

Nisar was saying they would remain in Lahore and visit heritage sites close by. Shalimar Gardens, Badshahi Mosque, Lahore Fort, Wazir Khan Mosque, Lahore Museum. He was also trying to get tickets for the Naseeruddin Shah–Ratna Pathak play at the Alhamra Art Center.

"Hijab's parents," Lady gloated, "already have tickets for when the play comes to Karachi."

"Good for you, my dear," Nona said. "Now, remember to behave there."

"Goodness, Aunty Nona, you're as boring as Aunty Alys. What are our plans for tonight?"

They went out to dinner at a new Thai restaurant, after which they picked up the latest Indian movie, *Dil Chahta Hai*. Alys declared it excellent for its blend of a serious topic with commercial flair, though her three seminal films remained *Dhool Ka*

Phool, Umrao Jaan, and *Insaf Ka Tarazu,* all judged by Lady to be much too gloomy to do anyone any good.

Overall, Alys decided that night, as she slipped into bed, she was glad she'd come to Lahore, though she wished Lady was not going to Karachi or that Jena was not sitting depressed in Dilipabad. Opening up *Sunlight*, Alys read a chapter on the protagonist, torn between a duty-bound life and her own desires, and gradually drifted to sleep.

The next morning, Nona and Alys dropped off a deliriously excited Lady at the airport. Once they returned home, they saw her note stating she'd "borrowed" Nona's designer sunglasses and blow-dryer but that she really, really needed them in Karachi. Together, Nona and Alys shook their heads at Lady's audacity and wished Karachi well.

They began to plan their excursions for the next two weeks. The first week passed in relaxation and merriment. Upon Nisar's insistence, each day was begun with a leisurely breakfast at home after which they'd visit the site of the day, enjoy dinner out, and end their evening back at home chatting over chai and a boardgame.

At the start of the second week, Nona had two final cake deliveries, after which, she assured Alys, she was truly all hers. Alys joined her in the kitchen to help prepare the cakes, a dark-chocolate globe and a rose-flavored rose garden. The cakes were ready to be delivered by late afternoon. Nisar, Nona, and Alys all got into the car because, after the deliveries, they planned to go for an early dinner. Alys volunteered to go into the houses, and she delivered the globe cake to the mother of an excited birthday girl. The second house was in a very posh area of town, and Nona read from the address, "Get ready for this, Alys: Buckingham Palace."

Alys chuckled. "Did I tell you Beena dey Bagh's humble abode is named Versailles of Pakistan?"

They arrived at Buckingham Palace, with its towering metal gates topped with ornamental spears and boundary walls lined with shards of glass glinting like the broken bones of crystal birds. A sleepy-eyed guard opened the gate to their honking, and they proceeded up the long driveway lined with sculpted conifers alongside a vast landscaped garden. Her father would love it, Alys thought as she got out of the car.

Alys carefully balanced the cake box in

her hands and made her way up marble stairs to an elaborately carved front door. She elbow-rang the doorbell. When no one answered, she tried the handle and entered an airy foyer with bright-yellow walls covered with black-and-white sketches of whirling dervishes.

"Hello?" Alys called out. She walked in farther, finally arriving at stained-glass double doors, and stepped into a large room. Sunlight poured in from a paneled skylight, and floor-to-ceiling windows looked out to a rock plunge pool with a waterfall. A broad-shouldered girl sat cross-legged on the marble floor with her back to the double doors. She was playing a sitar. Her music teacher, Alys presumed, sat before her, bobbing her head to the girl's strumming. The teacher stopped when she saw Alys. The girl turned around.

"So sorry to have barged in," Alys said, "but I'm here to deliver the rose garden cake from Nona's Nices. I rang the doorbell several times."

"I'm so sorry," the girl said. "My teacher, Rani-ul-Nissa *jee,* and I get so engrossed in practice, we hardly hear anything else."

The girl got up, her smile shy but warm as she asked Alys to set the cake on the octagonal coffee table. Alys had seen the girl's face before. But where? Dear God. She nearly dropped the cake. It was Jujeena Darsee. Not in a bathing suit in a Maldives resort pool with Bungles's arm around her but towering over Alys in simple cotton culottes and *kurti,* her hair cut in waves that framed her square chin, her wide feet clad in plush Gucci mules. Jujeena Darsee in the flesh.

"Do you have the receipt?" Jujeena asked.

Alys crammed it into Jujeena's hand. Was Darsee here? She needed to leave as soon as possible.

"Let me get my wallet," Jujeena said.

"Juju *beta,*" Rani-ul-Nissa said, slipping on her *chappals,* "I think enough for today. Also, I was hoping to see your brother. I wanted to thank him again for his tremendous help toward my husband's treatment and wheelchair purchase. The generosity has saved his life. A lot of people have money but do not have giving hearts. Your brother is a saint. God bless him."

"I'll tell him," Juju said. "But you know he'll only be embarrassed."

"I've yet to meet a man," Rani-ul-Nissa said, strapping on her motorbike helmet, "who's been blessed with so much and yet is so humble."

Alys was taken aback at this appraisal of

Darsee. She tried to reconcile "Darsee" and "humble" in the same sentence. She couldn't. Still, this praise was unsolicited and, she could tell, heartfelt. Alys watched Juju and the music teacher exit the room, and then she looked frantically for an escape route in case Darsee appeared. She wished Juju would hurry up with the payment.

Alys's eyes flicked over the expensive rugs on the floor, the decadent black-crystal chandelier, the ebony-and-silver floor lamps flanking ivory sofas arranged in semicircles on either side of the room, the forest green silk cushions, and glass vases with white gladioli everywhere. She looked at the huge sepia watercolor of two young women gossiping in what looked like the Thar Desert, the only dashes of color their ocher *dupattas,* and, on the opposite wall, the large abstract with swirls and shadows of coppers and russets suggesting a figure on a divan.

Jujeena returned with the remaining payment. Alys took it, sighing with relief that Darsee had not found her in his house. And then there he was, coming through the doors, dragging in a huge cardboard package.

"Juju, guess —" Darsee's voice faded.

"I didn't know this was your house. I came to deliver the cake. Rose garden.

Nona's Nices. She's my aunt. Nona is. I didn't know this was your house. I'm leaving, though, so, bye, thank you."

Alys was halfway to the car when she heard footsteps behind her.

"Wait, Alys," Darsee called. "Come back. I'd like you to meet my sister."

"I can't," Alys said. "My uncle and aunt are in the car and —"

"Ask them to come in too," Darsee said, "please. You can't come all the way here and then leave like this."

Why not? Alys thought as she tapped on the car window and apprised Nona and Nisar of the situation. Suddenly there was Darsee next to her, inviting them in, using a tone of voice she'd never heard, a tone in direct opposition to the cold tone in which he'd spoken when he'd handed her his letter in the park. While the contents of the letter had certainly softened her assessment of him, Alys wondered what was causing him to so respectfully invite her family members inside for chai. It was always polite, of course, to offer guests, invited or uninvited, a cup of tea, but Darsee was insistent. He was holding open Nisar's car door and leading him and Nona indoors and introducing them to Juju, who was putting away her sitar in a corner between two decorative tablas.

"Juju," Darsee said, "this is Alys Binat and her uncle and aunt."

"Nona and Nisar Gardenaar," Alys said. "My uncle Nisar is my mother's brother, the pulmonologist you may remember us mentioning when my sister twisted her ankle."

Darsee's blink was so rapid that no one save Alys noticed. And she only did because she was on the lookout for his disdain the second her mother and anyone related to her mother were mentioned. Instead, Darsee smiled at Nisar and Nona.

Alys was glad her aunt and uncle were doing her proud. They were not ones to be impressed by money and social status, and thus, instead of fawning over Darsee, they were treating him like an equal. Juju asked her to sit down. Alys sat down. Juju sat beside her and kept giving her shy glances.

Alys smiled at her. So this was the nervous young girl who'd been taken in by Wickaam and become pregnant and opted to have an abortion. Seeing Juju with her slumped shoulders and trusting smile and her gentle demeanor, Alys couldn't help but feel protective. Shame on Wickaam for duping this girl. And shame on him for duping the maids who hadn't even Juju's privileges.

But, then, Alys fully knew that the lure of a handsome face and flirtatious manners was one that could easily bridge class and prove equally irresistible to maid and mistress.

"I love your *kurti,*" Alys said to Juju. "The color suits you."

"Really?" Juju said. "Everyone always tells me that I look good in baby pink, so I wear it a lot. I like your T-shirt so much."

Alys was wearing white linen pants and a black T-shirt saying NOT YOUR AVERAGE AUNTY.

"Thanks. My sister Qitty makes these for fun. How long have you been playing the sitar?"

"A year," Juju said. "I'm not very good."

"I thought you were playing beautifully."

"Was I? I do try to practice every day. I wanted to learn the guitar, but my brother said first sitar and then the guitar, and I thought, why not listen to him for once?"

"How very kind of you!" Darsee smiled indulgently at Juju.

Alys looked from brother to sister and concluded that Darsee was most definitely not the envious sibling Wickaam had branded him.

"You live in Lahore, right?" Darsee said, turning to Nisar and Nona.

Alys braced herself for his grimace at the

441

answer, Jamshed Colony. Instead, Darsee mentioned a *dhaba* in Jamshed Colony that made the best chicken *karahi* in town.

"Don't tell our cook that, though," Darsee said. "Hussein is quite sensitive."

"We'll try not to," Nona joked. "In fact, that *dhaba* is one of the reasons we're reluctant to move from Jamshed Colony. We've been living there forever. I'm happy with the schools and my children are well settled, and to dislocate them for a bigger house in a more prestigious area makes little sense."

"I understand," Darsee said. "It's hard to let go of geography. Although — and I've told Alys this several times — I believe people like her and me have an advantage having grown up for a time period without any set roots, and so we are quite comfortable letting go of places. We're the sort of people who believe home is where you make it, and borders are ridiculous, and airports are the most harmonious places on earth."

Alys smiled. "You make the nomad's lifestyle sound so ideal, but depending on your personality, it can be really hard to get up and move, physically as well as emotionally."

"True," Darsee said. "What are you doing in Lahore? Is your family here too?"

Alys stared at him. He was asking about her family? With such congeniality?

"My family is in Dilipabad, except for my sister Lady, who's visiting a friend in Karachi. I'm here to tour Lahore with my uncle and aunt."

"Hoping to get tickets to the Naseeruddin Shah–Ratna Pathak play in town," Nisar said. "I had a friend who was supposed to purchase them, but by the time he got around to it, they were all pretty much gone."

"Ismat Apa Kay Naam?" Darsee asked. "In the Name of Ismat Apa?"

Nisar nodded.

"We're going to see that tomorrow evening," Darsee said. "Are you free? Were you looking for three tickets?"

"Four," Nona said. "Me, Alys, Nisar, and our nephew, Babur."

Darsee phoned someone named Pacman to ask if four more tickets for the play could be arranged. He was put on hold for a moment before being told yes. Darsee refused to take ticket money from Nisar. Next time it could be Nisar's treat, he said. Alys blinked. When exactly had Darsee learned good manners? And why was he going out of his way for them? Alys avoided Nona's glance: This is the rogue who robbed Wick-

443

aam of his inheritance?

"Alys," Darsee said, "Bungles and party are coming to the play tomorrow too."

Alys nodded as casually as she could. She turned all her attention to the maid rolling in a tea trolley with silver spoons resting on bone-china platters holding potato cutlets, chicken sandwiches, savory *dahi baray,* and the rose garden cake, which, it turned out, had not been ordered for a special occasion but because Juju was craving it.

"Daane daane pe likha hai khane wale ka naam," Nona said, grandly reciting the proverb — on every grain is written the eater's name — and she laughed as she took a sliver of her very own concoction. Juju rose to serve everyone tea and snacks.

How well mannered Juju was, Alys thought, as she accepted a delicate bowl and helped herself to the *dahi baray,* topping it with deep-fried crackers and fresh chopped coriander. After one bite, Alys declared the mashed white-lentil balls in cumin yogurt sauce superb.

"I have a friend Sherry who is an excellent cook," Alys said. "But your cook would give her a run for her money."

"Are you talking about the Sherry who recently married Farhat Kaleen, my cousin Annie's doctor?" Juju asked.

Alys nodded. She wondered how ridiculous Kaleen had been in front of Juju.

"I met Sherry at my aunt Beena's house. Sherry is so good-natured and kind."

Alys was delighted to hear the compliments.

"And Dr. Kaleen is so nice too," Juju said. "He takes such good care of Annie. A friend of mine tore his ACL, and he also sings Dr. Kaleen's praises."

Alys was pleased to see that Juju Darsee, far from being stuck up, instead shared Jena's propensity for finding good in everyone. The thought of Jena back in Dilipabad saddened Alys. She glanced at Darsee. He looked at ease, perhaps because he was home. But perhaps this persona was the real him, and that other persona, which had earned him the nickname Dracula, was someone else; he sounded nice and friendly, and certainly not like some busybody who would interfere in his friend's life. Dr. Jekyll and Mr. Hyde.

Darsee and Nona were talking about the paintings above the sofa sets. Nona admired both the geometric abstract and the women in the desert. She was familiar with the artists, she told Darsee, and she congratulated him on buying art that spoke to him.

"Aunty Nona's pet peeve," Alys said, "is

445

people who buy art to match the décor."

Upon discovering that Nona had attended the National College of Arts, Darsee had a question for her. He went to the cardboard package he'd dragged in. Nisar helped him open it and they took out a huge pastel in beiges and pale pinks of Lahore's inner-city rooftops and children flying kites.

"I either got it for a steal," Darsee said, "or I've been robbed."

"Why?" Nisar asked.

"Because," Nona said, smiling, "it's either real or an imitation. I wish I'd invested in a few of Iqbal Hussain's paintings back in the day before they became so expensive. Where did you find this?"

"Gallery," Darsee said. "Owner's private collection. He said it's authentic. Except the only art I've ever seen by this artist is of women from the red-light area. There is a signature at the back." Darsee tilted the painting so Nona could look at it.

"It's genuine," she said. "One of his earlier works. Iqbal Hussain was my professor at NCA; if you're interested, we can visit him and he can confirm it for you."

"I'd love that," Darsee said. "In fact, I'd love to meet him."

"I'll arrange it, then," Nona said. "I believe he's out of the country at the moment, at a conference, but as soon as he's back."

"Thank you," Darsee said.

"Can I come too?" Juju piped up. "He's a brilliant artist, the world knows that, but for me, it's that . . ." She stared into her lap. "It's that he doesn't shy away from who he is and where he comes from. He celebrates his origins. Actually, he thrusts them in the faces of society and says, 'Deal with my inconvenient truths.' And he's getting the last laugh, as his stock goes up and respectable women purchase his red-light-area paintings to hang in their drawing rooms, and so it is that women they wouldn't deign to sit with perpetually look down at them from their walls. I wish . . . I wish we could all find the courage to tell our truths."

Alys's and Darsee's eyes connected.

"Of course you can come too, Juju," Alys said. "You don't have to ask. In fact, that will be the first step in finding your courage."

Juju smiled shyly. Alys caught Darsee's grateful look, and she hurriedly looked away.

"Please stay for dinner," Darsee said, inviting them all.

"We were actually headed to the inner-city Food Street," Nisar said, "as part of our Tour Lahore. Alys is very fond of Lahori fried fish. Please, you and Juju must join us. But I warn you, this is my treat."

Darsee did not hesitate to accept, and they left, only to reconvene on a bustling street lined with open-air eateries, some established as far back as pre–1947 partition. They managed to find a table for their large party in front of a *tandoor* lit with a string of naked light bulbs and proceeded to order mango *lassi* and items on a menu they could smell long before they appeared — grilled meats marinated in spicy yogurts, freshly baked *naans* glazed with white butter, and onion, ginger, garlic frying in cauldrons, the sizzle and crackle and pop in the open air.

Soon their order was served, and Alys passed Juju the chickpea-batter deep-fried fish. She asked Juju her interests and hobbies besides music, even as she kept one ear on Darsee, Nisar, and Nona, who were munching away as they discussed the demand for bottled clean air given the rise in pollution worldwide — "Laugh, laugh," Nisar said, "people laughed at bottled water too, but I would advise investing in bottled air; fortunes to be made" — and the future of Pakistani art and music and its growing popularity internationally.

Alys could not recall a more pleasant

evening, and she was sad when dinner was over. She went to bed happy. Darsee's stellar behavior had surprised her and it also thrilled her, and she knew, suddenly, that had he always behaved like a gentleman, things might have been different. She snuggled under the quilt and caressed the spot on her hand where his fingers had so briefly touched hers at the NadirFiede wedding. She flushed. She thought of how he'd come running after her at his home, insisted he wanted his sister to meet her, how graciously he'd welcomed her aunt and uncle, how he'd gone out of his way for tickets, how animated he'd been at dinner, how carefully he'd heard everyone's views, especially hers, and how respectfully he'd disagreed if he had to, and, when dinner ended, how sincere he'd sounded when he told them that he was looking forward to seeing them the next day. Alys caught her breath as she recalled how he'd glanced at her at that moment.

A tremendously lovely day it had been, and tomorrow they were going to a play she'd been eager to watch, and she would see Darsee again, and she was not going to let anything spoil her evening, not even the addition of Bungles and party.

The next morning at breakfast, Nisar and Nona were still marveling over how Darsee was not the snob they'd been led to believe he was.

"Lady calls him Dracula," Nisar said as he poured milk into his oatmeal. "And Pinkie painted such a Frankenstein picture of him, I expected him to push us over a cliff for being middle-class professionals. Even Jena, who defends everyone, never defends him. Why you women insist on maligning perfectly first-rate men, I don't know."

Nona flicked a raisin at him. "Let's not canonize Valentine Darsee just yet. There is still the matter of Wickaam's accusations. However, I must say, even I was surprised by how nice he seems."

"It's my fault," Alys said unhappily. "I've always said one's opinion regarding anyone is only as good as how one is treated, but I confess, I'm to blame for the generally unfavorable impression of Darsee. I was biased after hearing him say mean things about me in private to Bungles. That, in turn, affected everyone's perception of him."

"But Wickaam?" Nona said. "Darsee

certainly does not seem the type to go around stealing inheritances. But, then, Goga didn't seem the type either."

"In Darsee's case," Alys said, blushing, "I have it on good authority that Wickaam is lying about the whole inheritance thing."

"What!" Nona and Nisar cried out simultaneously.

"I can't tell you how I know," Alys added wretchedly, "but trust me when I say that Wickaam is a liar and a deceiver and Darsee is innocent."

"We trust you," Nona and Nisar said. "But are you positive?"

Alys nodded.

Nisar whistled.

"Well, well," Nona said, raising her brows. "Alys, the *innocent* Darsee's attentiveness to us is due to you. He certainly seems to like you."

Alys stared at the black pepper sprinkled on her scrambled eggs. "He just likes that we've both lived abroad and that I actually read and don't just pretend to in order to come across as intellectual or unique. That's all it is, Aunty Nona. No need to give me that look."

Alys and Nona spent the afternoon at Liberty Market, going from boutique to boutique and checking out what new designs people were spending good money on. They also visited Redmon Book Gallery, where Alys spent her own good money. In fact, throwing guilt aside, she splurged. She leapt on a fresh copy of Jamaica Kincaid's *A Small Place* and also bought Leila Ahmed's *A Border Passage*, Jessie Fauset's *Plum Bun*, Rohinton Mistry's *A Fine Balance*, and Marjane Satrapi's graphic novel, *Persepolis*, which she knew Qitty would love to read too, and Mari would appreciate the pretty arabesque booklet with all of God's ninety-nine names explained.

They returned home well in time to get dressed for the play. Even fussing over attire was fun. Nisar settled on a smart *shalwar kurta*. Nona wore slacks and a floral blouse with a lapis necklace. Alys decided on a black *peshwas* with a black paisley print and mirrored bodice, matching *dupatta* and *thang pajamas*, black heels and accessories from Nona's silver jewelry, which she preferred to her mother's gold and precious stones.

Ajmer dropped them off at the main entrance to the Alhamra Art Center and then drove to the parking lot to wait. The play was in Hall One. Darsee was waiting for them in the entrance with their tickets.

He looked good, Alys couldn't help noting, in charcoal pants and a slim-fit black shirt. He greeted them as if they'd all been best friends forever, even Babur, who, upon Darsee's inquiry, informed him that he'd gotten into Cornell University and been offered a scholarship. Alys had not thought she could be any prouder of her cousin, but the look on Darsee's face proved her wrong.

They climbed up the circular stairs to the vast auditorium and stepped inside the carpeted amphitheater. Their seats were near the stage, and as they wound their way down the aisles, Darsee, Nona, and Nisar stopped to greet friends. When they finally reached their row, Alys saw that Bungles and his sisters were already seated. Bungles jumped up as soon as he saw Alys, his entire face a smile. He stepped over many toes to meet her and greeted her with such warmth that Alys almost forgot his weak will. She was delighted to see Hammy and Sammy looking ready to faint at her reappearance in their lives.

In order to annoy the sisters further, Alys hailed Bungles with jubilant camaraderie, even as she merely waved from the aisle at the sisters and Jaans, who was complaining loudly about being dragged here when he would have much preferred the invite to a weekend of boar hunting.

Alys was thrilled to see Juju stepping over shoes to welcome her with a giant hug. As Alys hugged her back, she caught Hammy squinting at Sammy. Good. Let her fret. Alys was also very happy to hear Juju use the tag "bhai" — brother — when she addressed Bungles. It was clear that the two shared nothing but a sibling-like camaraderie.

Darsee introduced Nona as the proprietress of Nona's Nices. Sammy shrieked. She loved Nona's Nices cakes! She congratulated Nona on the upcoming Indus Civilization Award. She and Hammy had received an award last year for their sanitary-napkins company, and this year they were presenters and had been sent the list of recipients. Hammy advised Nona not to be nervous during her thank-you speech, despite how prestigious an award the Indus Civilization was. After all, wonderful women like them deserved every accolade they received.

The second Hammy and Sammy became cognizant of Nisar and Nona's relationship to Alys, their expressions soured. Alys was sure that the prestige of the Indus Civilization Award must have fallen accordingly. Neither Nona nor Nisar missed the dynamics, and they were most bemused by the fluctuations in their social status. Babur too was mistaken for a somebody at first, and then his star also fell, only to be back on the rise at the mention of Cornell, though Hammy and Sammy looked as if they were about to ask to see his acceptance letter.

"Alys, it is so good to see you," Bungles said yet again. "How are you? How is your family?"

"Everyone is well," Alys said. "I'm in Lahore for a holiday with my uncle and aunt."

"Jena didn't come?"

"She was here for a few months a little while back."

"Jena was here?" Bungles frowned. "In Lahore? Why didn't she contact us?"

Before Alys could answer, Hammy asked, "Alys, how long are you in Lahore? You must visit us."

"But," Bungles interrupted Hammy, "wasn't Jena supposed to be teaching?"

"She was," Alys said, "but she wasn't feeling well and took some time off from work."

"Is it her ankle?" Bungles asked, alarmed.

"She's fine now," Alys said.

"How is Cherry?" Hammy called out in a thick Pakistani accent.

"Hammy," Darsee said, "have you changed your accent?"

"No," Hammy said.

"Then are you deliberately mocking Sherry's?"

"No," Hammy said, turning pink.

"Good," Darsee said.

Alys looked at him with yet-new eyes.

"Alys," Sammy said in a conciliatory tone, "are you the only fortunate one of your family to be getting a proper holiday?"

"No," Alys said, "my sister Lady is in Karachi."

Hammy said, "How very exciting for her. Lady's first time in K-chi?"

"First time staying with a friend in Karachi," Alys said.

"And who is that lucky friend?" Hammy said. "Jeorgeullah Wickaam? He's a close friend of yours, isn't he?"

Juju winced and Alys quickly replied, "Actually, that man is no friend of mine. And please, Hammy, do not be absurd. Of course my sister has not gone to stay with any man."

The lights began to dim, and Bungles returned to his seat and Alys slipped into hers. Next she knew it, Darsee was sitting beside her. Alys could smell his cologne.

"Thank you," he whispered, leaning into her. "Hammy has no idea about . . . how upset Juju gets at Wickaam's mention."

Alys kept her eyes straight ahead and muttered, "No problem."

The play began, and for the next couple of hours, she concentrated as best as she could on the three Urdu short stories by Ismat Chughtai that the three actors had chosen to recite as monologues. The first, "Touch Me Not," contrasted the pregnancy experiences of a prostitute versus a girl from a good family. The second, "Mughal Child," was about a dark-complexioned man married to a fair-complexioned lady and the effect on his self-esteem. And the third, "Housewife," explored class-based sexuality and domestic violence. When the lights turned on, the actors received a standing ovation and Alys glanced in Darsee's direction, sad that the evening was ending.

They exited the theater, chattering about their favorite stories. Jaans was boasting about napping through the play, and Darsee and Alys inadvertently exchanged a wry glance.

In the parking lot, Nisar and Nona thanked Darsee yet again for the excellent evening.

"Dinner?" Darsee suggested eagerly, but unfortunately Hammy complained of a bad headache and, since they'd all come in his car, Darsee called it a night.

In the car, Hammy's headache became bearable enough for her to hold forth on what a snob Alys Binat was about her aunt's award and Cornell-Babur, and didn't Juju agree that Alys was overly tanned and *junglee,* wild-looking?

Juju glanced at her brother and then said softly that she thought Alys was so nice and that she liked her tan and thought her unusually pretty.

Hammy laughed. Juju had no need to be civil about Alys for Valentine's sake.

"Remember, babes?" Hammy said to Darsee. "When you first met Alys you thought she was the most ratty thing you'd ever seen, and then, after she came stomping in from a walk in a public park without a *dupatta,* you generously decided her eyes were nice enough. I wonder where you stand now."

"No need to wonder," Darsee said. "Since then I've come to the conclusion that Alysba Binat is one of the most good-looking women, if not the most good-looking woman, I have ever set eyes on."

CHAPTER 23

The next morning Alys was curled up in an armchair in Nona and Nisar's living room, holding *Sunlight on a Broken Column* to her heart, when there was a knock on the door and a servant let in Darsee.

"Hello," he said. "I came to thank you again for diverting the conversation away from Wickaam last night."

"I'm glad I was able to," Alys said, slipping the book in her lap. She wished she'd bathed and that she wasn't in her peacock pajamas. She buzzed the kitchen and asked Ama Iqbal to bring chai.

"Where are your uncle and aunt?" Darsee perched on the armchair opposite her.

"We had so much to discuss about the play that we stayed up all night and then went for a *halwa puri* breakfast this morning. When we came back, they finally went to sleep."

"Why are you still up?"

459

"Life is short," Alys said joyfully. "I'm not sleepy."

"Lack of sleep is not good for your health," Darsee said. Then he flushed as if he'd said something he shouldn't have.

Alys felt a nervous flutter in her stomach. "I've been meaning to ask, how is Raghav? Did he conquer K2?"

Darsee smiled. "As much as K2 allows itself to be conquered."

"And how is Annie?"

"Trying to convince her mother to let her Nigerian boyfriend visit; otherwise she will pack up and move to Nigeria, which she just might do if Farhat Kaleen would agree to move with her."

Alys laughed. The book slid to the floor.

"So you are reading *Sunlight.*" Darsee picked it up. "I thought you might not read it after . . ."

They were silent for a second, each thinking of Islamabad and what had transpired there, his patronizing proposal, her condescending rejection.

"I just finished it," Alys said. "I was rereading the ending. What a beautiful meditation on memory and place. It so perfectly captures the nuance of the difference between houses and homes."

"You liked it, then?" Darsee said.

"I loved it."

"Me too. What exactly did you love?"

"Everything. The way Laila struggles between the secular and the religious, the way Abida and Nandi embody class and gender issues. The way Laila is forbidden to love a poor man."

Darsee's smile faltered. "Yes, the love sto—"

The door opened and Ama Iqbal brought in the cordless phone. It was for Alys. It was Jena.

"Jena," Alys said, "I'll call you back. What? Slow down. What do you mean she's run away? With whom? Of course I'll leave for Dilipabad immediately. Uncle and Aunty too. Have you called Falak Khala? We'll all be there soon."

Alys hung up. Tears dripped off her chin. When had she started to cry? Darsee was kneeling before her with a box of tissues.

"Is everyone all right?" he said.

"No one is all right." Alys took out a bunch of tissues. "My sister Lady has run away with Jeorgeullah Wickaam."

The color drained from Darsee's face.

"She was in Karachi, staying with a school friend, very respectable family. She left a letter saying she and Wickaam were eloping. I think you know what that means. They've

461

been together for four days, and if they were married I know Lady would've called home to show off. She just turned sixteen. She probably believes he loves her and will marry her. She will get pregnant, he will abandon her, and I don't know what we will do. My father left for Karachi as soon as he heard this morning. But what can he do? Why didn't I warn my family about Wickaam? Why?"

Darsee stood up abruptly. "I'm sure you want me gone."

Alys's heart sank, and after a moment she simply said, "Yes. Go."

As she watched him leave, Alys realized the depth of her feelings. She loved him. More important, she liked and respected him. As the fact of that admission settled within her, Darsee closed the door behind him and Alys knew that, had there been even a smidgen of a chance between them, it was gone forever. To be connected to a family ruined by Wickaam in the same way Juju herself had nearly come to ruin was not something Valentine Darsee would ever inflict on his beloved sister, and Alys was sure Darsee, at this very moment even, was thanking his lucky stars that she'd previously spurned his proposal.

CHAPTER 24

Alys, Nona, Nisar, and Falak arrived in Dilipabad by mid evening. Nona was going to miss the Indus Civilization Awards ceremony, but no honor any of them brought to the family could ever compensate for the dishonor Lady had dealt them. As they entered the front door, they could hear Mrs. Binat wailing. She was in the living room, laid out on the sofa, a thermometer by her side. Jena was wrapping up a blood-pressure monitor. Mari held a cold compress to her mother's head. Hillima rubbed the soles of Mrs. Binat's feet. Qitty was huddled in a corner.

"I keep getting panic attacks," Mrs. Binat said with a great sob when she saw her brother and sister. Nisar and Falak hurried to their baby sister's side with cries of not to worry, God would fix everything.

"I keep asking God, What did I do to deserve this? You should've seen Barkat's face when he found out. The last time he looked that way was when he discovered Goga had cheated him." Mrs. Binat clutched Falak's hands. She wouldn't let go of her big sister's grip. "My poor Lady. My poor Lady. Kidnapped by that *ganda aadmi,* dirty man."

"He did not kidnap her," Alys said. "She eloped."

"Oh, be quiet," Mrs. Binat said. "Oh, Lady, Lady, my innocent baby, where are you! Imagine that man, Wickaam, a python let loose in my den of bunnies, and now he is squeezing to death our *bachee,* our baby bunny, which would be perfectly fine if only he marries her."

"He's never going to marry her," Alys said. She tried not to think of Darsee and how fast he'd fled. "Wickaam is a fortune hunter and Lady has zero fortune."

Mrs. Binat's eyes welled up. "You were the one who brought Jeorgeullah Wickaam into our house."

"He was the lawyer assigned to us, remember?" Alys said guiltily. "For the Fraudia Acre case."

"The case is over, con man has run off again, not a penny will we ever see from that *manhoos* — accursed — land, and now Lady is being plundered for free. Someone hand me my tranquilizers. I want to be tranquil. Better yet, I want to be dead."

"Don't say that," Falak and Nisar said in distress.

"God has abandoned us," Mari said, gripping her inhaler. "If you ask me, we should all kill ourselves. Better that than endure society's taunts for the rest of our lives."

"Oh, Mari," Nona said. "Let us have faith that this will come to a good end."

"Nona *jee,*" Mrs. Binat said, "my sweet sister-in-law, someone has done *bura jadoo* — ill-will magic — on us. Useless Uterus Sherry married so well. Jena dumped by Bungles. Alys a failure. And now my Lady. Ill-will magic. No other explanation."

"The explanation," Alys said, "is that he targeted Lady and she likes to make you-you eyes at everyone, and this time she went too far."

"Alys," Mrs. Binat said, sitting up, "not everyone is content to live the life of an unmarried failure. Lady is bright and beautiful and soulful, and that is why that handsome devil targeted her. If I were him, I'd have done the same. Your father will find them and make them marry. That is what we should pray for."

"What we should be praying for," Alys said furiously, "are mothers who do not

465

preach marriage all day every day until —"

"Come, Alys," Hillima interrupted her. "Come help me make chai."

Hillima took Alys by the hand and pulled her into the kitchen. This was hardly the time for daughter and mother to have one of their fights. Alys sank into a chair at the kitchen table. Hillima gave Alys two painkillers. Minutes later Jena joined them. She sent Maqsood, the cook, out of the kitchen and to his room — he had a tendency to gossip.

Once Maqsood left, Alys asked Jena, "Does Mummy really believe Wickaam kidnapped Lady?"

"I don't know what she believes," Jena said. "Her beliefs keep changing every minute. If it wasn't for Hillima, the rest of us would have gone mad by now."

Hijab's mother had phoned that morning. Hillima had brought the cordless into the dining room, where the family was at breakfast. She'd given the phone to Mrs. Binat. Seconds later, Mrs. Binat had tossed the phone at her husband and proceeded to wail. Hijab's parents were distraught at their house being the launching pad for such a thing. They'd thought Lady belonged to a good family. Girls from good families did not do such things. She was a *Binat.* Otherwise they would have never allowed Hijab to invite her. Hijab was traumatized by this turn of events and completely innocent of any complicity. How dare Mr. and Mrs. Binat send an *awara badchalan,* a sex-crazed daughter, to their home.

After Hijab's mother hung up, a bewildered Mr. Binat informed them that Lady had run away with Jeorgeullah Wickaam. Only Qitty seemed unsurprised. In fact, she'd said, "I can't believe Lady actually went ahead with it. She always wanted romance."

Qitty had known this was going to happen and she'd said nothing. Mr. Binat looked as if he was going to hit one of his children for the first time in his life, and he told Qitty so.

Qitty had begun to cry. Lady had telephoned her to share her secret and had been so nice to her for once. Like a good sister. Lady had said there was a beach bonfire and Wickaam was there and everyone thought he was gorgeous but he had eyes only for her. Lady had also said that it wasn't as if Mummy and Daddy could ever afford to get any of them married with *phoon phaan* — a splash like NadirFiede — and she wanted an unforgettable splash of her own. Eloping was her way of getting it.

Hillima set mugs of chai in front of Jena and Alys.

"At least," Alys said, wrapping her hands around her mug and drawing as much solace as she could from its warmth, "we know Lady believed Wickaam was going to marry her. But you and I know he's not going to. That would take a miracle."

"Miracles don't happen to people like us," Jena said, her head in her hands. "We don't have the kind of money that can buy miracles."

It was decided that Nisar and Nona would join Mr. Binat in Karachi. Nona's parents could keep the children for another few days, and Nisar would take emergency family leave from work, because this was a family emergency. Alys would have liked to accompany them, but the school year was about to start and if she and Jena didn't return to work, their absence would confirm the rumors that were already circulating about Lady.

Alys had told her mother to please not entertain the neighbors or anyone with the details of what had happened, but Mrs. Binat required more of an attentive audience for her grief than just Falak, and to the delight of a neighbor who stopped by for a chat, she related the whole sordid tale.

The news spread overnight, and the next day throngs of neighbors arrived with their great concern. Bobia Looclus came armed with a platter of chicken *pulao* because, though grieving, one must eat. Mrs. Binat ate and held court, howling loudly about her ill luck, her poor Lady, that python Wickaam, and how this was all Hijab's parents' fault.

"People worry about servants gossiping," Mari said morosely to her sisters, "and here our mother is doing the job."

The next day, Nisar and Nona left for Karachi. Back in Dilipabad, everyone hovered around the phone. Mr. Binat called late at night. Nisar and Nona had arrived. To what good, though? Karachi was a sprawling metropolis; the couple, if that was what one must call them, could literally be hiding anywhere. The fact that they were hiding terrified him. Should they not have strutted back into society by now as Mr. and Mrs. Jeorgeullah Wickaam?

Nona got on the phone and assured Alys that her father was tired and dazed but otherwise all right and that, come tomorrow, they would go to every hospital, in case there'd been an accident. The hospital search proved futile and, the very next day,

Nona took over and sent Mr. Binat back to Dilipabad.

A despondent Mr. Binat took himself into his study and crept into his armchair. Jena brought him a strong cup of chai and Alys laid her head in his lap and he stroked her hair.

"You were right, Alys," he said. "You told me not to let her go. That she was immature and had no sense of right or wrong. But I was more worried about peace and quiet in this house, and now, because of it, we will never have any peace or quiet. This scandal will ruin Lady's prospects forever, but Wickaam may yet find himself an heiress. Today, for the first time, I am feeling the full fire of patriarchy."

"Women are never forgiven in our society, but men can be," Alys said.

"That seems to be the rule." Mr. Binat sighed. "Lady may get what she deserves, but I'm heartbroken for what that means for the rest of you girls. No, Alys, don't tell me not to be harsh on myself. Let me stew in my regrets. But have no fear. The Chinese proverb teaches us 'This too shall pass,' and make no mistake, it shall. I weathered my brother's betrayal and now I will weather my daughter's, and you girls will learn to weather it as well. It is your mother who will never learn to see what is what and what is not. Claiming Lady was kidnapped. That it is Hijab's parents' fault. Such preposterousness boggles the mind, but of course this too shall pass."

Farhat Kaleen's letter arrived the next morning at the breakfast table, where Qitty, Mari, Falak, and Mrs. Binat were tucking away while the rest stared at the food. Mr. Binat read the letter, then passed it on to his wife, who dissolved into hysterics. Falak told Alys to read it out loud.

My Dear Binats,

What I have to say concerns all of you and deserves the staying power of a letter rather than the ephemeral nature of a phone call, which, in my vast experience, often means in one ear and out the other, an affliction I strongly believe Lady suffers from to a great extent, as per Sherry's assessment of her. I am of course writing in regard to this elopement business. Is there even an elopement? Or is Lady living in sin?

I unfortunately had to break the news to Begum Beena dey Bagh — better she hear it from me rather than from rumormongers — and what she told me about

Jeorgeullah Wickaam was shocking. He is her nephew, but he is a disgrace. He was disinherited years ago. He has no money and, God help us, his law degree is fake! I ask again if Lady is living in sin? What will become of her when this scoundrel tires of her?

A woman is nothing and no one without her virtue. Her virtue is the jewelry of her soul. But this is forgotten by modern women, who march around in their *patloons* under the impression that wearing trousers means they are now men. A woman is a woman no matter what she wears and must behave like a lady.

Of course, this terrible business will affect all of you. Had I any doubts, then let me tell you that Begum Beena dey Bagh corrected me. I still pray that Jena, Alys, Qitty, and Mari may find someone to marry them, but Lady has permanently dimmed her sisters' prospects.

I heard that Lady is to set up shop and Wickaam to be the shopkeeper in charge of determining her price. God forbid this be true. One should pray for Lady's death before we should have to suffer such humiliation.

Given the situation, I'm sure you'll

understand why I think it unwise to visit each other at this time. I will also be most obliged if Sherry is not contacted and, if she contacts you, to please ignore her.

I wish you all the best in these trying circumstances.

I will pray for all your souls.

Fi amanillah, May God go with you,

Farhat Kaleen

"A loose woman is a flower every man wants to pluck and chuck," Mari said desolately. "That's what his letter means. I always said Jeorgeullah is no mullah, but none of you ever listen to me. And Lady is no lady. Lady *nay humari naak kaat dhi.* Lady has cut off our noses for shame. We, as a family, have no nose left."

"Should we write back?" Qitty asked in a tiny voice.

"What's there to say?" Alys said. She felt a persistent melancholy at how she and Darsee had parted without a friendly look or word, and she could only imagine Beena dey Bagh and Darsee's mutual congratulations over escaping any association with this strain of the Binat family.

"How can I show my face at the religious-club meetings?" Mari said, drowning her grief in buttered toast. "What will the members say? One sister so pious and the other practically a prostitute."

"Yes, Mari," Alys said. "We all sympathize that this situation has disrupted your social life. Believe me, we are all irrevocably impacted."

Alys expected Principal Naheed to fire her and Jena. She could well imagine parents up in arms at their daughters being taught by teachers whose sister had, as Farhat Kaleen put it, "set up shop." And so it was that Alys and Jena were fully prepared to be terminated on the first day of the new school year. The staff room was a hush and they were glad no one asked them if the rumors regarding Lady were true. In fact, the teachers were extra-sweet. That Lady was absent, coupled with Alys's and Jena's long faces, was proof enough to all that some disaster had occurred.

For the first time, Alys felt no joy as she gazed at her new batch of ninth-graders and gave them an overview of the semester and the books they would read. The students in Alys's and Jena's classes did not say a word. Later that day, Principal Naheed did summon them into her office. She shook her head and pursed her lips and remarked that teenage years could be very trying and that they were to keep her posted on the fragile situation.

Jena was grateful for Naheed's support and Alys was too, but she told Jena she would not be surprised if Naheed was frantically searching for teachers to replace them in case Lady returned home in disgrace, unwed and pregnant, even. Perhaps the Dilipabad Gymkhana would break its die-hard rule of "once a member, always a member" in order to expel the Binats. Such were the questions that, Alys was positive, entertained all Dilipabad.

Nona called daily for the next few days with an update to say there was no update. And then: They were found. They were staying at a cheap hotel in a cheap part of town. They were fine. Lady was glowing. Wickaam looked bemused. He had no answer for why they were not yet married, which, come to think of it, was his answer. And, brace yourself, Lady did not care that they were still unmarried. She said they'd be married soon enough and were having too much fun to break the "honeymoon."

Nona was sorry to report it, but Lady seemed incapable of seeing she'd done something wrong and that her decision was going to negatively impact her family. Nisar had prevailed upon Wickaam to tell him whether or not he meant to do the honorable thing, and Wickaam voiced his demand: one hundred thousand dollars.

It was an exorbitant sum. Nisar and Nona had some savings, as did Falak for sending Babur abroad. But even after they pooled their resources, their savings amounted to a pittance, for what was a grain of sugar to one who demands a cup?

Alys paced in front of her father in his study.

"We must give them the Lahore shop," Mr. Binat said. "The rent is always steady."

"That rent is the bulk of our livelihood," Alys said in horror.

"And it still won't be enough for that greedy fellow," Mr. Binat said. "We must sell the car, this house. What else have we got?"

"Where will we live?" Alys asked. "How will we make ends meet?"

Mr. Binat wrung his hands. "What a failure of a father I am."

"Don't say that," Alys said.

"An utter failure of a parent. My one job was to provide financial security to you girls and your mother, and I could not even do that. I should invest in a cart and sell the flowers and vegetables I grow. But wait —

with house gone, flowers and vegetables gone too."

"So we are to lose everything," Alys said, "to buy Lady her respectability, and thereby ours, whatever little respectability it will be."

A bleak evening it was at Binat House, with everyone mourning their lot and looking into the future with trepidation. Only Hillima reminded them that, ten years ago, they'd landed in this house with hardly a penny to their names and, look, they'd survived.

"We had this house," Mrs. Binat wept. "We had a roof over our heads."

"And now," Hillima said, "we have educated girls who can earn."

"This is true," Jena said. "We will never starve."

"We may never starve," said Mrs. Binat, hopeless at the thought of having to start over yet again, "but even on a full stomach one can lose the will to live. We will be forever hungry for better things."

"And dignity," Mari added. "And dignity."

And then, a reprieve. Nona called late that night. Such news could not wait for the morning. Must not wait when it would bring so much respite to all. Wickaam had agreed to marry Lady. No one was quite sure what had happened to change his mind. Perhaps Lady had wept and cried and begged. Perhaps Wickaam had decided he loved her after all. Perhaps — but who cared? They were to be married in the morning, as soon as four male witnesses were rounded up to take to the mosque. Nisar and three more men were needed; even strangers who were willing to sign their names to the marriage certificate would do.

And that was what was done, and Nona called to say: "They are married."

"Joy" would be too strong a feeling for what followed at Binat House. "Relief" was more appropriate. Only Mrs. Binat reveled as she put away the thermometer and blood-pressure cuff and began to plan a proper wedding for her favorite daughter, who was now married: Mrs. Lady Wickaam! *Oof* their children would be beautiful. Angels!

Mr. Binat put his hands over his heart and Alys, Jena, Qitty, and Mari panicked, but he told his daughters that he was perfectly fine. He couldn't be finer. At no financial cost to him, respectability and dignity had been restored.

"Wickaam must truly love her," Jena said.

"Don't be so gullible all the time, Jena," Mr. Binat said. "You think a greedy fellow like Wickaam will settle for a girl who loves him? I fear Nona has given him a huge share in her business and Nisar may have taken on debt. I dare not ask, because I can never repay them a hundred thousand dollars. All I know is that I am forever indebted."

"He is my brother," Mrs. Binat said proudly, "and this is how a loving brother comes to the rescue."

"Nisar and Nona have gone above and beyond loving," Mr. Binat said.

"Barkat," Mrs. Binat chirped, "at the very least we must throw the Wickaams a *mehndi* ceremony and a reception at the first available date open at the gymkhana. *Hai,* what will Lady wear? What will you girls wear? *Hai,* how exciting to have a daughter married! Finally! Finally!"

But Mr. Binat crushed Mrs. Binat's plans when he roared that, let alone throwing a *mehndi* or a reception, he was forbidding Lady and that *ganda aadmi* dirty man from setting foot anywhere near their home. If they dared show their faces in Dilipabad, he would shoot them.

Mrs. Binat began to cry. "You always begrudge me every happiness."

Mr. Binat was unmoved. He meant to keep this resolution, and he turned around and went into the moonlit garden, where he began to pull out weeds in order to calm his heart. This afternoon he had thought all was lost: shop, car, house, garden, jewelry, reputation. And now all was miraculously restored. He began to weep.

Alys and Jena found their father in the garden, weeding and weeping. They'd been sent by their mother to make him see sense, and he ordered them to return to her and make *her* see sense: Lady was dead to him, and Wickaam had never been alive.

"Daddy, she's not dead, God forbid," Alys said, "and she'll always be your daughter. You have to allow them to visit us at least once. If we abandon Lady, that man will treat her as shabbily as he wants, without any fear of consequences. Also, by inviting them here, by your making a show of accepting the situation, it will go from a big scandal to merely a messy situation and will put an end to much malicious gossip."

And so it was Mr. and Mrs. Wickaam arrived at Binat House for a week's visit, Wickaam driving a brand-new car and Lady, waving madly, decked out in a new designer outfit, Nona's "borrowed" sunglasses, and a fire-engine-red mouth.

"Your lipstick is *thabahi,* deadly," Mrs. Binat said, welcoming her married daughter with exhilaration. She held a Quran over Lady and Wickaam's heads for blessing.

"Enter, Husband and Wife. May God keep you forever sane, safe, and satisfied."

Mr. Binat tersely shook hands with Wickaam and barely acknowledged Lady. Alys, Jena, and Mari smiled as congenially at the couple as their natures allowed. Qitty hugged Lady.

"*Moti,* Fatty, you're crushing my clothes," Lady said as she hugged Qitty back. "Qitty, I wish you'd come to Karachi too. I wish you'd all come. So many hot men. Not like the losers in Dilipabad. Karachi is for winners, and, look, I won myself a husband."

"Not won exactly," Wickaam said, "but *phasaoed,* lassoed."

"Hahaha. How Wick wishes he was funny," Lady said adoringly. "But he is handsome! Could any of you have guessed that, out of all of us, I would end up Mrs. Jeorgeullah Wickaam?"

"And I, Mr. Lady Binat?" Wickaam said, scratching his head.

Lady basked and chattered nonstop. Wickaam smiled his usual smile. Both behaved as if nothing was out of place. Perhaps, Alys remarked to Jena, they believed it. Lady was awfully sorry to hear that the Dilipabad Gymkhana had no dates for a reception and neither did Lotus, Burger Palace, or Pizza Palace, and not even High Chai. But it was

481

understandable because of such short notice. She wouldn't have minded a big dinner thrown for them at the house, but next time.

This time she was going to visit each and every neighbor, school friend, and acquaintance, with Wick in tow. First she'd stop by and show off Wick to Mareea Looclus. That would put an end to fish-face Mareea's showing off about Sherry and Fart Bhai. Should she take Wick to the British School? Display him to former classmates and to Principal Naheed?

"No!" said Alys and Jena, and Lady was too giddy to argue.

Thankfully, Lady stayed true to her plans, and she and Wickaam were hardly ever home. Mrs. Binat, the proud mother, accompanied them on their visits, her arms linked between her beloved daughter and her dashing son-in-law. Dilipabad wasn't quite sure what to think. On the one hand, Lady had run away. On the other hand, she was home with *her lawfully wedded husband.* To the chagrin of gossipmongers, the vilest of the gossip was dying down.

On their last evening, Mr. and Mrs. Wickaam insisted on dining at home, and Mrs. Binat made sure Lady and Wickaam's favorite dishes were prepared.

"I wish you would settle down in Dilipabad," Mrs. Binat said, thoroughly upset that they were leaving the next day.

"That would be a death sentence, Mummy," Lady said. She and Wick wanted to travel. She'd been dying to go to Disneyland, and now they would go there for their honeymoon. And they planned to settle in Karachi when they came back to Pakistan. Wick had of late come into some money — Mr. Binat spluttered on his rice — and he wanted to invest in some business or other, maybe a bowling alley or a highly exclusive restaurant. Law was so blah, *naa.*

Wickaam looked up from his *koftas.* "Hated law. Long, boring, tedious."

"What is long, boring, tedious?" Alys said, unable to resist. "Walking through a college campus in New York?"

Wickaam gave her a slow, grudging smile. Alys returned it with a nod, and turned.

After dinner, which Mr. Binat gulped down as fast as he could, he went to bed, completely unable to stomach being in the same room as these two equally *bagaireth,* shameless, newlyweds. Neither one had shown one iota of embarrassment, and Lady especially was acting as if hers was a love story to equal Romeo-Juliet and Layla-Majnun and Heer-Ranjha, except, of course,

Lady and Wickaam were not star-crossed lovers who died. Mr. Binat expected no heartfelt apologies from Lady to them, but how he wished she had apologized properly to Nona for making her miss the Indus Civilization Award ceremony. Instead, the shameless girl told Nona that no doubt there was a reason God had not wanted her to attend and therefore found a way to prevent her from going.

Alys watched her father hurry out of the dining room. She very much wanted to follow him, except that all the sisters had promised Lady that, since it was her last night with them for who knew how long, they would stay up like old times and snack on pine nuts and chat. Thankfully, Wickaam declared he was tired and went to bed.

The Binat sisters and mother and Hillima traipsed into the living room and settled down. Lady wanted to know all the gossip at school.

"*Mashallah,* you were the gossip for a long while," Mari said dourly. "And with this visit you're the gossip again. You are notorious."

Lady clapped her hands. Better notoriety than invisibility. Who'd said what? And who was dying of jealousy that she'd married a man who looked like a movie star? In fact, Wick might star in a movie. A friend of his was making a movie and he'd asked Wick to be the hero, and Wick was seriously considering it.

"I thought 'Wick,' " Alys said, "was planning to write an earth-shattering novel."

"Oh, he will," Lady said. "He's just looking for the right person to write it for him."

Alys shook her head at Jena.

"I see you, Alys," Lady said. "You can make faces all you want, but I promise you, one day Wick and I are going to be rich-and-famous celebrities and socialites who appear in *Social Lights* all the time, and then you'll regret not believing in us."

"I hope so," Alys said. "For your sake."

"And I'm going to say I told you so," Lady said as she flipped through an issue of *Mode,* pausing at the pages where Qitty had turned the corners on obese models she thought resembled her. "I have so many people I'm dying to say I told you so to. And the number-one person is that yuck-*thoo* Dracula."

At Darsee's mention, Alys felt her stomach drop. She hated that it did.

"Don't mention that man's name on this perfect evening," Mrs. Binat said. She was dozing on the sofa, enjoying the voices of all her daughters drifting over her: If there was a heaven on earth, then being surrounded by one's grown children was it.

"I swear," Lady said, "Dracula nearly ruined my marriage. He spent the whole time standing on top of Wick's head as if Wick was planning to flee. If he wasn't Wick's first cousin, I swear I'd forbid Wick from seeing him ever again. I certainly don't want to see him again."

"Darsee was at your *nikah*?" Alys sat up.

"Oh Crapistan!" Lady said. "I promised Wick and Dracula I wouldn't tell. All of us promised Dracula we'd keep our mouths shut."

"All? Who 'all'?" Alys said.

"Me, Uncle Nisar, Aunty Nona. It was a stupid promise."

"What was Darsee doing there?" Alys glanced at an equally perplexed Jena.

Lady shrugged. "He was one of the witnesses. He frowned the whole time. *Bhalla* — imagine. Frowning at someone's nuptials. Such an ill omen. I hope his nose turns into a popcorn, just like Fart Bhai's. Qitty told me about the letter Fart Bhai sent, in which he said I should die of shame. That purity pervert married the best friend of the woman who rejected him — he should be the shameful one. What have I got to be ashamed of? Falling in love? Having a love marriage? *Lo jee!* I swear, all these men are so pompous, except Wick. He's a real catch. So down to earth. When I settle in Karachi, all of you visit me and I'll help you grab husbands. It'll be so much fun."

"Spare us," Alys said as she tried to make sense of Lady's revelation.

"I'd rather die a virgin," Mari said, "than resort to your tactics."

"Suit yourselves, then," Lady said, yawning. "But, seriously, my stupid sisters, think about the fact that I'm the only one married out of us. And on that note, I'm going to bed and to my husband, who is always Mr. Lonely Pants for me. Signing off for the night is your baby sister, Lady Binat, now also starring as Mrs. Lady Jeorgeullah Wickaam."

The next morning, Wickaam and Lady drove away from Binat House, but not before Alys pulled Lady aside once more to confirm that Darsee had been at her marriage ceremony, after which she wasted no time calling Nona. Nona was surprised that Alys did not already know. She'd thought Darsee was swearing secrecy because he wanted to tell her the sensitive news himself.

"Sensitive news?" Alys said.

"Alys," Nona said, "Darsee is the one who paid Wickaam a hundred thousand dollars to marry Lady. Of course, we shielded Lady from Wickaam's demand. Why break her heart? Darsee was at the marriage because he wanted to make sure Wickaam went through with it and didn't run off with the money. I'm so glad we've cleared this up. I would hate to think that any of you thought Nisar and I bailed Lady out. I mean, we gladly would have if we had that type of money. But who does? Well, Darsee obviously does, but you know what I mean. I wonder why he hasn't told you yet."

Alys hung up the phone. She headed toward the graveyard for some privacy. She paced the lanes between the graves. She walked by the grave of a Pakistani soldier who at the time of his death in World War II had been an Indian soldier; geography had converted his citizenship from one country during life to another after death. Darsee, with his romantic notions of being rootless, would have appreciated this observation.

Throughout her walk, Alys thought back to the last time she and Darsee had been together, in Nona's living room, about how they'd been talking about *Sunlight* until Jena's call had come, then Darsee had left abruptly, and she'd been convinced he'd have nothing to do with them ever again. Yet *he* was the one who'd paid off Wickaam to marry Lady. It was in all likelihood, Alys told herself, because he'd felt guilty. By asking her to keep Wickaam's sordid past a secret, he'd enabled Wickaam to manage yet another conquest, this time in the form of Lady. Perhaps, Alys also thought, Darsee believed that by marrying Wickaam off he would curb his cousin's carnal appetite once and for all.

The truth was, Alys had no idea why exactly Darsee had decided to spend a fortune on the cousin he despised. She would like to ask him, of course, but who knew if she'd ever see him again? Their paths were unlikely to cross; they had no reason to cross.

When Alys returned home, Binat House was in an uproar.

"You won't believe it, Alys!" Qitty said. "He just drove up and rang the doorbell and asked for her as if it was the most natural thing in the world. I said, 'Yes, she's home, in the living room,' and he went straight in and then he took her straight out and it's been over an hour since they left. But where have you been?"

"Who came in and who took who out?" Alys hurried to the living room, where both her mother and Mari were on prayer mats. "What happened?"

"Jena happened!" Mari looked up from the Quran she was frantically reading on Jena's behalf. "Bungles came and took Jena out. Mummy and I are praying for them."

"We are praying," Mrs. Binat said, "that this time the silly man gets it right."

"Oh my God," Alys said, and she rushed to find her father.

Mr. Binat was in the garden, transferring sprouting seeds from a pot into a flower bed. He was most amused at this turn of events but also had fingers crossed that this time Jena's heart would not be broken all over again.

CHAPTER 25

Jena had the shock of her life when Bungles came into the living room. She'd been sitting in the window seat, threading her mustache. Mari was holding up a magnifying mirror for her. When Bungles walked in, Jena stared for a long second and then hid the threading thread behind her back. Was her mustache area red? Then she decided, to hell with embarrassment. If anyone should be embarrassed, it should be Mr. Weak Will.

In fact, when Bungles asked her if she would please go on a drive with him, she agreed just so that she could tell him he was a weak-willed person and shame on him. Jena got into the car and hardened herself against the way his hair flopped over his forehead and the way he was nervously pursing his lips. They'd hardly turned the corner when Bungles parked under the mango tree that had grown not by design but due to littering. He turned to her and said, "Jena, will you marry me?"

"Are you here," Jena said, "because you've been given permission by your sisters and your friend?"

"What do you mean?" Bungles said.

Jena told him she knew that Hammy-Sammy and Darsee had previously been opposed to their match.

"They were," Bungles said slowly, "but the truth is, I honestly didn't know the difference between a crush and like and love. And when Hammy, Sammy, and Darsee kept telling me you were not interested, it was easier to accept that than to sort out my feelings. I'm so sorry to have hurt you. No, it wasn't a matter of a weak will, not at all. No, I'm not unduly influenced by others. I swear I'm not. Jena, I truly did not trust my own feelings. Jaans was the only one who always said he knew what I felt was true love. But Jaans. You know. Who listens to Jaans?

"But I didn't stop thinking about you for a single moment, and I finally admitted to myself that these feelings I have for you are it for me. As for my sisters and Darsee, while I value their opinions, this is my decision. I want to marry you. I hope you want to marry me. They told me that they'd known you were in Lahore and that they hid it from me. I was furious with them. They've apologized, profusely, and I hope you won't hold it against me that I've forgiven them. I hope you forgive them too, but if you can't, I'll understand.

"I told my parents of my decision to propose to you, and they flew in on the first flight out of California so that, if you say yes, there are no further delays for them to visit your house with a formal proposal. They came in last night, and here I am today to ask you if you will please marry me."

Jena returned home carrying a box of cream rolls from High Chai. She told everyone to sweeten their mouths, and then she broke into an ugly cry.

"I'm getting married to Bungles!" Jena said. "Mummy, you were right all along. He did propose."

"I told you so." Mrs. Binat chortled with joy. "I guaranteed he would propose, only none of you girls have any faith in me, not to mention your father prancing around insisting I eat my shoe."

Bungles's family was due to visit the Binats the next day with a formal proposal in order to ask for Jena's hand in marriage, as well as give her an engagement ring and set a wedding date. There was a great flurry of activity as residents of Binat House prepared for this event. In the morning, Mrs. Binat sent Jena to Susan's Beauty Parlor for a facial and to get her hair blow-dried. She was going to wear a simple pale-yellow cotton *shalwar kameez,* Jena had decided, and just lip gloss and her garnet earrings. This time she was getting dressed up for herself and not for anyone else.

Mr. Binat was dispatched to the *mithai* shop to order several kilos of *motichoor ladoos,* which would be distributed to the neighborhood and sent to the gymkhana and taken to school by Jena; oh, they were going to send celebratory sweets into every home in Dilipabad, such that no one would ever forget, cost be damned.

Bungles's parents turned out to be lovely. His mother kept kissing Jena's hands and telling her tales of Bungles's childhood and how naughty he'd been. For the first time in her life, Mrs. Binat did not have much to say, because she was so full of joy. She kept looking at the glorious diamond on Jena's hand and thinking it was exactly as she'd predicted: big and sparkling.

The Binglas had also given Jena a beautiful set of solid gold and diamond bracelets, as well as gifts and suit pieces to the rest of the Binats. Bungles's father and Mr. Binat got along well. They talked about politics and gardening and life in Dilipabad and life in California. Jena was very sweet to Hammy and Sammy. She was always sweet to everyone, but this time she was fully aware of her sisters-in-laws' duplicitous, cunning and manipulative capabilities.

Hammy and Sammy acted as if they'd always been madly in love with Jena and it was Bungles who'd been stalling. The fact was, they adored their baby brother, and if he wanted to ruin his life and marry 'senior citizen' Jena Binat despite their objections, then so be it. Such was their change of heart that they even declared D-bad a most charming and quaint town and High Chai hip and happening. Jaans behaved as best as he could and reminded everyone, every so often, that he'd predicted this coupling at first sight.

Darsee had accompanied them too. Alys watched him offer enthusiastic congratulations when Bungles slid the ring onto Jena's finger and Jena the engagement band the Binats had hurriedly procured for Bungles from a thrilled Ganju *jee*. Darsee discussed sports and politics with Mr. Binat. He ignored Mrs. Binat just as resolutely as she ignored him. He and Alys nodded hello to each other as if they were strangers. Alys wished she could thank him for paying Wickaam to marry Lady, but this crowded drawing room was neither the time nor the place.

After her future in-laws left Dilipabad to return to Lahore, Jena kept bursting into blissful tears. She'd truly given up hope of reconciliation with Bungles, for she'd believed that, even if he did reappear in her life, there was nothing he could say that would win her over or excuse his previous display of a weak will. But he had won her over and Jena's happiness knew no bounds, for herself as well as the fact that she was giving her family so much pleasure.

However, Jena supposed her favorite moment would be walking into the staff room the next morning with celebratory sweets and a ring on her finger. And it was. There was not a dry eye in the school or a moment of ill will; everyone loved Jena, and they hoped she would live happily ever after.

Alys was still smiling over the loving reception Jena had received in the staff room when Bashir, the peon, knocked on the classroom door. She turned to him with a knowing glimmer in her eyes.

"Let me guess," Alys said. "Principal Naheed wants to see me."

"Immediately," Bashir said, looking very scared. "There is someone here to see you."

It was Beena dey Bagh. When she saw Alys, she ordered Naheed to leave the office. Naheed had never been kicked out of anywhere, let alone her own office, but she walked out wordlessly onto the veranda. When the door banged shut, Naheed and Bashir crouched together by the keyhole.

"A pretty penny," Beena dey Bagh was saying, "your parents and relatives must have collected in order to buy my disastrous nephew Jeorgeullah for your sister, who, from all reports, is a girl of a disastrously loose character. As for this mess Bungles has gotten himself into by getting engaged to your sister Jena, well, he will face the consequences of such a rash decision. But that is not why I have come here."

"Why have you come?" Alys stood in the confines of the principal's office, matching, gaze for gaze, the towering Beena dey Bagh.

"You dare speak to me, an elder, in such a tone?"

"And your tone is justified because I'm younger?"

"I don't have time for your nonsense. I'm here to ask only one question, and the only answer I'd better hear is a no."

"What is your question?" Alys said. "I have a class to return to."

"I'll see how long you last in the teaching profession," Beena dey Bagh snarled. "My question to you, you rude, arrogant woman: Are you engaged to Valentine?"

"Engaged to Valentine?"

"It is a well-known fact that you Binat sisters are well versed in the art of bad magic and love spells. First you tried to grab Valentine's friend Raghav —"

"Raghav is gay," Alys said. "You know that."

"Nothing a nice girl can't fix, except you are not a nice girl."

"You can't 'fix' gay. It's a biological —"

"*Chup.* Silence. I was watching you at Versailles flirting with Raghav, and when you couldn't seduce him, you turned your attentions to my nephew. Girls of your class know exactly how to use their ways and wiles to grab men."

"Girls of my class!" Alys squinted. "I am happy to burst your bubble, but 'grab-it' transcends all classes. Class is immaterial to —"

"*Chup.* Silence," Beena dey Bagh said again. "Don't you dare lecture me on class.

498

Have you lost all sense of your place in the world?"

"What place would that be?"

"A place where you should not be able to open your mouth in front of me, let alone dream of being engaged to a dey Bagh. Who are you? Nothing and no one."

"I'm a Binat," Alys said, "from my father's side of the family, and in your worldview that is not nothing or no one."

"Yes, you're a Binat. Albeit a poor lowly Binat, pseudo-gentry," Beena dey Bagh sneered. "But your mother's family. Your grandmother. Let me be absolutely crass about it: Your maternal grandmother was a prostitute."

"There is no proof."

"Your sister Lady's actions have proved this genetic link beyond any doubt."

"You know what?" Alys said. "Maybe my grandmother was indeed a prostitute. Maybe she was the biggest, baddest, busiest prostitute in all of history. Hear me: I'm very proud of my prostitute grandmother. She was a working woman putting food on the table and a roof over heads, unlike women such as yourself who are born into an inheritance or luck out into marrying one."

"You have the audacity to compare me to

a prostitute!"

"I'm sorry you cannot celebrate all women and must denigrate some in order to feel good about where you come from. As a fellow educator, I find your sense of entitlement appalling, especially given that it stems from the hubris of inherited wealth and not one you've earned, not that self-made riches would make entitlement any more acceptable."

Beena dey Bagh had never in her life been spoken to this way.

"You dark-complexioned snake of girl," she said. "You're *no* girl. You're a woman. A *baigaireth aurat,* a shameless woman at that! You are *my* employee! A teacher in a backwater town! You slut! Who has allowed you the temerity to call yourself an educator? To put yourself on the same rung as me? Do you know who I am? I am Beena dey Bagh! I have founded an entire school system in Pakistan, English-medium no less. You *badtameez,* belligerent, bitch of a woman. If my nephew insists on marrying you, I will disown him. I will never speak to him again. He will rue the day."

"We'll see," Alys said.

"So you are engaged?"

"I'm not telling you."

"You are not engaged. Otherwise, a

500

woman from a whore background would readily admit to grabbing respectability. If he asks you, promise me you will refuse him."

"Let me tell you what I will promise," Alys said. "I promise that I'm only going to do what is best for me and not what is best for you or anyone else."

"*Chup.* Silence. You classless hussy."

"You *chup.* You silence," Alys said, and she walked out of the office and into Principal Naheed and Bashir and half the school gathered in the veranda.

"Hussy, how dare you turn your back on me?" Beena dey Bagh roared as she followed Alys. "How dare *you* walk away from *me*? Do you know who I am? I am Beena dey Bagh, descendant of royal gardeners and a luminary of this land."

Alys walked even faster while Principal Naheed's voice beseeched Beena dey Bagh to calm down and return to the office and she sent Bashir to *futafut* — instantly — bring chai.

For the rest of the school day, Alys could think of nothing but Beena dey Bagh's visit. Had Jena's and Bungles's engagement scared Beena dey Bagh into believing she'd "grabbed" Darsee? Had Beena dey Bagh any idea what her showing up at school would do to the rumor mill?

After Beena dey Bagh left Principal Naheed's office, Alys was called back in.

"Oh dear," Naheed said. "This is a right muddle. Beena dey Bagh wants you fired, but I reminded her that, as per franchise contracts, firing a teacher is largely my decision, and frankly, Alys, I have no desire to. You're a good teacher despite everything and, more important, thanks to you, students are able to bring their English accents up to standard. But now that I have chosen sides and Beena's wrath, please tell me it is true. Are you to be Mrs. Valentine Darsee?"

When the bell rang for home time, Alys gladly settled into the school van and shut her eyes, willing herself to relax. All day long she'd been bombarded by concerned students gawking at her (Rose-Nama was agape) and teachers asking her if she was okay, if there was any truth to the rumor. When the van stopped in front of the graveyard, she was dismayed to see a Pajero standing outside Binat House. Had Beena dey Bagh come to terrorize her parents?

Mr. and Mrs. Binat were in the foyer, anxiously awaiting her.

"Alys," Mr. Binat said, "what is going on?"

"It's Dracula," Mrs. Binat said. "He said

he'd wait for you in the garden."

Alys went straight to the garden. Darsee was by a pretty little wilderness with a tangle of fruit trees — orange, custard apple, tamarind — Alys's favorite area, not that he knew it.

"Hello, Alys," Darsee said. "Your mother called me Dracula."

"Oh." Alys looked sheepish. "My entire family calls you Dracula. It's a nickname from way back."

"I like it. Dracula."

"Good," Alys said. "They'll be so pleased to hear. Listen —"

"What?"

"I've been meaning to thank you," Alys said. "I must thank you."

"For what?"

"You know for what. I can only imagine how difficult it must have been for you to be in the same room with that man, let alone negotiate terms with him."

"I did it for you." Darsee cleared his throat. "I kept hearing you say how your sister's action had ruined the rest of you. I kept wondering what would have happened had I not had the resources to take my sister to Europe for a secret abortion. Also, writing that letter to you woke me up to several things. You see, Alys, you were right, I am a pompous ass" — Darsee smiled awkwardly — "but I'm a pompous ass with a heart of gold. Since birth I've been catered to by my parents, my aunts, by the help, everyone. When everyone pampers you, it takes super-human effort to remain levelheaded, and yet how much I abhor sycophancy, which is status elevation by association. What can I do for someone? How can my friendship benefit them? Could I put in a good word even though it's undeserved? Zero unaf-fectedness. Zero authenticity. Zero sincerity. Flattery will get you nowhere with me, but at first I thought you were playing the 'I'm not interested' grab-it tactic. But your disinterest couldn't have been more genu-ine. Never in my life had I thought anyone would refuse to marry me. Never had I imagined that what I was bringing to the table would not outweigh my flaws. Time had turned me into that person, but that is not who I want to be. Sometimes we lose sight of ourselves, but you see me, Alys, and you force me to see myself."

"You force me to see myself too," Alys said. "When I think of the things I said about you and your loyalty, I'm so morti-fied. You're the most loyal person I know. You're always courteous to Sherry — the way you called out Hammy for belittling her accent. You gave me a book that meant so much to you, and then you genuinely wanted to hear my views on it. You were so hospitable to my aunt and uncle. Juju's music teacher called you humble. All these things may have been enough for me to revise my opinion of you, but the way you dealt with your sister's predicament, the way you expressed sorrow for her situation without blaming or castigating her for it, the way you acknowledged your mother's sexuality without judging her harshly, as too many other sons would have, I came to admire you even more."

Darsee pulled Alys close as they walked deeper into the fruit grove.

"The things I said," he said, "about your family. Right or wrong, I shouldn't have said them, or at least not like that. And how ashamed I've been over suggesting you not meet them as much as you might want."

"You should be ashamed," Alys said, smiling sweetly, "but I accept your apology."

"So very kind of you," Darsee said playfully.

"You didn't give me any signal at Jena's and Bungles's engagement that you still had feelings for me."

"You didn't give *me* any signal," Darsee said. "The last I talked to you in Lahore in

Nona's living room, you brought up Laila from *Sunlight* and how she was in love with a poor man. I imagined you were trying to tell me that you loved some poor man. Clearly I am not poor."

"Clearly you are not poor." Alys laughed. "A nice bonus for me. I'm joking."

"I have something for you," Darsee said. "It was my mother's."

Darsee slipped a small sapphire ring onto Alys's finger. It was perfect. It was full of heart.

"I love you," Darsee said shyly. "I'm madly in like with you."

"I love you and I'm madly in like with you too," Alys said, equally shy. "When did you know you liked me?"

"From the very first look, and even more when you spoke."

Alys laughed. "I overheard you telling Bungles I was unattractive and not smart."

Darsee gave a guilty smile. "I was merely trying to get him to leave me alone and stop setting me up with anyone. I had no intentions of falling in love, and I resisted you as long as I could."

"Your Beena Aunty is going to have conniptions," Alys said.

"She's the reason I'm here," Darsee said. "She called me. She said she'd had words with you but, rude girl that you are, you refused to refuse marrying me if I asked you. I took that as my sign, and here I am."

Alys did not suppress her smile. "But why would she think we're engaged?"

Darsee reddened. "I may have inadvertently praised you one too many times."

"I see. Well, how very delighted Beena Aunty will be when she discovers she's played Cupid in our love story."

"She'll be thrilled." Darsee grinned.

"My Aunty Nona too," Alys said, "has, unbeknownst to her, played a role in our love story, as has Juju. If Aunty Nona didn't make cakes and Juju hadn't ordered a cake, I would never have turned up at your house — although, had I known it was for your house, I would never have even sat in the car, let alone delivered it."

"I know," Darsee said. "I'm so glad you didn't know it was my house and that you came, because, clearly, ignorance made all the difference. Although, in any case, I would have sought you out."

"It should have occurred to me that since your aunt's house is Versailles of Pakistan, then yours could very well be Buckingham Palace. What was your other aunt's house named, the White House?"

"Bingo." Darsee blushed. He took hold of

Alys's hands and he kissed them. "You win a lifetime's supply of anything you want."

"I have everything," Alys said. She loved her hands in Darsee's grip. She thought back to the all-too-brief moment when their fingers had connected, and now she finally allowed herself to fall into the full luxury of a touch she'd dreamed about but had thought impossible. "I don't think my life could be any more perfect than it is at this moment."

Chapter 26

"Dracula proposed and you accepted?" Mr. Binat said. "But you detest him."

"Over time, I've come to like Dracula very much."

"Alysba, my princess." Mr. Binat peered at her. "I don't have to say this to you, but I will. If you are feeling forced to accept this offer because of his assets, which I agree are hard to ignore, please do not. You of all my daughters will not thrive on money and prestige alone."

"Will you feel better if I tell you I respect him?"

"Respect Dracula!"

"We must stop calling him Dracula." Alys laughed. "I have discovered that he has the humility to admit to a mistake and the ability to change."

"Humility! That man?"

"Yes," Alys said. "That man."

The family was called in. Mr. Binat told

them all to sit down. Alys had an announcement.

"I'm getting married," Alys said.

"What!" Mrs. Binat yelped.

"To Valentine Darsee."

Mrs. Binat nearly fainted, and Jena rushed to the kitchen to get her water. She too was shocked. Everyone was shocked. Everyone said, "To Dracula! But! How!"

"When," Jena demanded to know, "did you first decide you even liked him enough to marry him?"

"Easy," Alys said. "When Aunty Nona told me how much he paid for the original artwork in his house. I thought, if he can pay that much to decorate his walls, imagine how much he'll spend to decorate his wife."

"Be serious, Alys," Jena said. "Marriage is not some joking matter. He disgusts you."

"You loathe him," Qitty said.

"Despise him," Mari said.

"Nafreth si," Hillima said. "You hate him."

"We all hate him," Mrs. Binat said feebly.

It was time, Alys decided, to tell her family that their Dracula was responsible for Wickaam marrying Lady. Mr. Binat could not have been more grateful. Long hours he'd spent contemplating how he was going to repay Nisar and Nona. He would offer to repay Darsee, of course, but Darsee, smitten by love for Alys and filthy rich, would, thankfully, be sure to decline repayment.

"Princess Alysba," Mr. Binat said. "Get ready for people to detest you. People can tolerate a woman being intelligent or pretty, and you are both. To be intelligent, pretty, and rich is an open invitation to enviable envy."

Mrs. Binat told Mr. Binat to stop cracking silly jokes at such a momentous time. Alys was not intelligent. Intelligent girls grew their hair long and did not sit in the sun. Clearly, Darsee lacked intelligence too, but his stupidity was their gain. Begum Valentine Darsee! Mrs. Valentine Darsee! *Hai!* Mrs. Binat kissed Alys on the forehead and proclaimed she'd always known in her mother's heart that God would not abandon her strange naïve frump of a daughter and that Alys would be able to grab it, and, look, she'd grabbed a prize.

"I told you to stay away from him," Mrs. Binat said, beaming. "Luckily, you never listen to me."

Alys listened with amusement, her mother recasting Darsee from ugly duckling to stellar swan and her sisters turning him from Dracula to Darsee Bhai.

The phone rang. Hillima left to answer. She returned and handed the cordless to

511

Mr. Binat. "*Fart Sahib da foon si.* It's Fart Sahib's phone call."

Mr. Binat literally took a step back as Farhat Kaleen blared an earful of congratulations. Was it true? Beena dey Bagh was livid. He'd called to warn his beloved family — Mr. Binat mouthed to his family, "We are beloved family today" — warn his beloved family that her wrath would be terrible and that perhaps Alys should reconsider, but, was it true, was she to be Mrs. Valentine Darsee? Was Alys there? Sherry wanted to speak to her.

Mr. Binat handed Alys the phone.

"Alys!" Sherry shrieked. "Is it true?"

Alys took a deep breath. "Yes."

"I told you," Sherry said. "I told you he was making mammoth you-you eyes at you. I also told you that you needed to grab him, and you did."

"Yes," Alys said. "Grabbing him has been my life's sole purpose this past year, as per your and Mummy's instructions."

But Alys's heart was doing funny things at the love in Sherry's voice. Their friendship had been in trouble for a moment, but now it was back on course. Sherry said she was leaving for Dilipabad — these were not celebrations she was planning to forgo. Kaleen could tend to Beena dey Bagh if he wanted, but tonight she and Alys had a date at the graveyard, where they would share a celebratory smoke.

CHAPTER 27

As per Mrs. Binat's fantasy, it was decided that Alys and Darsee and Jena and Bungles would have double *mehndi* and *nikah* ceremonies at the Dilipabad Gymkhana, while their *walima* ceremonies would take place separately in Lahore. Both the grooms-to-be were adamant that they were going to foot the bill for everything, and Jena and Alys had, after much deliberation, decided, Why not? It was going to be their money anyway once they married. They'd suggested a preposterous amount of *haq mehr,* but both men could afford it and they happily paid up. Also, the sisters insisted on the right of divorce being added to their marriage certificates, despite Mrs. Binat's protest that such a caveat was an ill omen.

"Life continues beyond happily ever after," Alys said. "Better safe than sorry."

People in the know were convinced that the eldest Binat girls practiced magic spells,

514

for not only had the two grabbed eligible bachelors younger than themselves, but Bungles and Darsee also obeyed their every command. It was widely whispered that Alys did not want children; the scandalized concluded that Darsee's acceptance of this proved that she was a highly accomplished witch. Beena dey Bagh was very unhappy at what was transpiring, but after Annie reminded her that Jeorgeullah was a catastrophe and to please not alienate Valentine, she accepted that he was marrying Alys, and she managed to find solace in the fact that a stellar educator was entering the family. Sherry was, of course, overjoyed, and Farhat Kaleen said no one could be happier than he and that no one could have prayed harder than he had for the Binat sisters to prosper. Ganju *jee* was ecstatic: The Binats were going from fake to real jewelry. The only person peeved was über-designer Qazi of QaziKreations, because Alys and Jena were not ordering their bridal outfits from him. Instead, they were going to have their mother design them, because Mrs. Binat had decided to give fashion designing a try: Pinkie Heirlooms, with an ecstatic tailor Shawkat at the helm. Still, Qazi was dressing their sisters, so there was yet a holiday or two for him in that.

One evening, as the Binats were discussing the wedding menu, the phone rang and Mrs. Binat went to answer it. When she returned, she was pale and Hillima was leading her by the elbow and seating her on the sofa.

"You won't believe who was on the phone," Mrs. Binat said.

"You're scaring me," said Mr. Binat. "Who?"

"Tinkle," Mrs. Binat said. "Tinkle was congratulating us on JenaBungles and Alys-Darsee. She said she'd always had full faith that the girls would do the Binat name proud. She said she was looking forward to their weddings. She said she wanted to host a big *milad* and *dholki* for each girl at" — Pinkie's voice trembled — "at the old house. She said: 'We will invite the whole of Pakistan. We will show them that nothing and no one can divide the Binat clan.' "

"No," Mr. Binat said loudly. Mrs. Binat, Jena, Alys, Mari, and Qitty jumped.

Mr. Binat cleared his throat. "I did not tell you, but when I was desperately looking for money to pay Mr. Jeorgeullah Wickaam to marry my daughter, I had no option left but to arrive at Goga and Tinkle's door."

Mrs. Binat gasped. So did the girls.

"It was not their meanness of spirit," Mr.

Binat said slowly, "that was displayed in those stale biscuits they served me, or that Tinkle did not even bother to appear, or that Goga took his time appearing. Rather, it was the smile that spread on my brother's face when I told him why I was there. Goga said he'd heard that one of my daughters had run away. He said he did not have money to spare on marrying off wayward girls. 'Bark,' he said, 'you obviously don't have the brains to make money, for men fall on their faces all the time and yet manage to get right back up. In business you are a known failure, but I did not expect you to be a failure of a father too.'

"I wanted to tell him about my kind and generous Jena, my fearless Alys, my artist Qitty, who holds her head up high no matter what anyone says to her, and my Mari, who just wants everyone to go to heaven. Even my silly, selfish Lady, who doesn't know what is good for her and just wants to have a good time all the time. But I didn't tell him about any one of my daughters. He doesn't deserve to know a single thing about my precious girls.

"As I was leaving that house, Pinkie, I realized that I'd spent this past decade there, if not physically, then in my heart by missing it and longing for it. But there was nothing there. It should have ceased to be home the minute we arrived in Dilipabad and you began to scrub clean this house. I should have rolled up my sleeves and joined you. They say blood is thicker than water. I say to hell with that. If blood mistreats you, better water. And if friends prove false, no matter, find better or be alone and be your own best friend."

"But, Barkat," Pinkie said carefully, "you have always dreamed of patching up with your brother. I know it."

"Goga is my brother biologically and Tinkle my cousin biologically, but in no other way have they earned those relationships. And the time for chances is over." Mr. Binat raised his hand. "I'm not retaliating, Pinkie. It is not a matter of retaliation. It is a matter of principle. They've treated us shabbily, as if we were enemies and not blood. I realized that you are correct: Our failure is their success. Since they broke the blood bond, I have no interest reviving it. We will not be inviting them to Jena's or Alys's wedding. We will not be holding any functions in their home. They are not welcome in my home or in my heart. My only regret is that I was unable to develop a relationship with my nephews and nieces or give my own children the gift of close cousins. But so be it. Not my fault. Not my problem.

"Pinkie, my love, I apologize to you for all the times I ignored your complaints about them, told you to get over their insults, to tolerate it, to compromise, to let it go. It was callous of me. It is not how a spouse should treat a spouse. Not how I, your husband, should have treated you, my wife, when I'd vowed to love and protect you. Forgive me."

Khushboo "Pinkie" Binat instantly forgave her husband everything, for this was every Pakistani wife's dream come true, that her husband should sincerely apologize on behalf of his family.

"And Jena, Alys, the rest of you," Mr. Binat said, "if your husband ever mistreats you, know that you have parents who support you and a home to return to here in Dilipabad, to rest and recover before you go back out into the world."

What Will People Say
Log Kya Kahenge

PRINCIPAL NAHEED: You know Alys and Jena were British School of Dilipabad teachers. In fact, I was the one who introduced Alys Binat to Valentine Darsee,

at the NadirFiede wedding. So sad —
Nadir's and Fiede's divorce. My daughters,
Gin and Rum, are so excited for Jena and
Alys, who will surely be among their first
clients when my daughters begin their
designer-clothing line. Expect brilliant
things from all BSD brands. I mean girls.

LADY: Hai, my only regret in eloping was
that I didn't get to wear QaziKreations at
my wedding. But I will be wearing Qazi
only at JenaBungles and AlysDarsee. Oh
God, not this question again! Who cares if
Wick was paid to marry me? Think of it
this way: Instead of a man buying a
woman, here is a woman who bought a
man.

MARI: Shakespeare says "All's well that
ends well." God says that too. So you
know what that means? Shakespeare was
Muslim.

QITTY: My sister Alys gave me the magazines. *Mode*'s last issue was published in
October 2001. They were forced to close
down. It wasn't circulation. They had
plenty of subscribers and were growing by
the day. They were forced to shut doors
because of lack of advertisements. Top

designers only wanted to design for skeletons. Their Loss. Fat Stocky Short Squat Women Are Here. We Exist. We Are Visible.

HAMMY: Marrying Jaans was Sammy's choice, and staying with him is her choice too. My ring? Two-carat solitaire. Yes, he is one of Jaans's good friends but nothing like him. My fiancé is a gem of a person. No, I was never interested in Valentine Darsee. Who is spreading this rumor? What will my fiancé think if he finds out? For God's sake, Valentine is one of my baby brother's best friends. I've always seen him as just another brother.

JAANS: Shaadi equals *barbaadi,* marriage equals misery, a socially constructed battleground. My wife, Sammy, agrees with me. *Chalo,* what to do, *bale bale.*

BEENA DEY BAGH: Jab mian biwi razee tho kya karey qazi. When the bride and groom are willing, nothing the priest can do to stop the wedding.

JUJU DARSEE: My brother couldn't have found anyone better than Alysba Binat.

ANNIE DEY BAGH: I'm so excited that my boyfriend is coming to attend the weddings. Yes, he's Nigerian. Why the face? What's bothering you? That I have a boyfriend? That he's black? Both?

MRS. SYEDA SHIREEN KALEEN NEE SHERRY LOOCLUS: Of course it is necessary to have an income of one's own beyond pocket money. I have never believed otherwise. But what a pity that homemakers are unpaid and so undervalued. Yes, Alys and I are planning to open a bookstore, and I will be in charge of translations. We are very excited. If my husband objects, my secret weapon, Annie dey Bagh, will have a word with him. That always works.

ROSE-NAMA: Miss Alys was always my favorite teacher, and I was one of her teacher's pets. My mother switched my schools because she didn't like the alternating uniform/free-clothes days. Or the new British School Group motto: "Home Is Everywhere on Earth. Be Honest. Be Kind." Or the introduction of a mandatory comparative-religion class. Or, as per new guidelines, a class on the history of marriage and sex.

TAHIRA: I'm so thrilled for Miss Alys and of course Miss Jena. Next on the list of duties is the good news that they are expecting. Thank you! My baby is due soon.

RAGHAV KUMAR: I knew something was up between those two.

HIJAB'S MOTHER: Of course my daughter is best friends with Mrs. Lady Wickaam. Did you know Jeorgeullah Wickaam is Valentine Darsee's and Annie dey Bagh's first cousin? Wickaam is such a humble boy. Wants to make it on his own merit, so prefers to keep a distance from his relatives.

HILLIMA: My girls. They are like family.

MOTHERS IN DILIPABAD AND OTHER "-ABADS," "-PURS," AND "-ISTANS" ACROSS PAKISTAN, TO THEIR DAUGHTERS: If Alys Binat and Jena Binat at their advanced ages can grab such catches, then you have no excuses.

DILIPABAD GYMKHANA VIPS: Pinkie Binat has exceeded expectations in training her daughters in the art of hook, reel, grab. All in favor of acknowledging her now and then? Done! Let's buy an outfit or two from her debut collection.

SOCIALITES IN SOCIAL LIGHTS: Congrats to AlysDarsee and JenaBungles. Wishing them all the best on their Happily Ever After.

EPILOGUE

One Year Later

Lady stood at the window in the Dubai apartment, looking at Jumeirah Beach in the moonlight. The glass was not as clean as she liked, and Wick did not take kindly either to smudges. They'd paid a pretty penny for this place, one of the finest in town, but you had to spend money to make money. You had to look the part. She would have an extra-sharp word with the maid about the windows. Lady patted her lips, pleased with the Botox, wondering if she should go plumper, bigger always being better.

"I'm bored," she said to Wick's reflection in the window. He was lifting weights. What a handsome man she'd managed to marry, Lady thought for the millionth time. Dracula and Bungles did not come close. But. Then. Their money. Wick had turned out to be an even bigger flop with finances than

525

her father. Alys and Jena had sent her some money to spend as she pleased and she was not going to tell Wick, because, unfortunately, he had the annoying habit of thinking the money her sisters and mother sent her was meant for him. She could make money modeling, but Wick, like her father, did not want her to model. However, while her father was controlling, Wick loved and respected her too much to bear the thought of other men doing the dirty with her pin-ups.

They'd had a rough patch for a while there, when she'd found out about his children, but that part of his life was behind him now. It wasn't even as if it was his fault alone — he was irresistible to women. They would have to learn to resist him, because there was only one lady for him now, she always reminded him, and that lady was Mrs. Lady Wickaam.

In fact, more than being upset with Wick, Lady was still annoyed with her family for barring him from Alys's and Jena's weddings. She would have boycotted in protest, except they really had been weddings of the year and Wick had encouraged her to attend. Best, he'd said, to stay in her sisters' good books.

"Let's go watch a movie," Lady said as

she turned away from the window. "Or eat out."

Wickaam mumbled something about their budget.

"Not to worry, Wick," Lady said, "we'll be rich and famous yet — this time our business idea is foolproof. Touch wood." And she touched the granite counter in the kitchen.

They were going to open up a lingerie boutique, Pakeezah Passions. Pure Passions. Their logo would be peacock feathers rising majestically out of what anyone with half a brain would be able to see was cleavage. Their tagline was "No more Mr. Lonely Pants. No more Ms. Lonely Panty." Pakeezah Passions would be the hottest lingerie ever, with a Pakistani twist. So Sindhi *ajrak* teddies and Baluchi mirror-work baby dolls and Punjabi leather bra sets and Pathan pom-pom panties. Also, on a separate note, Lady had insisted on a line devoted to brassieres of cotton and lace for those blessed with big busts. Wick was terribly excited. He was sure this business was the one to turn them from Wannabes to VIPs, and he grabbed his wife and she grabbed him back.

Mr. and Mrs. Binat lounged in bed, enjoying chai and *samosas* prepared on this Dili-pabad evening by Hillima, who was still elated at having received generous amounts of cash and gold earrings from both Alys's and Jena's bridegrooms, unlike Lady's use-less husband — looks, *ka aachar dalna hai,* was one supposed to pickle and preserve his good looks! — who had asked her what wedding present she was giving him.

"I still can't believe it," Mrs. Binat said to Mr. Binat, her eyes perpetually shining. "Three daughters married in one year, and so well, *duniya dekhti reh gayi* — the whole world watched in envy. Barkat, did I not always tell you I would only give birth to marriageable material?"

Mr. Binat looked up from his book on Mullah Nasruddin's sagely antics. The miracle was Alys and Jena finding the rarest of husbands: supportive, decent, rich, smart, caring, faithful, uncontrolling, kind, good-looking, healthy, funny, generous, polite, af-fectionate, respectful. Such men simply did not exist except in novels. Pinkie had her eye on Cornell-Babur for Qitty or Mari, whichever he preferred, but she was not as bothered as she would have been a year ago, because she had more-pressing issues to keep herself busy-busy.

Pinkie Heirlooms had taken off, thanks to

demand from gymkhana patrons, and she was adding a bridal line called Binat Bridals, and she had dreams of a vast empire under the umbrella House of Binat. Mr. Binat threw *samosa* crumbs to Dog and Kutta, new additions to the family. The puppies leapt off the rug, barking madly, happy to receive scraps.

Mari sat on the bed by her parents' feet. She'd been beaming so hard for the last year, her teeth ached. She was convinced each day anew that her sisters' outrageously good fortunes were the result of her piety and prayers. In giving thanks to the Almighty, Mari had taken to wearing a *burqa,* and whether Lady called her Ninja, or her mother called her Nut Case, or that brother in High Chai hissed, "Move it, Crow," she couldn't care less. The entire world was losing its way.

Mari flipped through brochures of the advanced Quran courses offered at the Red Mosque in Islamabad as well as of Harvard's comparative-religion courses. She'd apply to both. Though, really, going to Harvard would mean returning with prestige enough to set up her own Islamic school to rival all Islamic schools — *Al-Hira,* she would call it, after the cave in which the

Prophet Muhammad had hidden from the baddies who wanted to kill him. She would come back and she would rule and she would make people like Fazool and Moolee give up their New Year's parties — God willing, of course.

Qitty glanced at Mari browsing through the brochures. She returned to the drawing she was shading. She'd met a guy at Alys's and Jena's weddings, and it had been a perfect courtship. Then he'd said, "Jumbo, I'll marry you if you lose fifty pounds and promise to maintain the weight loss forever." When people would ask Qitty what it was about that particular moment, all she knew to say was that, suddenly, she was fed up. She'd yelled at him with all her might: "*Daffa ho,* get lost. If I'm happy loving myself just the way I am, then who are you to put conditions on accepting and loving me?"

That day, a lifetime of rage was unleashed at Lady, her mother, people who compared her to globular fruit, people who used "health" as an excuse to mock her; her anger poured out of her and onto paper. She'd sent her words to a national newspaper: She was not just fat; she was fat and intelligent, fat and funny, fat and kind, fat and fun, fat and beautiful, fat and a good friend, fat and creative, fat plus every lovely attribute in the world. She was fat and happy and did not care about being thin — imagine that.

Next Qitty knew, she'd been offered a weekly column on self-acceptance and talks all over the place. How she'd reveled in Lady's stunned shriek: "What! You've become *famous* for being *fat.* A fashion and beauty blogger." How she'd relished showing a silent Lady the thank-you letters she was continuously receiving for talking about living large and celebrating *all* of oneself. Never in her dreams had Qitty thought that she'd be called a role model or an inspiration. ("Never in my dreams either," Lady had said in a pinched voice as she'd wondered if Pakeezah Passions should design lingerie for fatties.) But it had been a dream of Qitty's to pen a graphic novel about a fat sister surrounded by four not-fat sisters and how the fat sister was the one who triumphed. And dreams came true, Qitty knew, as she inked in the final panel for *Unmarriageable.*

In Lahore, Jena was wrapping up a meeting with potential financiers to discuss funding for her dream organization — TWS, Together We Stand — which would provide educational scholarships to underprivileged girls in Pakistan. On the way home, she had the driver stop at Nona's Nices, Nona's flagship bakery, recently opened in Lahore, where she purchased her daily cravings, cream rolls. Bungles would monitor her gestational diabetes and they'd enjoy the dessert together in front of their wood fire as they debated girls' names.

Alys Binat — she'd chosen to keep her maiden name postmarriage — and Valentine Darsee walked hand in hand in Jane Austen's House Museum, in Chawton village, on their holiday in England. It was the cottage that Jane's elder brother had given his widowed mother and two sisters, Jane and Cassandra, to live in, and where Jane had written and revised many of her novels.

Alys ran her hand over the outside walls, the main door, the guest book, which she signed. She would never forget that Darsee had arranged this surprise visit for her birthday. Next they were going to Bath, Lyme Regis, Steventon, Winchester, and other Austen stops. Alys made a mental note to pick up souvenirs from each place, for her and Sherry's thriving bookstore.

Alys squeezed Darsee's hand and he

smiled at her as they moved from room to room. She thought of her favorite line in *Pride and Prejudice*: "For what do we live, but to make sport for our neighbours, and laugh at them in our turn?" She thought of Jane's mother and elder sister, both named Cassandra, outliving their beloved Jane, her father, George Austen, her brothers, James, George, Edward, Henry, Frank, and Charles, cousin Eliza, and of Martha and Mary Lloyd and Anne Sharp, Jane's friends. Of Harris Bigg-Wither, whose claim to fame was to be Jane Austen's fiancé of one night. She thought of Jane dead at forty-one and yet so very much alive in novel after novel.

Alys thought of the fictional Bennet daughters: Jane, Elizabeth, Kitty, Mary, and Lydia. She thought of Mrs. Bennet and Mr. Bennet. Mr. Fitzwilliam Darcy. Mrs. Lucas and Mr. Lucas and Maria and — her favorite character — Charlotte. Mr. Collins. Mrs. and Mr. Gardiner. Aunt Phillips. Of Charles Bingley. Caroline Bingley. Mrs. Hurst and her husband. Catherine de Bourgh and Anne de Bourgh. Colonel Fitzwilliam. She thought of the servants: Mrs. Hill and Mrs. Jenkinson and Mrs. Reynolds, the housekeeper at Pemberley, whose high praise of Mr. Darcy had made all the difference.

Alys thought of Jane Austen in this living

room, at this small round wooden table, her inkpot, her paper, the gliding of her fingers, her mind conjuring up lives, story after story, smiling, laughing even, at something Mrs. Bennet said, something she'd made Mrs. Bennet say. Mrs. Bennet, the world's worst mother but also perhaps the best mother because all she wanted was for her daughters to live happy, successful lives according to her times.

Alys looked up at Darsee and she wondered how this had happened, how he had gotten so lucky to have her marry him (oh, how lucky was she). Then they were in front of the cabinet displaying different editions of Jane Austen's novels. Her gaze rested on the first page of the universally beloved novel *Pride and Prejudice.* Alys took Darsee's hand and together their fingers traced over that most famous of first lines, the one she still assigned students in her literature classes to reimagine as they saw fit:

It is a truth universally acknowledged, that a single man in possession of a good fortune, must be in want of a wife.

PRIDE AND PREJUDICE AND ME

I first immersed myself in Jane Austen's *Pride and Prejudice* when I was sixteen years old. As interesting as its marriage plot was, I was spellbound, rather, by Austen's social criticism and how it was conveyed through her pithy wit. Here was a centuries-old English writer who may as well have been writing about contemporary Pakistani society. As a postcolonial child who grew up in the 1980s and was educated in Pakistan's English medium system, I was well versed in classic English poets and novelists. For fun, I read Enid Blyton, and because I studied for some years in an international school in Saudi Arabia, American authors such as Judy Blume. While these storytellers spoke of boarding-school midnight feasts and bras and busts, it was Jane Austen's wit and wisdom that first encouraged me to think critically about patriarchal society; a woman's traditional role; the ties of family,

535

friends, and frenemies; and the cost of keeping up appearances. As her stories skewered pretentious hypocrites, Austen's sharp pen drew a map for what marriage and compromise, silence and speaking up, meant, and her satirical insights on how to acknowledge drawing-room duplicity while still finding a way to laugh afforded comfort and solace.

Mrs. Bennet was like too many mothers I'd grown up around, those obsessed with getting their daughters married off because that was what "good mothers" did. As for "good girls," they obeyed their mothers, regardless of what they themselves wanted. But Elizabeth Bennet was a girl we wanted to be like, to arrive at a Netherfield Park in a muddy gown without a care for Pakistani society's quintessential cry of *Log kya kahenge?,* "What will people say?" In a country where marriages continue to be arranged on the basis of convenience, pedigrees, and bank balances, Elizabeth's spurning of the self-righteous Mr. Collins and the pompous Mr. Darcy were defiant acts we could look up to. According to Pakistani society, both "boys" would have made very suitable matches for Elizabeth, but — *gasp* — she said no, because *she* didn't believe they were right for her. Yes, Austen's novels end in the happily-ever-after of marriage, but these were marriages of the heroine's own choosing, after the hero had earned her respect, and they were based on both bride and groom *liking* each other. The marriages in Austen's novels gave me *hope* that there were good men to be found, and I wanted to pay tribute to that.

There were also other characters and situations in *Pride and Prejudice* that leapt out as mirroring Pakistani society. There was Lydia, who'd run off with Mr. Wickham, and whose whole family was terrified that if he didn't marry her, she'd be ruined and so would they. Was there any worry more Pakistani than the concern about what might bring a family honor or dishonor? There was sensible Charlotte Lucas, who made an expedient marriage for every reason but love. Was there anything more Pakistani than her calculated, "arranged" marriage? And there was Caroline Bingley, a snob disdainful of anyone who was not landed gentry or who hadn't inherited money — never mind that she herself was not landed gentry, since her wealth came via trade. Was there anything more apropos to Pakistan than class issues, snootiness, and double standards?

As I read and reread *Pride and Prejudice*, Elizabeth Bennet and every other character ceased to be English — to me, they were Pakistani. That I was imagining characters and scenarios in a Pakistani setting was nothing extraordinary. Ever since I could remember, I'd been engaging in literary transference/transplantation/translation from one culture to another. Growing up on English literature, I taught myself to see my daily reality reflected in my reading material, while plumbing its universal truths in search of particulars. Not just particulars in food and clothing, which were easily recast — *dupattas* instead of bonnets, *samosas* instead of scones — but rather in thematic content and characters' emotions. Thus Jane Bennet became just another Pakistani girl watching out for her reputation by being reticent instead of flirtatious, and her sadness at being spurned is no different from anyone's anywhere. In reading English literature through a Pakistani lens, it seemed to me that all cultures were concerned with the same eternal questions and that people were more similar to one another than they were different. As Alys Binat says in *Unmarriageable*, "Reading widely can lead to an appreciation of the universalities across cultures."

But Valentine Darsee says, "We've been forced to seek ourselves in the literature of

538

others for too long." In Pakistan there are seventy-four living languages, and Urdu and English are both official state languages. However, English, and a good accent, remains the lingua franca of privilege and opportunity. As an adult, I came across Thomas Babington Macaulay's "Minute on Education" (1835), in which he sets the colonized Subcontinent linguistic policy for creating "a person brown in color but white in sensibilities." It was then that I realized what the origins were of the emphasis in the Pakistani educational system on learning English and English literature at the cost of exploring our indigenous languages and literatures. History has made it such that my mother tongue, for all intents and purposes, is the English language. I wanted to write a novel that paid homage to Jane Austen and *Pride and Prejudice*, as well as combined my braided identification with English-language and Pakistani culture, so that the "literature of others" became the literature of everyone. Therefore, *Unmarriageable*.

NOTES AND RESOURCES

Dilipabad is a fictional town in Punjab, Pakistan, created by the author.

The play *Ismat Apa Kay Naam*, "In Ismat Apa's Name," was performed in Lahore in 2012. The author's setting it in 2001 is intentional.

For a list of books, authors, films, and people mentioned in *Unmarriageable*, go to the author's website, soniahkamal.com.

Charity Organizations in the Novel for Which Nona Bakes

Edhi Foundation (Edhi.org/usa/): A social welfare organization which also saves abandoned infants by placing "cradles" outside their offices for the babies to be put in.

Darul-ul-Sukun (Darulsukun.com): A welfare organization for people with disabilities.

Depilex Smileagain Foundation (us.depilex smileagain.com): An organization that provides acid-attack survivors with medical care, rehabilitation, and opportunities.

Literacy Organizations
Mirroring Jena's Venture

Developments in Literacy (dil.org): An organization that educates and empowers underprivileged students, especially girls.

The Citizens Foundation (tcfusa.org): A charity group that educates and empowers underprivileged students.

Jane Austen Literacy Foundation (JALF) (janeaustenlf.org): A foundation that supports literacy through volunteer programs, and funds libraries for communities in need across the world.

ACKNOWLEDGMENTS

To Jane Austen, for the stories you wrote that speak across centuries, for being blunt, impolite, funny, and honest. For skewering "good society."

To my husband, Mansoor Wasti, thank you for your support in every way. I simply would not be here without you.

Shikha Malaviya, kindred spirit, for chai-scones-*samosas,* old age on a beach, for reading this novel, email by email, as it was being written, all original 160,000 words of it, and then helping me see the trees for the forest. Your friendship is everything in every language.

My parents, Musarrat Kamal Qureshi and Naheed Kamal, née Pandit, whose joy and pride is everything.

My children: Indus, who has been reading my work and giving feedback since she was eleven years old; Buraaq, Indus, Miraage, my heartbeats, who really, at the end of it all, just want to know, Mom, what's for dinner? To the One who should have stayed but even went Unnamed, and to Khyber, and all lost to miscarriages — not a day goes by when your mother doesn't think about you: You are in this book, my babies, because you live in me.

My literary agent, Al Zuckerman: truly your belief in my writing has meant the world and is why I am still writing. Thank you for keeping faith and restoring mine; for loving and championing *An Isolated Incident* as ferociously as you do; you are my blessing. Thank you also, Samantha Wekstein at Writers House.

Anne Speyer, my wonderful editor, from your very first email I knew you got what I was trying to write with *Unmarriageable*. A billion *shukriyas* for making my vision possible and, in acquiring this novel, making my big fat dream come true, and for loving all these characters, and for your wisdom and guidance. Thank you, Jennifer Heuer, for a gorgeous cover. Thank you with all my heart to Janet Wygal, Melissa Sanford, Allison Schuster, Kara Welsh, Kim Hovey, Jennifer Hershey, Marietta Anastassatos, Kathy Lord, and everyone at Penguin Random House–Ballantine.

My niece Jahanara, thank you for being

my very first reader. I was so scared to hand it to you, and then you got back to me to say you'd read it twice, back-to-back, and it was your favorite novel in the world — there are no words to ever tell you what your words meant to me. My sister, Sarah, for literally letting me take your copy of *Pride and Prejudice* out of your hands because I needed to make notes that very moment, for your Iqbal Hussain painting story, and fact-check responses. My brother, Fahad, for grace under frantic fact-check emails, for your unwavering belief in my writing and this novel. Sobia, sister-in-law, also first reader of the epilogue and then the novel; your laughter at the characters, the situations; your encouragement — gifts that kept me going. Nephew Samir, you are my lucky star, born on the very day the cover was finalized and the launch date decided — your birth will be forever linked to this book. To my niece Ana for your input on the cover and for the cute — "but Soniah Khala, it's so long, I promise I'll read it when it's published." My Khalas and Mamoos — Tahira, Haseena, Mahira, Nisar, Mushtaq, you are in this book because you live in my heart, one way or another. My aunt Helen for giving me books as gifts, including my first *Pride and Prejudice*.

When I joined Georgia State University to embark on a four-year full-time academic MFA with closed-book exams, with three kids at home, I really did not know what I was getting myself into. This novel became my MFA thesis and was written in two months, and I truly believe that if it wasn't for that MFA-induced time crunch, I may still (perhaps forever) have been dreaming of writing it. Sometimes you can't help but believe that there is rhyme and reason behind every hard thing. To my inspirational creative writing professors: Josh Russell for your class on flash fiction, Sheri Joseph for your emphasis on novels; John Holman for your class on radical revision. Thank you all for your belief that this novel would sell. To Megan Sexton for being the best boss ever at *Five Points: A Journal of Literature and Arts* and for our fun conversations. My literature professors: Marilynn Richtarik for teaching me to write, which has made *all* the difference, and for William Trevor's *Felicia's Journey.* Jay Rajiva for postcolonial discussions and my soul text, Attia Hosain's *Sunlight on a Broken Column.* Tania Caldwell for talks on memory and Jill Ker Conway's *The Road from Coorain.* Scott Heath for *Harlem* and Jessie Redmon Fauset's *Plum Bun.* To the admin staff at GSU, for all you do.

To *all* my well-wishers — you know who you are — too many to name, who repeatedly cheered me on and kept asking when the novel was coming out. Hira Mariam for my beautiful website, so many jokes and laughs, and your love for *An Isolated Incident.* Meeta Kaur for your hospitality, passion, and encouragement. Zari Nauman for your feedback and giggles over Lahore. Manju Shringarpure, for your valuable texts: Get off Facebook and finish your novel! Sharbari Zohra Ahmed and Sadia Ashraf for weighing in on the cover and so much more. Kataryna Jakubiak for being the first to read the opening chapter and for your feedback. Devoney Looser for all your support and enthusiasm. Sonya Rehman for hope and more. Thrity Umrigar for hope and more. Sonali Dev for hope and more. To Pratima Malaviya for her delicious sketches of my Binat girls and more. Thank you: Kathleen A. Flynn. Jennifer S. Brown. Jessica Handler. Nandita Godbole. Dipika Mukherjee. Maheen Baqai. Rebecca Kumar. Nina Gangadharan. Saadia Faruqi. Kwan Holloway. Swati Narayan. Missale Ayele. Priya Nair. Connie Buchanan. Laurel Phenix. Reema Khan.

To Janeites the world over and Jane Austen Society members everywhere, especially

Jane Austen Society of North America (JASNA), where I first discovered fellow Austen fans and scholars. To JASNA Georgia Janeites: Erin Elwood. Renata Dennis. Kristen Miller Zone and everyone. To the Jane Austen Literacy Foundation, where I serve as a literacy ambassador.

To libraries everywhere, who are such a blessing, and especially to Fulton County libraries and Northeast/Spruill Oaks Branch, Georgia, for so much, and for weighing in on the cover: Laura Hoefner, Jayshree Sheth, Stephanie Gokey, Karen Swenson, Eva Mcguigan, and Gillian Hill.

To the baristas at Starbucks (store # 8202, Georgia), where much of this novel was so frantically written: Elise Watts, Brandon Ross, Emma Denney, Brittany Meekan, John London, Amberley Ferguson, and Beatrice — for keeping this immigrant writer in coffee (which is chai away from home), ice-cold water, and bright smiles daily for those two frightening, exhilarating months (for mothering me).

Thank you to all the following in Georgia and everywhere: independent bookstores and all others, literary organizations, book festivals, arts and culture magazines and websites for all you do for writers and for welcoming me into your fold.

Because there is always the kindness of strangers, to all in Georgia who I literally stopped on roads and in stores, who so willingly gave this author the time of day to weigh in on the cover: Thank you — we went with the teal one.

To: Sultan Golden, who makes his appearance in this novel as Dog and Kutta, and to Yaar, our cat, who made it to year nineteen.

To: Pakistan. Jeddah. England. America.

ABOUT THE AUTHOR

Soniah Kamal's debut novel, *An Isolated Incident*, was a finalist for the Townsend Prize for Fiction and the Karachi Literature Festival–Embassy of France Prize. Her TEDx Talk is about regrets and second chances. Kamal's award-winning work has appeared in numerous publications, including *The New York Times*, *The Guardian*, *BuzzFeed*, *Catapult*, and *Literary Hub*.

soniahkamal.com
Twitter: @SoniahKamal
Instagram: @SoniahKamal

The employees of Thorndike Press hope you have enjoyed this Large Print book. All our Thorndike, Wheeler, and Kennebec Large Print titles are designed for easy reading, and all our books are made to last. Other Thorndike Press Large Print books are available at your library, through selected bookstores, or directly from us.

For information about titles, please call:
(800) 223-1244

or visit our website at:
gale.com/thorndike

To share your comments, please write:
Publisher
Thorndike Press
10 Water St., Suite 310
Waterville, ME 04901

DATE DUE

10-23-08	

ITALY,
THE ROMAGNOLI WAY
A Culinary Journey

ITALY,
THE ROMAGNOLI WAY
A Culinary Journey

G. FRANCO ROMAGNOLI
AND GWEN ROMAGNOLI

GUILFORD, CONNECTICUT
AN IMPRINT OF THE GLOBE PEQUOT PRESS

Contents

INTRODUCTION

What prompted us to write this book is our obvious love for Italy. The two of us found each other in our mature years and soon discovered that our lives had run parallel courses. Franco—born and raised in Rome—was widowed, and Gwen—an American who had lived in Italy for many years—was divorced. In fact, it turned out that we had many friends in common on both sides of the ocean; that we had actually lived at one time, unknowingly, just a few blocks from each other in Rome's center; and that our children had bought their ice cream at the same gelateria. Now we are married (Gwen calls it "gray love") and travel frequently to Italy together, each time discovering that we share a love for the same places and same food, to our mutual delight. Although we may wax ecstatic about a particular place, we'll try to remain impartial and not be blind to its shortcomings. Sometimes our individual reactions to a place may have a different intensity, but, like a soprano and a tenor in a chorus, we sing the same song.

Even after many years of traveling, we are still perplexed by our fascination with unknown places, the roads less traveled, sites off the beaten path. Are we egotistic for striving to avoid typical experiences and cookie-cutter sightseeing? Do we, like explorers, harbor an inborn desire to discover what's on the other side of the ocean, or simply on the other side of the hill? Perhaps we simply hope to be able to say we were there first.

And yet, when it comes to Italy, this may seem overblown. Italy is a small country. How many out-of-the-way places are left anyway? From our experience, there are many—actually they can seem infinite. More than once, when we describe our experiences to friends, they say, "Good, you have seen Ninfa, but did you see nearby Sezze? And Norma just around the corner?" We have to admit to them that we have missed both. But only for now, because we will go back and search out Sezze and Norma, and in the process find Sermoneta. It never ends. There is always room for more.

In trying to avoid the beaten path, we do not mean to slight the big tourist attractions. After all, the treasures of Venice, Florence, and Rome are irreplaceable. But mass tourism has brought big changes to the otherwise spontaneous hospitality of these famous places. To be acceptable to all tastes, they have been homogenized and tailored to travelers' expectations. In Rome mock gladiators now prance in front of the Colosseum entreating tourists to be photographed with them for a fee. In Venice gondoliers serenade their fares with "*O Sole Mio*," the world-famous Neapolitan song. The places we write about are the ones largely unknown by the traveling masses. These are the places where the real Italy still exists.

Can you miss the Tower of Pisa, the Brunelleschi Dome, the Uffizi, or the Sistine Chapel? Impossible. These unavoidable sights are like the entree, the pièce de résistance of a sumptuous meal. Although these special main courses are rich and satiating, their fame has preceded them and deprived them of great surprises. Once you have partaken of them, you should take an emotional rest by going on the paths less trodden, tasting the smaller appetizing side dishes, less affected by fads and trends, but always delectable and often not anything that you would have expected.

Some years ago, we discussed with a friend the pros and cons of our travel philosophy and attitude. The subject came up while we were in Stresa, in the Lago Maggiore region. He asked us if we had seen the Colosso di San Carlone, a tourist attraction in the nearby town of Arona. Many, many tour busses were lined up for a visit there, shouldn't we go? We went.

Built in the 1700s the colossus honors Saint Charles Borromeo, a well-loved sixteenth-century cardinal and benefactor of the area. The statue is more than one hundred feet tall, a proportionate representation, in gigantic size, of the saintly cardinal blessing the crowd. The little finger of his blessing hand is seven feet long.

People throng, line up, push, and shove to pay to go through the gates leading to the San Carlone, "Big Charley," as it is known by locals. For the small admission fee, one can climb—or crawl— the body's inside stairs to the top and peep out from the two tiny windows that are his eyes. The immediate grounds are invaded by stalls, teeming with people buying a huge array of plastic trinkets and Italian soccer team pennants. It is really awful.

But then, if we had not followed this tourist path, we would have missed a sight so outlandish that it will stay with us all our traveling days. Or worse, we might not have fled and taken refuge at nearby Lake Orta, a hidden jewel that has become one of our favorite spots. The moral, then? Travel is rewarding. Visiting the "must-see" places can be as culturally illuminating as the lesser-known ones are fulfilling for the new insight of discovery, and, once in a while, introductions to foods that have not made it yet into the big leagues.

The paths—well trodden or not—are there, waiting.

One of the many rewarding elements of travel in Italy is its food, but while its gastronomy is known and appreciated the world over, lesser known is its incredible variety, which can be explained by Italy's geography. We have assembled these chapters to create an ideal itinerary from the north to the south of the peninsula. Because we have never planned our travels that rationally (we follow the seasons, the inspiration of the moment, no reason at all, or to write articles for newspapers and magazines) what we have compliled here is a collection of stories rather than an actual retelling of a north-to-south road trip.

GEOGRAPHY

Italy is a long, thin peninsula shaped like a boot, stretching from northwest to southeast. Including big and small islands, it is just about as big as California. It is fenced off from the rest of Europe by the Alps, which span uninterrupted from east to west, from sea to sea. They are forbidding mountains, the tallest in Europe, covered permanently with snow and glaciers. Just below the Alps is the Po River valley, the industrial center and agricultural basket of Italy, dotted with the largest lakes in the nation. Proceeding south we encounter the Apennines, a mountain chain that runs in the middle of the peninsula all the way to the tip of the boot and Sicily, effectively dividing the east from the west of the country. Italy is surrounded by about five thousand miles of coastline and, in addition to its two major islands, Sicily and Sardinia, it includes a myriad of small islands and archipelagos.

The climate reflects this geography, from the cold of the northern mountains to the temperate weather a few miles down the slopes and to the subtropical heat on the southern flatlands. But we can find warm spots in the north and cold ones in the south. Flowers bloom all year up north in Liguria, and in the south, Monte Etna in Sicily claims an extended ski season. Of course, some regions have more abundant resources than others do, but when it comes to agricultural production, most foods are as available in the north as they are in the south. The Po River valley is rich in cattle, dairy products, rice, and corn; the south favors wheat, olives, citrus fruit, and vegetables. In the south tomatoes are abundant; originally from the Americas, tomatoes have become the emblem of southern Italian cooking. All around the coastline, large and small fishing villages harvest and supply a large variety and quantity of fish. Grapevines grow exceedingly well all over the map, so much so that Italy was known by the ancient Greeks as Enotria, the land of wine. Hardly a village is without its own special wine, and Italy continues to rank among the world's biggest wine producers and exporters.

HISTORY

Italian history also contributes to this variety. Since prehistory foreigners have considered Italy the garden of the gods, and from all the directions of the compass they came to pluck its flowers. Through the centuries came the Franks, the Longobards, the Huns, the Spaniards, the Arabs, the Swedes, the Greeks, the Turks, the Saracens, and the Moors. Some stayed longer than others, but they all left their marks on the culture, traditions, ethnic traits, and character of the local people.

In fact, Italy became a single, united nation only in 1870. Before that it was a conglomerate of independent monarchies, republics, city-states, duchies, and papal states: a collection of self-enclosed bubbles in shifting conditions of allegiance or enmity with one another, all of them nursing and perpetuating their own dialects, traditions, tastes and, naturally, their own gastronomies. Practically every city, town, and village of today's Italy (which is divided into twenty semi-autonomous regions) has, despite today's climate of internationalization, fostered its own character and culture. It is not unusual to find distinctly different dialects and ways of cooking in two towns less than thirty miles apart or even in two villages on the opposite sides of a hill. To speak of one Italian cuisine is impossible, and that is why travel in Italy is so special. It is like an infinite number of differently colored tiles making up one magnificent mosaic.

The roots of all Italian family food, however, are planted firmly in peasant fare. Simple, satisfying food: The juxtaposition of clear, definite tastes, colors, and textures blending—*E pluribus unum*—into an unmistakably pleasing and comforting whole. Its ingredients are few, its cooking is simple, its techniques seldom elaborated. And yet, while its origins are generally humble, when power and money make their appearance (think of Renaissance Florence, of Rome of the Popes, of Venice of the Doges), Italian food becomes theatrical and grandiose, a command performance, an opera with a full orchestra and a great cast of fastidiously dressed singers.

What gastronomically unifies Italy is bread. The breaking of bread has more than its figurative biblical meaning. "Give us our daily bread" is not an abstract prayer but a basic need: A meal without bread is not a meal. A rich man at a table bereft of bread is poor;

a poor man will make a full meal out of a loaf of bread. Bread—the long, the short, the round, the flat, the crusty, and the smooth, all the thousand different kinds—is what makes an Italian meal. All the rest is *companatico* (from the Latin, *cum-pane*), all extras that come to the table to enrich the bread. In fact, the Italian's version of the expression "to call a spade a spade"—"to call bread bread, and wine wine" *(dir pane al pane, e vino al vino)*—beautifully illustrates where their hearts are.

For Italians gastronomy is more a way of life than a way of cooking. Food—the eating of it and the talking about it—is part of the texture of everyday life. Italian food even has a calendar of its own. Every city, town, and village has a special dish dedicated to a specific day, be it a day of the week or a saint's day. In Rome Thursday is when you eat gnocchi and Saturday is for *trippa* (tripe); Saint Joseph's Day is for fritters.

For Italians, like music, food is mood. Recognizable and friendly, sometimes it is like a Sousa march—loud, brassy, zesty, with a beat that asks to be shared; often it is sprightly and spicy like a Rossini aria; or it is soft and intimate, embracing and caressing like a Venetian barcarole.

Italian markets offer a daily cornucopia of colors and tastes, but more than by their appeal, cooks choose their menus based on their mood. On a misty, chilly Venetian day nothing will lift your soul like a bowl of *risi e bisi,* (rice and peas); the woodsy smells of a Tuscan autumn will suggest a *cacciatora* stew, for its aroma gives warmth to a pale sun and celebrates a crisp blue sky. Food is also about pleasure and conviviality: Italians can appreciate a few black olives and a loaf of bread as a full meal. Add a glass of wine, an orange, and a few friends, and it is a banquet. Throw in a song or two, and it's a feast. It is food with a heart and a soul, where *pane è pane e vino è vino*. This complexity of colors, textures, and moods is so intertwined with the Italian nature and landscape that together, place and food make an inseparable unit.

Italian food is tradition, what people hold onto in the midst of change. Italians carry it with them wherever in the world they go, and that is why Italian food is everywhere. Wherever there are a few Italians, there is going to be an Italian eatery. We found one in Ushuaia, *La Fin del Mundo* (The End of the World), the last, southernmost town in Argentina.

Italians travel with their forks.

Orta

THE CINDERELLA OF THE LAKES

*O*n a recent trip to Italy, we arrived at Milan's Malpensa Airport around eight in the morning, picked up our rental car, and drove straight to Orta, about a forty-five-minute drive. After settling into our hotel, we telephoned Franco's sister in Rome.

"We've arrived," we reported.

"Where are you?" she asked.

"We're in Orta."

"Orte?" She was referring to a little town, hardly more than a railroad junction, near Orvieto, barely an hour from Rome.

"No, Ort-a. We're up north at Lago di Orta."

"Where's that?"

"It's a little lake near Lago Maggiore."

"Mai sentito." Never heard of it.

Mirella, who has lived her whole life in Italy, is quite well traveled, but she had never heard of Orta. "Aha," we said to ourselves, "we are just where we want to be—off the beaten path."

This little lake can be described as a jewel set in the middle
of a crater. Its blue waters reflect the sparkle of snowcapped Alps,
and on a tiny island in its middle stands the church of San Giulio,
Orta's saint. In the glamorous lake region of northern Italy, Lake
Orta is the smallest of the lakes. The locals consider it the Cinderella of them all and resent that the notoriety of its big sisters (Lake
Maggiore, Lake Como, and Lake Garda) overshadow their lake's
natural attractions.

A mountain crest away (sixteen miles, as the twisty road
goes) from Lago Maggiore's fashionable Stresa, an international
resort and convention town, Orta's clear waters reflect the massif of the Alps. Eight miles long, one and one-half miles wide, the
lake is big enough to warrant a system of *vaporetti* (water buses)
and water taxis for the villages that dot its shores. The lake's main
town, Orta San Giulio, is named after the little island that fronts
it. The name of this fourth-century proselytizing saint pops up all
over because this region was once his stomping ground. Legend
says that floating on his cape and using his pastoral staff as an oar,
he plied the waters to the little island and freed it from a dragon
and an invasion of snakes.

Today there is no need for a cape. The water taxis, or even a
fisherman's rowboat, can ferry you to the island where no cars are
allowed. Isola San Giulio consists of only a few hundred square yards
of real estate, totally covered by buildings, over which the church of
San Giulio and its bell tower dominate. The church, which you can
inspect in a few minutes' walk, is the essence of peace and quiet—
the gentle lapping of water and your footfalls are all the noise you
will hear. Persimmon trees sprout from unexpected corners—a
handful of dirt seems sufficient for the sizable trees to thrive. In the

fall, when barren of leaves and laden with yellow-golden fruit, they look very much like naturally decorated Christmas trees, a common sight in the whole Orta area.

Since the seventeenth century, English and French artists and writers (Balzac among them)—all of whom obviously kept this little corner of paradise to themselves—have appreciated the peaceful beauty of the region, which includes the villages on the mountain slopes as well as the ones on the shores, and its gastronomy. For all its anonymity, today the area has several elegant multi-starred hotels and resort inns to satisfy the needs of a discerning clientele. The well-kept secret attractions of the place are many and range from sailing and windsurfing—there are several pocket-sized beaches around the lake—to leisurely strolls in and around the wooded hillsides. These strolls are particularly rewarding for mushroom hunters, especially for the prized porcini.

The hotel we chose to stay in was the San Rocco, which is situated right on the edge of the lake and offers rooms with enormous picture windows. We could see the water lapping at our window, making it seem as if we were in the middle of the lake. This kind of view makes you just want to stay put all day, watching the majestic swans, the fishermen that ply the waters, and the rowboats. But after a lovely lunch of prosciutto, *funghi* (mushrooms), and the best *grissini* (breadsticks) we've ever had, we were ready to explore. Our pricey accommodations proved that if traveling off the main road is generally less expensive, it isn't necessarily so.

The one and only main drag of Orta, Via Gippini, is lined with shops, cafes, and restaurants, but is barely wide enough for an infrequent car to get by. On our way to the main square, we found a steep set of wide steps on our left and decided to see where they led. After a zigzagging uphill walk of about fifteen minutes, there, overlooking the town, we came upon an unexpected sight. The path had opened up onto a gorgeous tree-and-flower-filled park that was dotted with twenty small chapels, each totally different in architecture and design from others.

We had discovered the Sacro Monte (Sacred Mount), a sanctuary honoring Saint Francis of Assisi. Each chapel contains a display of life-sized terra-cotta figures depicting a stage in his life. The Abbé of Novara founded the Sacro Monte in 1590 as a monastery, and in the following year, began to build this tribute to Saint Francis. More than a century would pass before the twentieth chapel was built, and during that period this impressive array of chapels kept sculptors, architects, painters, and builders busy. Huge kilns were built on the hillside to fire the sculptors' terra-cotta figures.

The twenty chapels are spread out over a five-acre area, so there is plenty of walking to do, but it's well worth the effort. The walls of the entrance to each chapel are covered with frescoes, while inside, behind massive wrought-iron gates, the dramatic sculptures are arranged in tableaux. Chapel I represents the birth of Saint Francis, and continuing through the numbers, artists have depicted all the stages of the saint's life, starting with his renunciation of the comfortable life of his wealthy family and ending with a celebration of his victory over temptation: His fellow monks lead him naked through the streets. Some of the chapels are stark and simple with few sculptured figures; others, such as the saint's canonization, are awesome in size, covering a large area and containing scores of massive terra-cotta bishops, cardinals, and other personages. They blend with other figures frescoed in the background walls, so that the tableaux appear much larger than they are in reality.

The hillside's beauty is further augmented by both the innumerable kinds of flowers that grow and embellish the area's botanical gardens, and the grand high view of the lake with, mirrored in the middle, San Giulio island. At sunset the whole scene—the surrounding hills and mountains, the island and villages on the shores—assumes a golden-red hue, all reflected on the calm waters in a spectacular panorama.

The idyllic character of this region might suggest that the local population has a relaxed attitude toward work. It turns out, however, that the region is a virtual beehive of artisanal activity. It produces a range of world-renowned brass and reed instruments, from trombones to saxophones, from tubas to piccolos. One would expect the bucolic quiet of the hills to be pierced at any moment by a blaring rendition of the Music Man's "76 Trombones," but apparently the instruments' testing and tuning is done out of earshot. Other handcrafted creations from the area include kitchen implements, from spoons and forks to mortar and pestles that are made out of local boxwood. This once-artisanal activity has developed today into the industrial production of copper and stainless steel pots and pans.

The ultramodern factories located around the town of Omegna on the northern shore of the lake are at the leading edge of industrial design for table and kitchen utensils. Largest and best known among them is Alessi, which has produced some famous creations permanently exhibited at New York's Museum of Modern Art. Alongside the factory is an outlet store where visitors can admire and shop the vast selection of culinary designs. The company is now headed by Alberto Alessi, an old friend and collaborator of Roberto Zola whose atelier/studio/foundry is located in Quarne, a small village on the hill above Omegna. Together they have designed and crafted the Alexofono, an updated, streamlined, ultraexpensive version of the saxophone, crafted individually for the virtuosi of the instrument, a real Rolls-Royce of the music world.

In addition, the industrious natives—taking a hint from an interesting peculiarity of the area between Orta and Lake Maggiore—have dedicated themselves to the making of umbrellas since the early eighteenth century. Here, the warm air rising from the lakes meets the cold air descending from the Alps, and creates a semipermanent, rain-promising white cloud stationed over the little town of Gignese. Umbrella making, which has made the fame and fortune of many enterprising locals, is celebrated in the town's Museum of Umbrellas and Parasols.

The Lake Orta area is one for all seasons. Only twelve miles from Orta San Giulio at 4,470 feet on Monte Mottarone, there are well-equipped ski slopes, but if skiing doesn't thrill you, you may enjoy the sweeping view of the Alps above and the Po Valley below that the top of the mountain offers.

One advantage of being outside the center-stage spotlight is the freedom that the local gastronomy enjoys from the pressures and demands of mass tourism. Moreover, Lake Orta and its province—in Piedmont, but just at the border with Lombardy— take advantage of the culinary traditions of both regions. A *Piemontese insalata di carne* (more fashionably known as carpaccio, paper-thin slices of raw sirloin, basted with olive oil and lemon and topped with bits of Parmigiano cheese) is just as much at home as a Milanese osso buco (veal shank), which you can now encounter all over the world. The freshest garden produce comes together in a Piemontese *bagna cauda* (fresh garden vegetables for dipping in an olive oil–anchovy-garlic sauce) as well as in a thick Lombard minestrone. The proximity to the rice paddies of Novara and Vercelli, which produce the superb arborio, Vialone, Carnaroli, and the new strains of exceptional rice, makes local specialties of all manner of risottos and any dish involving rice. These watery rice paddies are a perfect habitat for a large population of frogs who seem to be happily jumping directly to the local tables and their menus.

On an evening walk down Via Gippini, we were attracted by a small gate in the ivy-covered stone wall of a tiny alleyway. It looked as if it might be the entrance to a secret garden but, over the gate, half hidden by ivy, a sign identified the gate as the entrance to Taverna Antico Agnello. A set of stone stairs led us up to the intimate, family-style dining space consisting of a few small rooms— obviously once a residence—each with just five or six tables. The food consisted of local traditional specialties, carefully prepared and graciously served. With some variations, this bill of fare is repeated at the other few eateries in Orta: *risotto alle rane e porcini,* risotto with frogs' legs and wild porcini mushrooms; *Trota Affogata,* poached rainbow trout with a lemon-vinegar béchamel sauce topped with raisins; *anatra farcita,* duck stuffed with rice, sausage, mushrooms, and herbs; *costoletta di cervo,* a deer chop, tender but gamey. Some places offer *trot' e fava,* trout stewed with fresh fava beans; *frittata di rane,* a local frogs' legs omelette; and *luccio all'agro,* pike butter-braised with a grappa and wood-berries sauce. This all underscores the overwhelming use of local ingredients. And we washed it all down with the restaurant's house red wine, a wonderful Piemontese Dolcetto di Dogliani.

On Via Gippini we were confronted with even more astounding specialties of the region at Ristoro Olina. *Antipasto di carpaccio d'oca,* thin-sliced goose meat dressed in olive oil and lemon with shavings of pecorino cheese; *salame d'asino,* donkey-meat salami, a tasty and amusing combination, since in the vernacular, *salame* used as an adjective is the equivalent of "dumb" and *asino* means "stupid"; wild boar ham, prepared and cut like prosciutto, but leaner and stronger tasting; and a terrine of truffled braised rabbit served with quince jam. Olina makes its gnocchi in an unconventional way: Called *gnocchetti,* their version is made not with potato, but with crustless bread that has been soaked all night in milk then mixed with egg and flour and turned into dough. Shaped like small hazelnuts, these gnocchi are served with a butter, basil, and pancetta sauce that melts in your mouth. For main courses we ate a dish of veal medallions in a Gorgonzola sauce, and the vaunted local lake fish *corregone,* which, with its firm white flesh, we considered superior to trout. The leisurely proceeding began with a complimentary antipasto of *magrone,* a prosciutto with the fat removed (as many northerners like to serve it), and ended with a complimentary shot of grappa, offered as a digestive. A must.

Interspersed among the restaurants on Via Gippini are several *enoteche* (wine bars). In these cozy settings, people gather around rustic tables before dinner to enjoy an *aperitivo* or a taste of the local wines. We easily adopted that custom, finding it very civilized and warming in the misty air of the lake at dusk, most encouraging of conversation, and a good preparation for our walk to dinner. Being partial to reds, we sampled the Piemontese Ghemme and Gattinara and the slightly spritzy Barbera.

To keep the gastronomic tradition alive, the yearly *Riso e Lago* (Rice & Lake) competition prods the local restaurants to outdo each other in creating dishes based on products of the area. The rice

varieties, the frog population, the local fish— from carp to perch to trout to corregone—the special mountain-garden produce of crisp lettuces and chards, the wild mushrooms—from porcini to *ovoli* to *teste di drago*—the berries, and venison supply the ammunition for the contest.

Lago d'Orta: off the beaten track? Perhaps. But only metaphorically speaking. Lake Orta is twenty-six miles from the international airport of Milan Malpensa, and fifty miles from Milan Linate, the national airport.

RISOTTO ALLE RANE E PORCINI

Risotto with Frogs' Legs and Wild Mushrooms

1½ pounds (approximately) fresh or
frozen frogs' legs
2 fresh basil leaves
2 fresh sage leaves
3–4 sprigs fresh flat leaf parsley
1 small garlic clove
4 tablespoons butter
1 tablespoon olive oil
½ tablespoon salt

1 ounce dried porcini mushrooms
1 small onion
1⅓ cups arborio rice
¼ cup dry white wine
1 jigger brandy (optional)
4½ cups hot chicken broth (or
hot, lightly salted water)
Freshly grated Parmigiano
Reggiano cheese

WASH the frogs' legs and dry on paper towels. Soak the porcini in a cup of warm water. Mince together the basil, sage, parsley, and garlic. Sauté the mince in 2 tablespoons of butter and the tablespoon of olive oil until limp, then add the frogs' legs. Cook over low heat for 5 minutes, turning them a few times and making sure they do not stick to the pan. Stir in the salt. Remove the pan from heat and let cool.

MINCE the onion and sauté it on medium heat in a soup pot with the 2 remaining tablespoons of butter. When the onions are limp and golden, add the rice, raise the heat, and cook, stirring constantly until the rice begins to crackle. Stir in the wine and, if desired, the brandy. Stir in the hot broth (or the hot water), cover the pot, lower the heat, and let simmer for about 12 minutes, stirring occasionally.

IN THE MEANTIME, bone the frogs' legs, cube the meat coarsely, and return to its cooking pan juices. Lift the soaking mushrooms from their water, drain well, make sure they are free of sand, and chop them coarsely. Add the frogs' leg meat, its pan juices, and the mushrooms to the almost-cooked rice. Stir and cook for another 2 minutes or until the rice is done. Serve warm as a first course with a sprinkle of Parmigiano cheese.

Serves 4

TROTA AFFOGATA

Trout Poached in White Wine

2 large whole trout, or 4 small
  (3½–4 pounds total)
¼ cup golden raisins
1 small onion
6 fresh sage leaves
1 small garlic clove
1 tablespoon rosemary

Zest of half a lemon
¼ cup olive oil
⅓ cup white wine vinegar
⅔ cup dry white wine
1 teaspoon salt
1 scant tablespoon
  all-purpose flour

GUT the trout but leave heads and tails on. Rinse well in fresh water.

PLACE the raisins in ½ cup warm water to plump them up.

FINELY MINCE together onion, sage, garlic, rosemary, and the lemon zest.

PUT THE OLIVE OIL in a pan large enough to accommodate the fish in one layer. Add the mince and sauté over medium heat until barely golden. Remove from heat and place the fish on top of the cooked mince. Add the vinegar, wine, and salt, then add enough water to cover the fish. Bring it to a gentle boil, then cover the pan and simmer for about 5 minutes (more or less, depending on the size of the trout), or until the fish is cooked but not falling apart.

LIFT the fish from the broth and skin it while still warm. The fillets should come off the central spine easily. Assemble the fillets on a serving platter and keep them warm.

STRAIN the poaching liquid into a saucepan. Put ¼ cup of the liquid in a cup and stir the flour into it, turning it into a smooth paste. Pour the paste back into the poaching liquid, bring to a gentle boil, and stir it constantly until it turns into a creamy sauce. Drain the raisins and add them to the sauce; cook it for a few additional seconds, then pour the sauce over the trout. Serve immediately.

Serves 4

Val d'Aosta

A GEOGRAPHICAL HYPHEN

On our way to Monte Bianco, the highest mountain in Europe, we first headed south from Orta then northwest on the provincial Route 26, which follows the valley carved by the Dora Baltea, one of the rivers that flow into the mighty Po. We could have reached the same destination via the superhighway or the railroad, but neither would have opened up for us, slowly as in a magic show, the vistas of the countryside. This provincial byway runs in the middle of the Vale of Augustus—the Val d'Aosta—and as it approaches the mountains, the valley narrows and huddles next to the mountains' steep walls, shying away from the river as from a moody, unreliable wild animal. The Dora Baltea, after prolonged periods of rain or sudden thaws, can indeed turn into a roaring, murderous beast, trampling anything in the path of its rage. The Romans, well aware of the river's temper, carved their road up higher from its banks, chiseling away the mountain granite where it interfered with their path. The Herculean roadwork blazed one of the few gateways

across the western Alps. Today's roads parallel sections of the old
Roman road; the five-inch-deep ruts worn into the stone roadbed
attest to the traffic that for centuries carried Roman power and
commerce to and from Gallia, modern-day France.

A few miles from its southern border with Piedmont, the valley is choked by a gorge, and the road barely squeezes by. A formidable, imposing fortress was built there in the eleventh century to
close that natural gate against any incoming invaders. Bard is the
name of the village and of the fort. Destroyed in 1800 by the French
and rebuilt by the *Piemontesi* in 1830, the fort is a masterpiece of
military architecture, a gray monster hardly discernible between
the granite mountains' sheer walls. Across the river is Hone, a small
village with definite medieval tones. The tolling of the bell tower
clock and the aroma of cooking wafting along the stone-paved
alleys told us it was time for lunch. The welcoming open door and
the convivial sounds from within attracted us to the Hosteria della
Società Cooperativa, where a long-haired, chain-smoking chef held
forth. He and a young waitress welcomed us, told us to sit wherever
we wanted, and then practically abandoned us. Their total attention
was taken by a table of Alpine guides—eleven of them—celebrating
the eightieth birthday of the guide at the head of the table. Hanging
from a nail on the wall were his retired, well-worn mountain boots.
After the assembly got over its moment of surprise at the presence
of two obvious strangers, they invited us to participate in the general merriment. We joined the group in singing *"Tanti auguri a te"*
("Happy birthday to you") and partook of their food. The cheerful
wives, daughters, and friends, seemingly all very well versed in the
art of eating, helped the chef and waitress bring an unending flow of
dishes to the table. It started with *tomino,* a fresh goat cheese steeped

in olive oil and chopped chives; three types of dry salami, including a pork blood variety; ricotta with herbs, the cheese so fresh it still tasted of the nearby high pastures; sliced rounds of savory *cotechino,* a cooked fresh pork salami—whose principal element is the pork's skin—with potato puree; and a mixed salad of tomatoes and fennel. Then came *panzarotti verdi,* green ravioli filled with a spinach and cheese mixture in a melted butter sauce; *gnocchi in bianco,* potato dumplings with a walnut white sauce; and homemade *fettuccine al sugo* with a beef red sauce, enriched with walnut meat. And then there was a stew of *trippa e ceci,* calf tripe and chickpeas; and *stracotto,* a beef stew long simmered in red wine, accompanied by creamed spinach. To honor the guest, we tasted a little of everything, wetted by just a sip or two of robust house red wine since we planned to continue our drive.

A tenor voice broke the general din, singing aloud the opening lyrics of an alpine song; a baritone joined in, and then another. One by one the voices built up into a most melodious chorus, smooth and effortless, well lubricated by more than one bottle of that generous local wine. We left them at it and hit the road restored in body and spirit. The mountain song lingered in our heads and accompanied us.

The panorama changes with the whim of the road as we head further north. At times the cramped, limited horizon opens up to become a breathtaking vision of rugged, snowcapped mountains; at others it takes relief in small, sloping pastures as green and as big as emeralds. You can feel in your ears the road climbing with every turn and finally, fenced in by a crown of white mountains, it levels into a few square miles of flat land. It is here that, in the first century B.C., the Romans built a military camp and then a fortified city and, in honor of Emperor Augustus, named it Augusta Praetoria. It grew into today's Aosta, capital and namesake of the valley and of the autonomous region of Val d'Aosta. With a population of about forty thousand people, the city presents different faces: efficiently modern and yet with a pace that Italians describe as *da alpino,* with the relaxed, steady rhythm of a mountain walker climbing the Alps. Its vicinity to Monte Bianco's tunnel, connecting Italy with France, and to Monte San Bernardo's tunnel, connecting Italy with Switzerland, puts the city at the crossroads with Europe.

Our pre-dinner leisurely walk turns into a stroll into history. Just around the corner—still well preserved—stand the Roman defensive walls, the Roman theater and amphitheater (its twenty thousand seats give a sense of the city's historical importance), a Praetorian Gate, and the ruins of a forum. Medieval towers and buildings progressing in age through the centuries are tangible markers of its past and its ethnic heritage, showing how at one time or another Aosta (and the whole Val d'Aosta) belonged either to Italy or to France. In fact, the French and Italian languages have equal official usage, and all road and city signs are posted in both languages. Several hotels and many restaurants make the stay in Aosta a most pleasant one, and the base for excursions to the whole valley.

For its size—sixty miles long by forty miles wide—Val d'Aosta could be considered the Rhode Island of Italy, the smallest of Italy's twenty regions, and one of the five untouched by a sea. At the northwesternmost border of the peninsula, Val d'Aosta resembles two hyphens connecting Italy to France and Switzerland. Most of its customs, history, language, and gastronomy reflect its geographical position. Nestled among the highest peaks of the Alps—Mont Blanc/Monte Bianco (at more than fourteen thousand feet, it tops them all), Saint Bernard, the Gran Paradiso, Monte Cervino/Matterhorn, and the Monte Rosa—Val d'Aosta is a well-defined area not only by its geography but also by its character.

The stunning and unique beauty of the area is paralleled only by its strategic position. It is one of the few doors in the Alpine wall, a position that politically made it the lock and bolt, the gate-keeper, and toll-taker of all the traffic from northwest Europe into the Italian peninsula. It is through its steep, narrow passes that Hannibal the Carthaginian probably brought his army and its elephants to fight Rome in 216 B.C., a feat that Napoléon repeated in 1800 leading his French army, cavalry, and artillery on its way to victory over the Austrians at Marengo. (A brief aside: According to legend, in order to feed the general on the battlefield, Napoléon's chef collected whatever he could from the nearby farms and came up with the now-famous Chicken Marengo dish.) From prehistory, Val d'Aosta's key points were occupied and defended by the strong and powerful of the moment. In the Middle Ages, in a real game of "King of the Mountain," the commanding positions along the sixty-mile-long valley were held by seventy-two castles and fortresses, each within watchful eyesight of the other and each occupied by dukes who could open or close the valley at their whim. Many castles are now in ruins but many still exist, preserved and open to the public, even if we were frequently surprised to be their only visitors. Located an easy ride from Aosta are the Castles of Fenis, Verres, and Introd, just to mention a few.

The passage of different civilizations has made the people of the Val d'Aosta fiercely independent and consistently loyal to their creeds and beliefs. It explains the motto of the Alpine Division Aosta, the Italian mountain troops, which we heard uttered by our friendly guides in Hone: *"Che custa quel che custa,Viva l'Austa!"* ("Cost what it may, long life to Aosta!") It's the equivalent of *semper fidelis,* with the implication "to the bitter end." Above all, due to the nature of the land, the *Valdostani* are self-reliant: They nurse whatever soil has been left by the granite of the mountains to render the most over the longest period of time.

"We live," a Valdostano told us, "among mountains that are real mountains." He was suggesting that the mountains to their east—the Dolomites, or the Venetian Alps—as well as their people, are less "real mountain," more lacy and frilly.

"We are," he continued, "real mountain farmers. For us, all things have a measure of their own." For these mountain farmers, cold is colder, high is higher, work is harder. Fields are not measured in acres but in feet, and whatever grows, it grows tastier and is treasured more. In the mountain hamlets the Valdostani bake bread but once a year and then dry the loaves, which are made to last until the next bake. Sliced—or better, sawed—they will become the base for the famous local soup (*soupe* or *zuppa*). Here, in terraces facing south and as wide as a foothold, grow vineyards at the highest altitude in Europe. At night the grapes squeeze the warmth from the daytime sun that was stored in the stone columns that support their trellises. The wide, stocky pillars are made with the stones carved out of the mountain to make room for the terraces. Nothing is wasted in Val d'Aosta.

The wines from the grapes are not abundant, but they are good. Donnaz, Enfer d'Arvier, Pinot Noir, and Petit Rouge are produced in quantities barely sufficient to satisfy the demand of the local populace. Val d'Aosta is considered to be the highest per-capita wine drinking part of Italy. The region also keeps for itself the golden *renette* apples, the chestnuts, the small Martin Sec pears, and whatever else the soil lets go from its clutches. The gastronomic lineup includes an interesting mélange of dishes, a cross between French and Piemontese to the gain, in most cases, of both. The specialties are not many and not too elaborate. If anything—especially if we stick to the traditional fare—they supply the amount of calories required by the climate and work patterns.

It is difficult to describe the cuisine *Valdostaine* because it offers a different twist for each of the lateral valleys that, not unlike fish bones, join the central valley and from there climb to the high peaks. A classic example is the *zuppa.* Each valley has a variation on the same theme, relying on the local supplies. The common denominator of all is Fontina, the most prized among the many local cheeses. A Valdostano can discern in which season and in which valley the cows were at pasture, for the cheese is produced immediately after milking and varies in taste, aroma, consistency, and creaminess. Because of its international trademark, by law a cheese should not be called Fontina if it's not made in Val d'Aosta. On the list of local food, beside the ruling soups, is the *mocetta,* a highly flavored, thinly sliced cured meat of mountain goat (gamier, but not unlike a pig's *prosciutto di montagna*); *riso, latte, e castagne,* a soup of rice and dried chestnuts cooked in milk; the sturdy *carbonnade,* a dark stew of top-round beef marinated for at least twenty-four hours in red wine, then slowly cooked in its marinade and onions; and *civet alla Valdostana,* hare stewed in wine and spiked with fiery grappa.

This basic and limited lineup of dishes should not give the impression that life in Val d'Aosta is heavy, cheerless, and stodgy. After all, one local specialty that does not fit those adjectives is *costoletta alla Valdostana,* a lightly breaded veal chop, butterflied and filled with Fontina; another is *tegole d'Aosta,* Aosta "roof tiles," crisp and light almond cookies, similar to pralines. The same is true of the Valdostani character: Along with their dedicated seriousness and mountain-like solidity goes their love for camaraderie and conviviality. It is a rare occasion when a public place, be it a tony restaurant or humble eatery, does not host a group of Valdostani—young and old—having a glorious time together. Almost de rigueur, a postprandial, final toast with grappa triggers a burst of mountain songs. Even the local liqueur, Genepy des Alpes (alpine herbs steeped in grappa), takes the edge off the ninety-proof grape distillate.

We sampled Aosta's gastronomy and witnessed its conviviality at the Trattoria Praetoria, housed in an old restructured Roman building, and the next evening at the Borgo Antico, on the second floor of a medieval house—both right in the middle of town. When we expressed, half jokingly, our desire to work our way through the whole menu, the maître d' did not flinch but, with a smile, agreed to accommodate us with small samples of their specialties. Of course, being the season, they served us fresh porcini mushrooms prepared in all kinds of ways. Typically, both restaurants were hosting large groups of people, who, as a finish to their meal, passed around a *grolla.* Viva l'Aosta!

No other region's folklore is represented by the grolla (a word derived from holy "grail"), the cup of friendship: a finely carved pear-wood teapot-like contraption with at least four spouts—and up to as many as eight—from which friends sip as they pass it around the table. The contents? A hot blend of black coffee, red wine, and grappa, a mixture apt to melt away any enmity—as well as the ice on the roof.

Well represented by the grolla, wood is the medium of local

artists and artisans who extract out of it admirable artifacts, from statuaries to household implements, from intaglio to intarsio. We have seen their inspirations carved in a tree flanking a road, as if taken by an artistic impulse, an unexpected flight of fancy from an otherwise controlled temperament.

The local economy does not rely just on the sweat of the brow and the fruits of the land as in the past; it also takes ample advantage of another kind of natural gift: the absolute beauty of the land. Val d'Aosta is a winter-sports hub with some of the best skiing in Europe. With proud reasoning, the Valdostani boast of the fact that since their side of the Alps faces south, they enjoy sunnier slopes, still in daylight while the northern sides of the watershed, French or Swiss, are already in chilly shadow. The high trails of both Courmayeur at the foot of Monte Bianco/Mont Blanc and Cervinia at Monte Cervino/Matterhorn offer summer skiing, a great chance for bikini-clad beauties—and their Lothario counterparts—to show off their summer slaloming forms. Val d'Aosta's beautiful and rugged nature is four-seasonal: Spring, summer, and fall invite mountain hiking and climbing, white-water rafting and kayaking, fishing in the many Alpine lakes and streams, hang gliding from the high peaks into the valleys, or simply sightseeing. All done in a subdued, family manner.

The town of Aosta is the perfect spot to stay while taking day trips to the surrounding Alpine villages. The drive to Courmayeur takes only about an hour along a road filled with castles—Sarre, Aymavilles, Sarriod de la Tour, Saint Pierre—and amid forests of aspen and larch. In the fall when the larches' leaves turn, it seems as if the whole countryside is colored yellow gold. As the road winds closer and closer to Courmayeur, at each turn comes another glimpse of Monte Bianco as it looms bigger and bigger ahead. Cour-mayeur seems almost French, just like its name. Its pedestrian-only narrow streets are inlaid with perfectly aligned flat cobblestones, and bordered with exquisite shops. Every store, whether a ski shop or fashion boutique or the butcher or the baker, seems more ele-gantly appointed than the one before. Many cafes have (besides the usual stand-up bars for espresso) a cozy sitting area with comfort-able easy chairs surrounding a lit fireplace. High above, no matter where you are in the town, you see the splendid Monte Bianco, snow-covered all year long.

Driving along the road to Cogne, narrow and dizzyingly steep, at points its edges visibly crumbling down the precipice, made us marvel at those ancient Romans who managed to traverse this same way with their oxen-drawn wagons to collect iron from the mines. The same iron mines are still working today. Cogne is a slip of a vil-lage that does not show the elegance of Courmayeur, but it is also a major ski resort surrounded by magnificent scenery. Cogne lies at the entrance to the Parco Nazionale del Gran Paradiso—as the name implies, a paradise for sightseers and nature lovers. At the end of Val Savarenche and Val di Cogne, less than an hour's drive from Aosta, the park is a formidable mountain complex, home and ref-uge to a long list of mountain flora and fauna, their space shared by hikers who can follow marked paths from refuge to refuge.

Another destination for a day-trip from Aosta is the not-to-be-missed Cervinia. We took the road east from Aosta, and then north toward Mount Cervino or, as the Swiss call it from their side, the Matterhorn. Of all these Italian ski resorts, Cervinia is the one that looks most like a Swiss Alpine village (the real thing just a peak away), with its abundance of gaily painted log cabin-style condos, apartments, and hotels. If you stand in the center of town and turn around, you will find yourself surrounded on all sides by mountains covered with snow and glaciers. But the most eye-catching feature of the area is a distinctive single spike that shoots straight up into the crisp blue sky and immediately identifies this mountain as the Giant's Tooth.

On one of our recent visits to Cervinia, as we approached the town, the blue sky and the view of the mountains were suddenly swallowed by low banks of clouds. We had been warned about mountain driving. A breeze can blow the clouds up from the valleys and then—just a moment or two later—blows them away.

"Adjust your driving mode," we had read. "Be prepared for thick fog. Cattle tend to wander in the road." We had no such encounters, but we did reach the main square later then we had planned, almost at sunset. We parked, stretched a step or two, and had a look-around before our jaws dropped. A roundish hole had opened in the gray clouds, and in the middle of it, bathed in the pink gold light of sunset, stood Cervino's peak. A mirage? A miracle? An optical illusion? With camera in hand we clicked away until the curtains closed again and the vision was gone.

We just had to tell someone about this surprising experience. Who better than the staff of the local tourism office, half a block away? A young, elegant man there was a good sport trying to make sense of our babble. We stopped for a moment, then more quietly, one at a time, we described our sighting. "

"Oh," he said unperturbed, "it must be five o'clock." Calmly he explained that that phenomenon is no phenomenon at all: It is a command performance, happening every cloudy day at five on the nose. We left his office quite deflated, our excitement gone—and with the distinct feeling that the cool young man had pulled our legs. Later, when we had our photos printed, we had proof that our vision was real. The mountain peak glows in the hole in the clouds. The bell tower clock in the foreground marks five.

For those not inclined to outdoor activities, Val d'Aosta offers a gambling casino. Fifteen miles east of Aosta, Saint Vincent is a town totally out of Valdostano character, part fin-de-siècle spa (its Font Salutis, the old Fountain of Health, still offers miraculously curative waters), part 1980s modern, and all together totally dedicated to the hospitality industry. Its high-stakes gambling Casino de la Vallee, one of the few on Italian soil, attracts a great number of international players, now democratically interspersed by a slew of pedestrian slot machines. Although gambling is the main attraction, Saint Vincent also offers cultural and literary events of a national level (the Premio Saint Vincent is akin to the Pulitzer Prize). And, to complete the lively picture, Saint Vincent is home to many multi-starred restaurants. As in all of the Val d'Aosta, when it comes to food, there is no gamble.

ZUPPA VALPELLINENZE

Cabbage, Fontina, and White Bread Soup

The Valpelline is one of the valleys that from the tip of the Alps descends to join the central valley, close to Aosta. There are a few versions of this soup, each of which is the specialty of the low, mid or high Valpelline Valley. This version comes from the high valley, where it has been exposed to Swiss German influence.

1 small cabbage, approximately
   1 to 1¼ pounds
3 tablespoons unsalted butter
4–5 cloves
1 clove garlic
¼ teaspoon freshly grated nutmeg
Salt and pepper to taste
6 or 12 ½-inch slices Italian-style
   white bread, oven-toasted

4 ounces prosciutto, thinly sliced
   and cut into strips
5 ounces Fontina cheese,
   thinly sliced
1½ quarts well-seasoned
   beef broth, hot

PREHEAT the oven to 350°F.

PEEL OFF and discard the outer cabbage leaves. Cut out and discard the core. Separate the remaining leaves and boil them in salted water for about 5 minutes or until limp.

DRAIN the cabbage leaves, pat them dry with paper towels, and place them with 1½ tablespoons of butter in a soup pot. Stick the cloves into the garlic and add to the pot. Sauté over medium heat until the leaves are very tender and well cooked. Mix in the nutmeg, retrieve and discard the garlic clove, and add salt and pepper as desired.

LIGHTLY BUTTER an ovenproof soup tureen with a bit of the remaining butter. Make a layer of toast, followed by a layer of cabbage leaves, and topped with some strips of prosciutto and a slice of Fontina. Repeat the layering and finish with the last of the Fontina.

DOT THE FONTINA with the last of the butter. Pour enough of the hot beef broth over the layers to just barely cover them, and place the tureen in the preheated oven for about 10 minutes or until the soup has a thin, toasted crust on top. Serve immediately.

Serves 4–6 (depending on whether served as a one-dish meal or as a soup course)

COSTOLETTA VALDOSTANA
Veal Chop Stuffed with Fontina Cheese

4 veal chops, at least 1-inch thick	2 tablespoons milk
4–5 ounces Fontina cheese, sliced	Unflavored bread crumbs
Salt and pepper to taste	4 tablespoons unsalted butter
1 egg	White truffle shavings (optional)

PREHEAT the oven to 375°F.

BUTTERFLY the chops, up to their bones. Pound them to flatten them a bit, then fill each chop with a 1 ounce slice of Fontina. Seal the filled chops by squeezing their edges together. Add salt and pepper to taste.

BEAT the egg well, add the milk to it, then dip the chops in the mixture and pat them in the bread crumbs. Melt the butter in a skillet and once foamy, fry the chops in it. Cook on both sides, turning them when they're barely golden. Remove the chops to an ovenproof platter and bake them in the preheated oven for 3 or 4 minutes. Serve hot, with a few white truffle shavings if desired.

Serves 4

Torino and Piemonte

CRADLE OF THE NATION

*W*hen we think of a map of Italy as a page of a book, *Piemonte* appears to us in the upper left corner, as the very first word of the first paragraph to be read. This conforms not only with its geographical position but also with its prominence in the historical map of Italy. As a matter of fact, Piedmont boasts a long list of national firsts in many fields, from haute technology to haute fashion to haute cuisine . . . *pardon,* gastronomy.

The Gallicisms are not an affectation but are appropriate to the region, which has maintained a love/hate relationship with France since the time of Gaul, of which it was a province. Known as Gallia Cisalpina in Caesar's time, Piemonte has been independent from or tied to France on and off throughout history (the last annexation was from 1798 to 1814), with a stint as part of the kingdom of Sardinia under the House of Savoy. The French influence still manifests itself in the *Piemontese* dialect, just as much as the Italian influence is alive in the adjacent regions of France. It was Piemonte that sparked the movement that led to the Italian unification. In 1861 Torino (Turin) became a city of firsts: the first capital of Italy under Victor Emmanuel II of Savoy, first king of Italy, and the first to fly the first national flag, the Tricolor. Then in 1948, when the monarchy was voted off its throne, it was Piemonte that supplied the first president of the new Italian republic.

Torino, ex-capital of Italy and now capital of Piemonte, is one of the most elegant of Italian cities. Its aristocratic grandeur and formal lifestyle have gained the city the sobriquet "Italy's drawing room." And yet it is surprising how few people know it and how rarely they consider it a must-see. Perhaps this is because the *Torinesi,* known in Italy as industrious, solid, and not given to displays of emotion, will never toot their horn for themselves or their city. Torino did experience a sudden burst of renown in 2006 when it hosted the Winter Olympics in its stadium and in the surrounding Alpine towns, but since then the city seems to have retreated to its old reserved self.

The city was doted upon by the long line of dukes and kings of the House of Savoy that presided over its growth; there is something majestic and aristocratic in its architecture as if its whole core was designed for pomp and circumstance. Like Paris and unlike most Italian cities, it was built on a predetermined urban plan and with an eye to its future: Developed in an era of horses and buggies, the large tree-lined streets and avenues are of such spectacular size that they can still accommodate today's traffic. In return, the city invested heavily in the monarchy. Most of the streets, squares, and many parks (Torino is one of the greenest cities in Italy) are named after kings, queens, or princes, trunk and shoots of the Savoy genealogical tree, and there hardly exists a place in town without a monument to one of them. King Victor Emanuel II ordered many of the monuments at the end of the nineteenth century when the capital of Italy was moved from Torino to Florence and then to Rome. Having to be present at the monuments' inaugurations gave the bon vivant, jolly king a good reason to return frequently to his beloved Torino (and, as informed gossip went, to his many paramours).

But it is not necessary to be a king to fall for the city. Built on the banks of the Po ("majestic" is the most common adjective used to describe the Italian Mississippi) and of one of its tributaries, the Dora Riparia, hedged by rows of green hills, its horizon fenced by the nearby white-crowned Alps, this city has many things to offer besides its historic and aesthetic attractions.

Along with the firsts mentioned above, Torino can brag about being the birthplace of industrial Italy. Here the car industry took momentum with Fiat and Lancia; the Italian film industry began here; the fortified wine "vermouth" was concocted here; and a cocoa beverage was first turned into solid, exquisite chocolate here. Italian radio and the big band sound were born here, as was the fashion industry with the first Fashion Palace.

Friends, acquaintances, and mentors proudly revealed to us these and many other *Piemontesi* achievements. In an unexpected character reversal, their public official reticence turned, in private, into super-loquacity; they delivered facts, data, and dates with such fired-up enthusiasm that it was hard for us to keep up. Perhaps the austere character is changing with the new generations.

In a jesting mood, a friend told us that a writer once compared Torino to a beautiful Victorian lady who, with fashionable modesty, hid her voluptuous curves behind sober clothes.

"Finally now," he added, using as a metaphor the young ladies on motor scooters dashing around Piazza Castello, "the Old Dowager has lifted her skirts and given a cancan kick!"

Piazza Castello, with or without young ladies, has to be among the most beautiful squares in the world. The Piazza, its contour defined by the lace of its porticoes, is a truly magical space: It encloses the architectural marvels of the Royal Palace, the Royal Theater, the Church of San Lorenzo, the Prefettura Palace and, like an island in the middle of it all, Palazzo Madama and the castle, from which the square takes its name. Standing in Piazza Castello feels like being in the middle of a grand opera stage. It is the heart of the city, the appropriate spot from which to start a tour of the town.

Torino is an eminently walkable city and it is on foot that its graciousness is best savored. To get to know the city, all you need is an open, receptive mind and a good pair of walking shoes. From the porticoed embrace of Piazza Carlo Felice, walk down Via Roma and while your attention is totally taken by the elegant shops, cafes, and bookstores along the way, Piazza San Carlo will sneak up and surprise you. This square explains the image of the city as a "drawing room." It is huge, yet the pastel colors of the walls, the white stucco flourishes, and the decorative wrought-iron street lamps, make it a warm, comfortable environment. People stroll along or stand in small groups, engaged in conversation. It is all so polite and proper—even the car traffic is hushed—that soon your eyes might search for teacups and antimacassars.

Within a short walk, another piazza plays the same surprise trick: It is Piazza Carignano, dominated by the impressive, baroque palazzo of the same name. It is on this square that one of the city's major institutions, the Ristorante del Cambio, in operation continuously since

1757, opens its doors. In the midst of gilded and mirrored baroque, here met—and still meet—the city's aristocracy, industrialists, and merchants. Most notably, it was once the meeting place of the politicians from Palazzo Carignano, then the house of the Parliament. It is here at Ristorante del Cambio that Camillo Benso, count of Cavour, prime minister, and mastermind of Italy's unity in 1870, had lunch every day. From his table, Cavour could see Palazzo Carignano and, the anecdote goes, he would interrupt his leisurely, protracted lunch only if his assistant summoned him from his office window for some urgent reason—which just goes to show where priorities lie in Torino when it comes to food. Cavour's table is still there, marked by a bronze plaque. His favorite dish of *finanziera* (a delicate ragout of veal, beef, chicken livers and the essential cock's combs and wattles) is still on the menu, together with all the classic Piemontese wines and dishes, and his preferred dessert, *bunet,* a chocolate pudding with whipped cream.

Stroll on and turn left, following the invitation of an open doorway. Up a few marble steps, you'll be inside of the domed Galleria Subalpina, a rococo jewel. Filtered sunlight and the arrangement of flower beds give it the intimacy of an elegant parlor. Into it open the windows of fashion shops, bookstores, and Caffè Baratti, another of Torino's institutions, a century-plus-old coffeehouse where proper gentlemen still get together for an aperitif at midday (a Piemontese Vermouth, naturally) and proper ladies still meet in the afternoon for tea and pastries.

We wager that after the obligatory stop at Baratti, on your way out you will be carrying a small parcel tied with a ribbon; it's not easy to resist temptation and walk away from Baratti without some of its traditional sweets. But then, if you resist, it will be a short-lived victory: The town is strewn with *pasticcerie* (pastry shops), from which alluring aromas emanate. In any of these establishments, it is impossible to ignore the call of the *gianduia,* a chocolate morsel made with super-refined chocolate and hazelnut flour, This treat is so much the epitome of Torino that the term "gianduia" is also used to define a real, hard-core Torinese citizen. Traditionally, old established artisan families have made gianduia and other chocolates by hand, and they are considered of the highest quality, surpassing (in taste and price) the renowned Swiss chocolates.

When we meandered along Torino's main streets, we were constantly stopped in our tracks by an impressive palazzo. Whether medieval, Renaissance, or baroque, each one seems to shelter an internationally important museum or gallery. They range from the Egyptian Museum, second in importance only to Cairo's, and the Sabauda Gallery, rich in works by Flemish and Italian masters, to the unique Furniture Museum, with its vast collection of fifteenth- to seventeenth-century furniture, and the Gallery of Modern Art, which exhibits works by all the modern European masters. Not far from Piazza Castello is the Mole Antoneliana, a domed building with a slim, tall spire on top. The Mole (Italian for "huge") is visible from all over the city—at five-hundred-plus feet it is the tallest masonry building in Europe. Like the Eiffel Tower in Paris, it has become Torino's trademark.

But to be in Torino and only nourish the spirit would be a serious, unforgivable mistake. Here, food and wine are taken seriously. And for good reason: Many of its foods are unmatched outside of Piemonte. The white truffles from Alba seem to be born only to accompany a fondue of Fontina cheese. The rice paddies in the vicinity of the towns of Vercelli and Novara, the same ones that serve the Orta area, also provide Carnaroli, Vialone, or arborio rice to Piemonte for the making of a real risotto. A prosciutto of venison can be made only with Alpine deer and a *bagna cauda* (hot dip), perhaps the emblem of Piemontese food, should be made only with fresh vegetables from the area. Butter, oil, abundant garlic, anchovies, and truffles are turned into a savory dipping sauce and kept hot on a food warmer in the center of the table. Diners dip (*bagna* means "bathed") a mixture of raw vegetables in this warm sauce: the whitest cardoons; crisp red, green, and yellow bell pepper strips; tender celery stalks; carrot sticks; white hearts of lettuce. It is a convivial, warm-up event, accompanied by a robust red Barolo; if there is any hot bagna left after the vegetables are gone, it is an old peasant custom to mix eggs with it, then scramble it all and serve on toasts. Bagna cauda is loaded with garlic, and according to a local joke, this explains the laconic character of the Torinesi: They must keep their mouths shut or the garlic breath will be overpowering.

Local wines go with local food: unthinkable that a *stracotto*, a tender pot roast of beef, would be not cooked with a full-bodied red Piemontese wine. Some of the best and most prestigious Italian wines come from Piemonte. The hilly soil, sheltered by the Alps in a misty climate, produces the classy reds of Barbera, Barolo, Barbaresco, Nebiolo, Spanna, Gattinara, Grignolino, Dolcetto, and the noblest whites of Gavi and Cortese.

If there is any doubt about the respect that food and wine command here, amble along Via Lagrange, a street in the very heart of fashionable downtown. An unbroken succession of shops will bewitch the gustatory sense. A still-life window display of goodies in a *gastronomia* shop is matched, on the opposite side of the street, by the pasta store with fresh, dry, long, short, filled, wrapped, white, green, please-take-me-home pasta. A butcher shop follows, featuring *razza Piemontese,* meat from a Piemontese breed of cattle that is not only delicious but also special, they assure us—it has fewer calories and less cholesterol than flounder! And then, here comes another ubiquitous Pasticceria and a *Baita del Formaggio* (cheesemaker's mountain dairy hut), with all the cheese specialties you can dream of and then some. It is followed by the *Casa della Trippa;* Yes, tripe, in its many variations, is the only item sold there (it feels good to know there are kindred souls, somewhere). Next, a *Bottega del Maiale,* a monument to all that the humble hog produces for the human race, bacon to prosciutto, sausage to salami, tail to snout. Drag yourself away from the *Gelateria* window and be lured across the street by a *Frutta e Verdura* store; forbidden or not, its fruits and vegetables look so good they could have come directly from the Garden of Eden.

During our last visit to Torino, we stopped at the Hotel Venezia, an old-world-style establishment of fin-de-siècle vintage, with perhaps "old" being the operative word. Our room access was through ten-foot-tall double doors, opening onto a tennis-court-sized, fifteen-foot-high ceilinged room. Two enormous French doors overlooking the street took care of one wall; the rest were furnished with massive armoires and chests of drawers. The bed, although somewhat lumpy, was of imperial size, putting to shame a king-size one. The light from the central chandelier and two upright lampshades was at best crepuscular. A corner of the room, perhaps an eight-by-six-foot space, had been walled in and transformed into a bathroom; the open shower washed everything in sight with a touchy stream of now gelid, now boiling water. But then the moderate price and the excellent location of the *albergo*—just behind the magnificent Piazza Castello, in walking distance from everything—plus the friendly and cordial attitude of the personnel, from porter to concierge to manager, more than compensated for the room's quaintness.

Somewhat exhausted after our day of walking, we asked the concierge if he could recommend an eatery in the immediate vicinity, a trattoria where we could mix with the locals and partake of local food. He recommended, at less than a ten-minute walk away, the Ristorante Tre Galline located on Vicolo Tre Galline (Three Hens Alley). We found the name unusual in a city where most streets have historical names, but one never knows what Piemontese chickens are capable of. Moreover, the Tre Galline turned out to be quite a few tiers above the hoi polloi level we were expecting.

The place was quietly elegant, a white-linen, fresh-cut-flower kind of establishment. The young, refined waitresses (it's noticeable that most servers in northern Italy are women, while it would be rare to see a waitress in the south) were attentive and courteous. They served us a glass of bubbly white Prosecco and a basket of *grissini* (inimitable, thin, crisp breadsticks, another one of Torino's glories) to give us time to peruse the menu. One of its pages was dedicated to the day's specials with most of the entrees having a qualification, such as chicken *biologico,* or veal *biologico,* or beef *biologico.* We guessed it meant "organic." When we asked, the waitress kindly explained that it meant the animals were fed only *cose buone,* good things.

Considering the long walk we had taken, we really didn't need the help of an antipasto to tease our appetite. The theoretical role of the antipasto, as the ancient Romans devised, is as an *ante-prandium,* a kind of small exercise to stimulate one's appetite and taste buds in preparation for the real thing. A superfluous exercise, that evening.

Yet, we proceeded—purely in the interest of knowledge—with a *soufflè Torinese,* a small unmolded cup of creamed spinach and ricotta, with a whiff of nutmeg; and an equally small portion of caponet, the Piemontese way of disposing of zucchini flowers, stuffed with a mixture of minced meats and cheese, and then fried. As a concession to raw meat lovers, we had a sample of **Carpaccio,** a Piedmont classic: a preparation of thin slices of raw meat dressed with oil and slivers of Parmigiano or truffle. And then for main courses, a melt-in-the-mouth *agnello al forno,* baked milk-fed baby lamb, a real baby, butchered much younger than ever allowed in the United States. The *bollito misto* that followed not only gave sustenance to the dinner, but being one of our favorite dishes, we used it as comparison point with other regional bollitos. The recipe calls for slowly boiled beef brisket, veal cheek, veal tongue, guinea hen, and pork sausage which are served in steaming moist slices, with the condiment of two *bagnet* sauces, a green one (parsley, olive oil, anchovy) and a red one (spicier, with a tomato base). The waitress suggested a Barbaresco to accompany the entrees, "It's one of our great wines." We agreed—deep red, robust, somewhat austere, the wine definitely hit the mark.

We honored the old count of Cavour with bunet for dessert. It turned out to be a real Torinese dinner, and a memorable one. At the end we felt biologici ourselves, having been fed only cose buone.

:::::::

A boat ride on the Po offers a respite from walking and provides the traveler with the opportunity to see the city from another perspective. At one stop, you can transfer for a steep cable-car ride to the top of one of Torino's highest hills. It is there that the Basilica of Superga was built to celebrate the victory over the French in 1706, a turning point in the history of Piemonte.

The Basilica is certainly of special architectural and historical interest, but it is the view from its dominating position that makes the whole exercise rewarding. At your feet lies the city and beyond it emerge the hills, row separated from row by a faint mist, while above them, at the far horizon, the sweeping arc of the Alps rises and floats. On the high peaks of the Moncenisio, the San Bernardo, the Monte Bianco, and the Gran Paradiso mountains, the perennial snows glisten in a sight that will remain with you for a long time. It brings to mind the poem "Piemonte," by Giosuè Carducci (a star in the Italian poets' firmament):

> *Su le dentate, scintillanti vette,*
> *Salta il camoscio, tuona la valanga*
> *Dai ghiacci immani rotolando*
> *Per le selve croscianti . . .*
> *. . . Salve, Piemonte!*

> On the jagged, glistening peaks
> Leaps the antelope, thunders the avalanche
> From the immense glaciers rumbling
> Into splintering woods . . .
> . . . Hail, Piedmont!

The scene is like an embossed calling card, an open door, an irresistible invitation to come and meet the rest of Piemonte.

Heading east and south from Torino, in a triangular fashion, we stopped at Asti to taste the famous bubbly wine, the Asti Spumante; then on to Bra, the town where the Slow Food movement was founded in the mid-1980s by traditionalists in response to the proliferation of fast food (the McDonald's and their ilk); and ended up in Alba, world capital of the white truffle. The truffle, especially the white one, takes on legendary proportions in this little town where the famous *Fiera del Tartufo* (Truffle Fair) has been held every October for over seventy years. We were lucky to be there in November and therefore able to find a hotel room (an impossibility during the fiera), yet still be in the right season to partake of this extraordinary delicacy—extraordinary not only for flavor, but also price.

We spent more than an hour having a conversation with Angelo Feltrin, the head of tourism for the Langhe and Roero regions and, he proudly told us, a runner in New York marathons. We came away with an armload of books and pamphlets dedicated to the area's renowned specialty. There is even a National Truffle Study Center, a scientific institute whose aim is to learn more about the truffle and safeguard its survival. Huge banners across Alba's main streets laud Giacomo Morra, the "King of Truffles" and inventor of a folk cookery linked to the precious mushroom. Morra was such an ardent promoter of the truffle that in the late 1940s he sent a couple of kilograms to President Truman, who, being totally unfamiliar with this food, had them boiled (horrors!), and to Winston Churchill, who was so impressed he actually made a journey to Alba for a more thorough tasting.

Langhe and Roero, named for the nobles who once owned the land in the Middle Ages, together consist of a small area carved out of southern Piemonte, and are known for their production of the best red wines in Italy, such as Barbaresco, Nebbiolo d'Alba,

Barbera d'Alba, Dolcetto di Diano, Dolcetto di Dogliani, Barolo, and the sweet white Moscato. In fact, if you take a drive along the backroads of the area through the quiet and verdant country-side, you will come upon all these tiny towns: Diano, Barbesco, Dogliani, Barolo. . . . And, as we usually discover, the small off-the-beaten-track roads reveal the best scenery and most pleasant surprises.

On the agricultural scene the Langhe produces the tastiest of vegetables—a must for bagna cauda—as well as hazelnuts (Alba is home to the manufacturer of Nutella, that soft chocolate-nut spread all Italian children grow up on), and of course, the centerpiece of all, the truffle. The hills of the Langhe are also known for their myriad castles, not to mention some of the thickest winter fog in any part of Italy.

For our dinners in Alba, of course we wanted to try any dish that had truffles on it, which, naturally, are unavoidable entries on any menu of Alba's many restaurants. On our last evening, we chose Enoclub, a restaurant in a brick-walled cellar, with perfectly appointed tables covered by white linen tablecloths and vases of fresh flowers. You could get the thinnest shavings of truffle on top of just about everything, and though we wanted to try the famous appetizer, *fonduta*—melted Fontina, eggs, and cream, topped with a few shavings of truffle—the cost (practically half of the rest of the meal) seemed excessive. A cheaper alternative was the *uovo in cocotte con tartufo bianco,* a poached egg in a cup with stirred cream and Parmigiano, cooked in an oven with a sprinkle of grated truffle on top. For pasta courses, the ravioli *plin,* meaning "pinch," are a Piemonte specialty in which tiny ravioli have their edges pinched; *tajarin ai funghi porcini* is thin fettuccini with a wild, aromatic por-cini mushroom sauce.

Interestingly, the wine list here—in this center of the production of Italy's best wines—contained selections from all over
the world, including Australia, Chile, Israel, and even the United
States, the first time we had ever seen American wines on a wine
list anywhere in Italy. As rewarding as it was to see these wines on
the menu, we stuck to a Dolcetto d'Alba, a bright ruby red, easy-
drinking wine, and a favorite of ours. This one was just a tinge *friz-
zante* (sparkling), perfectly appropriate for a toast to ourselves. The
young waitress, pleased at our contented enthusiasm, refilled our
glasses: "This is on us," she said.

We walked back to the hotel, cocooned by a thick cold fog,
feeling very warm and cozy inside.

BAGNA CAUDA

Raw Vegetables with Anchovy / Garlic Dip

The success of a bagna cauda rests on the quality and (though not necessarily) the variety of the vegetables. Choose the freshest, most tender vegetables available on the market.

VEGETABLES:

1 red bell pepper	½ head of cauliflower
1 green bell pepper	3–4 small (tender) carrots
1 finocchio (anise or fennel bulb)	1–2 heads of Belgian endive
3–4 hearts of celery ribs	
(the whiter the better)	

WASH, CLEAN, AND TRIM the vegetables and cut into manageable, dippable strips. Keep refrigerated before serving.

SAUCE:

4 tablespoons unsalted butter	Salt and pepper to taste
4 garlic cloves	(Optional: To cut its sharpness,
8 anchovy fillets	soak the garlic in ½ cup of milk
¾ cup olive oil	for 2 hours, or overnight.)

MELT the butter in an earthenware casserole dish. Mince the garlic finely, or squeeze it with a garlic press, and sauté in the butter for 5 minutes.

MASH the anchovies into a paste and stir into the melted butter. Slowly stir in the olive oil and let the mixture bubble over low heat, stirring occasionally, for 30 minutes. Add salt and pepper to taste.

TRANSFER the sauce to a warming device on the table (or to individual candle- or oven-warmed cups) and dip the vegetables into the very warm sauce. You may also use long forks, fondue style.

SERVE with a good bottle of Barolo.

Serves 6.

CARPACCIO

Thin-Sliced Raw Beef, Dressed in Olive Oil, Lemon, and Parmigiano Slivers

The whole preparation should be done just before serving; the meat should keep its red color.

1½–2 ounces of beef per portion (approximately), sliced from a semi-frozen piece of lean beef (lean tenderloin or top round)	Parmigiano Reggiano cheese shavings White truffle shavings (optional) Fresh, thinly sliced porcini mushrooms (optional)
Extra-virgin olive oil, as needed	1 tablespoon minced flat leaf parsley
Fresh lemon juice, as needed	1 tablespoon capers, minced

SLICE the meat as thinly as possible (ideally using a meat slicer), and gently pound it paper-thin.

BARELY moisten the serving plates with olive oil; line the plates with the meat and dribble with olive oil and lemon juice. Distribute the Parmigiano shavings; add truffle shavings and mushroom slices if desired. Mix the minced parsley and the minced capers together and sprinkle over the plates.

SERVE as an entree for a spring/summer lunch or as an antipasto.

Serves 1

Trentino-Alto Adige

*S*kirting Lake Garda on our left, we entered Trentino-Alto Adige, the northernmost region of Italy and for a brief moment, fantasized that, if instead of a car we were driving a speed-boat, we would be trailing a rooster-tail of wine. It would have as many hues as the wines grown along the Val Lagarina, the valley that led us north from Verona to Trento. This colorful image was suggested by the sea of vineyards that flank the road on both sides and extend throughout the length and breadth of the valley, rising to the hilltops that border it. The vines are grown in pergola fashion, suspending leaves and grapes in an undulating carpet six feet or so above the ground. From the high perspective of the road, the wall-to-wall vineyards give the appearance of gentle waves, encouraging the illusion of navigating on a green sea.

The valley is daughter of the Adige, one of the great Italian rivers. Born in the Tyrolean Alps, the Adige flows past Bolzano and Trento, and then cuts through Verona to plunge into the Adriatic

Sea just south of Venice, joining the River Po in its delta. The Adige's fertile banks have been particularly hospitable to vineyards for more than three thousand years; testimony are discoveries of Etruscan wine vessels and other archaeological wine-cult troves, and the area has been producing wine since then. And very good wine, at that—about forty-two different kinds of reds, whites, and rosé, the appreciation of which was passed on by the Etruscans to the Romans, and then to Venetian merchants and Austrian lords, and currently to the world, through the exportation of superior Pinot Noir, Merlots, and Chardonnays and the fashionable Pinot Grigio.

To test this abundance of wines, we made a stop along the road near the town of Rovereto, not far from the upper tip of Lake Garda. Up a long steep hill, overlooking the vineyard-covered valley, is the Castel Noarna, owned by the Zani family which has established an up-and-coming winery there. Our host, Marco, and his elderly father showed us around their eleventh-century castle, part of which they have made into living spaces, and part of which is available for large parties. Throughout the castle are windows that open on the surrounding countryside. A visit to the cantina reveals barrel after barrel of wine, all made from the vineyards on the family's thirty-acre property. It was lunchtime, so along with our picnic of grilled chicken, *prosciutto di San Daniele* (the best-known prosciutto of the Veneto and Trentino regions), cheeses, and bread, we sampled as many of Marco's wines as he was willing to ply us with. The wine tasting turned into a blissful afternoon with a succession of flinty whites and a flowery rosé or two.

"Alto Adige is one of the major Italian sources of rosé," Marco told us.

But then he produced a fragrant red Cabernet Sauvignon that we particularly liked, even if he has named it "Mercuria" after a lady unjustly accused of witchcraft and imprisoned in the castle in 1648.

After a much-needed nap stretched out on lawn chairs conveniently located at the castle's entrance hall, we headed back on the Strada Statale from Rovereto to the city of Trento. A mountain, the first of the *Dolomiti,* rose dramatically in front of us, reminding us of the scene in Fellini's film *Amarcord,* when the huge ship, the *Rex,* startlingly appears out of the fog off the Adriatic coast. Our reverie was routed by glorious mountain views, crystal clear on an autumn day, which beckon us north. More and more of the Dolomites appeared until we were surrounded by mountains all the way to Trento.

The names of villages, towns, rivers, and mountain peaks tell us that we are treading on sacred Italian soil. This is the heart of *Italia Irredenta*—"Unredeemed Italy"—all those territories that by reason of geography, more than of culture, belonged to Italy but were under Austrian domination for most of the nineteenth century and into the early part of the twentieth century. The redemption of Trento and Trieste and of all the land in between, especially South Tyrol, was the battle cry that led Italy into World War I. In Italy the "Great War" was considered "our war," Germany and the Austro-Hungarian Empire "our" enemy. The generations that came of age between the two world wars were taught to give to this ground the value and the respect due to an altar. They were brought up to honor in deed and in thought all the martyrs and all the heroes and all the towns and all the mountains and rivers that were the actors and the stage for that conflagration. Valsugana, Bassano, Valgardena, Monte Stelvio, Monte Grappa, the Piave and Isonzo rivers, Ortigara, Cima Dodici, and Caporetto are the names of murderous battles, of bloody defeats and, after four years of trench-war mud and sacrifice, finally Vittorio Veneto, the name of the town where the rout stopped and the counterattack ended in the Italian victory. The Alps' watershed line was made to mark the new border, and all foreign lands south of it were 'redeemed' and became Italian. These battles became the inspiration for the now melancholy, now fiery Alpine chants, mournful poems, and triumphal songs, as well as a romantic heroic literature fanned by Gabriele d'Annunzio and, later, by Ernest Hemingway, who served here as an ambulance driver. Those Italian generations sang and recited and read it all, with bowed heads and overflowing hearts.

Today, Trentino-Alto Adige is an autonomous region formed by the two independent provinces of Trentino, with Trento as its capital city, and Alto Adige/South Tyrol, with Bolzano/Bozen as its capital. In this province, the widely used slash (/) may be interpreted as a unifying or, depending on the point of view, a dividing sign: After long fought and sometimes violent vicissitudes, in 1972 the 68 percent ethnic Austrian majority won the right to its own language, schools, and culture. Alto Adige/South Tyrol now has two legal languages, German and Italian, and every written document or sign has its ethnic mirror, separated (or united?) by a slash. Those who lose out are the *Ladini,* a 4 percent minority, the original inhabitants of the area even before the Etruscans. Given its proximity to the Brenner/Brennero pass, one of the few Alpine gateways between Italy and Central Europe, this border region has always been a transitional slash, its strategic value appreciated throughout history by invaders and defenders, by popes and emperors.

One testament to its tumultuous history—and an important visual element for us non-historians—is the incredible number of castle-fortresses and manors (three hundred fifty in Alto Adige alone) erected in the region, most of them in excellent condition, many turned into museums or hotels or *gasthaüser/ristoranti*. They are the gilding of the lily, an addition to the region's natural beauty, which is already exceptional and unique. The many mountain massifs, decorated by permanent sparkling snows and glaciers, are mirrored in and multiplied by the hundreds of emerald-green or sky-blue high mountain lakes, big and small.

Besides the pure enjoyment of peaceful beauty, or of sailing, fishing, or windsurfing, these lakes also offer unexpected rewards to the anthropologically and archaeologically inclined. Many of the lakes' shores are like archives of the evolutionary steps of man, which trace his comings and goings in this zone for over ten thousand years. It is here, in the Paleolithic era, that some primordial, upwardly mobile man moved his first abode out of the caves. He upgraded to huts built on stilts on the shore of a lake, Lago di Ledro, and created a lake-dwelling community. The discovery of ancient foundries and metal artifacts near Lago delle Piazze indicates that our ancestor then graduated into the Bronze Age. These lakes, valleys, and mountains are a living record of the eventful passing of human history. In this northernmost region, in this attic of Italy, it is fun to rummage in the old chests and find capsules of antiquity.

Trento is one of the large repositories of this history, even if it would hardly qualify as an "old chest." It is a city of about one hundred thousand, protected on one side by the rushing Adige River and on the others by the high pastures and rocky peaks of the Dolomites. Trento made the books of international history in the sixteenth century when it was the seat of the Council of Trent. Called by Pope Paul III, the council convened bishops of the church and high personages of the court of Emperor Charles V. The council lasted almost two decades and resulted in a number of milestones in church reform, still considered important today. Aside from the philosophical and ecumenical legislation reached, the powerful assemblage brought fame and, while the high times lasted, prosperity to the city.

You can find a good view of Trento from Dosso, the flat-topped hillock just across the Adige River. On its top is a neoclassical temple dedicated to Cesare Battisti, one of the three *irredentisti,* Italian heroes and martyrs hanged as traitors and spies by the Austrians in 1916 during World War I. The deed was done on the ramparts of the Castello del Buonconsiglio, making it—and Trento—a national shrine.

From the temple's belvedere the city below appears as a three-dimensional map, its architectural features like an open history book: the Roman Tower of Augustus, the Lombard-Romanesque cathedral, the massive thirteenth-century Castello del Buonconsiglio ("of Good Counsel"), the baroque fountain of Neptune, and the Renaissance church of Saint Mary Major and its campanile. The view should be a prelude to a stroll through the city, and in fact, just before the dinner hour, all *Trentini* seem to be doing just that—the *passeggio,* sauntering along the many streets, avenues, and squares open to pedestrians only, no wheels allowed.

The city of Trento does not make much official use of the bilingual slash, but the influences of Italy and of Austria are here; they mix subtly in the architecture, in the people, and in the gastronomy. The food is an elegant mixture of Lombard, Venetian, and

Austrian cuisines, borrowing a little from each and making it difficult, at times, to see where one begins and the other ends. It also reflects the roots of its people who, like the food, are a subtle mix, in character and physique, of the three ethnic groups. Although today the Trentini are for the most part urban and elegant, they are descended from mountain stock, as defined by the term *Alpini*, the name of the outdoors-ruddy, strong, and rugged people with their famous predilection for grappa.

So, when in Trento, do as the Trentini do: Promenade before dinner, make a stop once in a while to admire the buildings' unusual frescoed facades, take a rest at one of the many elegant cafes, and have a shot of grappa. It will not make an Alpino out of you, but—in moderation—it will definitely give a new spring to your step.

As in any other Italian city, restaurants abound. There are traditional *birrerie* (beer halls) and classic or modern restaurants. One such is Ai Due Mori, located in a quietly modern setting, and yet with a family-run feeling. Impossible to pass up are the **Canederli in brodo,** dumplings that are traditionally tennis ball–sized *knodel* but here are closer in size to golf balls, made with old bread, milk, eggs, calf liver, and a touch of nutmeg, poached and served in chicken broth. Other memorable first courses are *tagliolini con mirtilli e salvia,* very thin homemade fettuccini with blueberries mixed into the pasta, and a sage sauce with cream and a few more *mirtilli* on top—they are similar to blueberries, except that mirtilli are much sweeter and more fragrant; and a very creamy risotto with porcini mushrooms. For a main course we enjoyed a fork-tender *maiale in saor,* a loin of pork steeped in vinegar, then cooked in milk with mountain herbs and rosemary. To keep with local customs, it comes with a grilled—and fashionably thin—slice of polenta and a dollop of *crauti*. As in the Veneto region, polenta is a basic food staple of Alto Adige, as much as *crauti / krauts* is of the Tyrol. But, unlike the Veneto where polenta has a mushy consistency, the Trentini like it firmer and often grilled. In many Trento eateries, as a reminder of the closeness to Austria and the Viennese tradition, a cart of rich pastries is wheeled to the table, enough to fill one's allotment of sweet calories for at least a year. We indulged in a *Strudel di Frutta (Apfelstrudel)*, figuring that by choosing a fruit pastry, we were being more calorie conscious. Besides, we didn't want to offend the region by passing up its classic dessert.

As you travel north, you find the vineyards making more and more space for fruit trees and apple orchards, for which the region is famous. In spring when the orchards are in bloom and the mountain pastures are covered by wild flowers, the whole area competes for a spot as one of the Seven Wonders of the World. About thirty miles north of Trento, the Adige River takes a swift turn to the left just at the doorstep of Bolzano / Bozen.

Once in Bolzano / Bozen, the slash appears to be mostly a formality. The city is roughly the same size as Trento but, aesthetically, there is no mistaking that this one is in the heart of South Tyrol, a feeling promoted by the widely used German Gothic lettering and Tyrolese architecture. The citizenry is exceptionally and consistently hospitable, but in a more composed and formal way compared to that of the more instinctive and volatile residents of the Italian regions to the south.

"Tourism is one of our main industries," said Signor Giovannelli, "and ignoring it would be no less than killing the goose of the golden egg."

Signor Giovannelli is the manager of the Park Hotel and its

Belle Epoque restaurant. He has the poise and bearing of someone born to the task; his family name is Italian, but there must be a slash in his background from the way some of his consonants have a Germanic ring. And when speaking to his assistant, he reverts to fluent and rushing German.

"Actually we cannot ignore any of the aspects of our economy. Our province is not big and most of it is mountains. We have to take good care of whatever little we have. Quantity for us comes way behind quality." He paused, as if to underline that quality is a special local commodity.

"By focusing on quality," he continued on the subject of food, "we can take advantage of the many small-scale producers who will supply only first-class, locally grown ingredients."

The local cuisine, with its knodels, krauts, rich *goulash,* Wiener schnitzels, Apfelstrudels, and speck (a hog leg which has been smoked and cured, then pressed), remains faithful to the Austrian roots, but also doesn't disdain—and here comes a slash—using traditional Trentino dishes.

"Or at least," added Mr. Giovannelli with a smile, "we make a good interpretation of them. Here we are very attached to our traditions."

To illustrate, he mentioned that in many South Tyrol villages, on special days, people still wear the traditional lederhosen and dirndl skirts. Love for folkloric music is also very much alive. Each village has its own band and some have more than one. We could almost hear the windowpanes rattling at the sound of the happy, bouncy, cumulative "Oompah, oompah! Oompah-pah!"

The roads winding through Trentino Alto Adige are well kept and an invitation to travel, though a little bit less so during deep winter. At almost every turn and in every season, they deliver awe-inspiring scenery. Quantity here competes with Quality. The admirable cleanliness and tidiness of the landscape could appear staged: white-splotched brown cows choreographed in scrubbed-green pastures; wooden chalets and whitewashed villages positioned just so to counterbalance the majestic presence of the mountains; and waterfalls springing from high up, adding feathery motion to static scenery, with streams rumbling and foaming below. It all looks like a postcard-perfect picture, and one expects at any time to hear the echo of well-modulated yodeling reverberating down the valley.

Besides the many natural and urban attractions, a strong magnet to the region is the Dolomites. The jagged, pinnacled mountains, sprouting straight up from velvety pastures, are a treasure that Trentino-Alto Adige has to share with bordering Veneto. But, even so, nobody should begrudge a slice of a very rich cake. It has to be savored slowly. Heading west, we stopped at the top of the winding road at the Sella Pass, then slightly farther (or about two hundred white-knuckles hairpin turns later) at the Pordoi Pass. We got there around sunset; the mountains' vertical walls of pure Dolomite limestone, made of primordial algae and coral reefs, drank in the sun and took its color, snows and glaciers flashing its passage.

It is all quite heady. Like a shot of grappa. Or two.

CANEDERLI IN BRODO
Bread Dumplings in Chicken Broth

4 ounces unsalted butter
1¼ pounds day-old,
   crustless bread, shredded
2 cups of milk
4 large eggs, beaten
3½ ounces unbleached all-purpose
   flour (or as needed)

¼ teaspoon nutmeg
½ teaspoon salt
3 tablespoons minced
   flat-leaf parsley
10 cups chicken broth

CREAM the butter in a mixing bowl, add the bread, and blend well. Stir-ring, add a little milk, then the beaten eggs. Continuing to stir, slowly add the flour, alternating with the milk until you obtain a smooth paste of reasonable consistency, almost doughy. Add the nutmeg, salt, and parsley and blend well, kneading the paste/dough for a few minutes. It should be shapeable into little balls; if it crumbles, add a little milk, if too soft, add a little flour. Let the paste/dough rest for 30 minutes or so.

WHILE LETTING THE DOUGH REST, put the chicken broth in a pot and bring to a slow boil.

SHAPE the paste/dough into a little ball *(canederlo/knodel)* about 1¾-inch in diameter. Test one ball by putting it into the boiling broth: It should hold together, retaining its shape. If not, add more flour to the paste/dough and blend well. Test again, if necessary. Make canederli with the remaining compound, and cook them in the broth for 10 to 12 minutes. Serve warm in soup bowls with the broth.

AN ALTERNATIVE: With a slotted spoon, scoop the canederli/knodels from the broth and put in a serving bowl. Serve as accompaniment to goulash, in what is a common meal both in Trentino and Alto Adige.

Serves 6

GOULASH DI MANZO
Beef Goulash

1½ pounds onions
4 tablespoons olive oil (or lard)
2 pounds top round of beef,
    cut in 2½-inch chunks
1 cup dry red wine
2 tablespoons red wine vinegar
Salt and pepper to taste
2 tablespoons paprika

1 teaspoon cumin
2 bay leaves
2 cups water (or beef broth)
2 garlic cloves
1 tablespoon unsalted butter
Peel of half a lemon
Juice of half a lemon

CUT the onion in rings and sauté in a heavy pot with the oil (or lard). When translucent, add the beef and brown it. Stir in the wine and deglaze the pot, if necessary. Add the vinegar, salt, pepper, paprika, cumin, and bay leaves. Mix in one cup of water (or beef broth), cover the pot, and let it simmer for about 1½ hours. Check and stir once in a while, adding more water or broth if it's too dry. The consistency should be stew-like. In the meantime, mince together the garlic and lemon peel, mix with the butter, and add with the lemon juice to the goulash. Cook another 15 minutes or so—the meat should be tender enough to be cut with a fork— and serve with the canederli/knodel.

Serves 6

Veneto

THE THREE VENICES

*V*enezia is the capital of Veneto, that large area that used to go from Lake Garda in the west to the Adriatic Sea and Trieste in the east. Now it has been turned into three autonomous regions and renamed, with a touch of originality, *Le Tre Venezie*.

"The Three Venices" makes one think of those absurd, unsolvable mathematical puzzles: Take one Venezia, multiply it by three, equals . . . impossible. Like a Mobius strip, it would twist on itself and still come up "Venezia." Unique.

Venezia does not need an introduction. Venezia's unmistakable calling card is Venezia. It does not need adjectives or explanations, just as Everest doesn't need "Mount" and Sahara doesn't need "Desert." Venezia is always as new as today and as old as its first people who, seeking refuge from marauding barbarians, took over the one-hundred-odd islets of the lagoon and made it their residence. How it slowly emerged from the sea as a city, how it became a world power against which all other powers had to compare and compete, is a portent of nature and of history.

Venezia has no style—it *is* style. It has no art because it is art itself. More than art, it is an artifice, an intrigue of canals as shrewd as a labyrinth; an accumulation of marble and stones, of statues and columns, of arches and windows as implausible as perfection. It is, in a way, like snow and its flakes, always the same and yet continually different; of its hundreds of canal-spanning bridges, no one is like another. Its juxtaposition of architectural eras, of colors and textures, of water and sky, of things that in any other place would be formless and offensive here become elegant and radiant. All the sordid things of this city are obscured in our minds by the images suggested by Canaletto's paintings, as delicate as miniatures; or by the witticism of playwright Goldoni's characters, elegant and flittering as his crinolined ladies and courtesans, white-wigged and white-powdered as his *cavalieri* and dandies, and scheming and cunning as their servant Harlequin.

Venezia, "Queen of the Seas": a prodigious queen ruling over a court of admirals and soldiers, travelers and spice merchants, of artists and artisans, sculptors and painters, builders and architects, dramatists and musicians. Throughout its history, Venezia has presided over and influenced *Le Tre Venezie*. Politically, it has been divided and chopped up and passed from one potentate to another, from the Rome of Caesar to the France of Napoléon to the Austria of Emperor Franz Joseph, its various pieces reshuffled and renamed but always tied with Venezia. Today that area has become Trentino-Alto Adige, Friuli-Venezia Giulia, and Veneto. The various past and present provinces—even if clearly identified by their own dialects and customs, sometimes even by ethnicity—still carry a Venetian imprint. As a physical reminder, there is hardly a town in the Tre Venezie that doesn't show, in a predominant position, the Venetian winged Lion of Saint Mark, the Book of Law held firmly in its paws. Propped high either on a single column or on the wall of a town hall, relaxed and assured, it looks down on the populace. No other symbol—certainly not the rapacious Imperial Eagle of Rome nor the double-headed eagle of the Austro-Hungarian Empire—inspires such majestic confidence. Like a benevolent sovereign, "I am the Law," it seems to say. "I know the way. Obey, and I will protect you," the implicit "or else," always a strong incentive to behave.

Today Venezia is, understandably, a strong magnet. It attracts visitors from all over the world at all seasons, and is so overcrowded that it can barely keep up with the absurd influx of people. It is close to impossible for a visitor to fully enjoy all that the city has to offer. Many a *Cassandra* say that the city's fame is going to be its downfall.

Fortunately, like the sun at the center of its universe, Venezia has always cast a strong light, one that many of her neighboring cities and towns have basked in and absorbed. Theirs is a small constellation, so close at hand that to pass it up would be a mistake. The whole area is a high-intensity cultural and natural trove, a sampler box of all that Italy has to offer.

Barely twelve miles north, inland from Venezia, is historied Treviso, a town of about eighty thousand inhabitants. It is so compact and so colorful that it has been called a "pocket-size Venezia," built as it is around ancient, willow-bordered canals into which are reflected balconied, frescoed houses. It is also called *"la città dipinta,"* the painted city. Dating from early medieval times, the town was built with humble local bricks, covered with plaster for protection against the weather. In what must have been a communal sense of inferiority, the plaster was painted over in patterns to resemble more elegant bricks, marble, or other expensive materials. Many houses were frescoed, in various degrees of artistry, depicting mythological or sacred scenes. It is a pleasure to walk around town and discover the painted houses; they give the town a cheerful, sunny tone, mirrored in its canals and reflected in the general attitude of its gregarious and welcoming citizens. Sumptuous mansions and palaces attest to the past and present well-being of Treviso. Ever-present porticos run along spotless streets and old alleys that shelter elegant shops and then unexpectedly open onto bustling open-air markets.

Commanding the displays is the gastronomic flag of Treviso: the famous *radicchio trevigiano.* Unlike the round radicchio from Chioggia that we see in U.S. markets, Treviso's white and blood-red version is plume-shaped. The Trevigiani boast that they can prepare radicchio in 101 ways, and one of our favorites is *grigliato di radicchio,* the oblong leaves grilled with a little olive oil, almost crisped, its bitter taste a palate-pleaser. The fruits and vegetables at every produce stand are displayed in their bins like works of art: Green pears line up perfectly and alternate with red apples and yellow lemons; red tomatoes are laid out in zigzag fashion, interspersed with sprigs of parsley and basil; and green, yellow, red, and orange peppers form diamond patterns. It's hard to match the sights and scents of any Italian market, and a Treviso market lines up with the best.

The noisy fish market announces itself with its own clamor. Generations of fishmongers have been barking their wares on the same spot since the 1200s. Located on an island within the city, fenced in by canals, at day's end the market's remains are flushed directly into the canals and the place made clean and ready for tomorrow's commerce. Fish, rice, radicchio, and *luganega,* Treviso's special sausage, are the highlights of the local menu, and good food is the norm in Treviso.

The list of eateries is extensive, some with an outlandishly old pedigree. After a long meandering walk around town and in need of rest and sustenance, we settled on Toni del Spin, a trattoria that just happened to be there when we needed it; in a homey atmosphere, it offers a full list of regional specialties and wines. We were the first guests to arrive and the last to leave and, even if we only touched the tip of the iceberg, we were convinced of Treviso's reputation as a sanctuary of Italian gastronomy. A salad of slivers of fresh porcini mushrooms and shaved Parmigiano on a bed of arugula and radicchio opened our leisurely dinner of Treviso specialties, all guided by the suggestions of our friendly waiter. A first course of *zuppa di pollo* (the waiter rattled off at least twelve ingredients needed for the zuppa, including white wine) was as close to chicken soup as a Rolls-Royce is to a bicycle. We are tempted to put in that same class the next dish, *baccalà in umido,* a baked layered lasagna-like affair of baccalà (salt codfish) and thin slices of potatoes all moistened with milk and olive oil. Many people are put off by salt cod; it is an acquired taste, they feel, but in the Veneto it seems to be a genetic trait, to love it. Perhaps the word "salt" worries the non-Venetians, but the salt cod (dried and salted to look more like a board of wood than a fish) is rinsed in water for two or three days before being cooked, all traces of salt removed and the fish soft and plump again. Then came *trippa* (tripe), accompanied by excellent creamy polenta. Tre Venezie's ubiquitous cereal, made simply with corn flour and water, seems to come in infinite variations; this one had a somewhat coarse grain, just right for soaking up the sauce.

We are particularly fond of tripe and this *trippa alla Trevigiana,* tripe stewed in a tomato sauce, hit the mark. If not a Rolls, it was at least a Bentley. And the portions were big enough for four people.

Our comment was "Wow!"

"You must really like it. In all my career, it is the first time that foreigners ask for *trippa,* so I'm making up for it now," the waiter said, smiling.

We explained that at least one of us is not a foreigner and that the other is an honorary citizen.

"Even better, then," he quickly recouped, "so at least one of you will finish it all!"

He was wrong. We both finished it. And the polenta, too.

Treviso, like Venezia itself, comes with its own set of towns, villages, and must-see satellites, orbiting at no more than a forty-mile radius. They are all part of the Marca Trevigiana, the area around Treviso, and it will not take long to find among the green, verdant hills and foothills of the Alps some great masterpieces, such as the one at Maser—Palladio's Villa Barbaro with its cycle of frescos by Paolo Veronese—and then two miles away, Canova's house, hosting plaster casts of his most important sculptures. The whole area is filled with one magnificent Palladian villa after another, many frescoed by the likes of Tiepolo, Giorgione, and Tiziano. Among the glories of this itinerary, we include the many Prosecco vineyards. The white, cheerful sparkling wine is making big inroads internationally as an *aperitivo* or as a festive table wine, an affordable and good homegrown champagne.

On the way west to Vicenza, Palladio's own city, it's definitely worth the extra time to take the secondary road that goes through the towns of Asolo and Bassano del Grappa. Asolo comes first, a jewel of a little town, surrounded by cypresses and perched on a hill out in the middle of the Veneto plains. The whole town, with its porticoed streets and gorgeous shops, is encircled by landscaping so picturesque it seems to belong in a painting. The Villa Cipriani, a stately, historical hotel, is built among a labyrinth of gorgeous gardens.

Several are the eateries in Asolo, almost all with a view. Led by the aroma of chicken grilled over a wood fire, it didn't take us long to find I Due Mori, a lively *ristorante* whose grilled chicken is one of the house specialties. Gabriella, the owner and our waitress, looks as if she, too, has come out of a painting—most likely a Toulouse-Lautrec—with her mass of bright red curls and outgoing, vivacious manner. We, of course, followed all of her recommendations, starting with *gnocchi al radicchio,* potato gnocchi with strips of cooked radicchio trevigiano, and ravioli with zucchini sauce, both liberally laced with butter and cream. For main courses, *coniglio* and *capretto* (rabbit and baby goat) were slowly roasted on a spit over the embers of olive wood, and constantly basted in their melting fat until golden crisp outside and moist inside. Salads were a mix of the local heroes, porcini mushrooms and radicchio trevigiano, served—as our waitress reminded us—"to cleanse the palate." Thankfully, Asolo's up and down alleys are not made for easy car transit, and walking is a sure method to establish a balance between calories in and calories out.

It was difficult to take leave of this lovely town, but as aficionados of grappa we just had to head for the aptly named Bassano del Grappa, an enticing place just a few miles away at the foot of Monte Grappa. And we were right not to pass it up. The first thing we came to in Bassano was the Ponte degli Alpini, a wide, graceful wooden bridge designed by Palladio in 1569. The bridge has a particular lore for the Corpo degli Alpini, the elite troops identified by a long eagle feather in their hats. The *Alpini* are known not only for their expertise in climbing the harshest mountain peaks but also for their unlimited capacity for grappa, which, as they say in Bassano, is an Alpino's mother's milk. The crystal clear, fiery liquor's name, it turns out, has nothing to do with the name of the town or mountain. It is actually a corruption of *graspa,* the dregs left over from the pressing of wine, skins, pits, stems, and all. These are distilled into what has been described as liquid fire. Today, grappa has lost some of its rough attribute and has acquired a fashionable status, being distilled into mellower (a real Alpino would never go for that), differently flavored spirits—and much, much more expensive than the original, humble thing.

Bassano is considered the capital of grappa, and its main street is virtually one shop after another filled with bottles of it, bottles in every imaginable color, shape, and size. Whole shops sell nothing else, the sunlight sparkling and glistening off the intricate designs of the myriad vessels stacked on shelf after shelf, some more valuable for the pure artistry of their Murano blown-glass than for their contents. For some of us, however, that could never be the case.

This was borne out for us in a most unusual fashion. After leaving Bassano and later arriving in Rome, we realized we had left our prized bottle of grappa on a bus we had taken outside the town. We were actually able to reach the bus company and ask if a bottle had been found on a seat. Quite surprisingly, the answer was yes, and yes they would send it to our address in America. Many weeks passed and we had just about given up on seeing our grappa again, when one day it appeared in the mail. Excited, we opened it and began to pour—but nothing came out. Obviously, someone else along the way loved grappa as much as we do, but still felt it was worth shipping the empty bottle all the way across the ocean (and it wasn't even a fancy Murano one).

The Ponte di Bassano exceeds its historical and architectural fame, being the inspiration for one of the nationally best-known Alpine songs. It tells of an Alpino who, on the Bassano Bridge on his way to the murderous World War I front on Monte Grappa, says farewell to his *inamorata* with a last passionate kiss. It is a pretty melancholy song, even if, in the last refrain, it goes on to say that nine months later— guess what— "a pretty baby boy is born. Milk he doesn't drink, he drinks grappa because he's an Alpino's son . . . "

Obviously, the Bassano Bridge is not Andrea Palladio's major work. Starting as a humble stonemason, he became the most sought-after architect of the sixteenth-century Renaissance and inspired architectural works for centuries to follow. In the city of Vicenza (no more than thirty miles from Bassano), Palladio's most praiseworthy design is to be seen two miles out of town in the Villa Rotonda (from which Jefferson took inspiration for his Monticello mansion) and also at the Palazzo Valmarana. But the whole city is peppered with outstanding buildings and private and public palaces, a textbook of elegance in urban planning. You can walk down any street, especially Via Andrea Palladio, and ooh and aah over one splendid Palladio building after another. The other attraction that stirs admiration is the presence of many jewelry stores, their windows displaying fabulous gold bracelets, necklaces, broaches, and other expensive pieces. Vicenza's most renowned activity is the designing and making of jewelry, especially gold.

Perhaps the most famous treasure trove is Palladio's last work, the Teatro Olimpico, the oldest example of indoor theater existing in Europe. Unfinished at his death, it was completed by his pupil Scamozzi and opened its doors for a first performance in 1585. Following the master's design, the permanent stage set represents the Greek city of Thebes, built in a trompe l'oeil perspective that gives it, in a few short feet, the perception of incredible depth. The auditorium is designed to resemble a Greek outdoor amphitheater: A steep semicircle of wood benches (simulating marble) look up to the ceiling's frescoes of billowing clouds in the sky. The stage is flanked by toga-wearing statues, representations of the theater's benefactors. It is indeed a unique experience, and viewers can lose all sense of time and space. But not enough to forget to nourish the body as well as the soul.

Among the town's specialties is the classic *baccalà alla Vicentina*—a creamed dried cod, sometimes prepared with Italian cod and sometimes with Norwegian *stoccafisso* (stockfish). Unlike the Italian version, which uses salt to preserve the fish, this cod is dried in the cold Norwegian sun and air until it becomes as hard as a stick of wood. Before cooking, it is softened by pounding it with a mallet, soaked in water, then slowly poached in oil, milk, onions, and garlic, and turned into a creamy concoction. Served with polenta, the dish has become a symbol of the gastronomy of Vicenza. Polenta is a mainstay, either as one course or a whole meal, used as a carrier of sauces and stews, so much so that the citizens of Veneto (and by association, most Northern Italians) are nicknamed *Polentoni,* big polenta eaters. Of all Europe, it was Veneto that first adopted American corn as a basic alimentary staple, only a few years after Columbus' discovery. Veneto has returned the favor by giving the world polenta, as this once humble cornmeal mush has caught the fancy of international chefs.

From Vicenza we traveled thirty miles more to the west, to Verona. The town, thanks to Shakespeare and his Romeo and Juliet, has found its place in Veneto's firmament and shines its own light. (Few visitors go inside La Casa di Giulietta, the house with the famous balcony said to be Juliet's, but many have caressed her statue in the courtyard, judging from the dazzling brassy gleam of her left breast.) It's unfortunate that the fame of this city comes from the dramatist's tragic love story, because of all stages, this city is the least appropriate; mourning does not become Verona. Rain or shine, it would be impossible to find a more charming and more cheerful place. Its smiling people are so friendly that it is hard to imagine the perennially feuding Montagues and Capulets in their midst. It is a happy city that, indeed, could have been invented by a set designer. The open space of its first-century Roman Arena (almost as big as Rome's Colosseum); the umbrella-shaded, bustling open-air market of Piazza delle Erbe; the vast yet hushed and intimate Piazza dei Signori; the filigreed Scaligeri's Tombs; the luscious Giusti botanical and statuary gardens; the ornate Romanesque church of San Zeno with its incomparable sculpted bronze doors; and the brick-brown city streets and alleys are all an invitation to walk the boards of that stage. Do so, and you will join a cast of thousands on Verona's elegant main shopping street, Via Mazzini. In every season and at any hour of the day, but especially before dinner, the whole city is a continuous 'round and 'round promenade of chatting people in the quiet center, devoid of all motorized traffic.

The turn-around point for the *passeggiata* is the Liston, the wide sidewalk on one side of Piazza Brà, the huge unevenly shaped piazza facing the arena. Here you can stop at any cafe and have a traditional *ombra* (a "shadow," the name for a civilized glass of wine) and let most of Verona's people parade in front of you. Your ombra will be, or should be, a sample of the many *Veronesi* wines. All around the city and west to Lake Garda, the countryside is covered with vineyards: Valpolicella, Bardolino, Amarone, Soave, and Prosecco all have their place in the roster of classic Italian wines. After the ombra comes dinner, a Veronese occasion for appreciating food and enjoying friendship. Rarely do you encounter people eating alone in Verona; waiters encourage single travelers to share a table with others.

Many are the places for a convivial meal, covering the range from humble to sumptuous, but all equally welcoming and rewarding, and almost all with their special dish or particular way to prepare one. One of our favorites is Ristorante Greppia, which serves the most fabulous *bollito misto* we have had in all of Italy, the standard by which we compare all others. The waiter pushes to your table a huge cart filled with steaming platters of boiled brisket, veal, fowl, tongue, pork *zampone,* and *cotechino* sausage for you to select whatever and however much you like. Bollito misto is always served *con salse* (with a set of condiments) led by our preferred one, *mostarda di Cremona,* a spicy mixture of candied fruits in a mustardy syrup. Other sauces include *salsa verde,* in which parsley, capers, anchovies, and olive oil are blended together, followed by the more mundane horseradish mayonnaise and Dijon mustard. A pasta dish not to be missed while in the Veneto is *bigoli,* thick homemade whole-wheat spaghetti with an uneven, unsmooth texture; at Greppia it is served *in salsa* with an onion, anchovies, and olive oil sauce.

At our other favorite spot, La Bottega del Vino, part watering hole, part restaurant, they serve *bigoli all'anara,* bigoli with a sauce of duck stew. As its name indicates, La Bottega del Vino is an *enoteca,* a wine bar that has been expanded into a restaurant. At the front is a long bar and a few tables where the Veronesi gather at the end of the day for a glass of wine and camaraderie. As far as the eye can see are bottles of wine; every inch of every wall from floor to ceiling is covered with them. For those visitors who wish to stay for dinner, the back of the restaurant contains linen-covered tables and, of course, wine glasses of every shape and size.

Baccalà mantecato, salt cod with whipped cream; *sopressa,* Venetian sausage; and *ravioli verdi con ricotta e spinaci,* green ravioli with spinach and ricotta, are other regional specialties. Nearby Lake Garda provides Verona's tables with trout and lake perch; they generally appear on the table cooked simply, poached or grilled, so as not to alter the fresh taste of the fish. Finish it all with a slice of Veronese *Pandoro,* a light, golden sweet cake, and a glass of bubbly *Venegazzù Prosecco* and you will leave the table at peace with yourself, at peace with the world. So much so that in our mind's eye we see the Montagues and Capulets strolling together along the Liston.

From Verona, a sharp U-turn heading east led us back toward the lagoon. Only available time and stamina decided our next stop. From the sampler-box ahead of us, it was hard to take only one candy from each place: Giotto's frescoes of the Scrovegni Chapel in Padova, a 1305 work of essential influence on European art; Padova's basilica, the most lavish church built in honor of San Antonio and a fascinating mixture of minaret-like towers and Byzantine domes; the seventeenth-century masterpieces in the church of the Beata Vergine del Soccorso in Rovigo; and then, as a break from cultural interests, a mundane stop at Chioggia. Chioggia is at the southern end of the Venetian lagoon, an active port and principal supplier of fresh fish and shellfish to the Veneto. The moored, vivid-colored fishing boats and house facades kaleidoscope their images into the canals, a lively scene accompanied by the just as lively soundtrack of the fish market's barkers. For seafood lovers, Chioggia is a must: Numerous restaurants open their doors onto the canals, serving their specialties of *brodetto,* a soup made with at least seven different kinds of fish; and *risotto alla chioggiotta,* also based on fish; and then eels; cuttle fish, and *granzeola,* the spiny crab that is unique to the region.

The various gastronomic differences in the Veneto begin with the sophisticated cuisine of Venezia, using the spices of which the city was the main European trader. The subtle rice dishes— halfway points between soups and risottos, velvety with young vegetables and delicate fish—soon make room for a larger and sturdier cuisine as you move north. Beans, cabbage, potatoes, and pork are the basic ingredients of a humble larder. Soups dominate the mountain table—simple, direct, and satisfying, as a poor peasant cuisine makes obligatory. Due to their earthiness, the dishes of the northern part of the region seem to have a masculine appeal, as if prepared more by mountain men than women. Italy is, after all, a country whose language gives the feminine gender to softer, more delicate inanimate things. *Cucina* (cuisine) is feminine, a woman's thing. But this does not take into account that for centuries Veneto's male chefs have had a reputation for creativity and taste, often placed on the same level as artists. They are the very same who have given us *risi e bisi, pasta e fasioi,* granzeola, *fegato alla veneziana* (Venetian-style calf's liver sautéed in olive oil with onion slivers), tiramisu, *pandoro,* and the 101 different ways of using the red plume radicchio from Treviso or the red globe radicchio from Chioggia.

An expedition around Le Tre Venezie is like weaving between the sacred and the profane, between the rarefied pleasures of art and natural beauty and the worldly pleasures of the table. It is, to stretch an analogy, like a well-orchestrated meal, where textures, flavors, and aromas complement each other. All you have left to do is to say "Encore!"

FEGATO ALLA VENEZIANA

Calf's Liver Sautéed in Onion Slivers

This traditional Venetian dish appears in slightly differing versions. The following one, with the addition of wine and lemon juice, is a more modern one.

1 pound onions	3 tablespoons minced
4 tablespoons olive oil	flat-leaf parsley
3 tablespoons unsalted butter	¼ cup dry white wine
2 pounds fresh calf's liver, cut	Juice of 1 lemon
into 1-inch-wide, 4-inch-long strips	

CUT THE ONIONS into thin slivers. Heat the oil and butter in a pan and sauté the onions. Cook over low heat until the onions are limp and barely golden. Raise the heat and add the liver strips to the pan. Cook for 2 minutes on one side, then turn the strips and cook them for another minute. Add the parsley, stir in the wine and lemon juice, and cook for another minute. Remove the liver to a warm serving platter and pour the onions and pan juices over them. (If the juices are too thin, reduce them a bit over high heat, then pour over the liver.) Serve warm.

Serves 4

RISI E BISI

Thick Rice and Pea Soup

This is a traditional Venetian rice dish; it is served as a first course, and it's almost a risotto, but cooked *all'onda:* soupy enough for its surface to make a "wave" (a ripple) when served.

3 tablespoons unsalted butter	1 10-ounce package baby peas
3 tablespoons olive oil	(or 1 pound fresh)
1 small onion, minced	1 cup arborio rice
3 tablespoons minced flat-leaf parsley	1 quart chicken broth
3 ounces prosciutto, thickly sliced	Freshly grated Parmigiano
then cut in small squares	Reggiano cheese
or 3 ounces pancetta, cubed	

HEAT the butter and oil in a soup pot and sauté the onion and parsley.

WHEN THE ONION is translucent add the prosciutto (or pancetta). Stir for 1 minute, then add the peas and enough water to cover it; continue to cook on medium heat for 5 minutes.

ADD the rice and the broth and bring the mixture to a boil. Reduce the heat, cover the pot, and simmer for about 15 minutes, stirring once in a while, until the rice is done. The soup should be reasonably thick, but thin enough to be *all'onda*. Add a little more broth if needed or desired.

SERVE warm with a sprinkle of Parmigiano cheese.

Serves 4

Liguria

FIVE LANDS AND MORE

*S*een from the sea, Liguria appears to be a huge natural amphitheater. Alps and Apennines join in a mountainous embrace that entraps the warm breezes of the Ligurian Sea so that the whole region enjoys a semipermanent spring. Even the clouds are kept at bay by the mountains, and the clear sky is mirrored in the many hues of blue from the Gulf of Genoa.

The thin, sickle-shaped shore is practically the whole region of Liguria, the remaining real estate being a green, vertical strip of land that climbs from the sea to the top of the craggy mountains. Almost in the middle, the shoreline is split in two by the city of Genoa, a major Mediterranean port, capital of the region and fatherland of Cristoforo Colombo. West of the city begins the Riviera di Ponente that goes to join the French Cote d'Azur close to glitzy Monaco, while east of Genoa is the elegant Riviera di Levante that after sixty miles of perpendicular cliffs reaches Lerici at the edge of Tuscany.

We entered Liguria from France. A series of wet, gray days spent near Nice inspired us to pack up and move south. We pierced the fog on the superhighway and entered the tunnel that bores under the Alps. After a few underground miles, with France behind us, we resurfaced in Italy. A blue clear sky and a brilliant sun welcomed us like a blare of trumpets. "Well," we said to ourselves, "Old Lady Italia has done it again. Hello, Liguria!" And the gray disappeared from our souls.

The tall mountain chain protects Liguria from the cold northern winds and turns it into a natural greenhouse. Like Val d'Aosta and other Italian mountainous regions, most of its limited amount of soil is carved in land-hugging terraces. Whatever grows there has heightened, concentrated attributes; the sweat of man, the land, and the climate join forces to create exceptional produce. Even the flowers seem to be more intensely scented and colored. Liguria ships its flowers, especially flame-red carnations, all around the world. Romantic poets, from their vantage points in San Remo, Santa Margherita, Rapallo, and Portofino, have sung of this land.

Just next door to the south, overshadowed by these glamour places, is the town of Chiavari. An elegantly simple, relaxed, and pleasant city, facing a sheltered sea and untouched by winter, its lifestyle might make you think it's the Florida of Italy. Many retired people move here, finding it comfortable and affordable. If you should encounter a day with inclement weather, you can take your *passeggiata* anyway because all the streets are protected by graceful colonnades. A small pleasure-boat marina, a small fishing fleet, and a few small green (non-polluting) industries also keep its economy in a comfortable state.

The town's gastronomy appeals to us. Although obviously rooted in Liguria, Chiavari's tastes are mellower and less spicy than the rest of the region. Perhaps, we wonder, if that is because of the presence of so many older, retired people.

Minestrone con pesto may ring a Ligurian bell, but *corzetti* were news to us, and a local exclusive at that; They are embossed pasta medallions about two inches around and one-eighth-inch thick, made with flour, eggs, and a touch of red wine and served with a sage and butter sauce. A local woodcarver, we were told, is the only person left who produces the wooden coin-like molds used to form this pasta. They are one of our rare travel souvenirs and, on special occasions, we unwrap them and put them to work. Press one mold face to face against another with a thin layer of pasta in between and, voilà, you have a corzetto. A few corzetti make an unusual, and unusually textured, first course. Especially if aided by the super-aroma of Ligurian sage.

On the subject of gastronomy we talked to Roberto Dal Seno, the young chef of the restaurant at the Monte Rosa Hotel in Chiavari. How faithful is he to the traditional cuisine?

"I am more faithful to its philosophy than to the actual recipes." Then, by way of explanation: "Techniques change, new fashions, especially in presentation, take over and one has to be up-to-date. And, whatever I have learned, whatever I have grown up with, is 'filtered' by my own experience."

He did say "filtered" *(filtrato)* and it has a nice sound; it makes one think of rough traditions drip-dripping through young experiences and coming out refined and distilled. He hesitated a moment and then added with a smile:

"Perhaps my minestroni aren't exactly the same as my grand-mother's, but they are still Ligurian. It's the philosophy that counts!"

"And the taste," we concluded for him.

Right across the street from the Monte Rosa Hotel we found a tiny, rustic trattoria filled with local *Chiavarini* and clearly offering traditional fare, almost all in the form of fish dishes. Everything, the owners tell us, is part of that day's catch. We had a *brodetto con cozze e ceci,* a soup made with the unusual combination of mussels and chickpeas; *misto mare,* mixed seafood salad dressed with golden Ligurian virgin olive oil and lemon juice; a crisp, tender *fritto misto* consisting of deep-fried calamari and lots of shrimp; and a *stoccaf-isso* (stockfish) boiled with potatoes and moistened with that thick, golden olive oil. We sipped a local Vermentino, a very crisp white wine, the perfect foil for the seafood dinner.

Chiavari is a most suitable stepping-stone for things to come. We moved south past Sestri Levante, towards Lerici where the road crosses the Appennino Marittimo's mountains frequently in a sequence of spectacular—and stomach-churning, hair-raising—twists and turns. It switches back and forth from the Ligurian coast-line to the Tuscan inland, so that at times it is hard to know where one region begins and the other ends. Before Lerici, where the mountains plunge into the Tyrrhenian Sea, rest the five villages that make up the Cinque Terre, the "Five Lands." Strung along twenty miles of coastline, the villages cling to the cliffs as if rooted in them. Monterosso, Vernazza, Corniglia, Manarola, and Riomaggiore look painted on the mountain walls straight up from the coast.

You can reach the Cinque Terre by ferry from Sestri Levante on the north or from Lerici on the south, but the real thrill is to reach the area by land. For the high points of view encountered on the way, this is an experience closer to hang gliding than driving and, for the magnificent sights at every turn, worth every single yard and heart palpitation. There is also a more conservative way of travel: a commuter railroad, with frequent service. The train, going in and out of tunnels like a giant's needle, stitches the five villages together and connects them with the rest of the world.

The whole land looks scratched by horizontal lines, as if the work of huge nails. Only from close up do you realize that these are steep terraces, hewed out of the cliffs' walls and only two or three feet wide. There is not much room for growing things in quantity.

We wonder if the various villages have lost their individuality, if their people resent being generalized into Cinque Terrestrians. While each village is different, in many ways they are alike. They all have a medieval feel to them, and the houses are piled up one on top of the other in what seems a helter-skelter way. No reasonable architect would dream this kind of construction, and probably no architect designed it. A new room or a new house is built when needed and generally, given the lack of space, on top of another. The pastel colored houses are separated by alleys, most of which have the width of stretched arms. Some have an archway built between the houses—almost a tunnel—and the stone pavements are rarely on a level, their steep grade eased (for man or donkey) by ten-foot-wide steps. A shallow gully runs in their middle to let rain water flow into the sea. All the villages have a church on a little square (perhaps the only almost-level area around, and the only soccer space for young children and off-duty altar boys). The villages are clustered over and around small beaches and coves dotted with bobbing fishing boats. A few inns, small hotels, and trattorie take care of the hospitality activities.

The people's character reflects their environment: Having to live with a jealously measured land on one side and an ungenerous sea on the other, they are parsimonious and shrewd in the administration of their goods. Some people define this trait as innate stinginess, a downright miserly attitude. All *Ligurians* are master traders and barterers; as the saying goes, it takes three Levantine merchants to match one Ligurian. In reality they have a sophisticated ingenuity, born of necessity. In this land, majestic Mediterranean pine trees grow side by side with gnarled, centuries-old olive trees, along with intensely aromatic herbs and plants. Only a genius could judiciously balance the color, texture, and taste of pine nuts, golden olive oil, aromatic basil, and garlic and, with mortar and pestle, pound and squeeze their essence into *pesto.*

The old adage *"far di necessità virtù"* (making of necessity a virtue) well applies to the local gastronomy and, when it comes to handling vegetables, that virtue becomes virtuosity. Textures, colors, and tastes of different vegetables and greens become like colors on an artist's palette. This innate respect for all that the land offers shows up even before the produce reaches the kitchen. Market stalls are immaculately clean and their displays are juxtapositions of colors and shapes to match a still life. Each item is lined up to emphasize its best features, each is positioned so that its color catches the best light. Even on an overcast day, an open-air market appears blessed with sunshine. The customers are not in a hurry; they stop and go from stall to stall and from display to display in search of the best buy and of inspiration, letting the market dictate the menu for the day. Soon, conversations and exchanges of ideas between customers and greengrocers take on the tone of generals discussing an operation's strategy, and, by eavesdropping, you can figure out which of the produce will take the brunt of the frontal attack and which will be on the sidelines. The produce of the handkerchief-sized gardens mix and pair with the produce of the sea. The *ciuppin*—born here, the Ligurians say proudly, and emigrated to America as *cioppino*— is a thick potage of several kinds of fish, all that's available at the end of a market day, served either as a soup over toasted slices of bread, or depending on mood, thickened as a sauce for pasta. *Ravioli di magro,* ravioli filled with a mixture of cooked fish, ricotta, and local wild greens; black risotto, colored and flavored by squid ink; and **Trenette Verdi col Pesto,** the classic Ligurian homemade pasta cooked with beans and potatoes, seem to take advantage of the special chemistry of mountain air and sea.

Also exposed to sea-moist breezes and protected from inland cold winds, the terraced vineyards of Cinque Terre produce the strong, sweet Sciacchetrà, and the famous white, dry, delicately scented Cinqueterre wine. Experts say these wines seem invented to go with the local food; others say that their fame comes from their scarcity. So little is produced that only a few bottles leave the area, and the few that do are dearly priced.

Quite frankly we do not see why any should leave at all. To us, those few bottles are fine, consumed right where they are. They assuage quite well a visitor's thirst and appetite, brought about by the villages' steep streets, alleys, and stairways.

TRENETTE VERDI

Spinach Pasta

Trenette are as classic Ligurian as they can be. Classic, but with a twist, are the trenette verdi—spinach pasta. (In a pinch, the trenette can be substituted with commercial linguine.) The recipe for the pesto and the recipe for trenette verdi col pesto are below.)

10 ounces (fresh or frozen) whole leaf spinach	1 teaspoon salt
3½ cups unbleached all-purpose flour	3 medium eggs

WASH AND CLEAN the spinach, removing all thick and tough stems. Cook it in boiling water until well done. Drain thoroughly and squeeze as dry as possible. You should have a ball of cooked spinach as big as a large egg.

PUT the flour, salt, and spinach in the bowl of a food processor equipped with a knife blade; process until you have a homogeneously green-flecked flour. In an adequate container beat the eggs lightly and mix them slowly into the ingredients in the processor bowl. Process on-off until the mixture turns into rice-size pellets which, when pinched, cling together. Depending on the moisture of the spinach or the size of the eggs, a moist ball of dough may form at one end of the blade; if so, add more flour, a tablespoon at a time, until you obtain the pellets. If the pellets are too small and do not stick easily together, add a teaspoon of water.

TRANSFER the pellets to a pastry board and press them together into two or three balls of dough. Knead briefly, keeping what you are not working with under plastic wrap, and roll with a pasta machine to the thickness of a penny (about ¹⁄₁₆ of an inch). Roll all of the dough, then cut it into ribbons ¹⁄₁₆ of an inch wide (or as close to it as possible). Cut the ribbons about 9 inches long, and you have your trenette.

Serves 4

PESTO

Pesto means "pounded," hence anything that is pounded long enough could be called a pesto. But in the Italian (and absolutely in the Ligurian) food lexicon, pesto means only one pesto, made with only fresh basil as the leading ingredient. All the rest are pesto impostors and will be confiscated by the Gourmet Police. There is, nonetheless, some freedom in the proportions of the ingredients, adjusting them to personal taste.

If you do not have a mortar and pestle, this is the best reason to buy one now. (In an emergency, a blender or food processor may be used, but do it where nobody sees you. And the texture/color will be different.)

2 cups loosely packed fresh basil leaves	1 tablespoon freshly grated, sharp pecorino cheese
2–3 garlic cloves	1 tablespoon freshly grated Parmigiano Reggiano cheese
½ teaspoon salt	½ cup extra virgin olive oil
3 ounces pine nuts	

PUT the basil, garlic, salt, and pine nuts in the mortar bowl and mash and pound away until you have a pretty smooth paste. Stir the cheeses well into the paste, then add the olive oil. Taste for salt and adjust. The final pesto should be spoonable, of thick yogurt-like consistency. One tablespoon goes a long way; when used on pasta, it is diluted with some warm pasta cooking water.

ADDITIONAL NOTES: If you want to give a deeper green color to the pesto, you may add 2 or 3 fresh spinach leaves, or the leaves of 3 or 4 sprigs of Italian parsley to the basil leaves.

Adjust the amount of garlic to your taste; some pestos are very garlicky. For a less sharp garlic flavor, soak the cloves in a half glass of milk overnight.

The amount of pine nuts may be cut down by one third, and the same amount of walnut meat added.

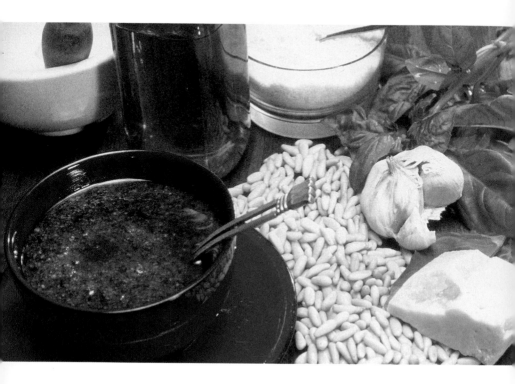

BLENDER PESTO

If you find your arm is aching too much from all that pounding, or if you just don't have that much time available, here is the easy way out:

Put the basil, garlic, salt, and pine nuts in the blender (the garlic should be lightly crushed first) along with the olive oil, and mix at high speed until you get the consistency you want. If you want the pesto coarser in texture, use a lower speed. When evenly blended, pour into a bowl and blend in the cheeses with a fork. Always keep some pasta cooking water ready in case the pesto is too dense, and, if you want, add a few pats of butter on the pasta for a creamier taste.

Both recipes serve 4

TRENETTE VERDI COL PESTO

Spinach pasta with pesto, potatoes, and green beans

For the real experience, homemade green trenette should be used. But even in Liguria commercial trenette show up either green or white, the latter being a slightly sturdier cut of linguine.

12 ounces homemade green trenette (or commercial linguine)	4 ounces fresh green beans (optional)
8 ounces (1 medium or 2 small) potatoes	4 heaping tablespoons of pesto
	Freshly grated pecorino Romano cheese

BRING A POT of at least 4 quarts of lightly salted water to boil. Peel the potato(es) and cut into small (¾-inch) cubes. Wash the green beans and cut into 1-inch pieces. Cook the potato cubes in the boiling water. After three or so minutes, add the green beans and the pasta. When the pasta is cooked al dente, drain it but reserve some of the cooking water. Distribute equally the pasta, potatoes, and green beans into four warm soup bowls. Add a good dollop of pesto and one or two tablespoons of hot reserved cooking water on each serving. Mix thoroughly and serve with freshly grated Pecorino Romano cheese.

Serves 4

Emilia-Romagna

OF HAM AND CHEESE AND MUSIC

As soon as word got out that we intended to spend six
months in Rome, the requests began pouring in. The
simple accommodations of our spartan apartment in the Trastevere section of old Rome were more than compensated for by the
panoramic view from its enormous roof terrace. The news of this
temporary address spread quickly among friends and relatives, supplying us with a queue of potential visitors from across the Atlantic.
Once our guests had made a quick study of the Forums, the Colosseum, Saint Peter's Basilica, and the Catacombs, some wanted to
branch out into the rest of Italy. Such welcome customers were
Gwen's sister, Ellen, and her husband Jack.

Jack's curiosity tended towards Ferrari and Maserati cars,
while Ellen's veered to prosciutto ham and Parmigiano cheese. She
had found a new supplier of these goods in Philadelphia, and now
she wished to compare them to the source. We were more than
happy to satisfy her wish, and on the spur of the moment, the four

of us took off for Parma in Emilia-Romagna on a quest to seek out the birthplace of these precious comestibles. There, while searching for ham and cheese, we ended up finding violins and Verdi.

Emilia-Romagna, lying just north of Tuscany, straddles the peninsula. On the east coast, it has a few fishing villages and a stretch of fashionable beaches along the Adriatic Sea, and on the western edge it almost dips its toes in the Tyrrhenian Sea, except it's fenced off by a thin sliver of Liguria. In simple map-speak, a traveler would be hard put to find a route going from north to south in Italy without crossing Emilia-Romagna. Julius Caesar had to when, coming from the Po River valley, he threw the dice and—Alea Jacta Est!—crossed the Rubicon and went south into the Tiber valley and Rome. For whatever reason, the crossing is always worthwhile: The region is one of the richest in Italy, industrially, agriculturally, historically, and gastronomically. The city of Modena manufactures Maseratis, Lamborghinis, and Ferraris; Reggio Emilia is at the center of a flourishing agricultural area; and Bologna is considered the culinary capital of the country.

Emilia-Romagna played a very important role in the Second World War, and in some places one still sees the results of bombing raids, left untouched on purpose as a memento of human brutality. The partisans were particularly active in the region, fighting on the side of the United States against the Nazi-Fascists. Tributes to the fallen heroes abound; the main square of almost every city and town has its marble or bronze memorial plaque, never without a bouquet of fresh flowers. One of the region's most appealing attractions—for food-trotters like us—is its reputation as the culinary mecca of Italy, a country where you'd be hard-pressed to find a bad meal anywhere.

We arrived in Parma at lunchtime on a sunny day in February, surprisingly warm enough for us to be able to eat outside in a cafe on the main square, Piazza Garibaldi, a popular meeting place for the townspeople. To stick with our intentions, we managed to sample prosciutto presented in various forms—in a sandwich made with focaccia bread, on a warm pizza, and in a salad with fresh mozzarella—all versions outstanding, as only true Parma prosciutto can be: moist and deep pink, not red, with a light salty-sweet taste. Real prosciutto di Parma is cured absolutely without the help of any chemicals, such as those used in pseudo-prosciutto, which make it red, dry, and salty. When we inquired about visiting a prosciutto factory, our aging waiter informed us that—unless we had a high-placed friend in the business—such a visit was nearly impossible without a reservation made way in advance.

"Moreover," he added by way of consolation, "when you have seen one prosciutto hanging from a rafter, you have seen two hundred thousand."

It has taken two or three generations for the prosciutto productions of family farms to become a huge, world-supplying industry. Traditionally, small family producers had their own particular formula, but the basic process is the same. The raw hams are put on a slanted board and covered in sea salt for one or two months, depending on size. To prevent spoilage, the fissures between the meat and the bone ends are caulked with ham fat. (By the way, now almost all hams are boned for easier slicing, even if, the old pros say, this leads to a diminished taste. This is a double loss since the leftover bone was an essential addition to many country soups.) The hams are then scraped of salt and hung on rafters, like bats on a cave's ceiling, to dry in a steady current of air. They are moved month by month to locales with decreasing air temperatures, until after about nine to twelve months the temperature is down to 50 degrees Fahrenheit. The hams are now full-fledged prosciutti and ready to travel the world. Fat pigs from the nearby Val Padana—the Po Valley—fed on special local grub (such as the whey left over from making Parmigiano), plus the particular breezes and seasonal temperatures are what it takes to make a Parma ham special. *Una volta,* once upon a time. Today, due to the enormous demand for prosciutti, a large quantity of raw hams are not from Parma at all. They come, carefully selected by the buyers, from many other parts of the world— including the United States—and, once transformed in Parma, go back where they came from with the prestigious label of "prosciutto di Parma."

Jokingly, we told Ellen that even though we were sitting right in Parma, the prosciutto she was eating could have come from a pig born just about anywhere.

"It is still excellent!" was Ellen's comment, and the agreement was unanimous. One thing our kind waiter did not do was to trim off—a frequent request from many tourists, he said— the creamy white fat portion of the prosciutto, a connoisseur's sweet delicacy now quite demonized by the calorie police.

One of the things we noticed in Parma was that, unlike Rome and other cities where the ubiquitous roaring noise of motors is deafening, the city was quiet. It's not that cars and motorcycles are banned in the city, it is just that Parmigiani of all ages love to get around on bicycles. It made it harder to tear ourselves away from the pleasure of an after-lunch basking in the warm sun, but as 3 p.m. approached, we decided on a visit to the duomo, the city's main cathedral. Since most churches and cathedrals in Italy are closed from noon or 1 p.m. until 3 p.m., our timing was just right.

The facade of the Romanesque cathedral, which dates to the eleventh century, has a porch supported by two large lions, a style developed in Lombardy. Even though we had already seen a virtually uncountable number of magnificent churches in Italy, the sight on entering the enormous duomo di Parma took our breath away. The dome, the ceiling, and the walls are completely covered with frescoes. Antonio Allegri da Correggio, Parma's most noted artist, painted the dome between 1522 and 1530; the rest is attributed to his pupils. Certainly it seemed to us a feat as complex as, and a great deal larger than, that of Michelangelo's Sistine Chapel.

The adjacent Romanesque baptistery is considered by many art historians as the most harmonious and best preserved medieval monument in Italy, a splendid octagonal building in rose-colored Verona marble. Its interior, which has sixteen sides, is literally covered with a jumble of sculptures, frescoes, and bas-reliefs, dating to the thirteenth century.

Other urban sights of interest are the ocher-colored opera house, Teatro Regio, famous for its operas, plays, and concerts; the collections of art and antiquities of Palazzo della Pilotta, a huge structure built in 1583 and badly bombed in 1943; and Casa Toscanini, the birthplace of the famous conductor, currently a museum for music lovers. In the city's Villetta Cemetery, Nicolò Paganini, the violin super-virtuoso and composer, is buried.

It was here that we began to change our goal from the initial search for gastronomy to a search for music. As hedonistic Romans said, once you have fed the body, you are ready to feed the soul.

Since Ellen had been a violinist, she was interested in visiting nearby Cremona—barely across the border in Lombardy—home of the legendary violin makers Antonio Stradivarius and the Amati and Guarneri families. Traveling northwest from Parma, we decided to take only country roads that passed through tiny villages and miles of the Po Valley's flat farmland, the most fertile region of Italy. This was a wonderful choice because we were just about the only car on the road, along with various horsecarts and farm machinery. The lush green farmland is sliced by long, narrow, straight roads that go on and on as far as the eye can see, bordered by deep irrigation ditches and lines of poplar trees. On the way, we happened upon the tiny town of Busseto, population seven thousand, once home to Giuseppe Verdi and just next to Le Roncole, the composer's birthplace. We had heard about a characteristic inn with an excellent restaurant in Busseto owned by the operatic tenor Carlo Bergonzi so, since dusk was approaching, we swung off the road and decided to stop for the night.

I Due Foscari could fool you: the medieval-style building is really only about thirty years old. On entering the lobby, we were pleasantly surprised to hear the voices of a soprano and baritone singing the famous duet from the second act of *La Traviata*. Unbeknownst to us, Signor Bergonzi, now well into his seventies and retired, holds master classes for promising young opera singers from all over the world right there in his inn, and we (luckily, opera lovers all) were to be the beneficiaries of free nightly concerts.

The walls of the lobby are covered with huge posters announcing Bergonzi's 1950s appearance in *Tosca* at La Scala, in *Aida* at the opera house in Parma, and in various other concert halls all over Europe. The poster of his twenty-fifth anniversary appearance at the

Metropolitan Opera in New York takes prominence at the entrance to the lobby. We were told that he was one of Pavarotti's teachers, and perhaps the enlarged photo of Bergonzi with "Il Big," as Pavarotti is known here, attests to that fact.

A walk around the town of Busseto (which cannot take more than ten minutes) reveals a town unsparingly devoted to its famous son. There is one delightful main street whose sidewalks are covered by porticos, the all-weather architectural constant of Italy's north. As we passed the various shop windows—from the butcher to the baker to the clothing store to the bookstore—looking inside, we saw giant photographs of Verdi himself at all ages and all stages of his life. Having our coffee at the Bar del Portico, we even discovered Verdi's bearded image on our sugar packets, so there was clearly no place where we could escape his gaze.

On our return to the inn, we passed the Teatro Verdi, recently renovated after being closed for twenty-five years in order to house the celebrations of the one-hundredth anniversary of Verdi's death. A large bronze statue of the master, seated in a big armchair, stands in front of the theater with a commanding view of the town's principal square. We couldn't help but chuckle on noticing that both the statue of Giuseppe Verdi and his theater are located on Piazza Carlo Rossi. (Which, loosely translated, would be Joseph Greens sitting on Charles Red's Square).

As we took our *aperitivo* in the bar at I Due Foscari, we continued to be entertained by operatic voices drifting up from the basement rooms where the master classes were being held. At the end of a tenor solo, we would see a young man loaded with music scores trotting up the stairs from his lesson, next a mezzo-soprano, and so on, until the classes came to an end. We learned from Bergonzi's son Marco that the corner bar where we were seated was originally a local restaurant that he and his father bought about thirty years ago, then expanded and enlarged in medieval style until it became the inn it is today. They chose the name "I Due Foscari"—a Verdi opera, of course, though little performed today—because the opera is about the close relationship between a father and a son, the two Foscaris.

The restaurant at I Due Foscari is known for its outstanding cuisine and elegant ambience, so it was our logical choice for dinner. Both the cuisine and ambience lived up to their reputation, with the prosciutto and cheese products being the shining stars, of course. We shared an enormous plate filled with varieties of cured ham from the region: prosciutto, *mortadella,* and the highly prized *culatello*, a specialty of Busseto. The best part of a pork hind leg, the rump, is aged like prosciutto for up to 18 months, packed in a natural casing like a round sausage and, when ready, is steeped in white wine. Culatello is handmade and is the aristocracy of cured meats, sweeter and smoother than prosciutto and much harder to find on the market. For most of our choices during the rest of the meal, Parmigiano held the stage in many roles, from soup to fruit.

The real Parmigiano is the Reggiano, from the area adjacent to Parma, and has to be made with milk collected between the first week of April and the first week of November, and then aged at least 18 months before it's ready. At two years of age it is called *vecchio* (old), and is perfect for serving with just fresh bread and a glass of red wine. The cheese should retain a certain moisture so that when cut, it exudes a *lacrima* (a tear). As it ages, at three years becoming *stravecchio* (ultra-old), it becomes better and better for cooking because it melts and blends without caking; at four years it becomes *stravecchione* (super-ultra-old), and is now perfect for grating. Any palate will discern the difference between Parmigiano Reggiano and run-of-the-mill Parmesan, which can be made anywhere at any time of the year. Here in Emilia-Romagna, prosciutto, culatello, and Parmigiano show clearly that good things shouldn't be hurried. Or, to rephrase it, that pedaling can be more rewarding than rushing by car.

I Due Foscari's restaurant has won international prizes for its own dish: *chicche della nonna* (grandmother's candy), pasta with a meat filling, like ravioli but shaped with twisted ends like candy and bathed in a sauce, naturally, of Parmigiano Reggiano and melted butter. Not to overlook the high-octane, one-dish meal *Timballo Emiliano,* a pasta casserole with cheese, prosciutto, and mortadella. Not only is the food excellent but the atmosphere is enchanting: We ate off fine china in candlelight and drank a delicious Sangiovese di Romagna from crystal glasses. Our only other dinner companions were the voice students who ate together at a long table and Carlo Bergonzi himself seated at his regular table in a corner of the room.

The next morning we headed to Cremona, a 15-minute drive north, again on country roads cutting through fields of wheat, corn, and dairy pastureland. Our first stop took us to the Piazza del Comune, the center of life in Cremona, where the 367-foot Romanesque Torrazzo, the tallest medieval tower in Italy, is located.

Just across the piazza is the Palazzo del Comune, or city hall. Posted on its doorway is the sign VIOLIN MUSEUM, SECOND FLOOR. And— especially for Ellen, our violinist—that is what we came for.

What we discovered was a heavily temperature-controlled room with six violins on display, each one hanging from the ceiling by a wire, contained in its own separate glass case. The only Stradivarius, dating to 1715 and made from only one piece of fine-grained fir, was exceptionally well preserved with its original varnish of a shining dark red color. The guard told us it is worth $3.5 million. One Guarneri dates to 1689 and the other to 1734, the latter having been played by the American violinist Pinchas Zukerman from 1972 to 1977 both in concert and for recordings. Three Amatis, dating to 1566, 1615, and 1658 and all in perfect condition, completed the collection.

But the best was yet to come. As we were examining the instruments amid a group of schoolchildren, the guard took us aside and said that, if we were interested, we could attend a playing of the Stradivarius in the adjacent hall. To keep their tone, violins must be played regularly, so the Stradivarius is played several times a week at 11:30 a.m. for ten minutes by a professor from the local music academy. (The other violins are played on different days at different times.) Normally, you need to make a reservation in advance for these brief recitals, but because we happened to be there at the right time, the guard allowed us to slip into seats next to the young music students. It was an enraptured audience listening that morning to the professor as he coaxed the rich notes of several baroque pieces from the instrument. The surroundings truly made us feel like we had been transported back in time: a baroque room, decorated with elaborate chandeliers and *putti,* where city councilors meet and civil wedding ceremonies are performed. At the end, Ellen expressed her amazement at how lush the old Stradivarius's tone was, full enough, she said, to fill a huge modern concert hall.

Cremona was the birthplace in the sixteenth century of the greatest violin and cello makers of all time, and the International

School of Violin Making continues to build instruments that are highly sought after by famous violinists today. On crossing the Piazza della Pace, with its bronze statue of Antonio Stradivari giving a violin lesson to a young boy, we found a small shop where two artisans, calling themselves "master lute makers of Cremona," carry on the tradition, carving out violins and cellos. Then, further on, we discovered a beautiful park that contained the tombstone of Stradivari as well as a statue of Amilcare Ponchielli, also a native composer whose "Dance of the Hours" is learned by most young piano students. Another famous Cremonan is the baroque composer, Claudio Monteverdi.

We could not afford to take a violin back to Rome, but we did bring back wonderful memories and bars of the classic Cremona *torrone,* a Christmas nougat specialty made with sugar, honey, almonds, and hazelnuts. This, too, should be aged, but in our hands it had no chance. The whole trip left us wondering, though, whether there was something about a diet of these luscious Emilia-Romagna delicacies that somehow contributed to the production of world-famous musicians. Ellen, who hoped there is some validity to that speculation, took back with her a few good recipes, along with chunks of real Parmigiano Reggiano and prosciutto di Parma.

On our way back to Rome, we could not help but make a stop in Bologna, long considered the master chef of Italy, but also abounding in other, perhaps lesser known, distinctions. In fact, we find it difficult to understand why Bologna is not a destination for interested travelers; it is a multifaceted city and definitely worthy of attention. And if you are in search of the fountain of youth, we have some advice for you: Come to Bologna. A visit to this city will shave years off your age, restore color to your cheeks, and give a new bounce to your step. Wherever you are or wherever you go in Bologna you are enveloped by age and, comparing it with your own, you feel younger.

The first contact with old age is made even before entering Bologna proper: Six or seven miles outside its doors is the village of Villanova di Castenaso. Artifacts brought to the surface prove that in the Bronze Age, in the first quarter of the last millennium B.C. during his slow migration west, Indo-European man stopped and made his home in this area. He was followed in the Iron Age by the *Italici* (the ancestors of the Italians) who established in Villanova an important agricultural/pastoral and metal production center, significant enough to give name to the "Villanovian civilization." Like layers in the big onion of time, they merged in the sixth century B.C. with the Northern Etruscans who, in the middle of the fourth century B.C. fell under the domination of the Boii Gauls. In turn, around the second century B.C., they were defeated by the Romans who, as was their habit, founded a town and called it Bononia, today's Bologna (pronounced "Bo-*lone*-ya"). Now, comparing your age and personal history with the above, you should feel younger already.

The Bologna of today shows its origins in its classic Roman urban plan: a grid made of streets running east to west (the *decumans*) that intersect avenues running north to south (the *cardi*). This master plan is clearly visible looking west from the top of the Asinelli Tower, in the town's center. At 332 feet, it is the tallest tower of the many in town; its top can be reached by climbing the 480 steps of the internal wooden stairs, and if you can do that, then you already have shed a few years off your age. From up there you can peel another layer of the onion of time by looking west: Now the streets diverge, like the fingers of a hand, from the center toward the countryside in the classic medieval urban layout. It is when looking below at the brick-red centuries-old buildings and towers (terra-cotta is the dominating color of the city) and then at the teeming activity in the streets between them that you feel the continuity of time, the sequence of centuries merging in a continuous renovation to the present. It adds up not to old age but to an ebullient young-blooded city.

This vitality is best represented by the attitude of it citizens, which can be described as *"gioia di vivere."* The inhabitants of Bologna, and of all Emilia-Romagna, exude a sense of dedicated enjoyment of life. "Sanguine" is the adjective that comes first to mind. The pulsating blood can be felt in the paintings of Guido Reni, in the music of Verdi, in the scientific research zeal of Galvani, in the intensity of Paolo and Francesca's love, in the daring technology of the Ferrari, the Maserati, the Lamborghini cars, in the vibrancy of Pavarotti's voice, in the poetry of Pascoli and Carducci, in the ingenuity of Marconi, in the artistry of Toscanini, in the imagination of Fellini, and in the uncompromisingly lusty cuisine. Walk the streets of the city and you will find this zest contagious   life in Bologna happens in public. Alleys, streets, avenues, and squares are all a common living room. It is there that, rain or shine, people walk and mingle and talk and shop and congregate and argue and laugh. Even the architecture of the city is tailored for this all-hours life: All the buildings are contoured by high-ceilinged, vaulted porticos, shaded by day, well lit by night. Of all the many porticoed cities we have traversed in Italy, Bologna outdoes them all with twenty-two miles of porticos, the greatest number of contiguous porticos in the whole world. You can conduct your life in public there and go from one end of town to the other without the need of parasol or umbrella.

Another symbol of this vitality is the University of Bologna, which was founded about a thousand years ago and is the oldest continuously active university in existence, the first and original *Alma Mater Studiorum*. It is because of its university that Bologna has been known through the ages as *La Dotta* ("The Learned"). Bologna's *Universitas Scholarum*—"universitas" meant a corporation of professionals—was the result of a free association of students with the unique arrangement that they chose and paid for their teachers. This system became a model for many universities that were to follow. From its inception, the university's School of Jurisprudence, which taught the philosophy of law, remained totally independent from the religious or civil authority of the period. The political independence of the "Doctors of Law" brought such great fame to the university that by the twelfth century, in Europe its name was synonymous with the teaching of law. Several of its other colleges—such as medicine, engineering, and liberal arts—had, and still have today, great reputations. Finally in the mid-seventeenth century all of the colleges were reunited in a centralized building, the Archiginnasio. Located in the heart of town, it is still a most elegant structure, used today as the civic library. Its portal is flanked by sculptures representing the arts and sciences; the walls and vaults of the interior galleries are decorated with the coats of arms of teachers and students who enriched the Archiginnasio with their minds. It also contains the beautiful seventeenth-eighteenth century Teatro Anatomico (Anatomical Theater), made entirely of wood and where anatomy lessons, open to the public, were held.

To see Bologna only as La Dotta, however, would be like seeing only one side of a coin. With equal value and status Bologna is also known as *La Grassa*. Envious outsiders tend to translate that term as "The Fat One," but proud *Bolognesi* will tell you that it means not only a lover of food but also of all that is rich and good and lively and lusty. And since they are known also for their loquacity, their interpretation of the meaning of "Fat One" could go on for a long while. It would include their love of caustic witticisms, frequently at their own expense when it comes to culture and gluttony. These double attributes come together in the local folklore's *maschera*.

In the Commedia dell'Arte the maschere were a set of stock characters identified immediately with a region or city: Arlecchino (Venice: witty, a schemer, an arranger always in search of his master's, and his, personal gains), Pulcinella (Naples: the smart underdog, the master of survival against all odds), and Rugantino (Rome: the king of malingerers, the practical joker against the powerful). Bologna is represented by hefty Dottor Balanzone, a know-it-all pseudo-doctor with a prodigious appetite and a motor-mouthed dispenser of free advice coined in phony Latin. "Full of baloney," as one would say today. As it happens, one of the city's gastronomic specialties is *mortadella di Bologna*, the huge sausage that once landed in America became simply "bologna" and commonly called "baloney."

The importance of food in the texture of life in Bologna and Emilia-Romagna is exemplified by another of the region's specialties. Where else in the world would a love-struck cook, inspired by his *inamorata*'s anatomy, shape out of thin pasta and spiced forcemeat a tasty morsel and call it "Venus' bellybutton"? Only misplaced prudery renamed that delight a *tortellino*, as it is now known the world over. And it is not alone: The region has given to the world so many creations, by now household words, that it should be given the place of honor in a gastronomic hall of fame, if one existed. Is there anyone who does not know lasagna? Or ravioli, Bolognese meat sauce, or homemade egg pasta?

As for eating places, the list of the "not to miss" suggested by friends, acquaintances, and taxi drivers is so extensive that it is impossible to stop at any restaurant and not come up with a winner. We ought to be satisfied with a statement like that, but we would feel remiss if we did not add that practically every restaurant has its own specialty. We are happy to say that this latest cultural pilgrimage throughout the region was wisely interspersed with gastronomic stops, and nary a single menu was repeated. (Actually, a small bowl of tortellini *in brodo*—broth—was ubiquitous and we cannot think of a more civilized way to begin a meal.) From *agnolotti* with a spinach and cheese filling in Ferrara to *tortelloni* with pumpkin filling in Reggio; from a fish *brodetto* (stew) in Rimini and *piadine* (flatbread) in Ravenna to a *cotechino* and *lenticchie* (salami and lentils) in Modena; and from the lightest of grilled *trippa* (tripe) in Forli' to *pappardelle* (wide noodles) with salmon and asparagus in Sassuolo, to a memorable pot roast *Stracotto al Sangiovese* in Ferrara, we had it all. A clarifying comment is now necessary: Love and robust appreciation of food in Bologna and environs doesn't justify the city's "La Grassa" moniker. It is very rare to find a fat person in Bologna.

Somehow correcting our theory about age and aging in Bologna, a congenial maître d', lifting a glass of ruby red, sparkling local Lambrusco, toasted us with a regional old saw: *"A tavola non si invecchia mai!"* At table one never grows old.

Well, if that saying is correct, we did not age a minute during our stay.

TIMBALLO EMILIANO ·

Pasta Casserole with Cheese, Prosciutto, and Mortadella

FOR THE BESCIAMELLA:

2 cups milk	¼ teaspoon freshly grated nutmeg
4 tablespoons unsalted butter	⅓ teaspoon salt
⅓ cup all-purpose flour	

WARM the milk to scalding (just under the boiling point).

MELT the butter in a saucepan. When it begins to bubble, add the flour all at once and whisk briskly until well blended.

POUR the warmed milk over it, always whisking; lower the heat and keep cooking until the consistency of a thin pudding has been reached. Stir in the nutmeg and the salt, and set aside covered.

FOR THE TIMBALLO:

10 ounces egg fettuccine (homemade, if possible)	2 cups besciamella
	¼ teaspoon freshly grated nutmeg
6 tablespoons unsalted butter (or as needed)	10 ounces mortadella, cut in ribbons like fettuccine
4 eggs	6 ounces mozzarella, shredded
10 ounces ricotta cheese	¾ cup unflavored bread crumbs
6 ounces Parmigiano Reggiano cheese	(as needed)

PREHEAT the oven to 375°F.

COOK the fettuccine in abundant boiling salted water. Drain when partially cooked or really al dente. Toss in 3 tablespoons of the unsalted butter, and set aside.

IN A MIXING BOWL, beat 3 eggs and add the ricotta, 4 ounces of Parmigiano, the besciamella, and the nutmeg; mix thoroughly. Combine the mixture with the fettuccine, the mortadella, and the mozzarella.

THOROUGHLY BUTTER a 9- or 10-inch springform pan. Pour the bread crumbs in it and shake it until the pan is evenly coated with bread crumbs. Pour out and save the ones that do not adhere. Fill the pan with the fettuccine mixture, tapping the pan gently on the counter so that the contents are evenly distributed.

SPRINKLE the top with the remaining Parmigiano and bread crumbs. Beat the last egg and dribble over the top, and dot with butter.

BAKE it for about 40 minutes, or until the top is golden and toasted. Let it cool for 10 minutes. Remove it from pan to a platter, cut into wedges.

SERVE WARM or at room temperature.

Serves 6–8

STRACOTTO AL SANGIOVESE

Pot Roast in Sangiovese Wine

1 3-pound boneless beef chuck or bottom round

2 ounces lean salt pork or slab bacon

6 cloves

1 medium onion

1 medium carrot

1 celery rib

1 quart Sangiovese wine *

½ stick of cinnamon (or ¼ teaspoon powdered)

Flour to dredge

3–4 tablespoons olive oil

3 tablespoons tomato paste, diluted in 1 cup warm water

1 jigger brandy (optional)

Salt and pepper

SLIT the meat here and there and lard it with strips of salt pork or bacon. Stick the meat with the cloves and tie it with butcher string.

MINCE together the onion, carrot, and celery.

PUT the meat, mince, wine, and cinnamon in a sealable plastic bag and let it marinate for a few hours or overnight.

WHEN READY to cook, drain the meat, pat it dry, and dredge it in flour.

CHOOSE a Dutch oven that will hold the meat snugly. Put the oil in the Dutch oven (with a good sealing cover) and brown the meat in it. Scoop the minced vegetables from the marinade and brown them in the pot, then add the marinade wine. Add the diluted tomato paste, the brandy (if desired), and, if needed, enough water to barely cover it. Add salt and pepper to taste.

BRING it to a boil, cover it with a tight fitting cover, reduce the heat, and cook at a low simmer for 3 hours, or until the meat can be cut with a spoon. Reduce the sauce to a thin gravy consistency.

SERVE the meat as a second course, with some of the sauce. The remaining sauce can be used to dress fettuccini or gnocchi.

Serves 6

* *If you are unable to find Sangiovese, you can substitute with any dry red wine.*

Republic of San Marino

PLEASE RING DOORBELL AND ENTER

*L*ooking west from Rimini, on the shore of the Adriatic Sea, you will be fascinated by an unexpected vision: Rising abruptly from the coastal plain, about fifteen miles away, a mountain juts almost perpendicularly 2,200 feet up in the air. Unusual as the appearance is, what really gets your attention is that the mountain's summit ends in three evenly spaced peaks, each topped by a castle tower. Even in a land where almost every hill is capped by a castle, this particular sight has an improbable artificiality to it, a storybook setting as if conceived by a Walt Disneyesque mind. What you are looking at is the Republic of San Marino.

Whenever we have a chance, we pay a visit to San Marino, the best antidote for end-of-the-trip blues. Generally, after a trip abroad, when it is time to go back home, the uplifting feelings of newly acquired knowledge, experiences, and tastes are mixed with a touch of regret for not having had more time, for having to leave something out, unseen, untasted. That is where San Marino comes in. It is a whole country you can see in two or three days—or one, if you are a fast walker. Foreign and romantic, the smallest internationally recognized, full-fledged sovereign state, it is the oldest republic in existence.

The Republic of San Marino is the size of Manhattan, 23 square miles, including the capital and the six villages that make up the whole real estate, and most of it is vertical. From whatever cardinal point you travel, you can spot San Marino from miles away, perched on top of Mount Titan, its three towers dominating the landscape. Legend has it that in the fourth century a Dalmatian stonecutter named Marino, fleeing from the hustle and bustle of the times (and the bloody anti-Christian persecutions of the Roman emperor Diocletian), retired to the very top of Mount Titan and made his home there. Other people joined him and shortly a small Christian community was thriving. At the end of a busy life, with "I leave you free from other men" as his last words, the old saintly man bequeathed to his followers a new country to which he gave his name and a motto: "*Libertas.*" Since then San Marino has been free and independent, a model of democracy, a miniature Switzerland in the bosom of Italy, ninety-six miles south of Venice and eighty miles southeast of Bologna. Over time, the little country grew and, to protect its freedom, built the defensive walls and the three impregnable towers, one for each of Mount Titan's peaks, aptly called (with rational originality) First Tower, Second Tower, and Third Tower. (Actually, their official names—only used on maps, it seems—are Rocca Montale, Rocca della Fratta, and Rocca Guaita.)

Throughout the ages, while wars were raging all around its territory, the republic maintained its neutrality and was recognized and respected as an impartial sanctuary. During World War II, San

Marino gave refuge from political and racial persecution to close to one hundred thousand people, about eight times its population at the time.

There is one major access road to San Marino, a four-lane highway that darts from Rimini along the valley of the Rubicon (of Julius Caesar fame) and then snakes up steeply toward the top of the mountain. And there it is: a sovereign state so small you almost expect to find a welcome mat and a doorbell at its gate instead of border and customs guards. The gate is there, though, and constantly open, manned by colorfully uniformed guards who look surprised if you attempt to stop or even slow down.

We each remember our separate trips to San Marino taken many years ago—probably thirty or more—when there was, as now, one major road of access. But then it was a narrow, one-lane country road winding endlessly up the mountainside, peculiarly bordered with rows of narrowly spaced signs shaped like huge marigolds, advertising nail polish. They reminded us of those old Burma Shave signs along the American highways in the 1940s and 1950s, but without the clever punch lines. It seemed as if the production of nail polish was San Marino's only industry.

Now, the old nail polish signs are gone, replaced by advertisements for a slew of international goods. A word of caution: San Marino is a duty-free state and the bargains that can be found in cameras, electronics, liquors, cigarettes, and perfumes have encouraged a proliferation of tourist shops replete with curios, trinkets, and all sorts of plastic junk. Fortunately, these are located on the lower part of the road before you reach the old town on top, but it can be a bit overwhelming at the start. You just have to keep on winding your way up the hill.

You can reach San Marino by train, bus, car, or any other contrivance, but you can enter the old town only on foot. During the summer months, the little country becomes a magnet for day-trippers vacationing at the nearby Adriatic beach resorts, so it is best to come off-season, or even better, during the winter months. Then, when San Marino's bricks and stones take soft hues and echo your steps in the empty alleys and stairways, it is easy to walk and feel transported back in time.

Once you have reached the old town, follow the cobblestone alleys and you will pass by excellent examples of twelfth-, thirteenth-, and fourteenth-century architecture; a museum with galleries of remarkable ancient and modern art; and an interesting Museum of Medieval Arms and Armor. If you are in a campy mood, you can also visit the Museum of Waxes and Instruments of Torture. The coupling is unfathomable; depending on whim, different historical personalities are on display at the entrance. On our last visit a waxy, scowling Winston Churchill was seated at the museum's door in front of a window displaying myriad grotesque metal implements devised for the infliction of pain. For the philatelist, a must is the world-class Museo Filatetico e Numismatico (Stamp and Coin Museum). Besides a scattering of tax-free small industries, postage stamps are a staple of San Marino's economy, the country having the distinction of being one of the first nations to join the Universal Postal Union. For more than a century its stamps have enjoyed recognition for their high quality, and the museum has a complete collection of San Marino and international stamps.

Soon your steps will lead you to the peaks of the mountains, the end of the line: the Towers. From their tops you will have a unobstructed 360-degree view. Some 2,200 feet straight down are the rooftops of the rest of the Republic of San Marino, a whole country at a glance. All around, as far as the eye can see, is the gentle, fertile Romagna countryside, a land of generous foods and wines. The *Sammarinesi* are ethnically, linguistically, and culturally of Romagna stock—and gastronomically, too, as you can easily guess by the tantalizing odors wafting from the various restaurants passed along the way. Many of the restaurants have tables set in terraces with views so stupendous that they cannot but enhance your appreciation of the food. There are no Michelin-starred restaurants in San Marino, but it is very hard to encounter a bad meal. The cooking adheres to the canons of the region: good, fresh ingredients cooked in a simple manner and served in generous portions. These ingredients include not only all that the best cultivated and richest farmland in Italy produces, but also the tasty fish of the Adriatic Sea. Its coast, so close by, is dotted with small fishing villages that assure the supply of a daily catch to San Marino.

One of our earliest visits gave us the basic indoctrination to the old republic's food and hospitality. Ristorante da Lino, family owned and run by Papà, Mamma, and their son Francesco, was representative of these characteristics. The establishment was also an inn, its few rooms big, uncluttered, and spotlessly clean with large windows overlooking the valley. The food served was traditional family fare: from minestrone (with as many vegetables as the local gardens could supply), baked lasagna (no ricotta cheese, but *besciamella,* white sauce, to bind all the goodies), *tagliatelle alla Bolognese* (the classic meat *ragù* enriched by chicken livers and gizzards served over homemade egg pasta), and fish *brodetto* (the regional fish stew that requires—to be the real thing—skate wing and many different kinds of fish and shellfish) to homemade desserts. The desserts include, naturally, the country's specialty, *Torta di San Marino*, a concoction of crisp wafers layered with dark chocolate, a torte's slice enough to justify a visit to San Marino all by itself.

Francesco filled many positions, depending where he was most needed: buyer, manager, cook, waiter. He was quite talkative, not an unusual trait—together with joviality—for Sammarinesi. After we commented on the ample size of the portions, Francesco asked: "Have you seen a fat person around?" And then: "Here, local or tourist, you have to march up and down, up and down all day. It gives you a San Marino appetite, good for San Marino portions!"

He had a point: Few are the level square feet of ground in the whole nation. The only level place we could think of was the main square, Piazza della Libertà.

Francesco was born in San Marino and, unlike other young people who emigrate in search of more elbow room and more opportunities, he told us he did not plan to leave. He visited New York once and liked it, but thought it too big, too noisy, too rushed.

"Real Sammarinesi are happy with what they have," he adds, and then, smiling, "mostly because what we have is good. If anything, what we miss is a little more space."

Yet San Marino passed on the chance to have more space. Legend says that Napoléon, in admiration for this small but indomitable bastion of freedom and democracy, wished to donate lands to the tiny republic. The offer was refused.

"If we had said yes, perhaps I wouldn't have been able to serve you this kind of prosciutto," added Francesco to that bit of historical —or hypothetical—information.

The prosciutto with fresh figs that he had just served was indeed excellent, lean and sweet, but we failed to see the connection. Francesco explained that he makes his prosciutto from pigs that, like the locals and the tourists, go up and down and down and up all day on small farms terraced on the mountainside, and thereby grow muscular and lean. The only land Napoléon offered was down in the plains, where the pigs would have grown lazy and fat, too fat. Local prosciutti are unusually sweet because they are hung to dry slowly in the cool, clean mountain breezes and not in the moist air of the plains. With thanks to Napoléon.

The cellar was Papà's dominion, and the wines served— a red Sangiovese and a white Trebbiano—came from the cool grotto below the house. They were both from local vineyards and made

under his supervision. Not much of a selection, admitted Francesco, but you can be sure they were not made with *la polverina*, meaning that they were pure and not made with the assistance of any chemicals. The dishes and the wines, even if standard fare, were good, genuine and satisfying. You eat and enjoy them without getting involved in intellectual gastronomic guessing games. As a matter of fact, after having eaten the food and drunk the wine, seen the sights and enjoyed the breezes, you can begin to understand why Francesco said he wasn't planning to leave and why a stonecutter named Marino chose the top of Monte Titano for some quiet and peace.

On a more recent stay, we stopped at the Hotel Cesare. Of a much larger scale than Da Lino, it has the advantage of being located just inside the main gate, a few yards away from the parking lot outside the fortified walls, where all cars have to be abandoned. Recently renovated, the hotel offers modern rooms with modern accoutrements, with some rooms overlooking the town and others overlooking the splendid panorama. Its restaurant, also independently accessible from the hotel, is a glass-canopied modern room, and here, too, the view is spectacular. A fireplace at one end of the restaurant doubles as a grill and barbeque ready to serve the house specialties. Here a local baby pig, who had been allowed to forage freely around the slopes, was turning slowly on a spit. Since it was winter and we were the only patrons in the dining room, we struck up a conversation with the husband-and-wife proprietors of both the hotel and the restaurant. Before long we found ourselves sampling their recommendations.

One delightful dish was homemade *tortelloni* in a basil and tomato sauce. Tortelloni are three or four times bigger than tortellini; the size gives you a more ample chance to taste the fresh pasta, which were stuffed with a mixture of ricotta and Swiss chard. Then we tasted the sausages, homemade from those neighborhood pigs and accompanied by turnip greens, which were sautéed in the same pan where the sausages are cooked and flavored by some of the melted fat and a whiff of garlic. It was a humble dish, a combination so appropriate that it makes you think that both pigs and greens were created just for this union. The slice of fresh *romagnolo* bread was icing on the cake. Then with a slight bow to a more modern cuisine, we have a light *Lombo di maiale all'arancia* (pork loin in orange sauce) accompanied by a colorful *Salad of radicchio and Belgian endive (insalata di indivia belga e radicchio).*

We tried another Sammarinese specialty, *passatelli,* homemade pasta made with flour, eggs, Parmigiano, and lemon zest, then cooked in a flavorful chicken broth. All these dishes were accompanied by the local wines of which the proprietors are particularly proud, and they urged us to taste them all: a Brugneto di San Marino, a Rosso dei Castelli Sammarinesi, a Moscato spumante di San Marino, and a Riserva del Titano, these last two semidry sparkling wines. The Moscato di San Marino and a slice of Torta di San Marino are a visitor's must.

On the way out of the honorable republic, barely outside its western border, at the small village of San Leo, the incredible sight of La Rocca ("The Rock") stopped us in our tracks. We marvel at how anybody could manage to build a fortified castle on top of a vertical stony spur. Besides offering a superb view, La Rocca is a classic example of a medieval castle, self-enclosed and self-sufficient. The custodian tells us that the dungeons are still used as jail cells by the local police, but we think this is a publicity stunt of the local tourism board. What is historically true, though, is that Giuseppe Balsamo, aka the Count of Cagliostro, died here in 1795. Welcomed into the richest European courts of the times, he turned out to be one of the most colorful rogues of the eighteenth century: adventurer, thief, pseudo-physician, alchemist, mesmerist, necromancer, all-around con man, magician, Freemason, and self proclaimed inventor of the philosopher's stone (which either turned lead into gold or gave everlasting youth). Unfortunately, he ran afoul of the Inquisition, which commuted his death sentence to life imprisonment and magnanimously let him finish his days in La Rocca's tiny cell, the *pozzetto* (the well hole). The cell's small window was shuttered in such a way that the only thing Cagliostro could see of the outside world was the church bell tower—the Inquisition's not-too-subtle reminder of who was who. And for us, a reflection on the nature of irony.

INSALATA DI INDIVIA BELGA E RADICCHIO

Belgian Endive and Radicchio Mimosa Salad

3 heads Belgian endive	2 tablespoons red wine or balsamic
1 head radicchio	vinegar
2 eggs, hard-boiled	¼ teaspoon salt
4 tablespoons olive oil	Freshly ground pepper

CUT the endive heads lengthwise, trim the bases, and remove the cores. Wash and dry the leaves and arrange 5 or 6 leaves in a star formation on each plate. Place medium-size leaves of radicchio at the center of star to form the inner petals of a flower. Julienne the remaining radicchio and set in the middle of "petals." Mince the boiled eggs into a "mimosa" and spoon over the salad. Blend the olive oil, vinegar, salt, and pepper (to taste) together and dribble over plates.

Serves 6

LOMBO DI MAIALE ALL'ARANCIA

Boneless Pork Loin in Orange Sauce

2½–3 pounds pork loin, boneless	2 bay leaves
6 tablespoons olive oil	½ teaspoon salt
1½ cups dry white wine	1 teaspoon freshly ground pepper
Juice of 2 oranges	4 tablespoons olive oil
2 tablespoons white wine vinegar	1 tablespoon soy sauce (or to taste)
1 tablespoon fresh rosemary	2 oranges, sliced (for decoration)
1 tablespoon juniper berries	

TIE the loin with butcher string. Make a marinade with 2 tablespoons of the olive oil and the wine, orange juice, wine vinegar, and rosemary. Put the loin in a plastic bag, pour the marinade into it, and seal it. Let stand refrigerated for an hour or two.

GRIND AND MIX together the juniper berries, bay leaves, salt, and pepper. Drain the loin from the marinade, pat it dry with a paper towel, and then roll it in the juniper berry mince.

Put the remaining 4 tablespoons olive oil in a fireproof casserole dish and brown the loin in it.

GRATE the zest of one of the squeezed oranges and add it to the casserole dish. Add the marinade and any leftover juniper mince. Bring it to a boil, cover tightly, and cook at a low simmer for 1 hour. Check that the loin does not get too dry; if so, add some warm water. The loin is done when, pricked with a tester, no pink juices run out—or when the internal temperature is 170°F. (Above 170°F the loin tends to lose its moisture.)

LET IT REST for 10 minutes before undoing the string and cutting in ¼-inch thick slices. Pour the pan juices into a small saucepan, add the soy sauce, and reduce to a creamy consistency. Adjust for salt if necesary, and pour over the loin slices arranged on a serving platter. Decorate with orange rounds and serve.

Serves 6

Toscana

NOT JUST FLORENCE

*M*ore than any other Italian region, Tuscany has achieved world status and become a buzzword, a Numero Uno destination point. For a foreigner, Tuscany is—and has been for the last couple of centuries or so—the coffer guarding all that represents Italian art and beauty. Once synonymous with Florence, Tuscany's reputation has now expanded well into the countryside, to include old villas and farmhouses, rehabilitated and turned into modern or rustic residences for sale, rent, or lease. The rich treasure trove that is Florence and the beauty of its surroundings justify their reputation. But we feel that they leave in the shadow an infinity of other Tuscan places, greatly deserving to be seen, felt, and lived.

Getting to Tuscany by plane, by the express train Settebello, or by the superhighways is to cheat oneself. Coming by plane is similar to skipping the slow, satisfying sequence of a meal and reaching for dessert right away, dipping one's finger in the rich creamy cake. The sleek trains and the fast *autostrade* stab the mountains, going in and out of tunnels; most of what you see is darkness interrupted by blinding flashes of countryside. Getting to the heart of Tuscany should not be easy. We like to work for it. We come to Tuscany by way of the harsh mountains that surround it from all points of the compass. This is how the Romans came, leaving trails and consular roads retraced today by the slow, secondary roads that go in and out of Tuscany.

Whatever way you enter Tuscany, you should do it slowly. Then Tuscany will reward the attentive traveler and open up to you, hill after hill, beauty after beauty, surprise after surprise. When you get there, you are better able to appreciate and understand Tuscany's heart. Or, rather, hearts, because Tuscany is the sum of many subregions, each with its particular name, topography, and individuality: Mugello, Pratomagno, Casentino, Val Tiberina, Val di Chiana, Chianti, Val d'Orcia, Garfagnana, Versilia, and Maremma. They exist independently of each other and yet in close symbiosis, all together spiraling around the Renaissance core: *Firenze,* Florence, *Fiorenza, città del fiore.* City of the flower.

The region would be just a set of artists' two-dimensional landscapes, or a sheet of rare parchment, unblemished and blank, if it weren't for its people. They are like the many illuminated letters that give a page its meaning. If for a better understanding of any place in the world, it's important to know the character of its people, when it comes to Tuscany, it is essential.

All the *Tuscans* we have known have told us that a single, homogeneous Tuscan character does not exist. They tell us that a *Fiorentino* is as different from a *Pisano* as a *Lucchese* is from a *Sienese* as they all are different from everybody else. They say so convincingly. But it's a lie.

Because Tuscans are liars. Their lies, however, are not bashful, blushing excuses for truth. Their lies sound more like boasts, challenges to the world to dare to question their veracity.

We have seldom heard a Tuscan whisper. Whatever he has to say, he will say it forcefully, for everybody to hear. Decibels are as important as content. Outsmarting is almost secondary to out-yelling the adversary. In 1494 during the siege of Florence, Charles VIII, King of France, threatened to sound his war trumpets to signal the final assault. In answer, the Florentine Captain of the People, Pier Capponi, yelled back from the ramparts: "Go ahead, play your bugles! We will ring our bells!" He knew that the pealing bells would drown out the bugles and summon the citizens to fight. Charles VIII understood what was coming and gave up. And Pier Capponi made history.

Tuscans have minds as nimble as an Olympic sprinter, as agile as a jester, and as difficult to hold as quicksilver. They will say they are the only real repositories of the pure Italian language. But, then, Tuscans will not use that language to speak or to converse; they will use it to engage in word duels, with feints and thrusts of witticisms as sharp as sabers and just as cutting. Tuscans love criticism—of others. They criticize other people's looks, speech, clothing, and reasoning. In short, they will criticize all the ways in which someone is not Tuscan.

"We are a difficult people to like," our friend Gustavo Francini, dedicated Tuscan by birth and by vocation, told us. "People do not like us very much," he continued. And after a pause: "*Perchè siamo meglio.*" Because we are better.

He said so with a wry smile, to make us think he was joking. But we knew better: He meant it. God bless him, he is gone now.

But he was a liar: Not only did we like him, we loved him. And he *was* better.

Tuscans love laughter; their smile is a quick flashing of strong teeth, clenched as in a bite. Their sense of humor also has a very strong bite. They are inventors and masters of the *beffa*. Meant to expose a foe to public ridicule, the beffa is a diabolically staged, orchestrated, and executed practical joke, with the same satisfying and sweet reward of a bloody revenge. In return, it can be paid back only with another beffa. Beffe go back and forth among families or villages, towns, and even cities for generations, keeping everybody in stitches and honing their Tuscan sense of bloody humor.

Who but a Tuscan poet could write (just possibly in jest), *"S'io fossi foco, io brucerei lo mondo / S'io fossi acqua, io l'annegherei ..."* ("If I were fire, I would burn the world / If I were water I would drown it ..."), and gleefully continue by saying that if he were death, he would go visit his stingy father and his whorish mother; if he were Pope, he would send all Christians to hell; if Emperor, he would chop everybody's head off? And if he were himself, as he is and was, he would take all the young and fair maidens for himself and leave the old and ugly to others.

That's the way Cecco Angiolieri—poet, soldier, and Tuscan —felt around the year 1300. Pope or emperor: You side with one or you side with the other, Ghibellines or Guelphs. But the self is always at the center: If *I* were fire . . . Tuscan leaders and politicos echoed Cecco's feelings. When the choice between emperor or pope became too taxing, they went off on their own and declared their cities independent communes or republics. At one time or another Pisa, Lucca, Siena, Florence, and Pistoia all went their own way.

Whatever a Tuscan does, he does fully. He does not believe in half measures or many shades of gray. Love or hate—indifference is not part of the Tuscan's lexicon. In Siena's Palio, the purpose is to have the much-valued horse of a city's contrada win the race at any cost, no holds barred. That some of the jockeys are too mauled to finish the race is inconsequential. It is essential to have the contrada's horse, with or without rider, cross the finish line. The jockeys are expendable; the only purpose of a confrontation is victory, a concept which for a Tuscan means "to excel."

We attribute this directness of thought and action to the Etruscan heritage. The Etruscans, for many centuries B.C., were the first and most highly civilized tenants of this beautiful land, lovers of the arts and sports, experts in architecture and engineering, superb farmers and winemakers. And teachers: They were the ones who taught the conquering Romans how to become Tuscans so thoroughly that the Romans, being quick learners, did them in. The Etruscans went, but the Tuscan soul remained.

It is this striving for excellence that makes Tuscan art incomparable. A work by Botticelli or Donatello not only has to be perfect, but also has to be better than anybody else's. Pygmalion, that romantic Greek, sculpted Galatea and fell in love with her. Similarly, a Tuscan sculptor yelled at his finished, lifelike creation, *"Perchè non parli?"* ("Why don't you speak to me?"), and when the statue refused to speak, he threw his mallet at it. Conceit? Yes, but with a name like Michelangelo, perhaps he could be justified in having a fit.

The Tuscan woman shares this "essential Tuscanity" with her man. Botticelli depicts her as the epitome of modesty: Naked or veiled, a Tuscan woman is the spiritual image of all that is pure. Boccaccio recognizes in her a bold carnality and brings her down to earth. Dante identifies his Beatrice with divine grace, source of all inspirations. Piero della Francesca depicts her fully pregnant, the most divine womanly woman. A host of Tuscan painters and sculptors see her as Mary, a flesh-and-blood Madonna nursing the Child, the essential mother. All of this is what a Tuscan woman is, and you will recognize her today: inspiration, partner, mother, and above all a vital counterpart to the Tuscan man. "Behind every great man there is a great woman" does not apply in Tuscany; she shares equal billing and presence on the Tuscan stage. Here, equal to equal, Catherine of Siena (the Saint) told Gregory XI (the Pope) what to do.

We wonder if there is something in the air, water, or soil of Tuscany that makes anything Tuscan unique. Even at table this distinction reveals itself: The Tuscan cuisine excels in ingredients cooked on open fire. On a grill or on a spit, there are no intermediaries between fire and food. Fire made of ancient olive wood, zesty and fragrant, sears in the essence of whatever is bred or grown on Tuscan soil or swims in its waters. With perhaps a touch of green-gold Tuscan olive oil and the scent of wild rosemary or juniper berries, it is a parsimonious cuisine—one that insists on substance and shuns complicated concoctions and sauces or elaborate preparations. Its flag bearers are the lofty *bistecca alla Fiorentina,* a big two-pound T-bone steak of Tuscan beef, grilled—or better seared—over olive-wood fire; and the modestly named *acqua cotta,* "cooked water," whose simplicity (wild mushrooms, raw eggs, tomatoes, Parmigiano cheese, old bread, and enough water to turn everything into a tasty soup) speak for unadorned, direct good food. The wines are also unmistakably Tuscan: From the most aristocratic Brunello di Montalcino and Rosso Nobile di Montepulciano to the hardy Chianti and the humble Pisciarello ("pissing wine"—its trip through your body will be brief, but delightful), they are red, generous, sincere, and full-bodied. Tuscan wines resent the swishing, sipping, intellectual interpretation of professional tastings; they are made to be drunk by the glassful. After all, as our friend Gustavo told us, *"Buon vino fa buon sangue"* ("Good wine makes good blood"). He knew—he was an expert enologist.

IL MUGELLO

We drove in from the north by old Route 65. It leaves Bologna deliberately, straight at first, then climbing in twists and turns, steady as a mountain mule, follows the watershed of the Tosco-Emiliano Apennines. By the time we reached the Raticosa Pass, at three thousand feet, the air was thin and clear and the breathing was easy; Emilia was behind us and Tuscany was around the next curve. Small villages went by, a few houses on each side of the road, one pasted on the side of the mountain, another rooted on the edge of the precipice. Covigliaio is one of them, its BENVENUTO sign almost back to back with its ARRIVEDERCI one. The village contains ten houses, one inn, and a small church. The church is modest; a few steps lead to its weathered, wooden door. It was closed, and a spray of weedy wild flowers growing in the cracks of the threshold's stones told us that it isn't open very often. Our eyes were drawn to a ceramic bas-relief in the lunette above the door: a Madonna holding the Child. The delicate design, the cerulean blues, the creamy whites, and the garland of fruits and flowers gave it away as a Della Robbia work. But is it? There was nobody around to ask, and it probably does not matter. The reality is that, signed or not, it is beautiful, even more so for appearing to us unannounced. In this unknown little church of this unknown village, the perhaps–Della Robbia is full of life. *Benvenuto in Toscana.*

We went back in our minds to one of the many conversations we had with Gustavo Francini. In the past we never had, or had the need for, what could be called a "serious" conversation. With his educated sense of humor and witticisms, the exchanges always turned into zany verbal tennis matches, enjoyable games in which he invariably scored all the points.

"Please, tell us: What is Tuscany?" we asked him.

"Tuscany is . . . " he said, and then caught himself short. He tried to mouth a reply, but stopped. He wanted to give his complete, truthful answer. He lifted his glass of wine and peered through it, as if to solicit inspiration from it. The wine gave deep-red reflections to his face; after a while, he said: "It is everything."

"It *has* everything?" we questioned him to confirm what we thought he said.

"No. It *is*," he repeated.

And we understood. "To have" has a possessive, materialistic, and hence decaying quality. "To be" is the essence of being; it encompasses all the attributes, good or bad, of life.

Tuscany is.

:::::::

We drove on a few more miles and reached the Futa Pass. From here it was all downhill, way down into the Arno Valley. On our left, the high, green hills of the Muggello region glided into sets of lower hills and then lower again in different shades of green, fencing in between them bowls of meadows and olive orchards and vineyards. The landscape is itself a work of art in a land of artists. As we continued the descent, the hills turn into wavy pastures and orderly farmland. We went slowly; here history hides behind every bump of the land. It is in one of these pastures that the master painter, Cimabue, discovered a young shepherd drawing perfect circles on fieldstones in a single stroke. He decided the boy deserved lessons, and today, Cimabue's name is not as well known as the pupil's: Giotto. The house where he was born is still here, hidden and isolated among olive tree orchards near the village of Vicchio, the same village where Fra Angelico, he of the spiritual and prolific brush, was born. On a slow road in the Mugello, you become acquainted with artists you met before only in art books. Here they become alive, acquire a body, become flesh and bone.

IL CASENTINO

To enter Tuscany from the east, we left the Adriatic at our back and crossed the Apennines again. The road rose, and then at the Mandrioli Pass it began its twisting descent and entered the Casentino. Within ten miles of the pass, as the crow flies, is the source of the Arno River; a few more miles to the southeast is the Tiber's. The slopes of the Casentino hills collect the waters and turn these puny brooks into the two most fateful rivers in Italy. They run south, parallel to each other until, three miles from Arezzo, the Arno turns west "its scornful snout"—as Dante said—and snubs the city. The Arno makes its way towards Florence and continues to find its sea, the Tyrrhenian, at Pisa. The Tiber continues its journey to Rome and, further south, to the same sea at Ostia. But while in Tuscany the two rivers flow in what are considered the two most beautiful valleys in Italy.

We followed the road south into the Alta Val Tiberina. From the very top of hills, medieval castles and walled villages watch our progress. One such diminutive town is Caprese, its walls sheltering a simple stone church whose bell tower points up to the sky like a finger. A simple plaque says that Michelangelo Buonarroti was baptized in this church and received his first blessing, a blessing he later shared with the whole world. It was humble Caprese, the Place of Goats, and not powerful Fiorenza, the Flower City, that gave birth to a Michelangelo.

Down the road, about fifteen miles from Caprese, is Monterchi. From its perch on top of its hill, it has a magnificent view of the valley, overlooking a double line of cypress trees that lead to the town cemetery. In the cemetery's mortuary chapel, Piero della Francesca painted one of his most moving frescos: *La Madonna del Parto,* the Pregnant Madonna. On the flat wall above the simple altar, Piero painted a domed circular tent. Two angels, one on each side of its entrance, lift the drapes much like the curtains of a stage. In the center, a beautiful, serene young woman, her blue gown unbuttoned below her bosom, reveals unashamedly and proudly her round pregnant belly. This most exclusively female condition, the beauty of the image, cannot fail to move you; it's an unmistakable proclamation of life in a chapel dedicated to the dead. The masterpiece, damaged by dampness through the years, has been expertly restored and is now housed nearby in its own little museum.

Piero della Francesca's hometown is twelve miles to the east, in Sansepolcro. Here in the town's museum resides "the best picture in the world." That is Aldous Huxley's judgment of Piero's *Resurrection,* and he says so more than once in his travel essay "Along the Road." He wrote it in 1925, and since then the fresco has been cleaned and cared for, so it should be even better today than it was then.

It is Huxley's unwavering admiration for *Resurrection* that is probably responsible for its salvation. In 1944, during the Second

World War, with the Allied forces pushing on the retreating Germans, a young artillery officer of the English Ninth Armoured Brigade was ordered to "soften" Sansepolcro by shelling it. Then when the occupying Germans were routed, his brigade would take the town. He obeyed but, after a few salvos, the name Sansepolcro began to ring a bell with him. He remembered a book he had read a few years earlier when he was eighteen that spoke of Sansepolcro's "best picture in the world." Risking court martial (in truth, it seems he had some information that the Germans were leaving town anyway), the young lieutenant gave the order to stop the shelling. Thus the *Resurrection*—and the town that sheltered it—was saved. Sansepolcro has a street named in honor of that young officer, Via Anthony Clarke.

Resurrection is indeed a beautiful, powerful fresco, and worth much, much more than the short trek from Monterchi to Sansepolcro. There are also other rewards for the trip, not least among them a good meal. At Albergo Fiorentino's restaurant, a good meal comes with a lot of good cheer. Alessio Uccellini, the tall, round, and impressive hotel owner and, at his pleasure, maître d'hotel, has perfected an astonishing way to serve and startle us. He brought what we ordered and, just before resting the plate on the table, he flipped it in the air and caught it again without spilling a drop of sauce or a strand of pasta. In faux circus jargon, he announced his acts: under *la jambe*, *double flippe* with turn, head over heels simple *et double* back-twist . . . *sans la net!* Plates twisted behind his back and sailed tumbling in the air, to be caught in one hand, bounced to the other, and finally deposited safely in front of us.

"I've been practicing for many years," said the jovial Signor Uccellini, "at first in the kitchen, with empty plates. When the breakage got to be reasonable, I began with solid foods on them, things I could drop without soiling the kitchen floor or ceiling too much."

"But why?" we asked.

"It's fun" was his answer. "Day in, day out, life in a restaurant can become a little monotonous. And the customers get a thrill, too!"

"What if one were to ask for, let's say, a cup of broth or a bowl of cherries?"

"Dear friends," he laughed, "monotonous yes, but not that much!"

The pleasures of the table that we happened upon in Sansepolcro proper can also be found in its environs at Castello di Sorci. A few miles away, in the middle of farmlands, the castello is more a large farmhouse than a castle, restructured into a restaurant or, more exactly, into a *locanda*. While "restaurant" suggests the existence of a menu where a customer has freedom of choice, "locanda" echos the historical function of a country inn where wayfarers could find comfort and hospitality if willing to accept *quello che passa casa,* "that which the house has to offer." Locanda di Sorci offers fixed price menus that change daily and are centered around the day's specialty.

"Tuesday: *tagliolini con fagioli,*" thin tagliatelle or fettucine with beans, "Wednesday: *quadrucci con ceci,*" little squares of pasta in a soup with chickpeas, "Thursday: gnocchi" and so on, each followed by three more courses. People have waxed poetic about the Sorci's *ribollita:* a thick soup of cannellini beans, black cabbage, and old bread, blessed at the end with green-gold Tuscan olive oil. It is supposed to be better one or two days after it has been prepared, hence *ri-bollita,* "boiled again." It's offered on Fridays. Other specialties are homemade pasta with *sugo di regaglie,* a sauce of chicken livers, hearts, kidneys, and coxcombs; and *grigliata mista,* mixed cuts of beef, pork, baby goat, lamb, rabbit, veal, chicken, and of any other four- or two-footed animal roaming the region, grilled on the embers of olive wood. And, if you are in luck, there's the famous *trippa alla Fiorentina,* veal tripe in a tomato sauce so delicious as to tempt the most picky, unadventurous palate. There is a large choice of wines at the Locanda, but whether white or red, the house pours only local, Tuscan ones.

Sansepolcro: the sacred and the profane.

Tuscany is.

::::::

VAL D' ORCIA

The Via Cassia is one of the seven Roman consular roads that, like spokes of a hub, converge on Rome from the outlying provinces. If "all roads lead to Rome," they also lead out: The Cassia will take you into Tuscany from the south. Here and there you can still see, just beside the new roadbed, the stones of the old pavement; you can touch the ruts left by history.

As soon as we crossed the border of the region of Lazio into Tuscany, the Radicofani Pass took us over the foothills of Monte Amiata, whose still-active iron mines supplied ancient Rome with steel, and then down into the Val d'Orcia. Even if the development of agro-industry has changed its traditional looks, the beauty of this valley is undiminished. Small farmers have sold out to corporations or joined together in cooperatives that can, with less labor, make the land more productive. The quilt of small farms is gone; large fields and whole hills are now plowed, sown, and harvested mechanically. What remains of the old farms are the farmhouses, lifeless in the middle of fields, like shipwrecks on a sea, abandoned in favor of the stark, anonymous but more comfortable urban dwellings. The landscape is painted now in bold strokes of color: emerald green, chocolate brown, sunflower yellow, silver grey. The vineyards' long rows of vines trace parallel lines, making the view more of a Mondrian than a Giotto. Thankfully, the lines of cypress trees that like so many exclamation marks outline the curve of a hill, the course of a brook, or the way of a road have been spared. They still give the land that exclusive Tuscan accent.

On its way to Siena, the Via Cassia comes upon a fork in the road. If the local hotels hadn't so heavily advertised the town in advance—*Avec Piscine,* "With Pool"—we could easily have passed it right by, the road signs dwarfed by the hotel placards. Bagno Vignoni is the town's name, thermal water is its game, known since antiquity for its curative power. If "quaint" is an overused adjective, it pretty accurately fits the description of this town: Its main square is not a square at all, but a large rectangular pool from which mineral water bubbles up at 130 degrees Fahrenheit. About sixty feet by one hundred feet, it is similar to a millpond. The water in the square holds the reflection of one hotel and some town houses that look on it from three sides; the fourth side reflects a medieval portico, named after Saint Catherine. A barely submerged stone ledge, once used as a settee for bathers, is no longer in use and it is now forbidden to enter the pool. As behooves a spa, the town is immaculately clean. In addition to the buildings that fence in the main watery square there are, at most, fifteen more houses and four hotels—plus the much ballyhooed Olympic-sized swimming pool, which, even if part of a hotel, has a separate entrance and a separate fee.

By the time the hot mineral water reaches the swimming pool, its temperature has gone down a few degrees but it's still capable of cooking a soft-boiled egg. Nonetheless, the piscina is crowded with people of all ages "doing the waters," recommended as beneficial for curing arthritis and rheumatism. For less affluent people, the town offers a natural solution: The main square's overflow water carves an uneven stream through the town, about three feet wide and two feet deep. We couldn't resist the temptation, so, along with a few other people, we took off our shoes, sat down on the stone banks, and immersed our feet in the running hot water. Others, more exhibitionistic and enterprising, stripped to their underwear and, arms crossed on their chest, lay down in the stream. The water soon reaches a cliff above a ravine, and spills straight down a good three hundred feet to form a small natural pool at its base. By then the water is lukewarm, and less hardy bathers take advantage of the more comfortable therapy at the foot of the overwhelming cliff. The whole scene, enveloped in a sulfur-smelling mist, has a definite Dantesque hellish quality.

Out of Bagno Vignoni, another fork on the Cassia leads us to Pienza, less than five miles away. The town is a unique example of Renaissance city planning and a single architect's showpiece. Enea Silvio Piccolomini, better known as Pope Pius II, assigned the Florentine architect Bernardino Rossellino to make over Pius' native village, Corsignano, and form it into something worthy of a pope. The outcome, renamed Pienza after Pius II, became an assemblage of *palazzi* and churches, their juxtaposition resulting in a balanced unity of volumes and spaces, of light and shadows.

Several food stores in Pienza display the many products of the Val d'Orcia in a hard-to-resist way—packaged as town souvenirs. Extra virgin olive oils, pecorino cheeses, wines of the Sienese hills, wild boar's sausages, and prosciutti: All cellophaned and beribboned, they make a superb and civilized alternative to the usual plastic trinkets for the tourists. At lunchtime we stopped at La Buca delle Fate, where we had a plate of wonderful cannellini, white Tuscan beans dressed only in gold-green Tuscan olive oil. To be cannellini, these white, fleshy beans have to have a Tuscan birth certificate; they are prepared in so many different ways they should be part of Tuscany's escutcheon. For us, they were perfectly accompanied by a luscious, tasty, barely grilled *bistecca alla Fiorentina*. We were assured that it was *razza chianina* beef, the unique cattle grown in the Val di Chiana. The bistecca looks very much like a Texan T-bone steak, but it is actually leaner and tenderer. La Buca, along with other restaurants in Pienza, still serves solid Tuscan food, accompanied by slices of the incomparable homemade bread, *pane casareccio* (country bread), crusty and hearty, the real staff of life. We believe it was a Tuscan who coined the word *companatico*, meaning "that which accompanies bread." The old road inns and post relays used to offer a full meal of *pane e companatico* for a fixed price. It meant that the bread was the star, the essential nourishment, and all that was served with it had second billing.

In a class of its own when coming right out of the oven, Tuscan casareccio bread (unsalted, as are all Tuscan breads) has no substitutes when used as an ingredient for a host of preparations. Try it with fresh figs and a slice of prosciutto. It is essential for the now world-famous bruschetta, which is a slice of casareccio toasted on a wood fire, rubbed with garlic, and dribbled with extra-virgin olive oil; and in *pancotto* and *pappa al pomodoro*, *ribollita*, *acquacotta*, and *minestra di pane,* all soups where toasted or dried-out bread is the main ingredient; and even in *panzanella*, a salad of diced onions, tomatoes, cucumbers, and cubed stale casareccio tossed together and slathered with olive oil. When in exile in Ravenna and forced to eat non-Tuscan bread, Dante, *il gran toscano,* complained, *"Oh, quanto sa di sal lo pane altrui"* ("Oh, how salty is other people's bread"), implying how painful it is to live away from home.

Here at La Buca, besides good food they also have a good sense of business. While waiting for our order to arrive, we became interested in the activity at a counter in a corner of the dining room. It was half deli, half bar: The waiters brought their orders there for wine, of which there were hundreds of bottles on display, or for cold cuts, beautifully displayed in a refrigerated case. Our obvious interest inspired our waitress to bring us a sample plate of cured meats, introducing us to each one of them with a brief description. Most remarkable was a generous slice of *finocchiona,* a tasty large salami spiced with seeds of wild *finocchio* (fennel).

"It is our pride," the waitress told us. "You can travel the world, but find this finocchiona only here, in Pienza."

She, and that sample plate, have made of us dedicated customers.

Pushing north, the Cassia enters deeper into the Sienese hills. When it comes to Tuscan topography, how poor is language: Italian has only one word, *collina* (hill), for the multitude of shapes and sizes and textures that is the Tuscan terrain. Here, the hills are gentle and soft like the body of a reclining woman; there, harsh like fists planted on the earth; now steep, dark, and pointed like a witch's hat; or smooth and bald, or craggy and gnawed, as though marred by a giant's bite; now green-silver and combed by rows of vines or dotted by olive trees; now clay, gray, dismal, and forbidding.

At Buonconvento, we turned off to the right; the hill rising high over a deep valley and across from barren clay slopes suddenly was thick with tall cypresses and eucalyptus trees. They almost hid from view the Abbey of Monte Oliveto Maggiore, a massive, pink brick complex. The abbey's church and its cloister rewarded our ascent; the cloister, its slim columns circling the flowering garden, has its walls brought to life with thirty-six frescoes. The work of Luca Signorelli and Antonio Bazzi, called il Sodoma, the panels tell the history of Saint Benedict. Like pages out of an illustrated book, the frescoes are populated by life-size saints and devils, heroes and rogues, and rich bishops and poor monks and tell of the life and times of the fifth-century saint. Depicted forcefully in Renaissance style—sometimes brutally by Signorelli, more delicately and gently by il Sodoma—the story unfolds on the walls, as vividly as in a moving picture.

Another work of art, just as astounding, rests in the penumbra of the church. Fra Giovanni da Verona, with a myriad of differently grained and colored woods—and a Carthusian monk's patience—created the beautiful intaglios of the chorus stalls and the wooden paneling of the church. Religious scenes, decorative motifs of fruits and flowers, and escutcheons of arts and guilds are all as vivid as brush paintings but with the sharpness that only a honed knife can give.

All this is under the benevolent surveillance of the white-robed Monaci Olivetani, a congregation of Benedictine monks who flutter around like huge doves but who will not hesitate to shake a severe, admonishing finger to reprimand noisy or immodestly clad visitors. Two young ladies in shorts and halter tops pleaded to be let in, but a monk, unmoved, adhered to the old rules and the girls had no chance. After all, the cloister's nineteenth fresco is captioned COURTESANS SENT TO SEDUCE THE MONKS, AND CHASED AWAY. The ladies lost then, and they lose now.

MONTE ALBANO

While roaming in Tuscany it is not unusual to encounter eye-catching signs; to the left or on the right of the road, black letters on orange-yellow placards announce HERE WAS BORN . . . or THIS IS THE BIRTHPLACE OF . . . The unassuming statements are completed by a name that we all know, or should: Galileo Galilei, Amerigo Vespucci, Della Robbia (a full family of them—at least five on a marker), Donatello, Michelangelo, Giovanni da Verrazzano, Giotto, Piero della Francesca, even Pinocchio. No detours are needed; their houses are right along your route.

This does not apply to the village of Vinci. Vinci is a destination; it does not rest near any major road. Coming to Vinci, Leonardo's birthplace, and standing on the same soil where he stood, seeing the same landscapes he saw, and recognizing in the locals' faces the ones he drew, we understand him more intimately and directly than through the mediation of a thousand books. Looking at the modest farmhouse of his birth, about a mile out of town, we rejoiced at the random and democratic way nature distributes genius. Leonardo came with no family name; he instead adopted the name of his village. Vinci now contains the Biblioteca Leonardiana and the Museo Vinciano where you can find, built precisely from his drawings and sketches, the working models of the incredible machines his mind conceived. Leonardo is officially described as painter, sculptor, architect, musician, engineer, and all-around scientist. From this list is missing what so clearly appears from his models and sketches: visionary. Who but a visionary could think of and design machinery—from airplanes to submarines—that was put to use and became essential only centuries later?

The museum overlooks the terra-cotta roofs of the village. Behind the roofs lie a deep green valley and the slopes of Monte Albano. Steep ramps lead from the museum to the small village, which is, like many others, clean, quiet, and unassuming. Young children were chasing a ball, zigzagging and chirping like the swallows in the sky. At a table outside the bar-cafe, four old men played cards; inside, two young men were leaning on the counter, laughing and showing off like two young roosters. Behind the counter an attractive young woman smiled faintly as if not to acknowledge openly their bold jokes. We were fascinated by that knowing, faint smile on her handsome face; we had seen it before. Mona Lisa? She produced hissing steam from her sleek espresso machine and we were amazed at her agility with handles and levers. "Leonardo's?" we asked her smiling, alluding to that mechanical marvel. She looked at us seriously, briefly, not dignifying us with an answer. Leonardo, in Vinci, is a serious matter.

During one of our Tuscan trips, while doing research for our food writing, we accepted an offer from an old friend: to take advantage of her Tuscan villa while she was in the States. There we could rest for as long as we wished, cool our bodies in the pool, collect our thoughts and notes, and give a vacation to our overworked taste buds.

Not far from Vinci, the villa is a remodeled Renaissance farmhouse at the edge of olive groves and vineyards. A double line of cypress trees leads up to it at the top of a hill; from there the house overlooks a panorama of undulating valleys, fringed by rows of cypresses and dotted by farms. Whoever remodeled the house saved the original lines, bricks, and stones as much as possible and still made of it a very comfortable dwelling. Its only concession to modernity is a working system of pipes and waterworks that include a partially enclosed swimming pool. We arrived after dark, found the house key where our friend said it would be, and in no time made ourselves at home. This, we told ourselves, is just what the doctor ordered.

The next afternoon, Marco, the caretaker, found us floating and splashing in the pool. He had been alerted to our arrival but eyed us with suspicion. He circled us and made unnecessary motions, pushing a flowerpot a few inches here, picking up a dead leaf there. The notebooks, maps, and photographs we had spread on the garden table near the pool intrigued him. Finally, he closed in on us and introduced himself as the *custode* and *mezzadro* (custodian and sharecropper) of our friend's property. We confessed to him that we were writers—or would be shortly, once we forced ourselves out of the pool. After the de rigueur how-do-you-do and small talk, he told us that other writer friends of the signora had also been here. Professors, no less, of Renaissance Art and History. The things you come to Tuscany for. We knew what was coming: What were *we* writing about? "A book," we said.

"Hmm. . . . History? Art?" He saw from our expressions that he was far off the mark, but he pushed on: "Then, a novel perhaps?"

"Better than that," we told him. "It's all of that and then some. It's about food."

He gave a short, coughing laugh, as if to recognize that he had been too nosy and now, as a comeuppance, we were pulling his leg.

To make sure, he squinted his eyes and tested us: "What food?"

"Italian food. From all over Italy. From Alto Adige to Sicily."
As proof we pointed to our notes for him to check, if he wished, as
our passport to credibility. "See, that is *Piemonte*. We are just coming
from there."

Now he knew for sure we were fooling him.

"Piemonte. I did my military service there. Nice place, elegant girls. But food? You call that food? Italian food is Tuscan. Tuscany is food."

He left us, shaking his head and mumbling to himself.

The sky was turning a Della Robbia blue, a single star prick-
ing a hole in it, the incredible quiet of the country laced by the bells
pealing an evening benediction, calling each other all over the valley. It was almost dinnertime when Marco's wife, Adria, came to
see us and introduced herself. She had heard that we had starved
our way through Italy, barely surviving Piemonte; we needed some
real food. We smiled our thanks to her, refraining from telling her
that to burn off the food intake of the prior month, we should have
jogged around the world. Twice. She uncovered the basket she carried under her arm and started producing containers and dishes,
displaying them, buffet fashion, on the table.

"Simple country food," she apologized, "just a taste of *cannelloni alla Fiorentina,* a little roast veal, a few fresh shelled beans *all'
uccelletto,* and barely a touch of Swiss chard with mushrooms. For
later, just in case, a small wedge of *crostata* of fresh fruit and some
pecorino cheese fresh from the farm."

The cornucopia of goodies kept coming out of the basket, and
we looked at it slacked-jawed like children at a magic show. She had
a warm smile and a motherly attitude.

"Don't let it get cold, now," she admonished us. Then, as an afterthought and with a final flourish: "Oh, and here is a bottle of Chianti. *Buon vino fa buon sangue!*"

The next morning, on the garden table by the pool, we found a tray with a round of freshly baked bread, a deep dish of butter, and a plate of fresh figs. The figs couldn't have left their tree more than a half-hour before; their stems still cried a milky tear of sap. A note on the tray, wedged under a jar of homemade *marmellata,* said "Buon giorno. Lucia." It was from Adria's daughter.

Somehow we managed to do some work, but our hearts were not in it. Shortly past noon, we dove into the pool and emerged to be confronted by a sizable, white-haired woman; she introduced herself as Marietta, Adria's neighbor. She was fidgety, shifting her weight from one foot to the other, but finally she came to the point. She did not know if Adria had reason to mention it, yes, Adria was a good cook, no question, but . . . well, she was almost like a niece to her, and she herself was the one who . . . well, after all . . . had taught Adria how to cook. So here was some real food for us: homemade fettuccine, a giblet sauce, a few slices of *porchetta* (young pig roasted on the spit), and a bunch of *misticanza* (a mixture of wild salad greens), about which she said, "You can travel the world, but find only in Toscana." She had heard that we were writing about food, so probably she knew what to do, but if we wished, she could help us out.

By the third day it was obvious that a fierce, generational competition had started and we were the targets. Lucia, who came to do the house chores, produced for our breakfast not only bread, butter, jelly, and figs but also some prosciutto and some *finocchiona* sausage. These, she wanted us to know, she had cured personally.

Even the wild fennel seeds for the big pork sausage she had picked herself.

"You can travel the world," she emphasized, "but this finocchiona you find only in Toscana."

Having heard the same thing in Pienza about finocchiona, we began to wonder how the notion of our being world travelers had spread around. World travel must have been associated, in their generous and fertile Tuscan minds, with an unlimited capacity for consumption. This belief had to be stopped, or it was going to stop us. Cold.

We found Marco tending the vineyard and told him of our plan: Since Tuscany was on our list of regional food to research and write about, we had an exceptional opportunity to do it right here with "experts." How about having everybody come in for one dinner, say tomorrow evening? Each family group could produce one, and only one, Tuscan specialty of its own, and one, and only one, wine. We would take notes and talk, just talk, about any other Tuscan dishes that might pop into their minds. Clean the slate in one controlled blow, we told ourselves, a scheme worthy of a Macchiavelli.

By the middle of the next afternoon preparations were well underway. Andrea, Lucia's husband, and Marco set up long planks on saw horses and arranged benches around the makeshift table. Adria, Marietta, and Lucia had taken over the villa's kitchen and made it into a staging station for the event. In the air's bluish haze, the setting sun looked like a huge ripe melon. It got redder as it descended behind the waves of hills, and the hills became diaphanous silhouettes fringed by lines of cypress trees. The sun finally sank, its last flame as red as the coals Marco and Andrea had nursed from olive wood in the *griglia* (they refused to call it a barbecue). Now they were setting a line of bottles on the table. Marietta's husband, Pietro, patriarchal in looks and age, orchestrated the serving order of the wines by arranging the bottles' lineup. He lifted one bottle, considered it, and replaced it with another—all with the concentration and deliberate motions of a chess player. On cue, the chorus of evening church bells joined the clattering of china as the first dishes appeared from the kitchen. The pop of the first cork, like a starter's gun, officially opened the event.

We should be able to relate forkful by forkful the progression of the gastronomic parade, but an exact recounting would carry us only through the first floats. Our notes grew disordered as the meal progressed and by the end became unreadable scribbles, with exclamation marks and asterisks doing the work of words: *agnello**** *al rosmarino!!!! Torta(?) Trota(!!)**! alla salvia!!* The pocket tape-recorder that we used as a backup to our note-taking recorded only the loud, choral, overlapping talk and a great clamor of dishes, glasses, and lots of laughter.

Some of our talk had to do with the pedigree of dishes: Was *gnocchi verdi,* definitely Florentine for its base of ricotta and spinach, more Tuscan than *salsicce di cinghiale,* sausages from a wild boar hailing from Maremma? Was a lean mountain prosciutto from the Garfagnana more or less valuable than a fatter, sweeter one from Val d' Orcia? Pithy queries these, but not as philosophically basic as: Is the lavish use of the grill in Tuscan cooking indicative of a refined cuisine, or is it only simple, peasant cookery? All issues for deep thought.

What we remember of that evening is *Coniglio in salmi* (the wild rabbit a spoil of Andrea's hunting, the stewing sauce Lucia's coup de grâce) and *fegatini,* morsels of pork liver wrapped in caul and bay leaves and, yes, grilled. We remember discussions of why foreigners crinkle their nose at the mention of tripe—mouthwatering for anybody in the know, either *alla Livornese* or *alla Fiorentina*— or of blood and liver sausages, or of veal spleen (without which there would be no *crostini toscani*). What would cannellini beans be if not stewed with pork rind? Ah, foreigners, foreigners!

It was agreed that Brunello di Montalcino (our contribution to the jollity of the dinner) is an excellent wine, but somewhat overrated.

"A wine for accountants," decreed Pietro, "who can add, subtract, and percentage every sip, weigh and analyze a year against another, and price it."

Much better, for folks like us, a Vino Nobile di Montepulciano: ruby, true and honest on the table year after year. Or any well-governed Chianti. Opinions flew as freely and colorfully as the flags thrust in the air at Siena's Palio: Up they go and twist and turn and fall in someone else's hands to be flung again and soar and arch in a streak of colors and flapping noise. Chianti? Are we talking Gallo Nero or Putto? From *colli senesi* (the hills of Siena) or *colline pisane* (the hills of Pisa)? But one thing was unanimously clear: Tuscan wine, to be wine, must be red. "White wine in Tuscany," said Marco, "is sissy wine." But then *Vin Santo* is something else. It is Holy Wine—to consider it white wine would be a sacrilege.

"It is a liquor of life," Adria waxed poetic. "Take early harvested grapes, hang them on trellises, and when only sugary humor is left in them, press them and seal the wine in small casks for at least three years. That's Vin Santo, that's holy."

Marco rushed away and reappeared with a well-aged bottle of sweet, dense, golden Vin Santo and a jar of Adria's *biscotti di*

Prato. Dunk a stone-hard almond cookie in a glass of Vin Santo to soften it: a bite of cookie, a sip of wine. Once you get started, this deceptively simple operation can carry you through the night. Your portions of cookies and wine have to end together; pour more wine if you have a cookie left, take another cookie if an amber drop still lingers in your glass. Marietta wrapped it all up with a ditty: "Fill the glass that's empty. Empty the glass that's full. Never leave it full, never leave it empty . . . "

With the appearance on the table of the final *zuccotto,* we made a faux pas. We compared the cake in appearance and artistry to Florence's Brunelleschi Dome and said that it is too big a work of art to have been baked with only a day's notice—it must have been store bought. Marietta didn't take the remark lightly. This and more she could do in a day. On this night we had only scratched the surface of what Tuscan food is. Whatever notes we had taken could barely fill a note of introduction. To back up her argument she produced a fat, well-worn book: Artusi's *The Science in the Kitchen and the Art of Eating Well.* The one she held was the 54th edition of a book first published more than a century ago, the bible for Italian cooks of Marietta's vintage. We know the book and its author well.

"A Romagnolo!" we protested to Marietta. "He was born in Romagna!"

She dismissed our comment: "An oversight of his, a youthful mistake. He speaks like a Tuscan and eats like a Tuscan," she added. "That's what counts."

She leafed through the pages, looking for her prophet's advice. She put her finger on the page with his suggestions for a late summer evening meal: a soup of *tagliolini in brodo,* homemade pasta in beef broth; a second course of *pollastro allo spiedo,* spit roasted pullet, with stuffed zucchini; and then a *ripieno di rigaglie e bracioline di vitella di latte,* cutlets of milk-fed veal stuffed with giblets; then a *tramesso* ("between-courses") soufflé of spinach; and then *insalata russa*, Russian salad that is a chilled mix of vegetables in aspic; and then *migliaccio,* a chestnut flour dessert; and then fresh fruit and local cheeses.

"And then," we tried to joke, "for the real meal . . ."

"And that's what I will make for dinner tomorrow," said Marietta seriously. "At my place. And don't forget your notebooks."

We had obviously met with her approval and had become part of her fold; her tone was schoolmarmish and firm. It didn't leave room for arguing. But the idea of another gastronomic cramming session made us pale.

"O.K., Macchiavellis," we said to each other, "let's see how we get out of this one."

We composed as diplomatic a note as we could for Marco. We begged him to explain to Marietta that we had been called away on important business. As grateful as we were to everyone for the previous night—we could write a full book about it—it was impossible for us to stay for her dinner. We sent regrets and our thanks to all, underlining "our thanks to all."

At dawn, we set out on the Siena-Grosseto road, which is like being in a fairy tale. Wisps of gauzy fog fill the valleys between hills; the intoxicating smell of moist earth mixes with that of woods and vineyards. The road heads west to Grosseto and then turns south. There the smell changes to a subtler one of wet grass and sea. Soon the Tyrrhenian Sea shimmers and, resting upon it, the rocky lump of the Argentario appears. It would be an island if nature had not tied it to the mainland with three thin, long prongs of land. It was our destination and shelter. At Porto Santo Stefano, one of the only two fishing villages on the Argentario, Giorgio was waiting for us at the main square's dock.

An old friend and host, he greeted us and then, gesturing to the fishing boats that were unloading, said, "Fish just got in. And I got all we need for a nice *zuppa di pesce*."

A nice Tuscan fish soup. Umpteen different kinds of fish, and mussels, and calamari, and wine-and-tomato sauce, and fried slices of good Tuscan bread, and a glass of crisp Pitigliano to go with it. We smiled wanly at each other: "A nice Tuscan fish soup," we said together. "Just what the doctor ordered."

A Tuscan doctor, undoubtedly.

VERSILIA

Entering Tuscany from the west is an easier task than coming from any other point of the compass—that is, if you are coming by boat. Not many people associate Tuscany with the sea, yet Tuscany has a long coastline that stretches about 150 miles from the southern border of Liguria to the northern one of Lazio. The Tuscan coastline satisfies the seagoing needs of central Italy. As a matter of fact you can touch Tuscan soil long before putting foot on the mainland: The islands of Elba, Montecristo, Gorgona, Giglio, as well as some minor islands, are part of the Tuscan archipelago, as rich in history and folklore as mainland Tuscany. Maritime Tuscany has written a few interesting pages of history on its own, stitched together, as it were, by the Aurelian Way. The consular road, built to lead the Roman legions from Rome to Gaul and beyond, still runs (revised and enlarged for modern traffic) along the Tuscan coastline, connecting old Etruscan settlements. The glorious name of Pisa, before becoming just "The

Leaning Tower of," struck terror all around the Mediterranean in the mean hearts of Saracen pirates. In the eleventh and twelfth centuries, Pisa, a maritime and very Tuscan republic, was a powerful rival to Genoa and Venice for supremacy on the seas.

One of the main features of the coast is the large strip of clean, golden beach that runs from the mouth of the Magra River, just outside of Marina di Carrara, to the mouth of the Arno at Pisa. The beach backs up against the thick woods of Mediterranean pines, their shape aped on the sand by the beach umbrellas that extend for thirty interminable miles. Versilia was born mostly to fulfill the wishes of fin-de-siècle small aristocracy and haute bourgeoisie for a fashionable, respectable—and undeniably beautiful—summer place. It had the elegance of a 1900s vintage spa: The salve for the body's health was a mere complement to the social need to see and be seen. The correct *habillement* was de rigueur for every hour and function of the vacation day, and vacation life had a set of strict etiquette rules. To expose even a glimpse of epidermis, on or off the beach, was unacceptable, a modesty matched by quiet public behavior. The town of Viareggio grew with this summer vacation fashion and was enhanced by the building of many elegant "grands," exclusive hotels dedicated to a refined and cosmopolitan clientele.

In the mid-1920s this summer destination was noticed by the growing middle class, which was acquiring spending power and social ambition. Elegant Viareggio was like a shiny pebble thrown into calm waters; the trend of coastline spas rippled throughout Versilia. For the families of new doctors and lawyers, small merchants, junior public servants, and government bureaucrats, a summer vacation in Versilia became the seal of acceptance into the *per bene* status, that nebulous "proper" rung on the social ladder where appearances are all-important. Families justified their summers in Versilia as mental and physical recuperation, but these summers were truly an excuse to display the family's new affluence. The transparent theater of a Versilian summer was a stage on which to enact small deceptions and spot those of others.

With the advent of the Fascist era, adults tried to fit the politically fashionable templates for looks and postures. Fascist men had to be smartly macho—a mix of pomaded Latin lover and Roman centurion—and Fascist women were supermothers of numerous intolerably obedient (or else!) Fascist-saluting children. In the brief season of a Versilia vacation, adults built their personae as creatively as their children built sand castles, both competitive constructions as ephemeral as the first wave of fall.

The rules of etiquette changed again with the boom of the post-war economy and the explosion of mass travel. Covering the full range of economic possibilities, every single foot of sandy beach and of forest shade in Versilia is now built over with cabanas and bathing establishments, restaurants and hotels, bungalows and villas, boardinghouses and campsites. Discreet elegance has been shouldered aside by loud mass taste. Among the new basic rules are maximum skin exposure during the day (*toppe-less* is basic), and attire and decibels as loud as possible through the night. For a few summer months these activities bring to many parts of Versilia a frenetic lifestyle that, although equated with youth, is avidly adopted by middle-aged time-fighters. At the first gray autumn sea, however, they will all give up the fight and go home. Then Versilia goes again into hibernation, its last signs of life given by the splashing of a few sturdy Nordic bathers, indifferent to the chilly waters. The area wakes up briefly in Viareggio for Carnevale, the pre-Lenten festivities that are celebrated all over Italy, but in no other place as spectacularly as in Viareggio. Elaborate fireworks light up the winter sky and a Mardi Gras run of gargantuan floats, forerunners of the Macy's Easter parade, attract a reveling crowd.

Heading south along the Aurelian Way, we came to Livorno (Leghorn), today one of the busiest ports in Italy. The commercial acumen of the Medici turned this town from little more than a fortified fishing village into a thriving city-port. With the fading of the Medicis' hegemony and the consolidation of the Grand Duchy of Tuscany, in the seventeenth century Livorno became an open city, refuge to all religious and political exiles, and a free port, making the city a great center for the commerce of goods and ideas. This enlightened move reinforced and enhanced native Tuscan traits in the *Livornesi*, so that today they are known as ingenious traders and merchants, as well as liberal, cosmopolitan freethinkers.

Events of unforeseen magnitude caused the biggest and darkest blot on Livorno's otherwise shiny history. Toward the end of World War II, Livorno became an important base for supplies needed for the Allied Armies' final push on Germany. The city outskirts became an enormous depot for all the needs of an army on the move. Amassing everything from toothpicks to tanks, jelly to jeeps, Spam to spades, canned goods to cannons, Band-Aids to blankets, and beef bouillon to bullets, the depot extended for miles. To a starving civilian population, deprived of everything after four years of war and bombardments (Livorno had suffered massive air bombings, both by the Allies and the Germans), the depot was a vision of the importance and size of a biblical reservoir of manna, kept from bursting by a lacy fence of barbed wire. But, burst it did.

In the nearby thick pine woods of Tombolo the goods began to trickle in, then to stream and finally to flood from the hands of unscrupulous guardians into those of greedy black marketeers. Anything was available in Tombolo, and everything was traded for windfall profits. In a brief time Tombolo became a new El Dorado, a magnet for profiteers, escaped military and civilian criminals, deserters of any and all armies, and merchants of female, male, black, white, and child prostitutes—a sinkhole turned into a separate, independent, armed sovereign state of anarchy. Neither military nor civilian police dared to enter its borders. Many people who did enter never came out. Tombolo was one of the most lurid by-products of war, a ghoulish carnival under the tent and protection of the centenary pines. Around its periphery sprung a midway of bordellos, eateries, and nightclubs that attracted a large clientele from all over Italy. This was slumming at its lowest, but many people, accustomed to the immorality of war, did not think of Tombolo as a moral slum. It became chic to be seen there, and for many personalities, being photographed reveling in Tombolo showed their open-mindedness, their being "with it" and attuned to the arrival of new times.

With the end of the war effort and the shipping home of the armies, the Livorno depot became obsolete. Police and politicians moved into Tombolo with crusading fervor and fanfare, but it was mostly a work of sanitation. Tombolo had died a natural death. The Aurelian Way still skirts the Tombolo woods on the way to or from Rome, sees the serene canopy of umbrella pines, and with the bored wisdom of millennia, passes by uncaring, as if nothing untoward ever happened there.

Livorno is still one of Italy's busiest harbors and a naval base, and as such, it has all the standard amenities of an active international

port. What is really special in Livorno is its cuisine. The large availability of Mediterranean fish—and the inventive way fish is used—make its cuisine Livornese first, Tuscan second. The *Livornesi* proclaim that theirs is the unsurpassed way (how boastfully Tuscan!) to prepare the tastiest fish dishes in Italy. Confronted with a *cacciucco alla Livornese,* few would argue. To hear a Livornese describe it, the making of cacciucco is more a ritual than a process and must follow traditional, unchangeable rules. Otherwise the results would be a normal fish soup, perhaps good, but not a cacciucco. A diversity of sea creatures—a dozen or so different species—is an acceptable beginning. The heads and bones of the bigger ones and some trash fish are cooked in a dense tomato sauce; once they are well cooked, they are ground, mashed, and sieved into a pot to become the thick base for the final broth. Wine and more fish broth are added and then, one at the time depending on their cooking times, the remaining fish, shellfish, clams, and mussels end up in the pot, each releasing its individual humor and essence to the soup which, being condensed, is more of a sauce than a soup. The cacciucco is then served hot in bowls, with or over toasted Tuscan bread.

There are several other Livornesi fish specialties, but why go on? Once you've got to the cacciucco, you've reached the pinnacle.

ALPI APUANE

We left the Tyrrhenian Sea, crossed the Versilian beach, crossed the pine woods, crossed the Aurelian Way and, there, the rest of Tuscany was facing us. What we saw, so close we felt we could touch it, was an almost perpendicular wall of mountains: the Alpi Apuane. They are steep but, as Alps go, not terribly tall—close to five thousand feet at their highest—and the "snow" that caps and streaks their sides is not snow at all. It is marble, Carrara marble. Quarried at the top, huge chunks of the mountains travel, at a truck's growling crawl, down steep tortuous roads to rest at the mountains' feet, in the marble manufacturing yards of Carrara, Pietrasanta, and Serravezza.

In these enormous yards the big marble cubes—blinding white, black, rose-veined, red, green, and any color in between—look like toy building blocks waiting for the hands of a playful giant. But what they are waiting for are the cutting blades of artisans or the chisels of artists. Then the Carrara marble leaves in different shapes and for different purposes, and travels the world in a centuries-old uninterrupted migration. With the new technologies, the marble artisans of old are now peerless industrial craftsmen. Valuable marble quarried in other parts of the world is sent here to be cut and prepared and then shipped to international markets.

Few roads connect the shore to the top of the Apuane and beyond. The main one is the Cipollaio Road out of Serravezza. It noses straight up and then zigzags on the carved flanks of the mountains, at times piercing them, tunneling into rock, leaving behind one ravine to resurface in another. Travel is slow and difficult, to be negotiated curve by curve, quarry by quarry. It is not hard to let the imagination leap from mountaintop to valley floor and back, and see these mountains as the womb of cathedrals and churches and—how truly catholic—of synagogues and mosques and pagan temples. Which of these mountains' open wounds, which quarry gave birth to which monument and statue and colonnaded building we know? How many more are still there, unborn, waiting to be carved out piece by piece and brought to life? Will there be another Michelangelo up here in the highest quarry of Monte Altissimo, waiting for months on end for that unique piece of marble, with the right veins, the right feel, the right soul for his creations? Which one of these monoliths hides within itself a statue waiting to burst out, its cocoon chiseled away by the vision of a master?

Within a quarry, near the sheared marble walls and the already carved huge marble cubes, the measure of man is ant-like, inconsequential. The long, lean arms of cranes, folding and swinging like the pincers of a mantis, lift their prey and deposit it on the flat backs of trucks. The sound of the trucks slowly reverberates in the cave-like emptiness as they haul their load down the steep road to the plain. One wonders: How did mere men garner the immense strength and courage five centuries ago to slice a mountain and carry it, block by block, five thousand feet down and miles away? We marvel at the miracle and honor the names of those who have shaped a masterpiece out of a chunk of marble, but why are the names of those who brought it to their hands not remembered?

GARFAGNANA

The imagination's questions subside, and so does the climb. Big vertical slabs streaked by whatever black humor is contained in the stone—define the sides of the road. The descent on the opposite side of the Apuane begins. The road parallels a white foaming torrent, then leaps over it and back, again and again. These streams feed the Serchio River; we are in Garfagnana, a piece of Tuscany as different from any other piece of Tuscany as the Alpi Apuane are from any other Alp. It was hard work to get here but the Garfagnana helps us to relax. We and our imagination have earned it.

The Garfagnana is geography's brief rest, a momentary relief between the jagged chain of the Alpi Apuane and the Tosco-Romagnolo Apennines. Even if the hills that rise on each side of the

Serchio's valley are crowded and steep, the mood of the region is mellow and cool. In the green seasons, the chestnut woods and the terraced vineyards cover the territory like a velvet blanket; even the air seems to have a green tinge and a taste, soft and easy to breathe. Here and there, the lakes of Villa, of Vagli, of Gramolazzo, and of Vicaglia give the region a blue sparkle, mirrors for the villages perched high on the hills. History, especially medieval history, has walked up and down the Garfagnana and left footprints; a traveler need not go far to encounter a village, castle, tower, or church with a story to tell. Any road that leads off the provincial road, which parallels the Serchio River, will take you up to the hamlets and villages that crown the hilltops or line the valley: Borgo a Mozzano, Barga, Gallicano, Coreglia, Castelnuovo. . . .

Our favorite route through the Garfagnana (we usually use the town of Lucca as our home base) is to start at the little town of Borgo and go north to the end of the narrow valley, where the road opens up onto splendid views of the marble quarries. At Barga, which is up a winding road, we stopped and stretched our legs and enjoyed some great food. There we could just wax romantic and let the views of the valley below feed our soul, but our more prosaic appetite is fed there, too. The food in Garfagnana is good and so is the wine. Garfagnana yields venison and wild mushrooms, stream trout and lake pike, pecorino cheese, chestnuts and wild strawberries and blueberries. Most of the restaurants and eateries around here come with a view; how easy to be a romantic gastronome!

We chose La Pergola and let ourselves be seduced by a steaming plate of *pappardelle alla lepre,* the long, wide strips of homemade pasta dressed with the sauce of a wild-hare stew. The gamey taste of the hare was subdued by the wine, tomatoes, sage, and thyme in the long-cooking dish. The offering was a double whammy: The pappardelle was the first course and dressed only with the stew's thick sauce; it was followed by the hare's meat and bones, whose added attraction, besides the taste, was to pick the bones clean with your fingers. This practice is not just local but accepted nationally—*fare la scarpetta* means using a morsel of bread to wipe the sauce from your dish. Although we haven't found anyone who can explain where the expression "make like a little shoe" came from, the custom is many an Italian's favorite way to end the meal's main course.

The local chestnuts supply the flour for a *castagnaccio* cake: The flour is simply mixed with water, olive oil, a few raisins, and pine nuts. It is a baked "peasant pie," the waiter warned us. The souffle-like middle is contained between a crusty top and bottom. Peasant, perhaps, but we promote it to "duke of a pie," just for a touch of deserved aristocracy. We kept this whole meal moist with a glass or two of Rosso delle Colline Lucchesi, a round, soft, and lively red not dissimilar from a good Chianti.

We followed the Serchio downstream and returned to Lucca, one of the most enchanting towns in a country full of enchanting towns, and one of our favorites. It is a walled city, but unlike the myriad walled towns of Italy, Lucca's wall is not built straight up to protect the inhabitants of a town perched high on a hill, as a defensive wall should be. Instead, it is squat and wide—possibly wide enough for several trucks to go side by side. But there are no trucks allowed on the wall, in fact no traffic at all unless you count bicycles and baby carriages. This elevated space is lined on both sides with old chestnut trees, lush green grass, and flower beds, and filled in the early morning with joggers, at midday with pensioners sitting on benches in deep conversations, around noon by people having lunch alfresco, and later in the afternoon by all manner of ice-cream-licking *Lucchesi* for the evening *passeggiata*.

We entered the walled city and let it charm us. The urban plan is typically Roman-medieval. Within blocks of the *città vecchia,* the accumulation of buildings from the Middle Ages has formed a complex of interlacing alleys, little winding streets, and inner courtyards, all connected to one another by passages and small squares. The whole old-city center is off-limits to motorized traffic, so you can saunter slowly and peacefully on the narrow streets lined with cafes and elegant shops. Then, suddenly an alleyway will open out onto one spectacular irregularly shaped piazza after another. Our feet led us to churches and towers, buildings and squares. Portals and windows surprised us at every turn; following a city map would be cheating, like unwrapping gifts before Christmas. And the town has many surprising gifts to offer. The impressive church of San Martino and its tall tower, several centuries in the making, is an architectural buff's delight for its many accumulations of styles; it is the city's cathedral, yet hidden on an out-of-the-way piazza. Gothic San Michele's elaborate four-tiered facade of slender columns is filled on the second tier with the busts of the great men of the time. Built of white limestone, the church glistens in the daytime like a delicate cake, topped by the statue of San Michele. At night it is softly lit, giving the illusion it is bathed in moonlight. Perhaps Lucca's most astonishing construction, though, is the piazza built on the footprint of a Roman amphitheater that was there centuries ago and now transformed into a large oval, surrounded by ocher-colored houses, cafes, and shops.

Lucca is full of favorite eating places, but the one in which we have the most fun is Da Leo. An inexpensive trattoria, its one large room is always filled with friendly, boisterous patrons. There is a large range of fare for such a small kitchen; the handwritten menu lists fifty entries, from antipasto to dessert. With the help of several friends, we put a reasonable dent in the abundant victuals, sharing a *Pappa al pomodoro,* a Tuscan soup (made classic by a children's ditty), based on tomatoes, olive oil, and old hard bread; and then *risotto al vino novello,* a risotto in which young wine is the basic ingredient. They were followed by a *coniglio in umido con olive,* rabbit stewed in wine with olives; *scaloppine tartufate,* veal medallions in a truffled sauce; and, naturally, a side dish of *cannellini all' olio e cipolla fresca,* white Tuscan beans with thin-sliced fresh onions dressed in extra-virgin Lucchese olive oil. *Cantucci,* almond biscotti for dipping, and Vin Santo made the dessert. While the fare is superior, it's the general conviviality all around that makes an evening at Da Leo special. We dispose of the Falstaffian affair with contemplative tempo; nobody rushes us, and as in most *trattorie,* once you are seated, the table is yours for the evening. Da Leo's fare and attitude are not unique—they can be found in various degrees of rusticity or of elegance in the many restaurants around town.

Less than an hour's drive northeast from Lucca is the small town of Collodi, childhood home of the author of *Pinocchio,* one of the most famous children's books ever written. Actually, the real name of the writer is Carlo Lorenzini, who took as his nom de plume Collodi, his mother's birthplace. It's an amusing stop for travelers of all ages, but especially for children, because the whole town has been turned into a sort of Pinocchioville. The entire main street is lined with stalls and shops that sell many different editions of the book and all sorts of puppet paraphernalia. And yet, the place has managed to avoid becoming Disneyesque. The literature at one of the stalls says that, after the Bible, *Pinocchio* has sold more editions and translations than any book in the world (possibly the precursor of Harry Potter?). In 1956, shining in reflected glory, the town dedicated a monument to the puppet. Then, more recently a green park was opened where, by following paths in a maze of bushes and evergreens, the visitor can follow all the adventures of Pinocchio as reenacted by a series of statues, culminating with a giant walk-in whale spouting water from the center of a pond. It is not Walt Disney World here, either; the statuary is inspired by the original illustrations of the book and not by the Disney cartoons. Generations of children have been brought up with the adventurous, funny, touching morality play of Pinocchio, a story that illustrates the rewards of virtue. Ironically, and sadly, Carlo Collodi's life shows the rewards of vice and gambling: He died in the street alone and destitute, never knowing the success of his masterpiece.

MAREMMA

Tutti mi dicon mare-maremma
E a me mi pare una maremma-amara.
L'uccello che ci va perde la penna
Io ci ho perduto una persona cara.
Sia maledetta mare-maremma
Sia maledetta maremm' e chi l'ama.

::::::

People call it mare-maremma
For me it's more like bitter maremma.
The bird that goes there loses its feathers,
But there I lost a good love of mine.
Be damned mare-maremma,
damn you and who loves you.

The voice is the voice of women working in the fields, singing with the slow beat of a thumping heart. It is a lament more than a song, a dirge of heartbroken women crying for themselves and their men "gone in Maremma." Someone could probably find a date for when it was first sung, but it would be irrelevant; the song remains one of mourning and rage, its inspiration valid since the beginning of Maremma's checkered history.

Maremma is the coastal region that begins shortly below Livorno and continues south well into Lazio, extending east from the sea to a good fifteen miles inland, toward the Apennines. It is the flattest strip of real estate in all of Tuscany and synonymous in the past with tidal marshes and brackish swamps, foul air, mosquitoes, and deadly malaria. Around the sixth century B.C., the Etruscans, good farmers as well as excellent engineers, couldn't let such a large area go to waste. They used the silt of rerouted rivers to fill the swamps; they dug earth from high lands and dumped it into low lands. The huge public works turned the land into a much more salubrious place and made of Maremma a fertile wheat-growing plain. The city of Grosseto became the Etruscans' granary, and around it minor settlements developed into flourishing centers.

With the arrival of the Romans, a people given more to sol-
diering than to agriculture, Maremma slowly reverted to swamps,
the dominion of murderous mosquitoes. Even more than in any other
low-lying land, the marshes' noxious effluvia were deemed bad to
breathe, *mala aria,* literally "bad air"—malaria, the debilitating and
eventually fatal disease. In the Middle Ages, during the hegemony
of the Medicis, Maremma assumed the function of a penal colony,
in theory a place where prisoners were sent to work in the salt flats,
but in practice to let them languish and disappear. For a long time
this state of affairs, besides inspiring sad songs, didn't do much for
the reputation of Maremma as a destination, the Tuscan equivalent
of Siberia, without the snow.

A change for the better, a reason for a more cheerful song,
happened around the sixteenth and seventeenth centuries. Ironically, it was a non-Tuscan who brought the change and rehabilitation to Maremma. Leopold II of Lorraine, enlightened head of
the Grand Duchy of Tuscany, took a personal interest in the fate of
Maremma. He oversaw the creation of a vast, permanent drainage
system of canals, regulated irrigation and tree planting, and performed a general reclamation of the area. Malaria, if not eradicated,
was brought under control, and Maremma developed again into a
productive agricultural region. In Grosseto, the rich center and
capital of the region, the grateful inhabitants of Maremma dedicated a monument to Leopold; it is a feature, along with the town's
cathedral, of the main city square.

After World War I, the reclamation (*la Bonifica)* of Maremma
was intensified and expanded and the land, divided into family-
sized farms organized as cooperatives, given to war veterans.
The lands' *Bonifica* turned out to be—even more than the trains

running on time—one of the early success stories of the Fascist regime.

Unfortunately, after the harsh conditions of World War II, Maremma suffered a deep malaria relapse. It was again brought under control, this time with a modern warfare-style campaign: Sprayed by helicopters with intensive doses of DDT, the miserable anopheles mosquitoes succumbed and so did malaria. If the chemical had not later been determined ecologically dangerous, today in Grosseto there might be a statue to the inventor of DDT alongside the monument of Leopold II.

Even with sporadic reclamation, many areas of Maremma have not remained suitable or profitable for cultivation. Abandoned to their original wilderness, they are shelters for many species of furred or feathered fauna. Besides being used as hunting preserves, these sectors have turned out to be ideal pastures for the breeding in the wild of a special sort of cattle, the *bue maremmano.* White, with large lyre-shaped horns—very much like the Texas longhorn—strong by way of natural selection, and accustomed to a difficult environment (hence in need of little care or shelter), the Maremmano cattle have been used throughout the centuries not only as an inexpensive source of meat and milk, but especially as an invaluable, essential aid to agricultural work. Thought by some to descend from the Asian herds left behind by the invading Huns, by others to be the same Taurus Silvester described long before by Pliny the Elder, and by still others as a mix of the two, Maremma cattle were for a long time a reservoir of brute force for all of Tuscany, and then for Italy.

The *coppia di buoi,* a pair of oxen tied to the yoke, became a popular symbol to represent the virtues of quiet, powerful strength, loyalty, obedience, and absolute dedication to work. In the mid-1800s, the Tuscan poet Giuseppe Giusti was even inspired to compose "Ode to the Ox": "I love you, humble ox; you imbue my heart with a feeling of vigor and peace." The arrival of tractors began to make the work of the noble ox obsolete, and by the end of the 1950s the sight of oxen working in the fields disappeared altogether—and with it, it is feared, the virtues for which the ox stood. Even if greatly reduced in numbers, the *bue maremmano* still breed freely near Grosseto, at Alberese, on the land set aside as the Parco Nazionale della Maremma.

To take care of the surviving cattle and to fulfill their historical duty as herders are the last of the *butteri,* a group that is similar to American cowboys. Created around the middle of the eighteenth century, the job of the *buttero* (a word derived from the Latin *Bos Ductor,* "ox driver") was to keep the herds safe in pastures and out of cultivated areas. The butteri worked for a few rich and noble families who had split the Maremma into large farm-ranches. The work of the butteri required superior horsemanship and the ability to remain glued to a saddle many hours a day, rain or shine, 365 days a year, along with the job of breaking and training maremmani horses. The horses' origin and breeding followed the same evolutionary pattern as that of the cattle: Born and raised in the wild, they closely resemble the wild mustangs of the American West. Out of the herd, the butteri selected the stallions that would sire fast cavalry horses, sturdy artillery horses, or elegant officers' horses for the Italian Royal Army. Real beauties but made obsolete by horsepower, quickly going the way of the noble ox.

To work as a buttero was an elite job with wages much better than those of the simple farmhand. Thus, it became a much-desired position in the hierarchy of the farm, kept as much as possible in the family, passed on from father to son. It was a position also sought after by many ambitious young men, so much so that during the yearly branding of the cattle (the *merca*), they would show up and display their riding prowess, hoping to be noticed by a farm supervisor and be hired. The merca turned into a self-styled rodeo, a day of work and a day of feast for pros and greenhorns to show off and compete in horsemanship.

The tradition is still alive; the merca takes place on a midsummer day in the town of Alberese, its popularity fed not only by the real but also by the legendary bravura of the riders. One such legend describes Buffalo Bill's arrival in Italy in 1890 with his circus, and how the *butteri maremmani* challenged and beat Bill's cowboys in "breaking" wild horses. In reality, it was more a comparison of two different ways of subduing the wild animals, with no winners or losers. The actual winners were the local dealers who supplied the wine for the unending toasts to each other. Today, the number of butteri is diminishing rapidly and their future is in doubt. With the purpose of their work disappearing, the next generation of butteri will be purely a symbolic one, sponsored by the local chamber of commerce for folkloristic performances at the merca.

Naturally, any Tuscan festivity would not be such if it did not involve the convivial consumption of food. Long tables are set up near the place of the merca and Maremma specialties are available for all, buffet style. Partaking of the food—and abundant wine—is a daylong affair lasting well into the night. Field kitchens with vats full of oil fry seemingly inexhaustible amounts of *crescentine,* hot and crisp fried dough, either salted or sugared. Larger vats of boiling water dish out the inevitable *pappardelle al salmi,* homemade pasta in a hare or rabbit stew sauce, or more simply *pastasciutta* (the term covers the whole gamut of pasta with a sauce) *alla Maremmana,* a sauce as close to a marinara as you can get. Ever present slices of *Sformato di Patate alla Fiorentina* accompany everything. Huge trays display all sorts of cold cuts—including slices of porchetta—to be made into scrumptious *pagnottelle* (sandwiches) with local casareccio bread. Long grills sizzle with all sorts of meats on skewers, from pork ribs to boar, from fowl to beef. Nothing particularly new, a general Tuscan fare encountered before—with the exception, perhaps, of steaks of *puledro,* young horse. An acquired taste. Sic *transit gloria equi.*

But Maremma remains. And so does Tuscany.

::::::

It is superfluous to reinforce in the traveler's mind that Tuscany extends from the high mountains of the Apennines to the shores of the Tyrrhenian Sea by way of innumerable hills. It is understandable, then, that in addition to all the shared Tuscan traits, there are also different ones for the valleys' farmers and the hills' winemakers, and the marble workers of the Apuane mountains—each with a character overlay as unique and different as the marble of Carrara.

Envious critics say that a shared, general Tuscan trait is frugality, thrift edging on full-blown avarice.

It is, again, a lie: No other people or country in the world has given, with such incredible disproportion, so much and so generously to the rest of the world.

PAPPARDELLE

Homemade Pasta for Salmi

3 cups unbleached all-purpose flour 4 large eggs, at room temperature
½ cup semolina flour   2–3 tablespoons red wine
½ teaspoon salt

PUT the all-purpose flour, semolina flour, and salt in the bowl of a food processor (with the cutting blade) and mix for a moment.

BEAT the eggs in a separate bowl and, while the processor is running, pour the eggs slowly into the flour and salt mixture. Process on and off for 10 seconds, then slowly add the wine, no more than necessary to form small pellets of dough. When pinched together they should form a reasonably dry dough. If too dry or too wet, adjust with small amounts of either wine or flour.

POUR the pellets in a bowl or on a working surface and knead them together to form a ball. Roll the dough into sheets by hand or by machine, then cut it into any size or shape needed. Pappardelle are strips about 1 to 1½ inches wide and may be cut on a slant into 2½ to 3-inch lengths or eaten in long strips.

Serves 6–8

LEPRE OR CONIGLIO IN SALMI

Rabbit in Savory Wine Sauce

Lepre (wild hare) is difficult to find in the market, but you can use rabbit. Rabbit, cleaned and ready to cook, can be found frozen in most supermarkets, or fresh in specialty butcher shops or Italian meat shops.

1 rabbit, approximately 2 pounds	6–7 whole cloves
Flour to dredge	2 tablespoons tomato paste,
1 small carrot	diluted in ½ cup warm water
1 small onion	1 cup dry red wine
1 celery stalk	¼ cup dry Marsala
3 tablespoons olive oil	2 tablespoons red wine
2 tablespoons unsalted butter	or balsamic vinegar
2 bay leaves	

WASH the rabbit and cut into 8 pieces, saving the liver and kidneys. Dredge the pieces in flour and let them rest.

MINCE FINELY together the carrot, onion, celery, and the reserved liver and kidneys.

IN A SAUTÉ PAN large enough to accommodate the rabbit, sauté the mince in the olive oil and butter until it's limp and golden, then add the bay leaves and cloves.

ADD the floured rabbit pieces and brown them. Stir in the diluted tomato paste, red wine, Marsala, and wine vinegar. Bring to a boil, then lower the heat, cover the pan, and cook at a very low simmer, stirring once in a while, for 40 minutes or until the meat practically falls off the bones.

TAKE the pan off the heat and when it's cool enough to handle, bone the rabbit. Put the meat back in the sauce, warm it up, and dress the pappardelle with it.

It may also be used to accompany polenta or served as a second course, with bones in, accompanied by a potato puree.

You may want to double the recipe, since, like all stews, it's even better the next day.

Serves 4

PAPPA AL POMODORO

Peasant Tomato Soup

1 pound day-old Italian bread	6 garlic cloves
(possibly a round loaf)	10 fresh basil leaves, chopped
4 cups peeled plum tomatoes	Salt and fresh ground pepper to taste
2 tablespoons olive oil	6 teaspoons extra virgin
4 cups chicken broth	olive oil (optional)

REMOVE the hard crust and then cut the bread into small cubes; put in the oven at 200°F for 15 to 20 minutes, or until it's totally dried out (but not toasted).

CHOP the tomatoes, put them in a soup pot, and cook them until they are soft and their juice is reduced a bit. Let them cool, then pass them through the fine disk of a food mill (or puree in a food processor). Put them back in the soup pot, add the olive oil, chicken broth, bread, the garlic cloves skewered on one or two toothpicks, and basil. Adjust for salt and add a generous amount of pepper. Bring the pot to boil, reduce the heat and let simmer, stirring once in a while, until the soup has reduced considerably and is of the consistency and smoothness of heavy cream. Retrieve and discard the garlic, and pour the soup into soup plates. (If desired, first dribble a teaspoon or so of extra virgin olive oil on each plate.)

SERVE either warm or at room temperature.

(In Tuscany pappa al pomodoro is prepared in larger batches because, they say, it is even better when reheated.)

Serves 6

SFORMATO DI PATATE ALLA FIORENTINA

Potatoes Florentine

1 pound potatoes	½ teaspoon freshly ground pepper
2 10-ounce packages of frozen spinach	1 cup grated Parmigiano cheese
3 tablespoons unsalted butter	Unflavored bread crumbs
½ teaspoon freshly grated nutmeg	⅓ cup of milk
½ teaspoon salt	

Preheat the oven to 375°F.

PEEL AND SLICE the potatoes into "potato chip" thickness. Cook the slices in lightly salted boiling water for 1 minute.

COOK the frozen spinach in salted boiling water for 4 minutes, then drain and squeeze it as dry as possible. Sauté the spinach in butter, then add the nutmeg, salt, and pepper.

BUTTER the bottom and sides of a 6x10-inch ovenproof casserole dish and dust it with bread crumbs. Make a layer with ⅓ of the potato slices, then sprinkle it with salt and cheese. Add another layer with half of the spinach and sprinkle it with cheese. Cover it with another layer of potatoes and sprinkled cheese, then another layer of spinach and cheese, and then the last layer of potatoes. Pour milk over it, sprinkle it with cheese and bread crumbs, dot it with butter, and bake in the oven for 40 minutes. Let it cool before cutting in squares and serving.

Serves 6

BISCOTTI DI PRATO

Hard Almond Cookies for Dunking

1 pound unbleached all-purpose flour	1 tablespoon almond extract
1 pound sugar	4 ounces whole peeled almonds,
4 large eggs	lightly toasted
2 teaspoons baking powder	4 ounces roasted unsalted peanuts
½ teaspoon salt	

PREHEAT oven to 375°F.

MIX the flour, sugar, eggs, baking powder, salt, and almond extract into a dough, and knead it. Add the almonds and peanuts.

ROLL OUT the dough on a lightly floured surface and cut it into thin (1½-inch) sticks as long as your cookie sheet. Keep flour handy—it is a sticky dough.

PUT the sticks on buttered, floured cookie sheets and bake for about 15 minutes, or until they are pale gold. Let them cool, then cut them on the diagonal into ½-inch slices. Return them to the oven at 300°F for about 10 minutes. Let them cool before serving them, to be dipped in Vin Santo, Marsala, or any other sweet dessert wine.

Makes about 4 dozen cookies

Le Marche

RAISING A CURTAIN

The early morning mist lifts from the valleys and reveals rivers and hills, well-ordered farms, orchards, and vineyards, a patchwork landscape of alternating green and beige squares, dotted with hilltop crenellated castles and walled-in towns. It is like a curtain rising on a play: Le Marche, the Unknown Italy.

If "unknown" is too strong a word, it is probably correct to say that the region of Le Marche (pronounced "lay *mar*-kay") is one of the least known abroad and least traveled. While villa-renting-and-buying Americans are filling up the towns and countryside of neighboring Tuscany and Umbria, Le Marche remains relatively undiscovered.

We have traveled in Le Marche many times and in every season, but for us, autumn is the best. The light, the colors, and the smells of the fields—some freshly cut, some just ready to harvest —the long parallel rows of grapevines that etch the hills and the plains, and the dots of olive trees outlining a farmhouse all make for a serene scenery, unprepossessing and yet whimsically theatrical. As an afterthought, a lonely tower stands slender and tall on top of a hill like an exclamation mark. The sky is a collection of majestic billowing clouds that leave most of the countryside in mottled shade. As in a Renaissance landscape, some of the hilltop villages are lit by a beam of sunshine, golden bricks glowing in their own spotlight, set apart from their shadowed surroundings. The sunbeam slowly fades out from one village and moves to another, a master's hand highlighting the magic view. We abandon the faster provincial road for the secondary road, following the crest of valleys into tunnels of greenery. Climbing and winding around the hills, each sharp turn opens vistas of the panorama below. It is like having surprised a beautiful woman in her casual housedress and no makeup. Natural. Naturally beautiful. No tricks.

Welcome to Le Marche, then. And this is only the southern part; the rest stretches west, shielded from Umbria and Toscana by the Apennine chain, and ends up north, after about one hundred miles, in Emilia-Romagna. West to east, valleys descend from the mountainous peaks of the Central Apennines and, like fingers reaching for the sea, in about fifty miles dip into the Adriatic. On the superhighway it will take you only an hour and a half to traverse Le Marche south to north, but you would miss all the splendor hiding among its country roads. All the charms that make Italy so appealing are contained in this small region: striking hilltop towns and castles, history, art and architecture, long sandy beaches, and rocky coves—without the crowds.

GRAPES

Our slow cruising speed was slowed even further by the long line of vans preceding us; more than vans, they were large open vats on wheels, heaped with grapes, chugged along by agricultural tractors. Sparkling in the sun, the freshly cut bunches of plump golden and blue-black grapes trailed an intense aroma. It took us no time to see that that river of grapes on wheels was going our way. It made no sense to run past it.

The convoy finally assembled unhurriedly in a holding space at the entrance of a large, white factory; thirty or so tall stainless silos were lined at its back. CO-OPERATIVA VINICOLA AGRICOLTORI DI OFFIDA said a sign in big letters on its facade. The smell of grapes has become the aroma of *mosto* (must, or juice) and is inebriating. We followed the convoy into the factory parking lot and approached the group of dismounted, chattering drivers.

"We would like to visit the cantina," we said.

"Out of the question," they told us.

Just in case we had not noticed, this is *la vendemmia* (the grape harvest), the busiest and the *most* important time of the year for them.

"Just look around," one driver told us, and, as if we couldn't figure it out for ourselves, with a sweeping gesture he pointed at the huge number of vans lined up, waiting to unload.

"You will need a permit anyway," said another driver, and with mock admonishment, added, "It will probably be denied. Nobody has time to show you around at this time of year."

"And then," continued the first, "it's past noon. The permit man will not be back for at least an hour."

Seeing our disappointment, they became good natured and apologetic.

"We are all just soldiers here," one of them chimed in. "The generals are at lunch."

Lunch!

That was our reason for coming to Offida. And we were late.

::::::

Several years ago when we were living in Rome, we decided to take a break from the eternally chaotic city and signed up for a cruise on the Nile. Relaxing and romantic, we were told. "Top class international," the travel agent assured us, "the best vacation you'll ever have." Unfortunately, the trip turned out to have more than its share of problems: interminable waits in 110-degree heat, cancelled flights, disappearing tour guides, skipped "gourmet" meals. When we finally reached our cruise ship, thirty-six hours late and past midnight, we found that our cabins were not even ready. The "esteemed passengers" (about fifty, all Italians) were told to wait in the bar for a get-acquainted cocktail. Given the state of tiredness, the complaining was subdued but general, punctuated by barbs and jests of revolt.

"Oddico! Siamo sicuri che questo è il Nilo?" a tenor voice cut through the general conversation. Say! Are we sure that this is the Nile?

"O fosse il Mississippi?" Or maybe it's the Mississippi!

"It's dark, and with this management . . . " added another.

Their accents were definitely *Marchigiani,* and their witticisms typical of the people of Le Marche.

"Tonino Lucarini," the tenor introduced himself to us along with his friends, Carla and Alfredo Gianuizzi.

"From Offida, Marche!" they said proudly.

For the next two weeks they made the "top class international cruise" much more palatable, the hot breezes of the Nile softened by the gentle tones of Le Marche.

We parted friends, promising to keep in touch and see each other again, sooner or later . . . here or there.

Several years passed before we traveled again to Le Marche, and when we wrote to our friends about our plans, they immediately invited us to lunch.

::::::

Just a few miles from the Adriatic coast, Offida is in the province of Ascoli Piceno. Seen from the valley, it looks like any other of the many villages nestled on top of the many hills. It would be a mistake to pass it by. It is a condensation of all the region can offer, surprisingly compressed and contained inside defensive walls. The town has very ancient roots, as displayed in its Archeological Museum, inside one of the old classic *palazzi* of Offida. Its artifacts go back to the early Paleolithic era and the settling of the Piceni, who probably sneaked in from Greece and the Middle East in the sixth or fifth century B.C. The Piceni were then displaced by the Romans, and the Romans, in turn, by the Longobards. Keeping things under one roof, the palazzo also houses the Museum of Popular Traditions (Folklore), The Municipal Picture Gallery, and, unique and prized above all, Il Museo del Merletto a Tombolo (The Lace Museum). The making of exquisite pillow lace is a proud local tradition, held aloft and passed on like the Olympic torch from mother to daughter for uncounted generations, and still very much alive. Pillows have nothing to do with it: The term defines a nimble technique that produces the most complex and elegant of all laces. In the museum you can watch the lace makers work on a cylindrical hard "pillow" called *tombolo,* on which the whole lacery develops.

Among the architectural gems stands the fourteenth-century Santa Maria della Rocca, an imposing Romanesque-Gothic structure looming huge and unadorned on top of an impossibly tall, straight, and vertical rock formation at the town's entrance. Renaissance, sixteenth-, and seventeenth-century buildings make the list of exceptional sites, rounded out by a Saint Augustine sanctuary, frescoed by master artists. All of these venerable structures in a small place could make Offida a pretty heavy, moldy, whisper-only museum. But, suitably located in a thirteenth-century Franciscan monastery, a renowned *enoteca* also sprouts here, containing a large collection of local wines to admire, taste, and buy. And then there is the jewel box of a three-tiered, frescoed, eighteenth-century theater, very much active during the theatrical season and essential for the madcap soirees of Carnival's masked balls. A long list of seasonal and religious events keeps the town, in spite of its prehistoric wrinkles, at a lively, youthful pace year-round. At one time, among the Mardi Gras events, there was an economy-sized, Pamplona-style running of the bulls when one single bull was left to run wild in the streets to chase and be chased by the citizenry. In 1819 after a harrowing accident, the live bull was substituted by a bull-costumed man, a humanitarian gesture that saved both blood and tradition.

All of this information gushed forth from Mario Biondi, a university student and dedicated historian of Offida. As a gesture of hospitality, our Offidian friends had engaged Mario for our enlightenment. The young city-historian was eager to perform as a guide for us and overflowed with names, dates, and a myriad of minor details. Unfortunately, this gushing wealth of information had to compete with the real highlight of the visit: lunch at the Gianuizzis, an event that turned out to be a hardly veiled euphemism for a midday pharaonic feast.

"*Qui si mangia bene, si spende poco!*" Carla singsonged with each offering, condensing, in theory, the whole region's gastronomical philosophy. She was also repeating a slogan used by family-run eateries all over Italy.

Without effort we agreed on the *mangia bene* ("eat well"), but the *spende poco* ("spend little") wasn't convincing in the least. The menu, served with deliberation (and equally savored with thoughtful meditation between mouthfuls), turned out to be a parade of just about every local specialty. So much for the small snack we had been promised and agreed upon by telephone. No way could we fake indignation for the betrayal, and so we kept toasting to the food, to each one of us, to the reunion. We even toasted to each of the wines. This necessitated a few trips to the cellar.

"After this, we will write *Eating and Drinking in Offida: A Gastro-Philosophical Treatise,*" was our comment about the festivities.

"You would be short a few things," said Carla.

"Mention one."

"Fish . . . "

"Two?"

"Shellfish . . . "

"Three?"

"Truffles. The season is just beginning."

"We thought you *Marchigiani* were generous but not show-offs."

"We *are* generous. And humble," Tonino wedged in. "We are workers; work to live—and live well, whenever we can—and not live to work. We like to save, like *formichine,* little ants. We keep an eye on the future, then we have fun."

"Generous, yes. Like Pius IX!" we teased him.

When Pius IX, a Marchigiano, was elected pope in 1846, he brought to Rome a bunch of tough countrymen and put them to work as tax collectors. This move prompted the Romans to coin the phrase *"È meglio un morto in casa che un marchigiano alla porta."* Better a death in the family than a Marchigiano knocking at the door.

"Aren't the Romans funny? Just like us: *Gente allegra, Dio l'aiuta!"* God helps cheerful people! was Alfredo's Confucian comment.

"Look around," continued Tonino, "look at those hills. Grapes, grapes, grapes. That's a lot of work. Digging, trimming, spraying, pruning and finally harvesting and pressing. That's backbreaking. But look what comes from it!"

Here Tonino settled back into the chair and looked at Alfredo, who did the same; with semi-closed eyes they drew inspiration from the ceiling, squeezing taste from their words:

"Verdicchio di Jesi," recited Tonino.

"Rosso Piceno . . . " added Alfredo.

" . . . Superiore."

"Vellutato, Riccaglio, Cabernasco,"

"Rozzano, Pliviano. Ruggiasco . . . "

" . . . di Offida, please! Rosso Conero . . . "

They continued in an inspired trance, the name of the wines taking a musical rhythm of their own, a heroic poem of glorious proportions.

::::::

"We are a co-operative of seven hundred members, more or less."

The next day on our way out of Offida, on impulse we drove again through the gates of the Cantina Sociale. This time nobody stopped us. The staging area was again full of grape-loaded vans, their drivers gathered together, talking. "Perhaps," we thought, "they don't notice us." Then one of them recognized us from the day before and came over to welcome us. He apologized for the abrupt behavior of the group the day before and, with an air of avuncular prominence, was pleased to satisfy our curiosity about the co-operativa.

"We are small farmers and pool our grapes because the co-operative has all the modern technology that we can't afford individually. It means more and better wine. And, we get paid for everything we produce, both for quantity and quality."

The farmer, a stocky, middle-aged, easygoing Offidian, gives a self-conscious smile. "The problem is that we don't get paid until the wines are sold, and that can take a year or more . . . " Another farmer overheard and nudged him in the ribs. "Well," he added, blushing, "we do get an advance."

"This promises to be a good year. Good quantity," interjected another, "but you know, wine is funny. Until it's ready and you can taste it, you never know how good it is. Some years are better than others.

We have been growing Verdicchio, Sangiovese, Falerio, Montepulciano, Piceno . . . our own vines, for centuries and longer. But now we have to go with the market. Pinot Grigio, Pinot Noir, Cabernet, Merlot, even Riesling . . . "

There is a certain sadness in his voice, a feeling of betrayal.

"But, *oddico!* I say, what's important for us is how they sell."

"The proof is in the pudding!" we interjected, but the idea of pudding falls flat on this audience.

A lanky young man wearing blue overalls introduces himself as Francesco Fortuni, the *enotecnico* (eno-technician), assistant to the boss enologist. He makes clear, however, that even though his title means he is the assistant, he is really in charge of the operations of the cantina. His boss only shows up once in a while, when he comes out of his cave, his chemistry lab. Francesco has been doing this work for three internship years; next year he will take his exams and become a full-fledged *enologo*. This is an awfully busy time, but if we don't mind some interruptions, he will guide us on a tour of the cantina. He assumes a take-charge attitude, and: *"Prima di tutto, facciamo il vino!"* First things first! Let's make wine!

He leads us through an arch-like structure. One at a time, the loaded vans stop under it and from above, a four-inch wide cylinder plunges into the pile of grapes, sucks up some, and in thirty seconds analyzes their acidity, water, and sugar content. Depending on the results, a worker directs the van—and we follow it—to a specific one of five stainless steel bins sunk in the pavement.

"This," says Francesco, "is a most important step: the selection of the grapes. Similar with similar. Their sugar content will determine the final alcohol content. The more sugar, the bigger the wine."

"Sweeter?"

"No. Bigger."

The vans unload their contents at their assigned stainless steel bins in which are contained huge screw-like affairs that rotate and crush the grapes; the mosto is piped one way, stems, seeds, and skins another. Francesco leads us through the high-pressure pressing, fermentation, filtering, temperature control, and control of alcoholic

content. He speaks of the wine with a sense of proprietorship—
it is his wine. He talks of hundred of thousands of *ettolitri* for the
same amount of *quintali* of grapes, his grapes. His scholarly, technical speech hardly hides his local accent, his warmth, his great pride.
He is boasting, even topping the assured attitude of the farmers we
met outside; it is out of character. *Marchigiani* are great storytellers,
witty, and generous, but definitely not boastful. Their character—
contrary to the national norm—is self-effacing, more interested in
diligent work and the cheerful appreciation of what life has to offer
than in self-promotion. A reason why, it is said, Le Marche is so
little known, even in Italy.

Francesco is on a roll. Fermentation, cold, warm, filtering,
aging in the stainless silos, in the huge oak barrels. Constant checking of acidity, alcohol, temperature. And then the grading: table
wine, reserve, special reserve, light, dry, *abboccato,* semidry. . . .

"A lot of decisions, gradations, density, are made by retorts
and pipettes, but at the end it's our palate that decides."

"What if something goes wrong?"

For a second Francesco's face becomes ashen.

"Rarely. No . . . " And then, recovering: "No. But some years
are better than others."

Finally, he wants us really to marvel. The bottling: five thousand an hour, six thousand an hour. . . .

Four people work full-time year-round in the cantina, and at
harvest time Francesco's boss hires four more temporary laborers.

With the hope that we'll see Francesco again next year, we
bid him good-bye and thank him profusely for taking precious time
from his busy schedule to be our guide for this vendemmia.

VERDICCHIO: ANATOMY OF A SIMPLE WINE

Nicola Baroni had his own co-operative and perhaps didn't know it. When he was young, he left his family's farm in Le Marche to move to Rome, where he became a government employee. He started as office boy at the Protocol Office of the Ministry of Foreign Affairs, and given his pleasant and courteous disposition, climbed the bureaucratic ladder to a position of a certain importance. When he retired Nicola bought a plot of land and a small vineyard in Frontale, a village of seven hundred souls, with most of the land in the sub-fraction of Coldigiogo, a place of seventy-three souls. It put him far away from the jurisdictional arm of the government, of which he had probably had enough. In Coldigiogo he built a farmhouse that served as a summer place for most of his clan and their friends. A large kitchen-refectory with a walk-in fireplace took care of his guests' appetites, and a sizable cellar took care of their thirst. It was, all told, a modest stone house but because it had indoor plumbing, it was exceptional enough to elevate Nicola and his cronies to elite status.

He had three bosom friends in Frontale, the best hunters in the world. The wild rabbits, the hares, the occasional fox, and the tiny birds had better stay away from the range of their shotguns and the bark of their dogs. Ancient, parchment-faced Don Girolamo, the ageless parish priest, all hellfire and brimstone, was the oldest. Domenico Viviani, gentle father of many children, superb wood carver (he transformed the entire forest of local boxwood into fruit bowls, bocce balls, and hills of white wood shavings,) was another. Nicola's son-in-law and Frontale's postmaster, Oreste Moriconi, huge as an oak tree, was the last and youngest to make the inseparable quartet. They each had a small plot of land and a few rows of vines they called vineyards. They were devoted to them, and, whenever they could, cared for each other's vines—leaf by leaf— and pooled their harvests.

During vendemmia, all the locals' disagreements big and small were put on hold and the village became one solid, integrated entity. Neighbors helped neighbors. From sunrise to sunset at harvest time, the whole area was a beehive of activity.

Ox-driven carts brought the grapes to the farms' threshing floors, where they were put into wooden vats. In the evening, neighbors young and old came, took their shoes off, and stomped on the grapes. The juices were channeled into pails and then poured into open-top barrels in the cellars. Food was shared, old bottles uncorked, asthmatic concertinas wheezed away, and the night became full of bonfires, singing and laughter, and bold tales. By dawn there were no more grapes and no more food. The singing had become hoarse and the tales all told. Harvest nights: the best nights ever. Until next year's. Memorable things happened on those nights, events that became part of the village lore—events that, like the wine itself, got better and better with age. Like that harvest night when the young priest, sent to help—or to check on—old Don Girolamo, ran away with the miller's pregnant wife on a motorcycle—the miller's.

When the must in the cellar stopped bubbling and started its wine career, it was filtered into three huge oak casks in Nicola's cellar and the foursome followed their proven winemaking protocol. The process could not be rushed, and its development had to be checked closely. The routine was quite fixed. At the end of a workday, the four sat in the kitchen, just above the cellar, at a table with a big candle stuck in its center; a greasy deck of cards was shuffled.

A small terra-cotta pitcher with the new wine was passed around and glasses were sipped slowly. Then the glasses were held against the candle and the wine's color examined. Another sip, a swooshing in the mouth. Silence. Then, with a pursing of lips, a first "'hmm . . . m." After four "hmm's," another glass was poured. Just to make sure. A hand of cards was played, silently. A bottle was uncorked and tasted to compare last year's with the new one.

These sessions happened every week. The card playing became noisy tournaments: Cards were slapped on the table, making the tray with bread slices, cheese, and salami jump. The terra-cotta pitcher took many trips up and down the cellar stairs, the stage and quality of each barrel assessed and marked with a piece of chalk.

When the stars were high in the sky and the candle began to flicker, the four left the kitchen and went outside, led by Don Girolamo singing a raucous prayer of thanks. On somewhat shaky legs they reached the back lawn and together pissed the new wine away.

Once in a while Nicola was left in charge of his vacationing eight-year-old grandchild and would let him sit at the table with the grown-ups and shuffle the cards. Sometimes, reluctantly, they let him have a tiny sip of wine. He dutifully gazed at the wine color against the candle flame, swished it around the palate, and said "Hm . . . hmm."

The grown-ups chuckled and smiled at his aping.

That child grew up, and with time learned quite a lot about wine. But Nicola will never know that that first sip is still the paragon against which his grandchild compares all wines.

Nicola Baroni was my grandfather.

::::::

Gwen had heard my stories of the land of my maternal ancestors, of the many happy summer vacations away from Rome I spent there as a child with aunts and uncles. She had also heard some of the not-so-happy stories of the time I spent there as a teenager working for the underground resistance during World War II.

The country road winds its way, snaking down a wild flow-ered side of a valley and up another, touching villages and towns that look like pearls set on the crown of hills. Even their names, strung together, could very well sound like poetry verses: *Castelplanio, Castelbellino, Cupramontana, Staffolo, Apiro, Cingoli, Poggio, Frontale* . . .

At the realization that we are so near to Frontale, Gwen urges me to stop. It was up in Monte San Vicino, the mountain near Frontale, where I, only a teenager, spent some months as a par-tisan in 1944. Seeking safety from a besieged Rome and to avoid being drafted into the Fascist army, I fled to my aunt, Zia Teresa (daughter of Nonno Nicola and wife of Oreste), the postmistress of Frontale, a village so small it was thought to be out of the war's maelstrom. Our thinking was proved wrong, however, when the Germans occupied Frontale on their retreat north, and set up their headquarters in Zia Teresa's house. I had to hightail it to the moun-tain, where I joined the partisans. My first warring action was to capture a prisoner, a stray white chicken lost on the slopes of San Vicino. After plucking the prisoner, I cut the bird in half with my Swiss Army knife (my only armament, before being supplied with more deadly weapons), and then pounded it—bones and all—as flat as two pancakes. I sprinkled it with wild rosemary and cooked it between two bricks made red-hot over the campfire embers. The fowl, passed into history as *pollo al mattone* (chicken on the brick), provided welcome relief to the partisans' scant diet. I was awarded my first cheers as a cook, but also a ferocious tongue-lashing from the group commander. The plucked white feathers, carelessly left to the wind, practically covered the side of the mountain with fluttering white dots. Not a smart move for people in hiding.

In Italy, *una frazione* is like a suburb, or a very small section, of a larger city or town. Small Frontale—itself a frazione of Apiro—has its own frazione, Coldigiogo, which consists of six houses, including my grandfather's, *la casa del ricco,* "the rich man's house," so-called because of the indoor plumbing.

Down a tiny road we find the house, almost unchanged from the days of my summer vacations there. Sadly, it is closed: we were hoping to visit it to see if its cellar is still cool and productive. Unexpectedly, the old house next door is brightly illuminated and bustling with activity. Our knock on the door is answered by Professor Alessandro Montanari, the director of the Osservatorio Geologico di Coldigiogo, a geology studies center. It turns out that the rock formations near Coldigiogo and Frontale are of great geological importance and students now come from all over the world to study them. The large central room is ringed with computers and other state-of-the-art beeping equipment. We can't help but wonder what Nonno Nicola, if he were alive, would think of these newfangled neighbors.

We take a short walk around Frontale, just a few miles up the road, and admired the view from the town's only piazza. More like a big rectangular terrace than a square, the piazza has one balustrated side overlooking the valley. Zia Teresa's green house, once the SS headquarters, is still there. A woman walks by, and at the sound of our voices, she turns and stares at the strange sight of foreigners. Then, she calls "Franco!" It is a childhood friend not seen in more than forty years. For a moment, all the past years seem to be erased as we smiled at each other. We are back kicking a ball made of tied rags around the square. Of those interminable games what is left is two pairs of moist eyes.

We two friends part with an embrace—it included Gwen—promising not to let another forty more years go by. And next time perhaps I will bring a real soccer ball.

::::::

Wine experts describe Verdicchio as "pale straw with greenish tints, fine nose, taut dryness, and good fruit/acid balance, with a lingering hint of bitter almonds." Our description is less educated but more to the point: It's a good, instantly likeable dry white wine, terrific with fish. On a summer day, we would walk a mile for a glass of chilled Verdicchio.

And on a recent hot summer day, we did just that. The simple sign over a door in Frontale, TRATTORIA—VINO, was inviting. It is as generic a name as can be but, since dinnertime was approaching, it had an irresistible appeal. The establishment is a simple square room; the light from its only window fell on a group of old men playing cards. Two younger men bent over them, kibitzing. The light, filtered by smoke, sparkled on the wine bottle and glasses on the table, making it seem as if Caravaggio had just passed by and arranged the tableau. A middle-aged lady, ruddy and rotund, drying her hands on her apron, approached us from the kitchen. At our wish to have a bite to eat, she replied that we would have to do with *quello che passa casa,* "what's in the house." We had heard that adage before, but she smiled and things looked promising. In a moment she was back with a terra-cotta pitcher of chilled wine and thick slices of country bread. "While you wait," she explained. In no time she returned with a bowl of *pasta e fagioli,* thick fresh-shelled bean soup; a few bits of penne floated in the thick, creamy soup.

"Peasant fare," she said as an apology.

With our consent, she poured a thin thread of olive oil on the warm soup. The oil caught the light and sparkled green-gold. It was the kind of food to be savored slowly, with eyes closed, as in meditation.

The wine that poured from the pitcher was clear and cool. We would not have been surprised if the lady told us she had stomped on the grapes herself. It was pale straw in color, with greenish tints. It had a taut dryness and a good fruit-acid balance. It even left on the palate a lingering taste of bitter almonds. It is Verdicchio, no doubt. And here, it was fantastic. Like none we ever had before.

COUNTRY LOVERS

"The name says it. Le Marche. Some ten or twelve centuries ago, the Germans called it *Der Mark,* 'the border area.' We are neither here nor there. We have no big cities, no Milans, no Romes, no Florences," said Tonino. "Florence? Milan? Think of huge frescos. Hundreds of characters messing around, swords, lances, horses, saints, angels, devils. . . . After a while you don't know what's what, and you don't care. You walk around with your jaws slacked, your eyes and your mind glazed over, but will never feel part of these places, a stranger. Le Marche? We don't try to impress."

Only a few days later, driving north along the Adriatic coast, Tonino's words kept floating in our heads. How inappropriately, shamefully modest. At Gabicce, a few miles north of Pesaro, the landscape becomes unique; under a crisp blue sky Gabicce's promontory plunges vertically into the rocky coast and into the bluest sea which, stirred by currents and breezes, turns into a palette of lazy blue swirls, from the lightest cerulean, to indigo, and emerald, and coal black blue. We had to stop and rest our eyes.

We *are* impressed.

On our left, a parallel chain of gentle hills parrots the blue display of the sea into a show of undulating greens, alternating fruit orchards, cornfields, and olive groves. There are few farms around, mostly hidden by clumps of ancient walnut trees. We start up a serpentine hill that leads to the beautifully preserved medieval castle of Gradara, closed in by fortified walls. At its feet, outside the drawbridge, is its very own village, once the residence of the castle's servants and keepers. Few visitors can keep a dry eye upon hearing the lore attached to this place. This is the stage of one the most romantic Italian soap operas ever, immortalized by Dante in the *Divine Comedy* and put to music by Tchaikovsky: the story of Paolo and Francesca. In the thirteenth century, Francesca da Rimini—an Italian beauty if ever there was one—followed the will of her father Guido da Polenta, and married by proxy Gianciotto Malatesta, the old, powerful, and mean hunchbacked lord of Rimini (a city about twenty miles east, at the sea). The proxy was Gianciotto's younger, gentler, and handsome brother, Paolo. At that time there wasn't much going on around the castle besides farming and sheepherding, and social life inside was pretty limited. Since it was a relatively

peaceful period, the boisterous soldiers' detail would be either playing cards in the armory or lending a hand outside in the fields. In
good weather, the two young people could frolic in the green fields,
but on rainy days life in the castle was pretty grim.

So the young bride and her only-by-proxy husband entertained themselves by reading to each other the love story of Lancelot
and Guinevere, a best seller of that time. Shortly the two beautiful
people's relationship, inspired by the book, went from platonic to
anatomical. Gianciotto the hunchback, stealthily back in the castle
and spying from a peephole, discovered the youngsters in mid—
ahem—reading, went ballistic, and did them in.

Dante put the two souls in the *Inferno* but, graciously, has
Francesca say, to excuse Paolo and herself, "The book was the cul-
prit and so was he who wrote it . . . . " Dante was so moved by the
lovers' story that ". . . as a dead man falling, down I fell."

Today, the unrepentant lovers' tale, even if graphically told
by a guide at the very scene of the crime, does not give anybody a
fainting spell. Modern theater, cinema, and media have the audience totally anesthetized to these kinds of events. But the location is
suggestive, the old guide very explicit.

From Gradara we wandered around the northern part of
Le Marche, weaving in and out of the early Middle Ages and the
Renaissance. The drive is easy as the roads roll along the gentle valleys among the hills. A turreted town sits on top of almost every
hill, and following their beckoning is like connecting the seemingly
random dots of a game that, at the end, reveals the complex historical design. Each place has its history, and all put together, they
spell the transition between the harsher Middle Ages and the gentler Renaissance.

URBINO

"I have a sister who teaches history in Rome," Alfredo Gianuizzi had told us at lunch. "She says that Rome has no great native Renaissance names. They all went to Rome from other places and flourished in Rome."

Once again, his subject was Le Marche: "We are a reservoir. Artists, architects, scientists, musicians. . . . They were born here, formed here, and went to spread their gifts in Rome, Florence, Venice."

The bountiful food and wine we had just consumed was a good lubricant for his eloquence. He stood up taking the declamatory posture of a poet, one hand on his heart, the other spread wide, and proclaimed: "Tis a nest of saints and of tyrants, of whores, of sculptors, of poets, and of popes and painters . . . . "

Urbino proves him right.

When we reached Urbino a soft rain was falling, giving the city misty edges and emphasizing its storybook look. All motor traffic stops at the city gates and, once inside, you feel in control of your steps: You do not have to share the public roads with cars or buses, or with anything that makes more noise than heels on cobblestones. As you near the center, you are aware that the sound of young voices fills the air. It is a happy sound that gives a smile to the old walls and turns the antique city into a living, contemporary entity. Urbino is the seat of a six-hundred-year-old university. Its students come from all over the world and are an important part of the city's life.

The rose-colored brick town sits on two hills that overlook the undulating, fertile valleys of the Metauro and Foglia rivers, with the backdrop of the tall pre-Apennine mountains. It is a beautiful sight, but it is the Palazzo Ducale that dominates Urbino's cityscape. Brainchild of Federico da Montefeltro—enlightened prince, mercenary captain, and *condottiere* of the fifteenth century—the enormous yet elegant construction was described by its architect, Luciano Laurana, as "a city in the shape of a palace." Even today, Urbino is considered a model of urban planning, a paragon for the ideal city. Unlike other noble families of the day who built forbidding castles isolated on hilltops or anchored on rocks, Duke Federico had his palace constructed as an integral part of the town. Urbino, along with Florence, Siena, Arezzo, and a few other enlightened places, was at the core of the birth of the Renaissance. Raffaelo, one of its most illustrious sons, was born in Urbino and was shaped by it, as was Bramante, the architect of the Rome of Pope Julius II. Many of the big names in the fields of science, history, letters, and juris-prudence developed and revolved around the Renaissance fulcrum that was Urbino. A visit to the Galleria Nazionale delle Marche in the Palazzo Ducale will confirm its glory days: Raffaello, Piero della Francesca, Paolo Uccello, the Della Robbias, Crivelli, Tiziano, Luca Signorelli, and many others—the Who's Who of Renaissance art— are represented and beautifully displayed there. A walk in the halls, corridors, and courtyards of the palazzo will define the meaning of "inspired grandeur."

Not much of the town is built on a flat surface; every street and alley is steeply inclined, and many graded stairways link one level of town to the next. In Urbino you do not encounter many flabby people, young or old, and you soon realize that even the simplest errand—going to the post office, let's say, or even the slow stroll of the ritual evening promenade—involves a considerable amount of exercise. Perhaps this is why *Urbinesi* seem to have healthy appetites, well taken care of by the city's food and its geographical position. High hills supply venison, wild mushrooms, and truffles; country orchards and gardens supply fresh vegetables and fruits, and the farms are rich in well-fed barnyard animals. The sea is only a stone's throw away, so whatever reaches Urbino's kitchens is no more than an hour away from its natural state. Moreover, local cooks are proud of their local ingredients and do not try to improve on them, avoiding complicated techniques and mixings; whatever reaches the table is simply cooked, and each element's character comes through pure and clear.

A sudden shower made us find refuge at La Vecchia Fornarina, a comfortable little restaurant in the center of town. We let our waiter orchestrate the menu. The weather being damp and chilly, he suggested we begin with warm, soothing *passatelli in brodo,* a smooth paste of spinach, ground tenderloin, beef marrow, cheese, and eggs, "riced" directly into boiling beef broth. He went to great lengths to explain that they were freshly made with a real passatelli instrument (similar to a potato ricer) and not a cheese grater, as some impostors do. Then, as our chill subsided, he brought us a plate of *assaggini* (little tastes) of house specialties; assaggini are a somewhat new addition to restaurants' table customs, not dissimilar from Spanish tapas. After the customer samples a bite or two of a menu's feature, he can decide whether to order the full dish. We try a few *cappelletti* in a meat sauce; a few *strangolapreti* ("priest-chokers," clergymen being a recognized class of dedicated gourmands), which are cheese and spinach gnocchi, baked in a cream sauce; and a few *garganelli,* twisted bits of pasta in a light cream-tomato-basil sauce.

"It is all very light," insists the owner-chef, who comes out of the kitchen to reassure us that we are still a way from overload mode. He is confident that we can easily deal with a *coniglio in porchetta,* a rabbit stew flavored by wild fennel leaves, accompanied by *cicoria in padella,* wild, bitter dandelion greens pan-sautéed with oil and garlic.

"A very good *digestivo*," the chef reassures us, "loaded with iron and chlorophyll!"

We should have stopped there, but the proffered fresh ricotta cheesecake topped with a couple of wild strawberries is too enticing to pass up—and quite evocative of the bosomy, unashamedly topless Fornarina, Raphael's model and *inamorata,* whose famous painting (a reproduction) looks down on us from the wall. The whole meal, helped along by the local Sangiovese d'Urbino, a cheerful red wine, and a white Bianchetto del Metauro, made the up-and-down, steep streets waiting for us seem much more level.

Outside the rain had stopped and the sun had returned, so for an even better digestivo, we made our way up the hill past Raffaello's house-museum. A long set of steps and cobbled alleys between stone houses took us to the top. Here we found Il Parco della Resistenza, a large grassy park filled with students engrossed in their books, lovers entwined on blankets, and children at play, all seemingly mindless of the others. From this vantage point the view of the town is total. The *palazzo ducale* with its two round bastions is still in command of the scene. The duomo, the spires, towers, and terra-cotta roofs form a panorama that is truly inspiring.

We felt that if we had available canvas and brushes we could perhaps join the roll call of local famous artists.

Urbino can do that to you.

PESARO

Taking a zag to the east, a fast twenty miles from Urbino, we came to Pesaro on the Adriatic coast. Besides a two-and-a-half-mile-long sandy beach, Pesaro has many things to boast about, special mementos of its rich history. There one can find many treasures— be it a portal, a palace, a square or a villa—reminiscent of each century, from pre-Roman times to the most recent one. But first among Pesaro's prides, and undoubtedly the most immediately recognized around the world, is the music of Gioacchino Rossini. It is said that only this city, for the sparkle of its air and sea, for the generosity of its food and wine, could have given birth to a Rossini. Master of the comic opera and of joyful compositions, his memory and his music are kept alive by the Rossini Opera Festival that takes place every summer. Then the strains of his *Barbiere di Siviglia, L'Italiana in Algeri, Semiramide,* and *La Gazza Ladra* fill Pesaro's air more than ever.

Good natured and happy as is most of his music, the rubicund Rossini also made history at table: qualified as *una buona forchetta* ("a mean fork"), he has lent his name to a few glorious dishes, of which foie gras and butter are the common denominators. The charge is led by *tournedos à la Rossini,* fillets of beef garnished with medallions of foie gras sautéed in butter with slices of truffle, and followed by *poulet à la Rossini,* a baked spring chicken again garnished by slices of foie gras and truffle, the baking pan then deglazed with Madeira wine. French cuisine was very fashionable in Rossini's time and lightness needed not apply.

Pesaro has some gastronomic specialties of her own, mostly revolving around fish, the most interesting being *arrosto segreto,* which consists of several kinds of small Adriatic fish pan-roasted on embers, "secret" because what's in the pan is kept hidden by the cover, also laden with embers.

ANCONA

Continuing our drive south along the Adriatic Sea, we come to Ancona, Le Marche's largest city with a population of around one hundred thousand. The region's capital, it has all the attributes of its status: large avenues, elegant buildings and shops, a state university, large commercial hotels, and a very active port. The city opens up for the visitor as a picture postcard, its bay protected and almost closed by the promontory of tall Mount Guasco, with one side facing east and the other west. From its top, one can admire both the sunrise and the sunset over the sea. A very active economy marks the town as a bustling center, but what warrants a visit is the old town, which, like others in Le Marche, reads like an illustrated history book of the city. Founded by the Greeks, it prospered under the Romans before becoming an independent seafaring republic. This emboldened the *Anconetani* to challenge the rich and powerful Republic of Venice. They lost. Later, Ancona fell under the control of the popes and was the last holdover of the Papal States until Le Marche joined the Kingdom of Italy in 1860. Among Ancona's many buildings and monuments is the incredibly well preserved Trajan's Arch, which was built in the second century to honor the emperor who set the city up as an important port. High up on Mount Guasco, overlooking the city, the twelfth-century Romanesque Cathedral of Saint Cyriac, with strong Byzantine and Gothic traits, is perhaps the most interesting church of all Le Marche.

Besides cultural duties, a good reason to stop in Ancona is to indulge in a bit of sybaritic abandon. Ancona has a lot of good eateries that cover the gamut from high class restaurants to trattorias (there are plenty of these around the port area). A traveler deserves a bit of extra pampering once in a while. The Passetto Restaurant is at the eastern high point of town, which affords it a magnificent view, and offers Old World courtesy with New World efficiency— two qualities that frequently are mutually exclusive. The service is impeccable and so are the settings, with enough silver and china to confuse a Tiffany salesperson. The view, though, takes second billing to the food. In addition to classic international menu items, Passetto also serves regional fish specialties, such as *spigola al cartoccio,* a sea bass baked and steamed in its own juices within a parchment paper pouch, and served with olives and porcini mushrooms. Brought to the table directly from the oven, the waiter makes a slit in its parchment bag, producing a puff of an aroma so intense that it could be a meal in itself. Another speciality is *pescatrice in potacchio,* the Adriatic cousin of monkfish, prepared in the classic Marche style. The *potacchio* is also Ancona's way of cooking rabbit, lamb, chicken, stockfish, beef—anything that can stew in a pan with olive oil, onion, garlic, rosemary, tomatoes, and, naturally, a good splash of dry Verdicchio. Ah, Le Marche!

Unlike most of the southern Adriatic coast, whose sandy beaches have become overdeveloped and overcrowded (mostly with northern Europeans), just a few miles south of Ancona, picturesque rocky coves take over the coastline. Little fishing villages like Portonovo, situated at the steep foot of Monte Conero, are quietly lapped by the sea. It is here that we discovered the Fortino Napoleonico, an actual Napoleonic fort now reconstituted as a small, plush hotel. The old military quarters have been transformed into a few elegantly appointed rooms and suites furnished with period pieces and super modern comforts, including minibars and Jacuzzis. The old mess hall is now a large and attractive restaurant dominated by a huge central fireplace.

The fare leans toward *cucina nuova* (nouvelle cuisine), redeemed—for us—by the regional dishes included in the menu. One such is the classic *brodetto,* a fish soup whose paternity is claimed by every town and fishing village of Le Marche. Nearby Ancona is the most vociferous, claiming the oldest and most authentic brodetto recipe. The basic requirements for brodetto are thirteen—no more, no less—different varieties of fish and shellfish, essential among them a skate wing, which gives the binding, gelatinous element to the soup, like okra to gumbo. All are cooked ever so slowly in a fish-tomato broth accented with vinegar and, naturally, a splash of Verdicchio. Linguistically brodetto is a diminuitive of *brodo* (broth), suggesting a lighter, delicate concoction, but it is misleading since a good brodetto can easily make a satisfying one-dish dinner.

The menu includes a selection of local wines that spans the whole meal, from a Verdicchio Spumante as an *aperitivo* to a still Verdicchio and a robust Rosso Conero for the meal proper. An after-dinner drink of fiery grappa, probably and deservedly well kept in the old gunpowder store, is a good close for the meal and a pleasant anesthetic for the bill.

We engaged in a discussion of the local wines with the young sommelier, who urged us to visit Jesi, hometown of Verdicchio, insisting that some wines are never as good as in their place of production.

"Go to Jesi. It will be worth your while. And it is not far at all."

In almost perfect Oxford English, he added: "On a good day, Joe DiMaggio could easily bat a fish from Ancona to a table in Jesi."

We find that unit of measure colorful but very baffling. Is there a game in Le Marche of which we are not aware?

JESI

From a distance Jesi looks like any other of Le Marche's walled-in towns on top of a hill. But as you get closer, you notice a difference. The old walls, dating from the eleventh century, are huge, but instead of being as forbidding and impregnable as defensive walls should be, they greet you with colorful bits of laundry hung out to dry. From a window here and a balcony there, they are like welcoming flags waving in the breeze. Through the centuries, the old military walls have been built upon and modified into habitations, turning them into a living part of the town. One enters through the old gates but, once inside the town, one-way streets discourage traffic and the center itself, mercifully, is off-limits to vehicles.

Jesi's history is just as colorful and varied as Le Marche's itself; a walk from the once fortified walls into the city will take you by the various landmarks of Jesi's path from Roman times to today. A land-mark that will not fail to impress you is the elaborate monument, baroque to a fault, in a town square that's dedicated to Jesi's favorite son, Giovanni Battista Pergolesi. A naked young violin player and a naked muse pay homage at the feet of the fastidiously dressed, eighteenth-century composer who died at the age of twenty-six. He is best known for his *Stabat Mater* for alto voices and violins and, above all, for his *Serva Padrona,* the opera buffa that set the standard for all to follow. More practical homage was paid by naming the local opera house after him, a jewel box of baroque art that occu-pies a central position on the town's main square.

Jesi is eminently livable and well-off, judging by the appear-ance of its citizens. On our *passeggiata* along the middle of Jesi's main street, we were struck by the elegance of our fellow promenaders and the luxuriousness of the shops that line the street. We realize that our way of evaluating a place's economy is a bit simplistic, but in the end our guesswork comes close to the mark. We keep track of the average mood of salespeople and customers at fashion shops and boutiques; we evaluate the prices and quality of the produce in the markets and of pastry shops and restaurants; and we check the percentage of Mercedes, Porsches, and Alfa Romeos in the parking lots. All things considered, by our judgment, Jesi fares quite well.

"Reasonably well-off" is a definition that can also apply to the whole of Le Marche. The once almost exclusively agricultural economy, made up of self-sufficient family farms, is now enriched by small- and medium-sized industries. Some, raised from the ranks of handicraft, have found a niche in the national—and some in the international—market. In keeping with the traditional background of the region, many of these enterprises deal with food and wine.

We found one that has obtained a particular national success: the Gabrini Company, producer of *polli ruspanti* (free-range chickens). A ruspante is fighting lean, athletic, dark-fleshed, and tasty, the opposite of the hormone-fattened, flabby industrial chicken. Some years back, the fear that eating hormone-fed poultry could undermine virility took over the country, and ruspanti were the only ones admitted on Italian tables. The logistics of breeding barnyard ruspanti in numbers big enough to make commercial sense was solved by Signor Gabrini by farming out ruspanti chicks, born from selected eggs, to a lot of small farmers. In their barnyards, the adopted chicks would grow into certified Polli Ruspanti di Razza Marchigiana, and after about two months or so—always under the control of Gabrini inspectors—they would be collected, processed at the central factory, and, with great success, sent to market.

On one of our earlier visits to Jesi, we toured the central factory, guided by the director of the marketing office. Housed in modern buildings, the factory was—from incubators to final wrapping—surgically clean and efficient. The marketing director, clad in a white smock, tall, and muscularly lean, could have been the poster child for the healthy ruspanti. At the end of the visit we could not resist asking that most nagging question. Without batting an eye: "Here," the director answered proudly, "the egg comes first!"

MACERATA

A wedding picture of Le Marche's marriage of Art and History would show us Macerata, with Commerce and Culture holding the white train. Macerata is a large town that bloomed with the Renaissance but its origins go back to Roman times, with perfectly preserved ruins scattered here and there.

Today the town is full of arcaded streets lined with shops, boutiques, and open-air bars. Streets and squares have the soft color of golden bricks and are pleasant, comfortable, and as predictable as an old aunt's parlor. The facades of many of the town's buildings display unusual textured designs unlike any we've seen in other parts of Italy. Macerata's best-known building is the extraordinary Sferisterio, built as an elongated handball arena in the 1820s in Palladian style, with elegant colonnaded stands and boxes. By the mid-1800s handball—a hard-to-imagine tennis played without racquets on a football-field-size area—was very fashionable and played anywhere there was enough space, fenced in or not. About one hundred years later, the game having lost its popularity, the arena was discovered to have superb acoustics and has been used as a concert and opera theater since then.

In Macerata they tell us *"simangiabene."* It is a phrase heard all over Italy, but here is said as one word, an adjective: "one-eats-well." It means that good food is a matter of fact, not an exception. It also defines the food itself: *Si mangia bene* does not involve quantity but quality, the kind that is immediately pleasing and does not need to be rationalized or explained.

If, while walking in Macerata, a rich aroma suddenly fills your nostrils, it could very well be from a *vincisgrassi* coming out of the oven. A specialty of the city, it is a glorified lasagna in which giblets, sweetbreads, beef marrow, and the blessings of Verdicchio are parts of the recipe. In it also appear Parmigiano cheese, butter, milk, Marsala wine, eggs, cream, and the shavings of a truffle or two. The high-octane ingredients all blend, surprisingly, into an incredibly light first course. It is this quality, it is said, that appealed so inordinately to Windish Graetz, an Austrian General of the Napoleonic

Wars of 1799, who gave the dish its Italianized name.

Ciavuscolo is another dish, so local that it is hardly found out-side the region: It is a very finely textured, soft, almost spreadable salami. Extremely flavorful and rich, it is considered an acquired taste. Served on a slice of fresh country bread, it is an acquisition easily made. But it wouldn't be fair to limit Macerata's gastronomy to vincisgrassi and ciavuscolo alone.

Years ago, to help us in our search for local specialties, the director of the Ente Turismo office in Macerata suggested that to have a deeper indoctrination we should make a stop in Montecosaro, only twelve miles away, and have lunch at La Luma. If we called ahead, Giovanni Bartolini—chef, owner, and expert in local and regional cuisine—could prepare a sample of his fare for us. And so, almost by chance, we discovered this tiny town. Little did we know then that Giovanni and his wife, Luisa, would become fast friends and that we would return countless times to La Luma.

Unsurprisingly, Montecosaro (population 4,884) sits on top of a hill and has its own bit of art and history. The beautiful eighteenth-century church of Saint Augustine, attached to the monastery of the Augustinian Order, dominates the village. The building, perfectly maintained, is used today as the city hall, and below in its high vaulted cellar is La Luma. It is an elegantly appointed dining room, large and roomy, with comfortably spaced tables covered with white linen, fine china, and fresh flowers. The clean, bare-brick architectural lines are softly lit; Persian carpets cover the floor, and paintings and prints adorn the walls.

On our first visit, Signora Luisa was expecting us; she showed us to a table and offered as an aperitivo a fluted glass of dry, sparkling Verdicchio. Giovanni will join us shortly, she said, but wouldn't we, in the meantime, try some *assaggini* that he has prepared for us? Her question mark was still hanging in the air as a young waiter in a black tuxedo wheeled in a small cart and transferred its goods, with methodical timing, to our table. A plate of assorted local cured meats was followed (the second of many trips of the cart) by *assaggini di stringhe all'arugola,* non-egg homemade fettuccini with arugula-based sauce; red ravioli (made with beet pasta) with zucchini and thyme filling; *baci di dama,* crepes of prosciutto, carrots, and cream cheese in a *besciamella* sauce. Luisa's soft voice announced each dish as it was set in front of us. We paced ourselves for what followed: *lumache in porchetta,* snails in a wild fennel sauce; *coniglio arrotolato,* boned rabbit rolled with celery, pancetta, and pine nuts; *furbi coll'abbiti,* a sauté of squid and Swiss chard; *trippa finta,* a casserole of fake tripe, actually a sturdy omelette cut in strips like tripe and cooked like the real thing; and *fricandò di verdure in crema di melanzana,* braised vegetables in creamed eggplant.

The wines that Luisa poured for us were elegant counterpoints to the dishes: a dry Rosato and then a fragrant Verdicchio, both of Montanello, from the hills near Macerata; and then a red, sturdy Rosso Conero. The last specialty of Macerata is a small plate of *scroccafusi,* crisp cookies the size and shape of walnuts; to complement them, a sip of semisweet Vernaccia di Serrapetrona, a red sparkling dessert wine.

The progression of foods and wines was impeccable, and it very well defined the term "assaggini," each dish served out of its own silver server but in tip-of-the-fork portions, and each wine poured in its particular glass.

Throughout the exercise, Luisa watched over the young waiter (and over us too, we suspected) to see that he used the right silver, china, and crystal with each serving. Finally, when the last customer in the house had left, she accepted our invitation to sit at our table.

"I left Sardinia to work as a nanny in Rome and met Giovanni when he was working at the Hilton Hotel. He had already worked for years as a chef in some of the best hotels in Italy and Switzerland before coming to Rome. Giovanni thought about striking out on his own, and I encouraged him because I could see his talent. He had always wanted to return to his hometown of Montecosaro, so when this place became available years ago, we took it. We remodeled and refinished, poured all our energy and worldly goods into it," Luisa recounted, somewhat wistfully.

Having a strong interest in wines, Luisa became a licensed sommelier and made the old wine cellar workable. The old traditional way to make light in a wine cellar was by using a *luma,* an oil lamp very similar to Aladdin's, and that's how the restaurant's name came about.

"Rub it and your wishes come true," Luisa added smiling. "It was a critical success from the start, and now after so many years it is also working out financially."

She is petite and looks barely thirty. We commented how all the years of hard work haven't done a gram of damage to her. She laughed and confided that she is the mother of a twenty-eight-year-old son and a thirty-year-old daughter.

Giovanni Bartolini arrived, wearing chef's whites; he is diminutive, natty, and as young looking as his wife. We felt somewhat embarrassed in offering our compliments; he obviously knows more about food than we will ever know. But he accepted them with a shy smile, almost blushing. Reticent at first, he warmed up as the conversation steered away from him and to the subject of food. The middle of the afternoon saw us still at table, talking, and sampling local wines that Luisa introduced with warmth and pride, as if they were her own children.

Giovanni regrets, like many other people we had spoken with before, that the younger generation is less interested in traditional cuisine, and so, it is up to those who love it to keep it alive.

"It is a pity that the young generations do not have, like us, memories of family dinners." Giovanni was serious and introspective. "My own son is a 'fast-fooder' and it saddens me."

He addressed me: "You must remember our grandmothers' dishes. They were done with nothing but lasted a lifetime."

I agreed with him and mentioned how many times I have told stories of old family meals to anybody willing to listen. "People don't believe me when I tell of the huge *polenta con gli uccelli* my Zia Teresa made." A big pot of scalding polenta was poured on a board as big as the dining table it rested on, and the polenta spread out like molten lava exactly to the edges. "We kids held our breath. The polenta never spilled over! Aunt Teresa really had an eye, a cupful more and there would have been a lot of polenta on the floor." When the polenta was reasonably cool, people would eat directly from the board, as at a communal plate, with a fork cutting a swath on the polenta in front of them, and keep going until they had enough. Giovanni and I chuckled at that once common event.

"But the part people think I'm really making up is the sauce that went over it." I looked at Gwen. I had told her this story before, and we both waited for Giovanni to say: *"Uccellini al sugo!"* The spoils of my uncle's hunting trips, a jumble of tiny birds—thrushes, sparrows—were plucked and cleaned, then cooked whole in a red sauce. People loved to chew them up, crunchy tiny bones and all, by picking up the birds by their beaks.

"Can't do that anymore," commented Giovanni. "Illegal. No more hunting of little birds. But we get around that."

He explained that now he makes polenta con uccellini scappati, polenta with birds-that-got-away sauce. The real birds are replaced by tender little veal birds.

"Must be delicious," I smiled, "but where's the crunch?"

"And what about freshly baked bread with a slice of prosciutto and fresh figs just off the tree?" Giovanni added. "Perhaps it was simple food, but so totally nourishing.

"I blame the new affluence," he continued. "People come here because we're known for our traditional food. But then, nobody wants pasta e fagioli anymore, they all want caviar." Giovanni smiled at the paradox. "It makes it difficult for me to satisfy trends and keep up with tradition at the same time. For old times' sake, I always keep ready a big *Frustingolo* cake. Old stuff, but children still love it."

He is very capable at nouvelle cuisine, presenting dishes that look like paintings, but that kind of food can be too intellectual, lacking the hearty appeal of "real food." He added that once in a while he prepares a real porchetta, a whole suckling pig boned and stuffed with wild fennel and herbs, then roasted slowly on a spit until it looks as if it was sculpted in gold, its skin so crisp that at the touch of a fork it cracks like crystal.

"Then I leave the kitchen door open and let the aroma fill the restaurant. On those days the traditional items on the menu fly out of the kitchen," he smiled proudly at his sly stratagem. But then, the next day, "Either a group of conventioneers, or a wedding party, or whatever, and what do they want?" He answered his own question in mock desolation: "Petit rice timbales in cuttlefish ink, flowers of filets of sole in a spinach mousse."

We parted and assured Giovanni and Luisa that we would be back for their porchetta. Just leave the kitchen door open: we will know when to come.

And, in fact, we have returned many times and now we can stay longer, because Giovanni and Luisa have opened Montecosaro's first hotel (twelve rooms at last count), also called La Luma. It was furnished by Luisa with the same exquisite taste with which she decorated the restaurant. Each room has a theme: music room, library, and fireplace room, all gorgeously appointed with appropriate period furniture and fittings. Half of the rooms have windows overlooking the broad valley below the town, revealing a panorama of the countryside that it's hard to take your eyes off. It's that brilliant Marchigiano patchwork of bright green alternating with squares of soft furry beige. A walk around the town's tiny square takes only five minutes, but after one of Giovanni's meals, it's necessary to do that walk over and over again.

On our most recent visit to Montecosaro, Luisa took us down into the valley where scores of new industries are blossoming. Now people come from all over the world to buy shoes and other clothing at the outlet stores. There is even a settlement of people who have come all the way from China to make their homes in Le Marche and work in the factories, something that would have been unseen and unheard-of anywhere in Italy in the past.

ASCOLI PICENO

The last town before leaving Le Marche is Ascoli Piceno. Its 2,500 years of history have been documented at every step by pre-Roman, Roman, medieval, Renaissance, baroque, and neoclassic monuments and buildings. Called the "travertine city," Ascoli is almost entirely built of the local travertine marble, which has a pale silvery-rose hue.

We arrived in Ascoli in the late afternoon, just in time to join the traditional passeggiata in the Piazza del Popolo, a square bordered by arcaded buildings that provide a sort of public living room for Ascoli's inhabitants. We found the piazza decorated for Carnevale and illuminated by chandeliers, suspended from wires strung between buildings on either side of the piazza. It looked like a ballroom, with the open sky for a roof. Since it was more or less teatime, we stopped for tea and pastries at the Caffè Meletti, an Ascoli landmark. For the last two centuries the Meletti Company has been renowned for its production of anisette liqueur. The cafe had undergone a complete restoration to its original Art Nouveau style, so as we sat at our window seats, surrounded by its highly polished dark wood interior, we felt as if we were in another century.

The square is the town's social center and is filled with groups of people of different ages, classes, and professions who, having staked out their corner, meet here at different hours of the day. The various groups, as in a patchwork quilt, are stitched together by children running around chasing pigeons and each other. The place is, indeed, alive and unique.

On one side of the square is the fourteenth-century Church of San Francesco, and upon entering it we were struck by the sight of a stained-glass window unlike any other we had seen before. Among all the traditional windows depicting scenes with religious figures is one showing a group of pale, emaciated people wearing the Star of David on their prison clothes, lorded over by a large man in a Nazi uniform. We decided to go to the sacristy to seek out an explanation. There we found an ancient monk, pale and thin, wearing a well-worn brown cassock. He looked ascetic, and could have easily come down from one of the church's old frescos. The window, he told us, commemorates the death in Auschwitz of a modern saint, the Polish martyr Maximilian Kolbe who was canonized in 1982. He could have found safety in his Catholicism, but he chose to comfort, aid, and share the fate of the Jewish prisoners in the concentration camp. We had never been in an Italian church whose stained-glass windows depicted modern events. But we soon discovered that this was not the only church in Ascoli that commemorated events of World War II. In the crypt of the duomo on Piazza Arringo is an entire series of mosaics depicting moments from the Second World War, including battle scenes with American soldiers, the fighting and death of partisans, and the cruelty of the fascists. It seemed almost incongruous to find on the main floor a traditional twelfth-century cathedral, dedicated to Saint Emidius, the patron saint of Ascoli.

We wrapped up our sightseeing and extended walking tour with dinner at the Gallo d'Oro restaurant. We asked the owner to characterize with a few words, if possible, the cuisine of Ascoli Piceno.

"One word: stuffed," he said. "Here, we stuff everything. We stuff olives, we stuff pasta, we stuff pigs and turkeys and rabbits and pigeons. Even fish we stuff."

To prove the point, we were served, to begin, *olive Ascolane ripiene,* the trademark of Ascoli's table: large pitted green olives, stuffed with a mix of meats, cheese, egg, truffle, and then breaded and fried. Next came *cannelloni all'Ascolana,* baked pasta stuffed with chicken livers and wild mushrooms, followed by cheese-stuffed turkey breast with truffles and accompanied by little drums of stuffed zucchini. Even dessert, the half-moon-shaped *calcioni*, were sweet ravioli stuffed with an improbably delicious mix of ricotta, sharp pecorino cheese, and chocolate. Signor Mazzitti had made his point.

"As for the wines," he added with obvious pride, "we have one of Italy's best kept secrets." Then, as if introducing a superstar in a theater, he proclaimed loudly: "Rosso Piceno Superiore!"

Ruby red against the table's candle, it was smooth and generously mouth filling. We also sampled a white Falerio, which, while not the greatest of wines, perfectly complemented the local brook trout (stuffed, naturally, with almonds and mountain herbs). To finish, he offered Anisetta Meletti.

"Many anisettes are produced in the world," Mazzitti told us, "but only the one made with wild fennel of the nearby Sibillini Mountains is the real one."

From Ascoli Piceno, take one step to the south and you are in Abruzzi; one step to the west and you are in Lazio, Rome's region. To travel in either direction is to leave Le Marche. Each time we visit, we know it a little more than before, but we continue to wonder why this region is so little known, perhaps even hoping that it remains so, unspoiled by mass travel and fast food. But a more difficult chore is ahead for us: to choose, among all the assaggini of places and food, which ones to return to and which ones to have more of. We know we're coming back for seconds—of everything.

VINCISGRASSI

Lasagna Le Marche Style

Vincisgrassi is a glorified baked lasagna. The major difference is the Marsala wine in the pasta and the addition of chicken livers, veal brains, and sweet-breads to the meat sauce. Sometimes, brains and sweetbreads are substituted by ground veal or ground beef—or even a mixture of the two.

FOR THE PASTA:

1¾ cups umbleached all-purpose flour	½ teaspoon salt
	3 eggs
½ cup fine semolina flour	2 tablespoons Marsala wine

MIX the flours and the salt in the bowl of a food processor with cutting blade in place. Lightly beat the eggs and Marsala together and, with the processor going, pour the mixture into the bowl. Keep processing, pulsing on and off, until the mixture turns into pellets. If the mixture is too dry, add some water a teaspoon at a time; if it's too moist, or if it forms a ball, add more flour.

POUR the pellets into a bowl and press them together into a ball. Knead it briefly and then, on a floured surface, roll the dough into a thin sheet. Cut it into 3x6-inch pieces and let it rest on kitchen towels. You can also run the dough through a pasta machine.

FOR THE SAUCE:

1 onion	½ cup tomato sauce
1 carrot	½ cup chicken broth
1 rib celery	1 cup milk (as needed)
12 fresh mushrooms	½ pound veal brains
2 tablespoons minced fresh flat-leaf parsley	½ pound veal sweetbreads (or 1 pound ground veal or ground
4 tablespoons unsalted butter	veal/beef to substitute for the
4 tablespoons olive oil	brains/sweetbreads)
10 ounces chicken livers, chopped coarsely	Salt and pepper Parmigiano Reggiano cheese as needed
1 cup dry white wine	

MINCE the onion, carrot, celery and mushroom stems (set the caps aside) together. Add the minced parsley and sauté in butter and olive oil until limp. (If using veal or veal and beef, add to the pan and brown.) Add the chicken livers and brown them gently. Add a little wine at a time until it is absorbed and/or evaporated. Stir in the tomato sauce and the broth and simmer for about an hour. Stir occasionally and add a little milk if the sauce thickens too much.

SLICE the mushroom caps. If using the brains and sweetbreads, blanch them, remove the thin pellicules, and cube. Add to the sauce together with the sliced mushroom caps. Simmer for another ½ hour, then set it aside and let cool.

FOR THE BESCIAMELLA:

4 tablespoons unsalted butter	¼ teaspoon freshly grated nutmeg
4 tablespoons flour	¼ teaspoon salt
2 cups milk	

MELT the butter in a saucepan over medium heat, then add the flour all at once and stir into a paste. Slowly add the milk, and using a wire whisk, stir and cook it for at least 4 minutes until you have a thick creamy sauce. Let it cool.

PUT the pasta pieces, a few at a time, in a pot of lightly salted, boiling water. Cook them briefly, to this side of the al dente stage, then fish them out of the boiling water with a slotted spoon and put them in a bowl of cold water. Drain the pasta well and place it on a plastic wrap–covered counter.

TO ASSEMBLE THE VINCISGRASSI:
PREHEAT the oven to 350°F.

BUTTER generously a 14x10x3-inch lasagna pan.

COVER the bottom with a layer of pasta, spread over it a coat of sauce, dot it with besciamella, sprinkle it with grated Parmigiano cheese, and cover it with another layer of pasta. Repeat the layering until all the prepared ingredients are used. Dot the top with butter and sprinkle with grated Parmigiano.

BAKE the vincisgrassi for 30 minutes.

Serves 6–8

POLLO IN POTACCHIO

Chicken Cooked in Wine and Herbs

Potacchio (prounounced "po-tah'-kee-o") is Le Marche's tasty way of cooking almost everything. Stockfish, salt cod, rabbit, baby lamb, even— in some villages—mixed vegetables are served potacchio style.

1 frying chicken, approximately 3 pounds	3 tablespoons red wine vinegar
¼ cup olive oil	1 cup dry red wine
1 medium onion, slivered	1½ cups basic tomato sauce
3 cloves of garlic, lightly crushed	½ teaspoon salt
3 tablespoons fresh rosemary	½ teaspoon cayenne pepper, or more to taste

CLEAN AND CUT the chicken into ten pieces (the six joints, plus the breast cut into four pieces). Trim and remove as much fat as possible.

PUT the olive oil, onion, garlic, and rosemary in a large sauté pan and stir-fry briefly. Add the chicken pieces, raise the heat, and cook, turning them frequently, until they're brown.

ADD the vinegar and wine, cover, and swirl the pan over the heat. After 2 minutes uncover the pan, scrape the bottom and sides with a wooden spoon, and stir in the tomato sauce. Add the salt, sprinkle in the cayenne pepper (to taste; the dish should turn out not spicy hot, but pretty zippy), lower the heat, and cover. Simmer for 40 minutes, stirring once in a while, then uncover and let it bubble away for another 20 to 30 minutes. The sauce should be reasonably thick and coat the chicken pieces well.

SERVE with warm, crusty Italian bread or slices of polenta.

Serves 6

FRUSTINGOLO

Fruit Cake

This is a traditional cake for vigil days, particularly Christmas Eve, in Le Marche.

2½ cups dry red wine	3 ounces unsweetened baking
4½ ounces sugar	chocolate, grated
10 ounces dried white figs	3 ounces unflavored bread crumbs
2 ounces golden raisins	3½ ounces flour
2½ ounces slivered almonds, blanched	1 teaspoon powdered cinnamon
2½ ounces chopped walnuts	½ teaspoon freshly grated nutmeg
2 ounces diced citron	Peel of 1 orange, grated
2 ounces honey	4 tablespoons canola (or olive) oil

POUR the wine in a small saucepan with about one ounce of the sugar and boil until reduced to ¾ of a cup.

PUT the dried figs in a small pan with enough water to cover them, bring to a boil, then simmer for 15 to 20 minutes or until the figs are moist and plump. Drain the figs, let them cool, and chop them coarsely.

WHILE the figs are cooking, put the raisins in warm water to plump up for about 10 minutes, then gently squeeze them dry.

OVEN toast the blanched almonds slightly at 250°F. When the almonds are barely golden, let them cool and chop them coarsely.

RAISE the oven heat to 375 F.

PUT the chopped figs, raisins, chopped almonds, chopped walnuts, and diced citron in a mixing bowl and mix well. Stirring, add the honey, grated chocolate, bread crumbs, flour, cinnamon, nutmeg, and grated orange peel. Stir in the oil and then add slowly the reduced wine, stirring constantly, to obtain a reasonably stiff mixture (when peaked in the middle of the bowl, it should slowly go back to level).

GREASE slightly an 8½-inch springform pan and pour the compound into it. Bake it for 40 minutes. Let the cake cool and rest before removing from pan. Cut into half-inch slivers. It is best served the next day. And the next.

Serves a multitude

::   ::

Abruzzi

HEAVY BOOTS, NIMBLE MINDS

*I*f you thought that Italy had exhausted its allotted share of tall mountains with the arc of the Alps, you should come to Abruzzi to reconsider. Here, at the geographical center of Italy, mountains are a constant, imposing presence. At 9,500 feet, the Gran Sasso d'Italia (literally, "the Big Stone of Italy") is the highest peak of the Apennines and the highest mountain outside the Alps, a sight that can't be missed from anywhere in the region. Geographers treat the whole area as a single mountain massif, a concept also embraced by historians to explain the area's long-standing isolation from the rest of the nation. The insularity of the region has influenced the character of the people and promoted a continuity of customs and traditions. Some of these can be traced back to prehistory through ancient artifacts, of which Abruzzi has the vastest collection in Italy. In addition to its undeniable beauty, the geographical variety of the mountainous complex—gorges, lakes, plateaus, wild rivers, and glaciers—offered shelter to prehistoric life both in the hot and the glacial periods when humans, elephants, rhinoceroses, and hippos had to share land and caves.

Only about an hour's drive away, Rome has made Abruzzi its playground for skiing in the winter and seashore vacations in the summer. Gran Sasso, besides being the tallest peak and a popular skiing area, is also of particular interest because of its historical importance. In July 1943 Mussolini was dismissed as prime minister by King Vittorio Emanuele III, arrested, and transported by *carabinieri* to the summit of Gran Sasso. The spot was chosen because it was so secluded that it was thought unassailable. There was no road up the mountain. The peak could be reached only by *teleferica* (cable railway), the irony of the situation being that Mussolini himself had built this ski resort and cable railway in 1934, inaugurating both with great fanfare. He remained as the heavily guarded sole guest at Campo Imperatore, the only hotel on the mountain, for two months until he was freed by a daring German rescue party who arrived in gliders, plucked Mussolini off the mountain in a short-take-off plane, and spirited him away to Germany. He later returned to head the Fascist puppet government in northern Italy where he was eventually killed by the partisans. The base of the mountain now contains several modern ski lifts and plenty of hotels and cafes, many in the style of an Alpine village.

The region is open as a natural history book for the intelligent traveler, the limited presence of humans during all eras having left the land unspoiled. Here one can enjoy a range of wild flora, from the velvety edelweiss to cerulean-blue saffron crocus, from primeval pine and beech to maple forests. There's also the fauna of the many parks: wolves, antelopes, wild mountain goat, deer, bears, and the soaring royal eagle, from which the capital city of L'Aquila takes its name.

These rugged conditions and the hardy climate have shaped the inhabitants' strong, tenacious, loyal, and feisty character. A people of shepherds, forced to pass through other tribes' turfs during the seasonal migrations of the herds, they developed a strong sense of self and an offensive-defensive warlike nature, national traits that convinced the ancient Romans to keep the Abruzzi people as allies and friends.

The *Abruzzesi* used vessels made of gourd or horn, clothing made of sheep or goat skin, and shoes made of heavy cloth bound with leather strips even in the industrial age and, in remote villages, even in more recent times. Some of this attire continues to be used for commemorative feasts, and in our memory we still see the *zampognari,* shepherds who come down to Rome each December to play Christmas carols on their *zampogne* (bagpipes). A remembrance, perhaps, of the shepherds who came to honor the Holy Child at the Bethlehem stable.

Here, shielded from outside influence more than in other regions of Italy, pagan rituals have sometimes resisted Christianity. Many churches and abbeys have been built on the foundations of old pagan temples, and many religious ceremonies show pagan origins. The old gods Pan and Ceres, protectors of harvests, have been replaced by saints. Saint Anthony Abbot assures a good slaughtering of pigs, while Saint Blaise protects against sore throats. In the village of Cocullo, as an echo of the ancient worship of reptiles, in the "procession of the snake-handlers" the statue of Saint Dominic and his courageous faithful are draped in live snakes, to protect against the bite and temptation of that other old snake, the Devil.

Throughout the historical vicissitudes of the Middle Ages and the Renaissance and following the steps of other Italian city-states or possessions of the emperor or of the pope, the cities and towns of Abruzzi—including L'Aquila, Teramo, Chieti, Pescara, Sulmona, and scores of family-owned villages—developed and accumulated a wealth of artistic and architectural treasures. With the unification of Italy, the political, religious, and economic climate changed quite drastically.

Only in the last three centuries (recently, by history's calendar) have easier transit and communications inside and outside the region brought Abruzzi abreast with the rest of Italy. In all seasons it is not uncommon to drive up to Abruzzi from Rome for lunch just to partake of its savory and fragrant cuisine.

The Abruzzesi are known as stubborn and cunning folks, or, as somewhat jokingly defined by friends and foes, *scarpe grosse, cervello fino* (heavy-booted, nimble-minded). Don't let the shepherd's mountain "heavy boots" fool you—the shepherding life is long gone—and the "fine mind" has produced many personalities of national fame. Yet neither hard work nor sharp thinking could stand up to the economic situation of the beginning of the nineteenth century. Abruzzesi emigrated in large numbers to the Americas, emptying entire towns and villages of their population. As a result, today a large number of Abruzzesi have close or remote relatives and active ties in the United States; visiting Americans are welcomed as members of the family.

We were recognized as such in the town of L'Aquila, where, at the restaurant Il Tetto, we were not allowed to order from the menu.

"For you we have something special," said the smooth maître d', "something only for special people. We cook it specially!"

We said to each other that we must be seeing the cervello fino at work, accompanied by a generous dose of diplomatic salesman-ship. Moreover, that the dish was being prepared just for us meant there would probably be a wait.

There was, but it was rewarded by the arrival of the waiter carrying aloft a silver platter covered by a silver dome. He was pre-ceded by the maître d'. The waiter lifted the dome like a magician as if, voilà!, to reveal the rabbit, whereupon the maître announced in trumpet-like tones, *"Tonnarelli della perdonanza!"* Below a cloud of steam and a powerful aroma, the tonnarelli appeared, strands of pasta the color of gold, shining in a delicate golden sauce. Why *perdonanza*—"forgiveness"? The maître reassured us that today there wasn't anybody or anything in need of perdonanza, of absolution.

"At one time in the Middle Ages," he explained, "a terrible disease took over L'Aquila. A plague. A man came with magic and cured the city, but expected a ton of gold as his reward." He took a storytelling pause. "The *Aquilani* were too poor to come up with the gold, so, instead, the men went out to harvest all the saffron they could find and the women made the tonnarelli with flour and lots of eggs. They produced a dish that looked like gold and tasted like heaven, so the man would forgive them their poverty and their inability to pay. Perdonanza!"

We waited for the punch line.

"That's it. That special man liked the gift more than the gold. And so, since then, we make it for special events and for special people."

The two of us have never had a ton of gold, but if we had, we'd probably trade it for those tonnarelli. Real gold corrupts, any-way, and forgiveness is better than gold. . . . We hope our heirs will see it that way.

Due to the tasty palette of available ingredients and the inspired way of using them, Abruzzi is a veritable nursery of famous chefs. Wherever in the world an Abruzzese cook is manning a stove, excellent food is assured. Cornerstones of the cuisine are the locally grown saffron, which is a cash crop of Abruzzi, and the ubiquitous red hot pepper *peperoncino,* affectionately named *diavolillo* (little devil), which definitely it is—and then some.

Our waiter explained to us that the local cuisine is inspired by a "never insipid, never spicy enough, never indifferent" motto. To have a tangible example of that, he recommended that we go to the nearby town of Amatrice, which throughout history switched alliances between Abruzzi and Lazio. Each region claimed, on and off, its political and cultural predominance over the other. One case in point is the famous *bucatini all'amatriciana:* A hollow, tube-like pasta (*perciatelli* in the United States), it is, in one version, prepared with a sauce based on pancetta, tomatoes, and fiery peperoncino. In the other version, the peperoncino is eliminated in favor of a light flavoring of onions and white wine. Each version proves the maxim "never spicy enough" and "never insipid" and, given the fighting ardor of the respective factions, "never indifferent."

We stopped at the Albergo Ristorante Roma in the center of Amatrice for a dish of bucatini all'Amatriciana and asked the waitress to which version the establishment subscribed. Obviously jaded by the question, she handed us without hesitation a printed recipe of their Amatriciana. No diavolillo, but excellent nonetheless. Later we suspected the existence of two recipes, one with and one without hot pepper. The locals, known for their fire-resistant palates, probably get the fiery one.

In a culture that historically handles all goods in a restrained, parsimonious manner, an incoherent culinary tradition is the *panarda.* It is an annual meal that the hosts spend months preparing for, since they are obliged to offer no fewer than thirty courses. The guests have to finish them all or risk great offense to the hosts. It is a tradition that is slowly being abandoned by the younger, more affluent generation, but justified by the older generation as a single day's liberation from a year of economic restrictions. Or it could be inspired by a saying from Roman times: *Una tantum, licet insanire*— "Once in while it's good to go nuts!"

Heavy boots, nimble minds and all.

BUCATINI ALL'AMATRICIANA

Pasta with Tomatoes, Salt Pork, Onions, and Hot Pepper

4 slices lean salt pork
4 tablespoons olive oil (or enough
    to cover pan bottom)
2 red pepper pods, seeded (less or
    more depending on how hot
    you want it)
1 medium onion, thinly sliced

⅓ cup dry white wine
3 cups plum tomatoes, peeled
1 teaspoon salt (approximately)
1½ pounds of bucatini (perciatelli)
    or the same amount of spaghetti
Pecorino romano cheese, grated

BLANCH the salt pork for 1 minute, then rinse and dry it. Pour the olive oil into a large frying pan over medium heat, and add the pepper pods. Dice the salt pork and add it and the onion to the pan.

COOK until the pepper pods are dark and then remove them (or leave them in, if you prefer hotter sauce). Continue cooking until the onion is limp and the fat of the salt pork is translucent and the lean meat is a pale pink. Add the wine and cook until the wine has evaporated.

ADD the tomatoes, crushing them as they go in. Bring the sauce to a boil, lower the heat, and simmer about 20 minutes, or until the liquid has reduced and the consistency has thickened. Add salt and adjust to taste.

WHILE THE SAUCE IS COOKING, drop the bucatini into a pot of rapidly boiling salted water and cook until al dente. Drain the pasta, put it in a deep platter, and cover with the sauce.

SERVE with grated pecorino cheese to sprinkle on top.

Serves 6

TONNARELLI DELLA PERDONANZA
Saffron Pasta

12 ounces homemade pasta, cut for tonnarelli, square spaghetti, or linguine (you can also use commercial spaghettini, thin spaghetti)
1 tablespoon olive oil
2 dried red pepper pods (or a few shakes of Tabasco)

1 cup peeled plum tomatoes
4 tablespoons unsalted butter
4–5 fresh basil leaves, roughly chopped
Salt to taste
1 packet *zafferano* (saffron)

SALT and boil the pasta water.

IN A FRYING PAN, sauté the pepper pods in the olive oil (the longer you sauté them, the hotter the sauce will get), or use Tabasco to taste. Mash the tomatoes into the oil and pepper. When warmed, add the butter and basil leaves. Add salt to taste, and let the mixture simmer while the pasta cooks.

WARM a serving bowl for the pasta; put the saffron in it and dilute it with one or two tablespoons of warm water.

DRAIN the pasta when cooked al dente, and immediately pour into the serving bowl on top of the saffron. Toss until the pasta is uniformly saffron colored. Toss in the sauce and serve.

Note: For the real thing, the homemade pasta should be made with the addition of ⅛ teaspoon of saffron.

Serves 4

::      ::

Puglia

LOVE AT SECOND SIGHT

*P*uglia: It may not be love at first sight. There is a definite difference between Puglia, called *Apulia* in Latin, and the other regions of Italy. For Puglia, one has difficulty applying with the same immediacy and liberality the adjective "beautiful." Only when you're comfortable with the deeper qualities of the region do you start giving in to the unusual allure of its land and its sea.

In other words, Puglia will grow on you, as it did for me when I lived there in the 1960s and as it has for both of us during several recent trips.

Puglia is in the southeast of Italy, forming the spur and heel of the Italian boot. It does not need a WELCOME, YOU ARE NOW ENTERING PUGLIA sign. As you approach the region from the northwest, it is as if nature itself had drawn a line on the ground, an unmistakably clear border. Your eyes will tell you that you are now in a bleached, tired old land, its face and body powdered by imaginary dust, reminiscent of a sunbaked Mesopotamia but without the Tigris or the

Euphrates. In fact, Puglia does not have any rivers at all, at least none that could reasonably apply for the job, and its rainfall is one of the lowest in Italy. Indeed, it is believed the origin of the region's name is *A-pluvia,* meaning "absence of rain" in Latin.

The traveler's first impression of the land is its flatness, even where it is not flat, and its dust, even where it is green. The Tavoliere, one of Italy's largest plains, covers a great part of the region, from the bony western Apennines to the Adriatic Sea. Once a deadly malarial swamp from which people either fled or died, the Tavoliere was slowly reclaimed and today has become Italy's largest wheat basket, a miniature Kansas.

At the edge of the plain, here and there the land rises in tentative "mountains," gritty and dried out. Among them, the villages look like a child's haphazard construction of chalky cubes balanced one on the other or strewn around, whitewash peeling away from sandstone. Traveling south, the calcareous sandstone piles up into the Murgia, the hilly central part of Puglia, parallel to the flat strip of land bordering the sea. The region ends in the Salento, the stiletto heel of the boot, where it dips into the Ionian Sea.

Weather, nature, and man, in an unholy alliance, have managed to strip most of this region naked of any major woods, depriving the earth of shade above and of moorings against erosion below. Cataclysms, fire, economic need and greed, wars, and invaders' rage have left the land shorn, letting the Mediterranean *macchia* (the brushwood, or tropical weedgrass) grow wherever it can. Through the ages the olives have survived, rooted deep in the harsh soil. Gnarled, centuries old, and much bigger than in other parts of Italy, with enormous trunks twisted and contorted into dramatic shapes, they grow for miles and miles along the country roads in central

Puglia. They are visually magnificent and widely nursed and cultivated, and their abundant, strong olive oil is a major source of revenue for the province.

On the northern edge of the region, perhaps in a spurt of rebellion against the monotony of the region's geography, nature has created the Gargano Promontory which juts into the Adriatic Sea and forms the spur of the boot. Rising in steep, harsh gradients from the land and plunging down on three sides almost vertically into the sea, the dome-shaped hunk of land looks more mountainous than, at 2,500 feet, it actually is. Its forbidding appearance and difficult access once segregated it from the rest of the land and made it the repository of mysterious forces and mystical legends. Supposedly the residence of malevolent spirits and generous gods, their respective prophets and oracles encamped there in sacred caves and temples.

For us, though, Gargano looked like a huge gray lump as we arrived from the north in a misty rain. Two lakes—one long and thin, the other round—are separated from the sea by a flat, half-mile-wide dune. Their flatness and pale color made the lakes blend so easily with the seascape that we almost went by without noticing them. A whirling flock of seabirds revealed them to us, and there they were, the Lago di Lesina and, separated by a hillock, the Lago di Varano. They are fed by freshwater springs and also by openings into the sea, so their water is brackish; for all purposes, they are seawater lakes. While a few kinds of fish have made their residence here, big and small *anguille* (eels) thrive exceptionally well.

The virtues of the eel were proven to us by the owner of Le Antiche Sere, a small trattoria we happened upon around lunchtime in the town of Lesina, on the shore of the lake. Its front door announced that the place served *Cucina tipica lesinese* ("typical food of Lesina"), indicating that even this tiny town had its own particular cuisine. Some of our best food discoveries have occurred just when our stomachs start to grumble; then, the first appealing eatery we encounter will do. Perhaps this is the moment to say that in Italy, no matter where you stop, rarely will you have a bad meal. Our Sunday lunch at Le Antiche Sere bore out that theory.

The room had a spartan simplicity with seven or eight tables, and the fact that each table was oversized told us that the place catered to groups. A knotted string curtain separated the room from the kitchen. When we entered, three of the tables were occupied by local multigenerational families: grandmothers apportioning food from the loaded serving platters, mothers feeding the small children, men wolfing down big forkfuls, pausing just a moment to discuss the Sunday soccer game, while older children chased each other around the room. All this activity gave us the opportunity to ogle at the fare being served and consumed. The owner came for our order, apologizing for the *confusione,* but we assured him that this was just the sort of activity we liked to be part of during our Sunday dinner. He proudly informed us that the specialty of the house—and his invention—was *cicatelli Antiche Sere,* a dish of small elongated pasta covered with a clam, mussel, squid, eel, and tomato sauce. It was delicious, and to top it off, a platter of eels followed.

Now, some people we know curl up their noses at the mention of eel. They do not know what they are missing, and at Le Antiche Sere they would be missing a lot. Eels are served stewed, fried, roasted, or grilled. The cook explained to us that their preparation depends on their size and kind. He stews or fries the smaller ones and roasts or grills the larger and fatter ones. Over live heat the layer of fat under the larger eels' skin melts away, leaving them crisp outside and moist inside.

After lunch we stepped outside and found that the rain had stopped. The sky was a more cheerful blue, dotted with white billowing clouds. Under that light and moving east toward the sea, Gargano looked gentler and rounder, with groves of olive trees and oak, chestnut, and pine trees. The air was green with shade, pierced by the blue sparkle of sea views. Our opinion of this southern land began to soften.

For centuries, people made pilgrimages to Gargano to seek protection against the evils that oppressed them. Even in recent years that strong element of mysticism was kept alive by Padre Pio da Pietrelcina, a monk who, early in his religious life, reputedly received the stigmata—the bleeding wounds resembling those inflicted on Jesus at the crucifixion. Believed to possess miraculous powers, Padre Pio turned the small village of San Giovanni Rotondo on Gargano into a destination for millions of faithful from all over the world around the 1950s. A sanctuary was built there next to an existing old temple, and Padre Pio was canonized as a saint in 2002. A few miles south, another large sanctuary competes for pilgrim traffic in Monte Sant'Angelo, a stunning town whose bright white symmetrical houses cascade to the sea. It is dedicated to the Archangel Saint Michael and built over the grotto where he appeared to the faithful on May 8 in A.D. 490. The sanctuary became an obligatory stop for the Crusaders on their way to the Holy Land.

The coastal road along Gargano's spur is as splendid as any you will drive in Italy, rivaling the Amalfi Coast and the Italian Riviera with its glorious panoramas. Many would say that it is a drive less spectacular than Amalfi's (it certainly has fewer hairpin turns), but it has more variety, with olive groves alternating with steep limestone cliffs and stone wall terraces—and all along, little white-washed villages jut from rocky cliffs that fall into the blue sea below. It's definitely less traveled, so you are not as likely to be harassed by giant tour buses and lines of cars prodding you on, incessantly honking their horns.

Nestled at the bottom of the cliffs are colorful fishing villages with ancient origins—Rodi Garganico, Peschici, Vieste, Mattinata —that are spaced clockwise around the periphery of the promontory. As we enter these towns, we are reminded immediately that we are in the south. Groups of black-dressed men, obviously unemployed, hang around on street corners, smoking and ogling the girls who walk past arm in arm, taunting them with comments in their local dialect—a sight rarely seen in similar towns in the north and just another reminder that in many ways, Italy is really two countries. Nowadays, the subsistence of these Gargano towns does not depend as much on fishing as it once did. Many of these locales have become summer resorts. First-class hotels, vacation villages, and convention centers in crystalline secluded bays are priming the resurgence of the hospitality industry of the area. The smiling spirits of fun and fashion have begun to replace the scary and austere spirits of old, making the coastal area feel almost like another planet compared to the mystical aura of Gargano's interior.

At the town of Manfredonia, Gargano ends and the rest of Puglia with its more typical *Pugliese* flatness resumes. Facing south, we can see the smooth blue sea on our left and flat land everywhere else. But we are beginning to see something else, too: All around are elements of a rich, fabulous, eventful past that, like threads of a tapestry in the works for millennia, weave and interweave to shape the Puglia of today. It is a permeating feeling that makes you look at the somewhat drab landscape with a better appreciation. Manfredonia was built by Manfred, the Swabian King, in 1256 to house the exiles of the nearby city of Siponto, which had been ravaged by war. Now a sea resort, this town grew from Roman times to achieve primary importance as a Pugliese port in medieval times.

West and south of here extends the Daunia, a region settled, legend says, by the Homeric hero Diomedes, who escaped from the pages of *The Iliad* with a few companions. At his death, his desolate followers were transformed by the gods into *diomedee* (albatrosses) so they could mournfully circle over and protect his tomb. They still fly high today, with hundreds of other species in the bird sanctuary of Gargano.

Venture forty miles to the west, and you will be in Foggia. Of Norman origins, throughout its long life the city was destroyed, rebuilt, pillaged, plundered, and rebuilt again by the French, the Spanish, the Saracenes, princes, emperors, bishops, and popes. In 1731, an earthquake almost managed to level it. Foggia is still a flourishing commercial-agricultural center, and no wonder—the *Foggiani* are among the most resilient and optimistic of people. Each event has left its mark, visible in the various styles (and conditions) of the churches, palaces, and urban monuments. Frederick II, King of Germany, Sicily, and Jerusalem, and father of Manfred, favored Foggia as one of his residences and built his Imperial Palace there. But then Frederick II left official buildings all over Puglia, the most famous and imposing of all being the Castel del Monte. The massive octagonal structure rises on top of a hill like an enormous, geometric rock sprouted from the earth. Elegantly naked, each of its eight corners is finished by an eight-sided tower of the same height (75 feet) as the main body of the castle. Since the year 1200 Castel del Monte has looked over the blank wheat plain that surrounds it. One needs to take a deep breath to absorb the sight. Hundreds of conjectures have been made about the reason for its unique construction: It is a showpiece of the emperor's might, or an imperial hunting lodge, or an enormous celestial observatory because of its perfect geometric harmony based on Arabian mathematicians' calculations.

Continuing southeast from Foggia, you will be in Cannae, the Tavoliere site where in 216 B.C. Hannibal and his Carthaginian army, elephants and all, crushed and chopped to pieces the Roman army, possibly the most humiliating defeat in Roman history. Between Romans and Carthaginians, twenty-five thousand lives were lost in the one-day battle, and Hannibal, sworn enemy of Rome, established his supremacy over all of southern Italy.

Every stone of the land appears to be a marker of history, from prehistoric burial dolmen and menhirs to the pockmarks of World War II; you feel the need to walk attentively and be careful of your steps. Puglia's geographical position makes it the bridgehead between Italy and central-northern Europe and the Levant. Albania, east across the Adriatic Sea, is within sixty miles, Greece slightly more; from there the door is open to the Middle East. The Romans built the Via Appia (Appian Way), more than 350 miles of paved road from Rome to the southern ports of Taranto and Brindisi—the "doors to the Orient"—and it carried all the traffic across Puglia for the best part of two millennia. Still there today, rebuilt and enlarged over the old road, the Via Appia still moves its cargo to Taranto and Brindisi, and in great part to Bari, the capital of the region.

This large city is the economical nerve center of the region

and, with its university, museums, and theaters of national importance, also a cultural center. In the last few decades the city has
developed into a modern metropolis, with all the advantages and
drawbacks that entails. Bari exists in three parts: It starts with central Bari Vecchia (Old Bari), with some spots dating to the eleventh century and earlier; this, in turn, is surrounded by Bari Nuova
(New Bari), the fin-de-siècle-style city with its well-planned grid of
streets, elegant shops, and apartment buildings; and then, in recent
years, further surrounded by the sprawling modern and industrial
city. Bari Vecchia—dusty, dirty, with its warrens of tiny alleyways
and no indoor plumbing—has been for centuries home for the
poorest *Baresi*. In its heart lies the Basilica of San Nicola, the eleventh-
century Romanesque church that is striking for its simplicity and
dedicated to Saint Nicholas. His bones are buried and revered there.
Once, citizens living outside the old town would tentatively venture
inside only to go to the basilica, but now the houses of Bari Vecchia
are gradually being renovated (with plumbing installed) and bought
at inflated prices by the affluent who enjoy the characteristic nature
of their new surroundings.

::::::

On one of our trips back to this city where I lived in the 1960s, I
found an increase of urban sprawl and traffic, but the friendships
formed way back then are as close and solid as if just made yesterday. As Franco already knew from the tales about our past lives
that we swapped when we first met, I lived in Bari for six years
and taught English at the American Studies Center. At the time, in
post-war Italy, English was replacing French as the lingua franca

and many adults came to the school to learn. Thus, most of my students were my age or even older, and many of them became good friends. Some even met their spouses in my classes! Anna and Umberto met there, and Maria Teresa married her classmate Giorgio. Through them, I met many other Baresi with whom I've remained very close even though we rarely saw each other after my return to the States. Most are grandparents now, but still as vital and lively as I remember them.

Bari is not a city that many Italians from the central and northern parts of the country find very appealing. But then, northerners tend to look down on the south of Italy. For me, though, Bari will always be a special place because my son was born there. In fact, my friends delight in reminding me that even if my son may call himself an American, he is really a fellow Barese.

I was eager for Franco to meet these dear friends I had been telling him about. On our first trip to Bari together shortly after we were married, everyone wanted to meet my *nuovo marito* and wine and dine us. Several sets of friends insisted on inviting us to their homes, each clearly wanting to outdo the other with a fabulous home-cooked meal in our honor. The first evening we all gathered at the home of Anna and Umberto Fiore—my devoted students of old—for a feast of memories and a typical Barese dinner. Umberto is a retired lawyer and has a fun-loving streak, teasing me about the fact that I had to go all the way to America to find my Roman. Anna is an excellent cook, as are all my women friends in Bari; they are, after all, the ones from whom I acquired my first Italian recipes. I used to stand in their kitchens to watch them prepare a meal and then copy in a notebook everything I had observed.

We started our feast, as expected, with the most famous of Pugliese pasta dishes, *orecchiette* (little ears or rounds sliced off a roll of dough and pressed with the thumb for a concave, earlike effect) *con cima di rape,* literally turnip greens, but also made with broccoli rabe or a kind of Italian cauliflower with tiny green flowerets, olive oil, garlic, *peperoncino,* and anchovies.

The centerpiece of the meal was *tiella di riso e cozze* (baked rice and mussels), a specialty so local it's not even Pugliese, only Barese. With escalating voices—all talking at the same time, Italian-style—Anna, Maria Teresa, and another friend, Nietta, each tried to explain why her recipe for this dish was the most authentic. The discussion became so heated it was practically impossible to understand anything they were saying. Finally, the following consensus was reached on the recipe: In a large baking dish you make a layer of olive oil and onion slices, then a layer of thin slices of potato, mussels, rice, and finally, tomatoes. Then comes another layer consisting of minced garlic, parsley, oil, and zucchini, and so on until the dish is full. The whole thing is topped off with a mixture of grated pecorino cheese and bread crumbs to make a nice crust.

Another specialty that became the subject of an animated discussion was *lampaggioni,* the bitter onions typical of Puglia, which can be boiled and dressed with olive oil, salt, and pepper, or boiled and then dipped in batter and deep fried along with artichokes, cauliflower, and ricotta. The breadbasket was brimming with *taralli,* a southern specialty shaped like a small unsalted pretzel and tasting like one. The conviviality was accompanied by various bottles of great local wines—including a well-aged Primitivo (ancestor of the California Zinfandel), red, big, and strong, defined by those present as "boisterous."

The next afternoon we met Umberto at a bar and were introduced to a brand-new afternoon drink concept. After we had ordered our *espressi,* he ordered an *espressino,* a word to which we both gave a blank stare. It turned out to be a tiny cappuccino served in an espresso-sized cup. Knowing the Italians' critical attitude toward foreigners who dare to order a cappuccino in the afternoon or, horror of horrors, after dinner (according to rigid custom, one should never order a cappuccino after noon), we could not help but tease our friend. How slyly Barese, we said, just by altering a name, one can change the rules of the game.

"Ah, we are at the forefront of new trends, you see," teased Umberto. Continuing his playfulness, he couldn't resist quoting for us a bit of drollery in Barese dialect that is the pride of Bari's inhabitants: *"Se Parigi avesse lo mare, sarebbe 'na piccola Bare."* Loosely translated: "If Paris had a sea, a little Bari it would be." Bari is the only place where we have encountered this new libation, and as far as we know innocent visitors to Italy are still frowned upon when they order a cappuccino in the afternoon.

That evening it was Maria Teresa's turn to host us at her and Giorgio's villa in the countryside south of Bari. Our group of eight was joined by their daughter, who is an exporter of Italian food (including her family's olive oil), so, naturally, vociferous opinions about the food and its preparation were heard throughout the meal. Maria Teresa served three different kinds of pasta and explained that this is not a new trend in Italian cuisine—one pasta dish is still the accepted first course to a meal—but she just wanted us all to have *assaggini* (tastes). Perhaps this was her way of demonstrating her prowess at the stove. Next, we had *ricci* (sea urchins), in remembrance of those Sundays forty years ago when we used to go to the pristine coves along the Adriatic Sea and pull the sea creatures right off the rocks, cut them open with a big knife, squirt with lemon, and suck them right out of their shells. We drank a wonderful Salice Salento, a wine that was known only in Puglia when I lived there, but now you can find it everywhere.

Our third and last evening was dedicated to another five-course meal partaken at the home of another pair of friends, Nietta and Sergio. They live in a gorgeous villa that is filled with the fabulous artwork they have collected through their years of traveling all over the world. (The affluence of our friends certainly seems to belie the belief that Puglia is one of the poorest regions of Italy.) My recollection from my early years in Bari was that Nietta was the best cook of them all, and the majority of the recipes in that old dog-eared notebook of mine are hers. She outdid herself, as usual, with a series of exquisite dishes all with a Pugliese flavor. We started with *minestra di fava, cicoria, e cipolle* (a soup of fava beans, dandelion greens, and onions), the first recipe I had obtained from her those many years ago. She remembered that I used to be fascinated by the sight of people picking cicoria in the fields near Bari, and that I had never seen anybody doing that in the States. After the minestra Nietta produced an amazing *zuppa di pesce* with all local fish and seafood, including eel. We finished off our feast with her homemade biscotti.

On the fourth day, after saying a reluctant good-bye to our friends, we staggered out of town, vowing not to eat again for days, and continued our Pugliese journey by heading south and inland to Alberobello. This town is known for its unique constructions, the *trulli*: circular white houses made from local limestone with black or grey cone-shaped roofs, all put together without mortar. The lower parts of the houses are whitewashed and many of the roofs are painted with white astrological or religious symbols. Architects come from all over the world to examine the trulli, but their origin remains a matter of speculation. The surrounding hillsides are dotted with the white trulli, making a lovely landscape. Unfortunately, the town of Alberobello itself has become Disneyfied, selling out to tourism with plastic trulli reproductions and other tacky souvenirs in knickknack shops.

That architecture—villages resembling a child's haphazard placement of white blocks on top of each other—continues as you go further south into Puglia. Locorotondo is a favorite, a beautiful bright white circular town sitting on a hill above the valley, with quiet alleyways for walking undisturbed and iron balconies from which flowers cascade. Another is Ostuni, also brightly whitewashed and sitting on a hillside with views of sea and countryside alike. In this area a number of *agriturismo* centers have recently popped up; old farmhouses have been made into inns and restaurants that serve excellent local dishes. Our preference when traveling in Puglia is to stick to the inner country roads because that's where the unique beauty of the region lies. Here is where you find those miles and miles of spectacular olive groves, vineyards, glistening hill towns, and very little traffic.

Toward the end of the heel in the Salento area, almost as a final surprise, is Lecce, a city largely planned and designed in one style: baroque. Because of its location and history one would expect a much more visible Byzantine influence; however, Emperor Charles V of Aragon built a defensive wall around the city that protected it against the marauding Turks and gave the city a reconstructive burst. In the following centuries the city turned into what

is considered to be one of the world capitals of baroque art. Praise must go to the local architects, artists, and artisans: They had the vision and the sharp chisels to turn Puglia sandstone into an elaborate tangle of facades and interiors throughout the buildings and churches in the city. From Lecce it is only a short drive to the sea and then down to the tip of the heel through the fishing villages of Otranto; Castro; Santa Maria di Leuca, the southernmost point of Puglia; and Gallipoli, where the Adriatic is still pristine and the towns are unspoiled.

From all of the above—indeed only a part of everything that is Puglia—one comes to understand that the region is shaped more by the imprint of man on nature than by nature itself. There are advantages to the general flatness and reasonably easy ways of communication in the region. While in other regions one can find substantial differences among the villages, towns and cities, Puglia has a unified character and dialect, a trait that is also reflected in its cuisine. The differences encountered from one province to the other are minor; the harvests of the sea and of the land make the basic staples.

The gastronomy, like the people, reflects foreign influences (especially Greek), and, stemming from a base of farmers, shepherds, and fishermen, it shows their resourcefulness and ingenuity in getting the most out of what's available. Local specialties are the result of invention and inspiration, or the use of local wild field greens and herbs, which the Pugliesi use traditionally. They are particularly proud of their olive oil, scented and thick—there is even an olive oil museum at the town of Fasano—and of their fish and shellfish. The abundant, sturdy Pugliese grapes, used until quite recently to give body to more refined wines, now make some remarkable and esteemed local Sauvignons and Chardonnays.

We said good-bye to Puglia in Taranto. It is a big city, both old and new, grown around its important port. We had our farewell dinner at La Fattoria, a place we're always drawn to whenever we visit Taranto. It is a quietly elegant restaurant, with mirrors and warm wood paneling all around. To welcome us, the attentive staff offered a glass of bubbly Rivera Brut—it's our own, they specified. It gave us time to examine a huge cart brought for our inspection, loaded with all sizes of fish, spiny lobsters, shrimp, and oysters. They looked as if they just came from the sea. We made a feast of them, from an *antipasto di mare* to a zuppa di pesce (oh, what glory!) to a *fritto misto mare* (mixed fish fry). A visually show-stopping dish concluded the sea parade: **Calamari Ripieni.** The stuffed squid appeared like smooth, glistening four-inch torpedos in their brown savory sauce. A Rosa del Golfo rosé helped us to toast Puglia, a renewed friend.

Our first impression seemed way in the past, and on second —and third—sight, Puglia had grown on us. It will grow on you, too.

CALAMARI RIPIENI

Stuffed Squid

12 medium-size squid,
  6–7 inches long
5 flat fillets of anchovy
2 garlic cloves
1 cup loosely packed flat-leaf parsley
2 tablespoons capers

4–5 tablespoons olive oil
3–4 tablespoons unflavored
  bread crumbs
1 cup dry white wine
Salt and pepper to taste

CLEAN the squids. Separate the tubes (bodies) from the tentacles.

MINCE together the anchovy fillets, 1 garlic clove, parsley, capers, and the tentacles of the squids. Put the mince in a bowl and add 1 tablespoon of olive oil and enough bread crumbs to form a paste.

STUFF the body of each squid with a scant teaspoon of the paste (don't overstuff or the squid will split open) and skewer it shut with a toothpick. Save any remaining filling.

PUT ENOUGH olive oil to cover the bottom of a sauté pan large enough to accommodate the squids in one layer. Put the squids in it with the remaining garlic clove and sauté at low heat, turning the squid around until lightly colored. Add any remaining filling to the pan and cook for another 2 or 3 minutes. Add the wine, raise the heat, and let the wine evaporate.

TRANSFER the squid (now shrunken) and the pan liquids to a smaller pot and add enough water to halfway cover the squid. Cover the pan and simmer on low heat for 10 minutes. Add salt and pepper to taste.

MOVE the squid to a serving plate and reduce the pan juices (if necessary) to sauce consistency. Pour the sauce over squid and serve warm as an entree or cold as an antipasto.

Serves 6

ORECCHIETTE CON CIME DI RAPE

Orecchiette with Broccoli Rabe

½ cup olive oil	1 pound broccoli rabe (or 1 pound
2 garlic cloves	green cauliflower)
1 dried red hot pepper	1 pound packaged orecchiette
(peperoncino)	Salt and freshly grated black
5–6 flat anchovy fillets	pepper to taste

HEAT the olive oil in a large saucepan, and sauté in it the garlic cloves and red pepper. When both are toasty brown, remove and discard them. Add the anchovies to the oil and mash them down with a fork into a paste. Set the anchovies aside in the pan and let them cool.

CUT off the larger stems of the broccoli rabe and coarsely chop the remaining stems and leaves, leaving the small broccoli flowerets untouched. (If using the cauliflower, separate it into the small flowerets, discarding the tougher stems.)

BRING a pot of lightly salted water to boil; add to it the prepared broccoli rabe (or the cauliflower flowerets) and the orecchiette. When these are cooked al dente, drain well and pour them into the saucepan with the anchovy sauce. Raise the heat and stir for a couple of minutes, until the pasta and broccoli rabe are well coated. Serve immediately with salt and pepper, if desired.

Serves 6

Calabria

THE TOE OF THE BOOT

Frequently, in late spring or in summer, a merciless heat is blown by African winds across the Mediterranean, and it envelopes Calabria. Loaded with desert sands and sea moisture, it is the dreadful, suffocating *scirocco*. If we happen to be in the region when the *scirocco* arrives, we always make it a point to pause at midday and take refuge.

On one such occasion, hoping to find cooler air, we left the coast of the Ionian Sea and headed for the higher elevations. We found no relief, and even our rented car seemed to pant going through the barren hills leading to the mountains. Finally, the top of a bell tower, appearing and disappearing around the curves, gave away the presence of a village, a place so tiny we might have passed it by, dismissing it as another pile of sun-baked rocks. The village looked very poor—a few stone houses huddled together—but it was now past high noon and we were as far from any urban center as we could be.

We reached the main and only square, a rectangle defined on three sides by houses and on the fourth by the church, all white-washed, all devoid of any traits apt to soften the starkness. Even the shadows seemed to glare in the reflected light. All windows and doors were firmly shuttered; not a soul was to be seen. It was there, in all that absence of color and sound, that a young man appeared. He was as surprised to see us as we were glad to see him. It was clear that this place was not on any Calabrian tourism itinerary, and the sudden influx of two visitors was quite an event for him. We explained that we were in search of shade and food. Was there any to be found nearby?

Smiling, he told us that—if our expectations weren't too high—both could be had at a small place nearby, a hole in the wall, really; it was easier for him to lead us there, if we wished, than to explain the way. He was barely past adolescence, neatly dressed in military fatigues; he told us he was home on a short furlough. No, he said, the village was not totally dead; at this time of day people were taking shelter inside, enjoying the coolness that the night had stored up within the thick stone walls of the houses.

After a brief walk we were where we wanted to be, in a cool, grotto-like eatery with four or five empty tables. There the young man announced to the owner that we were his *amici Americani* and deserving of his total attention. The owner, somewhat astonished by our unexpected appearance, conferred in confessional tones with our guide, and then consulted with a lady who had poked her head from the kitchen door. He told us that, since they weren't prepared for any customers, the best they could arrange would be some sort of *merenda,* a snack. We reassured him that we were not expecting much, and that the sheltered coolness of his place was already great sustenance. From the kitchen began to emanate noises of pots and pans and plates and whispered plotting. Then an eight- or nine-year-old boy rushed from the kitchen out into the street. By the time he came back carrying a basket, we had been served a carafe of white wine, cool, dry and sharp as a blade. Then the owner brought us an onion and zucchini *frittata,* super-fresh braided mozzarella, and just-picked garden tomatoes, followed by a warm loaf of country bread—unquestionably out of the boy's basket. The mixed juiciness of the mozzarella and tomatoes, together with a few basil leaves and some drops of olive oil made additional dressing unnecessary: a most unexpected *insalata caprese.* The young soldier would only accept from us our thanks and a small glass of wine. Together with the owner, he apologized for the scanty offerings. We reassured them that it had been, with the coolness of the place, a meal that will rate in our memory with the best we ever had.

For us, this brief experience in Firmo (the village's name, barely visible on a map) and our other visits to Calabria are like snapshots of the region's nature and history. Calabria is the very tip of the Italian boot. It straddles two seas: The toe dips into the Tyrrhenian, the instep rests in the Ionian. Altogether, the land has an amazingly varied beauty, all rocky cliffs, mini-bays, and coves on the Tyrrhenian side, a continuous stretch of white sandy beach on the Ionian side. Between the two the Apennine Mountains, ranging the whole length of Italy, come to die at the doorstep of Sicily. Although it has five hundred miles of coastline, the region's lifeline is attached to the land and not to the sea. The flat, defenseless Ionian coast made it inviting for outsiders' incursions, hence dangerous for the natives. For self-defense and safety, the *Calabresi* moved up to the high lands. As in the old game of "King of the Mountain," whoever made it up there was hard to budge out. Greeks came and flourished in Calabria, calling it their Magna Grecia (Greater Greece). In 550 B.C., Pythagoras founded his mathematical school in Crotone, one of the great learning centers of antiquity. Calabria was then not only learned but rich, too; seventy miles up the coast from Crotone is Sybaris. You would hardly know it today, but Sybaris was once a rich commercial center; its opulent citizens—Sybarites—dedicated themselves to expensive pleasures and refined sensuality.

During the third and second centuries B.C., at the time of the Roman Punic Wars, Calabria made the worst political decision it could make: It sided with Carthage, and that choice shaped its destiny. As retribution, victorious Rome shaved Calabria's land clear of trees, and many future Roman fleets floated on Calabrian wood. The victors added further injury by establishing the *latifondo,* confiscated small family farms that were collected into large land holdings. Roman absentee owners left the working of their huge farms to the enslaved natives, under the heavy thumb of hired supervisors.

The whole historical process sucked out Calabria's marrow and created in the populace an endemic poverty and a form of resigned submission. But also, on the other side of the coin, it pushed the few with red blood still in their veins to rebellion and banditry—an activity, which had the scope of an industry.

Around the beginning of the twentieth century, the demand for labor from North and South America opened the gates of the Calabrian cage: a very high percentage of the region's able men, with their women and children, fled the region in the first big emigration wave. Almost as in biblical terms, the Calabresi multiplied and populated the earth. But they also bled Calabria of its vital lifeline, leaving entire towns and villages unpopulated and dying.

Calabria, while much involved in contemporary Italian history, is still steeped in the heredity of Magna Grecia. Archaeological finds keep surfacing from the earth and the sea. One such discovery is the Riace Bronzes. In the early 1970s, found by accident near the town of Riace by scuba divers and fished out of the Ionian Sea, the six-foot-tall bronze statues of two Greek athletes, dating from the fifth century B.C., are considered paragons of virile power. When first exhibited, their perfectly sculpted, perfectly preserved bodies provoked quite a stir. It is said that many ladies, young and old, trekked from all over Europe to see them and to swoon and faint in their presence. The Bronzi di Riace are now exhibited in a room of their own in the elegantly modern Museum of Magna Grecia in Reggio di Calabria, the present-day and the antique making a striking contrast. Their magnetic appeal is irresistible, and whenever we are close to that city, we make a special detour to go pay homage to the Bronzi. We do not swoon or faint, but we definitely have mystical feelings, as if in the presence of men-gods arrived intact from old Greece.

When heading back to Rome from Calabria, we like to avoid the *autostrada* (superhighway), which could take us to Rome in about four hours, and instead drive on secondary roads. It may be a foolhardy choice, but actually, the Calabrian part of the autostrada can turn out to be a slow ride, since it seems to always be under construction and you never know when ROAD WORK or DETOUR signs will pop up. On the country roads we get to see and become acquainted with the face of a country.

On a recent visit, we took the shore road north from Reggio Calabria, and steeled ourselves for the encounter with the mythological sea monsters of Scylla and Charybdis. As Homer tells it in *The Odyssey,* Scylla and Charybdis face each other across the Strait of Messina, one monster in Calabria, the other in Sicily. They torment and toss weary voyagers in a gauntlet of terror and, finally, devour them in the churning waters. Let's face them in the daylight, we told ourselves, and planned to meet them at high noon. Face to face, the monsters were, to say the least, a letdown. Scylla is a delightfully quiet village, perched high over a long sandy beach; Charybdis was nowhere in sight, perhaps a faint shadow on the far Sicilian coast. Three hundred feet straight up, a large square and a promenade overlook the blue waters of the Bay of Scylla. Far away in the middle of it, long, thin oar-propelled boats were hunting swordfish in a centuries-old tradition, one man propped high on a mast scouting and pointing at the fish, another yielding a harpoon from the prow. Four other sailors manned the oars, indifferent to the monsters' danger. We approached two young men lingering in the square and timidly queried them about the whereabouts of Charybdis. We expected them to indicate for us the whereabouts of Monster #2. Instead: "Who . . . ?" they said with vacant eyes, telling us that, locally, the legend of Scylla and Charybdis isn't that big a deal at all. We recovered from the fizzled-out suspense at a local restaurant, sustained by a juicy steak of *pesce spada,* swordfish—freshly harpooned, we are told—cooked in a pan with peppers, capers, and lots of lemon.

Tropea was next, a town whose construction is so unusual it's hard to believe your eyes. Standing on the beach below, by a pristine sea, you look up at a sheer rock face on which are constructed houses that seem to rise straight up into the air. From above, if you are sitting in an outdoor cafe in the piazza, you look down onto a series of rocky coves, white sandy beaches, and a translucent green sea. Again we have the feeling of being bathed in mythology, this place evoking not sea monsters but sea nymphs and perhaps, in a regal cove, King Neptune himself. The reverie is so strong that a chilled glass of dry, sweet Greco di Bianco is a must. The barman tells us proudly that this wine is thought to be a descendent of the old Krimisa, one of the oldest vines of Europe; Calabrian winning athletes returning from the Olympiads were hailed with it. He is talking, he says, smiling, of many a thousand weekends ago. How mythically appropriate. A second toast is a must.

With the blue sea to the left, the seacoast road reaches the old town of Paola, a minor port. A remarkable number of crumbling baroque buildings are lined along little squares and steep, very steep, narrow alleys. Decayed noblesse tinged with proud poverty was all around us. It's not surprising that in the fifteenth century Paola gave to the world an austere saint, a hermit, Saint Francis of Paola. In the hierarchy of saints, he comes way behind Saint Francis of Assisi, patron saint of Italy, but he still rates high as the founder of the order of hermit monks, the Minis. This hermitic dedication seems to be lost on today's Paola. We stopped at a cafe and found ourselves surrounded by high school students who were having a great time playing hooky, eating pizza, and chain smoking right under a big sign reading VIETATO FUMARE. Perhaps as a demonstration of independence from authority, all posted orders in Calabria—from ONE-WAY STREET to NO PARKING—seem to have the value of a challenge. It is in Paola that we saw graffiti on the wall that declared in huge letters: *Maria, sei bellissima anche in divisa* ("Maria, you are very beautiful even in uniform"). The dislike of her uniform did not blind the writer to the policewoman's beauty. The graffiti, naturally, was written under the warning POST NO SIGNS.

The highlands of La Sila, the central part of Calabria, are a succession of green mountains, covered with maple, pine, and fir forests, and dotted with natural and artificial mountain lakes. The sight of cattle at pasture in the small valleys makes one think of a mini-Switzerland, an image hard to identify with southern Italy. But then, suddenly, the image reverts to a locally rooted one: In some villages like San Giovanni in Fiore, some of the older inhabitants wear traditional costumes and live in houses that have not seen a change in two centuries. It felt as if we had stepped into a nineteenth-century print or daguerreotype.

On another trip driving from Cosenza in the heart of Calabria to the coast, we again rejected the autostrada and took provincial roads through the interior, coming face to face with a most rugged and craggy terrain. It made us understand why during World War II, on its painful march through the boot, the American Fifth Army preferred to leapfrog this portion of Italy and risk the bloody landing at Salerno, more than one hundred miles to the north. Just to reach the coast at Cetraro, with sightseeing stops along the thirty-two mile pretzel-twisted roads, took us almost four hours.

Finally, from up high, we sighted the blue sea again with the same elation Columbus must have felt when he sighted land. By now it was way past lunchtime and, like Christopher and his crew, we were tired and starving. A few hours of rest were due. And then we saw it: the Grand Hotel San Michele. Enthroned on a natural terrace high above the sea, surrounded by Mediterranean pines and palm trees and trimmed with flowering bougainvillea, the place appeared foreign to its location like a transplant from the Belle Epoque. This was even more apparent inside when at the mahogany reception desk we were graciously told that the dining room was closed at this hour, and anyway, it was normally open only for hotel guests. Our dismay must have spoken volumes because the receptionist suddenly changed his mind and said he would open the dining room for us. Only for a light repast, however. What impressed us was that even though we had popped in without notice or reservations, at the wrong hour, in the wrong season, and, perhaps past presentability after our long drive, we were received with welcoming cordiality. A maître d' was summoned to take care of us and a waiter and a busboy pressed into service. The dining room, although large and formal, offered a relaxed sense of civilized comfort.

We stretched our fortuitous pause. We remained for four days.

On other occasions, we would have found the maître d's mother-hen flitting overdone, but we accepted with pleasure his concern for our comfort. He made us feel at home, even if at home we would never have used such an array of silver, crystal, and china, delivered by a traffic flow of serving carts.

We told the maître d' that we were traveling around on a search for regional foods. So, the next day he announced to us that, after consultation in the kitchen, the chef had agreed (the light work load of the off-season allowing him some freedom) to prepare some traditional Calabrian dishes for us and the other few guests. Moreover, he added, it was a great pleasure for the chef, the preservation of old traditional recipes being his avocation. Even if, here and there, now and then, he would add his own little twist. . . . After all, the chef continued, Calabrian cookery is composed mostly of interpretations of neighbors' cuisines.

An essay by the Academy of Calabrian Foods and Wines describes it as "not a poor cuisine, but a cuisine of poor people," echoing the diffuse canon of all Italian regions—richer or poorer—of doing the best with what's at hand. And its results always surpass the unpretentious ingredients that are used. In Calabria the humble pig dominates.

"Here, the pig is sacred!" the maître d' declared, "like the cow in India. In many villages it is left to roam free in the streets, piglets and all."

True to his words, our next meals were a random catalogue of "peasant" cuisine: *millecosedde,* "a thousand little bits," which is chickpeas, beans, lentils, cabbage, onion, celery, and mushrooms all cooked and mixed together with pasta to make (in theory) a one-dish meal; *macco di fave,* a mixture of fava beans, onion, tomato, and spaghetti; *mariola,* an omelette-like concoction cut in small diamond shapes and warmed in broth; *sagne chine,* a lasagna in which the filling is mostly pork meat and cheese; *braciole di maiale,* thin slices of pork loin, wrapped around sheep cheese and herbs and pan-cooked in their own fat. A series of small-fish (sardines) and big-fish dishes (tuna, swordfish) rounded out the list. All courses were accompanied by the robust red Cirò of ancient renown from the vineyards close to the Ionian coast.

The meals were simple perhaps, but once we got to *dolci* (sweets), invention and imagination were set free to roam. It seems that each town, village, or family has its own particular recipe for a traditional sweet, each one celebrating a special saint's day. Most recipes revolve around honey, which is abundantly produced in Calabria and, perhaps, a Greek culinary memory. Almost ubiquitous, with slight differences, are the sweet-pillow **Bocconotti.**

It was not just the food but also the place's uniqueness that made us stay. Even if it is roughly thirty miles from Cosenza—as the crow flies—the Grand Hotel San Michele is a zillion miles from anywhere in Calabria.

Even more distinctive is the hotel's ecologically self-sufficient operation. The water of a nearby river is channeled, filtered, and purified for all the needs of the hotel and its Olympic-size pool. The outflow of the pool water is refiltered, purified naturally by vegetation, and used to water the nine-hole golf course, which in turn is grazed and fertilized by a flock of sheep. The sizable farm attached to the hotel supplies fruits, vegetables, grapes for wines, vinegars, olive oil, jellies and marmalades, milk, cream, and cheeses. Meats come from animals bred on the farm; fish comes from the sea and a large artificial pond.

Our experience at the San Michele contrasted sharply with the Calabria we were previously acquainted with, and until that visit, we had been unaware of the region's complexity. It's a region that ought to be put on the map of Italian places to visit and appreciate: the worldly modern and the traditional. Can the two coexist? And if so, for how long? Will the desire—or need—to bring Calabria in line with modern economic and social structures overpower the old, colorful traditions and lifestyles?

For a sober judgment, we will have to come back—and find both, we hope.

MARIOLA

Consommé with Diamond-Shaped Crepes

1 egg yolk
3 egg whites
3 tablespoons low-fat milk
2 tablespoons minced flat-leaf parsley
½ teaspoon marjoram
¼ teaspoon salt

5–6 tablespoons unflavored
bread crumbs
9 cups chicken (or beef) broth
Freshly grated pecorino romano
cheese (optional)

WARM a well-seasoned omelette pan, or a non-stick sauté pan, over medium heat.

PLACE in a bowl the egg yolk, egg whites, milk, parsley, marjoram, and salt and beat well. Add the bread crumbs a tablespoon at a time, and continue beating until a reasonably smooth batter is obtained.

RAISE the heat under the pan and pour in some of the batter. Tilt the pan all around to make a crepe. Do not overcook: The final cooking will be done in the broth. The crepes will be somewhat sturdy; the bread crumbs tend to absorb the liquids in the batter and thicken it, so you have to operate quickly. If the batter becomes too thick, beat some more milk into it.

WHILE the crepes cool, put the broth on to boil. Cut the crepes into ½-inch strips, and then cut them again at a 45-degree angle into diamond shapes. Drop them into the boiling broth, turn off the heat, and serve in consommé bowls. Garnish with grated Pecorino Romano cheese, if desired.

Serves 6

Note: The diamonds can be prepared days ahead—they refrigerate or freeze well. The same is true for the broth.

BOCCONOTTI

Sweet Turnovers

Bocconotti are small sweet turnovers, filled with a mixture of ricotta, honey, and pecorino.

FOR THE PASTRY DOUGH:

1 cup all-purpose flour	1 egg yolk
¼ cup granulated sugar	1 whole egg
Grated zest of ½ lemon	1½ tablespoons vegetable oil
3½ tablespoons unsalted butter, softened at room temperature	

MIX together the flour, sugar, and lemon zest, then work into it the butter. Beat lightly the egg yolk and whole egg with the oil, and knead it into the flour/butter mixture. Knead it gently on a floured surface into a soft, unsticky ball of dough. Do not overwork it. Chill the dough.

FOR THE FILLER:

1 egg yolk	10 tablespoons pecorino cheese, freshly grated
¼ cup honey	
1 tablespoon flour (or as needed)	½ teaspoon powdered cinnamon
1 cup ricotta (not too wet)	

BEAT the egg yolk, honey, and flour until light and fluffy. Mix in the ricotta, pecorino, and the cinnamon. Depending on the egg size, the amount of moisture in the ricotta, and the density of the honey, the consistency of the mixture may vary; it should hold its shape when spooned. If not, add a little more flour.

PREHEAT the oven to 350°F.

ON A WELL-FLOURED WORK SURFACE, roll out the chilled dough to ⅛-inch thickness, and cut in 3-inch-diameter rounds. Put a small teaspoon of filler in the center of each round and fold them over in half; seal the edges together by pressing with the tines of a fork. Put the half-moons on a buttered and floured cookie sheet and bake for approximately 20 minutes or until lightly golden.

Makes approximately 12

Sicily

OF CUSCUSU AND OTHER MARVELS

*W*hen we arrived at Punta Raisi, Palermo's airport, a warm breeze rippled the sea at the end of the runway, bounced off the mountain at the other end, and made the air shiver, giving to all things soft, blurred, dream-like outlines. As we stepped off the plane, the mixed scents of sea and of wild flowers and herbs and orange blossoms enveloped us. Sicily, where oranges, lemons, passionflowers, and a thousand other wildflowers grow, is a Garden of Eden. A sunny garden. Sun, Sicily's escutcheon: a round, smiling orange sun, sprouting three legs. Trinacria was the Greeks' name for the three-pointed island.

For this trip, Sicily was to be our springboard to its satellite islands: the Eolie, the Egadi, and the farther away Pantelleria. Italo, a dear Roman friend, insisted that during our short stopover in Sicily we had to, we simply had to, meet a close friend of his. If she ever knew we had stopped by without seeing her, ah, then Italo would have to pay dearly for it, for years be the target of her Sicilian ire. And so, we met Rosalia: petite and wiry, barely past middle age, and free from family duties since her children had grown up and moved away. She was a writer, a gastronome, an expert of all things Sicilian and, above all, a poet. She spoke Italian in romantic, poetic, declamatory—and, we found out quickly, very contagious—turns of phrase. After brief contact with her, we had the communal tendency to speak as if on a baroque stage. She had a take-charge, no-nonsense, no-excuses attitude. When we told her we had planned to stay in Palermo just long enough to recover from jet lag and then we would leave for the islands, she informed us that our plans, as of that moment, had changed: She would be our guide and mentor and show us something of Sicily, her Sicily, as nobody else could.

"*Sicilia,*" our newfound mentor recited, to set the tone, "where Jupiter buried the hundred-headed dragon, where wild grows the laurel, where one moonlit night seems as long as life, a day of sunshine as brief as happiness."

We agreed to get in touch by phone next morning, then we would see.

Rosalia showed up unannounced at breakfast. She accepted, pro forma, a cup of coffee. But she made it understood that there was no time to waste.

"Sicily!" She was on a roll, her hands moving as if playing castanets. "Sicily, two days: something. Ten days: something more. A month will barely suffice to tell of Sicily to your friends. A lifetime not enough to understand it all. Let's begin with now."

She drove us from one corner of town to the other, her driving as florid as her speech and as imaginative—even for Palermo—in the many liberties she took with the rules of the road.

"Palermo, where the sacred and the profane meet: It is the city of Rosalia the Saint and of Roger II, conqueror and king."

And we saw Palermo, no stone unseen: "Every corner, every stone of Palermo is history!" A beautiful, bewildering city, changing its mood, its pace, and its colors with the shifting hours and light of day or night. A magic that touches everything: the baroque churches, the Moorish palaces, the Norman castles, the grim alleys and the fragrant gardens, the stalls and the markets. It's all enveloped in a loud cacophony of sounds and voices that carries from dawn well into the night. It could very well be the voice of life.

It is a voice that becomes deafening at the Ucciaria fish market. Every species of fish, shellfish, or mollusk that swims or crawls in the Mediterranean waters congregates on the metal-surfaced stalls of this market, their quality and prices hawked at full throat by the fishmongers. The silvery-black swordfish, swords up-ended, gleam like the armor of heroes wrenched from the sea and now up for the spoil. Their blood, hosed from the benches, drains in rivulets between the stones of the pavement.

"In the twelfth century," our guide yelled to make herself heard, "an Arab described this market as sordid and fabulous, just like a pipe of hashish."

Time with Rosalia is two breathless days, forty-eight hours, 2,880 minutes with no stone unturned and lunches, dinners, and snacks at open-air stalls.

"Here in Mondello, *arancini* are medals we give ourselves!"

And well they could be: As big as tennis balls, the fried golden spheres of rice with a core of meat ragout, still hot from the boiling oil, scorched our fingers and our palates. But they were delicious.

Our time is up, we told her. But she made us promise that we will not leave Sicily before going to the western tip of the island to see Trapani.

"Trapani is where Arabia meets Sicily," she told us. "To this tip came the Arabs. Accustomed to the burnt desert, they made of this land their enchanted garden."

She gestured to enrich her speech: "It is here that the Arabian couscous speaks Sicilian and blossoms into *cuscusu*. *Cuscusu co'a ghiotta 'e pisci:* couscous with a gluttony of fish!"

We had met couscous before, in North Africa. It left memories of strong mutton fat, overcooked porridge, and greasy fingertips, having eaten it the Arabian way. Probably the worst couscous ever made, but our first and, Allah willing, we hoped our last. Allah, however, could do nothing against our Rosalia's rhapsodizing: "Cuscusu in Trapani is robed in legend. I will alert this little place at Pizzolungo and they will be ready for you. You can't say no."

We couldn't, and we didn't.

We moved west from Palermo, skirting the incredibly blue-green gulf of Castellammare, the town's fort dominating the miles-long, half-moon-shaped sandy beach, and continued through rolling hills, olive groves, and past the Greek Temple of Segesta, the best preserved outside of Athens. Once we reached Mount Erice, high above Trapani, we were out of Sicily. From the top of the mountain, from the spot where the Phoenicians built a temple to Astarte, rededicated by the Greeks to Aphrodite and then by the Romans to Venus, all of Sicily was behind us. In the town of Erice on pavement of elaborately laid stone, our steps echoed among a labyrinth of alleys and stairways, leading to incredible, far-reaching views. Below us, 2,500 feet straight down at the edge of the sea, was Trapani, the city born from the sickle lost by Ceres while in search of her daughter Proserpina. Down we went to our rendezvous at the shore. Pizzolungo, a quiet village lapped by the bluest of seas, is at the doorstep of Trapani, a sizable city and busy port. It is also the location of large salt flats that have been producing sea salt since Roman times.

It was not difficult to find the restaurant—it was the only one. Perched on the beach, it consisted of a large whitewashed room with a few simple tables and chairs. At one end French doors framed the seascape; outside the doors was a shaded veranda with two other tables. Another door led to the kitchen. The proprietress, cook, maître d', and waitress (whose beauty and girth were themselves mythological, leading us to nickname her "Juno") was waiting for us there, ready to produce a cuscusu for our enlightenment. In spite of her size, Juno moved with incredible elegance; she spoke strict Sicilian dialect, a handicap for us, as our straight Italian was for her. When we spoke to each other, we focused on her lips and she on ours. But gestures and smiles carried the day. She motioned: Ready? Yes! we smiled back.

With saffron water and a few drops of olive oil she wet a large shallow dish: a mafaradda, she said. With one hand she let semolina flour rain delicately on the dish while the other pinched and glided through it, turning it into rice-sized grains. The two massive hands were engaged in a dance of their own, following a sensual rhythm: sliding, bending, rising, then disappearing behind the tenuous falling curtain of flour. An odalisque could have learned a thousand secrets. As the flour turned into couscous, she put it to rest on a board in the sun, gold bathed in gold.

She flavored the grains with cinnamon, salt, pepper, and a few drops of olive oil to ready them for the couscous steamer. An obvious heirloom, her steamer was made of two fitting terra-cotta vessels: the bottom one to contain some water; the top one, its base perforated by tiny holes, to hold the couscous. She made a paste with water and flour and used it like putty to seal the two containers together. Tightly covered, the steamer went on the fire and performed with nothing more than a hissing of vapor once in a while.

"And now for the broth," said Juno, as if up to now it all had been a warm-up exercise.

She produced a broth by putting garlic, almonds, parsley, cinnamon, and pepper in a mortar and reducing them all to a paste with a few powerful twists and blows of the pestle. She sautéed onions and added the paste and some tomato puree to them. Then she added warm water, stirring ever so slowly.

"Now the broth has to boil," and realizing our agony, "only a few minutes!" she smiled.

The aroma of the broth, catalyzed by the puffs of steam from the steamer, permeated the kitchen. Juno was seducing our nostrils.

She danced on. For the ghiotta of fish, "you need all kinds of fish," she said. The more, the better. And fresh. "The fish know when I make cuscusu." One of her hands made like a fish jumping out of the sea and landing on the other, her pan. She laughed at her imagery, but we believed her.

Whole or in pieces, heads and bones in, grouper, monkfish, snapper, mullet, and sea bass and shrimp and squid went to cook in a covered copper pan. While the fish poached in their own humor, the steamed couscous was poured into a bowl and moistened with some broth. Then she wrapped the bowl in a blanket. To keep it warm, like a baby.

Finally the couscous and the ghiotta came together: the golden, plump, moist couscous turned into a cradle for the fish, and again bathed in broth. Steamed clams and mussels decorated the top's edge. Land and sea finally united, a living invocation of the Koran: "Nourish thyself, oh believer, and rejoice in the food you receive from the generosity of Allah." A generosity that humbly, gratefully we accepted: It

changed our opinion of couscous forever. This cuscusu was a dish for
the gods. Perhaps, in reality, it was only fish surrounded by a crown of
couscous, but the fragrance and flavor were ambrosia, brought to the
table by Juno herself. Yes, at Trapani, Arabia meets Sicily. But it's an
uneven match: When it comes to couscous, Sicily wins. Hands down.

From Trapani we headed east toward the Aeolian Islands, but to
stretch our Sicilian stay a little longer, we took the island's southern
shore on the way to the ferry. Our time left in Sicily, as Rosalia had
put it, would be like "an hourglass filled with the sands of time, dis-
pensing a marvel with each grain. . . ." Time here, we proclaimed to
ourselves, echoing Rosalia's voice, "is made of seconds and of eons."
The Aeolians will keep another day or two, and wait for us.

And marvel indeed followed marvel: the intense blue of the
coast replaced inland by the gold of the wheat fields and the emerald
green of the rolling hills; the chiaroscuro of ashen-hued village squares
dotted by black-clad people, alternating with the explosion of colors
in the almond and cherry orchards; and the shivering silver of the olive
trees. Colors in the decorated carts and in the mosaics of churches,
color when one least expects it. If Trapani's cuscusu is a gluttony of
fish, the rest of Sicily is a gluttony of colors, flavors, and scents.

And then we heard Rosalia's voice guiding us in Agrigento, "called
by the ancients the pearl of Magna Graecia, the most beautiful city created not by gods but by mortal man. . . ." In its Valley of the Temples,
"the fluted columns rise to the sky like prayers to Jupiter Olympus, to
Juno Lacinia, to Hercules, to Castor and Pollux. . . ." The size and the
location of the temples prove their purpose: "Compared to the beauty
of nature and the majesty of the gods, man is miniscule." Yet standing at
the base of one of the huge columns, we considered the irony: The sheer

artistry and size of the constructions put their ancient builders on the same footing with their magnificent gods.

Next was Siracusa, "where the memory of Greece arrives with every wave of the Ionian Sea," and Mt. Etna, the largest live volcano in Europe, "regal in its ermine white, snow-robed shoulders and with, at its feet, the homage of a thousand blossoming almond trees." Further along was Taormina and its old Greek amphitheater where "with the endless sea as background, all the human comedies and all the human tragedies could be played."

And then, island rounded, we were at Milazzo to meet our ferry. Rosalia, our host, guide, and poet came from Palermo, and with a last wave of her hand, said Godspeed, good-bye.

On the ferry we watched Sicily slowly recede. Memories of this short trip break through the surface of our minds like the dolphins piercing the sea in the ferry's wake.

From the island disappearing behind the sea mist, a fragment of a poem emerges from ancient memory depths. (Was it a remembered quote from our hostess? Or was it the imagined voice of *The Odyssey*'s Circe, the enchantress?) We seem to hear a voice recite it, in a whisper:

> "Leaving you are now, but to return.
> If you don't wish to love me,
> Love me I will make you,
> Because by magic
> I make myself loved."

Gwen insists it was Franco's voice.

Franco still thinks it was Sicily's own.

CUSCUSU CO' A GHIOTTA 'E PISCI

Fish Couscous

FOR THE FISH BROTH:

4–5 tablespoons olive oil

4 garlic cloves, peeled and mashed

1 large onion

4 anchovy fillets, chopped

3 bay leaves

2–3 sprigs flat-leaf parsley

4–5 fresh basil leaves

¾ cup almonds, lightly roasted,
    then powdered

2 pounds fish "racks" (fish heads
    and bones of cleaned fish from
    following fish recipe) or
    chowder fish

Reserved shrimp shells (see
    following fish recipe)

1 cup dry white wine

7 cups warm water

1 cup tomato sauce (can be canned)

2 tablespoons tomato paste

2 teaspoons salt

PUT the olive oil in a soup pot and sauté in it the garlic cloves, onion, anchovies, bay leaves, parsley, basil, and almonds. When the mixture is golden, add the fish racks (or chowder fish) and the reserved shrimp shells; stir and cook for a few minutes over high heat. Add the wine and stir until it has almost evaporated. Then add the water, tomato sauce, tomato paste, and salt. Bring the mixture to a boil, cover the pot, reduce the heat and let simmer for 45 minutes or so. Skim the top if necessary halfway through the cooking. Let the broth cool a bit, then filter it through a fine sieve or cheesecloth.

FOR THE COUSCOUS:

1½ cups fish broth

1 cup water

⅛ teaspoon powdered saffron

⅛ teaspoon powdered cinnamon

⅛ teaspoon powdered cloves

⅛ teaspoon powdered nutmeg

1 10-ounce package
    instant couscous

PUT all ingredients except the couscous into a soup pot and bring them to a boil. Then add the couscous, stir well, and cover the pot. Turn off the heat and let it rest for 5 minutes.

FOR THE FISH:

Fish broth
2½ pounds (approximately) of at least 2–3 kinds of fish (e.g., swordfish, monkfish, halibut, grouper, black sea bass, grey mullet, or any solid-fleshed, non-
  oily fish) cleaned, deboned and cut into pieces
½ pound shrimp, shelled and cleaned, shells reserved
½ pound squid
½ pound mussels, mostly for presentation

PUT the remaining broth in a pan that will accommodate the prepared fish in one layer. Bring the broth to a boil, then add the fish: the ones with the sturdier meat first, then, as soon as the broth comes back to a boil, the next and so on, finishing with the shrimp and squid. Cover and cook for another 2 minutes. Turn off the heat and keep warm.

IN A COVERED skillet, steam open the mussels.

TO SERVE:

FLUFF the couscous and arrange it in a ring on a warm serving platter (or in warm soup plates). Scoop out the cooked fish from the pan and put in the center of the couscous. Decorate with the mussels. Put the hot broth in a tureen and ladle it on the individual servings, as desired.

Serves 6-8

Egadi Islands

THE LAST MATTANZA

*A*s if by intercession of all the fertility goddesses, from the barren sea sprout the Isole Egadi (the Egadi or Aegadian Isles), a three-island archipelago: Favignana, Levanzo, and Marettimo. As an afterthought to Sicily, they are a stone's throw from Mount Erice, the westernmost corner of Sicily. A Cyclops' throw, anyway: translators of The Odyssey insist that Erice is the place from which Poliphemus, the Cyclops, pitched boulders at Ulysses, who then took shelter on the Isle of Goats, today's Favignana. As if to prove it, the island has a cove named Ulysses' Landing, but nobody knows who named it or when the name was given. Of the three islands, Favignana is the largest and most populous with about 2,500 permanent residents.

FAVIGNANA

"Holy Savior, You who created the sun and the moon, the fish in the sea, the tuna and who fishes it, You made promises, and don't forget it! Now, God, You must help us!"

The chant of the *tonnaroti*—the tuna fishermen—rises in the moist sea air from a boat that is approaching the *tonnara* (tuna nets). It is a guttural chant, more like a lament, echoing in the silence of dawn with the slow rhythm of the swell of the sea.

"Our Lady of the Rosary, Saint Joseph and Saint Teresa, Saint Anthony and Saint Peter, tell the tuna to come, help us get a good catch. Listen to us, listen to God's orders!" answers the crew of another boat.

The words are in a strict dialect that even many Sicilians fail to recognize. Some say they are Greek or Phoenician pagan invocations to the sea gods, passed on through the centuries and adapted to the going language and religion. The haunting chant goes back and forth from boat to boat, in a strange mix of prayer, reverence, and veiled threats, like admonitions to the heavenly protectors to behave correctly for this special occasion, or else. . . . There is an implied familiarity between tonnaroti and the deities. They have known each other for a long time, bound by a symbiotic relationship; poor fishermen need the protectors as much as these deities need the fishermen's constituency.

In the waters facing the port of Favignana, a half-mile or so out at sea, we see the *tonnara*: a six-mile-long stretch of nets anchored to form a set of chambers, one feeding into the other, with no return. The last chamber, a square of 150 feet by 150 feet and 90 feet deep, is closed on three sides by heavy stationary barges fixed to the nets and, on the fourth side, by a strong movable net—the door of the trap. The tuna will pass through the opening, and then the fourth side will be brought into place, sealing the fish in this final chamber, *la camera della morte* (the chamber of death).

The stage is set for the *mattanza*. Rooted in Spanish, the name means "the killing." Actually, it is a slaughter—the slaughter of the huge bluefin tuna caught on the way to their spawning grounds. Every May and June, the tuna enter the Mediterranean at Gibraltar, leaving the frigid waters of the Atlantic for the warmer ones of Sicily and Turkey. On the way they encounter the tonnara barrage of nets and are caught in the labyrinth. Spectators on the boat with the tonnaroti view the mattanza as a mythical performance, a Cretan duel of man against beast. Anybody willing to show up at the dock before dawn and who will fit in the fishermen's boats is a welcome guest.

The tonnaroti have reached their position on the barges, lined side by side like soldiers ready for battle. They are waiting for the Rais' orders. The name "Rais" explains who he is: Either from the Latin *Rex* (king) or the Arab *Ras* (boss of bosses), Rais is the admiral, the absolute capo, the architect of tonnara and mattanza, supreme commander of every aspect of the operation, from the setting and repairing of the nets to the transportation and disposition of the catch. As soon as he arrives, the mattanza, its choreography unchanged in obeisance to millennia-old rules, takes place. And then, in time, repeated again.

Or perhaps not.

"Do not miss this one," the tourist agent in Trapani had warned us, "because it is going to be the last mattanza."

Whether the last of this season or forever, it wasn't clear.

The Egadi Isles, even though quite different from each other, have generally been considered a unit in geographical and historical terms. It was in the Aegadians' sea that in 261 B.C. during the First Punic War, the Roman fleet annihilated the Carthaginian's. It established Rome as a sea power and put the Egadi Isles on the map. The legend goes that as a result of the murderous sea battle, the waters of a cove in Favignana turned red with blood: It is called *Cala Rossa* (Bloody Cove).

The islands belong to the same administrative district and shared in the same economy until the recent decline in their traditional activities of farming and fishing, causing the islanders to look to tourism for their subsistence. For years the islands—especially Favignana—were totally self-sufficient, sustained by agriculture, coastal fishing, sheep and cattle herding, dairy activity, and tufa-stone quarrying. The inhabitants boast that these quarries supplied the stone blocks that were used to build everything that was ever built in Sicily, even the Greek temples. But, with pre-mixed cement, who needs tufa blocks anymore? As for agriculture, that's hard work, so it's easier to let the land lie fallow and build on it. Houses can be rented for good money in the summer season.

Ironically, the islands' biggest appeal is good simple food and a quiet lifestyle (the islands have been called "The Islands of Silence"), which will be the first thing to go if mass tourism takes hold.

The owner of the Hotel Egadi is outspoken against this trend. She—and she is not alone in her way of thinking—has the fire of a crusader when defending the traditions and culture of the islands, referred to as the *cultura del tonno.*

"They call me a rebel, but I just call it as I see it. Look at what's happened to places that have gone after tourists' money. Fool's gold, I say," she declares.

We point out the peculiarity of her position: her hotel and restaurant have an excellent reputation in town. Isn't she catering to and profiting from tourism?

"I am careful," she smiles. "People come to me. We go with the tradition. We are not planning to put up golden arches."

The dinner we had at her restaurant confirmed it, with tuna taking the lion's share of the menu. *Raù di tunnu* (ragout of fresh tuna) is a thick steak marinated in white wine, flavored with garlic, fresh mint, and cloves, and then slowly stewed in a light wine and tomato sauce. Served as an entree, the tuna was flavorful and moist, and the stew's sauce dressed the homemade pasta, which was served as a first course. A second entree was *cipollata di tonno,* sweet-and-sour fresh tuna steak covered by caramelized onions and raisins. Perhaps it was the atmosphere or the earlier lecture about the *cultura del tonno,* but we agreed that this is the best tuna we had ever had—and of course, the freshest. *Caponata,* the islands' ubiquitous all-around vegetable concoction, came with the tuna. It can be served hot, cold, or at room temperature; as a snack on toast triangles; as an antipasto; or as a side dish. Eggplants, tomatoes, onions, celery, and any other vegetable at the whim of the cook join raisins and pine nuts in a sweet-and-sour blend.

A major activity on the island used to be the tonnara factory (the word "tonnara" means both the fishermen's nets and the tuna processing). In the large complex of buildings, the tuna were processed in an activity that turned the two-month tuna-fishing season into a yearlong affair. Tuna is the sea equivalent of a pig: Nothing is wasted. (Only the tuna liver is thrown away: Old sailors say that it makes hair, all hair, fall out). The butchering of a tuna is an art in itself: Every single part of its complex anatomy has a particular use and value, from the top-rated *ventresca* (the belly portion), to the cuts that are best used fresh and those for canning, down to fins and bones that end up as fish meal and fertilizer. Connoisseurs search out the *buttarica* (bottarga), dried and pressed tuna eggs, and *lattume,* the milky tuna sperm, with the same zeal—and spending almost as much money—as caviar hunters; it's perhaps because, besides their gastronomic qualities, both have been considered powerful aphrodisiacs since Roman times. The tuna factory gave work to a lot of people and shaped their lives and their culture. Favignana, more than the other islands, followed this "culture of the tuna," which involved every aspect of daily life, including its tuna-based gastronomy.

Graffiti dating back to the neolithic era, discovered on the walls of a grotto on the nearby island of Levanzo, attest to the islands' age-old dependence on tuna. The graffiti show men and beasts, and, appearing among them for the first time in man's history, a tuna. The old, glorious factory has been closed for years; the traditional tuna artisanship cannot hold a candle to the modern, more efficient, more profitable industrial methods. Now that the land tonnara is gone, how much life is left to the mattanza in the sea?

At the beginning of the century there were more than a hundred tonnare in the Mediterranean Sea. Today you can count them, perhaps, on the fingers of two hands, and each year some disappear. There are several reasons for the decline of the tonnare: They are too expensive to run and the schools of tuna are getting smaller.

Above all, the blame lies with the *Tonnare Volanti* (Flying Tonnare), the new invaders of the Mediterranean. The Flying Tonnare are fast fishing vessels, mostly Japanese, that, with the help of electronic devices, can spot a school of tuna, encircle it with nets, haul everything up, process the catch right on board, and call it a day. While the traditional tonnare, with appropriate net sizes, let the smaller tuna escape, free to proliferate and multiply, the Flying Tonnare suck up everything from the sea. The old tonnaroti hate the Flying Tonnare with a vengeance; they are killing off both the tuna and the tonnaroti with one blow. But here is a bitter irony: The Japanese are exceptional buyers of tuna, and they pay top dollar for the best catch of the tonnaroti.

The morning sun is rising higher in the sky, and the tonnara has not seen much action yet. "The Rais' boat has been delayed. He will be here soon." It is the Vice-Rais speaking, in answer to a spectator's query. He is a Greek statue come to life, with the build of someone who can take care of a mattanza all by himself.

"And then, we are also waiting for the tuna . . ." he adds, as if to say that there is no rush. The tuna are on their way, going chamber by chamber, down a dead-end street.

"In the last mattanza we caught 580 tuna, each around 900 to 1,100 pounds. Not bad, but not as good as when we would get almost twice as many. Even so, there are about sixty families who depend on this mattanza, and they will earn more in two months from tuna than from a year of tourism."

Voices have been raised throughout Italy against the tonnara method of catching the beautiful fish: an anachronistic, cruel, medieval way, infused with primitive, unnecessary savagery, they say. The tonnaroti answer is that they are aware they do violence to nature, but it is a violence necessary for survival, their survival. It is not a sport and there is no wanton cruelty. The prayers and the invocations are exorcisms to cleanse and to absolve the tonnaroti's guilt.

"And then, killing tuna does not pain your heart. . . . Tuna's blood is cold. On your hands it's like no blood at all . . . and tuna do not yell and scream and kick like pigs do. That's painful," says the Vice-Rais in an attempt to justify his occupation.

The Rais has arrived. His small boat, three sailors at the oars, is positioned in the middle of the chamber of death. The spectators hush and the morning is suddenly quiet. The Rais raises his hands in a messianic gesture and gives an order. The barge with the tonnaroti moves and closes the last side of the chamber. Its sides and bottom are lined by the net that the tonnaroti, chanting, begin to pull up, hand over hand, until it almost reaches the surface. With every hauling in of the net, the louder the chant, the smaller the chamber. It now looks like a large pool, its waters as blue and clear as the sky, almost festive. Then a lightning-fast shape appears and goes by, and then another. Like shadows they appear below the surface and disappear. They multiply, running crazed around the pool; a fin cuts the surface like a knife through silk, then two, three, many. One big tuna jumps up out of the water, remains suspended in the air for an infinite moment, sucking salvation from the sky, then in a flash of shiny black and silver plunges back in. And then another and another. The surface is not silk anymore; it is churned white by tails beating it to a boil, to a foaming boil.

The Rais' boat looks as if it is floating above the churning and trashing. He gives an order and the tonnaroti start their work. They are divided into squads of six: Two long harpoons bring a tuna close to the barge, two shorter harpoons bring it up to arms' reach, and two short hooks plunged into its belly heave it up and into the barge. The timing is perfect: The bleeding monsters shake and twist and their tails thrash and beat, and it is this motion that helps the tonnaroti lift the huge weight, letting the tuna slide between them, dodging the powerful, murderous blows of the tail as it goes by. The killing has reached a frenzy. The squads—we count eight in the melee—work in unison: four, five, six tuna at a time go into the barge, their blood reddening the pool. More are twisting and churning in the red water, their glassy eyes reflecting the sky. Someone has described the mattanza as a mano-a-mano duel between man and beast, comparing it to a bullfight. It is a most romantic vision, but the bull has a chance in a fight, the tuna none.

There are 124 tuna in the bottom of the barge, none left in the blood-red camera della morte. The Rais lifts his arms to the sky and says: "Jesus! Jesus! Jesus!" The tonnaroti mark themselves with a quick, approximate sign of the cross: "Amen and thanks!" they say. The shiny bodies of the tuna are covered with ice; the barge will be towed to Trapani, to market. There Japanese buyers select the tuna and a crew of specialized Japanese butchers cut it as specified by the Japanese market. The best cuts—or even a whole tuna, if an exceptional specimen—are flown to Japan. Amen and thanks.

One hundred and twenty-four tuna is not a great catch, and none of them is particularly large. But the tuna have made their spawning runs for the year.

This is the end of the season, the last mattanza.

There are rumors abroad that if the revenue from the tuna is not worth the work involved, perhaps the mattanza will be performed only for the benefit (and the money) of tourists. But nobody wants to contemplate this ignominious end of a millennia-old tradition.

The tonnaroti will be involved for a little longer in tonnara work, pulling up the nets, storing the good and repairing the torn, hauling the hundreds of heavy anchors and floats and taking them ashore. Their work done, they will return to civilian life, the life of Favignana, and wait for the next mattanza.

If and when, only God and the accountants know.

CIPOLLATA DI TONNO

Fresh Tuna in Onion Sweet-and-Sour Sauce

2 or 3 onions (approximately 1 pound)
5–6 tablespoons olive oil
3 tablespoons unsalted butter
¼ teaspoon salt
¼ cup water
½ cup red wine vinegar
1 heaping teaspoon sugar
Dash of Tabasco

2 tablespoons golden raisins,
plumped up in warm water
2 bay leaves
4 fresh tuna steaks, 1-inch thick
(approximately 2 pounds)
Salt and pepper to taste
½ cup dry white wine

CUT the onions into thin slivers and sauté them in 2 or 3 tablespoons of olive oil and 1 tablespoon of butter. Add the salt and stir until the slivers are limp. Add the water and cook until it evaporates.

STIR in the vinegar, sugar, and Tabasco and cook over low heat until the vinegar is almost evaporated. The sauce should retain a creamy texture. Drain the raisins and add to the sauce. Cover the sauce and set it aside.

PUT remaining olive oil and butter and bay leaves in a sauté pan. When it's warm (not hot), add the tuna steaks and sauté for 2 or 3 minutes per side, depending on thickness. Do not overcook: Tuna tends to dry out, and it should be cooked on the outside but still moist inside. Raise the heat, add the wine, and cover the pan for a second or two, until the wine stops steaming. Deglaze the pan with the pan juices if necessary.

TRANSFER the tuna steaks and their pan juices to a warm serving platter or plates. Spoon the warm onion sauce over the tuna and serve.

Serves 4

CAPONATA

3 medium eggplants (about 2 pounds)
Salt
2 medium onions
Olive oil
20–24 ounces peeled plum tomatoes
   (ripe fresh or canned)
2 celery stalks (as white as possible)
12 cracked green olives
   (Sicilian or Greek)

2 tablespoon capers
1 tablespoon *pignoli* (pine nuts)
1 tablespoon raisins
½ cup red wine vinegar
1½ tablespoons sugar
1 teaspoon unsweetened chocolate
   (optional)

CHOP the eggplants into ¾-inch rounds, salt them liberally, and put in a colander to drain their bitter moisture for 20 to 30 minutes.

PEEL AND CUT the onions in thin slivers or small squares and sauté them in olive oil until limp. Chop the tomatoes roughly and add to the onions; stir and cook for 5 minutes.

CHOP the celery in ½-inch slices and add them to tomatoes and onions. Pit the olives and chop them coarsely, then add them with the capers to the pan. Bring the mixture to a boil, then reduce the heat and let it cook at a very low simmer.

SCRAPE the salt off the eggplants and rinse them thoroughly. Cube them and sauté them in olive oil until golden and slightly limp; add them with the pignoli and the raisins to the cooking sauce. As soon as the sauce bubbles again, add the vinegar, sugar, and the chocolate (if desired). Cook for another 5 minutes, until everything is cooked but still retains some texture. Serve warm or cold.

Serves 6

Aeolian Islands

ON ULYSSES' TRACKS

*W*hen you enter the Italian Southern Seas, you enter a world of mythology. The shipping line that goes through the Strait of Messina, between Italy and Sicily, and past Scylla and Charybdis, the two all devouring sea monsters, is named *Caronte* (Charon), the ember-eyed skipper of the ferry to hell. The Aeolian Islands' sea is the dominion of old Aeolus, master and ruler of all winds. There, a poor man's *Odyssey* tour can retrace the steps of Ulysses.

LIPARI

The Isole Eolie, an hour-and-a-half ferryboat ride from Milazzo, off the northeastern coast of Sicily, are an archipelago of seven islands: Alicudi, Filicudi, Salina, Panarea, Vulcano, Lipari, and Stromboli. The largest is Lipari, the name frequently used for the whole archipelago. Although the volcanic islands all have the same geological mother, there are no twins in this family. They all are different and, each in its own way, strikingly beautiful.

Homer gave status to these islands by having Ulysses wander around their seas, and it was in Lipari that Aeolus entrusted him with the sealed Jar of the Winds to be opened only for a fast return to Ithaca, his home. The jar came with a caveat: If it were needlessly opened, the winds would gush out and be untamed forever. Ulysses did not abide by the warning, and that is why, according to knowledgeable local meteorologists, the islands are constantly windy, even today.

In the neolithic age, the eruptions of local volcanoes produced a large quantity of glass-like, shiny, black obsidian stone. With the correct blow, the obsidian breaks into razor-sharp chips ideal for all sorts of cutting tools. For more than a millennium, the Aeolians successfully exported their black obsidian—in the rough or manu-factured—to many parts of primitive Europe. With the advent of the Bronze Age, they lost their monopoly on "edges" and had to make a living just like the other less enterprising islanders, by fish-ing and agriculture.

In spite of their stark volcanic nature, the islands appear luxuriantly green. From every crack of the black, tormented, and gnarled volcanic rock, from every fistful of dark soil spring forth all sorts of wild flora: cadmium-yellow broom, fire-red wild gera-niums, purple bougainvillea, orange-red wild roses, pink dwarf orchids, and Day-Glo green cacti. A collection of shapes and colors to match the palette of a painter gone berserk.

An infinity of big and small coves of transparent waters, well stocked with fish, surrounds the islands. Hidden sea caves and grot-toes abound, along with hot mineral springs chock-full of healing powers. These, the natives inform us proudly, have been known since the Romans, who came here to mend whatever damage was provoked by their high-living excesses.

But all the beauty and local resources do not make for a rich economy. It is an economy of subsistence, and many young people leave the islands for more promising shores.

"These are poor islands, and theirs is a poor cuisine," says the manager of the Hotel Giardino sul Mare in Lipari. She is a self-appointed and dedicated curator of the local culture and gastronomy. From our table at the Hotel Giardino we can easily see Sicily's coastline.

"We have an abundance of few ingredients; we make good music with only a few notes." Compared with the cuisine of the *continente,* she says, referring to Sicily and peninsular Italy, the islands' cuisine is less rich and elaborated.

The basic ingredients come primarily from the water. From the high seas, there is *tonno* (tuna), *pesce spada* (swordfish), *cernia* (grouper), and *arricciola* (amberjack), and from closer to shore all the variety of small rockfish. From the land come the plump, flavorful capers, eggplant, and bell peppers, tasty lentils, and aromatic wild herbs such as rosemary, fennel, sage, and thyme. There's also garlic that, due to some attribute of the land, has a strong aroma but a much milder, less acidly pungent taste than continental garlic. Scarce trees produce olives good for curing and for producing just enough olive oil for local consumption. Fruits and nuts include the much-valued Malvasia grapes (especially on the island of Salina) to make raisins and the Malvasia Passito dessert wine; thick-skinned, strongly scented lemons; super-sweet apricots; figs; almonds; and the prickly pears of the ubiquitous cactus. There is no cattle for meat, but some sheep, poultry, and wild rabbit make alternatives to fish.

The conversation continues while we taste an array of dishes: fusilli with *pesto isolano* (different from the classic basil/garlic pesto of Liguria for the presence of tomato); *risotto con sugo di seppie,* rice with squid ink; *cotoletta di pescespada,* breaded swordfish cutlet; and *merluzzo al salmoriglio,* baby cod. We finish up with the classic "poor cuisine" dessert: fresh fruit and local *ricotta salata,* a hard, salted sheep's cheese ricotta similar to feta.

The gastronomy of Lipari is representative of the whole archipelago, with minor variations due to the imaginations of local cooks, and availability of ingredients.

"Actually," our mentor says, "improvisation is very much part of the islands' cooking: You take the basic theme and you run with it. You still recognize it, but will be amazed by all the possible variations."

She suggests a few other places for us to try Aeolian food. We gladly followed her advice, ready and willing to face the music.

"I have never eaten anything that wasn't grown on the island or that wasn't cooked at home," says Angela Cusolito Buongiorno, a signora introduced to us as one who could shed light on the local food and called "Lina" by her friends.

"I never touch anything that is commercially prepared, or preserved, or frozen," she continues unwaveringly. "I even make the pasta myself. And I do not go much for meat, either."

What's left in her repertory are fish and vegetables—and baby squid, big squid, inkfish, baby octopus, and papa octopus, all of which she wraps into the friendly family of mollusks. Mollusks, she said, are very good for you: nothing but good protein, no fat; much better and tastier than steak. We told her that we are masters at squid but not always successful at octopus—what's her secret?

"Bring lots of water to boil, with no salt. Salt toughens the octopus. Briefly dunk the *polpo* in the boiling water three times using tongs, then set the heat to simmer, cover the pot, and let the octopus bubble for twelve or twenty minutes, depending on size; then you can fish it out, or leave it in until the water cools. Cut it in pieces and dress it like a salad or even *al salmoriglio*. It's good." *Salmoriglio* is the classic Aeolian Islands way of dressing all fish.

"Grill, poach, broil, or even fry fish, any fish, then dress it with salmoriglio: olive oil, lemon juice, minced parsley, a good touch of oregano, salt, and pepper cooked in a double boiler until velvety. Some even put in a few capers, but not too many or they overpower the fish. And there you are."

A specialty of Signora Lina is *pasta cui vruoccoli arriminata:* cooked cauliflower and chopped *maccheroni* stirred in a pan with an anchovy, tomato, basil, raisin, and pine-nut sauce. *"È da morire,"* something to die for, she describes it. Unfortunately, these days, she just takes a little bite and lets the family devour the rest. Why? She is very conscious of her waistline, her weak spot, she blushes under her heavy make-up. Signora Lina is eighty-one.

"But," she says, "I still drive a mean stove!"

If Ulysses' Penelope had cooked like Signora Lina, we wondered, would he have ever left home?

In Lipari, volcanic pumice stone—much used in industry to make abrasives—is quarried in great quantity, and exported. The quarry is blinding white under the sun and smooth, in sharp contrast with the tormented volcanic black rock mixed with a riot of flowers of the rest of the island. When Aeolus doesn't blow too hard, a boat ride around the island can be a memorable experience. Otherwise, you can travel by car on the road that circles the island, in spots at sea level, in others at the edge of high cliffs offering new vistas. If you have to share the road with an oncoming car, prepare yourself for some heart palpitations at every hairpin turn.

To reach Ristorante La Ginestra we had to zigzag our way out of town by the pumice quarry and up the road to one of Lipari's high peaks. From La Ginestra the view is glorious: Edged by *ginestra* (bright yellow broom), the cliffs plunge a thousand feet into blue-green waters to form a craggy, rugged coastline. Two *faraglioni,* one a tall thin rock, and the other a short and squat one, rise out of the sea and provide an exclamation point and a period to the view. The story continues across the half-mile straits with the semi-barren island of Vulcano and, to the right, with the green island of Salina. Farther away, the shadows of Alicudi and Filicudi float above the shimmer of a sunset sea.

Around this peak rests the best agrarian part of Lipari. There are a few flat squares of land but, where it is too steep, the land is terraced and sustained by walls of black lava blocks.

Salvatore Morales, owner and chef of La Ginestra, represents the younger generation of cooks dedicated to local cuisine. Salvatore explained that, even if it seems paradoxical, the small island has two somewhat different cuisines: Near the coast, fish commands the table, while upland, pasta, vegetables, poultry, and rabbit have primary importance. To stay with our musical metaphor, the cuisine plays variations on frugality. Commercial pasta, imported and therefore expensive, plays second fiddle to the homemade pasta, which is made only with hard-wheat flour and water, no eggs. Local vegetables, such as chickpeas, eggplant, dried fava beans, and lentils, are traditional and common in upland dishes. Nevertheless, some cross-pollination exists between mountain and sea cuisines: It is not unusual for farmers to barter with fishermen, trading fresh garden products for fresh fish. Both farmers and fishermen enrich their menus with no money changing hands.

Salvatore tells us that his kitchen likes to mix sea and country in a new generation of dishes. Fishermen on the coast appreciate a dish made with a common kind of calamari, *totani al sugo,* and he has brought it up to the country and created *totani alla campagnola* (calamari farmer's style), using landlubber ingredients such as potatoes, bell peppers, and tomatoes in a stew. We settle in for a sample of La Ginestra's fare, and Salvatore brings us *involtini di pescespada* (swordfish birds), which he makes by wrapping thin slices of swordfish around a mince of bread crumbs, fish meat, raisins, pine nuts, and herbs. The birds are then breaded and skewered three at a time, and cooked on a grill or, more frequently, on a griddle. They are served straight or with a *ghiotta,* a tasty tomato sauce with capers and olives, an island sauce as ubiquitous as salmoriglio. He proceeds with a sample of Lipari's *maccheroni con melanzane* (macaroni with eggplant), which turns out to be homemade pasta with a sauce of tomatoes, eggplant, a few crumbs of ricotta salata, and just a sprinkle of chopped capers and parsley. It is remarkably *appetitosa,* which means something light and tasty to prod the taste buds to ask for an encore.

On a roll, we continue with Salvatore's way of preparing *coniglio agrodolce,* rabbit in a sweet-and-sour sauce. It is neither too sweet nor too sour, again a very appetite-teasing way to enhance the white, tame meat of the rabbit. For a finale, Salvatore introduces us to what he says is the accompaniment to every island meal: *insalata isolana* (island salad), a balance of crisp lettuce, onions, olives, capers, ricotta salata, and garden fresh tomatoes. The dressing is supplied mostly by the juice of the cut tomatoes and a few drops of olive oil and wine vinegar.

Local fruit and a sip of aged *Passito di Malvasia* (a good, semi-sweet Madeira comes to mind) put a close to our dinner. At the end, we applaud La Ginestra for its performance, an elegant concerto made exclusively with local notes.

A counterpoint to the relatively young La Ginestra is the Ristorante Filippino: It is the oldest—and the first ever—restaurant on Lipari. Started in 1910 "as a shack with a few chairs and tables," it has grown into the most elegant and prestigious eatery on the island.

"It began with our family serving whatever was cooked at home," confides Antonio Bernardi, grandson of the founder and, with his brother Lucio, present owner of the restaurant. "The menu was perhaps five dishes. Now the list is much longer, but the spirit is the same. We carry on the tradition: We serve what the island serves us, frugally. We use our tomatoes to make the sauce for our fish, and then we use the same sauce for our pasta. Swordfish or tuna steak we simply cook on a griddle, accompanied with our onions sautéed and moistened with our vinegar. We use our capers, olives, and wild fennel to flavor thin slices of swordfish and then we grill them and serve them with our ghiotta. We make a sauce with some of our sweet peppers, a bit of eggplant, and a few bits of fresh tuna and put it over our homemade pasta. It is *mangiare onesto,* an honest cuisine, wrapped in local aromas and flavors."

He goes on, waxing poetic about his food, the islands' food. It is a contagious affair and we are not immune.

One late afternoon during our daily *passeggiata,* we happened upon Pasticceria Oscar, the town's main pastry shop, where Oscar's wife, Signora Angela, saw us peering tentatively through the glass-enclosed counters and shared with us the history—and a tasting—of Aeolian biscotti. First was the popular *spicchitedda,* made with flour, cooked wine, and cinnamon, then twisted into brown pretzel-like shapes. It was followed by *nacatula,* a pie dough cooked with almonds, bits of tangerine, and cinnamon, formed into many different cookie shapes. It was all consumed with the island's sweet Malvasia wine. Signora Angela is as proud of her *dolci* as she is of the shop's prominently displayed photograph of her with the king and queen of Belgium, who partake of her wares in the summer when their yacht is anchored at Lipari.

VULCANO

The *aliscafo* (hydrofoil) grumbled its way out of port, then the grumble became a growl. It picked up speed, lifted itself from the water on its skinny legs, and glided quickly over the sea. From Lipari it reached Vulcano in ten minutes. Vulcan, the god who made armor for the gods, resided here, but eons ago he put away his hammer and anvil and retired. The Cyclops, his gigantic one-eyed assistants, have also packed up and left. All that remains of his forge are a few embers smoldering deep inside the island, smoke escaping from a few fumaroles. It is not difficult in this atmosphere to fall under a spell: The aliscafo's steward is an illustration who has come alive right out of an *Odyssey* schoolbook.

"Please, forgive our staring, but," we were compelled to ask, "are you, by any chance . . . Ulysses?"

"Sorry," he told us, "I am Rutilio Taranto, mate first class."

We struck up a conversation and told him how our autosuggestion could be justified: Not only because of his curly black hair and beard, piercing eyes, straight Greek nose, and shining smile, but also his job—wandering continuously around these islands like Homer's hero.

"Yes, I get around," he laughed, "but every night I'm back home!"

Our stay in Vulcano will be short, just long enough to leap from Homer to Dante. The island has many mineral hot springs—above and under the sea—and one famous hot-mud pool, surrounded by monstrous lava formations. As we approached the island, the smell of sulphur was strong. The noon sun beat down white-hot and left no shadows; a few people were immersed in the hot mud up to their chins, their heads appearing severed and floating on the white surface. It was a scene straight out of Dante's *Inferno*. Once out of the pool, the bathers let the hot sun bake the mud on their skin, turning themselves into terra-cotta statues. Then they jumped into the nearby crystal-clear sea and washed away the hard mud and, with it, any of the malaises that prompted them into the hot pool. Doctors order the treatment to benefit skin, liver, kidneys, ovaries, lungs, and obesity. Many come for *la cura* from far away and return year after year, attesting to the powers of the bubbling mud. At the end of day, some commute back to the *continente*, while others remain in Vulcano or go to Lipari. Honest good food, they say, is part of the therapy.

FILICUDI

Out of loyalty we take the same *aliscafo* so that Rutilio, our Ulysses, can take us with him on his wanderings around the islands. Alicudi, Filicudi, Salina: all beautiful, and, if you are searching for tranquillity and good food, each is worth a stay.

Now it is my turn to recount to Franco an old odyssey of my own. I am curious to return to Filicudi, because my first and only journey there happened more than thirty years ago. It is the tiniest and least populated island, and, along with Alicudi, the farthest away from the main island of Lipari. The two islands look like huge black rocks, jutting straight up from the sea.

As soon as we arrive at the dock in Filicudi, I see that it looks exactly the same as it did back in 1972 when I first discovered the island under the most unusual circumstances. When I was working at the NBC News office in Rome, I traveled to Filicudi with the correspondent, Doug Kiker, and a camera crew to cover what appeared to be a hot story. The night before, government authorities had rounded up the ten men they considered to be the biggest Mafia chiefs in Italy and sent them to this desolate island. Prosecutors had been hoping for years to gather enough evidence against these mafiosi to bring them to trial, so it was decided to keep them in a kind of exile while witnesses were sought to testify against them.

Our group flew to Messina then drove to Milazzo, where the ferry leaves for Lipari. On the dock at Milazzo we encountered the ABC News reporter, Peter Jennings, then based in Rome, and his crew who were obviously after the same story. Reaching this tiny island was no easy task back then; there was no aliscafo, not even a ferry, no public transportation of any kind from Lipari to Filicudi, or for that matter, from anywhere to Filicudi. So in Lipari, our two competing news groups decided we'd better join forces to find a way to reach our destination. Luckily, we found Beppe, a fisherman, who was willing to take us in his fishing boat. The next morning, after a two-hour ride in his brightly painted Sicilian boat, Beppe dropped us on a tiny patch of sand at Filicudi and promised to return for us in an hour and a half. After straggling up the rocky beach carrying innumerable pieces of camera equipment, we found ourselves in the company of ten mafiosi and a large contingent of *carabinieri* (state police). Except for the ten exiles and their guards, not another soul was to be seen on the island, and not a sound heard except for the bleating of sheep and goats and the incessant clanking of the bells around their necks.

I was brought along as an interpreter, as was Kay, the woman traveling with the ABC crew. Since the two of us were the only Italian speakers in the group, we were assigned the task of interviewing the Mafia chiefs on the slim hope they might divulge some aspect of their activity, a morsel for the evening news back in the United States. Young, attractive women, it was thought, would encourage the mafiosi to relax and talk. (This is Italy, after all!)

"Quite a naïve thought," says Franco. "Didn't anybody mention to you the Mafia's rule of omertà? Death for opening their mouth, and with *il sasso in bocca,* a stone stuck in it."

"Well, we did know that," I assure Franco, "but, you see, the American news offices in Rome were starved for stories in those days. Our bosses in New York were busy reporting important news from all over the world and were hardly ever interested in what was happening in Italy. The only events they ever had us cover were Christmas and Easter with the pope. So I guess we were just hoping to get a story on the air."

A run-down, deserted *pensione* was being used as the temporary quarters for the mafiosi and inside each *capo* had his own tiny room furnished with a cot and nightstand. I was to interview the men in the five rooms on one side of the building, and Kay the other five. With great trepidation, I approached the first door, knocked, and called out a tentative *"Buongiorno."* The voice of my first mafioso invited me to enter.

"Io sono padre di famiglia." I am an honorable family man, he told me as soon as I walked in. "My children need me," he said, picking up a large framed photograph from his nightstand.

There he was, surrounded by an array of beautiful olive-skinned dark-haired sons and daughters, and balanced on his knee, his adorable first grandchild.

"Can you imagine a man with a family like this being associated with the Mafia? How can anybody, how can you?" He was extremely offended and would talk to me about nothing except his wonderful family.

I didn't fare any better in the second room occupied by one Signor Sinatra. (No relation, he said.) He would speak only about his well-to-do family in Naples and the degradation he felt at this outrage. How humiliating that the papers were connecting his name to the Mafia!

In the next room, where Salvatore was residing, still no results. Salvatore quite rightly pointed out to me that if the government really had anything on him, they would have indicted him properly instead of coming up with this half-baked solution. The mission continued until Kay and I had met every mafioso and failed to elicit even a single morsel of information—and, of course, they absolutely refused to be filmed. As a matter of fact, by the time we had finished, I had heard so many sad stories that I had become quite sympathetic to the plight of these seemingly wrongly accused, upstanding members of society.

That is, until the carabinieri pulled out the dossiers of the ten prisoners, revealing that these dear sweet family men were responsible for hundreds of deaths, dismemberments, and injuries. But, since none of them would grant an interview or agree to be filmed, there was obviously not going to be any news story here. Just to make the trip worthwhile, when the mafiosi emerged from the pensione for their "exercise period," the cameramen started filming, capturing nothing more for their efforts than close-ups of the backs of bald and stringy-haired heads of ten totally nondescript men wandering among bleating sheep and goats.

We all sat on the beach and waited for Beppe and our return trip to Lipari. And waited and waited. With nothing else to do on the island, the TV crews and the carabinieri began to quench their thirst with the bottles of local wine that the guards had stored in their tent. As the hours passed, and everybody became more and more soused, Kay and I exchanged nervous looks. We realized that we were the only women on the island, and decided that of the three groups of males—journalists, carabinieri, and mafiosi—it was the mafiosi we would want as our protectors. It got so late that we thought we might have to stay overnight, so the guards showed Kay and me the makeshift cells they had prepared to use if a mafioso got out of hand. Each dark, dank cell contained a straw mattress on the floor and a bucket in one corner, but the scariest part was that the padlocks were on the outside. Luckily, we were spared that fate when at ten o'clock that night we heard the putt-putt sound of Beppe's fishing boat approaching the beach. That's Sicilian time for you.

Just as we were boarding the boat, we heard a chorus of *"Arrivederci"* and looked back to see our mafiosi all waving from their windows. *"Buon viaggio,"* they shouted, "and tell your TV stations that we are innocent!" We were sure they would miss us, since we were probably the only contact with the outside world they would have for a long, long time. Our two crews made it back to Lipari under

a gorgeous starry sky, and returned to Rome with no story at all—
but with a never-to-be-forgotten venture onto the tiny, deserted
island of Filicudi.

Six weeks later, in a few lines tucked on an inside page, Rome's
newspapers reported—just as Salvatore had predicted—that the
mafiosi had been released from custody in Filicudi for lack of evidence to indict them for any crime.

Except for a few daily arrivals and departures of the ferry and aliscafo, today Filicudi has hardly changed a bit. On this trip together,
Franco and I could not help but notice the unmistakable aroma of
freshly baked bread on the aliscafo. We knew there were no cafes
on the aliscafo, so following our noses, we came upon several huge
burlap sacks, marked ALICUDI and FILICUDI in large black letters. Sure
enough, the sacks were unloaded on the dock at each island and
carted up to the one tiny grocery store. These islands have no bakery, no butcher shop, not even a bar-cafe, and remain semi-deserted
even in summer months.

Filicudi has only one hotel, the Phenicusa, the same one
where the mafia chiefs were lodged for a brief time before being
transferred to the abandoned pensione. A fisherman mending his
nets at the dock recalled the event and told us that the residents of
Filicudi protested vehemently when the mafiosi were sent to live
among them, and many left the island for good. The present population of a few hundred permanent residents is augmented slightly in
summer when some Italian celebrities and journalists come to stay
in their fancy villas built in the island's rugged hills, to retreat from
the stresses of urban life.

STROMBOLI

At the northernmost point of the Aeolian archipelago is the island of Stromboli, connected with the others by ferry and aliscafo. On these seas, this sleek craft is the counterpart of the old stagecoach on land, making the rounds of the islands, loading and unloading passengers and goods. Stromboli is the most striking of the volcanic islands, at first sight reminiscent of an elementary school child's representation of a volcano: a black cone resting on the sea with a hole on its top from which gushes a plume of smoke. By adding a scattering of white houses at sea level, the picture becomes quite accurate. There are two villages on the island, Stromboli and Ginostra, and small groups of fishermen's cottages, all of which comprise a population of less than one thousand.

Stromboli is the oldest continuously active volcano in the world and, precise as a metronome, it keeps time of millennia: Every twenty minutes or so, red-hot lava and burning stones erupt from its belly. At night the eruptions light up the sky in a wondrous display, visible even from the farthest islands. During the volcano's normal activity, local guides, mandatory for viewing the crater, lead groups of visitors to the top. But, our own guide, Rutilio, tells us that every once in a while Stromboli erupts violently, spewing giant rocks and boulders so far away that it is dangerous to go near the island. Walking tours are then prohibited, and even sailing is restricted to a distance of not less than 1,200 feet, or even further if necessary to avoid the boulders. His information adds a sense of adventure to our trip.

Geologists and volcanologists come from all over the world to study Stromboli, a fact that Jules Verne took advantage of in his mid-1800s classic, *Journey to the Center of the Earth*. The protagonists,

Professor Otto Lindenbrock, a geological whiz, and his nephew Axel travel to the center of the earth and after infinite adventures, they resurface, spewed out of Stromboli. The island's more recent claim to fame is the romance in 1950 that erupted between Ingrid Bergman, the actress, and Roberto Rossellini, the director, during the filming on location of the movie *Stromboli*—a fiery affair that reverberated past the islands and around the world.

SALINA

Salina is named after the little salted lake of Lingua lying in the island's southeastern tip, where inhabitants once used to gather the salt needed to preserve capers and fish. The aliscafo arrives at Santa Maria Salina, Salina's main port, and on a bus ride lasting little more than an hour, you can circle the whole island, then leave from Rinella, the other port town, or return to Santa Maria. Salina is greener than its rocky sisters and full of spectacular scenery. Roads even more narrow and precipitous than Lipari's follow the island's coast and offer dramatic views of towering cliffs that plunge onto tiny white beaches and deep green water.

We were the only passengers on the rickety local bus, which careened around tight turns and hung onto the side of precipices as we made our way around the island. Our driver, Paolo, decided to become our tour guide, pointing out characteristics of the local architecture. The principal town of Malfa is filled with gorgeous summer homes. Many of their exteriors are decorated with an architectural oddity called *merli,* which are scallop-shaped borders on the roofs. Paolo told us that the more merli you see on a house, the richer the owner. As we approached the far end of the island, he beckoned us to look down over one of those dramatic cliffs to the pristine beach below—the site where the Nobel Prize–winning Chilean poet, Pablo Neruda, walked with the postman in the film, *Il Postino*. Then Paolo showed us the house used as Neruda's in the film which, he told us, people have offered millions to buy, but the owner, a writer who lives in Rome, refuses to sell. Paolo was obviously extremely proud that his tiny, gorgeous island was chosen for the filming of such a world-renowned movie.

As for food, all our previous information turned out to be right. Simply prepared, *onesto* good food is available on each island, but without striking new notes: The whole archipelago plays in harmony.

We can see now why it took Ulysses twenty years to return home.

PASTA CUI VRUOCCOLI ARRIMINATA
Pasta with Cauliflower Sauce

2 ounces golden raisins
10 ounces (approximately)
   cauliflower, cored and separated
   in flowerets
1 small onion
4 tablespoons olive oil
2–3 flat anchovy fillets

3 tablespoons tomato paste
   dissolved in 1 cup warm water
2 ounces pine nuts
1 pound spaghetti
¾ cup of sharp pecorino
   cheese, grated
5–6 fresh basil leaves, minced

SOAK the raisins in a cup of hot water.

COOK the cauliflower flowerets briefly (just enough to soften them a bit) in salted boiling water; drain them and set aside.

CHOP the onion into thin slivers and sauté them in the olive oil on medium heat in a saucepan large enough to hold the cauliflower and the cooked pasta. When the onion is transparent and golden, lower the heat and add the anchovies; break them with a fork and dissolve them in the oil. Stir in the tomato paste dissolved in a cup of warm water, bring the sauce to a boil for a minute or two, then cover it and simmer for 10 minutes. Drain the raisins, dry them a bit, and add them with the pine nuts to the sauce. Put the cauliflower into the saucepan with the sauce, stir with a wooden spoon without breaking the flowerets, and cover and cook over low heat.

COOK the spaghetti in abundant boiling salted water. Drain it well when al dente, and transfer it into the saucepan with the cauliflower. Raise the heat and mix the pasta and sauce well for a couple of minutes. Serve immediately, with a sprinkling of pecorino cheese mixed with the minced basil leaves.

Serves 4

CONIGLIO AGRODOLCE

Rabbit in Sweet and Sour Sauce

Rabbit, cleaned and ready to cook, can be found frozen in most supermarkets, or fresh in specialty butcher shops or Italian meat shops.

2½ cups dry red wine

2 basil leaves

½ teaspoon freshly
    grated black pepper

1 rabbit (about 2½–3 pounds),
    cut into several pieces

1 onion

¼ cup olive oil

Flour to dredge

1 cup canned tomatoes,
    with juice

Salt to taste

⅓ cup wine vinegar

4 tablespoons granulated sugar

2 ounces peeled almonds, toasted
    and crumbled

MAKE a marinade with 1 cup of the wine, the basil leaves, and the pepper. Put the rabbit in a leakproof plastic bag, add the marinade, and refrigerate for a couple of hours.

CUT the onion into thin slivers and put in a pan large enough to hold the rabbit. Add the olive oil to the pan and sauté the slivered onion on medium heat. Drain the rabbit from the marinade, reserving it; dredge the rabbit pieces in the flour. Pat them well, shaking off excess flour, then brown the pieces in the oil.

WHEN THE RABBIT is well browned, lower the heat and add a cup of the wine. When the wine has almost evaporated, add the tomatoes, mashing them with a fork. Bring it to a boil, then lower to a simmer and add the remaining wine. Continue to cook it over low heat. If the rabbit gets too dry, add a little warm water.

IN THE MEANTIME, put the saved marinade, the vinegar, and the sugar in a small saucepan and reduce the mixture until it's as dense as cream. Add it to the simmering rabbit. Test the meat for doneness and salt; when it's done, transfer it to a serving platter. The remaining sauce should be dense enough to coat the rabbit; if not, reduce it to a creamy consistency. Pour it hot over the rabbit, sprinkle with the almonds, and serve.

Serves 4

Ponza

SMALL, BUT BIGGER THAN CAPRI

The 110-seat aliscafo floated quietly out of Anzio and, once clear of port, lifted itself up and skimmed the sea at high speed, like a giant waterbug. It cut a foamy wake on forty miles of Tyrrhenian Sea and in seventy minutes docked in the blue-green harbor of Ponza. Ponza is the largest of the five islands in the Pontine archipelago, part of the string of volcanic gems that begins geologically with the islands of Capri and Ischia in the south and ends with the uninhabited island of Palmarola in the north. Administratively they belong to the region of Lazio, whose coast they face and of which Rome is the capital, but ethnically they are securely anchored to Naples.

A living proof of this duality is Salvatore, the young man who was our guide and mentor during our stay on the island. He is a student of scenic design in Rome and is deeply interested in the past, present, and future of Ponza, where he was born. He was waiting for us at the pier. We had never met before and had only spoken on the phone, but with his easy welcome, he opened an immediate, friendly channel of communication as only Neapolitans can do, with their unhurried, elegant way of talking and of moving. And first things first, as a proper Neapolitan would suggest, we had our obligatory morning cappuccino at a sidewalk cafe. The place offered a commanding view of the half-moon harbor and of the white and pink houses perched around and above it like spectators in a Greek amphitheater. An ancient show was acted out once again by the fishermen who were landing the catch of the night, lining the decks with row after row of shining, metal-black swordfish. A light breeze carried the aroma of the sea and swept the air clean, giving clear edges to light and shadows. The whole view seemed etched with a sharp point by a master artist.

"Spectacular. Breathtaking," we hazarded.

"Just nice," commented Salvatore matter-of-factly. "Breathtaking comes later."

For years a Roman friend of ours had been extolling the beauty of Ponza, and finally, we had come to see for ourselves. Why, we asked Salvatore, is this island, whose beauty allegedly challenges Capri's, kept a secret? Why, besides those in the immediate neighborhood, do so few people seem to know of its existence?

"We are a paradox," answered Salvatore. "Nobody knows of us, but everybody has been here as far back as you can think. Prehistoric man came here to fetch obsidian rocks to make stone knives and arrowheads to take back to the continent. Phoenicians and Greeks made port in Ponza. Here Ulysses encountered the Maga Circe, she of the love potions, and then sailed by Ventotene, his ears stuffed with wax, not to be lured by the song of the Sirens. We gave Rome gold and ships and men to fight Carthage. And of what do people talk? Capri! Always Capri!"

Cappuccino over, we moved along; from the port there is only one way to go—up. Seen from its highest peak the island resembles a lizard basking in the sun, head pointing south. It is about five miles long, a little more than a mile at its widest and a little less than seven hundred feet at its narrowest. Capo Guardia, the highest point at 1,050 feet, is the lizard's head. From there we got the full cyclorama view: To the north, on the green sea, floats the island of Palmarola; to the east is Zannone; and, farther away, to the southeast is the silhouette of Ventotene, the second largest island of the archipelago. But the real view was at our feet: Ponza stretched below, every inch of usable land terraced to the edge of precipitous cliffs; left and right, the long body is scalloped by harbors and bays carved away by sea and wind, their waters crystal clear and with the colors of tropical seas.

"Breathtaking?" we asked, seeking confirmation from Salvatore.

"Almost, but not yet!" he smiled in answer.

On the way down he told us of another paradox "historical," he called it—of the Pontine Islands. In spite of their exceptional beauty, they have been used not as resorts but primarily as places of exile (if not as outright prisons) from Roman times to the more recent Fascist era. Emperor Augustus started the trend with his *Lex Julia,* a law that prescribed exile for adultery: Julia Augusta, his own daughter, deemed "not too thrifty with her honor," was exiled to the island, a gilded cage. Sumptuous villas were built for her and her retinue, and tattletales of the times said that even in exile, unfazed by the sentence, she continued to be quite prodigal with her honor. The long arm of the *Lex Julia* tapped the shoulders of Ottavia (wife of

Nero), Vispania Agrippina (wife of Germanicus), and also a chip off the old block, Julia Minor, daughter of Julia Augusta. With time the interpretation of the law became more flexible and was used mostly to put political opponents out of the way. This custom was revived centuries later by the Fascists who, from the late 1920s to the early 1940s, shipped out to Ponza and Ventotene political undesirables from Italy as well as from Yugoslavia, Albania, and Greece, countries that fell for a short time under the Fascists' grip. To assuage a sense of local guilt, Salvatore added that the exiles were treated humanely, quartered in clean barracks or single homes, free to roam the island and even to receive periodic visitors, and the islanders made all sorts of efforts to make the exiles' lives easier.

Not so lucky were the common prisoners sent for life to the penitentiary of Santo Stefano, a small island not much bigger than Alcatraz and located a mile off Ventotene. The only building on the island (there isn't much room for anything else), the penitentiary was built in 1795 on the order of Ferdinand IV, King of the Two Sicilies. The architect, Francesco Carpi, designed it on the general scheme of Dante's *Inferno,* adding a few circles of his own. At a time when prison was a synonym for "abject punishment," he spared nothing to make the prisoners constantly aware of the purpose of these dungeons. In an unbelievable and unexplained twist of fate, Carpi himself became an inmate in his own miserable prison and died there.

Just as unbelievable is that this place was operative until 1965 when, following an attack of national shame, the Italian government closed it down. Today the island prison is deserted, and anyone with a boat and strong stomach can visit. It is difficult to forget the inscription stenciled large on the wall of the dank mess hall: A

TRUE GENTLEMAN IS RECOGNIZED BY HIS TABLE MANNERS. If not much else, the wardens surely showed a sick sense of humor.

Thank God those times are over, Salvatore commented. Now that the prison image has disappeared, people are appreciating Ponza for what it is: a quiet enclave of fishing villages, with an incredibly mild and constant climate, most interesting flora and fauna, and ever-changing bewildering seascapes, ideal for all sports above and below the sea as well as for family vacations. An accessible, affordable paradise.

Walking down from the top, we met Antonio Balzano, a young man of Pavarottian bearing. The meeting, in appearance fortuitous, had been craftily arranged by Salvatore, a car-less student, to take advantage of Antonio's minivan for the land tour of the island. Antonio displayed the same easiness and friendliness as Salvatore: We were barely underway and we felt as if we had known each other for a long time. He spent fourteen years in Stamford, Connecticut, operating his family's successful restaurant (*Ponzesi* seem to have a knack for restauranting all over the world, above all in the United States), but he missed the island too much and came back. Now, in his late thirties, he has become a developer and is building apartments around the island, but he still finds time to show off his beloved Ponza. Antonio's tiny Fiat van fit him tightly like an old jacket; we were told that there are some thirty miles of paved roads on the island, and this car knew them intimately, blind curves, bumps, potholes, and all. Salvatore and Antonio carried on a loud duet, at times a chorus, rattling off in an exuberant rhapsody the scenic points along the way: Punta Capo Bianco, Cala (Bay) Feola, Punta di Capo Bosco, Cala dell'Acqua, Punta del Papa, Le Forna, the natural pools. The road circles the island high over the coast,

offering aerial views of bays and inlets, the color of their waters
deepening with their depth, from crystal clear to intense blue.

We stopped here and there and, once out of the car, our
words were whispered, as if loud voices would intrude on the eloquence of nature. Cala Caparra is the end of the line. Here you turn
around and go back by the other side of the island: Cala Gaetano,
Punta Nera, Cala d'Inferno, Cala del Core. To us every corner, bay,
inlet or beach topped the beauty of the last, but we had stopped
asking Salvatore if we were allowed to call any of them "breathtaking." We mimicked the Neapolitan silent way of questioning with
a combined arching of eyebrows and lifting of chin. He answered
"no" with a slow shake of the head, indicating that this sightseeing
was only the prologue of what was to come: the tour of the island
by sea. Many of the beaches and bays can be seen and reached only
by boat, and Antonio had borrowed one for tomorrow, just for that
purpose. Antonio would have liked to continue his guided tour, but
our eyes were satiated and we suggested calling it a day. The sunset
was beginning to flame and the pale, full moon was starting to rise.
Tomorrow was another day. Dinner, anybody?

"I soak the swordfish in water and vinegar," said Valerio Soriani,
"then I cut it paper thin and I dress it with lemon, olive oil, a brushing of garlic, capers, and parsley."

He was explaining the *pescespada alla marinara,* the dish he
had just served us as an antipasto, a dish he has been preparing
for a long time, he told us, long before it became fancied up into
carpaccio. We had reconvened at his restaurant, Da Valerio, of
which Signor Soriani was also the chef, though not for long. He
had decided to retire and had sold the restaurant; at the end of

the month he would move on and the place would be under new management. But at that moment, he was serving us his specialties and those of the island: *spaghetti alla granzeola,* a dish of pasta with local king crab, its meat steamed, scooped out, and spiced with hot pepper and dry white wine; and, swordfish being a special catch of Ponza, *pescespada brodettato,* swordfish poached in tomatoes and wine, enlivened at the end with a creamy lemon sauce. Fresh bread, still warm from the oven, was essential to sop up the juices. Valerio pointed out that his swordfish was not only the freshest but also *di coffa e non di rete,* caught on the hook and not in the net. It was also smaller, not like the huge ones harpooned around Sicily. In somewhat morbid terms he explained that on the hook the fish dies fighting-mad which, for some reason, makes its flesh firmer and tastier. If fish and other delicacies from the sea are obvious island food, what Valerio offered next was not: *cicerchie,* halfway between small chickpeas and navy beans. Because of the unique qualities of Ponza's soil they have an intense earthy flavor and are super-packed with vitamins and iron. So are the local *lenticchie,* lentils, tiny, dark, and flavorful. We asked him about the historical specialty of Ponza: the moray eel. Valerio looked at us with a sly smile.

"For that, you will have to come back another time," he said, as if another of his dishes that night could overload our taste buds. And it probably would have.

It was another clear morning, as all October mornings should be. We met Salvatore at the same cafe overlooking the port. He was dangling the keys of a borrowed boat: It was a powerful 80 hp. inboard motor job, whose owner was away on the continent for a few days. The craft was bobbing at the dock, not big but with lines so sleek it seemed to be speeding even at rest.

"A great boat," said Salvatore, "but there is a hitch."

It turned out that for that kind of boat a special license was needed, and so he had broadcasted a call for a licensed operator. Soon a volunteer materialized, a slim gentleman in his late fifties called Ernesto, nattily attired in yachting clothes, captain's hat included. Like all the other islanders we had met, he was very friendly and talkative. By the time we had finished a cappuccino, boarded the boat, cast off, and taxied out of port (he seemed very familiar with this craft, flicking switches on and off without any hesitation or doubt), he had told us all about his recent tour of the United States, visiting many Ponzesi who live there. Most of them own one or more restaurants and are very successful, so much so that they can afford to come back every year for the feast of San Silverio, Ponza's patron saint, and contribute munificently to the biggest festivity of the island.

The boat was plot-plot-plotting, idling along under the whitewashed village hanging high on the cliffs. The first stop, just a short distance from the port, was the Cave of Pontius Pilate. On the water, at the base of a 150-foot perpendicular wall of rock, is a natural cave named for Pontius Pilate of New Testament fame. There are two opinions about his appellative, neither substantiated: One says that Pilate was born in Ponza, hence Pontius, the other that he bloodily suppressed the island's revolt against Rome and hence, as was Roman custom, added the name of the victorious campaign to his. But the cave's interest rests not in its name but with its erstwhile function: a moray eel–breeding fishery. The Romans, it seems, were inordinately fond of the eels, so they created a system of breeding pools in the natural cave and in adjacent manmade grottoes; connected by passages, the sea water circulated and renewed itself with the changing tides. As the eels grew, they were moved from one pool to another and when they reached the last one it was good-bye Charlie for the fat ones.

Some features of the grottoes' pools, such as the small altars carved in the rock, suggest a religious meaning of the complex and possibly, since the vicious morays were as gluttonous for Romans as Romans were for them, a strong sacrificial connotation. Legend has it that some masters, displeased with their slaves, sent them "to feed the eels," an order literally meant. On the ceiling of the main breeding pool, a small chimney-like tunnel opens to the sky and, at the right time, frames Orion: It seems that the eels mated most happily and prolifically under that constellation.

As we continued the voyage around the island, we had to agree with Salvatore: The view from the sea was even more spectacular than from land. There is no end to the different formations of rock, shapes, color, and textures, a continuous display of wonders created by volcanic fire, carved by the sea, and etched by the wind, a stage set changing with every turn of the coast. Adding to the marvel are the colors of the water, changing like the reflections in a kaleidoscope's mirror. Their transparency makes them paradise for scuba divers, and paradise enough for us.

"Time for the 'b' word yet?" we asked Salvatore.

"No, not yet, but getting there," was his sibylline answer.

Ernesto had been piloting expertly in the glass-like waters on the lee side of the island, jockeying the boat in and out of grottoes, so close to the rocks protruding from the sea like tall columns that we could touch them and feel their texture. We congratulated him on his expertise as we rounded the tip of the island. We must have stumbled on some magic word, because, a diabolic smile breaking on his face, Ernesto pushed the throttle to full and the craft sprang forward with a roar. We stumbled backward and held on to the gunwale for dear life. The machine surged up and then flapped down with every wave of the windward sea, piloted by a man possessed who, with each back-wrenching thump of the keel, emitted a blood-curdling rebel yell. Perhaps to give purpose to the performance, he started aiming the crazed vessel at unsuspecting fishing boats and swerving away from them at the very last moment, drenching them in foaming water. He knew every single fisherman by name and waved wildly at them with his captain's hat. In no time at all, we were drenched to the bone by the flying sea spray and could do nothing but look at each other in consternation. We tried to think of a word that could exorcise the sea devils out of the wretched man; finding none, we decided philosophically not to fight destiny, musing that if we had to have an appointment with our maker, we couldn't think of a better place to meet Him. Sanity clicked back into our skipper as suddenly as it had clicked out: He cut the power to idle and let the boat stream to a stop on a quiet bay. The silence became, as they say, deafening.

"This," said Signor Ernesto in the most natural of tones, "is Cala Spaccapolpi and that rock is the Parson's Breeches."

Drenched and finding no good reason to dry ourselves at this stage of the game, we slipped into the green sea and went for a swim; the water, so clear we could count the pebbles on the bottom, was reasonably warm, especially considering that it was way past summertime.

We had dinner with Antonio and Salvatore on the terrace of our hotel, the Chiaia di Luna. It seemed our two guides had already interceded with the chef to make sure he prepared a dinner made only with local ingredients, which of course absolutely had to include moray eel. As an opener, he served poached tiny shrimp, squid, and baby octopus (no bigger than a thumb) on a bed of arugula, drenched in olive oil and the juice of aromatic local lemons, followed by the famous moray eel in three different ways: *fritta dorata,* floured, dipped in egg, and fried; *al sugo,* stewed in an intense, thick tomato sauce imbued with the moray juices; and *alla griglia,* grilled and basted with olive oil scented with sage and oregano. The third one *(anguilla grigliata, grilled eel),* we decided, was the best; the layer of gelatinous fat melts on the fire, leaving the skin crackling crisp, the meat moist and smoky. We can now understand the Roman emperors' predilection for the mean beast: It is delicious. Its milk-white firm flesh is as close as you can get to lobster but without its stringiness, or, even more accurately, to a cross between lobster and monkfish.

The Chiaia di Luna is modern and well appointed, having been designed according to the canons of Mediterranean resort hotels: a central building for common areas and facilities (reception, restaurant, piano-bar, reading and TV room, swimming pool) and separate whitewashed buildings terraced around the hill, holding one or two apartments or small suites, all with balconies. The unique feature of the hotel is its location: Up above the town, close to the highest spot of the island, it has a far-reaching view for each point of the compass. The one from the terrace overlooks the Chiaia di Luna, perhaps the island's most spectacular beach. A half-mile long, shaped like a sickle moon, the sandy beach lies at the bottom of a

330-foot perpendicular cliff; the wind has etched it with all sorts of patterns that appear to change in depth and color with the changing light. At sunset, it was a deep red that, as time progressed, turned to blue-violet. The stars were out, the full moon had risen again; we were sipping an after-dinner cognac and enjoying the spectacle in front of us. The moonlight had turned the cliff into spun silver and at its base the waves, rippling on the shore, trimmed the cliff with phosphorescent lace. We knew, at this moment, that there couldn't possibly be a sight on all of Ponza that could top this one.

"Breathtaking," we said to no one in particular, "breathtakingly stupendous!"

Neither Antonio nor Salvatore commented on that, so we take their silence, for once, as assent.

The next morning we left Ponza on our way to Capri.

But, somehow, our hearts weren't in it.

Pantelleria

DAUGHTER OF THE WIND

*A*s the plane circles the island for landing, steep cliffs— craggy, dark, and foreboding—appear at the wingtip. Then, suddenly the landscape turns flat, green, and reassuring, just what you would wish for a smooth landing. What attracted us to the island was the promise of a quiet vacation and its isolated position. Seventy miles southwest of Sicily, Pantelleria is Italy's southernmost point. At forty-four miles off the North African coast, it is geographically and ethnically closer to Tunisia.

Once in the main town and port, also named Pantelleria, we are impressed right away by its unassuming, quiet appearance; there are no noisy traffic jams or the buzzing of motorbikes so irritatingly common in Italy today. It is a refreshing start, especially for those who appreciate tranquillity. The following days confirm our first impression. We are won over by the direct simplicity of its hospitality, the heartiness of its food, and the unspoiled, ruggedly unique beauty of the island.

There are several hotels on the island and many private homes and condominiums available for visitors to rent. The Mursia Hotel is modern and efficiently elegant, but not overbearingly so. We immediately like the gracious, smiling hospitality of the staff (this trait is in evidence throughout the island) and the hotel's one-stop practicality. If we need a car or a boat, one will be available, and the food at its restaurant "Le Lampare" is excellent and affordable. It is there that we are introduced to the island's gastronomy with a light lunch of an *insalata pantesca,* a mix of local greens, capers, potatoes, and tuna.

The hotel's architecture, like most of the island's, is white-washed, arched Moorish; the recall of North Africa is immediate. Through the open French doors of our room the perennial breezes bring in the sound and the moist fragrance of the sea, which is just a few steps away. But do not expect a sandy beach: There is hardly one on the entire island. Cement steps, or steps carved in the rock, lead to landings by the water. It is impossible to resist the sea's invitation and not jump in. The water changes color like a kaleidoscope with the slant of the sun, yet its transparency is absolute: water like a liquid sky. With diving masks we marveled at how far down the light penetrates. That swimming-in-the-sky experience can be had in hundreds of the coves and inlets all around the island.

Pantelleria, in a formative geophysical spasm, bubbled to the surface 300,000 or so years ago. Its black volcanic appearance explains the name the Phoenicians gave the island: Black Pearl of the Mediterranean. Live *favare,* or mini-geysers, continue to puff boiling-hot steam here and there from cracks or tiny craters in the volcanic rock, and several warm mineral springs attest to the still active geology. But then, the whole area is mischievously unrestful, puzzling geologists today as it did civilian authorities of the recent past. In 1831 an island about three miles in circumference surfaced a few miles off Pantelleria's coast facing Sicily. It was immediately made part of the territory of the Kingdom of the Two Sicilies and named Ferdinandea in honor of King Ferdinand II. French scientists intent on studying it called it Julia (the surfacing happened in July); sailors from a British frigate in the vicinity, who had been sent to plant Her Majesty's flag on the still-wet rock, named it Graham. Much ado about nothing: After five weeks the islet sank again, performing the same trick it had done in 10 B.C. and A.D. 1200. All that remains today is a volcanic shallow bank, a magnet for a multitude of fish and the scuba divers who go after them.

On Pantelleria itself, volcanic eruptions have piled lava upon lava, creating grotesque constructions here and there: Arches plunge into the sea, rocky columns sprout from it, and one famous formation looks like a huge elephant dipping its trunk into the sea. This is L'Elefante, the landmark most closely identified with Pantelleria. In the Khaggiar (Place off the Black Rocks), an area that stretches from the sea almost to the center of the island, the locals prod visitors to discover animal or human figures in the volcanic rocks, a game not dissimilar to searching for characters in the billowing of clouds. One is definitely recognizable: On a huge rock, fire and wind have sculpted a figure. Protruding beard on its chin, crown on its head, it is the King of the Khaggiar.

Standing erect above all the other configurations, it has indeed the authoritative posture of a king. As an extra trick of nature, at the level of the eyes, a perforation cuts across both sides of the face; the sunset light shines through it and gives a lively sparkle to the king's eyes.

Among the gnarled and tortured black rocks a multitude of indigenous plants grow. Botanists from the world over come to admire and study the 569 varieties of plants divided into 73 families, 306 genuses, and 429 species. These cover a full dictionary of botanical terms and names, coldly technical and Latin, and hardly evocative—to our ears—of the beauty of these plants and flowers. One plant that is ubiquitous, and particularly appealing for the contrast of its lily-white blossoms sprouting from cracks in the harsh black rock, is the caper. It takes so well to this soil and climate that its edible buds are first quality, and capers are grown commercially here, generating a sizable income for the island.

We had made our reservations at the Hotel Mursia while in Palermo, and when we arrived at the Pantelleria airport, Rosario Di

Fresco, the hotel's co-owner, was there waiting for us with his mini-van. In his late thirties, Rosario is jovial and talkative with an open, smiling demeanor. It took about thirty minutes to reach the hotel and by the time we got there, we felt as if we had known each other for a long time. He moved energetically and carried on a conversation uninterruptedly while loading and unloading luggage or going through papers on his desk, his voice sonorous with barely a tinge of Sicilian accent. Rosario is also president of the local archaeological club, a defender of all that is Pantelleria, and the animator of much that it will be. He suggested all the activities we could pursue under his tutelage—sailing, scuba diving, snorkeling, swimming, nature walking, spelunking—and offered to show us around the island, including its restaurants. His sturdy build made us suspect that he has a strong appreciation for food.

"As for all those activities," we told him, "let us wait a moment for those. But we would love to be shown around."

And so he did, driving us in the minivan along the island's twisting roads, a joyfully witty, most knowledgeable guide.

Rosario explained that human settlement on the island began some five thousand years ago with the arrival of the Sesioti, who were probably a tribe of entrepreneurs from Sicily. They quarried and exported the obsidian, that black gold of the neolithic era, found in great quantity on Pantelleria as on the Aeolian Islands. Several archaeological sites are marked on Rosario's map, including the Sesioti's large neolithic tombs, impressive stone constructions peculiar to Pantelleria, called *Sesi*. Other sites, such as a huge defensive wall and the house foundations of a neolithic village, have been generally left alone to age without much intervention. To us this added to their interest, for they have escaped the embalmed, preserved feeling of the fenced-off official archaeological grounds found in most of the rest of Italy.

The position of the island as a stepping-stone between Africa and Sicily, at the intersection of sea-lanes in the Mediterranean where sailors could rest and restock their ships, made Pantelleria strategically very appetizing, Rosario explained. Phoenicians, Carthaginians, Greeks, Romans, Vandals, Byzantines, Moors, and Normans (who finally annexed it to Sicily) took over the island in turn, all leaving cultural, ethnic, and architectural traces of their presence (a historical routine not different from all the Italian peninsula). The island's location in the sea routes gained it the Greek name of Kossyros, "The Smaller One," probably because as a navigation reckoning point it came after the larger Malta. It was known to the Romans as Cossyra.

"This is why I like to think of Pantelleria," rhapsodized Rosario, "as the heart of the Mediterranean. All the people that shaped Western civilization stopped and nested here." He thought for a moment, then added: "Heart because it is in the center, because it pulsates. Pantelleria is a concentrate of Mediterranean."

Other foreign marks—actually scars—were left during the Second World War. Mussolini called Pantelleria the unsinkable Italian aircraft carrier in the Mediterranean (the Italian Navy having no real aircraft carriers) and also, unwisely, boasted that it concealed a secret submarine base. These *pronunciamenti* were taken seriously by the Allied air forces, which bombarded the island heavily, softening an already soft landing target. Pantelleria was the first parcel of Italian soil to fall to the Allies with essentially no casualties. The most distressing incident, as Winston Churchill tells in his memoirs, occurred when a local donkey bit a Tommy, the moniker for a British soldier. Nonetheless, the bombs added many man-made craters to the natural ones.

Of all the leftover ethnic influences, Arabic is the foremost: The local language retains some Arab-derived words, and many locations have names in or from Arabic. Even the name of the island is a corruption, say local archaeological buffs, of the Arabic *Bent El Rion,* "Daughter of the Wind," a sobriquet that couldn't be more appropriate. The winds that sweep the Channel of Sicily hit the island from all four cardinal points on an average of 337 days a year. The wind is truly one of Pantelleria's shaping forces. It is the wind that keeps the vegetation close to the ground. Since time immemorial, farmers have protected their plantings by growing them inside hollows dug in the earth. Much of the land has been carved into farming terraces in order to take advantage of every single foot of soil not taken by volcanic rock or swept by the wind. In spite of this natural drawback, the island has a population of farmers, not fishermen.

"For work we farm the land," say the islanders. "For sport we fish the sea."

The good news for the visitor is that there is nearly always a protected leeward side somewhere on land or sea. And generally the wind is warm: The average temperature is about 68 degrees. Of course, it is warmer in summer, or when the southern *scirocco* blows up from the Sahara, and slightly colder with the northern *libeccio* during the short—and still mild—winter months.

By car you can circle Pantelleria in a few hours, though many people choose to take the trip on foot, boasting afterward of the rewards of the adventure. The road runs sometimes at sea level but mostly up at the edge of high cliffs, at points rivaling the beauty of the Amalfi Coast. Other roads lead to the interior, to various hamlets, and up to Monte Grande, the top of the island.

On the eastern part of the island lies the fishing village of Gadir. Off its diminutive port are mineral springs that form hot bathing pools on the edge of the sea. The village is a compact set of *dammusi,* the traditional constructions peculiar to Pantelleria, which derive their name from the Arab *damus* (domed edifice). Large or small, built of volcanic stone blocks, these one-story houses are unique for the squashed-down domes that form bumps on their otherwise flat roofs. Each room has one dome; count the bumps and you know how many rooms a *dammuso* has. In a water-poor land, the purpose of this design is to collect rainwater and channel it through spouts into holding cisterns. *Dammusi* also have thick walls that efficiently retain warmth in winter and coolness in summer. By now many old spartan dwellings have been made modern and comfortable. Hidden from view is the large complex of *dammusi* Giorgio Armani has built at Gadir as a vacation retreat for him and his many guests.

An admirable case in point sits high on a hill not far from Gadir, in the village of Tracino. Here Aldo Volpi, a native of Milano, has transformed an abandoned windmill *dammuso* into a series of elegant dining rooms with windows and terraces offering wide-angle views of sea and sky. More important than the architectonic feat is the fact that Volpi has created a superb restaurant, I Mulini (The Windmills), whose menu of strictly researched traditional local dishes is enriched with (very few chefs can resist the temptation) modern interpretations. Memorable are Volpi's *ammogghiu,* a garlicky sauce of grilled tomatoes, herbs, and local first-pressing olive oil; the *ravioli amari,* "bitter" ravioli filled with local sheep cheese and mint; and the ancient *mustazzoli,* where almonds, honey, and sugar come together into sweet cookies, accompanied by a glass of Moscato Passito di Pantelleria wine.

The island produces some excellent grapes, for which it is famous. Once used almost exclusively by the Arabs for producing the sweetest of raisins—their religion forbidding the pressing of grapes into wine—the Moscato and the Zibibbo grapes now produce the Moscato Passito di Pantelleria and the Tannit, strong-bodied, sweet dessert wines, and the Solimano, one of the very few officially recognized sparkling wines of southern Italy.

Pantelleria's food marries different gastronomic heritages and products of land and sea, a union that creates a family of culinary delights proudly offered by the many eateries around the island. Herbs, vegetables, fruits, and olives seem to squeeze all the essences out of the soil they grow in and all the aromas out of the wind to achieve an intense, concentrated flavor. Even milder fish, such as sole or *flounder (rombo ai capperi)*, get an intense flavor boost from the combination. Capers and the local fragrant basil and tomatoes combine in *pesto pantesco*, a winning rival to the well-known Ligurian pesto; *insalata di arance* is an astonishing—and unforgettable—combination of round slices of blood oranges, black olives, and slivered red onions; and *sciakichouka*, a mix of local vegetables, is a version of ratatouille, but much spicier and more flavorful. The list is long and covers the whole range from soup to sweets, but for us the best is *couscous di pesce*, the essence of land and sea linked together in one dish. The couscous is steamed in the aromatic broth of, and served with, a stew of many different fish (local grouper presiding), and, unlike the Sicilian *cuscusu*, also contains peppers, zucchini, and eggplant.

South of Gadir and down from Tracino we saw, in seemingly unending procession, spectacular sea coves and grottoes, a feature common to all volcanic islands. Because they are at the bottom of perpendicular cliffs, they can be admired and explored only from the sea. Boats can be chartered for the purpose and we chose the Green Divers, based at the Hotel Mursia, to take us around the island. The young sailors on board (none of them looking more than twenty-five years old) expertly guided us in and out of the grottoes, all the while filling us with the lore and myths of caves and cliffs, tales which, like the caves themselves, became more colorful as the tour progressed. Their names are evocative: Turks Landing (Turkish pirates landed here for their frequent murderous raids), Old Lady's Leap (an 800-foot perpendicular plunge, the reason for its morbid name is not explained, but we could figure it out), and the Cheese Grotto (the walls are reminiscent of Swiss cheese). Just around Pantelleria's southern tip, which is aptly named Dietro Isola (Opposite Side of the Island), are the waters most frequented by scuba divers for the abundance and variety of the fish. Prized above all, the local *cernia* (grouper) as ugly and unappealing in the deep as its white, firm flesh is good on the plate. The local lore continues to the northwest with the Grotta di Sataria (Cave of Good Health), where legend has it Ulysses, although pining for Penelope, spent seven years with the lusty nymph Calypso. As real estate goes, compared with the beauty of other grottoes, Calypso could have done better, even if her grotto sports three successive pools with water temperatures progressing from tepid to warm to decidedly hot.

The cruise ended at sunset, and the crew, encouraging us to come again, promised that no matter how many times we circumnavigate the island, the experience will be a new one each time. It is so for them. We believed them.

The day before our departure, we walked again with Rosario, taking on the challenge of the uphill road to Monte Grande at the top of the island. The view opened on a mosaic of green cultivated patches separated by walls of black rocks, white cubes of dammusi, farmhouses dotting the terraced landscape, and shielded orchards hugging olive trees and grapevines. Below us, at the edge of an emerald sea, a sweet-water lake: Lo Specchio di Venere (Venus' Mirror). Mythology says that Venus used the lake as a mirror before her encounters with Bacchus, here on location for the sweetness of the wines.

In more recent times, Rosario told us, Gabriel García Márquez was very much taken by the island and chose it as a place to work in solitude. He was in Pantelleria when the astronauts landed on the moon in 1969, and he wrote in his memoirs, "There is no better place than this to think about the moon . . . " —elusive, poetic, mysterious. "But," comparing it with the island, "Pantelleria is more beautiful," he concluded.

From the lookout point at the summit on a clear day, as the song goes, you can see forever, which is really Tunisia on one side and Sicily on the other.

"Pantelleria, a concentrate of Mediterranean," Rosario had said a few days before.

Now at our parting he asked us how we would encapsulate Pantelleria.

"The blue of the sea, the color of the flowers, the old stones and the cliffs, the food, the wine: a concentrate of Italy." After a pause, we added: "But without the crowds and the noise."

And we reflected that although the island has many names— Black Pearl of the Mediterranean, The Smaller One, Daughter of the Wind—if we had our way, we would call her "The Unspoiled."

:::::::

The small plane took off, skirted the island again as in a good-bye, then pointed its nose north. We were leaving behind yet another friend, yet another place. This one is the last tip of Italy, we told ourselves. It was as if we had reached the last page, the back cover of an illustrated book. But we would not close it and put it away. We knew that once we reached Rome and then Boston, we would want to open it again and start over from page one. It is a big book with many pages, some of which we will want to visit many times. Others, brand-new ones, are still to be explored. Maybe next time.

INSALATA DI ARANCE
Orange Salad

24 black olives (Sicilian or Greek style)
½ red onion, finely slivered
Juice of ½ lemon
6 seedless oranges (preferably blood oranges)

6 tablespoons extra virgin olive oil
½ teaspoon salt, or to taste
A few drops of soy sauce (optional)

MARINATE the olives and the onion slivers in the lemon juice for 10 to 15 minutes.

PEEL the oranges, removing as much of the white pith as possible. With a very sharp knife, slice the peeled oranges into thin rounds and spread out on a serving plate. Sprinkle with the olive oil and the salt. (Add a few drops of soy sauce, if desired.) Press gently on some of the slices to release some juice; tilt the plate, scoop up the juices with a spoon, and dress evenly all the slices. Distribute the olives and onion slivers around the plate and serve.

Serves 6

ROMBO AI CAPPERI

Flounder in Parsley and Caper Sauce

(As a substitute for flounder, you can use swordfish or halibut steaks, cut no more than ¼-inch thick.)

1 onion, peeled and halved	2 tablespoons minced capers,
1 carrot, scrubbed and halved	well drained
1 celery rib	4 tablespoons finely minced fresh
1 bay leaf	flat-leaf parsley
5–6 black peppercorns	Juice of 1½ lemons
1 teaspoon salt	2 tablespoons of unseasoned fine
2 pounds fresh flounder fillets	bread crumbs
1 tablespoon olive oil	2 tablespoons dry sherry
1 tablespoon unsalted butter	

PUT the onion, carrot, celery, bay leaf, peppercorns, and salt in about two quarts of water in a poaching pan or a large sauté pan, and boil for 15 to 20 minutes. Let it cool to a simmer and then poach the flounder fillets in it for 3 minutes. Turn the heat off and let the fillets rest in the water for another 5 minutes. Lift the fillets out of the pan, drain them well, put them on a serving platter, and keep them warm.

PUT the olive oil and butter in a saucepan, and when sufficiently warm, add the minced capers and parsley. Stir in the lemon juice and then the bread crumbs. Add the sherry and stir over low heat for a second or two until everything is well amalgamated and of saucelike consistency; if it's too thick, dilute it with a little warm water. Pour the sauce over the flounder fillets, decorate it with lemon wedges, and serve.

Serves 6

RECIPE INDEXES
Recipe Index by Region

Recipe Index by Category

CARNE (*Meat*)

Coniglio Agrodolce (Game) :: Rabbit in sweet and sour sauce 315

Coniglio in salmi (Game) :: Rabbit in savory wine sauce 172

Costoletta Valdostana :: Veal chop stuffed with Fontina cheese 27

Fegato alla Veneziana :: Calf's liver sautéed in onion slivers 76

Goulash di Manzo :: Beef goulash 59

Lombo di Maiale all'Arancia :: Boneless pork loin in
  orange sauce 121

Pollo in potacchio (Poultry) :: Chicken cooked in wine and herbs 220

Stracotto al Sangiovese :: Pot roast in Sangiovese wine 109

PESCE (*Fish*)

Anguilla Grigliata :: Grilled eel 331

Cipollata di Tonno :: Fresh tuna in onion sweet-and-sour sauce 292

Cuscusu co' a ghiotta 'e pisci :: Fish couscous 278

Pescespada Brodettato :: Swordfish in lemon sauce 330

Rombo ai Capperi :: Flounder in parsley and caper sauce 345

Trota Affogata :: Trout poached in white wine 11

VERDURE & INSALATE (*Vegetables & Salads*)

Caponata :: Eggplant, tomato, onion, celery, raisin,
  and pine nut dish 293

Insalata di Arance :: Orange salad 344

Insalata di Indivia Belga e Radicchio :: Belgian endive and
  radicchio mimosa salad 120

Sformata di Patate alla Fiorentina :: Potatoes Florentine 174

DOLCI (*Sweets*)

Biscotti di Prato :: Hard almond cookies for dunking 175

Bocconotti :: Sweet turnovers 266

Frustingolo :: Fruit cake 221

G. Franco Romagnoli was born and brought up in Rome, Italy. In 1952 he married Margaret O'Neill, the American head of the Marshall Plan radio section in Italy. The Romagnolis moved to the United States in 1955 where Franco was hired to set up the film section for WGBH-TV, Channel 2, Boston. He remained as Director of Photography and, subsequently, as Director of the Film Department until 1960. Then, as a freelance producer-director-photographer, he made documentaries for Channel 2 and for the Public Broadcasting System (PBS) in the United States, as well as feature films and commercials in Europe (through 1975). During this time, Franco's still photography was exhibited in New York, Boston, and Rome, Italy.

In the mid-1970s Franco was the writer and co-talent with Margaret, of the television series on Italian cookery "The Romagnolis' Table." The first U.S. television show on Italian cooking, the series covered, in a light but informative way, the interaction of Italian regional culture and its gastronomy; it was aired nationally on PBS stations throughout the 1970s and early 1980s. Franco and Margaret toured extensively to all major cities in the United States, lecturing and demonstrating Italian cooking. Nine cookbooks followed, including *The Romagnolis' Table* and its sequel, which sold more than 400,000 copies.

From 1979 to 1989, the Romagnolis supervised the operation of their restaurants, "The Romagnolis' Table" in Faneuil Hall

Marketplace, Boston, and in Salem and Burlington, Massachusetts.

Franco's travel and gastronomy articles have been published in the *New York Times,* the *Boston Globe,* the *Christian Science Monitor,* the *Los Angeles Times, Eating Well* magazine, *Gourmet* magazine, *Food and Wine* magazine, *Cook's Illustrated,* and *Expressions,* the American Express magazine. Two of his short stories, as well as a travel piece, have appeared in *The Atlantic Monthly.* For many years Franco conducted seminars on Italian culture and cuisine at Boston University, and led enogastronomy tours to various regions of Italy. Margaret died in 1995.

Gwen O'Sullivan Romagnoli is Franco's second wife. She was born and raised in Philadelphia, Pennsylvania, and in the early 1960s went to live in Bari, Italy, where she taught English for six years. In 1970 she moved to Rome, where she worked for the NBC News Bureau and also wrote monthly fashion bulletins for the Rome High Fashion Institute and articles about the Roman show business scene for *Variety.* After returning to the States in 1976, she attended law school, practiced law, and wrote articles for the *Massachusetts Lawyers Weekly.* Gwen and Franco met through a mutual friend, and they married in 1998. Gwen has traveled extensively in the United States and Europe, especially in Italy (on her own and with Franco). Her food and travel articles have been published in the *Los Angeles Times,* the *Boston Globe,* and *Expressions,* the American Express Magazine. They include pieces on *trattorie* in the Trastevere and Testaccio sections of Rome, the Italian regions of Le Marche, Emilia-Romagna, and the restaurant scene in Boston and Buenos Aires.